PRAISE FOR JAYNE ANN KRENTZ
AND HER MARVELOUS BESTSELLERS

Grand Passion

"Filled with the kind of intelligent, offbeat characters . . . [who] are so fun to get to know that it's hard to close the book on them. . . . Jayne Ann Krentz is one of the hottest writers in romance today."

—*USA Today*

"Krentz at her best. . . . [*Grand Passion* has] the snappy dialogue that has become her trademark and a cast of characters you want to know personally."

—Sandra Brown

"Charming, suspenseful, and downright steamy. . . . Pure and unabashed fun."

—*West Coast Review of Books*

Absolutely, Positively

"[A] cheerful escapist package combining sex and mystery. . . ."

—*Cosmopolitan*

"Combines whimsy and mystery with a touch of the paranormal . . . [and an] unusual and particularly intriguing hero."

—*Library Journal*

"*Absolutely, Positively* pushes all the right buttons—and it always works."

—*Kirkus Reviews*

"A delight. . . . Krentz's leads are engaging and believable."

—*Publishers Weekly*

"Insightful and entertaining. . . . Jayne Ann Krentz outdoes herself."

—*Affaire de Coeur*

Also by Jayne Ann Krentz

Absolutely, Positively
Deep Waters
Eye of the Beholder
Family Man
Flash
Golden Chance
Grand Passion
Hidden Talents
Perfect Partners
Sharp Edges
Silver Linings
Sweet Fortune
Trust Me
Wildest Hearts

Written under the name Jayne Castle

Amaryllis
Orchid
Zinnia

Published by POCKET BOOKS

JAYNE ANN KRENTZ

Grand Passion

Absolutely, Positively

POCKET BOOKS
New York London Toronto Sydney

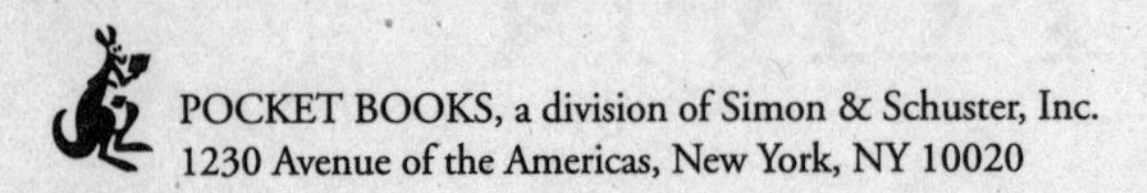

POCKET BOOKS, a division of Simon & Schuster, Inc.
1230 Avenue of the Americas, New York, NY 10020

ISBN: 1-4165-0734-5

This Pocket Books trade paperback edition January 2005

10 9 8 7 6 5 4 3 2 1

Manufactured in the United States of America

For information regarding special discounts for bulk purchases, please contact Simon & Schuster Special Sales at 1-800-456-6798 or business@simonandschuster.com

These titles were previously published individually by Pocket Books.

GRAND PASSION
1

ABSOLUTELY, POSITIVELY
283

Grand Passion

For Claire Zion, editor and friend:
You believed in me from the beginning—
My thanks.

Prologue

Max Fortune sat alone in the hidden chamber of the old brick mansion and contemplated his collection. It was something he did frequently. He had learned long ago that his paintings and books were the only things that truly belonged to him, the only things that no one could take away from him.

Most of the masterpieces that hung on the walls of the secured, climate-controlled vault had been created by modern artists who were only just beginning to achieve the recognition they deserved. A few paintings were already acknowledged as works of genius. Some of the artists were still undiscovered, except by Max.

Although he knew their present and future value, Max had not collected the paintings as an investment. Savage, bleak, and technically brilliant, the canvases reflected something inside himself that he could not put into words. Many were the stuff of the old nightmares that he had had as a child.

He had no doubt that one day every painting in his possession would be acclaimed as the unique creation it was. His instincts were unerring when it came to art. He had the inner eye.

With the exception of the complete works of Dr. Seuss and several tattered volumes of the Hardy Boys series, the rare books in the glass cases would have fetched enormous sums at any auction. Max coveted books almost as much as he coveted paintings.

He especially valued old and rare books, books that had a history, books that had meant something to someone. When he held an old book in his hands, Max knew a fleeting sense of connection with people who had lived before him. He felt as though he shared a small part of someone else's past. It was as close as he got to feeling like a member of a family.

The elegant old house, which Max occupied alone, sat on Seattle's Queen Anne Hill. It commanded a sweeping view of the city and Elliott Bay and was considered a prime piece of real estate. Everything in the mansion, from the 1978 California Cabernet Sauvignon that Max was drinking to the exquisite Oriental rugs on the polished hardwood floors, had been chosen with great care.

But Max knew better than anyone that all the money he had lavished on the great brick structure had not accomplished the impossible. It had not turned his house into a home.

Max had not had a home since the age of six. He was fairly certain now that he would never have one. He accepted that stark fact. He had long ago learned that the secret of surviving was not to want the things he could not have.

Max's philosophy of life worked quite well for the most part because there were very few things he wanted that he could not have.

Among the many things that Max had acquired for himself was a formidable reputation.

People described his reputation in different ways. Some said he was dangerous. Others said he was brilliant and ruthless, utterly unrelenting in his pursuit of a goal. Everyone agreed on one thing, which was that when Max Fortune set out to do a job, the job got done.

Max knew that his legendary reputation was based on one very simple fact: He never screwed up.

Or, almost never.

One

It had taken Max Fortune nearly a month to locate Jason Curzon's mistress. Now that he had found her, he didn't know what to make of her. Cleopatra Robbins was definitely not the sort of woman he had been expecting to find.

Max stood quietly near the roaring fire and surveyed the chaos that filled the cozy lobby of the Robbins' Nest Inn. In spite of her evocative first name, Ms. Robbins certainly did not look like a sultry charmer who made her living by seducing wealthy men old enough to be her grandfather.

She looked exactly like what she purported to be: a cheerfully harried innkeeper trying to deal with a flood of new arrivals.

Max glanced at the series of insipid seascapes hanging on the walls as he listened to the hubbub going on around him. He smiled with faint derision. It was obvious that Cleopatra Robbins was not only not a typical seductress, she was not much of a connoisseur of art. Anyone who would hang those bland views of storm-tossed seas would be incapable of appreciating the five Amos Luttrell paintings that had been left in her care.

It was just as well she preferred the seascapes, because Max intended to take the Luttrells from her. They belonged to him. They constituted his inheritance from Jason Curzon, and Max had every intention of claiming them.

He was prepared to use whatever tactics were necessary to recover the legacy. Having to fight for what was his would be nothing new for Max. Since the age of six, he had done battle for everything he had ever wanted in life. Sometimes he lost, but more often he won.

Max rested both hands on the intricately carved hawk that formed the grip of his cane. With an effort of will that was second nature to him, he ignored the persistent ache in his leg. The old wound was acting up again tonight, bringing back memories he had no intention of indulging.

He concentrated instead on Cleopatra Robbins as she bustled about behind the front desk.

Max remembered that Jason had called her Cleo. The nickname suited her much better than the more dramatic Cleopatra.

Trust Jason to choose a mistress who did not fit the stereotype. But, then, Jason had always had a gift for looking beneath the surface. He'd had the discerning eye of an intuitive collector, a man who trusted his own instincts rather than the opinion of others. The stunning array of paintings he had bequeathed to his favorite art museum in Seattle bore testimony to his unerring taste. But the five Amos Luttrells had formed the centerpiece of his collection.

Curzon had owned close to two hundred paintings at the time of his death. As far as Max knew, Cleopatra Robbins was the only mistress Jason had ever collected.

An unexpected sense of wrongness rippled through Max as he tried to envision the woman behind the desk in bed with Jason Curzon. Jason was the closest thing Max had ever had to a father. He told himself he should have been glad that the old man had had some feminine companionship during the last year and a half of his life. God knew, Jason had had many lonely years after the death of his wife.

But for some reason Max didn't like the idea that the female providing that companionship had been Cleo Robbins.

Max concluded that she was somewhere in her late twenties, perhaps twenty-seven or twenty-eight. He studied her precariously listing topknot of thick, dark, auburn hair and found himself wondering what it would look like tumbled down around her shoulders. There was no particular style to the design of the topknot. The rich mass of hair had obviously been twisted into position in a hurry, anchored with a clip, and left to flounder under its own weight.

Instead of the exotic kohl her namesake might have used to outline her eyes, Cleo Robbins wore a pair of round, gold-framed glasses. Max realized that in an odd way they served the same purpose as elaborate makeup, concealing the real expression in her wide, hazel green eyes.

The lady he had been hunting for the past month looked out at the world with the professionally friendly gaze of a successful innkeeper, but he sensed something deeper and more compelling about her.

Max had an inexplicable urge to try something that he knew from experience rarely worked. He looked into Cleo Robbins the way he looked into a painting.

To his surprise, the commotion and noise around him receded, just as it did when he was transfixed by a work of art. The world and his focus narrowed to include only Cleo Robbins. He felt the familiar stirring deep inside himself almost immediately. It made him uneasy. He was accustomed to feeling this sense of fascination and longing only when he was in the presence of the things he collected.

Jason had told Max that the talent could be applied to people as well as art and books. But Max had discovered the hard way that the ability to see beneath the surface had its limits when it came to dealing with other human beings. People were more complex than art, and all too often they had an ability to hide the deeper truths about themselves.

Nevertheless, there was no denying the kick-in-the-gut feeling he was getting now as he studied Cleo with what Jason had called his inner eye.

"Just one moment, Mr. Partridge. I'll have someone take your luggage up to your room." Cleo gave the irritable-looking Mr. Partridge a spectacular smile as she banged the silver bell on the desk.

"About time," Partridge muttered. "Took me nearly three hours to get here from Seattle. Don't know why in hell the company had to pick an inn way out here on the coast for this damn fool motivational seminar. Could have held it at one of the big hotels in the city."

"I'm sure you'll find that at this time of year the Washington coast provides a wonderful setting for an educational retreat." Cleo glanced anxiously toward the staircase. "I'm afraid my bellhop is busy at the moment. I'll give you your key, and you can go on up to your room. I'll have the luggage brought up to you later, if you don't mind."

"Forget it. I'll carry it myself." Partridge snatched up the suitcase at his feet. "Can I at least get a drink somewhere around here?"

"An excellent selection of Northwest wines and beers is available in the lounge, Mr. Partridge."

"Damn. What I really need is a martini." Partridge snatched up his key and stalked toward the staircase. The next three people in line behind him surged forward in a wave.

Max watched as Cleo braced herself for the onslaught. He saw her glance again at the stairs. When the missing bellhop did not materialize there, she turned back to face the wave with a warm smile of welcome.

The lobby door slammed open with a crash. Max saw lightning crackle across the night sky. Rain, wind, and two more drenched inn patrons blew into the hall. They joined the crowd milling around in front of the hearth.

"Lucky Ducky go swimming."

Startled by the high, squeaky voice that came out of nowhere, Max looked down. A small boy with a head full of blond curls looked up at him. He was dressed in a miniature pair of jeans and a striped shirt. He appeared to be no more than five years old, and he had a thumb stuck in his mouth.

"I beg your pardon?" Max could not recall the last time he had conversed with a child.

The small boy yanked his thumb out of his mouth long enough to repeat his statement. "Lucky Ducky go swimming." Jamming his thumb back into his mouth, he gave Max an expectant look.

"I see." Max sought for a suitable response. "It's a cold night for swimming, isn't it?"

"Uncle Jason said ducks can swim anytime, anywhere."

Max's hands tightened around the hawk-headed grip of the cane. "Uncle Jason?"

"Uncle Jason's gone," the child confided with a wistful expression. "Cleo says he's in heaven."

"Jason Curzon in heaven?" Max contemplated that. "Well, anything's possible, I suppose."

"Did you know Uncle Jason?"

"Yes."

The boy took his thumb out of his mouth again and gave Max a bright, toothless smile. "My name is Sammy Gordon. Did you know my daddy, too?"

"I don't think so." A staggering thought occurred to Max. "Not unless your daddy was Uncle Jason?"

"No, no, no," the child said, clearly impatient. "My daddy isn't in heaven like Uncle Jason. My daddy's lost."

Max realized he was beginning to lose the thread of the conversation. "Lost?"

Sammy nodded quickly. "I heard Mommy tell Cleo that he had to go find himself."

"I see."

"He never did, I guess."

Max did not know what to say to that. He glanced across the crowded room and saw a pretty woman with short, honey-blond hair emerge from the office behind the front desk. She went to give Cleo a hand.

"That's my mommy," Sammy volunteered.

"What's her name?"

"Sylvia Gordon." Sammy eyed Max's cane with deep interest. "Why do you have to lean on that? Did you hurt yourself?"

"Yes."

"Will you be all better soon?"

"I hurt myself a long time ago," Max said. "This is as good as I'm going to get."

"Oh." Sammy was intrigued.

"Sammy?" Cleo came around from behind the desk. "Where are you?"

Max's head came up swiftly. Jason's mistress had a rich honey-and-cream sort of voice, perfectly suited to a Cleopatra. Another jolt of awareness went through him. He could almost hear that warm, sensual voice in bed.

"Here I am, Cleo." Sammy waved a wet thumb at her.

Max's eye was caught by a glimpse of silver as Cleo emerged from the crowd. He glanced down and frowned when he saw that Jason's mistress favored shiny, silver-toned sneakers with glittering, metallic laces. The rest of her attire was not nearly as tasteless, but it wasn't particularly inspiring, either. It consisted of a yellow oxford cloth button-down shirt and a pair of faded jeans.

"I wondered where you were, Sammy." Cleo smiled at the boy, and then her eyes met Max's.

He saw the startled expression that appeared in her soft hazel gaze. For a few seconds her gold-framed glasses afforded her no protection at all. In that brief moment she was as open to him as a work of art, and he knew that she was as aware of him as he was of her.

The impact of the flash of raw intimacy stunned Max. It was a dangerously disturbing experience, completely unlike anything he had ever known with another human being. Until now the only things that had had a similar effect on him were extraordinarily fine paintings and very old books. Desire, fierce and completely unexpected, swept through him. He fought it with all the willpower at his command.

Cleo's gaze slipped briefly to Max's cane, breaking the spell. When she looked up again, she had her professionally hospitable expression firmly in place. Her eyes were still very lovely, but they were no longer as clear and readable as they had been a few seconds earlier. The lady had stepped back behind her veil, and Max had himself under control once more.

"We'll be right with you, sir," she said to Max. "As you can see, we're a little busy at the moment."

"He's a friend of Uncle Jason's," Sammy volunteered.

Cleo's eyes widened. The professional politeness in her expression disappeared. It was replaced by a brilliant, welcoming warmth that made Max's insides tighten.

"You're a friend of Jason's?" Cleo asked eagerly.

"Yes."

"That's *wonderful.* Don't worry, I'm sure we can find room for you. Make yourself comfortable while Sylvia and I finish the check-in. I didn't catch your name."

"Max Fortune."

"Right. Sammy, show him into the solarium. He can wait there."

"Okay." Sammy looked up at Jason. "You can follow me."

Max kept his eyes on Cleo. "If you don't mind, I believe I'll wait here. I wanted to speak with you."

"Of course," Cleo said easily. "Just as soon as I have a free minute." She glanced down at Sammy. "Honey, do you know where Benjy is?"

"Benjy's gone."

Cleo was clearly nonplussed. "Gone?"

Sammy nodded. "That's what Trisha says."

"She must have meant he was busy," Cleo said.

"Nope." Sammy shook his head with grave certainty. "He's gone."

"Good grief. He can't be gone," Cleo said. "He's supposed to be here tonight. He knew we had this group arriving."

"Cleo? Where are you?" A young woman who appeared to be no more than nineteen or twenty approached with a stack of towels in her arms. She, too, was wearing jeans. She also had on a loose-fitting plaid flannel shirt. Her light brown hair was tied back in a ponytail, and her attractive features were marked with fine lines of tension.

"Right here." Cleo frowned in concern. "Are you okay, Trisha?"

"Sure, just real busy."

"Where's Benjy?"

"I don't know." Trisha's eyes slid away from Cleo's. "We've got a problem in two-ten. The toilet's stopped up."

"Just what I needed," Cleo muttered. "Benjy's the master plumber around here. Where is he when I need him?"

"Want me to work on it?" Trisha asked.

"No, you finish making up the rooms. I'll get someone else on it." Cleo swung back around and pinned Max with a hopeful look. "What did you say your name was?"

"Max Fortune."

"And you were a friend of Jason's?"

"Yes."

"A good friend?"

"Yes."

Cleo gave him a dazzling smile. "Then that makes you practically one of the family, doesn't it?"

"I don't know," Max said. "Does it?"

"Of course it does. Jason would never have sent you out here to meet us unless he considered you family. At times like this, family pitches in around here. Jason always did his share when he was staying with us. Do you mind?"

"I'm afraid I don't quite follow, Ms. Robbins."

"No problem. I'm sure you'll figure it out soon enough. This way."

"Ms. Robbins, I'm here to talk to you."

"Later. Like I said, I'm really swamped right now." Cleo led the way down a short hall.

A strange sense of disorientation gripped Max. "Ms. Robbins, if you don't mind, I'd rather wait out here."

"Everyone helps," Sammy said. He took his thumb out of his mouth again and grabbed a fistful of Max's Italian-designed, hand-tailored jacket. The fine silk-and-wool-blend fabric crumpled beneath the devastating assault of the little fingers.

Max gave up trying to argue and allowed himself to be tugged down the hall. Cleo was already well ahead of him. She had a closet door open at the end of a corridor and was peering inside.

"Aha. Here we go." She reached into the closet, hauled out a plunger, and held it triumphantly aloft. "Trisha said it was room number two-ten. Sammy can show you the way, can't you, Sammy?"

"Okay," Sammy said happily.

Max eyed the plunger. It dawned on him just what was expected of him. "I think there is a misunderstanding here, Ms. Robbins."

She gave him an inquiring look. "You did say you were a friend of Jason's, didn't you?"

"That's what I said." Max eyed the plunger grimly.

"Jason was always terrific about lending a hand when one was needed," Cleo said encouragingly.

Max looked at her. He didn't know what to make of Jason's mistress, but he knew that until he found the five Amos Luttrell paintings, he was going to have to bide his time. "I'll see what I can do."

"Wonderful. I really appreciate this." Cleo thrust the plunger into his hand and gave him a smile of deep gratitude. "Run along with Sammy, now. I've got to get back to the front desk." She turned and hurried down the hall without a backward glance.

"This way." Sammy yanked on Max's jacket. "There's stairs in the back."

Max set his teeth and allowed himself to be dragged off, plunger in hand, toward an unknown destiny. He felt as if he'd accidentally stepped into another world, where the laws of nature were slightly altered. *Jason, what the hell were you doing out here,* he asked silently as Sammy led him up the back stairs to the second floor.

"In here." Sammy pushed open the door marked two-ten.

The room was empty. Max swept the frilly, fussy, overstuffed furnishings with a single glance and dismissed everything, including the picture of the spaniels that hung over the bed. It was a classic example of Victorian sentimentalism and extravagance at its worst.

Max walked across the ugly flower-pattern carpet and glanced warily into the white-tiled bath. He was willing to acknowledge that the Victorians had known how to do bathrooms. He approved of the huge, white, claw-footed tub.

He did not, however, like the way water lapped at the edge of the toilet bowl, threatening to spill over onto the floor. At least it appeared to be clean water, he thought. He supposed he should be grateful for that much.

"Lucky Ducky go swimming," Sammy reminded him again.

Realization dawned on Max. "In this particular toilet?"

"Ducks can swim anywhere."

Max resigned himself to the inevitable. He leaned his cane and the plunger against the wall while he shrugged out of his expensive jacket. He hung the jacket carefully on the hook behind the door. Then he unfastened his gold cuff links, put them in his pocket, and rolled up the sleeves of his handmade white silk shirt.

Family pitches in at times like this.

It was an odd thing to say to a man who had not been part of a real family since the age of six. As far as Max was concerned, the series of foster homes he had lived in after his mother was killed in a car accident did not count.

He had never known his father, a faceless figure who had walked out of his life before he was even born. Max had never bothered to search for him. He had no interest in locating a father who did not want to claim him.

It was after he had been shunted off to the second foster home that Max had begun collecting things. *Things* didn't reject you, he had discovered. *Things* didn't walk away from you. *Things* didn't tell you in a thousand subtle ways that you weren't good enough to be a member of the family. *Things* could be taken with you when you moved on to the next temporary location.

It had been books at first. Surprisingly enough it was easy to collect books, even if you couldn't afford them. People were astonishingly eager to give them to you. Teachers, social workers, librarians, foster mothers—they had all been delighted to give books to young Max.

For a long while he had worried that someone would eventually ask for them back. But no one ever did. Not even the librarian who had given Max his very first volume of Dr. Seuss.

Most of the other children had quickly grown bored with their free books and had traded them to Max for what seemed to him like ridiculously low prices: a candy bar, a toy, a couple of quarters. Each book had been a rare bargain as far as Max was concerned. It was something that belonged to him. Something he could keep forever.

When he was young he had hoarded his treasures in his suitcase. They were always packed and ready for the next, inevitable move. He had asked his social worker for a lock and key for the dilapidated piece of luggage. She had smiled an odd, sad smile and given him one without question.

Max was sixteen when he discovered what was to become the grand passion of his life: modern art. He had skipped school one afternoon to wander through Seattle's Pioneer Square. For no particular reason he had walked into several of the galleries. In two of them he had seen paintings that had reached straight into the secret center of his being. For the first time he understood that there were others in the world who had nightmares and dreams that resembled his own. He had never forgotten the experience.

When he was in the presence of paintings that touched the raw core inside himself, Max did not feel quite so alone.

Max had been twenty-three when he and Curzon had met. That had been twelve years ago. Max had just gotten out of the Army and had taken the first job he had found. It was manual labor for the most part, but Max had liked it right from the start. The work consisted primarily of crating, transporting, and hanging the paintings that an art dealer named Garrison Spark sold to his clients.

Max hadn't particularly liked Spark, whose ethics were questionable at best, but he had been transfixed by some of the art he was allowed to handle. Spark, in turn, found Max's unerring eye for art extremely useful. The two made a pact. In exchange for the job, Max promised not to voice his opinions on the authenticity of certain paintings that Spark sold unless the client asked for that opinion.

Max had delivered two paintings, both genuine, to Jason Curzon before the event occurred that had changed his life. The moment was still crystal clear in his mind.

He had just uncrated a large canvas, a dark, abstract picture purported to be the work of a new and rising artist whose paintings Jason had been eager to collect. Max had stood politely aside, allowing Jason to examine the picture in silence.

Jason had gazed into the painting for a long time before he had turned to Max with an enigmatic expression.

"What do you think?" Jason asked.

Max hid his surprise. In his experience clients never solicited the artistic opinion of the man who delivered their purchases.

Max looked at the painting. He had seen three other works that had been created by the same artist. He had been immediately compelled by the others. This one left him unmoved. He weighed his answer carefully. He knew Jason had paid a huge sum for the picture.

"I think it's a fake," Max finally said.

Jason gave him an appraising look. "So do I."

"A very good fake," Max said quickly, mindful of his treasured job. "After all, it fooled Mr. Spark."

Jason had merely arched his brows at that remark. He sent the painting back to Spark with no explanation other than that he had changed his mind. But the following month he had invited Max to view his private collection.

Max had been enthralled by the visions that hung on Jason's walls. At the end of the tour Jason had turned to him.

"You're smart and you think fast on your feet. Most important, I think you've got the inner eye," Jason said. "You ever think of doing something a little more intellectually demanding than crating and uncrating art for Garrison Spark?"

"Like what?" Max asked.

"Like coming to work for me. I'll put you in charge of buying art for Curzon hotels. You'll report directly to me, and you'll answer only to me. It will mean travel, an excellent salary, bonuses, and mingling with the corporate hierarchy. Interested?"

"Why not?" Max said. He knew a turning point in his life when he saw one, and as usual he had nothing better waiting for him in the other direction.

Jason surveyed Max's cheap brown suit, permanent-press shirt, and frayed tie. "First we're going to have to polish you up a bit."

Jason was as good as his word. He taught Max everything he needed to know in order to move in the rarefied circles of the international hotel business. Max learned quickly. He copied Jason's exquisitely polished manners and wore his expensive new clothes with natural ease.

After having fought his way through the foster care system and the Army, he was not intimidated by the high-powered corporate types with whom he came in contact. Jason wryly observed that the situation was just the opposite. Most people were intimidated by Max.

"An extremely useful talent," Jason said a year after Max had been on the job. "I think we should make use of it."

Max knew how to make himself useful when it suited him. It suited him to please Jason Curzon.

Within six months he had become much more than the curator of Curzon International's art collection. He had become Jason's right-hand man.

His responsibilities had evolved swiftly. Someone else was eventually appointed to manage the art collection. Max was put in charge of gathering intelligence on the competition and reporting on the suitability of potential hotel sites. From the beginning he made it his goal to learn in advance everything Jason needed in order to make far-reaching decisions regarding potential acquisitions: local politics in foreign locations, including the names of the specific officials who expected to be bribed before construction could begin on a new hotel; the reliability, or lack thereof, of certain members of Curzon management; sites that were ripe for development or, conversely, needed to be abandoned before they started losing money. Max had made himself an indispensable authority on all of those things.

For all intents and purposes, he had been second-in-command at Curzon.

In the process he had learned the correct way to drink tea in Japan, coffee in the Middle East, and champagne in France. He bought his shirts in London, his suits and shoes in Rome, and his ties in Paris. And he bought art and books wherever he found them.

Curzon Hotels was a family-owned business that had been bequeathed to Jason and his brother, Dennison, by their father. Jason had always held the reins of the company, not only because he was the elder brother, but because he had the savvy intelligence required to manage the business. Dennison had not liked being relegated to second place, but he had tolerated it because there was no doubt that Jason was the natural leader in the family.

Now, with Jason gone, Dennison was determined to demonstrate that he had as much business acumen as his brother.

While he was alive, Jason had given Max the illusion that he was almost a member of the Curzon family. Three years ago Max had made the mistake of thinking he was going to become a real member, but that promise had dissolved in the ruins of his relationship with Kimberly Curzon, Dennison's daughter.

Six weeks into the engagement, Kimberly had come to her senses and realized she could not marry a man with no background or family connections. She had married Roarke Winston, instead, the heir to a large industrial empire.

Max had realized then that he would never be a member of the family.

He had handed in his resignation the day after Jason had died of a massive heart attack. A week later he had set out to find the legacy Jason had spoken of on his deathbed.

"Five Amos Luttrell paintings," Jason had whispered after ordering his brother's family from the hospital room for a few minutes. "They're yours, Max. They don't go to the museum with the others. I wanted you to have them. Your inheritance from me. You understand? It's in my will."

Max had gripped the old man's hand, hanging on to him as if he could draw him back from the brink. "Forget the Luttrells. You're going to pull through this, Jason. You're going to be okay."

"Bullshit. I'm eighty-three years old, and this is it. Better to go out this way than some of the ways a lot of my friends have gone. Been a good life for the most part. I had a fine wife for forty years, and I had a son I could be proud of."

"A son?" Max had been startled by the revelation. He had been told that Jason and his wife had never had children.

"You, Max. You were the son I never had. And you're a damned good one." Jason's gnarled fingers bit into Max's hand. "Those paintings and everything else you find out there on the coast with them are yours. Promise me you'll go get them."

"Take it easy, Jason." Max could feel the unfamiliar dampness in his eyes. It was the first time he had cried since his mother had died. "You've got to rest."

"Left 'em with Cleo."

"What? The paintings? Who's Cleo?"

Jason's answer had been lost in a wracking, wheezing cough. "Met her a year and a half ago. Amazing woman." His frail fingers grasped Max's with unnatural strength. "Been meaning to introduce you. Never had a chance. You were always off somewhere. Europe, the islands. Always busy. Too late now. Time goes by so fast, doesn't it?"

"Jason, try to get some rest."

"You find her, Max. You find her, and you'll find the paintings and everything else."

"Jason, for God's sake. . . ."

"Promise me you'll go after them."

"I promise. But don't worry about that now. You're going to be all right."

But Max had no longer been able to keep Jason back from the edge. Jason's hand had gone limp then, and the ghastly wheezing had finally stopped.

Max pushed aside the memories. He had found the mysterious Cleo, and soon he would find his Luttrells. He picked up the plunger and took aim at the toilet bowl.

"I'll help," Sammy said.

"I think it would be best if you supervised."

"Okay. I'm good at that. Cleo lets me supervise a lot."

Max went to work. Five minutes later, amid a great deal of gurgling, a yellow plastic duck popped to the surface.

"Lucky Ducky," Sammy exclaimed in delight.

Max eyed the plastic duck. "Very lucky. From now on Lucky Ducky had better do his swimming somewhere else."

"Okay."

Cleo appeared in the doorway, breathless and more disheveled than ever. She was heavily burdened with luggage in both hands. Several tendrils of hair had escaped the topknot and were hanging down in front of her eyes. She blew them out of her way. "How's it going in here?"

"Max saved Lucky Ducky," Sammy said.

"My hero," Cleo murmured.

"I believe the toilet will flush properly now," Max said coldly.

The bathroom light sparkled on the lenses of Cleo's glasses as she grinned at him. "I'm really very grateful to you. This is Mr. Valence's regular room, and I was afraid I'd have to shift him to another one. He doesn't like to be shifted around. He's kind of fussy. Tends to get upset when things deviate from the usual routine."

Max held the dripping plunger over the toilet. "Look, if you don't mind, Ms. Robbins, I would very much like to speak with you now."

"Just as soon as I've got this lot settled and dinner has been served. In the meantime, I seem to have lost my bellhop. Any chance you could lend a hand?"

"He hurt himself." Sammy pointed to the cane leaning against the wall.

Cleo's gaze darted to the cane. A deep, embarrassed blush rose in her cheeks. "Oh, sorry, I forgot. Never mind. I'll get someone from the kitchen staff."

For some reason that rankled. "I can handle a few suitcases, Ms. Robbins."

She looked skeptical. "Are you sure?"

"Yes, Ms. Robbins, I'm sure."

Her smile was brighter than the fluorescent light over the mirror and infinitely warmer. "Terrific. By the way, please call me Cleo. I like to be on a first-name basis with anyone who can unstop a clogged toilet in a pinch."

"Thank you," Max said through his teeth.

Cleo looked at Sammy. "Maybe you'd better see if they need any help in the kitchen, dear."

Sammy assumed an air of grave importance. "Okay, Cleo." He looked up at Max. "Family always pitches in at times like this."

"Well, I'm off," Cleo announced. "Got to get this luggage to the right room. See you later, Max. Grab dinner in the kitchen when you get a chance." She whirled about and disappeared around the edge of the door.

"Bye, Max. Thanks for finding Lucky Ducky." Sammy dashed out of the room in Cleo's wake.

Alone in the bathroom, plunger in hand, Max looked down at the plastic duck floating in the toilet bowl. "What the hell have you gotten me into, Jason?"

For the next three hours, Max was fully occupied. He carried countless suitcases, straightened out a logistics problem in the tiny parking lot, poured after-dinner coffee and sherry for guests in the lounge, and replaced a burned-out bulb in one of the rooms.

He didn't get a chance to go in search of Cleo until after eleven o'clock. When he finally tracked her down, she was alone in the small office behind the front desk.

She was seated with her back to him at a table that held a computer and several piles of miscellaneous papers and notes. His trained eye skimmed appreciatively over her. It was not the first time that evening that he had found himself intrigued by the subtly graceful line of her spine and the sweet, vulnerable curve of her neck. Her feet, still clad in the silver athletic shoes, were tucked under her, toes resting on the chrome base of the swivel chair.

He stood silently in the doorway for a moment, watching Cleo as she concentrated intently on a printout spread out on the desk. Without taking her eyes off the figures, she absently reached up to unfasten her hair clip. The simple feminine gesture triggered a heavy, pooling sensation in Max's lower body.

He stared, enthralled, as Cleo's hair fell free around her shoulders. The glow of the desk lamp highlighted the red fire that shimmered in the depths of the thick, dark stuff. Max had a sudden, urgent need to warm his fingers in the flames. Unconsciously he took a step forward. His cane thudded awkwardly on the floor.

"What?" Startled, Cleo spun around in her chair. She relaxed when she saw Max. "Oh, there you are. Come on in. Have a seat. I thought you were George."

"Who's George?" Max regained his self-control in a heartbeat.

"My night desk man. He phoned and said he'd be a little late tonight."

"I see." Max moved across the small space and lowered himself onto the chair near the window. With cool precision he positioned the cane in front of himself and rested his hands on the hawk. "I think it's time we talked, Ms. Robbins."

"Cleo."

"Cleo," he repeated.

She smiled. "I suppose you're wondering if you can have the same arrangement that Jason had."

Max gazed at her uncomprehendingly. "I beg your pardon?"

"It's okay. I don't mind. You're a friend of his, after all. Heck, it's the least I can do. I'm sure Jason would have wanted you to enjoy what he enjoyed here."

Max wondered if he was hallucinating. He could not believe that Cleo was offering to let him take Jason's place in her bed. "I am overwhelmed by your generosity, Ms. Robbins. But I'm not sure Jason would have wanted that."

"Why would he object?"

"Jason was a good friend," Max said. "But there are limits to any friendship."

Cleo looked briefly bewildered. "You're an artist, just as Jason was, aren't you?"

Max lowered his lashes slowly, veiling his gaze while he digested that comment. Jason had freely admitted he could not draw a straight line, let alone paint. He had collected art, not created it.

"Not exactly," Max finally said carefully.

Cleo gave him a sympathetic, knowing look. "Say no more. I understand completely. You haven't been able to sell yet, so you're reluctant to call yourself an artist. I know how you feel." She hesitated. "I'm a writer."

"You are?"

She blushed. "I've got a book coming out this spring. It's called *A Fine Vengeance*. It's a sort of woman-in-jeopardy thing. Suspense and romance."

Max eyed her thoughtfully. "That's very interesting, Ms. Robbins."

"I haven't told anyone except the family about it," Cleo said quickly. "I'm waiting until it actually shows up in the stores, so I'd appreciate it if you wouldn't mention it."

"I won't say a word about it," Max promised.

"Jason knew about it, of course. So I don't mind if you know, too. The point I was trying to make is that it isn't whether or not you sell your work that makes you an artist or a writer. It's whether or not you work at your craft."

"That is a point of view, I suppose."

"Sometimes a person can be very good and still not sell. Take Jason, for instance. He never sold a single painting, and he was a wonderful painter."

"He was?"

"Certainly." Cleo tilted her head to one side and gave Max a curious look. "You must have seen his work. Those are his paintings hanging out there in the lobby. Didn't you recognize his style?"

Max turned his head sharply and stared through the doorway at the series of uninspired seascapes. "I didn't recognize them."

"Didn't you?" Cleo looked briefly disappointed. Then she smiled again. "I love those paintings. They'll always remind me of Jason. In a way they're his legacy to all of us here at Robbins' Nest Inn. Who knows? Maybe one day they'll be worth a fortune."

Never in a million years, Max thought. "And if they do turn out to be quite valuable," he asked softly, "what will you do? Sell them?"

"Good heavens, no. I could never bring myself to sell Jason's work. It belongs here at the inn."

Max cleared his throat cautiously. "Ms. Robbins . . ."

"Cleo."

He ignored the interruption. "Jason owned five Amos Luttrell paintings. Before he died he told me that he had left them here at the inn."

"Who's Amos Luttrell? Another friend of Jason's?"

She was either the most accomplished liar he had encountered in years, or she was a naive idiot, Max decided. His money was on the former. He could not imagine Jason having an idiot for a mistress. In which case he was up against an extremely clever opponent.

"Luttrell was a master of neo-expressionism," Max said blandly.

"Expressionism? That's modern art, isn't it?" Cleo wrinkled her nose. "I've never really liked modern art. I prefer pictures that make sense. Dogs, horses, seascapes. That kind of thing. I don't have any modern art hanging here at the inn. It wouldn't fit in at all."

A cold anger raged through Max. There was only one conclusion. Cleo was obviously aware of the true value of the Luttrells and had decided to play dumb. She was going to pretend she knew nothing about them. She must have realized that Max had no proof she had them in her possession.

It was a clever tactic, he admitted to himself. And one he had not expected to encounter. But, then, nothing was going quite as he had anticipated here at Robbins' Nest Inn.

"Now, then, as I was saying," Cleo continued blithely, "if you're an artist like Jason, you'll probably enjoy the arrangement I had with him."

Max raised one brow. "What, exactly, are you offering?"

"The same salary I gave Jason plus room and board any time you're staying with us in exchange for the kind of odd-job work you were doing tonight. I promise you'll get plenty of time to yourself to paint. You can have Jason's old room in the attic. It's quiet and comfortable. Jason liked it."

Room and board but not her bed, then. At least not yet. "I'm not exactly a starving artist, Ms. Robbins."

"I know that." Cleo smiled gently. "But there are a lot of different ways to starve, aren't there? You're a friend of Jason's, and that's all that matters."

"I'm not sure I would make a good Antony," Max said dryly.

"Huh?" A second later Cleo's face turned a charming shade of warm pink. "Oh, I get it. I'd better warn you that we have one ironclad rule around here. No Cleopatra cracks and absolutely no asp jokes."

"I'll try to remember that."

"So? Are you interested?" Cleo gave him an inquiring look.

The sense of unreality that had gripped Max earlier returned. He stared at Cleo for a long while, and then he made his decision.

What the hell, he thought. He had to find out what had happened to his Luttrells, and it wasn't as if he had anything or anyone waiting for him in Seattle. Jason had sent him in this direction for a reason. Max decided he might as well follow the yellow brick road to the end.

Another turning point, he thought. And as usual, he had no reason to go back.

"As it happens," Max said, "I've just lost a job. I'll take the deal you gave Jason."

Two

"Andromeda, these muffins are out of this world." Cleo popped the last of the hot muffin into her mouth and chewed happily. "As usual."

Andromeda, the head chef of the Robbins' Nest Inn, smiled serenely. All of Andromeda's smiles were serene. She was heavily into metaphysical studies. "I'm glad you like them, dear. It's a variation on the corn bread recipe Daystar's been using for the past few months. You know Daystar. She can't stop experimenting."

"The old recipe was terrific, too, but this one is even better. The guests are going to love these little suckers." Cleo scooped up another corn bread muffin and slathered it with honey.

She hastily devoured it as she surveyed the busy kitchen. Andromeda's staff, all middle-aged and all members of the Cosmic Harmony Women's Retreat, were an industrious crew.

The arrangement between the inn and Cosmic Harmony was simple and lucrative for both sides. Andromeda and her team provided first-rate seafood and vegetarian cuisine for the inn's guests that was unmatched anywhere else on the coast. In return Cleo paid the Retreat a portion of the inn's profits and agreed not to force the women into standard white kitchen uniforms.

Andromeda and her friend, Daystar, were the cornerstones of the inn's kitchen staff. Other members of Cosmic Harmony came in at varying times, depending on who was available and what skills were needed. This morning Cleo recognized Nebula and Constellation hard at work. One was preparing muesli, and the other was slicing sourdough whole wheat bread. The women at Cosmic Harmony generally adopted new names when they came to the Retreat. Some stayed for a few days, weeks, or months. Others, like Andromeda and Daystar, were permanent residents.

All of the women at work this morning had the sleeves of their long, jewel-colored gowns secured above their elbows. Their bright head scarves and strange bronze and silver necklaces added an exotic touch to the kitchen.

The latest editions of the guidebooks had recently begun citing the cuisine at the Robbins' Nest Inn as one of the best reasons to visit the Washington coast in winter or any other time of the year.

For Cleo, the women from Cosmic Harmony provided something much more important than a money-making restaurant; they provided friendship and a place to go when she needed peace and serenity. She often went to the Cosmic Harmony meditation center after one of the recurring nightmares that plagued her from time to time.

The Retreat, situated on a magnificent stretch of land overlooking the ocean, had once been an exclusive golf resort. The resort had failed years earlier and had slowly rotted into the ground.

Five years ago Andromeda and Daystar had conceived the notion of turning the abandoned site into a commune for women. Initially they had leased the grounds and buildings. But three years ago, together with Cleo's assistance, they had pooled their limited resources and purchased the old resort at a foreclosure sale.

Andromeda and Daystar, who formed the core of Cosmic Harmony, had not always been involved in metaphysics and philosophies of self-realization. They had, in fact, started out as members of a Seattle bridge club that had met every Tuesday for years. As time went past, each had found herself on her own due to divorce. The bridge club had been the only thing that had remained stable in their lives.

Andromeda's name in her former life had been Mrs. Hamilton R. Galsworthy III. She had helped create Cosmic Harmony six months after her husband, a doctor who was board certified in gynecology, had run off with his aerobics instructor. Dr. Galsworthy had had an extremely capable lawyer who had managed to ensure that Andromeda did not get more than a token amount in the divorce settlement.

Andromeda had explained to Cleo that she bore no ill will toward her ex-husband, who wound up being divorced by the aerobics instructor within a year. "It was really very sad, dear," Andromeda had once explained. "The poor man was sixty at the time, and they say she had him doing an hour of high-impact aerobics twice a day. With ankle weights, no less. He hasn't been the same since, I'm told. One assumes his karma finally caught up with him."

But there was no going back for Andromeda, not even when Hamilton R. Galsworthy III, M.D., showed up at her door, a broken man, offering to come home. Andromeda had already launched herself on a new path of cosmic enlightenment. In addition, she and her bridge partner, also recently divorced, had discovered that their friendship for each other was a stronger, more enduring bond than the relationship either had had with her ex-husband.

Andromeda sipped a cup of herbal tea in a slow, ceremonial manner. "I wanted to speak to you about one of our new guests," she said to Cleo. She was nearly sixty, a cheerful elf of a woman with a halo of curly gray hair and bright, inquiring eyes. When she moved, the small bells attached to the hem of her gown tinkled merrily.

Lately, every move Andromeda made had an air of carefully cultivated grace and ritual about it. She was currently studying the traditional Japanese tea ceremony and its implications for daily living. It was the latest in a never-ending series of such philosophical explorations for Andromeda.

"We got twenty-five new arrivals last night," Cleo responded. "Another Seattle company is sending some of its employees through one of Herbert T. Valence's three-day motivational seminars."

"Oh, dear. Another one of those, eh?" Andromeda shook her head. "Hard to imagine that anyone really believes there are five easy steps to wealth, power, and unlimited success."

Cleo grinned. "I get the feeling good old Herbert does. The guy must be making money hand-over-fist with these seminars."

"True. He does seem to be doing rather well, doesn't he? This is the third seminar he's booked in here this winter," Andromeda observed.

Cleo laughed. "Just be grateful he's decided the inn makes a suitable setting for his uplifting and inspiring messages."

"I am, dear. I am well aware that the inn is doing very nicely this winter because of Mr. Valence. However, when I mentioned the new guest, I was not referring to one of the seminar attendees."

Cleo smiled wryly. "Let me guess. You're talking about Jason's friend, right?"

"Yes. Are you certain he was a friend of Jason's?"

Cleo glanced at Andromeda in surprise. "He says he is. He certainly knew about Jason having stayed with us from time to time during the past eighteen months. And he knew about the arrangement Jason and I had worked out." Cleo wolfed down the last of the muffin. "At least I think he did. I offered him the same deal, and he took it."

"He's working for you now?"

"Uh-huh."

Andromeda frowned delicately. "I told you when Jason first started to show up around here on the weekends that he was not exactly what he seemed."

"I know, but I liked him. You said you liked him, too. We both agreed we could trust him."

"Well, I knew he was not a threat, of course. In his own way Jason needed us. I am not so certain about this other man."

"You only met him briefly last night."

Daystar swooped down on Cleo before Andromeda could respond. "Saw his car in the parking lot." She hoisted a spatula in a warning manner. "My ex-husband bought a Jaguar like that right before he married his secretary. Your Mr. Fortune is no starving artist, Cleo."

Cleo smiled at her. Daystar was a sturdy, competent-looking woman whose shrewd, no-nonsense eyes reflected her assertive, inquisitive attitude toward everything and everyone. She was the airy, ethereal Andromeda's natural opposite. Cleo had often thought the two made a perfect pair.

"Jason wasn't exactly starving either," Cleo pointed out. "At least not in the literal sense. But he needed a place like Robbins' Nest Inn in order to paint. And he wanted to help out around here."

Andromeda gave her a gentle smile. "You mean he wanted to be part of our extended family."

Cleo shrugged. "Maybe Max Fortune wants the same thing."

"Or perhaps he wants something else," Daystar said darkly.

"I doubt it," Cleo murmured. "Don't forget, I saw him with a toilet plunger in his hand. You learn a lot about a man when you see him in action like that." She popped the last bite of muffin into her mouth. "Besides, what else is there for him around here except the same kind of family thing that Jason found?"

"I don't know," Daystar said. "I'm just suggesting that you be cautious. The fact that he knew Jason does not automatically make Mr. Fortune a member of the family."

Andromeda nodded in agreement. "Daystar is right, dear."

"Don't worry, I'll be careful," Cleo promised.

She was about to pick up the teapot when a flash of awareness made her pause. There had been no telltale sound above the clatter of pans and the hum of conversation that filled the kitchen, but Cleo knew without turning around who was standing in the doorway. A small thrill shot through her, leaving her tingling from head to foot.

Apparently her strange reaction to Max Fortune last night had not been just a curious by-product of the stress she had been under at the time. She was perfectly relaxed this morning, and yet she was experiencing the same unsettling sensation. She took a deep breath and braced herself.

"Good morning, Max." Cleo swung around, pot in hand, and smiled at him. She would not make a fool of herself, she vowed silently. She would be calm and dignified. She struggled to keep her expression limited to one of polite welcome, but inside she was bubbling with the delicious, unfamiliar excitement.

It was clear in the light of the new day that her imagination had not been playing tricks on her. Max Fortune's impact on her senses was devastating. She found herself staring in spite of her determination to be casual and cool.

He was the man in the mirror. She had never seen his face clearly in her dreams, but the moment he had materialized, she had recognized him.

Cleo gave herself a small, imperceptible shake in an effort to free herself from the disorienting sensation that was sweeping through her. She forced herself to concentrate on facts, not fantasy.

Max was obviously in his mid-thirties but definitely not in any danger of going soft. There was a lean, hard quality to his body. His boldly carved face bore a disquieting similarity to the hawk on the handle of his cane.

The subtle fierceness that marked him gleamed clearly in his gray eyes. There was an air of unrelenting watchfulness about Max Fortune, as if he trusted no one and depended on no one. Cleo sensed that this was a man who took nothing for granted. He looked as though he expected to have to fight for whatever he wanted in life.

But the hard-edged, potentially ruthless element in him was overlaid with a tantalizing air of polished civility. It was a powerful, compelling image for Cleo; one that was straight out of the deepest, most secret recesses of her imagination. There was no doubt about it; the well-hidden, carefully contained, very sensual aspect of her nature recognized Max Fortune.

He was the man who lived in the shadows of her secret fantasies.

Perhaps it was not so strange that she knew him on sight, she thought ruefully. After all, she had written a book about him. She just hadn't known his name at the time.

The cane should have had the effect of making Max look at least somewhat vulnerable. Instead it only served to reveal another hard edge. It hinted at pain that had been subdued by the force of sheer willpower and self-control. Cleo found herself wanting to touch and soothe that old anguish in him.

She gripped the handle of the teapot, completely at a loss to explain her reaction to this stranger who had walked in out of the storm last night and made a place for himself near her hearth.

"Good morning." Max examined the kitchen and its unusually garbed staff. His expression showed no particular reaction except mild interest. "Is this where I get breakfast?"

"Definitely." Cleo jerked herself out of the thrall that had enveloped her. "Andromeda can fix you up, can't you, Andromeda?"

"Of course." The tiny bells on the hem of Andromeda's gown chimed as she turned away to put two corn bread muffins on a plate. "There is also muesli with fresh fruit and yogurt over on the counter. Take whatever you want."

Max's gaze was on Cleo. "I'll do that."

Cleo felt a tremor go through her. "Tea?" she asked quickly.

He glanced at the pot in her hand. "Any coffee available?"

"Right over there." Cleo nodded toward the freshly brewed coffee that was sitting on the counter. "Have a seat at the table, and I'll get you a cup."

"Thanks."

Cleo ignored Daystar's speculative frown. She scooped up the coffee pot and another muffin for herself and hurried to follow Max to the nook where the staff of the inn grabbed meals during busy times.

"Don't expect service like this every day," Cleo said lightly as she slid onto the bench on the other side of the table. She poured coffee into a cup. "Around here, everyone fends for himself when the inn is full."

"I'll remember that."

"We're going to be swamped for the next three days with this motivational seminar crowd," Cleo observed.

"I saw the audiovisual equipment being set up in the parlor. What's this seminar stuff all about?"

"Herbert T. Valence's Five Easy Steps to Wealth, Power, and Unlimited Success," Cleo explained.

Max looked up. "There aren't five easy steps to all that."

"No?"

"There's only one step."

Cleo was intrigued. "What's that?"

Max shrugged. "You fight for it. And when you've got what you want, you fight again to defend it."

"Not according to Herbert T. Valence. He says the trick is to think positive and affirm your goals every day. I gather he started giving these seminars a couple of years ago. He's got quite a reputation."

"The man's either a fool or a con artist."

"Mind your tongue." Cleo chuckled. "Thanks to Mr. Valence, I have a full inn. Try a muffin." She tore hers apart, heedless of crumbs. "I've had two already, and I swear this is going to be my last one."

Max picked up a knife and went to work on one of his muffins as if it were an uncut diamond.

Cleo stopped chewing and watched in fascination as he methodically split the muffin in half. Next, he cut off a quarter of the muffin with grave precision.

He put down the knife, picked up a spoon, and dipped it into the honey pot. When he had collected a quantity of the thick, golden stuff, he gave the spoon a deft twist. Not a single drop of honey fell back into the pot or onto the table as he gracefully transferred it to the muffin on his plate.

It was like watching a Borgia or a Medici eat, Cleo thought. One had the feeling that behind the polished manners, there was a sheathed sword tucked politely out of sight.

Max's eyes met Cleo's just as he was about to take a bite. He stopped with the muffin section halfway to his mouth. "Something wrong?"

"No, not at all." Cleo grinned. "It's just that Jason was the only person I ever saw who ate Daystar's muffins so neatly. Most people inhale them."

"I'm sure they're excellent." Max glanced at the women who were preparing breakfast. "Your kitchen staff is a little out of the ordinary."

"I'll say. They're fantastic." Cleo leaned forward and lowered her voice. "Someone's always trying to steal Andromeda and Daystar. Every restaurant owner and inn manager on the coast would kill to get them."

"Where did you find them?"

"I didn't. They found me." Cleo sat back. "They're from the Cosmic Harmony Women's Retreat. The Retreat is about a mile and a half from here, on the other side of the cove. You can see it from your window."

Max looked up from his muffin. "I saw something that looked like an old resort."

"It was at one time. The resort folded. It wasn't the right kind of establishment for this section of the coast. At any rate, after I opened the inn, Andromeda and Daystar decided I needed a first-rate kitchen to attract business. They, on the other hand, needed a stable source of income to run the Retreat. They waved a contract in my face, and I signed."

"Just like that?"

"Sure. I tend to make most decisions on the spur of the moment. For instance, I bought this place within twenty-four hours of looking at it. Of course, if I'd gotten a good look at the antique plumbing I might have hesitated a bit. It gave me nothing but trouble for the first two years. But Benjy wandered into my office one day a year and a half ago looking for a job, and my maintenance problems were solved."

"Until Benjy disappeared last night?"

Cleo frowned. "I wonder where he is. I'm getting a little worried. It's not like him to just up and vanish like this. He and Trisha . . ." The phone rang before Cleo could finish the sentence. She snatched up the kitchen extension that hung on the wall of the nook. "Robbins' Nest Inn."

"Cleo? Thank God. This is Nolan."

" 'Morning, Nolan. A little early for you to be calling, isn't it?" Cleo relaxed back against the wall and braced one foot on the bench. She saw Max's gaze go to her bright, gold-toned sneakers. She thought she detected disapproval in his cold gray eyes.

"Sorry." Nolan's voice was uncharacteristically sharp. "Cleo, I need to see you as soon as possible."

She groaned. "I told you I couldn't have dinner with you until the weekend. I've got an inn full of guests."

"Forget dinner. I want to talk to you right away. This is important."

Cleo took her foot down off the bench and straightened. She had never heard this particular edge in Nolan's voice. "Is something wrong?"

"You tell me."

"You're not making a whole lot of sense here, Nolan."

"Damn it, Cleo, I have to talk to you."

"Take it easy," Cleo said soothingly. "We'll talk. Do you want to come by the inn now?"

"No," he said swiftly. "I can't do that. Look, can you meet me down at the beach?"

"Nolan, this is February, not August. It's cold outside. Why do you want to meet at the beach?" Cleo was acutely aware that Max was listening to every word.

"The beach, Cleo. Fifteen minutes. You owe me that much, at least."

"I *owe* you? Nolan, have you gone nuts? I don't owe you a thing."

"You do now. I'll see you in a few minutes."

"Wait a second, I've got the breakfast crowd to deal with. I can't just dash out of here."

"This won't take long," Nolan said. "And it's really important. It affects both our futures." He hung up the phone.

Cleo made a face as she replaced the receiver. "He sounds a trifle upset. Guess I'd better go see what he wants."

"Who's Nolan?" Max picked up the knife again and started in on the second muffin.

"Nolan Hildebrand is the part-time mayor of Harmony Cove. I think he has bigger political aspirations, but I try not to hold that against him. I mean, somebody has to go into politics, right? At any rate, I've been sort of seeing him for about five months."

Max's gaze was hooded. "Sort of seeing him?"

Cleo blushed. "You know. Dating him. It's not like either one of us has a lot of choice around Harmony Cove. It's a very small town, in case you didn't notice."

"I noticed."

"Well, anyhow, Nolan and I go out to dinner a couple of times a week when I'm not too busy here at the inn." Cleo didn't know why she was feeling awkward. Perhaps it was because Nolan was one of only a tiny handful of men she had dated since the death of her parents four years earlier.

It had taken a long time to get over the searing trauma that had shattered her life the day she had walked into the blood-spattered living room of her parents' home. It was that same terrible room that she still saw in the occasional nightmares that brought her awake in a cold sweat.

The authorities had called it a case of murder-suicide. For some reason no one could explain, perhaps in the heat of a passionate quarrel, successful businessman Edward Robbins had killed his wife and then turned the gun on himself.

Cleo had never been able to accept the reality of it. Six months of therapy had done little to help. She was gradually able to deal with the loss, but not the reasons behind it. They made no sense to her and never would.

She had been an only child, and she alone knew how deep the bond had been between her parents. It was not inconceivable to her that one might have chosen to follow the other into the grave, but it was impossible to believe that one would have murdered the other. The authorities had explained that such things happened, even in the best of families.

When she had eventually surfaced from the state of numbed shock into which she had been plunged on that day of horror, Cleo had found herself alone in the world. She had been twenty-three at the time.

Slowly, painfully, she had begun putting her life back together. She had gone to the coast frequently during that period, drawn by the eternal, soul-soothing appeal of the ocean. It was there she had discovered the Cosmic Harmony Women's Retreat and the strength to rebuild her world.

With the money left from the trust fund her parents had established for her, Cleo had purchased the old Victorian inn that sat on the bluff high above Harmony Cove. Slowly but surely, she had gathered a clan of friends around her.

It was a loose-knit group, and some of the members changed from time to time, but there was a central core that consisted of Cleo, Andromeda, Daystar, Sylvia Gordon, and her son, Sammy. Trisha Briggs and Benjy Atkins had both been added to the clan somewhere along the line. So had Jason Curzon. An extended family had been created, albeit a nontraditional one.

Although she had needed the closeness of her friends, Cleo had felt no need for a lover. She did not think she was cold or frigid, but there was no denying that a part of her seemed to have gone into hibernation somewhere deep inside her. Her therapist had suggested that Cleo had become deeply wary of intimacy because of the manner in which the close bond between her parents had been so shockingly severed.

On the one hand Cleo longed for the sort of relationship her parents had enjoyed, the therapist explained, but on the other hand she was fearful of what might lie at the heart of it. Only a dark sickness of the mind could have made Edward Robbins turn the gun on his beloved wife. The therapist was convinced that Cleo now feared that such a powerful love might be based on an equally powerful and very dangerous obsession.

The only thing Cleo knew for certain was that she could not give herself to a man unless she loved him the way her mother had loved her father. Cleo understood that for her it would have to be a grand passion or nothing at all.

She had been dating Nolan Hildebrand for some time now on a casual basis, but she had not gone to bed with him. She knew she never would.

Max watched her intently. "Did Jason know about Hildebrand?"

Cleo was surprised by the question. "Of course. I told you, Nolan and I have been seeing each other for quite a while."

Max put down the last, unfinished bit of muffin and folded his arms on the table. He leaned forward, his eyes cold. "Are you telling me that Jason didn't mind sharing you with the mayor of Harmony Cove?"

"Sharing me?" Cleo blinked, astonished. "What on earth are you talking about?"

"You know damn well what I'm talking about. I knew Jason for twelve years, and I know that he was not the kind of man who would share his woman with another man."

A warm tide of embarrassment flooded through Cleo as she finally understood what he was talking about. "Are you crazy? Jason and I were friends."

"I know."

"Good friends. Not lovers. For heaven's sake, Max, he was old enough to be my grandfather."

"So? You wouldn't be the first woman to latch onto an older man in hopes of getting your hands on some of his money."

"So that's what this is all about." Anger surged through her, driving out the embarrassment. "For your information, Jason didn't have much money. He never even managed to sell one of his paintings. He was an old man who was living on a pension and Social Security."

"Is that right?"

Cleo slid out of the booth and got to her feet. "I don't believe this. I thought you were a friend of Jason's. I thought you knew all about him and about his family here at the inn."

"Are you telling me you weren't Jason's mistress?"

"I don't think I'm going to tell you a damn thing, Mr. Fortune. I'm afraid you'll have to excuse me. I've got to race off and meet another one of my many lovers. When I get back, I'll expect to find you checked out." Cleo spun around on her heel and stalked out of the kitchen.

She refused to glance back over her shoulder as she left the room. But she could feel Max's cold eyes on her all the way to the door.

Fifteen minutes later, still seething from the small but extremely unpleasant scene in the kitchen, Cleo parked her car in the unpaved lot above the beach. Nolan Hildebrand's Jeep was the only other vehicle in sight. Few people came to the beach at this time of year.

A cold, rain-soaked blast of wind struck Cleo as she got out of her car. It tore her hair free from its precarious moorings and whipped it into a froth around her face. There was a storm boiling out over the ocean. It would arrive within the hour. She intended to be back at the inn by the time it hit shore.

And Max Fortune had better be gone when she got there, she told herself. She shook her head in disgust, unable to believe that she had misjudged him so badly. Usually her instincts about people were highly accurate.

The Jeep door opened, and Nolan climbed out. He hurried toward her, the collar of his leather jacket turned up to shield his neck from the wind. The brisk breeze ruffled his light brown hair, accenting his handsome features. He carried a brown paper sack in one hand.

Cleo contemplated him with a sense of affection. She had known from the beginning that Nolan was not fated to be the great love of her life. At the start of their relationship, he had made a few determined attempts to seduce her, but when she had declined the invitations to his bed, he had seemed oddly content.

Nolan was a pleasant dinner companion, and Cleo genuinely admired his efforts as town mayor. He worked hard at the part-time position while practicing law at the small firm his father had established.

"I was afraid you wouldn't show up." Nolan came to a halt in front of her. He jammed one hand into the pocket of his jacket and regarded her with troubled eyes.

A flicker of real concern went through Cleo. Something was obviously very wrong. "What's this all about, Nolan?"

"I just want to know one thing." Nolan thrust the paper sack at her. "Did you write this?"

"What in the world?" But Cleo could feel the familiar shape of a book inside the sack. Her blood stilled.

She opened the bag and glanced inside. She found herself gazing at a familiar stark white cover. The title, *The Mirror,* was embossed on it in the same shade of white. A length of scarlet ribbon curling evocatively across the bottom of the white cover was the only note of color.

"Oh, dear," Cleo murmured.

"Did you write that?" Nolan bit out.

"Well, yes. Yes, I did, as a matter of fact. It was published a couple of months ago." She smiled tentatively. "My first book, you know."

"You published it under a pen name?" Nolan asked, sounding as though he wanted to be very certain of his facts.

"Yes." Cleo gingerly reclosed the bag. She cleared her throat. "It's, uh, considered a rather fine example of women's erotica, you know."

"Erotica."

"It actually got very well reviewed in several literary magazines and one or two feminist journals."

Nolan gave her an outraged look of disbelief. "It's porn, that's what it is."

"Oh, no, definitely not." Cleo clutched the book protectively to her breast. "I told you, it's erotica. There's a big difference."

"Not to the media, damn it. Not to every right-wing newspaper columnist who decides I'm too liberal on First Amendment issues. Not to the conservative, small-town voters of Harmony Cove."

Cleo bit her lip. "I don't understand."

"Christ, Cleo." Nolan ran an exasperated hand through his wind-tossed hair. "I'm starting to build a political career. Don't you know what this kind of thing could do to me?"

"I wrote the book, not you."

"Don't you see? It's bad enough that I've been dating you. What if we'd gotten married? I'd have been ripped to shreds as the husband of a porn queen."

Cleo stared at him. "You never said anything about marriage."

Nolan scowled. "Well, I was starting to think about it."

"Nolan, that's ridiculous. We're not in love, and you know it."

"I was beginning to think we would have made a good team." Nolan gave her an aggrieved look. "You know what it's like for a politician these days. The media dissects everything under a microscope. Your background seemed perfect for a wife."

"Perfect?"

"No scandals, no radical politics, no previous marriages."

"And a nice income of my own from the inn?" Cleo suggested dryly.

"Money had nothing to do with it," he said with righteous indignation. "It was your character that attracted me. Hell, I even know for a fact that you don't sleep around. The only thing that bothered me a bit was your friendship with those weird women at Cosmic Harmony."

"My friends are not weird." Anger flared inside Cleo. "You think I've got a pristine past? What about my parents?"

"What about them? I know they're dead."

"But you don't know how they died, do you? I never told you that."

Nolan scowled. "I got the impression they were in a car accident."

"That's the impression I've let most of the people around here have. It's easier to explain than the truth."

Nolan looked wary. "What the hell's the truth?"

Cleo lifted her chin. "They say my father shot my mother and then killed himself. How's that for a skeleton in the closet? Do you think the media would have ignored a juicy tidbit like that?"

Nolan's shock was obvious. "Are you serious? You should have told me."

"Why? I have a right to my privacy. Besides, it's hardly the sort of thing one discusses over dinner at the Crab Pot Restaurant." Cleo pushed her glasses higher up on her nose and took a steadying breath.

She was furious with herself for having allowed Nolan to goad her into telling him the painful facts of her parents' death. It was something she rarely talked about with anyone.

"We might have been able to finesse the stuff about your parents, although it would have been difficult. But we'd never have been able to explain that damn book you wrote." Nolan's gaze turned bitter. "You really had me fooled."

"Sorry about that. I didn't know you were considering me for a position as a politician's wife. You might have mentioned it earlier. I would have told you all the lurid details of my past right up front."

"Is that right?"

"Damn right." She widened her eyes in mocking derision. "You don't think I'd actually want to be a politician's wife, do you?"

Nolan's face reddened. "Look, I'm sorry about this, Cleo. And about your folks. About everything. Hell, I know I'm not handling this very well. It's just that the business with that damned book came as a shock."

"I can see that."

"Look at it from my point of view," Nolan pleaded. "I didn't know you'd actually published anything, let alone a book like *that.*" He looked at the paper sack she was holding as if it contained a snake.

"I didn't tell you about *The Mirror* because I didn't want anyone outside the family to know that I'd written it."

He snorted. "I'm not surprised."

"I'm not ashamed of it," she stormed. "It's just that this book was a very personal thing for me. I knew no one around here would understand. I didn't want the kid who works at Bennington's Drug Store leering at me every time I went in to buy shampoo. I didn't need the attendant at the gas station making snide remarks. I didn't want to have to explain it to Patty Loftins down at the beauty shop."

"I can sure as hell understand that." Nolan turned away to gaze out over the choppy ocean. "Patty's got a mouth the size of the Grand Canyon."

Cleo looked down at the brown paper sack she was clutching. It was impossible to explain *The Mirror* to anyone. It was too intimate. Too much a part of her most secret self. She had poured all her most private fantasies into the book, baring her deeply sensual soul.

The passion that was trapped inside her had combined with the aching loneliness to form a searing account of a woman on a quest for emotional intimacy and physical release. The tale had literally cascaded out of her a year and a half earlier. The book had been published a month ago.

The critics had, generally speaking, responded very favorably to *The Mirror.* Only Cleo knew that none of them had really understood it. They had thought the book was a work of autoeroticism, that the female narrator was locked in a fantasy of startling intimacy with the masculine elements of her own nature.

They did not comprehend the significance of the man in the mirror.

Writing *The Mirror* had been a cathartic experience for Cleo. It had also taught her that she wanted to keep on writing, although she knew she would never again need to write a book like *The Mirror.*

"I wish I could explain this to you," she said quietly. "*The Mirror* was a one-of-a-kind thing for me."

"I should hope so. I read some of that stuff last night. I couldn't believe you'd written it. You wouldn't even go to bed with me." He shot her a fulminating look. "Just as well, I guess. I'd never have been able to compete with the fantasy in that damned book. No man could. That woman in the book is making love to herself. She doesn't need a man, does she?"

"Nolan, you don't understand."

"Sure I do. Now I know why you wouldn't sleep with me. It wasn't because you were so damned pure, was it? It was because you've decided no mere male can give you what you can get from your own imagination and a good vibrator."

"Stop it right now." Cleo took a step back. "I don't want to hear another word about this. I told you, you don't understand."

"I understand what that book could have done to my chances for getting elected to the state legislature next fall. It would have turned me into a laughingstock in the press."

Cleo had had enough. "Relax. You're saved. As far as I'm concerned, we never have to see each other again unless our shopping carts collide in the aisles of the grocery store."

"Damn it, Cleo, I didn't mean to have it end this way. It's just that I was really getting serious about our relationship."

"Don't worry. You've had the good sense to break things off before I could do any damage to your brilliant political career."

"It wasn't just that," he muttered. "I liked you, Cleo. I mean, I really liked you."

Cleo sighed. "I liked you too, Nolan. Believe it or not, I still do. Heck, I'll probably even vote for you when you run for office next fall."

"Thanks." He suddenly seemed at a loss for words. "Look, I won't say anything about that book to anyone else."

"I'd appreciate that."

"Well, I guess that's that, then. No hard feelings, huh?"

"Sure. Right. No hard feelings." Cleo turned around and started toward her car. Halfway there, a thought struck her. She turned back. "There's just one thing I'd like to know."

"What's that?"

"How did you find out about *The Mirror?*"

His mouth thinned. "Someone left it in my mailbox along with a note."

A chill went through Cleo. "A note?"

"Yeah. I left it in the book."

Cleo nodded and walked on to her car. She opened the door and got inside. For a moment she sat behind the wheel, watching as Nolan started up his Jeep and took off down the narrow road toward town.

When the other vehicle was out of sight, Cleo slowly opened the paper sack. She gazed at the cover of *The Mirror* for a long time, and then she opened the book and took out the folded sheet of paper inside. The note was brief and to the point.

> The Queen of the Nile is The Queen of Filth. A man with an important future ahead of him cannot afford to be seen with a whore.

The tone of the note was uncomfortably familiar. It bore a remarkable resemblance to the anonymous letter Cleo had received last month.

After the initial shock of receiving it, Cleo had dismissed the letter. It had been forwarded through her publisher, after all, and she had assured herself that the sender had no way of knowing her real identity.

But now she had to confront the fact that someone not only knew her identity as the author of *The Mirror,* he or she was apparently determined to punish her for having written it. And that person knew who she was and where she was.

Cleo's hand shook as she turned the key in the ignition. She suddenly wanted to get back to the safety of the inn as quickly as possible.

Three

Max paused beside the open door of the large parlor. The quaintly furnished room was filled with seminar attendees. At the front of the parlor a man with silver, blow-dried hair, a chunky gold watch, and a massive diamond ring held forth. He was wearing a jacket and a pair of handmade leather shoes that Max knew had cost at least as much as the ones he, himself, owned. There was obviously money to be made in the motivational seminar business, Max decided.

"My name is Herbert T. Valence, and you know something? I am incredible." Valence radiated intensity. He practically bounced on his toes as he gazed expectantly around the room. "I am amazing. I can do anything I want to do. And you know what? So can you. Say it after me, everyone. *I am incredible.*"

"I am incredible," the audience repeated as one.

"I am amazing," Valence said. He looked as if he were about to burst with excitement and enthusiasm.

"I am amazing."

"I can do anything I want to do," Valence prompted.

"I can do anything I want to do."

"The power of positive thinking is literally out of this world," Valence announced with a triumphant smile. "It's pure energy. It's raw fuel, waiting to be poured into your creative engines."

Max watched with interest as Valence seemed to levitate back across the room to his wall chart.

"I am here to teach you the secret of having it all," Valence told the audience. "Money, power, success, and self-esteem. They can be yours by following my simple Five-Step Program. You want to wear clothes like mine? Drive a Porsche like mine? You'll be able to do just that when you've finished my program. I guarantee it."

Max lost interest and walked on toward the lobby. He stopped in front of the first of the series of seascapes that hung there and stood looking into it for a while.

There was nothing to see beyond the surface image of a storm-tossed sea. The technique was poor, the design was static, and the colors were dull. It was the work of an amateur. Jason had been right in his own estimate of himself as a painter.

"There you are, Max. I've been looking for you." Sylvia Gordon waved from the office doorway. "There was a phone call for you a few minutes ago. I rang your room, but there was no answer so I took a message."

Max turned away from the seascape he had been studying and walked over to the front desk. "Thank you."

"No problem." Sylvia smiled. "Sorry I couldn't find you when the call came through." She handed him a piece of paper. "Whoever she is, she sounded very anxious to get hold of you."

Max glanced at the note. *Kimberly called. She wants you to return her call as soon as possible. Very important.* The *very important* had been underlined three times.

"Just a business matter," Max said. "It's not really important."

He crumpled up the note and tossed it into the wastebasket, just as he had the half dozen other urgent messages he had received from Kimberly Curzon during the past month. He wondered absently how she had managed to track him down here at the coast.

"Is Cleo back yet?" he asked.

"No." Sylvia glanced at the wastebasket where the note had disappeared. When she looked at Max again there was speculation in her eyes. "But I expect her any minute. She won't be away long. Not with this crowd filling up the inn."

A roll of thunder drew Max's attention to the window. It had grown dark outside. The blustery wind was howling beneath the eaves. The rain would hit at any minute. Even as Max watched, a shaft of lightning arced across the sky.

"Another storm," he said.

Sylvia shrugged. "It's that time of year. Listen, I wanted to thank you for finding Sammy's duck last night. He really treasures that thing."

"It was no problem."

"Lucky Ducky means a lot to him because Jason gave it to him." Sylvia smiled tremulously. "Sammy's at that age when he's looking for a male role model. You know how it is."

"Sammy said his father's lost. He says he went off to look for himself."

Sylvia grimaced. "Children take things so literally, don't they? But he's not entirely wrong. Doug came home from the office one day and announced that he couldn't handle the responsibility of a wife and child. He said our marriage had been a terrible mistake. He packed up his things and left. Sammy was only a year old at the time."

"I take it your ex doesn't come around to visit Sammy?"

Sylvia shook her head. "Doug went back east, where he apparently decided he was ready for responsibility after all. The last I heard he had married again and started a new family. He's never contacted Sammy and me since, except through his attorney. He does occasionally remember to pay child support."

The lights went out just as another flash of lightning lit up the darkened sky.

"Darn," Sylvia muttered. "There goes the power again. I hope it's just a blown fuse this time. Last month a tree went down across the lines, and we were without electricity for hours."

Max seized the opportunity. "I'll check the fuse box, if you like."

Sylvia gave him a grateful look. "Thanks. Hang on a second." She reached under the front desk and produced a flashlight. "We keep one handy, as you can see. This sort of thing happens a lot around here."

Herbert T. Valence stormed out of the parlor just as Sylvia handed the large flashlight to Max. His expression of intense enthusiasm had been replaced by a look of intense agitation.

"What is going on around here?" Valence demanded. "I'm trying to run a video in there. What's happened to the power?"

"I'm going to check on it," Max said mildly. He took the flashlight from Sylvia.

Valence scowled. "Well, hurry up about it, will you? I've got a seminar to teach. I've got a reputation to maintain, you know. I can't do my best work without my audiovisual equipment."

"Try being creative," Max said. "Just think positive. Positive thinking is the fuel that runs the engine of creativity, remember?"

Sylvia turned away, but not before Max saw that she was struggling to bite back a laugh. Valence's face tightened with outrage.

"Is that supposed to be funny?" Valence asked coldly.

"I'm just giving you some of your own advice." Max stepped around him, heading for the basement stairs. "And I'm not even going to charge you for it."

"Now see here," Valence sputtered, "I don't have to put up with that sort of rudeness."

The lobby door opened at that moment. Max glanced back over his shoulder as wet wind and a disheveled-looking Cleo swept into the room.

Cleo was clutching a brown paper sack protectively under one arm. He saw the strained expression on her face as she swung around to close the door. Apparently the meeting with Hildebrand had not gone well.

"Whew." Cleo shut the door and ran her fingers through her wet hair. "It's pouring out there. Everything all right in here, Sylvia?"

"No, everything is not all right," Valence said before Sylvia could respond. "The power is off. I want it fixed immediately. I'm trying to run a seminar, as you well know, Ms. Robbins. I've got a reputation for flawless performance, and I simply cannot work without electricity."

Max watched as Cleo summoned up her innkeeper's soothing smile. "Yes, of course, Mr. Valence. We'll get someone on it right away."

"I'm already on it." Max held up the flashlight.

Cleo's gaze flashed to his face. "I thought you'd be gone by now."

"Whatever gave you that idea? You just hired me."

Cleo looked as if she badly wanted to respond to that, but Valence's presence forced her to restrain herself. "What do you think you're doing?"

"I'm going down to the basement to check the fuse box. Any objections?" Max waited politely.

Cleo set her jaw. "I'll come with you."

"I think I can handle this on my own," Max said.

"I said I'll come with you." Cleo managed another serene smile for Valence. "Just give us a few minutes, Mr. Valence. I'm sure we'll have everything back under control very soon."

"I should hope so," Valence muttered. "My time is extremely valuable. I can't afford to waste it sitting around waiting for someone to turn on the electricity." He shot one last annoyed glance at Max as he stalked back down the hall to the parlor.

Max watched Valence disappear. "Did you know he's incredible?" he said to Cleo. "Also amazing."

"What on earth are you talking about? Here, give me that." She snatched the flashlight out of his hand and strode down the hall to the door that opened on to the basement stairs. "Why aren't you gone?"

"There are a number of reasons." Max opened the door and surveyed the inky depths of a vast basement. "One of which is that I haven't apologized for the small misunderstanding we had at breakfast."

"It was not a small misunderstanding." Cleo switched on the flashlight and started down the basement stairs. She still had the paper sack tucked under her arm. "You were rude, crude, and obnoxious."

"You may be right." Max's cane tapped softly on each step as he followed Cleo downstairs. "However, I'd like the chance to apologize for assuming you were Jason's mistress."

"A *gold-digging* mistress." Cleo reached the foot of the stairs and swept the beam of light around the crowded basement.

"All right," Max said patiently. "I apologize for assuming you were his *gold-digging* mistress."

"Okay, you've apologized. Now you can leave."

Max took a tight grip on his hawk-headed cane. She was not going to get rid of him this easily. She still had his Amos Luttrells. "I'm afraid I can't leave just yet."

Cleo crossed the room to the circuit-breaker panel. "Why not?"

"I told you last night. I need the arrangement you're offering. I don't have another job."

She turned away and concentrated on opening the panel cover. "That's not my problem."

Max could tell that she was wavering. He decided to change tactics. "What happened with Hildebrand?"

Cleo flipped a switch, and the overhead light came on. Her smile was grim. "Nolan came to the same conclusion about me that you did. He thinks I'm a fallen woman. As a budding politician with a career in the White House ahead of him, he can't afford to be associated with the likes of me."

Max was surprised by the jolt of anger that went through him. He studied Cleo's set face. "This was a sudden conclusion on Hildebrand's part?"

"Very sudden."

"What prompted it?"

"I can't imagine." Cleo closed the panel door and switched off the flashlight. "You'll have to excuse me. I've got a lot of things to do, and you've got a long drive ahead of you."

Max positioned himself directly in her path. "Cleo, wait. I meant what I said. I'm sorry about the misunderstanding, and I don't have anywhere else to go. I'd appreciate it if you'd let me stay for a while. I'll earn my keep."

She hesitated. The uncertainty was plain in her eyes. "Look, I'm sorry about your situation, but you really can't expect me to give you the same arrangement I gave Jason. Not after what you said this morning."

"Jason was your friend," Max said quietly. "He was my friend, too. What did you expect me to think when he talked about a mysterious woman named Cleo? He was on his deathbed. He didn't have the strength to give me a detailed explanation of just how you fit into his life. All I knew was that he—" Max broke off, searching for the right words. "Cared for you."

Cleo's expression softened. She lowered her eyes and was silent for a long minute. Finally, she met his gaze and said, "All right. For the sake of our mutual friendship with Jason, I'll let you stay."

"Thanks," Max said. It had been easier than he'd anticipated. The lady was obviously a sucker for a hard luck story.

"But only through this long weekend," Cleo added, just as if she'd read his mind and suspected she'd been had. "There's still no sign of Benjy, and I could use an extra hand around here for the next three days. But I'll expect you to leave on Tuesday. Understood?"

"I understand."

Three days was a long time, Max thought. A lot could happen. He'd been known to make and break multimillion-dollar deals in a period of three days. He'd once orchestrated in less than three days the ransom and rescue of an entire contingent of Curzon executives who had been kidnapped by terrorists. With any luck he would find his Luttrells in the next three days.

And if not, he'd find a way to stay on longer at Robbins' Nest Inn.

Herbert T. Valence was right. The trick was to think positive.

Cleo glanced into the lounge around nine o'clock that evening. Max and Sylvia were pouring after-dinner coffee and sherry for the inn guests. A pleasant fire blazed on the hearth, creating a scene of warm contentment. A low murmur of conversation wafted across the room.

Cleo had been chiding herself for her lack of willpower all afternoon. She knew she should have sent Max packing as soon as she returned from the meeting with Nolan. She had told herself she would kick him out if he was still hanging around the place. But somehow Max had managed to make her feel sorry for him.

She could not escape the feeling that she had been manipulated.

"You'll have to admit that Max adds a certain style to the place," Sylvia observed as she paused beside Cleo. "Jason used to have that same aristocratic air when he poured coffee and sherry. The guests love it."

"He acts like he owns the place," Cleo muttered. "Look at him. Every inch the gracious lord of the manor."

"Face it, Cleo. Put a man like Max to digging a ditch, and he'd manage to make it look like he owned the ditch and a hundred thousand acres surrounding it."

"Maybe he does. He drives a Jaguar. And those clothes he's wearing didn't come from any bargain basement."

"He's trying to be helpful," Sylvia said. "He's done everything you asked him to do this afternoon. He even hauled logs in for the fire, which was probably not an easy task with that cane of his."

Cleo winced as a shaft of guilt lanced through her. She sincerely regretted having asked Max to fetch the firewood. The truth was, she hadn't even considered his bad leg when she'd issued the order. Something about Max made it all too easy to forget his cane and everything it implied. Max simply did not look as if he had any weaknesses.

"There's something about him that bothers me," Cleo grumbled.

"Like what?"

"I'm not sure," Cleo admitted. She hesitated. "He thought I was Jason's mistress."

Sylvia glanced at her in surprise and then grinned. "No kidding?"

"It's not funny."

"Yes it is. Do you know what your problem is? You've been in a lousy mood ever since you returned from seeing Nolan."

"Nolan thinks I'm a porn queen."

Sylvia's mouth fell open. "What?"

"He found out that I wrote *The Mirror.*"

Sylvia stared at her. "No one knows you wrote it except members of the family. I didn't tell a soul, I swear it, Cleo. I can't believe anyone else did, either."

"I know. Don't worry about it. I guess the secret was bound to leak out sooner or later."

Sylvia frowned. "I know how important it was to you to maintain your anonymity with that book."

"It's such a personal thing," Cleo said. "I won't mind people knowing I wrote *A Fine Vengeance.* But *The Mirror* has too much of me inside it."

"I understand," Sylvia said gently.

Cleo shifted restlessly. "I told Nolan that I don't want to deal with the snide remarks people will make, but the truth is, I don't want to deal with their rude curiosity. I had too much of that kind of thing after my parents died. People asked me the most awful, personal questions about what it had been like to find them—" Cleo broke off abruptly. "There's no telling what kind of questions they'd ask about *The Mirror.*"

Sylvia put a comforting arm around her. "It's all right, Cleo. Take it easy. The most important question at the moment is, who told Nolan?"

"I don't know," Cleo admitted. "Someone put a copy of the book into his mailbox, along with a note saying I'd written *The Mirror.* The note also said that I'd make a very unsuitable wife for a man with political ambitions."

"My God, that's downright weird. No wonder you've been upset all afternoon. What did Nolan say?"

Cleo smiled wryly. "He said I was no longer a viable candidate for the position of Mrs. Nolan Hildebrand. Said my pornographic past could seriously jeopardize his political career. He hoped I'd understand why he was dumping me."

"Why, that little slimeball," Sylvia muttered. "I trust you told him to take a long walk off a short pier?"

"It's over, and it really doesn't matter. My relationship with Nolan never amounted to much in the first place." Cleo met Sylvia's worried gaze. "I don't want the rest of the family to know about the note. It would only upset everyone."

Sylvia nodded in agreement. "All right. I won't mention it. But what about Nolan? Won't he tell everyone you wrote that book?"

Cleo smiled wryly. "I doubt it. He doesn't want anyone to know he associated, however briefly, with a woman of doubtful virtue."

"No offense, Cleo, because I know you liked him, but the guy's a jerk. He's probably got a brilliant political career ahead of him."

Cleo started to respond and stopped short when she saw Sammy running toward them down the hall. The little boy was dressed in his pajamas. He grasped Lucky Ducky firmly in one small fist.

"What are you doing up, honey?" Sylvia asked in concern. "You're supposed to be asleep."

"Can't sleep." Sammy clung to his mother's hand and pressed close to her leg.

"A bad dream?" Cleo asked gently.

"No." Sammy hugged Lucky Ducky close. "Trisha's crying."

"She is?" Cleo frowned. Trisha slept in the room next to Sammy's.

"Won't stop." Sammy turned his face into Sylvia's skirt.

"I'll go up and see what's wrong," Cleo said. "Don't worry about her, Sammy. I'm sure she'll be fine."

Sammy nodded but did not raise his head. Sylvia picked him up and hugged him tightly. "Cleo will talk to her, honey. Everything will be okay."

"Trisha's probably unhappy because Benjy's gone," Cleo said. She exchanged a glance with Sylvia. "Keep an eye on things here."

"Right," Sylvia said. "Max and I can handle the lounge crowd."

Sammy brightened suddenly as he caught sight of Max behind the bar. "There's Max. Hi, Max." He waved Lucky Ducky in greeting.

Max glanced toward the door. His gaze went to Sammy and then to Cleo. He put down the bottle of sherry he had been wielding and walked over to join the small group in the doorway.

"Something wrong?" he asked quietly.

"Trisha's crying," Sammy explained. "Cleo's going to go make her feel better."

"I see." Max watched Cleo intently. "Do you think it's serious?"

"From Trisha's point of view, yes," Cleo said. "She's worried about Benjy. There's been no word from him. I'll be right back."

Cleo turned away and hurried toward the back stairs. She was not surprised by the announcement that Trisha was in tears. She had been concerned about her since last night, when they had all discovered that Benjy had vanished.

Trisha's room was on the third floor. She had moved in two years earlier when she had taken the job at Robbins' Nest Inn. Trisha and Benjy had been drawn together from the moment they had met. Cleo knew they had a lot in common. Too much, perhaps. Both came from badly mangled, nonsupportive families. They had become close friends within the framework of Cleo's extended clan. About six months ago, Cleo knew, they had become lovers.

Cleo had watched the inevitable romance spring up between Trisha and Benjy with some misgivings. She was not at all certain that either of them could cope with the responsibilities of a committed relationship, yet she knew that was exactly what both desperately wanted. There had been an odd sense of fate about the pair. It was as if they were two lost waifs clinging to each other in a storm.

Cleo stopped in front of Trisha's door and knocked softly. "Trisha? It's me, Cleo."

"Cleo?" Trisha's voice was muffled. "I'm in bed. Please go away."

"Trisha, you know I can't do that. Sammy says you've been crying. Let me in. We'll talk."

"I don't want to talk."

"Not even about Benjy?"

"Especially not about Benjy." Trisha suddenly burst into wracking sobs.

Cleo couldn't stand it any longer. "Let me in, Trisha, or I'll use the master key."

There was a moment of painful silence. Then the door opened slowly to reveal Trisha's tear-blotched face.

"Oh, Trisha," Cleo whispered. She opened her arms.

"I know why he left," Trisha wailed. She flung herself into Cleo's comforting arms. "It was because of me."

"Of course it wasn't because of you." Cleo patted Trisha's shoulder. "Benjy's got problems of his own, you know that. He's got a lot to deal with."

"I know," Trisha sobbed. "And I gave him one problem too many."

"Trisha, it's not your fault that Benjy left."

"Yes, it is," Trisha said in a choked voice. "I'm pregnant."

Cleo closed her eyes briefly, her worst fears confirmed. "Oh, Lord."

"I told Benjy, and he couldn't handle it. That's why he left. Cleo, what am I going to do? I'm so scared."

"It's all right," Cleo said quietly. "Everything's going to be all right. You've got family now, remember? You're not alone."

It was nearly midnight before Cleo wearily made her way to the tower room on the third floor. She had chosen her small sanctuary with care immediately after she had moved into the inn.

Her private quarters were tucked away out of sight of the guests' rooms. Her small suite in the tower afforded privacy and a view of the sea. There were times when Cleo badly needed both. Being surrounded by family and inn guests was all very well most of the time, but there were occasions when Cleo needed the protective solitude of her own rooms.

She unlocked the door, her mind still on Trisha's unhappy situation, and let herself into the lovingly overstuffed domicile. It was furnished, as was the rest of the inn, in the most flowery expression of Victorian style. Every item, from the chintz wallpaper and the canopied bed to the ceramic clock on the table, had been carefully chosen by Cleo.

She flipped the switch on the wall, leaving the door still open behind her. The bedside lamp cast a warm glow over the frilly white pillows arranged on the bed.

The light revealed something else on the bed: a length of red satin ribbon curled like a scarlet snake on one pillow.

Cleo stared at the ribbon in stunned shock. She suddenly felt lightheaded. Her fingers, still clutching the doorknob, started to shake.

"Cleo?" Max materialized behind her in the open doorway, looming over her. "I've been looking for you. I wanted to talk to you before you went to bed."

"Not now," she got out in a hoarse whisper. She could not take her eyes off the red satin ribbon.

"What the hell?" Without apology, Max shouldered his way past her into the room. He swept the surroundings with a single glance and then swung around to face her. "What's wrong?"

"Please," she whispered. "Go away."

"You look like you've just seen a ghost."

"Go away," she hissed.

Max ignored the command. Instead he calmly closed the door. "Don't faint. I'm no good with fainting women." He put an arm around Cleo and pulled her tightly against his chest.

"I'm not going to faint. I've never fainted in my life." Cleo wanted to resist the compelling heat of his body, but it was soaking into her, driving out the chill that had gripped her a moment earlier. She stood there, leaning against him for a few minutes.

The man in the mirror.

Eventually she started to relax. Max felt solid and strong and he smelled good. Cleo inhaled the enticing combination of soap and maleness. She had never before found herself captivated by a man's scent, but Max's fascinated her. Surreptitiously she tried to bury her nose against his chest.

"Are you okay?" Max asked.

The question broke the delicate thrall that had begun to form around Cleo. Embarrassed, she raised her head, straightened her glasses, and pushed herself away from him. "I think so. Sorry about this. I was a little startled by something. I'm okay now."

Slowly he released her. His eyes never left her face. "What was that all about?"

Cleo knew she should keep her mouth shut. But her defenses were down because of the shock of seeing the ribbon on the pillow and because of the way Max had held her. She knew she owed him absolutely no explanations. But she suddenly needed to talk to someone. If Jason had been there, she would have told him the whole story.

Max had been Jason's friend. Max was not a stranger. Not really.

"That ribbon shouldn't be there." Cleo didn't know where to start. She went over to the bed and stood looking down at the coiled length of satin. "Someone put it there."

"A gift from Sammy?"

"No." Cleo hugged herself. "God, no. Sammy wouldn't know anything about the significance of a red satin ribbon left on a pillow."

"But you do?" Max did not move.

"It's a scene out of a book I wrote." Cleo shivered. Then she spun around and went to the bookshelf. She took down the copy of *The Mirror* that Nolan had given to her that morning. "It's from this. Chapter three."

Max took the book and glanced at the cover. "You wrote this? It says the author's name is Elizabeth Bird."

"That's me. Elizabeth Bird is a pen name. Until recently it's been a deep, dark secret known only to members of the family. But today it has become painfully obvious that someone else knows it."

"Why did you try to keep yourself anonymous?"

Cleo watched his face. "Take a look at the book."

Max flipped open the cover and scanned the inside flap. He looked up after a moment, his eyes unreadable. "You write women's erotica? I thought you wrote romantic-suspense."

Cleo lifted her chin. "I wrote one book of erotica before I started writing romantic-suspense. *The Mirror* is that book." She bit her lip and could not resist adding, "It was actually rather well received. Even got some good reviews." Of course, Max wouldn't believe that, Cleo thought. She wished she hadn't sounded defensive. She wished she'd kept her mouth shut.

"I see," Max said. There was absolutely no inflection in his voice.

For the life of her Cleo could not tell what his reaction was to the news that she had written *The Mirror.* "That book you're holding in your hand is the chief reason Nolan decided I was unsuitable company for a rising politician."

"Ah, well. Politicians tend to be a rather dull bunch, don't they? No imagination."

Cleo smiled dangerously. "I suppose it confirms your earlier opinion of me as a loose woman."

"It confirms my impression that you are a very unpredictable woman." Max sat down on a small, chintz-covered chair without waiting for an invitation. He leaned his cane against a table and started to massage his thigh with an absent movement of his hand. "Why don't you tell me what this is all about?"

Cleo sighed and flopped down into a wingback chair. She stretched her legs out in front of her, shoved her hands into her pockets, and eyed Max thoughtfully. She was already regretting her impulse to confide in him.

"There's not much to it, objectively speaking," she admitted. "All I know is that some disgruntled reader has apparently decided to punish me for writing that book. He or she sent a really nasty letter to me last month."

"What did you do about it?" Max asked.

"Nothing. What could I do? There was no signature. It was forwarded from my publishers, so I assumed the person who wrote it didn't have my real name and address. But this morning Nolan told me that someone left a copy of my book in his mailbox."

"Anonymously, I assume?"

"Yes. Along with the warning that I wouldn't make a good date for a politician. And tonight I walk in here and find that ribbon on my pillow."

"You suspect you're being pestered by an outraged reader?"

"Who else could it be?" Cleo shuddered. "Some weirdo is out to harass me, I guess. And he or she was right here in my bedroom tonight. It's creepy." It was more than that; it was frightening. But Cleo was not about to admit it. Not yet, at any rate.

"I might be able to help," Max said quietly.

Cleo stared at him. "How?"

"I know a man who runs a firm that specializes in corporate security and investigations. If you like, I can ask him to check out a few things."

"Forget it. I don't want to get involved with a private investigator."

"Why not?"

Cleo set her teeth. She'd been burned once by a private investigator who had taken her money and done nothing for her. She didn't intend to get conned again. "It's not worth it. I don't want to blow this up out of all proportion. Whoever it is will get tired of the game after a while and go away."

"You think so?"

"This sort of thing happens to writers sometimes," Cleo said defensively. "There's not much a person can do."

"I'm not so sure about that. Look, I can at least have O'Reilly check out the guests who are staying here this weekend. We can find out if any of them have a reputation for being rabid censors."

"I told you, I'm not going to pay a private investigator to look into this."

"You won't have to pay him," Max said softly. "O'Reilly is a friend of mine. He owes me a couple of favors. He'll be glad to do this for me."

Cleo hesitated. "You think so?"

"Yes. There's no harm in running a quick check." Max looked thoughtful. "It will take some time, though. I doubt if I can get O'Reilly to do it in just two days."

Cleo eyed him with instant suspicion. "Is this a pitch designed to convince me not to kick you out on Tuesday?"

"Yes." Max shrugged. "I don't have anywhere else to go. Jobs are hard to get these days."

She groaned. "I knew it wasn't going to be easy to get rid of you."

Four

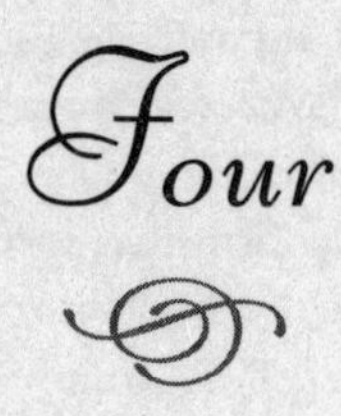

I recognize him even though I cannot see his face clearly in the mirror. He's a phantom in the glass, confined forever in a silvery world, but I know him instantly when he touches me.

His fingers are warm, not cold, although he is locked away in that frozen place behind the mirror. He wants me as no one else has ever wanted me. I want him. In some way I cannot explain, I know that he is a part of me. Yet he is as trapped in his prison as I am in mine.

When he comes to me tonight he will put his hands on my breasts, and I will shudder in response. The heat will rise within me. He will watch my face and see the desire in me. I do not have to hide it from him. He alone will understand the need and the longing and the passion inside me that no one else has ever seen. In his arms I will be free.

But what about him? Will I ever be able to release him from the mirror?

Max closed *The Mirror* and put the book down on the small nightstand beside the bed. He took a slow breath and concentrated on controlling the deep, sexual ache that had settled into his groin. He should have had enough sense to stop reading after he'd finished chapter one.

But he had been unable to resist continuing on to chapter two, even though the sensual fantasies in the book were so vibrantly female in nature that they felt alien. The fact that they were Cleo's fantasies was what had compelled him, seduced him, captivated him. In *The Mirror,* Max knew he had found another window through which he could view her.

The glimpses he'd gotten tonight were going to keep him awake for a long time.

He pushed back the covers and swung his legs over the edge of the bed. Old pain, familiar and unpleasant, lanced through his left thigh when he got to his feet. Automatically he glanced down at the scar. It looked as ugly as it always did, and it called up the usual memories.

Memories of one of the few times that he had screwed up royally.

Max reached for his cane to steady himself. He waited a minute, and gradually the pain eased. He made his way over to the window and looked out across the night-shrouded cove. Through the steady fall of rain he could see the lights of the Cosmic Harmony Women's Retreat winking in the distance.

Max gazed at them for a long while, and then he glanced back over his shoulder at his newest temporary home. He had stayed in a lot of places over the years, from cheap, thin-walled trailers to European castles, but this was the first time he had lived in an attic.

The large room under the eaves of the old inn was surprisingly cozy. It was also comfortable, so long as he remembered to duck the steeply sloped roof beams near the walls. Luckily there had apparently not been enough frilly Victoriana left over to waste on this portion of the inn. To his infinite relief, the furnishings up here were worn, rustic pieces that suited his taste for clean, straightforward shapes and forms.

Max envisioned Cleo asleep in her canopied bed one floor below and immediately regretted it. The image only served to intensify the heavy feeling in his lower body. It was going to be a long night.

His gaze fell on the coil of red ribbon lying on the desk, and his mouth tightened.

He'd made a tactical error this morning when he had confronted Cleo with his assumptions about her role in Jason's life. He was rarely so clumsy.

Having neatly wrecked his chances for insinuating himself easily into her odd household, Max had realized immediately that he'd needed a new pressure point. He'd had to find a way to convince Cleo to let him stay on at the inn. The incident with the red ribbon had provided him with a perfect excuse for hanging around.

He had told her he'd have O'Reilly check out the guests who were staying at the inn, and he fully intended to do just that. But he was going to tell O'Reilly not to rush the check. Max needed time to search for the Luttrells.

He scooped up the scarlet satin ribbon and let the ends trail through his fingers. The realization that someone had invaded Cleo's bedroom in order to deliberately frighten her sent a frisson of cold anger through him. Literary criticism had its place, but this particular critic had gone too far.

He was definitely not in a mood to sleep, Max decided. It sounded quiet downstairs. This would be a good opportunity to take a look around the inn's basement. He'd already prowled through several upstairs rooms and found nothing. The basement was the sort of place someone like Cleo might have chosen to conceal five valuable paintings.

Max shook his head in disgust at the thought of the magnificent Luttrells stashed in a damp basement.

He crossed the room to the closet. As usual, he had brought a fully packed carryall with him. The habit of being ready to leave at a moment's notice had been formed when he was a boy and was too well entrenched to be broken now.

Max tugged on a pair of dark trousers and one of the new white shirts he had recently received from his London tailor. For no good reason that he could think of, he stuffed the scarlet ribbon into his pocket. Then he headed downstairs.

The inn was quiet. Each floor was well lighted, but no one was about. Herbert T. Valence's intensive training in motivational techniques had apparently exhausted the seminar attendees.

Max saw the light on in the small office behind the front desk as soon as he walked into the lobby. He paused, listening intently for a moment. Then he went forward soundlessly, careful to keep the tip of the cane on the carpet so that it would not announce his arrival. He expected to find George, the inn's night desk man, at work.

A loud snore rumbled through the lobby. It emanated from the inner office. Max's brows rose. He took another few steps and glanced through the open doorway of the inner office. A thin, bald man somewhere in his mid-sixties was seated in Cleo's chair. He was fast asleep, his head down on his folded arms.

So much for night security at Robbins' Nest Inn.

But what was bad for security created a convenient situation for Max. He could take his time exploring the basement. He started down the hall that led to the basement stairs.

When he went past the glass-walled solarium, a tingle of awareness made him hesitate. He stopped in the doorway. The lights were off inside the room, but there was enough of a glow from the hall to reveal a familiar, graceful figure lounging in one of the regal fanback wicker chairs.

She sat alone in the shadows, gazing pensively out into the rain-soaked darkness. Cleopatra contemplating the fate of Egypt.

The throbbing sense of urgency that still swirled deep within Max flared back into life once more. Instinctively he brushed his hand across the pocket that contained the length of red satin.

"Hello," Max said quietly. "I take it you couldn't sleep either?"

Cleo's head came around very swiftly. She blinked at Max's backlit figure, as if trying to make out who had invaded her private realm. He could see that the soft, dark cloud of her hair had worked its way free of the clip that was supposed to keep it in place. She was wearing her usual uniform of snug, faded jeans and an oxford cloth button-down shirt. Her gold sneakers gleamed in the shadows.

The faint hall light revealed Cleo's wary, shuttered expression. An emotion other than desire stirred inside of Max. He recognized it vaguely as concern. He had not seen that particular look on Cleo's face before, not even when they had discussed the significance of the red ribbon on her pillow.

"I had an unpleasant dream," Cleo said quietly. "I get them sometimes. I thought I'd come down here for a few minutes to get rid of the cobwebs. What are you doing up?"

Max wondered what sort of dreams it took to awaken Cleo and cause her to seek refuge in the solarium.

He walked into the darkened room and sat down in the wicker chair across from her. For a moment he said nothing. He could hear the burbling of the water in the shallow, tiled fountain that was the centerpiece of the room.

"I had nothing better to do, so I decided I'd come down and see how easy it was to get hold of a master key or the key to your room," Max improvised carefully.

"The key to my room?" Cleo looked briefly startled.

"Someone must have used one or the other to open your door earlier tonight."

"Oh, I see." Her fingers clenched around the arms of the wicker chair. "It wouldn't have been that hard to get hold of a key, I'm afraid. I suppose you saw George?"

"He's asleep."

Cleo wrinkled her nose. "He usually is. The thing is, we've never had much of a security problem here at the inn."

"I noticed that the front desk is frequently unattended for several minutes at a time during the day, too," Max pointed out.

"Yes. We're always a little short of staff. Everyone pitches in when we're full. Sometimes that means whoever is at the front desk has to help out in the kitchen or check on a problem in one of the rooms."

Max gingerly stretched out his leg and absently massaged his aching thigh. "The bottom line here is that almost anyone could have entered the inn sometime today, swiped a key for a few minutes, used it to unlock your door, and left the ribbon on your pillow."

"Yes." Cleo's brows drew together. "Believe me, from here on out, we'll make certain we keep a much closer eye on the keys."

"I think that would be a good idea," Max said dryly. "For openers, the keys should be kept inside the office at all times, not left on the hooks behind the front desk. No one but members of your staff should be allowed into the office, and the door should be locked if the front desk is unattended, even for five minutes."

"I'd already figured that out for myself," Cleo muttered.

"Tomorrow morning you can get me a complete list of everyone who is staying at the inn this weekend," Max continued.

Cleo leaned back in her chair, rested her elbows on the arms, and steepled her fingers. She gazed at him, brooding. "You're serious about having your friend O'Reilly check out my guests, aren't you?"

He was surprised by the question. "Did you get the impression that I wasn't serious about it?"

"Not exactly. You look like the type who takes most things seriously."

"In my experience it's the things which don't get taken seriously that cause the most problems," he said.

"So you take everything seriously," Cleo concluded. "Sounds like a rather grim way to go through life."

"It's the way I am."

"I'll bet you're a real fun date."

The flash of humor in her eyes disconcerted him. Max forgot about his aching leg for a moment as it struck him that she was laughing at him. It was an odd experience. People reacted to him in a variety of ways, but virtually no one found him amusing. "I've never had anyone comment on that."

"You're a strange man." The amusement faded from Cleo's eyes. "I don't know what to make of you, Max. I thought I did when you arrived, but now I'm not so sure."

"I can prove that I was a friend of Jason's, if that will make you feel more comfortable around me."

Her eyes widened. "I believe you were Jason's friend."

"And I apologized for thinking you were Jason's mistress."

"Yes, I know." She waved a hand in a magnanimous gesture. "I've decided not to hold that against you any longer, by the way."

"Thank you," Max said humbly.

"I mean, I can sort of see where you might have gotten the impression that Jason and I were . . . well, never mind." Cleo blushed. "I can see where you got the idea."

"When you decide what it is that's still bothering you about me," Max said gently, "let me know."

"I'll do that." She watched intently as he rubbed his thigh. "What's wrong with your leg?"

"It aches a little sometimes. Especially after a long day."

"How did you hurt it?" Cleo asked. "Were you in an accident?"

"You could say that."

"How long ago did it happen?"

He was amused by her sudden fascination with the topic. "Three years ago."

"It looks painful."

"Occasionally it is."

She bit her lip. "I suppose it's bothering you tonight because of all that firewood you lugged into the lobby this afternoon. You should have said something when I asked you to do that."

"It's got nothing to do with hauling firewood around. Sometimes it just aches, that's all."

"Does massage help?"

Max shrugged. "I don't know. I've never tried professional massage."

"I give a good therapeutic massage." Cleo's smile was tentative. "I learned how to do it when Andromeda hired a massage therapist to teach the women of Cosmic Harmony. Andromeda's into holistic medicine, you know."

"I'm not surprised."

"Want me to work on that leg?"

Max abruptly stopped rubbing his thigh. He flexed his fingers slowly as he imagined what it would feel like to have Cleo's hands on his leg.

"All right," Max said. He was going to regret this, he was certain of it. But he seemed to be lacking in willpower tonight.

Cleo got slowly to her feet. She took two steps to close the distance between them and knelt on the floor beside his chair. Her eyes were huge and luminous behind the lenses of her glasses.

"Tell me if I hurt you," she whispered.

"I will." Max took a deep breath and waited for the exquisite torture to begin.

Cleo put her hands on his thigh. For a while she did not move at all. She simply let the warmth of her palms soak through his trousers into his skin.

Max was startled by the amount of soothing heat she was generating. He looked down at Cleo's bent head. She was concentrating intently on her task. The delicate, sensual curve of her neck was within reach. All he had to do was move his hand a scant six inches or so, and he would be touching her. Max gripped the arms of the chair.

"You're very tense." Cleo frowned as she pressed her fingertips gently into his hard, muscled flesh. "Try to relax. According to the massage therapist who taught me how to do this, the chief cause of soreness in the muscles is tension."

"I'll try to remember that."

She began to knead his thigh with long, smooth strokes. "How does that feel?"

"Good." It was true, Max realized, surprised. No one had ever offered to massage his leg for him since his "accident." He hadn't realized how soothing it would feel to have someone else work on the knotted muscles of his thigh.

"Andromeda is very good with herbs. I'll ask her to mix up something you can use as a muscle relaxant," Cleo said.

Max winced at the thought. "Never mind. I generally use brandy when things get bad."

"I think you'll find one of Cosmic Harmony's herbal teas will work just as well. The guests love them."

Max didn't feel like arguing. He closed his eyes and focused on the sensual touch of Cleo's hands. Another window, he thought. Another glimpse into the intriguing depths of Cleopatra Robbins.

Long minutes passed during which Max's leg began to feel infinitely better. But the massage did nothing to diminish the driving need inside him. The sense of urgency was growing beyond control.

"Cleo, I've been reading *The Mirror,*" Max said.

Her hands stilled. Max swore silently, wishing he'd kept his mouth shut.

"I suppose you think it's pornography, just like Nolan did."

"No," Max said. "I think it's beautiful."

"Beautiful?" Her voice was little more than a whisper.

"More than beautiful. It's fascinating."

Cleo's hands began to move again on his thigh. "Really?"

Max opened his eyes and looked down at her averted face. "Reading it is like looking into a fine painting. There are hundreds of layers to see. Some are obvious, others aren't. Some can be described, but the most important ones can't be put into words at all. You have to feel them."

Cleo flashed him a misty smile. "You sound like Jason when you talk like that. He said some people see art with another eye."

"He called it the inner eye."

"That's right." She tilted her head a little to one side. "Is that how you see art?"

"Yes."

"It sounds strange. Can you see into people the same way?"

"Not usually," Max admitted. But I'm learning to see you that way, he thought. The knowledge went through him like wildfire. The more he knew about Cleo, the more he wanted her. This was exactly how he felt when he was in the presence of a fine painting that spoke directly to him.

He wanted her.

"You're lucky you can't see into people the way you do art." Cleo continued to stroke his leg. "I can sometimes, and it's very frustrating for the most part."

He studied the sweet, vulnerable line at the nape of her neck. "Why do you say that?"

"Because it doesn't do much good. Even when you can see things about people, you usually can't change them."

"You sound like you're talking from experience."

"I am." Cleo looked up, her eyes troubled. "The reason Trisha was sobbing her heart out tonight is because she just found out she's pregnant. She says Benjy left because she told him about the baby."

"I see. I'm sorry about Trisha, she seems like a nice enough kid. But what does her situation have to do with what we were talking about?"

Cleo's shoulder rose and fell in a small shrug. "I knew the first time I saw Trisha and Benjy together that they would cling to each other. They're two of a kind. Two orphans in a storm. I wasn't surprised when their friendship turned into a romance. But I also knew it could lead to disaster."

"Why?"

"Because both Benjy and Trisha have had to be so strong in order to just survive, that they're both very fragile when it comes to dealing with other people. Does that make sense?"

"I don't know," Max said.

"Take my word for it. Adding a baby to the equation was just too much stress. Especially for Benjy. He's never had a father of his own, and I imagine the thought of becoming one himself terrified him. No wonder he disappeared for a while."

Max touched a stray lock of Cleo's hair. She did not seem to notice. "You're not to blame for Trisha's situation."

"My point is that I could see deeply enough into both Trisha and Benjy to know that this mess Trisha's in was almost bound to happen. But I couldn't do a thing to stop it. Knowing what was coming didn't do any good, did it? I couldn't avert the catastrophe."

"It wasn't your responsibility to avert it," Max said.

Cleo smiled wryly. "Trisha and Benjy are both part of the family. I should have been able to do something about the situation before it got out of hand."

"I thought I was the one who took things too seriously."

Her smile faded. "This is serious. Trisha and Benjy are both family. I care about them."

He couldn't think of anything to say to that. Cleo obviously had an odd definition of family. On the other hand, Max thought, he couldn't think of a better one. He decided not to comment.

Cleo worked for a while in silence. Her fingers probed gently, seeking the depths of his taut muscles. "I'm glad you didn't think *The Mirror* was pornographic," she said after a moment.

"It's just the opposite." Max closed his eyes.

"You sound very certain of that."

"You know what they say about pornography." Max smiled faintly. "You know it when you see it. *The Mirror* isn't it."

"What makes you so sure?"

He searched for a way to put his inner knowledge into words. *"The Mirror* is alive. It generates a variety of responses, not just a sexual reaction. It's an affirmation of life and the future. Pornography is static."

"Static?"

He spread the fingers of one hand wide and then let them relax. "It's one-dimensional. No past, no future, no depth, no emotion, except for a short-term sexual response which wears off very fast. I'm not saying it's good or bad; it's just boring after about ten minutes."

"Ten minutes?" Cleo repeated very innocently.

Max heard the laughter in her voice. He raised his lashes and gazed at her through narrowed eyes. "Okay, fifteen, if it's really well-done pornography."

She laughed softly. Her fingers continued to move on his thigh. "How is your leg feeling now?"

"Much better." It was the truth.

"You're not an artist, are you, Max?"

"No."

"So what did you do for a living before you came here?"

"This and that," Max said. "Odd jobs for the most part."

"What kind of odd jobs?"

He hesitated, uncertain of how much to tell her. If she knew he had worked for Jason she might think that he had merely been an employee and therefore had no real claim to the Luttrells. She might even conclude that she had more of a right to them than he did. Max preferred her to know only part of the truth, that he had been Jason's friend. It put him on an even footing with her. After all, Cleo had been no more and no less than Jason's friend, too. She would not be able to salve her conscience by telling herself that her relationship with Jason was closer than Max's had been and that therefore she had more of a right to the Luttrells.

Max realized at that moment that somewhere along the line he had decided that Cleo did have a conscience.

"I worked for an art dealer once," Max offered as an example of the odd jobs he had performed.

"It must have paid very well," Cleo said.

"Yes." He knew she was thinking about the Jaguar and probably about his expensive clothes. He decided it was time to change the topic. "But I'm not in that line of work anymore."

"How did you meet Jason?"

"We shared a mutual interest," Max said.

"Art?"

"Yes." He hoped she would stop there.

Cleo paused. "Max, were you telling me the truth when you said that Jason was rich?"

"Yes." He wished he could read her mind. For the life of him he could not tell if she was playing the innocent brilliantly or if she really was innocent. He'd had very little experience with innocence of any kind. He didn't trust himself to recognize it on sight.

Cleo pursed her lips in a thoughtful expression. "I always sensed that there were a lot of things we didn't know about Jason. But he didn't seem to want us to know them, so I never asked. I figured he'd get around to telling us in his own good time."

"Perhaps he would have. But time ran out for him." Maybe she really was what she seemed to be, Max thought, irritated at not being able to decide.

It was then that he realized with stunning clarity that he wanted her to be as innocent as she appeared. He did not want to discover she was nothing more than the conniving little art thief that all the available evidence indicated she was.

He wanted something more, too. He wanted her to want him.

Max had been certain last night that Cleo was aware of him in a deeply sensual way, just as he was aware of her. He had seen the unguarded reaction in her eyes during those first, fleeting moments. But he detected nothing overtly sensual in the way she touched his thigh tonight. Her fingers were gentle and soothing, not deliberately seductive.

He tried to reconcile the picture of the woman who knelt beside him with the image he had of the woman who had written *The Mirror.* There was a paradox involved here, and it fascinated him. Max had a mental vision of fire frozen in ice.

All his male instincts told him that Cleo Robbins was not very experienced, and yet *The Mirror* had burned with a searing, passionate sensuality.

Max was suddenly, intensely aware of the length of satin stuffed into his pocket.

"Cleo?"

"Yes?"

Max could not think of a way to put the question he wanted to ask into words. Instead he reached into his pocket and slowly drew out the length of scarlet ribbon.

Cleo's hands stopped moving on his leg. She stared, transfixed, at the ribbon in his hand. Max saw the sudden, deep stillness in her. He wondered if she was afraid of him.

The abrupt need to protect her was so strong, it caused his hand to shake. "Don't be frightened."

She looked up at him, her eyes filled with silent questions. "I'm not afraid of you."

"I'm glad." The ribbon dangled from his fingers, almost touching the floor. He caught hold of the loose end with his other hand. The satin gleamed softly as he stretched it out to form a gentle loop. "I told you I'm reading *The Mirror.*"

"Yes." Her voice was only a whisper.

"I'm on chapter two."

"Are you?" Cleo touched the tip of her tongue to the corner of her mouth. She glanced at the ribbon again.

"I know that the woman in *The Mirror* thinks she will recognize her phantom lover when she sees him, even though she has never seen his face clearly in the glass."

"Yes, she'll know him." Cleo's eyes were deep, fathomless pools of uncertainty and yearning behind the lenses of her glasses.

"What I don't know yet is how she will let him know that she recognizes him," Max said softly.

"She won't have to tell him. Not with words, at any rate."

"But he'll know that she knows?"

"Yes," Cleo breathed.

The blood roared, wild and hot, through Max's veins. He could not recall feeling so intensely alive in his entire life, not even when he contemplated his magnificent collection of books and art. He was balanced on the dangerous edge between joy and agony.

Without a word, because there were no words, Max raised the loop of red satin. He slipped it slowly down over Cleo's head.

She did not move. *Fire frozen in ice waiting to be freed.*

Max settled the length of inexpensive scarlet ribbon around Cleo's throat as if it were a necklace composed of priceless rubies. He tugged gently on the ends of the ribbon, drawing her to him. Cleo leaned forward as if caught in a spell.

Max released the ends of the ribbon and plucked Cleo's glasses from her nose. He set them down on the floor beside his chair. His eyes never left hers.

Cleo blinked once or twice as if she were inside a cave gazing out into bright sunlight. With a soft, low groan, Max lowered his mouth to hers.

Cleo shuddered at the first touch of his lips, but she did not pull away. She tasted him as if sampling a new, exotic wine. The nibbling sensation at the edge of his lips nearly sent Max beyond the reach of his self-control.

He brushed his mouth lightly across hers, teasing forth a tentative response. There was feminine eagerness shimmering just beneath the surface. He could feel it.

But he could also feel the hesitation in her. She wanted him, he realized, but something was holding her back. It was as if she was not quite certain how far she wanted to go down this particular road.

He also sensed that there was an awful lot of ice between him and the flame that burned inside Cleo. But the fire was there, waiting to be set free.

He opened his mouth on hers. Cleo hesitated a moment longer, and then she gave a small, murmuring sigh and put her arms around his neck.

Max suddenly realized that he had been ravenous for a very long time. Cleo's mouth was sweet and ripe, incredibly fresh. After the first taste, he wanted to devour the fruit. Never had anything tasted so exquisitely good.

He urged her lips apart. She followed his lead, allowing him into her moist warmth.

There were two ways to deal with ice, Max reminded himself. One could melt it or one could chop through it with an axe. The latter was far and away the fastest method, and he was in a hurry.

He started to haul Cleo up off the floor and into his lap.

She gasped softly under the assault. Max felt the incipient panic in her. So much for the fast approach. He took a deep breath and kept a savage grip on his clamoring need.

He lifted his mouth from Cleo's reluctantly and looked down into her bemused eyes.

"I'm sorry," Cleo whispered.

He smiled slightly. "I'm the one who probably should be saying that." Except that the only thing he was sorry about was that she had drawn back before he could finish what he had started.

She smiled tremulously. "Don't apologize. It's just that I wasn't prepared to have a very private fantasy come to life."

"Fantasy?"

Cleo eyed him warily. "Don't pretend that you haven't read chapter three."

"Chapter three?" Max was getting confused.

"That's the chapter in my book in which the man in the mirror puts a red ribbon around the woman's throat and draws her into the glass. She steps into his world, and he makes love to her there."

"Just as I did to you?" Max was pleased with himself.

"Yes. Just as you did to me. Except that you didn't exactly make love to me, did you?" She touched her full, soft mouth. "You only kissed me." Cleo scowled briefly. "Are you sure you didn't read chapter three?"

"Very sure. But I will definitely read it before I go to bed tonight," Max promised. "And possibly chapter four as well."

Cleo's cheeks burned a brilliant shade of pink. "Maybe it would be better if you didn't. I think you've read far enough to get an idea of what *The Mirror* is all about."

Max held her eyes. "There's no way I can stop now."

Cleo gazed at him with a disturbingly serious expression. "Maybe we'd better get something clear here. If you're looking for an entertaining interlude out here on the coast, forget it. I don't do entertaining interludes."

"Neither do I," Max said.

She picked up her glasses and pushed them firmly onto her nose. Her face was flushed, but her eyes were steady and clear. "To be perfectly blunt, I don't do interludes at all, entertaining or otherwise."

"Not at all?"

"No."

"Never?" Max persisted, curious.

Cleo got to her feet and retreated to the shadows of her fanback chair. She gazed out into the night for a long while.

"Once, a long time ago, when I was twenty-three, there was a man. But we broke up after my . . . after my parents died. There hasn't been anyone since."

"Why not?" Max asked, greedy for every scrap of information he could collect. He wanted to learn everything there was to learn about her, he realized. He had to dig down through the layers and find all the closely guarded secrets.

"I don't know why not." Cleo's eyes flashed with a sudden shower of angry sparks. An instant later the fireworks vanished as quickly as they had appeared. "That's not entirely true. A therapist told me that I've never been able to cope with the way my parents died."

"How did they die?"

Cleo looked down at her clasped hands as if debating how much to tell him. She appeared to come to some sort of decision. "They say my father shot my mother and then turned the gun on himself."

"Jesus," Max muttered.

"The theory is that I can't reconcile the fact that they loved each other with the way they died. It's impossible for me to believe that the bond my parents shared was tainted by some sick obsession of my father's."

"There's a certain logic to that," Max said quietly. "Look, Cleo, I'm sorry I pushed for so many answers. I had no right to do that."

"Damn." Cleo shot to her feet and walked to the glass wall. "I don't know why I'm telling you all this. You're the second man I've confided in today. I guess this business with the anonymous notes and the ribbons has me more rattled than I thought."

Max narrowed his eyes. "You told Hildebrand about your parents?"

"He made me mad when he said I wasn't pure enough to be a politician's wife." Cleo sighed. "I got kind of mouthy, I guess. Told him I had another skeleton in the closet besides *The Mirror.* I couldn't resist pointing out that the press would probably have a field day with the facts surrounding my parents' death."

"I see. How did he take it?"

Cleo shrugged. "Oh, he was well and truly shocked. Max, I'm sorry I got into all this with you tonight. It's a very private matter. Until today no one but the family has known what happened to my folks."

"I don't intend to discuss it with anyone else."

"I didn't think you did." She bit her lip. "I just wanted you to realize that I'm not a good candidate for a quick fling or even a long-term affair."

Max reached for his cane and got slowly to his feet. He folded his hands on the hawk and stood watching Cleo. "I won't push you into anything you don't want."

Her answering smile held a curious blend of uncertainty and relief. "Thanks for understanding. I'm sorry about what happened here tonight. It was my fault."

Max smiled to himself and headed for the door. "Don't be too sure of that. See you in the morning."

"Max?"

"Don't worry, Cleo. From here on out, we'll do it by the book. Your book."

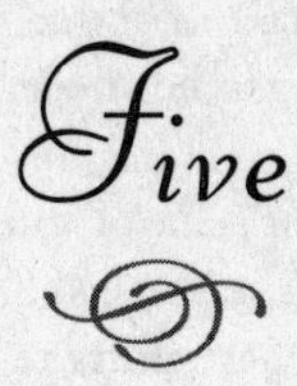

Five

Shortly before dawn the next morning Cleo gave up trying to sleep. She pushed aside the quilt, got out of bed, and crossed the room to cast an appraising eye at the weather.

The dark sky was overcast, but it was not yet raining. There would be plenty of time to get in a brisk walk along the top of the bluffs before the next storm struck.

After the restless night she'd just spent, she needed to clear her head with the crisp, cold sea air. Perhaps later in the day she would go to the meditation center at Cosmic Harmony. Unfortunately there wasn't time to do that this morning. Cleo wanted to be at the inn when the morning rush started in the kitchen. As Jason had once observed, there was no substitute for close supervision in a small operation such as the Robbins' Nest Inn.

Cleo felt a twist of sorrow at the memory of her friend. She eased it aside as she stepped into a pair of jeans and put on a blue oxford cloth shirt. Jason would not have wanted her to dwell too long on his passing, she reminded herself as she laced up her gold sneakers. Jason Curzon had believed in living for the future, not the past.

She grabbed her hunter green down parka on the way out the door. She made her way downstairs and walked through the still slumbering inn. Gentle snores from the vicinity of the office told her George was still on duty and as alert as ever.

She let herself out through the door at the back of the kitchen.

Andromeda, Daystar, and the morning crew from Cosmic Harmony had not yet arrived. And the guests would certainly not be stirring for a while.

The chilled air hit her like a tonic when she stepped outside. The night was giving way slowly to the gray light of the new day. The biting cold made Cleo abruptly aware of the fact that she had forgotten her gloves. She stuffed her hands into her jacket pockets and started off along the bluff overlooking the sea.

She wanted to think about a lot of things this morning: the dream, Benjy's disappearance, Trisha's problems. She needed to deal with all of them. But her mind resisted her efforts to concentrate on any of those issues. No matter what she did, it kept spinning back to the one, single event that had dominated her thoughts for most of the night: Max's kiss.

It was the first time she had kissed a man since her parents' death and not felt the subtle sense of wrongness that had tainted every other relationship she'd had.

All she had experienced with Max last night was a wondrous sensation of exultant joy. She had wanted him, *really* wanted him.

The passion that she had known lay buried inside her had awakened and responded to the touch of a real man at last. Relief soared through her at the realization that she had found the one who could help her free herself.

The man in the mirror had finally walked into her life.

But to Cleo's chagrin, things were not as clear as she had expected them to be if and when she found the right man. There were so many unknowns about Max Fortune, so many uncertainties.

One of the factors that troubled her the most was that he did not seem to be responding to her in the same way that she was responding to him. She had been so sure that if she ever encountered the man in the mirror in the real world, she would not only recognize him immediately, he would also recognize her. She knew from the things her mother and father had said that they had known they were meant for each other from the first moment they met.

But when Cleo had looked into Max's eyes last night, she had seen not just sexual desire, but a disturbing element of calculating control. She sighed unhappily at the thought. She had to face the fact that although her response to him had been instantaneous, pure and unfettered, Max Fortune apparently had his own agenda.

That made him dangerous. Theoretically it should have set off her finely tuned alarm system.

So why wasn't she getting that old, familiar feeling of wrongness about him? she wondered.

She recalled the way he had put the red satin ribbon around her throat and drawn her to him in a perfect imitation of a scene in chapter three of *The Mirror.*

A little too perfect, she thought wryly. She'd be willing to bet that Max actually had read that chapter before seeking her out last night.

The feeling that she no longer had the dawn to herself made Cleo turn her head and glance back over her shoulder. She managed a polite smile of greeting for Herbert T. Valence, who was striding briskly along behind her.

Valence was nattily dressed as always in an expensive-looking camel coat, paisley print silk scarf, and a pair of taupe leather shoes. Whatever brand of mousse or spray he had used to anchor his silver locks into place was impervious to the snapping breeze. Not a single hair was moving in the brisk breeze. The diamond on his pinky sparkled in the early light.

She appeared to be inundated with spiffy dressers these days, Cleo reflected, amused. The combined sartorial elegance of Max and Herbert T. Valence was definitely elevating the inn's image this weekend.

"Good morning, Ms. Robbins." Valence bobbed his head with bird-like speed.

"Good morning," Cleo said. "I didn't hear you coming up behind me. Out for a morning walk before your next seminar session?"

"I make it a point to walk one mile every day," Valence informed her. "Proper aerobic exercise is essential to a successful attitude."

"It's always nice to meet someone who practices what they preach."

"I have a reputation to maintain, Ms. Robbins. I can only do that if I live by my own five basic rules of success."

"What are your five rules, Mr. Valence?" Cleo asked curiously. "Or don't you hand those out for free?"

"As we have a professional relationship, I don't mind giving you my five rules."

"How kind of you." Cleo wondered if the list would include clicking his pen exactly five times before replacing it in his coat pocket and always staying in the same room at the inn. During the course of her so-called professional relationship with him, Cleo had had occasion to observe a long list of such eccentricities in Valence.

Valence held up his hand and pointed to his thumb. "The first rule is to concentrate on the objective." He pointed to the next finger. "The second rule is to prepare a plan to meet that objective. The third rule is to resist the impulse to deviate from the plan. The fourth rule is to pay attention to every detail and to make certain it is covered before proceeding with the plan."

"And the fifth rule?" Cleo asked.

"The fifth rule is to always think in terms of success, never in terms of failure."

Cleo considered that. "But what happens if one does fail, Mr. Valence?"

Valence tilted his chin at a proud angle. "Failure is not an acceptable outcome for those who orient their lives toward success. I assure you that I did not acquire my reputation by making mistakes, Ms. Robbins."

"Must be kind of tough having to live up to that kind of reputation," Cleo mused.

"The rewards more than outweigh the effort involved," Valence said. "You should know what I'm talking about, Ms. Robbins. Look at what you've accomplished at your age. You're the owner and proprietor of one of the most successful inns on the Washington coast. How did you talk a bank into loaning you the kind of money it must have taken to open Robbins' Nest?"

Cleo looked out over the steel gray sea. "I had some money of my own."

"Ah, I see. Family money, then."

Cleo thought of the trust fund she had inherited after her parents' death. "Yes."

"I apologize for my questions," Valence said a bit gruffly, as if he had suddenly realized he might have intruded on Cleo's privacy. "Didn't mean to pry. The thing is, I'm always interested in success stories. I guess you could say I collect them."

"You collect them?"

"Yes, indeed. Whenever I find an interesting one, I like to dissect it. Find out how it happened. I learn things from it that I then incorporate into my seminars."

"Well, there's not much to my story, Mr. Valence," Cleo said. "I bought the inn with my inheritance. With the help of some good friends, I've made it work. That's all there is to my tale."

Valence bobbed his head again. "You've certainly got an unusual group of employees. Your kitchen staff all look like they're from some New Age commune, and that new one, the man with the cane, doesn't dress or act like hired help."

"Well, he is hired help," Cleo said shortly. "But I don't know how long he'll be staying." That realization made her catch her breath. The thought of Max leaving sent a flash of pain through her. She realized she did not want to lose the man in the mirror now that she had finally found him.

"In my opinion, his manner is far too arrogant for his position."

Cleo smiled to herself. "I'll speak to him about it."

"I suggest you do that." Valence glanced at his chunky gold watch. "I should be getting back to my room, I suppose. I want to go over my notes. Before I bid you good day, however, Ms. Robbins, there is something I wish to discuss."

Cleo stifled a groan. "What's that, Mr. Valence?"

Valence gave her a disapproving look. "I trust there will be no more upsetting occurrences such as the loss of electrical power that I was obliged to endure yesterday afternoon."

Cleo smiled wryly. "I'm afraid that sort of thing is beyond my ability to control, Mr. Valence. We'll do our best, but I can't guarantee anything, especially during a storm."

"If you cannot promise a reliable power source, I may be forced to select another location for my seminars," Valence warned.

"As I said, Mr. Valence, we'll do our best to keep you up and running."

Valence grunted a rather dissatisfied response. "Well, that's that, then. We shall just have to see, won't we?"

"I guess so," Cleo said. "Have a good day, Mr. Valence."

"Thank you. Same to you."

Valence stopped, made a neat one hundred and eighty degree turn, and started back toward the inn.

Cleo watched as he tucked his chin into the warmth of his expensive coat and leaned resolutely into the crisp breeze. Then she continued on her way along the bluffs. She thought about what she had just told Valence about Max. *I don't know how long he'll be staying.*

An excellent reason for being extremely cautious, Cleo thought. Max was definitely an unknown quantity, even if she did have the distinct sensation that she had been waiting for him all of her life.

Cleo delayed the family meeting on Trisha until after the last of the crowd of seminar attendees had checked out the following day. She held it during the lull that ensued in the afternoon before preparations began for the evening meal.

Andromeda, Daystar, Trisha, Sylvia, and Cleo sat down on the benches of the kitchen nook. Trisha looked at the others and burst into tears.

"There now, dear, don't fuss so." Andromeda handed her a napkin to blot her eyes. "You aren't the first woman to find herself in this sort of situation, and you won't be the last. The important thing to remember is that you aren't alone."

"I thought he loved me," Trisha whispered.

"I think he does," Cleo said gently. "But Benjy's confused about a lot of things."

"Too confused to use any birth control, apparently," Daystar muttered. She gave Trisha a severe look. "I seem to recall mentioning the subject to you a while back, young lady. What went wrong?"

Trisha started to sob heavily. "I'm sorry. I just wasn't thinking. You don't know what it's like."

"Don't I?" Daystar snorted. "I'm sixty-two years old, my girl, and I didn't spend those years in a box. Believe me, I know what it's like. Passion is no excuse for stupidity. A woman has to use her head. She has to stay in control of the situation."

Trisha cried louder.

Cleo glared at Daystar. "For heaven's sake, this is getting us nowhere."

Andromeda gave her friend a scolding look. "Cleo's right. There's no point lecturing poor Trisha now. The damage is done. We have to go forth from here. As that Mr. Valence has been telling everyone all weekend, we have to think positive. Problems should be looked upon as opportunities."

"You're right. I'm sorry." Daystar patted Trisha with gruff affection. "Don't worry, Trisha. We're going to survive this."

"It was all my fault," Trisha wailed.

"It takes two," Cleo said firmly. "Benjy had just as much to do with this as you did."

"The difference is that Benjy can walk away from it," Daystar said bluntly. "Trisha can't."

"You know," Andromeda mused, "I'm surprised that Benjy did walk away. I thought that boy was finally getting his act together, as they say. He was working hard here, attending classes at the community college part-time. He was even starting to talk about the future in a positive manner. I really believed he was going to make it."

"He was trying," Trisha said loyally. "I know he was."

"I agree," Cleo said. "And I know he cares for Trisha. I imagine he's feeling pretty scared at the moment."

"Maybe we should have gotten some professional counseling for the boy," Andromeda said.

Daystar shrugged. "Don't know if that would have done any good."

Cleo decided to take charge before the discussion degenerated into a what-went-wrong-with-Benjy session. "I've been doing some thinking. We've known Benjy for a year and a half. He's a good kid, and I can't believe he's really run out on his responsibilities. I'll bet he's just gone off someplace to think for a while."

Trisha looked up from the napkin. There was a tiny flicker of hope in her eyes. "Do you really believe he'll come back?"

Cleo pursed her lips in thought. "I'm sure Benjy is very confused and shaken at the moment. He probably needs someone to talk to."

"Well, why didn't he talk to one of us?" Daystar demanded. "We're his family."

Cleo grimaced. "Have you noticed that with the exception of Sammy, we're all female? Poor Benjy probably felt we'd be so busy sympathizing with Trisha that we wouldn't understand what he was going through."

Sylvia's brows rose. "That's a possibility, I suppose."

"It's important to remember that Benjy does have a responsibility in this, whether he wants it now or not," Daystar said. "A financial responsibility."

"I agree," Sylvia said. "Benjy may not be able to handle his moral and emotional commitments yet, but he can and should be required to handle his financial responsibilities. At least Doug still sends some child support once in a while. Benjy should do the same."

Cleo held up her hand. "Before we start pressuring Benjy to honor his financial obligations, I think we should try another tactic. I think we should convince him to come home where he belongs."

Trisha gave her another desperate look. "But he's gone. I don't know where he is. How can we find him?"

"Maybe Max can find him," Cleo said slowly.

"Max?" Trisha stared at her. "But how can Max find him?"

"Max says he has a friend who runs an investigation firm," Cleo said. "I don't have much faith in private investigators, but Max seems to think his friend is very good. Benjy hasn't been gone long, and he probably isn't trying to hide."

Trisha bit her lip. "Do you think Max's friend can find Benjy?"

"I suggest we find out." Cleo got to her feet with sudden resolve. As soon as the idea had occurred to her, she had sensed it was the right approach to the problem. "Stay here, I'll be right back."

She whirled around and headed for the door. She did not look back, although she was aware of the others staring after her in bemusement.

Cleo went down the hall to the lobby. There was no sign of Max. She tried the parlor next. It was empty except for three guests who were reading quietly in front of the fire. In the hallway she encountered one of the maids who came in on busy days and was helping clean up after the seminar guests.

"Darleen, have you seen Max?"

"I think he's in the solarium with Sammy," Darleen said.

Cleo changed direction and went down another hall. A moment later she walked into the solarium. Rain was beating pleasantly on the glass roof. The steady patter and the gurgle of the fountain were the only sounds in the room.

Max was seated in a fanback wicker chair, his left leg propped on a matching wicker footstool. His cane was leaning against the wide arm of the chair.

It struck Cleo that Max looked oddly at home in the exotic surroundings. Something about the scene made her think of an elegant pirate who had retired to a South Pacific island. She winced when she saw that he was reading *The Mirror.*

Sammy was seated beside Max in the miniature wicker chair that Cleo had bought him for Christmas. He had Lucky Ducky and a picture book in his lap. He had his thumb stuffed contentedly in his mouth and seemed as intent on his reading as Max was on his.

"Hi," Cleo said softly.

Sammy took his thumb out of his mouth. "Hi, Cleo. Me and Max are reading."

"So I see."

"Max says books are special. He's got lots and lots of 'em. He keeps 'em in a secret room in his house where no one can see 'em except him."

"Is that right?" Cleo wondered what else he kept in that secret room. His heart, perhaps. She crossed the tiled floor. "Max, I wondered if you would mind joining me and the others in the kitchen."

Max looked up warily from *The Mirror.* "Why?"

Cleo cleared her throat cautiously. "We, uh, wanted to ask you to help us."

He gazed at her with a brooding stare. "Help you do what?"

"Find Benjy."

"Damn," Max said very softly.

Sammy yanked his thumb out of his mouth again. "You're not supposed to say words like that around me."

Max looked down at him. "I apologize. I don't know what came over me."

Sammy nodded. "It's okay. Just don't tell Mommy."

"I won't," Max promised.

Cleo waited hopefully. "Do you think you could find him, Max?"

"Max can find anything," Sammy announced. "He even found Lucky Ducky."

"O'Reilly might be able to locate him," Max said carefully. "What do you intend to do with Benjy if you do find him?"

"I'm not sure," Cleo said. She gave him her most winning smile. "But I think I'd like you to talk to him."

Max looked completely taken aback. "You want *me* to talk to him? I don't even know the guy."

"I realize that," Cleo said earnestly, "but you're a man, and I think Benjy will feel more comfortable talking to a man at this stage."

"What the hell do you expect me to talk to him about?"

"Not supposed to say hell either," Sammy said.

"Sorry," Max said brusquely.

Cleo kept what she hoped was a persuasive smile in place. "Ideally I'd like you to talk him into coming home. I want him to shoulder his responsibilities toward Trisha. But at the very least he needs to realize he has a financial obligation to her."

"You don't ask much, do you?" Max said grimly.

"What's an obligation?" Sammy asked.

"That's what people say a person has when they want that person to do something." Max didn't take his eyes off Cleo.

"Oh." Sammy appeared placated by the answer.

Max studied Cleo. "This is way outside my area of expertise. I am definitely not a social worker."

"But you said your friend O'Reilly was good at tracking down people," Cleo reminded him.

"Finding Benjy is one thing," Max said. "Talking him into coming back here is another."

"We've got to try."

Max looked at her. "I'd rather you left me out of this."

Sammy took his thumb out of his mouth. "I bet you could make Benjy come home, Max."

Cleo gave Max a searching glance. "Would you mind if we finished this discussion in the kitchen?"

"Something tells me I can't avoid it." Max took his foot down off the stool.

He started to reach for his cane, but Sammy jumped to his feet, picked it up, and handed it to him.

"Thank you." Max took the cane politely. He tucked *The Mirror* under his arm and looked at Cleo. "All right. Let's go."

Sammy sat down in his small fanback chair. "Are you going to come back and read some more with me, Max?"

Max glanced down at the boy. "Maybe."

"Okay. I'll wait here for you."

Cleo smiled ruefully as she led the way out of the solarium. "Sammy has really glommed on to you, hasn't he?"

"He does seem to be underfoot every time I turn around."

"I think he's trying to turn you into a sort of honorary uncle, just as he did Jason," she explained.

"It's okay," Max said. "I'm getting used to it."

Cleo pushed open the kitchen door. Trisha, Sylvia, Andromeda, and Daystar turned to stare at them. The expressions on their faces ranged from anxious and hopeful to grim and determined.

"Well?" Daystar beetled her brows at Max. "Are you going to help us locate Benjy?"

Andromeda and Sylvia watched Max with an ill-concealed expression of appeal. Trisha sniffed into her napkin and gazed at him uncertainly.

Max surveyed the group sitting in the nook. His face was unreadable. "I can probably find Benjy for you."

The women traded relieved glances.

"That's wonderful," Andromeda said. "Will you talk to him? Try to get him to come home?"

Max's jaw tightened. "I'll talk to him for you, but I'm not making any promises."

"We understand," Cleo said quickly.

Trisha stirred uneasily. "I'm not sure this is a good idea. I mean, I don't know if Benjy can handle this kind of pressure. What will I say to him if Max does find him and bring him home?"

"For one thing," Max said, "you will stop calling him Benjy."

A startled silence fell on the group. Cleo and the others gazed at him in mute astonishment.

Cleo got her mouth closed first. "What are you talking about? Benjy is his name. Benjy Atkins."

"Not if he comes back here willingly and shoulders his responsibilities," Max said. "If you're going to ask good old Benjy to become a man, the least you can do is to treat him like one. From now on, his name is Ben."

"Sure, Max, I can run that list of names through the computers," Compton O'Reilly said on the other end of the phone. "But what the hell's going on? Is it true you've left Curzon International?"

O'Reilly sounded amused, but that was nothing new, Max thought. He always sounded that way. Max was one of the few people who understood that O'Reilly's humorous approach to life was a facade. Since the death of his beloved wife and daughter in a plane accident five years ago, O'Reilly had retreated into a place where nothing seemed to bother him. Max would have envied him if he hadn't sensed that, for O'Reilly, the relentless amusement was a way to cover up the pain that still burned hot inside him.

"I'm through with Curzon." Max cradled the phone between his shoulder and his ear as he reached for a pen. "I've got a new position."

"No kidding?" O'Reilly said. "There've been some rumors, but I didn't believe them. Thought sure the Curzons would make you an offer you couldn't refuse after the old man died."

"I'm not open to offers from Curzon." Max winced as he leaned back in his chair. He rubbed his leg and gazed out the window of his room. It occurred to him that he was starting to enjoy the view from the attic.

"I can't say I'm totally surprised to hear that some other big chain got you. Was it Global Village Properties? They've been after you for a long time."

"I didn't go with Global Village or any of the other big chains." Max tapped the pen idly against the pad of yellow paper sitting on the desk. The names of all the guests who had stayed at the inn that weekend were listed alphabetically on the first page of the pad. He had noted addresses and phone numbers beside each name.

"Picked a small independent, huh?" O'Reilly sounded briefly thoughtful. "What's up? Looking for a challenge? Going to buy out a small operation and start your own hotel chain? I can see you doing that. You're the one person who could give the Curzons a run for their money. Should be fun to watch."

"It's just a small inn on the coast, and I don't have any plans to buy it out and turn it into a chain."

O'Reilly chuckled. "Come off it, Max, I can't see you running a folksy little bed-and-breakfast place on the coast."

"You don't understand. I'm not running the place at all. I'm working for the owner."

"Doing what?" O'Reilly demanded.

"Odd jobs. Unclogging toilets, hauling firewood, tending bar. At the moment I'm trying to handle a small security problem," Max said. "Do you think you can stop laughing long enough to check out that list of names I just gave you, or shall I call Brindle Investigations?"

"Hey, no need to call the competition. I can handle this. Who do I bill?"

"Send the bill to me."

"Something I don't understand here," O'Reilly said. "You've already got the addresses for those people. What, exactly, do you want me to look for?"

"I'm not sure." Max scanned the page of names. "See if anyone on that list has connections with ultraconservative groups or off-the-wall religious organizations. You might also check on whether or not any of them have a record for getting arrested for making right-wing social protests or causing disturbances over First Amendment issues. That kind of thing."

"You think you're dealing with some morally outraged fanatic?"

"It feels like that," Max said. "My employer wrote a book that's just been published. I think what we've got here is a self-appointed censor who's decided to mete out his own brand of literary criticism to an author."

"Sounds like a guy who's got a couple of screws loose, is that it?"

"Whoever he is, he's the type who would go out of his way to frighten an innocent writer."

"There's no shortage of people who feel called upon to censor what other people read, Max, you know that."

"I know, but I'm hoping that the number of people who would take the trouble to track down an anonymous author and leave weird warnings around will make a much shorter list."

"I'll see what I can do," O'Reilly said. "I should have the info in a few days."

Max eyed the storm that was forming out over the sea. "There's one other name I want you to check out for me, while you're at it. I want to find a young man named Benjamin Atkins."

"Is he connected to your security problem?"

"No, I don't think so. Separate issue. He's a former employee of the inn. Left in the middle of the night with no forwarding address."

"I get the picture. What did he take with him?"

"It's not what he took, it's what he left behind," Max said.

"Okay, be cryptic. What do I care? Give me what you've got on Atkins."

Max read off the few meager facts Cleo had given him. Ben's young life was all too easily summarized. Parts of it reminded Max of his own past. At least he hadn't gotten a young woman pregnant when he was barely twenty-three, Max reflected. He'd always been very careful not to get any woman pregnant.

That thought brought to mind a strangely tantalizing image of how Cleo would look ripe and round with his baby. A surge of possessiveness and wonder twisted Max's insides. *His baby.* It struck him that this was the first time he had actually thought about having a kid of his own.

"I'll get back to you as soon as I've got something," O'Reilly said.

"Thanks." Max hesitated. "By the way, there's no great rush on that Atkins situation."

"What the hell's that supposed to mean?"

Max kneaded his left leg and studied the sea. "It means that I'm in no great rush to get answers. Take your time." He hung up the phone.

The reason he was in no hurry to locate Atkins was that once he did he would have to carry out the mission that Cleo and the others had assigned him. It was almost certainly going to be Mission Impossible. Max was ninety-nine percent sure he wouldn't be able to talk Atkins into returning to the inn's odd family.

Hell, Max thought, he didn't have the slightest idea of how to go about convincing a young man to accept his responsibilities.

The Atkins situation was shaping up to be one of those exceedingly rare, but very memorable, occasions when Max knew he was almost bound to screw up. He hated failure, hated it with a passion. The price was too damn high.

When he failed to talk Atkins into coming back, Max knew he would not find a warm welcome waiting for him back at Robbins' Nest Inn. People treated you differently when you didn't give them what they wanted. An outsider was welcome only as long as he was useful.

It was a pragmatic issue, Max told himself, not an emotional one. Being edged out of the inn's cozy family would make it difficult to continue searching for the Luttrells. That meant he had to find the paintings before he left in search of Ben Atkins.

Max continued to massage his aching thigh. The answer was obvious. He would have to seduce Cleo. That would be the fastest, easiest way to get the answers he wanted.

Cleo was the key to recovering his inheritance. She had to know more than she'd admitted. There was no reason for Jason to have lied to Max on his deathbed.

Cleo knew where the paintings were, and Max knew from reading *The Mirror* that she was vulnerable to passion. Now that he had discovered the fire in her, he was almost certain he could make her want him.

Max stopped rubbing his thigh and contemplated the pot of herbal tea Andromeda had sent upstairs with him earlier.

"Cleo says you're having a bit of trouble with that leg of yours," Andromeda had said as she'd bustled about the kitchen, preparing the concoction. "Try a cup or two of this and see if it doesn't help."

"Does wonders for my arthritis," Daystar had volunteered.

"Try it, Max," Cleo had insisted. "Andromeda's teas are great for headaches and sore muscles."

The stuff tasted like essence of weeds, as far as Max was concerned. But the novelty of having Cleo and the rest of her "family" fuss over him had proved irresistible for some reason. He'd already gotten one full cup of the stuff down. Maybe it was his imagination, but his leg did seem to feel better, just as it had last night when Cleo had massaged it. He decided to try a second cup.

Hot images of the previous night flooded back, sending another rush of desire through his veins. Max sipped the tea as he allowed himself to savor the memory of Cleo's mouth under his. Sweet, fresh, and trembling with a shy eagerness.

His instincts told him that he could satiate himself with the warmth of her body as he had never been satiated before in his life. All he had to do was unlock the flame inside the ice.

But time was running out. O'Reilly was good. Max knew that even taking his time about it, his friend would come up with the answers he had been sent after fairly quickly. At that point Max would be forced to track down Atkins and talk to him. He had given his word.

That meant he had to find the Luttrells before he left in search of Atkins. Max knew that after he'd had his little man-to-man chat with Atkins, things would never be the same for him here at the inn. He would be an outsider once more.

No big deal, Max thought. He was used to the role of outsider. But he wanted those Luttrells.

Two days later Cleo popped into the kitchen to check on dinner preparations. She saw Daystar hovering over a large pot of what looked like Cosmic Harmony's very special bean and vegetable soup.

"Have you seen Andromeda?" Cleo asked.

"She'll be here any minute." Daystar added fresh basil to the pot. "Got delayed at the Retreat."

"Did something happen?" Cleo sniffed the soup appreciatively.

"Some man in a gray suit and a silk tie drove up just as we were leaving. He insisted on talking to her. Said it was important. I came on ahead to get dinner started." Daystar ground some pepper into the soup. "Any word yet on the whereabouts of Benjy?"

Cleo arched her brows. "You mean Mr. Ben Atkins?"

Daystar chuckled. "Oh, that's right. We're supposed to start calling the boy by his new name, aren't we?"

"Max says if we don't, he won't bother to even try to bring Ben back. And, no, as far as I know, there's been no word on his whereabouts."

"Trisha doesn't think Max can find him," Daystar said. "Or that Ben will agree to come back even if Max does locate him."

"We'll see." Cleo turned her head as the back door opened and Andromeda bustled into the room. Water drops sparkled on her iridescent blue rain cape.

"It's pouring out there." Andromeda peeled off the shimmering cape and hung it in a closet. "Thought I'd never get rid of that silly man. What a waste of time. He simply wouldn't take no for an answer."

Daystar closed an oven door. "Salesman?"

"You could say that." Andromeda frowned. "Except that he wanted to buy, not sell. His name was Garrison Spark."

"Hah. I knew it," Cleo muttered. "He was probably trying to steal you and the others for his own restaurant, wasn't he?"

"Not exactly, dear." Andromeda tied her apron around her waist. "He said he was an art dealer. He's looking for some paintings by a man named Luttrell."

Cleo widened her eyes. "Amos Luttrell?"

"Yes, I believe that was it. Why? Have you heard of him?"

"Uh, yes. As a matter of fact, I have." Cleo frowned. "Max mentioned him."

Andromeda picked up a knife and went to work slicing red peppers. "Mr. Spark claims there are five paintings by this Luttrell person floating around out here on the coast somewhere. Says they're worth a fortune."

Daystar glanced at her. "How much is a fortune?"

Andromeda shrugged. "Fifty thousand dollars."

Cleo's mouth dropped open. *"Fifty thousand dollars.* Are you kidding?"

The kitchen door swung open at that moment. Max loomed in the doorway. Sammy was right beside him, Lucky Ducky in hand.

"We need another tray of hors d'oeuvres in the lounge," Max said.

"With olives," Sammy said with an air of grave importance. "All the olives are gone."

Max glanced down at him. "That's because you ate them."

Sammy giggled. "Lucky Ducky ate them."

"I've got another tray ready to go," Daystar said. "I'll send it right out."

Max glanced at Cleo. "Something wrong?"

"Someone named Garrison Spark is looking for those paintings you mentioned the first night you arrived."

Max went utterly still. "Spark is here?"

"Not here," Cleo said. "He went to Cosmic Harmony. Andromeda talked to him. Max, Mr. Spark says those paintings are worth fifty thousand dollars."

"He lied," Max said quietly. "They're worth a quarter of a million. In five years' time they'll be worth a million."

"Good lord," Daystar breathed.

Cleo was dazed. "A quarter of a million?"

"Yes," Max said. He looked at Andromeda. "What did you tell Spark?"

Andromeda looked surprised by the edge in his voice. "I told him I had never heard of Amos Luttrell, let alone the paintings."

Cleo scowled at Max. "What's going on, Max? How could anyone think that Jason owned such valuable paintings?"

His eyes met hers. "I think it's time I explained a few of the facts of life as they relate to Jason Curzon. I told you he was not a poor man. That's putting it mildly. He was Jason Curzon of Curzon International."

"The hotel chain?" Cleo was stunned. "Are you certain of that?"

"Yes," said Max. "I should know. I used to work for him."

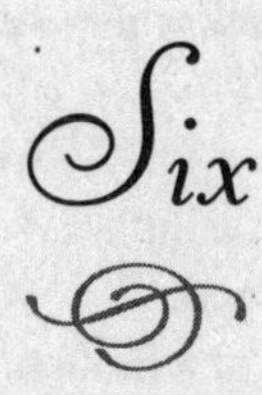

Six

"So our Jason Curzon was really one of those Curzons? The head of the big hotel chain?" Cleo asked again later that night.

She was perched on a stool at the bar, a cup of Andromeda's herbal tea in front of her. It was a typical, slow, midweek night in winter. It was late, and the low hum of conversation in the shadowed lounge had a relaxed, sleepy quality.

Max was behind the bar, looking as professional as if he had spent his entire working life making espresso drinks and serving after-dinner sherry. He was, Cleo reflected, an amazingly adaptable man. He'd handled every task he'd been given with a calm, totally unruffled aplomb.

"That's probably the twentieth time you've asked me that question." Max picked up a newly washed glass and dried it with a white linen towel. "For the twentieth time, the answer is yes."

"He never said a word. Guess he didn't want us to know." Cleo shook her head in silent amazement. "We always knew his last name was Curzon, but we never dreamed he was connected to the hotel family."

"He obviously liked being treated as just another member of your family," Max said quietly. "He was apparently living out a pleasant little fantasy here on the coast. There was no harm in it."

"Of course not, it's just that it's so hard to believe that the head of one of the world's biggest hotel chains spent his weekends here at Robbins' Nest Inn. Sheesh." Cleo made a face. "I had him unclogging toilets, too.

He used to help Benjy—excuse me, I mean *Ben*—with the plumbing all the time."

Max slanted her a strange glance. "You really didn't know who he was, did you?"

"Never had a clue. Not even when we got the letter from a Mrs. Singleton telling us he had died."

"Roberta Singleton was his secretary. Knowing Jason, he had probably left her a list of people to notify in the event something happened to him."

"And we were on the list." Cleo recalled the many long talks she'd had with Jason here in the lounge. "At least I know now why he had so many good suggestions about running this place. I nearly doubled my profit this past year, thanks to him. It was Jason's idea to put in the computerized billing system."

"Jason knew what he was doing when it came to running hotels." Max picked up another glass. "He was the best in the business."

Cleo watched him closely. "No wonder you thought I was some kind of gold-digger when you first got here."

"Let's not reopen that subject."

"Suits me." Cleo took a sip of her tea and frowned as she remembered another topic he had brought up that first night. "So you worked for him?"

"Yes."

Cleo studied his expressionless face and knew intuitively that the single-word answer covered a lot of territory. "What exactly did you do for him?"

"Odd jobs. Same as I do for you."

"Somehow I can't envision you tending bar and handling luggage for Curzon International," Cleo said.

"Why not? I do it here."

"You do have a knack for making yourself useful." Cleo decided to abandon that subject. "What about those paintings you mentioned? Those Artie Lutefisks or whatever you called them."

Max gave her a pained look. "Luttrells. Amos Luttrells."

"Right. Luttrells. The night you arrived you seemed to think Jason might have left them here."

"That's what he told me." Max's eyes were completely shuttered now. It was impossible to tell what he was thinking.

Cleo tilted her head to one side. "Now this Garrison Spark person is looking for them. He must think they're here, too. Know anything about him?"

"He owns a gallery in Seattle. Very exclusive. I worked for him for a while."

"Him too?" Cleo elevated one brow. "You do get around, don't you? What did you do for Mr. Spark?"

"Crated paintings. Transported them. Delivered them to their owners. Strictly manual labor. I didn't work for Spark very long." Max studied the reflection in the glass he was polishing. "He and I had a few differences of opinion on a couple of matters."

"What matters?"

Max looked at her, his gaze steady. "Spark is very smart, and he knows a great deal about contemporary art. But he's not bothered by pesky little nuisances such as honesty and integrity. If he thinks he can pass off a fake to a client and get away with it, he'll do it."

"Really?" Cleo was fascinated. "I've never met a crooked art dealer. He sounds kind of exotic."

"He's got all the ethics of a snake." There was a rough edge to Max's voice. "You heard what Andromeda said. He claimed the Luttrells were only worth fifty thousand."

"You're sure they're worth more?"

Max's mouth tightened. "A lot more."

"And you're sure they belong to you?"

"I'm damn sure they belong to me," Max said very softly.

"Did Jason actually *give* them to you?"

"Yes."

"He just up and gave you a bunch of very valuable paintings?" Cleo persisted.

"Yes."

"The two of you must have been awfully good friends," she observed.

"You could say that." Max stacked the dried glasses in precise rows on the counter. "On his deathbed he said—" Max broke off abruptly and concentrated on arranging the glasses. "Forget it."

Cleo nearly lost her balance on the stool as the deep emotions emanating from Max washed over her. She could also feel the equally powerful waves of the self-control he was exerting.

"Max?" she prodded gently. "What did he say to you?"

Max's eyes were stark when they met hers, but his voice was perfectly neutral. "He said something about me being the son he'd never had."

Cleo looked at him and knew beyond a shadow of a doubt that Jason's dying words constituted the most important words Max had ever heard in his life. "Oh, Max. . . ."

Max's mouth curved with cool self-mockery, but his eyes did not change. "I knew at the time that Jason was exaggerating. Hell, I was his employee, not blood kin. Nobody knew that better than me."

"Yes, but if he called you his son he must have cared for you a great deal."

Max's smile vanished. He concentrated on polishing another glass. "He was dying. Deathbed conversations are probably always a little melodramatic. I'm sure he didn't expect me to take him literally." He paused briefly, his gaze hardening. "But he did give me the Luttrells. There was no mistake about that."

She knew then that it had been a very, very long time since anyone other than Jason had told Max even indirectly that he was loved. She thought about the great love of her parents, which had bonded her small family together, and knew a searing sense of sorrow for all that Max had missed.

"Those Luttrell paintings are more than just a valuable gift, aren't they? They're your inheritance from Jason," Cleo said. "He wanted you to have them."

"He sent me out here to find them," Max said in the same dangerously neutral tone. "He said he'd left them in your care."

"Hmm. I wonder what he meant by that." Cleo glanced at the paintings of English hunt scenes that decorated the walls of the lounge. "Jason never even mentioned them to me."

"Is that right?"

Cleo glowered at him. "What's that supposed to mean?"

"Nothing." Max smiled coolly, his expression speculative. "I'm just wondering what he meant, that's all."

"Well, I haven't got the foggiest idea," Cleo said. She was about to pursue the point when she realized that Max's attention had shifted to the door of the lounge. Cleo turned her head to see what he was looking at.

A man with the sharp, angular features of a tormented poet sauntered into the room. He was wearing a black pullover, black jeans, and black boots. His dark brown hair was swept straight back from his forehead and hung down to his shoulders. There was a distinctly smoldering quality to his heavy-lidded gaze.

Cleo smiled at him.

"Friend of yours?" Max asked softly.

She leaned slightly across the bar. "That's Adrian Forrester. Harmony Cove's great unpublished writer. He arrived in town a year ago and told everyone he was an author, but so far he hasn't made a single sale. He comes in here once or twice a week."

Max's brows rose. "I take it you haven't told him about your success?"

"Are you kidding? I seriously doubt that he would want to hear about it. I think it would depress him." She sat back as Adrian approached.

Adrian reached the bar and took the stool next to Cleo's with languid grace. He gave her the world-weary smile he had practiced to the point of perfection. A jaded Lord Byron consumed by ennui.

"I thought I'd drop in for an espresso," Adrian drawled. "I've been doing battle with a crucial scene in my book all day. Can't seem to get it the way I want it. Thought some caffeine and a change of atmosphere would help."

Cleo smiled consolingly. "Sure. Max, here, makes great espresso."

Adrian flicked Max a brief, dismissive glance. "Make it a double, pal. I need a jolt."

"I'll see what I can do," Max said. "But I'm warning you, if you say 'Play it again, Sam,' I won't be responsible for the results."

"Huh?" Adrian's brow furrowed in confusion.

"Forget it." Max went to work at the gleaming espresso machine. Steam hissed.

Adrian swung around on his stool to face Cleo. He nodded toward Max without much interest. "Someone new on staff?"

"Yes," Cleo said. She knew from experience that the only thing Adrian really liked to talk about was himself, so she changed the topic. "How's the writing going?"

Adrian gave an eloquent shrug. "I've got a proposal out to a couple of major publishers. I'm expecting to hear from one of them soon. They're going to go wild for it. I'll probably find myself in the middle of an auction. I suppose I'll have to see about getting an agent one of these days."

"Another mystery?"

"Yeah. It's called *Dead End.* Classic, hard-boiled detective fiction. It's the purest form of the genre, you know. Very few people are doing it these days." Adrian's mouth twisted in disgust. "Too many women writers out there doing romantic-suspense."

"Is that right?" Cleo asked.

"Yeah. They're ruining the genre with a bunch of female detectives. Even in the books where the protagonist is a man, they give him a female companion." Adrian grimaced. "Everybody's doing *relationships.*"

"What's wrong with that?" Cleo asked, thinking about the very romantic relationship she had put into *A Fine Vengeance.* "I like some romance in a story."

"Give me a break, Cleo. Romance is women's stuff. I'm writing real books."

"Are you implying there's something wrong with what women like to read?" Cleo asked very politely. She tried to be patient with Adrian, but there was no getting around the fact that he could be a real pain.

"I'm saying that the modern mystery novel has been ruined by female writers who have insisted on making the relationships in the story more important than solving the crime," Adrian stated grandly. "Who the hell wants a relationship in a mystery?"

"Women readers, maybe?" Cleo suggested.

"Who cares about them?" Adrian gave her a dark, brooding look. "I'm writing classic mystery. Lean and mean. The tough stuff. My work is pared down to the essentials."

"The essentials, hmm?"

"I'm creating something important, something that will endure, something that the critics will love. I'll be damned if I'll cater to a bunch of women readers who are looking for *relationships* in a story."

Max set the espresso down in front of him. "I'm not so sure that's a smart move, Forrester. People have always read for character rather than plot. And good characterization requires a relationship of some kind."

Cleo smiled approvingly.

Adrian gave Max an annoyed look. "What are you? Some kind of literary critic?"

"Not tonight. Tonight I'm a bartender."

"Take some advice and stick with that job. Something tells me you aren't going to make it in a more demanding field." Adrian picked up the small cup of espresso, took a deep swallow, and promptly choked.

"Aaargh!" He sputtered wildly and grabbed a napkin.

Alarmed, Cleo reached over to pound him on the back. "Are you all right, Adrian?"

Adrian glowered furiously at Max. "What the hell did you put in this espresso?"

"I used French roast and doubled the shot." Max looked innocent. "You said you wanted it strong."

"Damn it to hell, that's downright lethal," Adrian growled.

Max smiled politely. "I make coffee the way you write mysteries. Lean and mean. The tough stuff."

Max was deliberately seducing her.

The day after the scene with Adrian, Cleo sat quietly on the mat in Cosmic Harmony's spare, tranquil meditation center and absorbed the full impact of what was happening.

Max was making it clear that he wanted to take her to bed.

It was a subtle form of seduction. Since that one kiss in the solarium, there had been no overt moves from Max. But Cleo could feel the mesmerizing desire in him whenever he was in the same room. It flowed over her and around her, enthralling her as nothing else had ever done.

Usually Cleo sought out the calm of the meditation center after one of the unpleasant dreams, but this afternoon she had come here to think about Max.

She gazed into the large yellow crystal that was the only object in the room and knew that she had reached a turning point in her life.

The crystal caught the pale light of the cloudy day and glowed a soft, warm gold. Cleo stared into the amber depths and thought about the past and the future.

She had always been very certain that if and when the right man showed up in her life, he would fall in love with her just as she would fall in love with him. She had been sure that the bond would be there between them from the moment their eyes met.

But Max Fortune knew very little about love and probably trusted the emotion even less.

He did, however, know a great deal about desire.

Soon, Cleo knew, she would have to make a choice. She could either surrender to the powerful sensual thrall of desire that Max was forging, or she could draw back to the safe place within herself.

She could draw back and wait.

Wait for what? she wondered. There would be no other man like Max. He was the man in the mirror.

But she had created the mirror, she reminded herself. The only things she saw in the glass were the things she, herself, projected into it.

The truth was that when she looked into the mirror of her mind and heart, she never saw a clear reflection of the man for whom she waited. Yet she was sure that Max was that man.

Earlier this afternoon she had confronted the fact that she was very probably in love with him.

The incident that had triggered the knowledge was a small one, but it had had a devastating impact on Cleo. It had made her realize that she had reached a point of no return.

It had all come about innocently enough. Sylvia had been busy when the time came to pick Sammy up from kindergarten. Max had offered to fetch him. Cleo had invited herself along for the trip because she had wanted to pick up some things at the drugstore in town.

She and Max arrived at Sammy's school a few minutes early and sat in the Jaguar in the parking lot, waiting for the children to come pouring out of the gate.

"One of us is always very careful to be here when Sammy gets out of school," Cleo had explained. "He gets very anxious if there's no one waiting."

"I see," Max said. He rested one arm on the wheel and watched the school entrance.

At that moment the door opened, and a dozen screaming kindergarteners dressed in rain coats and hoods raced out onto the sidewalk. Cleo spotted Sammy in his little yellow slicker. The boy was scanning the cluster of waiting vehicles, searching for his mother's car or, perhaps, Cleo's familiar red Toyota. He didn't recognize the green Jaguar immediately. His small face crumpled with alarm.

"He doesn't see us," Cleo said. She reached for the door handle.

"I'll let him know we're here." Max opened his door and got out.

Sammy saw him at once and broke into a happy, relieved grin. He dashed toward the Jaguar, heedless of the rain puddles. Max opened the back door.

"Hi, Max," Sammy said as he scrambled into the back seat.

"Hi, Sammy."

Sammy looked at Cleo. "Hi, Cleo."

"Hi, kid." Cleo turned in the front seat to smile at him. "How was school?"

"It was okay." Sammy opened a folder. "We made pictures. I did one for you, Max. Here." He removed a crayon drawing and held it out to Max.

Cleo realized that she was holding her breath. She knew in a moment of stunning clarity that if Max failed to properly appreciate Sammy's picture, he was the wrong man for her. It was that simple.

Max eased himself slowly back behind the wheel and closed his door. He took the crayon drawing without comment and examined it for a long moment.

Silence filled the Jaguar.

Then Max looked up, his gaze gravely serious. He turned in the seat to face Sammy. "This is one of the most beautiful pictures I have ever seen, Sammy. Thank you."

Sammy glowed. "Are you going to put it on the wall in your room?"

"Yes. Just as soon as we get home," Max said.

Cleo let out the breath she had been holding. She knew then that her fate was probably sealed. She had fallen in love with Max Fortune.

Cleo felt another presence in the meditation room at the same moment that a shadow fell on the yellow crystal. She pulled her mind back to the present and waited.

"Andromeda said I would find you here." Max's cane thudded softly on the hardwood floor.

Cleo looked up at him. His eyes held the same shimmering intensity that she had seen in them when he had examined Sammy's drawing that afternoon. He held a single red rose in his right hand.

"Hello, Max." Cleo did not dare look at the rose. "What are you doing here?"

"I came to give you this." He dropped the rose lightly into her lap.

Cleo picked it up as if it might explode in her hands. Chapter five, she thought. The man had, indeed, been studying *The Mirror.*

The red rose in chapter five had symbolized seduction. Cleo wondered what Max would think when he got to the last chapter in the book. That chapter featured a white rose as a symbol of love.

Cleo wondered if Max could only go as far as the red rose.

"I don't know what to say," she whispered.

Max smiled. "You don't have to say anything."

Her eyes met his, and she knew that he spoke the truth. There was no need to say anything, because Max knew exactly how close she was to falling into his arms.

The inn's lounge was quiet again that evening. The handful of guests were clustered around the hearth sipping espressos, lattes, and sherry. Cleo sat on her favorite stool and watched Max wash and dry glasses. Neither of them had referred to the small scene in the meditation center that afternoon.

"You know, you're really good at that," she said as Max rinsed another glass and set it on the tray. "You're good at everything around here. Remind me to have you take a look at one of the water pipes in the basement tomorrow. It's leaking."

"Something is always leaking around this place," Max said. "One of these days you're going to have to put in new plumbing."

Cleo sighed. "That will cost a fortune."

"You can't run a place like this without making occasional capital investments."

"Easy for you to say," she grumbled. "You're not the one who has to come up with the money. I wish Benjy would come back."

"Ben."

"Right, Ben. He had a knack for handling the plumbing."

Max seemed to hesitate. "Speaking of Ben—" He broke off abruptly and glanced toward the door. "Ah, I see we are about to entertain another one of your gentlemen callers."

"My what?" Cleo glanced around in surprise. "Oh, that's Nolan."

"The budding politician?"

"Yes. I wonder what he wants."

Nolan walked purposefully toward the bar. He was wearing a handsome leather jacket, a discreetly striped shirt, and a pair of dark slacks. His light brown hair was attractively ruffled and slightly damp from the rain. He smiled broadly at Cleo, just as if he hadn't labeled her book pornography a few days ago.

"Hello, Nolan." Cleo peered at him warily. "What brings you here?"

"I wanted to talk to you." Nolan sat down on the stool next to Cleo's. He glanced briefly at Max. "You're new here, aren't you?"

Cleo stepped in to make introductions. "Nolan, this is Max Fortune. He's a new employee. Max, this is Nolan Hildebrand."

"Hildebrand." Max inclined his head and continued drying glasses.

"Fortune. I'll have a double decaf nonfat grande latte," Nolan said.

Max elevated one brow, but he did not respond. He turned to the espresso machine and went to work preparing the coffee drink.

Cleo idly stirred her tea. "Gosh, Nolan, I hope you're not jeopardizing your chances of getting elected next fall by being seen here with me tonight. I'd really hate to have that on my conscience."

Nolan had the grace to look abashed. "You've got a right to be annoyed with me, Cleo. I handled that scene at the cove very badly."

"Was there a good way to handle it?" Cleo asked. She was aware that Max was listening to every word.

"I shouldn't have come unglued just because you wrote that book," Nolan muttered. "It wasn't that big a deal. I want to apologize."

Cleo widened her eyes in surprise. "You do?"

Nolan nodded his head with sober humiliation. "Yeah. I behaved like an ass. Will you forgive me?"

Cleo relented instantly. "Sure. Don't worry about it. I know it must have been a shock to find *The Mirror* stuffed into your mailbox along with that note."

"You can say that again." Nolan gave her a rueful smile. "It's still hard for me to believe you wrote something like that. I mean, it just seemed so unlike you, Cleo. All that stuff about ribbons and mirrors and scarves and so on."

Max put a small paper napkin down in front of Nolan and positioned the latte glass in the center. "A fascinating tour de force in the neoromantic style, don't you think?"

"Huh?" Nolan blinked and turned to scowl at Max.

Max picked up another wet glass and went back to work with the dish towel. "I think *The Mirror* offers a unique and insightful perspective on the interior landscape of female sexuality."

Nolan scowled. "Who the hell did you say you were?"

"It varies. Tonight I'm the bartender," Max said. "But getting back to *The Mirror*, I have to say that I was very impressed by the intricately layered depths of many of the scenes. Weren't you?"

Nolan stared at Cleo. "You said no one else around here knew you'd written that book."

"Excepting family, of course," Max murmured.

"Family? What family?" Nolan demanded.

"Never mind," Max said. "Didn't you find that there was extraordinary shape and substance to the eroticism in the book? It goes far beyond the overtly sensual and into the realm of the philosophical."

"Look, I didn't come here tonight to talk about Cleo's book," Nolan ground out through set teeth.

"A definite sense of far-flung resonance pervades every chapter, every scene of the book," Max continued. "The fluent narrative voice conjures up an alternative reality that takes on a life of its own. For the male reader, it creates an alien world, a distinctly female world, and yet I'm sure you found that there was a strange sense of familiarity about it."

"Christ, I don't believe this," Nolan muttered. "Cleo, I wanted to talk to you about something very important."

Cleo gulped the last of her tea, nearly choking on her own laughter. "Sure, Nolan," she sputtered. "What's on your mind?"

Nolan shot a wary glance at Max and lowered his voice. "This is sort of personal."

"The portrayal of a female view of sexuality in *The Mirror* was nothing short of riveting," Max offered as he poured more tea into Cleo's cup. "The reader has the sense that the narrator is both the seducer and the one who is seduced. It brings up several interesting questions about the matter of reader identification, as far as I'm concerned. What was your conclusion?"

"Can't you shut him up?" Nolan asked Cleo.

Cleo looked at Max and saw the gleam in his eyes. "Probably not."

"The reader must ask himself, for example," Max said in measured, pedantic tones, "just who is the seducer in *The Mirror?* Is it a work of autoeroticism? Is the narrator actually seducing herself when she looks into the mirror?"

That was certainly what the reviewers had believed, Cleo thought. She waited with a sense of impending fate to hear what Max had to say about it.

"I'm trying to have a private conversation here," Nolan said in a tight voice.

Max ignored him. "Personally, I think something far more complex is going on. Women writers, after all, are interested in relationships. I believe that the figure in the mirror is the *other,* and that, initially, at least, he is actually the seducer. But there's another problem in the book. I think the man in the mirror is just as trapped in his world as the narrator is in hers."

Cleo froze. None of the reviews that had appeared on *The Mirror* had understood that fundamental fact. Her eyes met Max's, and she nearly fell off the bar stool when she saw the deep, sensual understanding in his gaze.

She gripped the edge of the bar and held on for dear life. That shattering moment of silent communication did more to melt her insides than anything her imagination had conjured up when she wrote *The Mirror.*

Max smiled slowly at her. Instead of giving her a fresh napkin to accompany her second cup of tea, he put a playing card down beside the saucer. He reached into his pocket, removed a small object, and set it down on top of the card.

Cleo was afraid to glance at the face of the card. But in the end she was unable to resist.

When she looked down her worst fears were confirmed. The card was a queen of hearts. Lying on top of the card was a small, familiar key. She knew it was the key to the attic room. Cleo jerked her eyes back up to meet Max's. What she saw there stole her breath.

"What's going on here, Cleo?" Nolan glared at the card and the key. "What's this all about?"

"I don't know," Cleo admitted. But the admission was made to Max, not to Nolan. Nolan seemed to have faded somewhere into the distance. Max was the only person who mattered.

"There's only one way to find out, isn't there?" Max said softly. "You'll have to use the key."

It was a scene straight out of her book. Like the red rose, the key had been another symbol of seduction. Cleo was light-headed. It was as if she had stepped into a dream that she, herself, had fashioned but that Max now controlled. Nothing felt quite real. She wondered if Andromeda had been experimenting lately with the formulas of her herbal teas.

Nolan was looking confused and angry. He scowled at Max. "What's with that key and the card?"

"Cleo's been looking for them for a long time," Max said gently. "I found them for her."

Nolan turned back to Cleo. "Damn it, I'm trying to talk to you about something that involves a lot of money. I don't know who this guy is"—he jerked a thumb at Max—"but I've had about enough of his interference."

Max smiled dangerously. His eyes gleamed.

Cleo wrenched herself momentarily free of the silken web of sensual promise that was swirling around her. She tried to concentrate on Nolan's annoyed face. "What did you say about a great deal of money?"

Nolan apparently decided that he finally had her full attention. He leaned forward intently. "A man named Garrison Spark came by my office today. He's looking for some very valuable paintings that he thinks may have been left here in Harmony Cove. He says that old guy who used to stay here at the inn was actually a very wealthy member of the Curzon family."

"I know."

"Spark says Curzon owned the paintings but that he had sold them to Spark just before he died."

Cleo stared. "Mr. Spark told you that Jason sold him the Luttrells?"

Nolan leaned closer. "You know about them?"

"I know that the Luttrells, if they're ever found, belong to Max, here."

Nolan's knuckles were white. His eyes narrowed. "The hell they do. Spark said Fortune might try to claim them, but he says Fortune has no proof of ownership."

"And Spark does?" Cleo asked.

Nolan nodded quickly. "Spark can produce a bill of sale."

Max set a glass down very casually and picked up another. "Spark is very good at producing forgeries of all kinds."

Nolan ignored him. "Cleo, the paintings belong to Spark. What's more, he's got a client who will pay fifty thousand dollars for them. Spark says he'll pay a finder's fee if we can figure out where Curzon stashed the paintings."

"A finder's fee?" Cleo repeated. "You mean a commission?"

"He'll go fifty-fifty." Nolan was barely able to contain his excitement. "Whoever finds those paintings and turns them over to Spark will collect twenty-five thousand dollars. I could really use that kind of money for my campaign fund."

"I could use it to fix the plumbing here at the inn," Cleo mused.

Nolan's smile held a hint of satisfaction. "We'll split the twenty-five grand, Cleo. Deal?"

"Afraid not," Cleo said. "For openers, I have no idea where the paintings are."

"They've got to be around here somewhere," Nolan insisted. "Spark is convinced that Curzon hid them here in Harmony Cove. He talked to someone at Cosmic Harmony first because he'd heard that Curzon was friends with some of the women there. But I know how much Curzon liked you."

"Jason was my friend."

"Right," Nolan agreed swiftly. "And I'll bet that if he left those paintings anywhere, he left them here at the inn. Level with me. Do you know where they are?"

"No."

"Are you sure? Because there's a lot of money involved here. I know how sentimental you are. You're the type who would hang on to those Luttrells just because they reminded you of an old friend. But they're too valuable to be kept around as mementos."

"I'm not keeping them around as mementos," Cleo said patiently. "I have no idea where they are. And if they do turn up, Max has first claim to them."

"Not according to Garrison Spark." Nolan shot Max a disgusted glance. "According to Spark, Fortune was just a professional gofer. He did odd jobs for Spark for a while. Then he quit without any notice to do odd jobs for Curzon International, where he apparently managed to ingratiate himself with Jason Curzon. He says Fortune is an opportunist who always has an eye out for the main chance."

"A man's got to make a living," Max said.

Cleo stirred uneasily on the bar stool. She was still feeling disoriented. Out of the corner of her eye she saw the key to the attic room glinting in the soft light. "Nolan, I don't know anything about the paintings. You're wasting your time."

"Okay, so maybe you don't know where they are," Nolan said quickly. "But Spark thinks they're around here somewhere, either at the inn or at Cosmic Harmony. I propose we join forces to find them."

"Forget it," Cleo said.

"You heard the lady," Max said.

"Why don't you just shut up and tend bar?" Nolan muttered.

Max's smile was dangerously benign. "If you don't want to talk business, I suppose we could go back to *The Mirror.* Did you notice the allusions and metaphors that permeate the book? The use of the scarlet ribbon was especially interesting. It creates both a threat and a bond. A brilliant commentary on the different ways in which men and women view sex and sensuality, don't you think?"

"Goddammit, I've had enough of this." Nolan got to his feet and turned to Cleo. "I'll talk to you some other time when he isn't around."

"I'm sorry." Cleo felt a pang of regret. Until the other morning at the cove, Nolan had been a friend. She jumped down off the stool and took his arm. "I'll walk you out to the lobby."

Nolan was immediately mollified. "This business with the Luttrells is important, Cleo. There's a lot of money involved."

"I understand." Cleo refused to look back at Max as she guided Nolan out of the lounge. "But I really don't know where the paintings are. Jason never said a word to me about them."

"You're sure?"

"Absolutely certain."

"They've got to be around here somewhere. Spark is sure of it." Nolan's mouth thinned in frustration. "Listen, Cleo, Spark says Fortune is a two-bit con man. He says the guy has no legal claim to those paintings."

"I think Max does have a claim to them," Cleo said quietly.

"Don't be a fool. Spark has a bill of sale. Damn it, it's obvious Fortune is trying to charm you into telling him where the paintings are. I don't want to see you get hurt, Cleo."

"Thoughtful of you."

"I mean it," Nolan said. "Cleo, in spite of what happened, we're old friends. I only want what's best for you."

"Thanks for coming by, Nolan." Cleo opened the front door. "I accept your apology. I'm glad we're still friends."

"Sure." Nolan came to a halt at the door. His brows drew together in a frown. "Why the hell did you let Fortune read your book? You said you didn't want anyone to know you'd written it."

"It's okay, Nolan. Max is one of the family." Cleo shut the door gently in his face and leaned back against it with a long sigh.

Max had behaved outrageously. She would have to speak to him. The trouble was, she wasn't sure quite what to say. All she could think about was the key to the attic room that he had given to her.

Cleo took a moment to regroup her forces. Then she straightened away from the door and stalked back into the lounge. The last of the guests were leaving to go upstairs to their rooms. Max was busy closing down the bar.

"I want to talk to you," Cleo said.

"Watch out for Hildebrand," Max said coolly as he shut off the lights behind the bar. "Spark has obviously gotten to him."

Cleo frowned, distracted. "What are you talking about?"

"You heard me." Max came around from behind the bar. He was leaning more heavily than usual on his cane. "Spark has convinced Hildebrand that it will be worth his while to find the paintings. Hildebrand has decided you can help him collect the twenty-five grand. That's the only reason he showed up here tonight."

"It wasn't the only reason. Nolan apologized to me," Cleo said stubbornly.

"Don't be a fool, Cleo."

"Funny, that's what Nolan just said. I'm getting all kinds of good advice tonight."

Max gave her a strange look. "Maybe you ought to take some of it."

Cleo took a deep breath. "Max, I'd like to talk to you about something important."

"I've got something I want to talk to you about, too," Max said. "O'Reilly phoned this afternoon. None of the guests who stayed here at the inn the night the ribbon was left on your pillow checks out as obviously weird."

Cleo was disconcerted. "I'd almost forgotten that your friend was running a check on those people."

"It doesn't mean one of them didn't do it, only that there's no obvious suspect."

"I see."

Max slanted her a brooding glance. "O'Reilly thinks the best way to handle the situation is to ignore it. He says whoever is behind the incidents will grow bored with them if you don't give him the response he wants."

Cleo thought about it. "Do you agree with Mr. O'Reilly?"

Max shrugged. "I'm not sure. But he's the expert on this kind of thing, not me. He says that, based on his experience, he thinks it's most likely someone from the local area who found out about *The Mirror* has decided to play some bad practical jokes on you."

"Some sour-minded malcontent who has nothing better to do, I suppose."

"His advice is to go to your local police chief if there are any more incidents."

"All right." Cleo made a face. "I told you private investigators weren't very useful."

Max paused. "I wouldn't say that. O'Reilly also told me that he found Ben Atkins for you."

That stopped Cleo in her tracks. She smiled at Max in delight. "He did? Where is Benjy? I mean, where is *Ben?* Is he all right?"

"As far as I know. According to O'Reilly, Atkins is working at a gas station in a little town south of here." Max walked toward the door.

Cleo hurried after him, bemused by Max's strange, new mood. It was as if he regretted the fact that his friend had found Ben. "Did he contact him?"

"No." Max went through the door and started toward the stairs. "I thought I'd drive down and see him in person."

"Yes, of course." Cleo climbed the stairs beside him. "That would probably be best. It's really nice of you to do this, Max."

"Don't get your hopes up, Cleo. If he doesn't want to come back to Trisha and the baby, I can't force him."

"I know. But I really think Ben will want to come back home once he's had a chance to get over being scared. He just needs someone he can talk to, Max."

"Maybe." Max halted on the third-floor landing and turned to walk Cleo to her room.

Cleo glanced down at his cane. "Your leg is bothering you tonight, isn't it? We should have taken the elevator."

"I'm fine, Cleo."

"I could make you a batch of Andromeda's special tea. I know the recipe."

"I've got some pills I can take." Max halted in front of her door and held out his hand.

Cleo reached into her pocket for her room key. Her fingers closed first around the key to Max's room. It burned her hand. She quickly dropped it back into her pocket and yanked out the right key.

Max said nothing. He simply took the key from her and unlocked the door.

Cleo stepped into the cozy safety of her room and turned to say good-night. "Max . . ."

His mouth curved faintly. "If you want to talk to me any more tonight, you know where to find me. All you have to do is use the key."

He turned and walked toward the narrow door that opened onto the attic stairs. He did not look back.

Cleo stood in the doorway of her room and watched until Max vanished. Then she slowly closed her door and went to stand in front of the window.

Beneath the scattered clouds, the ocean was a black silk cape that stretched out to the horizon. Moonlight gleamed on its folds as it shifted gently over the mysteries below. Cleo gazed out over the surface of the dark sea, trying to imagine what it concealed.

All you have to do is use the key.

It was another line from her book, of course. Max was apparently memorizing every chapter.

She thought about the way he had been leaning on the hawk-headed cane as he went up the stairs. Her instincts had told her from the start that the recurrent ache in Max's leg mirrored the darker, deeper wound in his soul. He was a man who had survived without much love, and he had found ways to do without. But that did not mean he wasn't hurting.

Five Amos Luttrell paintings, no matter how beautiful or how valuable, were never going to fill the empty places in Max's life. She knew what Max needed, even if he didn't. He needed a home, just as she had needed one after her family had been destroyed.

Cleo opened her fingers slowly and looked down at the key and the card he had put into her hand.

She dropped both into her pocket and went to the door. She let herself out into the hall and went downstairs.

When she reached the kitchen she found a stainless steel kettle, filled it with cold water, and set it on the stove.

A few minutes later Cleo poured the boiling water over the herbs she had placed in a ceramic pot. She put the lid on the pot and added a cup and saucer to the tray.

She carried the tray down the hall and took the small elevator to the third floor. Then she walked to the attic staircase door.

She climbed the darkened stairs to the attic and paused in front of Max's door. The floorboard in front of Max's room squeaked. She knew he could hear the sound from inside the room. Cleo put the tray on the floor and knocked hesitantly.

"Max?"

There was silence for a moment. Then Max's voice came softly from inside the room. "What is it, Cleo?"

"Open the door. I brought you some of Andromeda's tea."

"Use the key that I gave you."

Cleo took a step back as if the door had suddenly become red-hot. "Max, I didn't come up here to play fantasy games with you. I brought you something for your leg."

"I don't need anything for my leg."

"Yes, you do. Don't be so darn stubborn." Cleo dug the key out of her pocket, shoved it into the lock, and opened the door before she lost her nerve.

The only light on in the vast room beneath the eaves was from the small lamp beside the bed. It revealed Sammy's crayon drawing neatly pinned to the wall beside the desk. It also played over Max's dark, shadowed figure near the window.

Cleo saw that he had taken off his shirt and shoes. The only clothing he had on was a pair of trousers.

There was power in the smooth, muscled contours of Max's shoulders. Cleo stared at the dark, curling hair on his chest, fascinated by the way it formed a vee that plummeted beneath the waistband of his pants.

Max's eyes met hers. "The riddle of *The Mirror* is who is the seducer and who is the seduced."

Cleo's fingers trembled as she dropped the key back into her pocket and reached down to pick up the tray. "I didn't come up here to be seduced."

"Did you come up here to seduce me?"

"No."

"Then what are we going to do?"

"Drink tea. At least you are." Cleo kicked the door shut behind her and marched into the room. She put the tea tray down on the desk and poured a cup of the herbal brew. She held the cup out to Max. "Here, have some of this. It will make you feel much better."

"Will it?" Max's gaze was filled with a dangerously disturbing sensuality as he obediently took the cup from her hand. His fingers brushed hers.

"Yes." Cleo rubbed her damp palms on her jeans. "At least I hope it will. You're in a strange mood tonight, aren't you?"

"Am I?" Max took a long swallow of the tea. Then he put the cup down on the desk. "The only mirror in this room is that one over there. I wonder what we'll see in it when we look into it together."

Cleo's gaze went to the old-fashioned full-length mirror on the wooden stand. A shiver of excitement stirred the hair on her neck. As if he knew exactly what she was feeling, Max reached out and took her by the hand. He led her toward the mirror.

Cleo couldn't speak. She waited one last time for the crashing tide of uncertainty and wrongness to wash over her, but nothing happened. There was no fear with Max, no desire to pull back from the brink. She floated across the room as if she were a balloon on the end of a string that he held in his hand.

Max drew her to a halt in front of the mirror. He stood behind her, his hands on her shoulders. His eyes met hers in the silvered glass.

Cleo felt the heat in him. A gathering sense of urgency welled up inside her in response. She was shaken to the core by the force of her own desire. She had not felt this way since she had written *The Mirror.*

"I'm glad you used the key tonight, Cleo." Max unfastened the clip that bound her hair.

She watched the thick mass of her hair tumble down around her shoulders. Then she felt Max's thumbs slide beneath the weight of it. His fingers touched sensitive skin at the nape of her neck.

"Max?"

"Beautiful," he whispered. He bent his head and dropped a kiss into her hair.

Cleo looked into the mirror and saw the face of the man inside the glass. For the first time the reflection was crystal clear.

The man inside the mirror was Max.

Seven

Max removed Cleo's glasses and set them down on a small table. He managed to invest the small action with a startling degree of intimacy. It was as if he had just removed a protective veil. She felt naked and vulnerable.

She could still see well enough to make out her own reflection and that of Max looming behind her, but the images were gently blurred. It was like looking at figures trapped in a silvery mist.

Max's eyes met Cleo's in the mirror. His mouth curved slightly. "Who is the seducer and who is the one who is seduced?"

Cleo shivered. The reflection in the mirror allowed her to see Max's hands move on her shoulders even as she felt the weight of them. The sensual power in him captivated all her senses. "I don't know. I never knew."

"Maybe there isn't an answer." Max flexed his fingers gently. He watched her face. "Maybe it's supposed to be like this."

"Like what?" Cleo could not tear her eyes away from the mirror.

"Like looking into a spectacular painting. Becoming a part of it. Seeing some of the layers and knowing that there will be no peace until you've seen them all."

"What happens when you've seen them all?" Cleo watched his hands slip slowly down her arms. "Do you grow bored with the painting?"

"No. It's impossible to see all the layers. So you keep looking, reexamining the ones you've already seen and searching out new ones. The hunger is always there."

Cleo touched one of his hands with her own. "Hunger?"

"You can satisfy it temporarily, but you know it will return, and you know you will need to look into the painting again. And again." He lifted the heavy weight of her hair aside, bowed his head, and kissed the side of her throat. "And again."

"It sounds painful." But the urgency in her that was generated by his warm, tantalizing kiss was not painful at all. It was exquisitely exciting.

Max's eyes gleamed in the shadows. "The hunger is part of the pleasure. But you know all about that, don't you?"

"No. Yes." She trembled as he traced the line of her jaw with his fingers. "I don't know." The eyes of the woman in the mirror were still veiled in mystery, even though she no longer wore the protective glasses.

"You described the sensation in *The Mirror,*" Max said. He threaded his fingers through her hair as if it were so much precious silk. "There is hunger on every page. The book is filled with it. It's a hunger so deep it has the power to make the reader hungry, too."

"*The Mirror* is a fantasy," Cleo said breathlessly.

Max reached around from behind and started to unbutton her oxford cloth shirt. "A fantasy like the fantasy we're watching in the mirror. A fantasy which is also reality."

"No." But she was no longer certain of that. He was right, the fantasy was rapidly becoming a reality. Max was making it happen. It was disorienting and disquieting. It was also incredibly thrilling.

"You're the woman in the book, and you're the woman we're watching in the mirror, aren't you, Cleo?"

A light-headed sensation swept through her, leaving her a little dizzy. "If I'm her, who are you?"

"You know who I am. I'm the man in the mirror. And I'm the man who's touching you. The brilliance of *The Mirror* is that in it seducer and seduced become one."

She wanted to explain just how much of a fantasy *The Mirror* really was, but she could not find the words. He would never believe that she had an extremely limited acquaintance with the kind of sensuality she had described in her book. No man would believe that *The Mirror* had been created almost entirely from her imagination.

Cleo watched the image in the mirror as Max slowly and steadily undid the buttons of her shirt. She was riveted by the sight of his fingers as they slipped into the shadowed valley between her breasts.

The woman in the glass could not really be her, Cleo thought. She looked mysterious and exotic and sensual; she looked like a Cleopatra, not a Cleo.

Max's fingers touched her bare skin, and she sensed herself start to merge with the woman in the mirror. The man in the misty reflection looked at her with knowing eyes, eyes that saw the many layers waiting to be revealed. Eyes that were filled with a hunger that matched and perhaps exceeded her own. That knowledge shook her.

"Max, I think I'm getting a little scared," Cleo said.

"Of me?"

She looked into the mirror and saw the stark need etched into every line of his face. She also saw the control and self-discipline that governed that need, and she knew that she was safe.

"No," Cleo said softly. "I'm not frightened of you."

"Of yourself?" He had the shirt undone now. Slowly he parted it, revealing her breasts.

"Of the unknown, I think."

"But you know what's waiting for us, Cleo. You wrote a whole book about it." Max eased the shirt off her shoulders and let it fall to the floor. He circled her waist with his hands and slid his palms upward to cup her breasts. "I'm the one who's going into the unknown."

He meant it, Cleo thought, deeply intrigued. Not in the literal sense, of course, but she knew that in some way tonight would be a new experience for Max, too. The knowledge touched her deeply.

Wordlessly she lifted her fingertips to the side of his face. The movement caused her breast to glide upward. Max's thumb skimmed across her nipple, sending a searing jolt of sensation through her.

Cleo cried out softly and closed her eyes for a brief moment. She leaned back against Max, seeking the heat and strength of his body. He was as solid as a rock behind her. The heaviness of his arousal pressed into her buttocks.

Cleo opened her eyes when she felt Max's fingers go to the button of her jeans. He dropped soft, persuasive kisses into her hair as he slid the zipper downward. Cleo stared into the mirror as he eased the jeans and her panties down over her hips. It was like watching a dream unfold. She was part of it and yet still apart from it. The real Cleo was still hovering uncertainly between the image in the mirror and the woman who stood in front of it.

"Look at you." There was primitive male awe in Max's voice. "You're beautiful."

She wasn't, and she knew it, but part of the magic of the night was that Max could make her feel beautiful. Cleo smiled dreamily and put her hands on top of Max's.

He eased his fingers downward into the dark triangle of curls that concealed Cleo's most secret places. She leaned her head back against his shoulder. When he slid one finger into the liquid warmth that had gathered in the folds between her legs, she moaned.

The right man.

Cleo turned abruptly within the circle of Max's arms and splayed her fingers across his chest. Without any hesitation she lifted her face, offering him her mouth.

Max groaned and crushed her lips beneath his. The full force of his own hunger broke over her. Cleo felt like a small, supple tree in a gale.

This kiss was not like the other one that Max had given her that night in the solarium. It was darker, more demanding, and far more blatantly erotic.

Cleo shuddered beneath the sensual onslaught, but she had no wish to pull back from it. Instead, she craved more of Max's brand of hunger. It was, in turn, making her insatiable.

Max cupped her buttocks in his hands and pressed her against his aroused body. She tasted his mouth with her tongue, and he, in turn, shuddered.

"I don't know if I'm going to live through this." Max covered her lips once more with his own and drew her back toward the bed. "And I don't care so long as I have you tonight."

Cleo pressed herself closer. She felt Max stagger a little as he worked to balance her weight as well as his own without the aid of his cane. Cleo heard his sudden, sharp intake of breath and knew that his leg was protesting the added burden. She started to draw back.

"No." Max caught her hands and put them firmly around his neck. His eyes gleamed with passion. "Forget the damned leg. Hold on to me. Tight."

She clung to him and felt the heat that was radiating from his skin. Max was burning up with desire. She wondered if she felt as warm to him.

He collapsed back onto the quilt, dragging Cleo down on top of him. Cleo sprawled across his chest and burrowed into his warmth. She couldn't seem to stop kissing him. She wanted to touch him everywhere.

She showered him with kisses as he lay beneath her. His throat, his chest, his belly; she savored every inch of him. He was so beautifully, powerfully, inexpressibly *male.* The potential they shared was so vast that it almost frightened her. He was the exciting *other,* the one who would set her free and whom she, in turn, would free.

Max sucked in his breath again, but this time, Cleo knew, it wasn't because of the pain in his leg. He wrapped one hand around her head and gently pushed her mouth against the skin of his flat stomach. "Yes," he muttered. "So good."

He reached out, captured her hand in his, and settled her palm over the fierce bulge in his trousers.

Cleo stilled as she cautiously explored the size of his erection. She forced her head up against the weight of his hand. "Max?"

His fingers trembled as he touched her breast. His eyes were shadowed with dark excitement. "I want you."

Cleo smiled tremulously. "I want you, too."

"Then there isn't any reason to stop now, is there?" He searched her face.

Cleo took a deep breath. "No. There isn't any reason to stop."

Max moved, turning onto his side and easing Cleo onto her back. He covered her body with his own and kissed her.

Cleo speared her fingers through his hair and arched herself against him. The reality of what she was experiencing transcended everything she had imagined when she wrote *The Mirror.*

Max tore his mouth free from hers and sat up reluctantly. He unfastened his pants and worked them off. Then he leaned over to open the small drawer in the nightstand. Cleo heard the rustle of a foil wrapper. When he was finished, he turned out the lamp and came back to Cleo.

"You're more beautiful than I had imagined," Cleo whispered. "And bigger." She blushed furiously. "I mean all over. What I meant to say was . . ."

Max smiled slightly as he fitted himself between her legs. "Yes? What did you mean to say?"

Cleo saw the humor in his gaze and shook her head impatiently. She reached up and caught his face between her palms. "Max, what I'm trying to say is that although in some ways you're different from what I expected, in other ways I know you in a way I can't explain. It was you I fantasized about when I wrote *The Mirror.* I don't understand it. How could I have known about you?"

"There's no need to understand it." He brushed his mouth across hers. "You seduced me the first time I saw you. Open for me, Cleo. God knows I need you."

She felt him probing gently, dampening himself in the moisture between her legs. She gripped his shoulders very tightly and braced herself. She was not quite certain what to expect, but the anticipation was threatening to overwhelm her.

Max raised his brows as her nails bit into his skin. "Don't worry, I'm not going anywhere tonight."

"I know." Cleo tried to unlock her fingers. "I'm sorry, I can't help it."

His soft laugh held a world of masculine satisfaction. It also held a tenderness that made Cleo feel safer than she had at any point since the death of her parents. She was in good hands, she told herself.

"It's all right," Max said. "I'm not complaining. It's just that no one's ever held on to me the way you're holding on to me."

"How am I holding you?"

"As if you'll never let go." Max took her mouth again. At the same moment he drove into her swiftly, filling her completely with one long, powerful stroke.

Cleo closed her eyes and gasped in astonishment.

Max went completely still, his entire body suddenly rigid.

Cleo cautiously opened her eyes and found him staring down at her with an expression of stunned shock on his face. Neither of them moved.

Max recovered first. "Don't tell me this was—" He broke off, struggling for words. "Was this your first . . . ?"

"Yes." She smiled up at him, aware that her body was rapidly adjusting to the strangeness of having him lodged within her. "Remind me to drop a note to my therapist in the morning. I want to tell her that it was worth waiting for. I think she thought I was just being picky."

"Damn." Max rested his damp forehead on hers. "I didn't realize."

"I know." Cleo tightened her already fierce grip on his shoulders. She was acutely aware of the aching fullness inside her. "Do you think we could get on with it now?"

"I don't think we could stop it now."

"Good."

Max started to move within her. He was slow and careful and very, very thorough. He made love to her until his back was slick with sweat and his muscles trembled beneath his skin. Cleo felt her body clench around his with each stroke. She could not seem to get enough of the hot, thick feel of him inside her. She lifted her hips off the bed.

"My God, Cleo." He reached down and touched her with slow, knowing fingers.

"Max." Cleo surrendered to the climax with a small, startled shriek.

"Don't be afraid. It's all right. This is how it's supposed to be." Max surged into her one last time on a ragged groan that signaled a surrender as great as her own.

Max was silent for a long time. He lay sprawled on the pillows, his arm around Cleo.

"Why didn't you say something?" he finally asked.

"What was there to say?" Cleo snuggled closer. She was feeling incredibly content and a little sleepy. All she wanted to do was close her eyes and glue herself to Max's warm strength. Unfortunately she was going to have to get dressed and traipse back to her tower room in a few minutes.

"How about, 'Say, Max, I've never done this before, and I'd appreciate it if you'd take your time and do it right,' " Max muttered.

Cleo smiled against his chest. "You didn't seem to need instructions or advice. You did it just right. By the book, as a matter of fact." She paused, remembering his words the night he had put the scarlet ribbon around her and kissed her. "As promised."

Max winced. "About that book," he said ominously. "Do you mind telling me how someone who is, uh . . ."

"Handicapped by the lack of personal experience?" Cleo offered helpfully.

"Let's call it romantically challenged," Max said diplomatically.

Cleo raised her head to look down at him. "Romantically challenged?"

"I was searching for the, uh, politically correct phrase."

Cleo started to grin. "Romantically challenged? *Romantically challenged?"*

"If you don't like that phrase, think of another."

"Let's see." Cleo considered carefully. "What about *relationship deprived?*"

"All right."

"No, no, wait. I've got a better one." Cleo sat up, holding the sheet to her breast. "How about *sexually impoverished?*"

"Whatever. Cleo, what I'm trying to ask is . . ."

"Hold it." Cleo held up a hand. "I've got a better one. *Differently experienced.*"

"Damn it, Cleo . . ."

"Wait, wait, I've got an even better one. How about *sensually impaired?*"

"Enough with the political correctness jokes," Max said. "I'm trying to carry on a serious conversation here."

"You started it. *Romantically challenged.* I love it." Cleo started to laugh.

"So how about answering the question?"

"Romantically challenged." Cleo laughed harder.

"It's not that funny," Max said grimly.

"Yes, it is." Cleo was giggling so much now she could barely speak. "Especially coming from you."

Max gave her a quelling look. "Do you mind telling me how you managed to impart such an interesting note of realism to *The Mirror?*"

Cleo doubled over in another fit of giggles. "I relied entirely on my imagination."

He stared at her in disbelief. "Imagination?"

"If you think about it, you'll recall that most of *The Mirror* is taken up with the feeling of anticipation, not the actual experience."

"The hunger," Max said softly.

"Exactly. The hunger." Cleo savored the rich, warm feeling that filled her. More laughter bubbled within her. "Believe me, I understood that part very well."

Max's expression was bemused. "I won't argue with that. All the same . . ."

"For crying out loud, Max, you don't have to jump out of a plane to guess what it would do to your insides."

"You said that just before your parents died there was a man," Max said carefully.

"There was. Actually there were two or three. Not at the same time, of course. But I never went to bed with any of them."

"Why not?" Max persisted.

Cleo shrugged. "None of them was Mr. Right, even though I have to say that numbers two and three were really terrific kissers. Then, after my parents died, my therapist said I developed that psychological block or whatever it was I told you about."

Max stared at her and slowly shook his head. "It's incredible."

"What is?"

"That you wrote *The Mirror* using just your imagination."

"Talent," Cleo said without a shred of modesty. "Pure talent."

"I've always had a lot of respect for the creative imagination," Max said.

"I'm not surprised. You are, after all, a connoisseur of fine art." Cleo's joy was threatening to explode in another burst of laughter. She didn't know if she would be able to contain it. "Tell me, oh, great expert, how do I compare to the average Van Gogh?"

Max narrowed his eyes. "More colorful."

"Colorful." The laughter overcame her again. She thrashed about in the throes of it and managed to tumble over the edge of the bed. She landed softly on the carpet and burst into a fresh peal of giggles. "How about Picasso?"

"You're a little more unpredictable than Picasso." Max propped himself on his elbow and looked over the side of the bed. His gaze was enigmatic. "You seem to be in an unusually good mood tonight."

Cleo widened her eyes. "Gee, Max, do you really think my mood is unusual under the circumstances?"

"Let's just say I've never heard of anyone who fell out of bed laughing after having sex."

"How many people do you know who waited this long to experience sex?" Cleo countered.

"You have a point." Max paused. "Forget what your therapist said. Tell me what you think you were waiting for all these years."

"The right man, of course."

Max stilled. "The right man?"

"Uh-huh." Cleo's giggles faded at last into a smug smile. She folded her hands behind her head and gazed happily at the ceiling. "My therapist said he'd never come along. That I was using the fantasy as an excuse not to get involved."

"What did you say?"

"I said I sure hoped he wandered into my life sooner or later, because I didn't have any choice in the matter. I *had* to wait for him. All the others felt *wrong*. She didn't understand that, and I couldn't explain it to her. It was one of the reasons why we parted company. That and the fact that she cost a fortune."

"Cleo," Max asked very softly, "how did you know I was the right man?"

She looked up at him from the floor and realized that he was deadly serious. She stopped chuckling. "I don't know. The same way you know a fine painting when you see one, I guess. Some sort of inner eye."

Max gazed down at her for a long while. Then his mouth quirked in a strange fashion. "Speaking of paintings, you really don't know where my Luttrells are, do you?"

"Nope." Cleo sat up. "I'm sorry, Max, but Jason never said a word about them to me."

"I believe you."

"Good, because it's the truth." Cleo smiled as she got to her feet. She found her glasses and pushed them onto her nose. "Holy cow, look at the time. I'd better get dressed and get to my room."

"Stay here with me tonight."

She gave him a wistful look as she pulled on her shirt. "I wish I could, but I can't. George might need to get in touch with me for some reason. He'd call my room, not yours."

"Call him now and let him know you're here with me."

Cleo blushed as she tugged on her jeans. "That would be a little awkward, don't you think?"

"No," Max said. "It would be honest."

"It isn't a matter of honesty, it's a matter of privacy." Cleo stepped into her silver sneakers and leaned down to tie the laces. "And it isn't just him. Anyone else who needs me would look for me in my own room, too. People would worry if they couldn't find me."

Max sat up slowly. "If that's the way you want it, I'll walk you to your room."

"You don't have to do that." Cleo glanced up as Max shoved the sheet aside. The light of the bedside lamp revealed the jagged white scar on his thigh. "Oh, Max," she whispered.

He looked at her and saw the expression on her face. His eyes hardened as he reached for his trousers. "Sorry. I know it's not a pretty sight."

"Don't be ridiculous." Cleo hastened over to him and knelt beside the bed. She touched his leg with light, questing fingers. "No wonder it bothers you so much of the time. Does Andromeda's tea help?"

Max looked at her hands on his thigh. "Surprisingly enough, it does. But not as much as your massage technique."

Cleo stroked and squeezed gently. "My God, when I think about how much it must have hurt. . . ."

"Don't think about it," Max said dryly. "I don't."

"It must have been a terrible accident."

"It was my fault," Max said. "I screwed up."

Cleo studied the odd, puckered scar. "Were you driving?"

He smiled faintly. "Yes." He pulled on his trousers and levered himself to his feet. "Sure you don't want to stay?"

Cleo stood. "I'd love to stay. But I don't think it would be a good idea." She glanced at the tea tray. "Promise me you'll drink the tea before you go to bed."

"It'll be cold."

"It doesn't matter," Cleo insisted. "Drink it anyway."

"All right." He traced the outline of her mouth with his finger. "I promise. Come on. We'd better get you to your room. You've got an inn to run, and I've got a long drive ahead of me in the morning. We both need some rest."

She closed her fingers around his wrist. "Thank you for finding Ben for us."

Max's jaw tightened. "You're welcome. But you do understand that I can't guarantee I'll be able to talk him into returning, Cleo."

"I know." She smiled. "But somehow I think it will all work out. I'm sure that deep down Ben wants to come back to Trisha and the baby."

"I wish you and the others weren't so damn optimistic about it." Max picked up his cane and started for the door. His hand closed almost violently around the knob. "What happens if I can't convince him to come back here?"

"He'll come back with you," Cleo said, feeling extraordinarily confident.

Max said nothing in response. He walked her down the attic stairs and along the corridor to the tower room. When they reached her door he stopped and turned to face her. He tipped her chin up with his finger.

"Cleo," he said slowly, "about tonight. I'm not quite sure what to say."

"It's all right, Max." Cleo stood on tiptoe and brushed her lips across his cheek. "You don't have to say anything." She opened the door to her room and stepped inside. "Good night."

Max examined her in silence for a long moment, as if memorizing every detail of her face. "Good night, Cleo."

He turned and went down the hall to the attic stairs.

Cleo closed the door and leaned back against it. The glorious euphoria was still flowing in her veins. The whole world looked warm and rosy tonight. The future had never seemed so bright and full of promise.

She raised her eyes heavenward and smiled. "Jason Curzon, I don't know what you did with those paintings Max wants so badly, but thanks for sending him out here to look for them."

Everyone gathered in the kitchen the next morning to say good-bye to Max.

"Another stack of buckwheat pancakes?" Daystar asked when she saw that Max's plate was empty.

"No, thank you." Max folded his napkin with great precision and placed it on the table beside the plate.

"More coffee?" Sylvia hovered over him with the pot. "You've got a long drive ahead of you."

"I think I've had enough." Max glanced at his watch. "I'd better be on my way."

Cleo smiled at him from the other side of the table. "Promise you'll drive carefully."

He looked at her with the same unreadable expression that had been in his eyes last night. "I promise."

"We'll be waiting for you," Cleo said softly.

"Will you?" he asked.

Before Cleo could respond, Sammy darted forward and grabbed a fistful of Max's trousers. He tugged on the expensive fabric to get his attention. "Remember to fasten your seatbelt," he said earnestly.

Max glanced down at him. "I'll remember."

Sammy was clearly delighted that his instructions would be followed. He giggled, turned, and dashed out of the kitchen.

Sylvia smiled as the door swung shut behind her son. "You've been good for him, Max."

"We have mutual interests in common," Max said. "We both like books and fine art."

"Take your time driving back tonight," Andromeda advised. "There's another storm on the way. We'll hold dinner for you."

Max looked at her. "I might be very late."

Andromeda smiled serenely. "That doesn't matter. Dinner will be waiting."

Trisha gave Max a misty smile. "Tell Ben I love him," she whispered.

Max got to his feet. "I'll tell him."

"Thank you, Max," Trisha said.

He glanced at the ring of expectant faces that surrounded him. "I'll talk to Ben if I can find him. But there are no guarantees. Do all of you understand that?"

Cleo and the others nodded obediently, if impatiently.

"We understand," Cleo said cheerfully.

Max's mouth twisted. "Like hell you do," he muttered. "You all think I'm going to pull this off, don't you?"

"Nothing is for certain," Andromeda said. "But I think Cleo's right. You're the best man for the job."

"I'll walk you outside to your car." Cleo fell into step beside him. "What time do you think you'll be back?"

"I don't know."

"Well, it doesn't matter." Cleo opened the front door. "We'll be waiting for you."

Max said nothing. When they reached the Jaguar, he took his keys out of his pocket and opened the door. He hesitated before he got behind the wheel.

"Are you okay, Cleo?"

She stared at him curiously. "Sure. Why do you ask?"

He glanced past her toward the others who were standing in the doorway, ready to wave farewell. "You waited a long time for last night. You must have had a lot of unrealistic expectations. I just wondered if you had any regrets this morning."

Cleo smiled slowly. "As it turns out," she murmured, "my expectations weren't unrealistic in the least. In fact, the actual experience far exceeded the most creative flights of my imagination."

Max looked as if he didn't know what to say next. "I, well, I just wondered."

Cleo batted her lashes outrageously. "Was it good for you, too?"

A dull red blush stained Max's high cheekbones. He fumbled briefly with his keys and dropped them on the seat. "Damn." He leaned down quickly to retrieve them. Then he straightened again. "Yes," he said. "It was very good. The best it's ever been."

Cleo grinned. "Right. Well, that's settled."

"I'd better be on my way."

She waited until he got behind the wheel. "Remember what Sammy said. Be sure to fasten your seatbelt."

Max buckled the belt and shoved the key into the ignition. His eyes met hers. "Good-bye, Cleo."

"Good-bye." She bent down to kiss him quickly on the mouth. "Hurry home." She closed the car door.

The Jaguar's engine purred behind her as she walked back to the lobby entrance where Andromeda, Daystar, Sylvia, and Trisha were gathered in the doorway. They all waved at Max.

Cleo turned to wave, too. Max did not wave back. She couldn't tell if he saw them in his rearview mirror or not. "Well, he's off."

Trisha dragged a hankie out of her pocket and blew into it. "Do you really think he'll bring Benjy—I mean, Ben—back?"

Cleo smiled at her reassuringly. "I think if anyone can do it, Max can."

"Cleo's right," Andromeda said. "Max seems very competent."

They all watched in silence as the Jaguar disappeared from sight.

"He's gone." Sammy came running down the hall into the lobby. He was clutching Lucky Ducky, and his eyes were huge.

Cleo and the others looked at him in concern.

"What's wrong, darling?" Sylvia asked gently.

"Max went away for good." Tears formed in Sammy's eyes.

"No, dear, he just went to look for Benjy." Sylvia grimaced. "I mean, Ben. He'll be back tonight."

Sammy shook his head with solemn despair. "He went away forever."

Cleo went down on one knee beside him. "How do you know that, Sammy?"

" 'Cause he took everything with him," Sammy sobbed. "I went upstairs to his room, and all his stuff is gone. Even the picture I gave him."

"You must be mistaken, honey." Cleo stood up quickly. "I'm sure his things are all there."

"They're gone," Sammy whispered. "His door was unlocked, and everything's gone."

"I'll go check," Cleo said.

She dashed up the three flights of stairs to the third floor and paused to catch her breath before she went down the hall to the attic stairs.

Sammy had to be wrong. Max was coming back. He'd said so.

Or had he? Cleo tried to recall his exact words. But the more she thought about it, the more she realized that although Max had implied he would return that evening, he hadn't actually promised to do so.

Cleo opened the narrow door at the end of the hall and took the attic stairs two at a time.

The door to Max's room was unlocked, just as Sammy had said.

Cleo opened it cautiously, aware of a cold feeling in the pit of her stomach.

The room was as neat and orderly as it had been the day Max had moved in. Cleo went through it methodically. Not a single one of Max's expensive white shirts hung in the closet. The dresser was empty. The black leather carryall was gone. So was Sammy's picture, and the copy of *The Mirror* that Cleo had given to Max.

It was as if Max had never been there.

Cleo sank slowly down onto the bed and clasped her hands very tightly in her lap. She remembered the question Max had asked her last night after he had seduced her.

Speaking of paintings, you really don't know where my Luttrells are, do you?

Eight

He would remember her joyous laughter for the rest of his life. Max could still see Cleo clearly in his mind, shimmering first with passion and then with delight. And he had been the one responsible for giving her both.

Max savored the unfamiliar pleasure that coursed through him. Even the pouring rain that partially obscured the highway and the knowledge of what lay ahead could not dim the warmth that welled up inside. He was not accustomed to being viewed as a man who could make someone else happy. He certainly had never seen himself in such a light.

But last night he, Max Fortune, had made Cleo Robbins happy.

She said she had waited all her life for the right man, *for him,* and she claimed she had not been disappointed. Last night, for the first time in his entire life, he, Max Fortune, had been someone's Mr. Right.

And this morning the bizarre little circle of friends that orbited around Cleo had treated him like an important member of the family. To them he had been a hero setting forth on a quest. Everyone had fussed over him, fed him homemade buckwheat pancakes, urged him to drive carefully, told him to hurry home, reminded him that dinner would be waiting.

Dinner would be waiting.

Max contemplated that notion for a long time. He could not remember anyone ever holding dinner for him. The closest he ever came to the experience was when he ordered room service at a Curzon hotel. Max decided that room service definitely didn't count.

Too bad he would not be able to enjoy arriving late at Robbins' Nest Inn to find a hot meal and a family waiting this evening. But he had known from the start that his odds of returning to a warm welcome were vanishingly small. After all, everyone would be waiting for a hero, and Max knew he probably would not qualify for the role.

Returning to Cleo and her family as a hero tonight meant returning with Ben Atkins in tow. There was little chance of that.

He had known the quest was doomed from the start. He should have refused it. But somehow, what with everyone from Cleo to Sammy expecting him to do something, he had been unable to say no.

After a long, sleepless night he had made his decision. He would go back to Harmony Cove this evening because he had to face Cleo and the others. He had to see their faces when he acknowledged that he had failed them.

When he saw the disappointment and the rejection in Cleo's eyes and in the eyes of her friends, he would leave. He had learned a long time ago that people only wanted him around as long as he was useful.

He wouldn't even have to waste time packing, he thought as he glanced at a road sign. Knowing what lay ahead, he had risen at dawn this morning, folded his belongings into the carryall, and stowed the bag in the Jaguar's trunk. Being packed and ready to leave was an old habit. He had picked it up at the age of six, and he had never really lost it.

It was easier, somehow, to have one foot already out the door when someone was about to tell you that you would have to leave, anyway.

Max slowed for the exit ramp marked Garnly. According to O'Reilly there were only three gas stations in Garnly. Ben Atkins was reportedly working at one of them.

Max cruised slowly through the drab little town. The rain was still falling steadily, a wet, gray veil that managed to conceal some of Garnly's less attractive aspects. He glanced down at the address he had written on a sheet of paper.

It was the second gas station on the left. Max eased the Jaguar into the small parking area and switched off the engine. He sat quietly for a moment, staring through the rain at the figure working in the service bay.

The young man moved with a quiet certainty, as if he had been working on cars all his life. He appeared tall and thin in the stained gray coveralls. His lanky blond hair needed a trim. He seemed huddled in on himself, a man who communicated better with mechanical things than he did with human beings.

Max opened the door and got out of the Jaguar. He walked through the rain to the shelter of the service bay and waited until the mechanic noticed him.

"Be with you in a minute." The mechanic hunched over an alternator.

"I'm looking for a man named Ben Atkins," Max said.

"Huh?" The mechanic looked up with a wary expression. His face was like the rest of him, thin and closed in on itself.

"Ben Atkins," Max repeated.

The mechanic frowned in confusion. "I'm Benjy. Benjy Atkins."

"Guess I made a mistake," Max said. He turned to walk back to the Jaguar.

"Wait." Metal clattered on metal as Ben tossed aside his tools. "I told you, I'm Benjy Atkins. What's this all about? Who are you?"

Max halted and turned around again. "Like I said, I'm looking for a man named Ben Atkins."

Ben stared at him as he wiped his hands on a dirty rag. "That's me. I mean, I'm Ben Atkins. But everyone calls me Benjy."

"Not anymore," Max said. "I hear you're going to be a father. In my book that makes you Ben, not Benjy."

Ben looked stunned. "You know Trisha?"

"Yes."

"Is she okay?"

"No. She's scared to death."

Ben's face tightened into a sullen mask. "Who are you, mister?"

"My name is Max Fortune."

"Yeah, but who are you? How do you know about me? And about the baby."

"Let's just say I'm a friend of the family."

"I ain't got a family."

"That's not the way I heard it." Max glanced at his watch. "It's almost noon. You plan on eating lunch?"

Ben blinked. "Well, yeah. Sure."

"You're in luck. I'm buying."

* * *

"He'll be back," Cleo said with a stubborn confidence that she was not really feeling.

"If he planned on returning," Sylvia said patiently, "why did he pack his things?"

"I don't know." Cleo propped her silver sneakers on top of her desk and glowered down into the dregs of her coffee. "I think he's used to being packed and ready to go. I have a feeling it's second nature for him. An instinct or something."

"Instinct?" Sylvia asked dryly.

"You saw how easy it was for him to move in here when he arrived. Max obviously travels light."

Sylvia wrinkled her nose. "You think he just sort of instinctively put his bag in the trunk of his car this morning?"

"Yes."

"Before anyone else was up and about?"

"Yes."

Sylvia lounged on the edge of the desk and sipped her own coffee. "Cleo, my friend, you might as well face facts. He's gone."

Cleo closed her eyes. "God, I hope not."

Sylvia was silent for about three full seconds, during which she examined Cleo's face intently. "Damn," she finally whispered.

Cleo opened her eyes. "What's wrong?"

"You and Max." Sylvia waved her hand meaningfully. "The two of you."

"What about us?"

Sylvia groaned. "You fell for him, didn't you? I knew something was happening. I could feel it. We all felt it. Thank goodness he wasn't around long enough to seduce you."

Cleo said nothing.

Sylvia cleared her throat. "I said, thank goodness he wasn't around long enough to seduce you."

Cleo swallowed the last of her coffee.

"That bastard," Sylvia muttered into the stark silence.

Cleo put her cup down on the desk. "He's not a bastard."

"Yes, he is. This makes me so mad. I liked Max. Sammy liked him. Andromeda liked him. Trisha liked him. Even Daystar liked him. Why did he have to be such a bastard?"

"He'll be back," Cleo said evenly. But deep inside she could feel the cold wind that was chilling her bones.

Sylvia was right. Facts were facts. Max had come to the inn in search of his precious inheritance from Jason. Last night he had at last appeared convinced that Cleo didn't know what had happened to the Luttrell paintings. This morning Max was gone. The conclusion was obvious.

But she could not quite bring herself to accept the obvious.

"Poor Trisha," Sylvia said wearily. "I think she was really beginning to hope that Max meant it when he said he would find Benjy."

"He did mean it," Cleo insisted. The man who had made love to her last night was not a liar.

The inn door swung open, interrupting Sylvia's next disgusted comment. Cleo glanced through the office window and saw a tall, blond, elegantly slim woman stride into the lobby. The woman moved with the singular air of confidence and muted disdain that indicated the sort of wealth and social standing that reached back more than one or two generations.

"Uh-oh," Cleo said. "Something tells me that, yes, indeed, once again our humble little inn has been mistaken for a five-star hotel in the south of France."

Sylvia grinned reluctantly. "Boy, is she in for a disappointment. She looks like she just stepped out of *Vogue,* doesn't she? That little silk suit must have cost a bundle. I'll handle her, if you like."

"No, that's all right." Cleo swung her silver shoes down onto the floor and rose from the chair. "I need something to take my mind off Max."

She put on her most polished innkeeper's smile and went out to the front desk. "May I help you?"

The woman raked Cleo with an assessing glance. She did not appear to be impressed with what she saw. "I'm looking for Max Fortune."

Cleo sucked in a small, startled breath. "You and everyone else." So much for distracting herself with non-Max thoughts. "I'm afraid he's not here at the moment. We're expecting him this evening."

"I'll wait."

"Late this evening," Cleo said carefully. *Like maybe never,* she added silently.

"In that case," the woman said, obviously annoyed, "perhaps you'd better give me a room for the night. I don't intend to sit out here in your quaint little lobby for the next few hours."

"Certainly." Cleo whipped out a registration card. "If you would just fill this out for me, I'll get you checked in immediately. Will you be using a credit card?"

Without a word the woman reached into a discreetly expensive black leather bag and produced a credit card that looked as if it had been stamped out of solid gold. She handed it to Cleo.

Cleo glanced at the card. *Kimberly Curzon-Winston.* She took another look at the middle name. "Curzon?"

"Yes." Kimberly scrawled her name on the registration form.

Cleo swallowed. "Any relation to Jason Curzon?"

Kimberly frowned. "His niece. You knew my uncle?"

"Sort of." Cleo smiled wryly. "But not as well as I thought, apparently. He seems to have had a much more interesting family background than we realized."

"I can't imagine how you came to know Jason Curzon, but I suppose it doesn't really matter." Kimberly put down the pen. "You said Max Fortune would be returning late this evening?"

"As far as we know." Cleo crossed her fingers behind her back and smiled bravely. He would return, she told herself. He had to return.

"Would you mind telling me where he is at the moment?" Kimberly's patience was obviously wearing thin.

Cleo glanced at the tall clock. "Right at this moment he's probably in a little town called Garnly."

Kimberly looked startled. "Why on earth did he go there?"

"A family matter," Cleo said smoothly.

"That's nonsense." Kimberly's eyes were cold. "I've known Max for several years. He doesn't have any family."

"He does now," Cleo said, "although I'm not sure he realizes it. Look, Ms. Winston . . ."

"Curzon-Winston."

"Ms. Curzon-Winston," Cleo repeated obediently, "perhaps I can help you."

"I doubt it."

"The thing is," Cleo said politely, "Max works for me. If something is wrong, I should know about it."

"What did you say?"

"I said, Max works for me."

A strange expression appeared in Kimberly's blue eyes. "We are talking about the same Max Fortune, aren't we? Tall. Black hair. Rather fierce-looking. Uses a cane?"

"That's our Max," Cleo agreed.

"Then he couldn't possibly work for you. He's a vice president with Curzon International." Kimberly's smile was glacial. "Max Fortune works for me."

"I didn't know what to do." Ben gazed despondently down at his half-finished burger. "It really took me by surprise, you know? I screwed up one time, and Trisha got pregnant."

"It happens," Max said. "Only takes once."

"Shit, you ever had a woman tell you that she's pregnant and you're the father?"

"No." Max reflected briefly again on how he would feel if Cleo told him she was pregnant with his baby. But that would never happen. He had been careful last night. He was always careful about such matters. After all, he had a reputation for not screwing up. "I can see that it would be something of a shock."

"You can say that again. I told Trisha I needed a little time to think things through." Ben ran his fingers through his hair. "I got to figure out what to do, you know?"

"Yes."

Ben raised haunted eyes and gazed helplessly at Max. "I don't remember anything about my own dad. He left when I was a baby. How am I supposed to know what to do with a kid? I don't know anything about being a father."

"You remember Jason Curzon?"

Ben frowned. "Sure. He was a neat old guy. Helped me out with the plumbing at the inn. I liked Jason."

"So did I," Max said quietly. "Jason used to say that a man learns most things by doing them. When it comes to figuring out how to be a father, men like you and me have to depend upon on-the-job training."

Ben's expression was bleak. "I already made enough mistakes in my life."

"You know how to hold down a job, don't you? Everyone at the inn says you're a hard worker."

"Well, sure. Work's one thing. Raisin' a kid is another."

"The way I look at it," Max said, "a lot of the same rules apply."

Ben stared at him. "You think so?"

"Yes." Max looked out the window and wondered when the rain would stop. "Look, the most important thing about holding down a job is to show up for work on a regular basis. Seems to me the same thing applies to being a father. You get points for just being around."

"Yeah?" Ben slitted his eyes. "What do you know about being a father?"

"Not much," Max admitted.

"So maybe you shouldn't be giving me advice," Ben said belligerently.

"Maybe not."

A long silence descended on the booth.

Ben scowled. "Is that all you got to say?"

"No," Max said. "There was one other thing I wanted to discuss."

"What's that?"

"I was wondering if you could give me a couple of hints on how to handle the leaking pipe in room two-fifteen. I've tried everything I can think of, and the sucker just keeps on dripping on the floor of the sink cabinet. It's getting worse."

Ben blinked in obvious alarm. "Those pipes under the sink in two-fifteen are just about rusted out. You got to treat 'em with kid gloves. One wrong move, and the whole dang thing is gonna go."

"Ms. Robbins?" The urbane man on the other side of the front desk smiled aloofly. His hair was a distinguished silver-gray, and his gray suit was the last word in sophisticated tailoring. His eyes were ice cold.

Cleo eyed him warily. "I'm Cleo Robbins. Can I help you?"

"I sincerely hope so," the man said in a smooth tone that held just the barest hint of condescending amusement. "Allow me to introduce myself. My name is Garrison Spark."

"I was afraid of that." Cleo took the card that Spark handed to her. It felt heavy and rich and ever so tasteful in her hand.

"I would like to talk to you about five very valuable pictures."

"Sorry." Cleo tossed the card into the wastebasket. "Can't help you. For the last time, I know nothing about the Luttrells."

Spark smiled coolly. "I sincerely doubt that you know much about Max Fortune, either. If you did, you would be extremely cautious. The man is dangerous, Ms. Robbins."

"Look, Mr. Spark, I'm getting a little bored with this hunt-the-missing-picture game. Jason Curzon did not leave those paintings here at the inn. Believe me, if he had, I would have run across them by now."

Spark looked even more amused. "The question in my mind is not whether Curzon left those paintings here, but rather how much do you want for them?"

"What?" Cleo stared at him in amazement. "I just told you that I don't know where they are. And if I did know, I would give them to Max before I gave them to you. He's got first dibs."

"I see the clever Mr. Fortune has charmed his way into your good graces." Spark shook his head ruefully. "Either that or he has played on your sympathies with a hard-luck story. I fear I must tell you quite frankly that giving the pictures to Max Fortune would be an extremely foolish thing to do."

"Why?" Cleo shot back.

"Because he has no legal or moral claim to them. He's after them simply because they are brilliant works that he wishes to add to his collection. I should warn you, Ms. Robbins, that Fortune will stop at nothing when it comes to obtaining a painting he desires for his private collection. He can be quite ruthless."

"What about you, Mr. Spark? How far will you go?"

Spark's eyes mirrored reluctant respect. "I can be just as tenacious as Fortune, my dear, but I tend to take a rather different approach."

"What approach?"

"I shall be quite happy to pay you a fair price for the Luttrells."

"Really?" Cleo eyed him skeptically. "Max says they're worth a quarter of a million."

Spark chuckled indulgently. "Fortune always did have a flair for exaggeration. Fifty thousand is a much more realistic estimate. Although I'll grant you that in five years the figure could be much higher. However, five years is a long time to wait, isn't it? I am prepared to give you twenty-five thousand for those paintings today."

"Forget it."

"You're a hard bargainer, Ms. Robbins. Very well, make it thirty."

"Don't you ever give up?"

"No," Spark said. "I don't. And neither does Max Fortune. How much has he offered?"

"He hasn't offered a cent," Cleo said honestly.

"He will," Spark said. "Unless, of course, he can talk you out of them for nothing. He's not above trying that tactic. Presumably you will not allow him to do so, however. Call me when he makes his final offer. I will top it."

"There will be no final offer, Mr. Spark, because there are no Luttrells lying around Robbins' Nest Inn. In case you hadn't noticed, I prefer a different sort of art."

Spark glanced disparagingly at Jason's seascapes. "So I see."

"It's all in the eye of the beholder, isn't it, Mr. Spark?"

Spark turned back to Cleo. "Ms. Robbins, if you are by any chance holding out because you believe that you can sell the paintings yourself on the open market, allow me to disabuse you of that notion. It takes contacts to sell that kind of art. I have those contacts. You do not. Please keep that in mind when you make your decision."

Spark turned on his heel and walked out.

The lights of Robbins' Nest Inn glowed with welcoming warmth through the sleeting rain. Max studied them as they drew closer. He was aware of a strange sense of unreality. If he used his imagination, he could almost make believe he really was returning home after a long, exhausting, but successful journey. Home to a hot meal, a loving family, and a woman who would fly straight into his arms the instant she realized he had arrived.

But that kind of unrealistic imagination was not his strongest suit. He was far better at envisioning the logical, pragmatic consequences of failure. And there was no getting around the fact that he was returning as a failure. Ben was not with him, and there was no guarantee that he would return on his own in the near future.

Max slowed the Jaguar as he turned into the inn's parking lot. He was not eager for what awaited him. But at least he was packed and ready to leave, as always. The difference this time was that he would be leaving something important behind him.

The inn's lot was nearly full. Max glanced curiously at the vehicles that filled it. This was Thursday. By rights it should have been a slow night, but there was a surprising flurry of activity going on in the pouring rain. Men hurried back and forth between the parked cars and the lobby entrance, transporting bags and suitcases.

Max finally found room for the Jag behind the kitchen. He parked, got out, and made his way toward the back door with a sense of bleak inevitability.

The fragrant aroma of fresh bread and a curry-spiced stew enveloped him as he opened the kitchen door. Max allowed himself a moment to savor the warmth. Almost like coming home.

Andromeda, intent on a pan full of steaming vegetables, looked up as the back door opened. A welcoming smile lit her eyes.

"Max, you're home. Thank goodness. We're in a real panic here. A bunch of men who are supposed to be engaging in something called a Warriors' Journey on the beach got rained out. They all showed up here about an hour ago."

"Hi, Max." Daystar brushed flour from her fingers. "How was the drive?"

Trisha walked into the kitchen through the swinging door that opened onto the dining room. Max steeled himself against the hope in her eyes. Better to get this over with quickly, he decided.

"I'm sorry, Trisha," he said into the thick silence that had suddenly descended on the kitchen. "Ben's not with me."

Trisha's eyes glistened with tears. She nodded, as if she had already guessed the truth. "You saw him? He's okay?"

"Yes. He's fine." Max sought for something more to say. "He was worried about you."

"But not worried enough to come home."

"Cleo's right." Max gripped the handle of his cane. "He's scared."

Trisha's smile was watery but real. "He's not the only one, but I'm luckier than he is. At least I've got family around me. He's all alone out there."

"Yes." Max waited for her to blame him for his failure.

"Thanks for driving all that way to talk to him." Trisha crossed the room and put her arms briefly around Max. "If anyone could have talked him into coming home, it was you." She hugged him quickly and stepped back. "You're a good friend, Max."

He searched her eyes and found no sign of rejection. "I don't know what Ben's going to do," he warned, just in case Trisha had not fully understood that he had screwed up.

"Well, it's up to Ben, isn't it?" Andromeda said calmly. "You spoke to him and let him know that his family wants him to come back. Now we'll just have to wait and see what he decides to do. In the meantime, we've got an inn to run."

"Max needs a cup of tea to warm him up before he leaps into the fray," Daystar declared. "He must be chilled to the bone after that drive."

"I'll get you a cup, Max," Trisha said. "Sit down."

Max glanced back toward the door. The Jaguar with his packed carryall in the trunk was waiting outside.

Sylvia pushed open the kitchen door. "Everything okay in here? Looks like we're going to need dinner for twenty tonight. Mr. Quinton, the chief honcho of this bunch, said all his guys want red meat, can you believe it? I told him we don't serve red meat." She stopped short when she saw Max. Her slow smile was filled with satisfaction. "Well, I'll be darned. You did come back. How was the drive?"

"Wet. What made you think I wasn't coming back?" Max asked.

"Sammy came rushing downstairs right after you left this morning and informed us that all your things were gone," Sylvia said dryly. "Some of us naturally assumed that you had no intention of returning."

"I'm here." Max started toward the kitchen nook where Trisha had set a cup of tea for him. "But I didn't bring Ben with me."

Sylvia sighed. "Can't say I'm surprised. But it was worth a shot. Thanks, Max. You went above and beyond the call of duty on this one. I'll bet you could use a shot of whiskey rather than a cup of tea. George keeps a bottle behind the front desk."

Max looked at Trisha. "Tea will do fine."

The kitchen door banged open again, and Sammy dashed into the room. He skidded to a halt, his eyes widening when he saw Max. "Hi, Max." He dashed forward and seized Max's leg in a quick hug. "I was afraid you wouldn't come back."

Cleo appeared in the open doorway. "What's going on? I could use a little help with this crowd of manly males out here. They're milling around like so many bulls in a china shop. I think one of them is toting a spear—" She broke off when she saw Max. Her eyes glowed with sudden joy. *"Max.* You're home."

He stopped beside the nook and folded both hands over the hawk on his cane. "Hello, Cleo. I couldn't talk Ben into returning with me."

"Oh, Max." Cleo flew across the room toward him. "I was so afraid you weren't coming back."

At the last instant Max realized she intended to throw herself into his arms. He hastily put the cane aside and braced himself.

Cleo landed squarely against his chest. His arms closed around her as she burrowed against him. She was warm and soft, and the scent of her filled his head. Memories of the previous night flared in his mind, sending waves of heat through his body.

"Let's save the mush for later," Sylvia said, sounding amused. "We've got twenty hungry warriors to feed and shelter."

"Right." Cleo raised her head. The laughter faded from her eyes. "Good heavens, I almost forgot. There's someone here to see you, Max."

He released her reluctantly, still struggling to shift gears in his mind. He had spent the past few hours convinced that he would not be staying at the inn any longer than it took to announce his failure. Now he was having to adjust to the notion that no one was blaming him or rejecting him for the fact that Ben had not returned.

Max frowned at Cleo. "Who wants to see me?"

"Kimberly Curzon-Winston. She says Jason was her uncle."

"Damn."

"That's not all she says." Cleo pushed her glasses more firmly into place on her nose and eyed Max with speculation. "She says you work for her. I told her she was wrong."

The possessiveness in Cleo's voice made Max smile. "Did you?"

"Yes. I told her you work for me. What's going on here, Max?"

Max picked up the teacup and swallowed the contents. "Just what you said. I work for you."

"But you used to work for Ms. Curzon-Winston?"

"No," Max said flatly. "I told you, I worked for Jason. When he died, I resigned my position with Curzon International."

"I see." Cleo's eyes gleamed behind the lenses of her glasses. "Well, then, that settles it, doesn't it? Who gets to tell Ms. Curzon-Winston that you are no longer her employee?"

"I'll tell her."

"Good idea. Oh, by the way, your old pal Garrison Spark showed up today, too. Never a dull moment around here."

Max went still. "What did Spark want?"

"What do you think he wanted?" Cleo raised her brows. "He offered me a measly thirty grand for the Luttrells. I told him the same thing I told you. I don't have the stupid paintings, and if I did have them, I'd give them to you."

Max stared at her. He couldn't think of anything to say. The sound of raised masculine voices from the lobby caught his attention. He picked up his cane. "I think we'd better get your unexpected arrivals settled."

"Right. I just hope they don't start shooting arrows or tossing their spears around. This is a respectable establishment." Cleo whirled and rushed to the door. "Sylvia, give me a hand with the front desk. Trisha, call George and tell him we need him to come in early tonight. Then give Andromeda a hand here in the kitchen. Max, there's a leaking shower head in one-ten. Can you take a look at it?"

"Yes," Max said.

"I'll call George," Trisha said. She gave Max a quick, misty smile. "Thanks again, Max."

It was the first time in his life that anyone had thanked him for just trying, Max reflected. He nodded at Trisha, unable to think of anything to say.

He left the kitchen wondering what kind of tools one needed to fix a leaking shower head.

"What in hell is going on around here, Max?" Kimberly paced the shadowed solarium, the only place in the inn that wasn't overrun by warriors.

Max stretched out his legs and absently rubbed his thigh. Kimberly was as stunningly beautiful as ever, he thought, but he experienced absolutely no reaction to her now. Whatever he had once felt for her had died three years ago.

"What does it look like?" Max said quietly. "I've found a new job."

She shot him a disgusted look. "Come off it, Max. You and I have known each other too long to play games. Why did you leave Curzon?"

"Let's just say that I felt like a change."

"If you wanted more money, all you had to do was ask. For God's sake, you know that." The heels of Kimberly's gray suede pumps clicked loudly on the tiles, betraying the tension that was evident in every line of her body. "If this is some kind of ploy to get the seat on the board that Uncle Jason promised you, I assure you, you didn't need to stage this dramatic little scene."

Max arched a brow. "Come off it, Kim. We both know your father would never allow anyone but a member of the family to sit on the board."

Kimberly flushed. "I know my father has a thing about that, but I might be able to talk him into reconsidering his decision. He wants you back at Curzon. He'll do just about anything to get you back, Max."

"Forget it. Things have changed. I don't give a damn about the seat on the board. Not any longer." Max listened to his own words with silent amazement. At one time he would have seized the offer with both hands. A seat on the board would have meant that the Curzons as a group had really accepted him. It would have been the next best thing to belonging to the family.

"What are you trying to do?" Kimberly asked tightly. "Why the shock tactics? What's your agenda? Just tell me, Max. We can come to terms."

"I don't have an agenda. At least not one that concerns Curzon."

She shot him a quick, suspicious glance. "Don't tell me you've decided to go with Global Village Properties? If that's the case, I can guarantee you we'll match whatever offer they make. You know as well as I do that Curzon can't afford to have you go work for our chief competitor. You know too much."

"I'm not going with Global Village."

"What is it then? You can't be serious about working for that odd little innkeeper in the tacky running shoes."

Max smiled slightly. "Why not? The pay's good."

"Don't be ridiculous. She can't possibly pay you anything close to what you were earning at Curzon." Kimberly swept out a hand to indicate all of Robbins' Nest Inn. "We both know you could buy this place with less than one year's salary. Not to mention bonuses. How much is she paying you?"

"Minimum wage."

Kimberly stared at him. "I don't believe you."

"It's not such a bad deal. I've got my own room in the attic and three hot meals a day. I also get to keep all the tips I make in the lounge. Some guy left me a ten-dollar bill last weekend."

"You sleep in the attic? You're working for tips? This is insane. Why are you doing this to me?" Kimberly came to a halt in front of him. "You know Curzon needs you. I need you."

Max rested his head against the back of the wicker chair. "You don't need me, Kim. Neither does the company. In a few months you'll realize that you and your family can get along just fine without me."

"We've all depended on you for years. You know that, Max."

"Dennison is probably a little nervous at the moment. After all, this is a transitional period. But he's got you." Max narrowed his eyes faintly. "You've got what it takes to handle the company, Kim."

"You know my father would never turn Curzon over to me,"

Kimberly said bitterly. "I'm not the son he always wanted, and I never will be."

Max said nothing. There was nothing to say. Kimberly was right. Her father, Dennison Curzon, intended to take the reins of Curzon International and prove that he had the same talent his brother had had. It was unfortunate for all concerned that he was not the brilliant corporate strategist that Jason had been.

The only one in the family who could lead Curzon International into the future was Kimberly, and they all knew that her father was highly unlikely to entrust her with the task. Dennison believed the job required a man.

It was probably going to turn into an unholy mess, but Max figured that was the Curzons' problem now.

Kimberly watched Max for a moment. Then she turned away and walked to the fountain. She stood looking down at the bubbling water, her head bowed. "I think I should tell you something, Max."

"What?"

"Roarke and I are having problems. I'm thinking of leaving him."

Max eyed her classic profile. "Why?"

"Does it matter?"

Max shrugged. "No."

Kimberly touched the blue tiles that formed the highest pool on the fountain. "I made a mistake three years ago, Max. I allowed my father to talk me out of marrying you."

"He didn't have to talk very hard. You started having doubts right after I put the engagement ring on your finger."

"I was a fool."

"Let's not get melodramatic about this. I'm in no mood for it." Max reached for his cane. "It's been a long day, and I'm tired."

Something bright gleamed in the open doorway on the other side of the room. Max turned his head and saw Cleo standing in the shadows. The light from the hall reflected off her metallic sneakers. He could not see the expression on her face.

"Max?" She took a step into the room. "I've been looking for you. I think we'd better close down the lounge. This is a rather strange crowd. All those men who arrived earlier are sitting around telling each other about their divorces. Some of them are starting to cry. It's very depressing for the other guests."

"I'll take care of it." Max rose from the chair, grateful for the interruption.

Kimberly looked at him in open astonishment. Then she swung around to confront Cleo. "I don't believe this. Will somebody please tell me what's going on?"

"I need Max," Cleo said quietly.

"Do you really?" Kimberly gave her a scathing look as she started toward the door. "The real question here is why does Max need you? A word of warning, Ms. Robbins. Max Fortune is not playing bellhop and bartender without a damn good reason."

"Is that so?" Cleo angled her chin. "And what would you know about his reasons for doing anything?"

"A great deal." Kimberly made to brush past her. "Max and I go back a long way together. Or hasn't he told you about us?"

"What's there to tell?" Cleo challenged.

Max swore softly.

Kimberly smiled coldly. "I think I'll let Max give you the details, Ms. Robbins. You might start by asking him how he got that limp."

Half an hour later, with all the inn's guests safely tucked in their rooms and George in command at the front desk, Max went up the stairs with Cleo. He was aware that some part of him was still waiting for the other shoe to drop.

"Sheesh." Cleo pushed hair out of her eyes. "No offense to the male of the species, but I'll be glad when Mr. Tobias Quinton's gang of manly warriors checks out. It's unnerving having a bunch of men around who are trying to get in touch with their emotions."

"We can kick them out tomorrow morning," Max suggested. "Tell them you have another group checking in or something."

"Yeah, but I don't have another group checking in," Cleo said glumly. "In fact, we're going to be fairly empty this weekend. There's no getting around the fact that Mr. Quinton and his crowd are paying customers. I suppose we can put up with them for a while."

"Spoken like a dedicated innkeeper," Max said as they reached the third floor.

He hesitated, waiting to see if she would invite him down the hall to her room or put her hand in his and let him lead her up to the attic. She did neither.

"Well, good night, Max." Cleo gave him a bright little smile, but her eyes were wary. "You must be exhausted after that long drive. I'll see you in the morning."

She stood on tiptoe and brushed her mouth against his cheek. Then she turned and went down the hall alone to her tower room.

Max did not move for a long while. He just stood there, staring after her until she disappeared. A dark, seething desire twisted his insides, but that was not the worst part. The worst part was that he did not know what Cleo was thinking.

She had not said a word to him about Kimberly since the confrontation in the solarium. He could not tell if she was angry or hurt or simply cautious. He knew she had questions. He could feel them simmering inside her.

In the meantime he had a big question of his own, and there was only one way to get it answered. Max tightened his grip on his cane and went down the hall to Cleo's room.

He came to a halt in front of her door and lifted his hand to knock. He paused, gathering his courage. Asking his question of Cleo was going to be just as hard as returning to the inn without Ben Atkins in tow. Perhaps harder. Max knocked twice on the door and waited.

It seemed to take forever before Cleo slowly opened the door and peered out through the crack. The hall light glinted on the lenses of her glasses, concealing the expression in her eyes.

"Is something wrong?" she asked politely.

"I would like to clarify the sleeping arrangements," Max said with great care.

Her brows snapped together in a frown of concern. "Is there a problem with one of the room assignments?"

"Yes," Max said evenly. "Mine."

Cleo's fingers clenched abruptly around the edge of the door. She looked as if she needed to hold on to it in order to keep from collapsing. "Yours?"

"I was just wondering where I'm supposed to sleep tonight."

Cleo stared at him. "Where do you want to sleep tonight?"

"Here." Max wedged the toe of his shoe into the narrow opening between the door and its frame. "With you."

"Oh."

He braced his hand against the door frame. "Is that all you can say?"

Cleo flushed a vivid shade of pink. "I wasn't sure what you wanted to do. I mean, I didn't know how you were feeling about the situation. I thought you might need a little time to get in touch with your emotions."

"You're starting to sound like Tobias Quinton."

Cleo smiled weakly. "I am, aren't I? Well? Are you in touch with your feelings?"

"I know what I want." Max flattened one hand against the door and pushed gently inward. He would not force his way into her bedroom, he told himself. He would just lean a little and see if she leaned back. If she didn't, he would have the answer to his question.

"Max."

The door gave way abruptly as Cleo released her grip on it and stepped aside. Max realized at the last instant that he was leaning a lot more heavily against the door than he had intended. He lost his balance. His bad leg started to give way. He almost fell into the room.

He was saved from sprawling ignominiously on the floor by the counter force exerted when Cleo slammed into his arms. He staggered once and managed to get a firm grip on both Cleo and his cane. He steadied himself as she hugged him very tightly.

"I didn't know what to think this morning when I realized you had packed all your things," Cleo said into his chest. "And then when that Kimberly Curzon-Winston person showed up and told me that you worked for her, things got more confusing."

"I know. It's all right. I've been just as confused today." Max caught her chin on the edge of his hand, tipped up her face, and kissed her. Hard.

Cleo put her arms around his neck and returned the kiss with sweet fervor. Without lifting his mouth from hers, Max eased her back against the edge of the bed. They collapsed together on top of the old-fashioned quilt.

This was what it meant to come home, Max thought.

An hour later Cleo stirred in the darkness. "Max?"

"Umm?" He barely heard her. He was drifting on the edge of sleep, his body satiated, his mind at ease. Cleo was cradled against him, her lushly curved derriere pressed against his thighs. The peaceful feeling that consumed him was so unique that he wanted to savor it until he fell asleep.

"Were you and Kimberly lovers?"

"Hell." Max was suddenly wide awake.

"What did you say?"

"Nothing important." Max opened his eyes, folded one arm behind his head, and contemplated the frilly canopy overhead with a brooding glare.

"So what about you and Kimberly?"

"We were engaged for a while."

"Engaged." Cleo shot straight up into a sitting position. "Are you telling me you almost married her?"

"It was a very short engagement." Max gave her a cautious glance and saw that she was glowering down at him.

"How short?" Cleo demanded.

"Uh, six weeks, I think." Five weeks and four days. Not that he had been counting at the time.

Five weeks and four days of thinking that he had finally muscled his way into the inner circle of the Curzon family. Five weeks and four days of believing he had made a secure, permanent place for himself in Jason's world.

"You think? Can't you remember?"

Max groaned. "It was three years ago, Cleo."

"What happened?"

"Nothing happened. We got disengaged, that's all."

"Did you change your mind?"

Max yawned. "She changed hers," he said before he stopped to think. As soon as the words were out of his mouth, he knew he'd made a grave tactical error. "I mean, it was a mutual decision."

But it was too late. Cleo pounced. "She's the one who called off the engagement? Not you?"

"We decided we weren't meant for each other," Max said.

"Why not?"

"There were a lot of reasons," Max said.

"What reasons?"

Max began to feel hunted. Instinctively he drew a line, just as he always did when someone tried to apply pressure. "Stop pushing, Cleo. My relationship with Kimberly was finished three years ago."

"But you've been working for her all this time?"

"I told you, I worked for Jason, not Kimberly. Now I work for you."

"Hmm." Cleo considered that. "Why did she call off the engagement?"

Max drummed his fingers lightly on the bed. "She decided that we came from two different worlds. She was right."

"Which two different worlds?"

"She came from old money, good schools, and a long line of socially acceptable ancestors. She was the heiress to Curzon International. I came from nothing. The only money I have is what I earned working for Jason. Her father did not approve of me. Hell, Kimberly didn't approve of me, herself. Not really."

"So she married somebody named Winston?"

"Roarke Winston."

"Let me guess," Cleo said. "Old money, good schools, a long line of socially acceptable ancestors?"

"Right. He's in charge of his family's business empire."

"What did Kimberly mean when she said I should ask you about your leg?"

Max gave Cleo another sidelong glance. He had a feeling she was going to prove tenacious. It figured. That quality went right along with the other Girl Scout attributes. "We got engaged shortly after I injured my leg. While I was in the hospital recovering, as a matter of fact. Kimberly was"—he searched for the correct word—"somewhat emotional at the time."

"She was worried about you?"

"I think she was feeling a little guilty."

Cleo frowned. "Why? Did she have something to do with your accident?"

"In a way. She had insisted on flying down to a potential hotel site in South America. I was already on the scene and had decided that it wasn't a good location. I advised her not to come, but she wanted to check it out for herself."

"What happened?"

Max shrugged. "I picked her up at the airport. On the way back into town we were stopped by a bunch of guerrillas who had gotten word that a member of the Curzon family was expected. They were planning to kidnap her and use her as a bargaining chip in their ongoing battle with the local government."

"My God." Cleo was shocked. "What did you do?"

Max slanted her a strange glance. "When I worked for Jason I spent a lot of time in places where the potential for that kind of thing existed. I routinely carried a gun. Shots were exchanged when I ran the roadblock. One of the shells came through the door of the car and hit my leg."

"That's how you got hurt?" Cleo's voice rose to a squeak. "Rescuing Kimberly?"

"Yes."

Cleo clutched his arm. "You could have been killed."

"Look, Cleo, this is ancient history, and I don't think there's much point discussing it."

"But you could have been killed," she whispered again. Her nails dug into his arm.

Max heard the old horror buried in her barely controlled voice. He realized she was no longer concerned about his relationship with Kimberly, but was thinking about her parents' death and her own past.

"It's all right, Cleo." He rolled onto his side and pulled her into his arms. "Take it easy. I'm here."

She curled into his warmth and clung to him. "I'm okay."

"Good." He stroked her back soothingly. "It's late. Try to get some sleep."

She relaxed slightly against him. "You said that your engagement only lasted six weeks?"

"Give or take a few days." He strove to sound disinterested. "I've forgotten the exact length of time."

"And now Kimberly's married to someone else."

"Yes."

"She wants you back, Max." Cleo's voice was bleak. "I can tell."

Max smiled into her hair. "Only for business reasons. Her father thinks the company needs me."

"Does it?"

"I don't particularly care if it does or it doesn't. I don't want the job."

"You're sure?"

"I'm sure." He kissed her throat. "I've got another job."

Cleo looked up at him through her lashes. "I'll bet Curzon International pays a heck of a lot better than Robbins' Nest Inn."

"That all depends on how you look at it." Max kissed the sweet, scented curve of her breast and laced his fingers through the soft thatch of hair between her legs. "I'm satisfied with what I'm getting here."

"Are you?" Cleo put her hand on his shoulder. "Max, do you still love her?"

Max was startled by the question. He had never thought about loving Kimberly. He had never thought about loving anyone. "No."

"You're sure?"

"I'm sure."

"You say that awfully easily."

"It's easy to say." Max took one nipple into his mouth. It was as firm and ripe as a raspberry. The taste of it sent a shudder of excitement through him. Sexual tension seized his insides.

"Why is it easy to say? Didn't you love her three years ago?"

"Cleo . . ."

"I just wondered," she said softly. "I know how strong love can be because my parents were deeply in love. It's not the kind of thing a man like you could dismiss easily if he had experienced it."

That stopped him. He raised his head. "A man like me?"

Cleo stroked his cheek with gentle fingertips. "You're like one of those paintings you say you collect. Very deep. Lots of layers. I think that if you ever fell in love you would stay in love for a very long time. Forever, probably."

"I'm not a work of art. Don't romanticize me, Cleo." Max caught her fingers and held them against his chest. "I don't know anything about that kind of love. I don't think it really exists."

"My parents had it." She smiled. "It's the kind of love I want for myself."

Max got a sinking feeling in the pit of his stomach. "You could spend your whole life looking for it and never be satisfied with what you find."

"That's what my therapist said." She stirred against him. "So you really weren't in love with Kimberly?"

"I think it's a safe bet that the kind of feeling Kimberly and I had for each other was nothing like the bond you say your parents had." He slid his leg aggressively between Cleo's warm thighs. He could feel her responding to him, and the knowledge reassured him. Cleo might have an unrealistic view of love, but her body had a very pragmatic reaction to his. He intended to nurture that reaction until it was more important to her than the search for an elusive, mythical grand passion.

"I don't understand." Cleo braced her hands against his shoulders and searched his face. "What sort of feeling did you have for Kimberly?"

Max tried to contain his impatience. He was thoroughly aroused, and Cleo was warm and sultry and ready for him. "Cleo, it's a little hard to explain. Kimberly represented a lot of things I thought I wanted at the time. I guess I thought that if I got her, I'd get those other things, too. I was wrong. She did us both a favor when she broke off the engagement."

"What things did you want?" Cleo whispered.

"It doesn't matter. I don't want them any longer."

"Are you certain of that?"

"Yes," Max said. He moistened the tip of his finger with his tongue and then reached down to touch the taut little bud hidden between her legs.

Cleo flinched in reaction and then lifted herself against his hand with a soft moan. He cupped her gently and eased one finger into her damp heat. She was burning for him. He couldn't wait to lose himself in her again.

"What do you want now?" Cleo asked.

"You."

She sighed in soft surrender and brushed her lips across his shoulder. "I want you, too."

A few minutes later when he buried himself deep inside her, Max realized he had spoken a greater truth than he had realized. He wanted Cleo in a way he had never wanted any other woman in his life. He did not question the need; he simply accepted it.

The distant thuds brought Cleo up out of a dreamless sleep. She lay quietly for a moment, trying to identify the sounds. They stopped after a moment.

She concluded that George, or perhaps one of the guests, had walked down the hall outside her room.

Cleo yawned and tried to turn on her side. She realized she could not move because Max was pinning her legs to the bed. He had one muscled thigh thrown over her calves.

In addition to being trapped, she was much too warm. The heat from Max's body made the quilt superfluous. Sharing a bed with Max was a very strange experience, Cleo thought. It was like sleeping with a blast furnace.

The thuds started up again. They reverberated softly through the walls in a primitive, unrelenting, extremely irritating rhythm.

Thump. Thump. Thump.

Cleo came fully awake in a hurry. She jackknifed into a sitting position.

"Good lord, Max. Someone's drumming down there."

"What's wrong?" Max asked from the depths of the pillow.

"Don't you hear it? Someone's got a drum downstairs." Cleo pushed aside the quilt and struggled to get herself free of Max. "He'll wake up everyone in the whole inn."

Cleo managed to get out of the bed. She raced to the closet and reached for a pair of jeans and a shirt.

"Hold on, Cleo. I'll go down with you." Max got out of bed, yawning.

The distant murmur of men's voices mingled with the drumming. Cleo listened intently and then yelped in disbelief.

"They've started chanting." She grabbed her glasses and pushed them onto her nose. "It must be some of the men from Mr. Quinton's Warriors' Journey group. That does it, I'm going to throw them all out. I don't care if it is raining cats and dogs."

"If you throw them out, you'll have a hard time collecting for the rooms," Max reminded her as he zipped up his trousers.

"Right now all I care about is getting that damned drumming stopped." Cleo was at the door. "I knew I should never have taken them in tonight. I didn't like the looks of that Tobias Quinton from the start. I'm too darn soft-hearted, that's my problem."

She yanked open the door and raced out into the hall, aware that Max was following more slowly behind her.

The drumming was a lot louder when she reached the second floor, louder still when she got to the first floor. It seemed to be coming from the solarium.

Cleo went to the front desk. George was nowhere in sight. Assuming he had already gone to investigate the drumming, Cleo started to turn toward the solarium. Then she heard the snores emanating from her office.

"George?"

"Your ever vigilant night clerk is sound asleep," Max observed as he came up behind her.

"For heaven's sake." Cleo ducked into the office and saw that George was, indeed, sprawled in her chair, eyes closed, mouth agape. His feet were propped on her desk.

"Forget it," Max advised. "He wouldn't be much help, anyway."

"I suppose you're right." Cleo squared her shoulders and stalked past him. "I'll just have to take care of this myself."

"Cleo, maybe you'd better let me handle this."

"I've been running this inn for three years." Cleo turned the corner and went down the hall to the solarium. The drumming and the chanting got louder.

"You've got me to help out around here now, remember?"

"That doesn't mean I can't deal with a few rude guests." Cleo stopped in front of the French doors that opened into the solarium. The doors were closed, but through the glass panes she could see that the lights were off inside the room. An orange glow from the fireplace told her that Quinton and his crowd had built a fire on the hearth. "Of all the nerve."

"I think you'd better let me go in there first," Max said. He started to step around her, reaching for the doorknob.

"Nonsense." Cleo threw open the doors.

The thunder of a drum and the roar of masculine voices lifted in a primitive chant boomed out of the solarium. In the light of the leaping flames Cleo could just barely make out the shapes of several men seated on the floor. They formed a half circle in front of the fire.

A majestic, white-maned figure sat in their midst. He had the drum in front of him. His arm was raised to strike the next blow.

"That will be quite enough, Mr. Quinton." Cleo swept out her hand and hit all the switches on the wall in one slashing blow. The solarium was abruptly flooded with light.

Twenty stark naked men turned to gaze at her in stony-faced disapproval.

Cleo stared back in stunned amazement. Not one of the men was wearing a single stitch of clothing.

Cleo was speechless. She swung around and found Max standing directly behind her.

"I told you to let me go in first," Max said. His eyes were gleaming with amusement.

Cleo finally found her voice. "Do something."

"You bet, boss." Max moved aside so that she could step past him into the hall. "I think it would probably be best if you went back upstairs. I'll get the warriors back to their tents."

"Yes, leave us, woman," Quinton intoned in a deep, graveled voice. "This is a matter for men."

"She's just like my ex-wife," one of the participants called out. "Diane never let me have any fun, either."

"This is a time for men to come together," Quinton chanted. He thumped the drum. "This is a time of male power and strength. A gathering time for warriors."

Cleo glared at Max. "I don't want them put back in their rooms. I want them out of here, do you understand? Immediately!"

"Think of the income you'd be losing if you throw them out tonight, Cleo."

"I don't care how much profit I lose. I want them off the premises."

"You are welcome to join us," Quinton said to Max. "This is a place and a time for men."

"Thank you," Max said very civilly.

"Max," Cleo hissed, "I swear, if you take off your clothes and start chanting in front of the fire, I am going to throttle you."

Max's mouth curved. "Is that right?"

Quinton rose to his feet. He held the drum discreetly in front of himself. "Don't let her intimidate you," he said to Max. "You are a man. It's time to get in touch with your own maleness. You must reach down inside yourself and discover the strength of the warrior who resides within you."

Cleo swung around once more and confronted her unwanted guest. "I do not want to hear another word out of you, Mr. Quinton. I took you in tonight out of the goodness of my heart when you and your group showed up on my doorstep. You begged me for shelter, and this is the thanks I get."

"We were not begging for shelter," one of the seated men said in a disgruntled tone. "We could have spent the night on the beach."

"Then why didn't you?" Cleo demanded.

"Because we didn't feel like it," one of the other men declared.

"No kidding? What's the matter?" Cleo asked. "Were all you macho, manly warriors afraid of a little rain?"

Max's hands descended firmly on Cleo's shoulders. "I think this is degenerating into a farce." He turned her around and marched her out of the door. "Take yourself off, boss. I'll handle this."

"You do that. I'll go make sure we've got all their credit card numbers before they leave tonight. We're billing them for a full night's lodging. And breakfast, too, even though they won't be here to eat it."

Max smiled. "Good night, Cleo."

Cleo ground her teeth and started back down the hall. Behind her Quinton began to beat his drum. She could not recall when she had been so incensed. She rounded the corner and stormed into the lobby. She was just in the mood to chew George out for dereliction of duty.

A familiar figure came out of the office. He had a key in his hand.

"Hi, Cleo," Ben said sheepishly. He held up the key. "George was asleep, so I helped myself. I was going to go on upstairs to my room. What are you doing up?"

Cleo instantly forgot about Tobias Quinton and the nude warriors in the solarium. She stared at Ben in delight.

"Benjy—I mean, *Ben*—you're home!"

"Yeah."

"It's so good to see you again." Cleo ran forward and hugged him. "We've been so worried about you."

"Sorry for getting in so late. I just sort of decided to get into my car and start driving." Ben hugged her back a little awkwardly. "I probably should have waited until morning, huh?"

"Absolutely not." Cleo released him and stepped back. "This is your home. You were right to come straight here. Wait until Trisha finds out you're back."

"Yeah." Ben looked down at the key in his hand. "You think she'll be mad at me? I didn't mean to hurt her. I just needed to think things over, you know?"

Cleo smiled. "She's going to be very happy to see you, Ben. She knows that you got scared when she told you about the baby."

Ben flushed. "Yeah. Well, I guess she was probably even more scared. Max said that it was easier to be scared together than alone."

Cleo tilted her head slightly to one side. "Max said that?"

Ben nodded. "He said Trisha needs me. He said the baby is going to need me, too, even though I don't know nothin' about being a father."

"He's right. Ben, I'm so glad you came home."

"Is that you, Ben?" Max called impatiently from the hallway behind Cleo.

"Yes, sir." Ben's voice held an unmistakable edge of respect. He glanced past Cleo to where Max was standing in the shadows. "I'm back."

"So I see." Max's eyes gleamed with silent approval. "Good timing. I was about to wake George and ask him to give me a hand, but something tells me you'll be more useful than George."

Ben straightened his shoulders. "What do you want me to do?"

"Cover my back while a guy named Tobias Quinton and I play a couple of hands of poker. I don't think there will be any cheating, but you can never tell."

Cleo snapped out of her short-lived good mood. "Poker? What are you talking about?"

"Relax, Cleo." Max smiled blandly. "Quinton and I have reached an agreement. We're going to settle this matter in a manly fashion. If I win, the warriors will go peacefully upstairs to bed."

Cleo was outraged. "What happens if you lose?"

"Then they get to drum and chant until dawn."

Cleo was flabbergasted. "This is insane. You might lose."

"Don't worry." Max winked solemnly. "I won't lose. Trust me."

Cleo wanted to scream. "Who came up with this stupid idea?"

"I did," Max said.

"Oh, my God." Cleo sagged against the front desk. "I don't believe this."

"Relax, Cleo," Max advised. "This is a male thing. I wouldn't expect a woman to understand it."

Ten

It was pleasant being a family hero, Max reflected the next morning after the breakfast rush. Trisha thought he walked on water because Ben was back. Ben seemed to be in the process of turning him into a role model. Andromeda and the rest of the Cosmic Harmony crowd thought he'd finessed the situation with Quinton's group of rained-out warriors brilliantly. Sammy thought he was great simply because he was back.

The only one who was still grumbling was Cleo.

She stalked into the kitchen shortly after the dining room had been cleared. Most of the staff were drinking coffee or tea and nibbling on the latest version of Daystar's muffins.

Cleo came to a halt in the middle of the floor and stood facing everyone with her hands on her hips. Her expression was a cross between surly and triumphant.

"That's the last of them," she announced. "Tobias Quinton and his bunch are finally gone. As I live and breathe, it is my most profound wish to never see a manly warrior male for the rest of my natural life."

Max met Ben's eyes. Neither said a word. They both turned to look at Cleo.

Max cleared his throat politely. "Just out of curiosity, how do you classify Ben and me? Wimpy weenies?"

Cleo had the decency to blush. "Don't be ridiculous. You know what I mean."

"Does this mean I'm not getting a drum for Christmas?" Max asked.

Sylvia, Andromeda, and the others burst into laughter. Cleo endured the reaction stoically. She went over to the counter to pour herself a cup of tea.

"Go ahead, laugh," she muttered. "But I'm here to tell you that it's just the sheerest good luck that Max and Ben were able to get those characters off to bed last night. What if Max had lost that stupid card game?"

"How could I lose at cards with a name like Fortune?" Max asked equably.

Andromeda was immediately intrigued. "Of course, Max. There's probably some harmonic connection between the name you were given at birth and your luck. Do you always win when you play?"

Ben grinned. "I'll bet he always wins when he deals the way he did last night. I watched him. Cleo had nothing to worry about. Tobias Quinton never had a chance."

Cleo gave Max a sharp glance over the rim of her mug. "Did you cheat, Max?"

"There are some things we manly macho men do not discuss in front of females," Max said with lofty disdain. "It's a male thing, you know."

Cleo shuddered. "Speaking of male things, I certainly hope I never see another collection like the ones displayed in the solarium last night."

Everyone fixed Cleo with deeply inquiring looks.

Max recalled the ring of nude men sitting in front of the fire. He smiled politely at Cleo. "Disappointed, were you?"

Cleo gave him a goaded look. "Let's just say that none of them compared to the strikingly superior specimen I have recently been privileged to view in a private showing."

Max choked on his coffee. "Glad to hear that."

Sammy tugged on Cleo's jeans. "What's a male thing?" he asked with the persistence only a five-year-old can muster.

Cleo glanced down and smiled benignly. "Sometimes it doesn't amount to much, dear. But occasionally it can be a work of art."

"Oh." Disappointed by the answer, Sammy went over to the counter to help himself to another muffin.

Everyone else started to grin. Cleo turned pink again and helped herself to more tea.

Yes, there was a lot to be said for being a hero, Max thought. But the best part was learning last night that he didn't really have to do anything except come home in order to get the job.

At midmorning Cleo halted in the middle of her walk and watched as Kimberly strode toward her across the rocky beach.

Today Kimberly looked tastefully stylish in expensive penny loafers, heather gray trousers, and a houndstooth jacket. Her blond hair was in an elegant chignon. Cleo was suddenly very aware that her own hair was a windblown tangle.

"Good morning, Ms. Curzon-Winston," Cleo said, determined to be polite. "I thought you'd left."

Kimberly stopped in front of her. Her eyes were cool and watchful. "I wanted to talk to you before I go."

Cleo folded her arms across her chest. "About Max?"

"Yes."

Cleo gave her a quizzical look. "There isn't much to say, is there?"

"I want to know what's going on between you two."

"Why?"

Kimberly's mouth tightened. "Because Max is acting very strangely. Completely out of character, as a matter of fact. He's up to something, and I want to know what it is."

"I really don't think I owe you any explanations," Cleo said as gently as possible. "My relationship with Max is personal."

Kimberly looked briefly amused. "Relationship? With Max Fortune? Trust me, Ms. Robbins, Max doesn't know the meaning of the word *relationship*. He's a robot. A very brilliant, very clever, extremely useful robot, but a robot, nonetheless."

Cleo was stunned. "That's not true."

"I've known him a lot longer than you have, Ms. Robbins. Did he tell you that we were engaged for a time?"

"Yes."

"Did he tell you that he got that limp saving my life?"

Cleo tightened her arms across her chest. "He told me."

Kimberly looked out at the cloudy horizon. "He asked me to marry him while he was lying in a hospital bed. He was well aware that I was feeling guilty. It was my fault he'd been shot, and both of us knew it. He used that knowledge in a very cold-blooded way to push me into an engagement."

"Why would he do that?"

Kimberly shrugged. "Because he wanted me and he wanted Curzon International. I'll admit I was physically attracted to him. I tried to tell myself at first that he loved me, but I knew all along that he was just using me to get what he wanted. When Max wants something, he does whatever it takes to get it."

"I think you're wrong," Cleo said.

"Am I?" Kimberly's mouth twisted. "You haven't seen him in action the way I have. Max has a certain reputation."

"What sort of reputation?"

"Once he's made up his mind that he wants something, he's almost unstoppable. Whenever Uncle Jason needed a business deal pulled out of the fire or had a problem at one of the hotels, he sent Max in to handle it. Max never failed. As far as he was concerned, whatever Uncle Jason wanted, Uncle Jason got."

"Max was very close to your uncle," Cleo said stiffly.

"Max isn't close to anyone. Not in the way you mean." Kimberly smiled bitterly. "He used Uncle Jason, just as he uses everyone else. Max deliberately set out to make himself indispensable to Curzon. As usual, he succeeded."

"If Max is so ruthless, why do you want him back?"

"Curzon International needs him." Kimberly's gaze was grim. "At least my father seems to think it does."

"What do you think?" Cleo asked quietly.

Kimberly looked out over the cold sea. "I think Max would be extremely useful to Curzon, but I also think he would be dangerous. If we pay the price he'll probably demand in exchange for his return, we'll be taking an enormous risk."

Cleo studied her intently. "What do you think Max wants from you?"

"A seat on the Curzon board. Uncle Jason promised that he'd get it eventually. But Jason died before he could force the rest of us to accept someone on the board who was not a member of the family."

"Max doesn't seem to want to go back," Cleo said cautiously. "He thinks you and your father can run the company without him."

Kimberly gave a short, brittle laugh. "That's not what my father believes. He says we need Max. At least for a couple of years."

Cleo looked down at the toes of her silver sneakers and then raised her eyes to meet Kimberly's. "How do you feel about it?"

Kimberly shot her a swift, unreadable glance. "I think that my father is in charge of Curzon, and if he wants Max back, I'll do my damnedest to get him back. There, Ms. Robbins, I've put my cards on the table. You know exactly where I stand."

"You just want to use Max. You're no different than you say he is."

Kimberly mouthed a disgusted exclamation. "You don't understand, do you? Max relates to people in one of two ways. He either wants something from them, or he uses them to get something else that he wants."

Cleo stared at her. "Did you ever love him, Kimberly?"

Kimberly hesitated. "I will be perfectly blunt. There was no possibility of loving Max. He and I were attracted to each other from the moment we met. But physical desire is the limit of what Max can feel for a woman."

"Are you sure of that?"

Kimberly smiled coldly. "Very sure. I was surprised to learn that he's involved with you. Max is as discriminating in his taste in women as he is in his taste in art. Quite frankly, you're not his type."

"And you are?"

"Yes." There was no arrogance or challenge in Kimberly's voice. She made the statement with simple certainty. "Uncle Jason turned Max into a very sophisticated connoisseur of art. Max picked up the technique, and he applies it to everything he wants, including women. He has the finely honed instincts of an extremely selective collector."

"If you don't believe that he's genuinely interested in me, what do you think he wants from me?" Cleo asked.

"I don't know yet. But I suppose you'll find out soon enough. We all will."

"What's that supposed to mean?"

Kimberly turned her head, her eyes hard with warning. "Just that Max obviously has his own reasons both for working for you and for seducing you. My advice is that you bear that in mind."

"What do you want me to do?" Cleo smiled bleakly. "Fire him?"

"That might not be a bad place to start. You're in over your head, Ms. Robbins." Kimberly turned and walked off down the beach.

"The thing about hardware stores," Ben said to Max as they walked into Harmony Cove Hardware the following afternoon, "is that you got to know what you want before you walk through the door."

"Why is that?" Max glanced around curiously. He had never spent much time in hardware stores. Hardware stores were for men who had real homes of their own. Mansions didn't count. You called someone else in to do repairs in a house such as the one he owned in Seattle. He'd rarely had occasion to fix a leaking faucet, paint a bedroom, or put up wallpaper until he'd moved into Robbins' Nest Inn.

"Because if you don't know what you want and stay focused on it, you get sidetracked." Ben paused beside a display of gleaming steel wrenches. He picked one up and fingered it lovingly.

"Do we need a wrench for this job?" Max picked up one of the wrenches and examined it with interest.

"Nope." Ben put the wrench down. "But you see what I mean? It's easy to get sidetracked. There's so much really great stuff in a hardware store."

"These are nice." Max paused beside a counter full of shiny power drills. He hefted one, testing the weight and feel of it in his hand.

Ben peered at it with admiration. "Real nice. Look at the price on that sucker."

Max glanced at the price tag. "Probably worth every penny."

"Yeah." Ben grinned. "Think I could convince Trisha that I need one to fix up the baby's room?"

"You could try." Max put the drill back down on the counter.

"Something I've been meaning to ask you," Ben said as he examined a neat arrangement of nails.

"What's that?" Max looked at a rack of colorful screwdrivers.

"You planning on sticking around the inn for a while?" Ben concentrated intently on the nails.

"Yes," Max said. "I'm planning on sticking around until someone throws me out."

"Yeah. Well, okay," Ben said. "That's all I wanted to ask. Hey, will you look at those clamps. I've been meaning to get one for my workbench down in the basement."

Max continued to study the screwdrivers. "I could use one of these."

"You never know when you're going to need a screwdriver handy." Ben picked up a clamp. "They're busy planning the wedding, you know. Trisha says that even though we're going to get married right away, the family wants to do it up real formal. Tuxes for the guys and a fancy gown for her."

"I know." Max had heard the discussions in the kitchen that morning.

Cleo, Andromeda, Daystar, and Sylvia intended to pull out all the stops for Ben and Trisha's wedding. It had already been decided that the event would take place in less than two weeks at Cosmic Harmony. Daystar had pointed out in her usual pragmatic fashion that under the circumstances, there was not a lot of time to waste.

"I've never worn a tux," Ben said hesitantly. "Didn't go to a senior prom or anything. I don't even know where to get one."

"Nothing to it," Max assured him. He selected one of the screwdrivers and took it down from the rack.

"You sure?"

"I'm sure," said Max. "Don't worry about it. I'll show you how it's done."

Ben nodded, looking vastly relieved. "Okay." He flashed Max a quick, searching glance. "So what do you think about being my best man or whatever it is they call it?"

Max slowly put down the screwdriver he had been examining. He looked at Ben. "I'd be honored."

Ben turned beet red. "Yeah, well, it probably isn't that big a deal to you. But thanks."

"You're wrong," Max said. "It's a very big deal. I've never been anyone's best man."

Ben smiled, and the two men returned to their shopping.

An hour later Max reluctantly walked out of the hardware store with Ben. He had a shiny new screwdriver in a paper sack.

"We didn't do too bad," Ben said cheerfully as they strolled toward the Jaguar with their purchases. "Been needing that clamp for a long time. And you can't have too many needle-nose pliers lying around. They're always disappearing. Hell of a sale on those toilet float balls. I wonder if we should have picked up more than three."

"Damn," Max said, as he came to a halt beside the Jaguar. "We forgot the washers for the faucet in one-oh-three."

Ben groaned. "I told you that hardware stores were dangerous. You wait here. I'll go back and get them." He tossed the sack to Max and hurried back toward the store.

Max leaned against the Jaguar's fender to wait. It had finally stopped raining for a while, but a heavy fog was condensing just offshore. It would soon be moving inland. In another hour the roads would be shrouded in a heavy cloak of gray mist. Driving would be hazardous.

Max hoped Ben would not get captivated by a display of power tools. He wanted to be home by the fire when the fog settled in over Harmony Cove this evening.

Home by the fire. Hell, he was turning into a regular home-and-hearth kind of guy. What have you done to me, Jason? Max asked silently. Did you know what would happen when you sent me out here in search of those Luttrells?

Two men got out of a nondescript Ford that was parked across the street. One was slightly taller than the other. He was also a few years older, with thinning hair and a slight paunch. The younger one wore GQ glasses and had a mouthful of very white teeth that had clearly been labored over by an orthodontist. Both men were out of place in casual Harmony Cove. Their business suits, expensive ties, and highly polished wing tips identified them as outsiders as clearly as the fact that they were coming straight toward Max.

"Max Fortune?" The older man stuck out his hand. "Phillip Sand. This is my associate, Hamilton Turner. We represent some people who would very much like to get you on our team."

"Global Village Properties," Max said.

Turner smiled, displaying his beautiful teeth. "How did you guess?"

"I wondered when you'd get around to talking to me." Max glanced toward the entrance of Harmony Cove Hardware. There was no sign of Ben.

"Why don't we have a cup of coffee while you wait for your friend?" Sand suggested smoothly.

Max shrugged. "Why not?"

Cleo sat quietly, her legs folded tailor-fashion, her hands resting on her knees. She gazed into the large yellow crystal, willing her mind to focus. She was the only one in the meditation room at Cosmic Harmony this afternoon.

She was not sure why she had felt the need to seek out the refuge again today. There had been no nightmares recently. But around three o'clock, she had realized that she was feeling unsettled and restless.

The sensation had not disappeared after she had fixed herself a cup of Andromeda's tea, so Cleo had gotten into her Toyota and driven the mile and a half around the cove to the Cosmic Harmony Retreat.

Now, gazing calmly into the crystal, Cleo acknowledged to herself what she had not wanted to confront earlier. The truth was that the conversation with Kimberly had bothered her more than she had been willing to admit.

He has the finely honed instincts of an extremely selective collector.

Max obviously has his own reasons both for working for you and for seducing you.

Physical desire is the limit of what Max can feel for a woman.

Cleo closed her eyes and drew a slow, deep breath into the pit of her stomach. Kimberly was wrong about Max. She had to be wrong about him. Max had been Jason's friend, and Jason had been a kind, compassionate man.

Max was patient with Sammy. Whatever he had said to Ben had been responsible for making the younger man want to come home to Trisha and the others.

And when Max made love, Cleo reminded herself, he gave as much as he took. Perhaps more. Cleo knew her experience was extremely limited, but instinct told her that Max was a very generous lover.

Her instinct also told her that in bed, at least, he needed her in a way he would probably never be able to put into words.

Cleo opened her eyes again and stared at the light inside the yellow crystal. Sex wasn't all Max needed from her. He was hungry for other things as well, the same kind of things she had grown up with and that she had deliberately set out to recreate after the death of her parents.

Max needed a family. Whether he knew it or not, he wanted one. Surely that was why he was hanging around Robbins' Nest Inn even though he knew the Luttrell paintings were not there.

He's a robot. A very clever, very brilliant, extremely useful robot, but a robot nonetheless.

"No," Cleo whispered. Her hands closed into small fists. Max was no robot. But she suspected Kimberly had been right when she implied that Max didn't know much about relationships.

Cleo blinked, setting herself free from the gentle thrall of meditation. She took another slow, deep breath and uncoiled from the position she had been holding for the past half hour.

As always she was a little stiff after sitting still for so long. She went to the bank of floor-to-ceiling windows and looked out, startled to see how thick the fog had become.

It was time to go home. Preparations would be starting for the evening meal, and with any luck, there would be a smattering of new guests checking in for the night. Heavy fog sometimes induced cautious travelers to spend the night at the first available inn rather than drive on to their destinations.

A woman dressed in a Cosmic Harmony gown and wearing the familiar necklace waved to Cleo as she walked up the path toward what had once been the main lodge of the old resort.

"Better hurry, Cleo. That fog is going to get worse before it gets better."

Cleo lifted a hand in acknowledgment. "I'm on my way, Nebula. Don't worry about Andromeda and the others. They can stay the night at the inn if the fog doesn't clear up later."

"Of course, dear. Have a good evening."

Cleo nodded at a small group of women who were hurrying from the indoor pool back to the lodge. They waved back. Some were familiar faces, others were visitors who had come to spend a few days at the retreat.

By the time Cleo reached the parking lot, the fog had partially obscured the trees that lined both sides of the road. Luckily there was rarely any traffic on the narrow strip of pavement that led from the retreat back to the inn.

Cleo turned on the lights and eased the Toyota out of the small parking lot. The heavy mist ebbed and swirled in front of her, revealing and then concealing the white line. By the time Cleo was halfway back to the inn, she could barely see the road at all. The fog had not been so heavy along this stretch of coastline since mid-January. She slowed the Toyota to a snail's pace.

The Toyota began to slow still further of its own accord.

Cleo pressed her foot down on the throttle. Nothing happened. She glanced down at the gauges in concern. With a shock, she saw that she was out of gas.

But that wasn't possible, she thought, annoyed. She had filled the tank just last week. Someone else had either borrowed her car or siphoned the gas out of it.

"Damn."

It was going to be a cold walk home.

A few minutes later, bundled up in her hunter green parka, flashlight in hand, car keys in her pocket, she got out of the Toyota and started to walk along the edge of the road. There was less than a mile to go, she assured herself.

The fog had become an icy gray shroud. It blanketed everything with an eerie stillness. Cleo kept to the far edge of the pavement and listened intently for the sounds of automobile engines. Anyone approaching in a car would be unable to see her until he was on top of her. The safest thing to do would be to get off the road entirely if she heard a car coming.

All she heard was the cold, relentless silence.

The gray mist grew heavier. The early night of a Northwest winter was closing in quickly. In another half hour it would be dark.

Cleo concentrated intently on listening for an approaching car. What she heard was the soft echo of footsteps on the pavement behind her.

She stopped and whirled around. The fog formed an impenetrable gray wall behind her.

"Is someone there?"

The footsteps stopped.

"Who is it?" Cleo dug out the small flashlight she had brought with her and aimed it into the dense mist. The beam did not penetrate more than a few feet. It revealed nothing.

Wondering if she had been mistaken, Cleo turned around and started walking more quickly down the road. She kept the flashlight on, even though it didn't do much good. Something about the light was reassuring.

She had not gone more than a few yards when she heard the ring of footsteps on pavement again. Cleo halted once more and turned around.

"Who's there?"

The footsteps ceased.

A chill that had nothing to do with the weather shot down Cleo's spine. She was suddenly acutely aware of the fact that the flashlight beam made her location more visible in the fog. She flicked the switch, dousing the light.

The dark mist closed in on her. So did the footsteps.

Cleo did not question her next move. She reacted instinctively. She started to run.

When she heard the muted thuds of her own soft-soled sneakers hitting the pavement, another wave of fear went through her. *Idiot,* she thought. Now she was announcing her location by sound.

She stopped and listened. The footsteps behind her were louder. Whoever it was would burst through the fog any minute.

She spun around and plunged into the trees beside the road. The soft, damp earth absorbed the impact of her shoes. Whoever was playing the cat-and-mouse game on the road would be unable to find her by sound alone.

Cleo worked her way carefully through the trees. She knew she had to be careful about straying too far from the road. If she lost her bearings in this gray soup, she could end up wandering around in the forest until she succumbed to hypothermia.

She stilled as the footsteps drew relentlessly closer on the road. Afraid to move farther into the undergrowth, she crouched down behind a thick fir and pulled the hood of the parka down over her face. She was very glad the coat was dark green rather than a vivid orange or red.

She prayed she was overreacting.

She prayed the footsteps would continue on down the road.

The taste of panic was in her mouth. She recognized it immediately even though she had not felt anything this intense outside of her nightmares for nearly four years.

The footsteps were directly opposite to her now. They paused for a moment.

Cleo stopped breathing.

A few seconds later the stalker continued on down the road.

Cleo did not take a deep breath until she could no longer hear him.

Several minutes passed before she eased back the hood of the parka. She allowed a little more time to creep past before she risked getting to her feet.

She did not dare switch on the flashlight as she made her way back toward the road. For an instant she thought she had gone in the wrong direction. The pavement was not where it was supposed to be.

Then she felt the graveled shoulder beneath her shoes. Relief poured through her, leaving her weak and jittery.

When she reached the blacktop, Cleo stopped and listened intently again. The growling purr of a sophisticated automobile engine sounded in the distance. The driver was moving slowly along the road, either out of respect for the blinding fog or because he was searching for someone.

Cleo started to retreat back into the woods, but at the last minute she hesitated. There was something familiar about the muted roar of that particular car engine.

A few seconds later Max's green Jaguar emerged from the fog like a sleek beast of prey. The low beams of the headlights sliced through the thick mist.

Cleo switched on the flashlight and waved it about wildly. The light bounced around, dancing on the gray fog. "Max, stop," she yelled. "It's me."

The Jaguar halted swiftly. The door on the driver's side slammed open and Max got out, cane in hand. Cleo could not see the expression on his face, but she could hear the steel in his voice.

"Cleo. For God's sake, what do you think you're doing?"

"Walking home." Cleo ran toward him. "Max, I've never been so glad to see anyone in my whole life. I was so scared."

She threw herself against his chest and clung to him like moss on a log. Max grunted under the impact, but he kept his balance with one hand on the top of the car door. He wrapped his other arm around her and pulled her close.

"What's wrong?" he asked harshly. "Are you all right?"

"Someone was following me. At least, I think he was." Cleo realized she sounded breathless and unnerved. "I could hear footsteps in the fog. I think they were footsteps. They sort of echoed. And there was no other sound and . . . oh, God, Max, I'm not sure if I really did hear them. But I hid in the woods, anyway. And then you came along."

His arm tightened around her. "Are you sure you're all right?"

"Yes, yes, I'm fine. Just a little shaky." Cleo made a valiant effort to pull herself together. "I'm sorry, I'm acting like an idiot, aren't I?"

"No. You're acting like someone who's had a bad scare."

Cleo straightened, but she couldn't bring herself to pull away from the comforting warmth of his arm. She found a hankie in her pocket and blew into it. Then she took a deep breath.

"The car ran out of gas," Cleo said in what she thought was a firm, controlled voice. "Only it shouldn't have, because I had just filled the tank. I started walking home. Then I heard the footsteps. I called out. No one answered. I got off the road until whoever it was had passed. That's really all there was to it. I don't know why I freaked."

Max cut through the rambling explanation. "Where's your car?"

"Back there somewhere. Not far." Cleo waved vaguely to indicate the road behind her. "I think some kid must have siphoned the gas out of my tank or something."

"We'll worry about your car later. Right now I want to get you home. Sylvia, Trisha, and the others are starting to get worried." Max opened the Jaguar's door and ushered her into the warmth.

"I'm sorry everyone's upset," Cleo mumbled as she relaxed into the warmth of the front seat. She reached for her seatbelt. "I really do feel sort of stupid. I'm sure my imagination just got the better of me."

"Maybe." Max got in beside her and started the engine. He put the Jaguar in gear and eased it back onto the road.

"Aren't you going to turn around and drive back to the inn?" Cleo asked.

"I want to make sure your car is far enough off the road. We don't want anyone hitting it in this fog."

Cleo didn't argue.

A short distance down the road, the Jaguar's headlights picked up the ghostly shape of the Toyota wreathed in fog.

"Let me have your keys."

"What are you going to do?" Cleo asked as she handed him the keys. "You can't start it. There's no gas."

"I just want to take a quick look. I'll be right back."

"Is this another one of those male things?"

Max closed the door without deigning to answer. Cleo sat watching as he went over to the Toyota, opened the door, and got behind the wheel. She waited for the engine to sputter to life and then die, but Max made no move to start the car. He just sat behind the wheel for what seemed like a very long time. She could not tell what he was doing.

Cleo was about to get out of the Jaguar to see what was keeping him, when the Toyota door opened again. She saw that he had a piece of paper in his hand. The uneasiness stirred back to life within her.

Cold air and tendrils of fog swirled into the Jaguar when Max opened the door.

"I found this on the driver's seat." His eyes were grimly intent as he handed the piece of paper to Cleo. "I assume it wasn't there when you left the car to start walking back to the inn."

Cleo read the typewritten message on the piece of paper:

> The first Cleopatra was a whore. She died the death she deserved.

Eleven

"O'Reilly, I don't want to hear any more about the lack of results." Max's voice was low and harsh as he spoke into the phone. He was sitting at the small desk in the attic room. His cane was propped against the back of the chair. "I know you didn't find anything interesting when you ran those names through your computers. I'm telling you that we need a whole new angle on this thing."

There was a short, taut silence as Max listened to whatever his friend was saying on the other end.

Cleo sat in the middle of Max's bed, her arms wrapped around her knees. She was still fully dressed and feeling chilled, although the room was pleasantly warm. Max had hustled her straight upstairs to his room the minute they had reached the inn. On the way through the lobby he had told Sylvia, Ben, Trisha, and the others that he would explain everything later. Cleo was starting to fret because she knew the family was downstairs worrying.

"That's right, for all intents and purposes the note sounded like a death threat," Max said. His jaw tightened as Cleo shuddered. "No, I don't know of anything going on out here that would push some local crazy over the edge. Yes, I'm going to keep an eye on her. No, she's not going to go anywhere alone from now on."

Cleo opened her mouth to protest that statement, but Max only looked more grimly determined, so she shut it again.

"Yes, I think the case needs a little more in-depth work, myself," Max said, not bothering to hide his sarcasm. "And I don't want it put on the back burner. I want top-of-the-line service. All right. We'll see you sometime tomorrow. Make it before noon, O'Reilly."

He hung up the phone and regarded Cleo with brooding eyes.

Cleo moistened her lower lip. "What did Mr. O'Reilly say?"

"He said, and I quote, 'You always want top-of-the-line service, you son of a bitch.' "

"Oh." Cleo smiled ruefully. "I'll bet you always get it, too. There was no need to be rude to Mr. O'Reilly. I'm sure he's doing his best."

"I wasn't rude, I was firm. He's turned up absolutely nothing so far."

"He found Ben."

"That has nothing to do with this other matter." Max paused thoughtfully. "At least, I don't think it does."

Cleo straightened her spine, alarmed by the tone of his voice. "Of course it doesn't. How could it?"

"Damned if I know. None of this makes any sense at the moment." Max grabbed his cane and got to his feet. "Come on, we're going downstairs to let the others know what's happening."

"Max, I told you, I don't want everyone worrying about this."

"Too bad. They're going to have to worry about it. I'm going to see to it that everybody worries."

Cleo frowned. "I think we should keep this between ourselves."

"I want everyone in the family to know what's going on so that everyone can keep an eye on you."

"I'll feel like a prisoner."

"That's the whole idea." Max crossed the room, reached down, and caught her hand in his. He yanked her lightly up off the bed. "Let's go."

"I would like to remind you that I'm the one in charge around here." Cleo went to the door and threw it open with a defiant flourish. It was much easier to feel defiant when you were once again feeling quite safe, she discovered. "I don't recall giving you permission to run things."

"It must have slipped your mind." Max herded her out the room. "You've been busy lately."

"Max, this is not a joke."

"Christ, Cleo, you don't have to tell me that. You gave me a hell of a scare today. By the way, don't worry about me being in charge for a while around here. I'm good at running things."

"That's what Kimberly said."

"Speaking of Kimberly, when did she leave?"

"Right after we had a cozy little chat on the beach."

"What did you two talk about?" Max urged her down the second flight of stairs.

"You, for the most part."

"Sounds dull."

"I assure you, Max, you are never dull."

They had reached the first floor. Sylvia looked up from behind the desk. She glanced first at Max's set face and then gave Cleo a concerned look.

"Everything okay?" she asked.

"No," Max said. "Everything is not okay. Call the others. I want everyone in the kitchen in five minutes."

Cleo rolled her eyes. "Honestly, Max. You're carrying this a little too far."

But Sylvia was already hurrying around the edge of the desk. "I'll find everyone."

Cleo threw Max a disgusted look as Sylvia dashed down the hall. "No one around here jumps for me like that."

"It's the difference between our two different management styles," Max explained. "You operate with what is generally called the consensus style."

"What do you call your style?" Cleo shoved open the kitchen door. "A dictatorship?"

"Don't knock it. It works."

"Where did you learn it?"

"From Jason."

"I don't believe it," Cleo declared. "I think it comes naturally to you."

One by one the others gathered in the kitchen. Sammy clung to his mother's hand, his eyes widening as he realized how serious the grown-ups were behaving.

"I don't think we should include Sammy in this," Cleo whispered uneasily to Max. "He'll be scared."

"He's part of the family," Max said. "He already knows something is going on, and if we don't tell him what it is, and that it's under control, he'll be frightened. This way he'll feel included, and he'll know that action is being taken. That should reassure him."

"Since when did you become an authority on child psychology?" Cleo asked.

Max looked at her. "I was a child once, myself."

"I find that extremely difficult to believe."

"I'm not surprised. So do I."

Cleo watched the expressions on her friends' faces as they gathered around the nook table. Andromeda, Daystar, Trisha, Ben, Sylvia, and little Sammy all glanced first at her with deep concern. They then turned and looked expectantly at Max.

Max wrapped both of his hands around the handle of the hawk-headed cane. He regarded the family with a considering gaze.

"Someone has been threatening Cleo because of the book she wrote," he said.

Everyone stared at Cleo.

"Good heavens, I don't believe it," Andromeda said softly. "Cleo? Are you all right?"

"Yes, Andromeda," Cleo said soothingly. "I'm fine. Max is making a big production out of this."

Ben put his arm around Trisha and frowned at Max. "What's going on?" he asked.

"Did someone hurt Cleo?" Sammy demanded anxiously.

Max looked down at him. "No," he said quietly. "And no one is going to hurt her. We are all going to keep an eye on her."

"Even you?" Sammy asked.

"Especially me," Max said.

Cleo listened with a growing sense of unreality as Max gave everyone a quick, concise summary of events. They all paid close attention. It was obvious that they were looking to Max for leadership in this crisis. No one questioned his authority.

It occurred to Cleo that somewhere along the line Max had become a very important part of the family. Today he had even begun to challenge her own role as the head of the clan. She realized that she would have to make some adjustments if Max stayed on at Robbins' Nest Inn.

In a flash of rueful insight Cleo suddenly understood why Kimberly and her family had refused to give Max a seat on the Curzon board. He would have ended up running the company in short order.

Forming a partnership with Max was going to be an interesting challenge, Cleo thought.

She watched, impressed in spite of herself, as Max took complete control of the situation in the kitchen and managed to reassure everyone, including Sammy.

"O'Reilly will arrive tomorrow," Max concluded. "He's a first-class private investigator. He'll want to interview everyone, including all of us."

"But we don't know anything about these strange incidents," Andromeda said unhappily. "What can we tell him?"

"Just answer his questions," Max instructed. "O'Reilly knows how to do his job. In the meantime, we all have a job to do, too. From now on, Cleo is not going to leave the inn alone. Clear? I want someone with her any time she steps foot outside the inn's front door."

Cleo roused herself for another weak protest. "Max, that's taking things too far. I'll be careful, I promise."

"The way you were this afternoon?" he asked bluntly.

Cleo glared at him. "I didn't know the situation was going to get this bad."

"Exactly." Max turned back to the others and surveyed them with the air of a commander sending troops into battle. "Is everyone straight about this? Cleo does not leave the inn alone."

"Got it," Ben said. "We'll keep an eye on her."

Sylvia nodded. "Don't worry, we'll make sure she's never alone."

"What happens if she goes outside by herself?" Sammy demanded.

Max raised a brow. "If you see Cleo disobeying orders, you come and tell me right away. Understand?"

"Will you make her go into her room for a time out?" Sammy inquired with grave interest. "That's what Mommy does to me when she gets mad at me."

"I might do just that," Max said. "Only I think I'll make her go to my room instead of her own room."

For some reason that sent Sammy off into a gale of giggles.

"Sheesh," Cleo muttered. "I'm going to go crazy."

Trisha smiled at her. "Don't worry, we won't let you go crazy alone."

The blood was everywhere. So much blood. It had soaked into the carpets and spattered against the walls. It had saturated her mother's dress and pooled beneath her father's head. Too much blood. The smell of it made her sick to her stomach. The sight of it drove her to the edge of sanity.

Cleo opened her mouth to scream and discovered that she was voiceless.

She struggled to escape the evil room and realized she could not move. She was trapped.

"Cleo. Cleo, wake up. You're dreaming."

Max's voice cut through the gossamer strands of horror that had been used to weave Cleo's nightmare. She opened her eyes and saw him looming over her. He had his hands on her shoulders, pinning her against the pillows.

Reality emerged from the whirling mist of red that clouded her mind. She was safe in the attic room with Max. She was not alone.

For the first time, she was not alone when she awoke from the dream.

"Max?"

"It's all right, Cleo. I'm here."

"Oh, God." She closed her eyes and took several deep breaths, just as she did when she was meditating. "Sorry. I don't get the dreams very often, but when I do, they make me a little wild."

"What dreams?" Max released his grip on her shoulders, but he did not move away from her. He remained where he was, half covering her with his warm, comforting weight.

"I don't like to talk about them. I tried that with the therapist. But talking about them only makes them seem worse." Cleo shuddered beneath Max's weight. The heat and strength of him enfolded her in a snug, secure haven. She was not alone tonight. Max was with her.

She made a soft little sound and closed her arms around his neck. Then she turned her face into his bare shoulder and let the tears fall.

Max said nothing. He simply held her close and let her cry until the storm had passed. When it was all over, he kept her cradled against him. His hand moved slowly along her arm.

"Your parents?" he asked at last.

"Yes." Cleo hesitated. "I was the one who found them. Sometimes I dream about it."

"Jesus, Cleo." Max continued to stroke her gently. "I'm so damned sorry."

"It's been four years. But the dreams, when they come, are just as bad as ever. My therapist said I might have them occasionally for the rest of my life, especially if I'm under stress."

"Which you are right now, thanks to whoever is leaving those notes around." Max's voice was gritty with suppressed anger. "I'm looking forward to getting my hands on the bastard."

"Max?"

"Yes?"

"Thanks for coming after me this afternoon."

"Next time you get into the car, check the gas gauge."

Cleo smiled wryly. "My father used to do that."

"What? Check the gas gauge?"

"No, lecture me or my mother after the crisis was past. It was as if he was angry at us for having gotten into trouble in the first place. I remember my mother had her purse snatched once. Afterward Dad chewed her out something fierce for not being more careful."

"He was mad at himself, not her," Max said quietly. "He hadn't been able to protect her, and it scared him."

"That's what Mom said."

"When men get scared, they usually get mad," Max said.

"A male thing?"

Max smiled faintly into the shadows. "Probably."

Cleo snuggled closer. "Max, there's something I've been wanting to ask you."

"I hope this is not about my relationship with Kimberly," he warned. "Because I really don't want to talk about that anymore."

"It's not about that." Cleo wrinkled her nose. "I told you, Kimberly and I have already had a long discussion on that subject."

"Why do women always have to get together and talk about their relationships with men?" Max asked, disgusted.

"Who knows? It's a female thing, I guess. Are you going to lie there and tell me men never talk about their relationships with women?"

"Never," Max said. "I think it's against the code or something."

"Like heck it is. Never mind. What I want to know is, why did you pack your things and put them in your car before you left to find Ben yesterday?"

Max was very still. "I didn't think I'd be staying here unless I brought Ben back with me."

That was not the answer Cleo had been expecting. She turned on her side and levered herself up on her elbow to look down at Max. In the shadows it was difficult to read his expression. "What do you mean? What did Ben have to do with whether or not you stayed with us?"

Max looked up at her, his gaze shuttered. "Coming back without Ben meant I'd failed."

"So?"

Max threaded his fingers lightly through her hair. "I knew how much everyone had counted on my being able to convince Ben to come back. I knew the odds were against it, even if the rest of you didn't. I figured I'd never pull it off."

"So?"

Max shrugged. "I wasn't sure how you and the rest of the family would feel about me if I screwed up that badly."

Cleo was horrified. "Are you telling me you thought we wouldn't want you to stay with us just because you weren't able to bring Ben back?"

Max gave her an unreadable look. "It's been my experience that people only want you around as long as you can do something for them."

"Of all the ridiculous things to say." Cleo was stricken by a sudden thought. "Is that how things worked at Curzon International?"

"That's how things have worked most of my life. Curzon was no exception."

"I can't believe Jason ran his business that way."

"I hate to shatter your illusions about Jason Curzon. But I can guarantee that he didn't run Curzon International with a sweet, gentle, consensus style of management. He was one tough son of a bitch."

"Jason would have given people a second chance. I know he would have."

Max's mouth curved slightly. "Sometimes, if there were extenuating circumstances, and if he needed whoever had screwed up badly enough to keep him around. But second chances were rare at Curzon. And there was no such thing as a third chance."

"You got along with him."

"I made it a point not to screw up when it came to getting things done for Jason."

Cleo touched his arm. "Are you saying that you think Jason would have kicked you out if you'd failed him in some way?"

Max hesitated. "Let's just say I didn't want to put it to the test."

Cleo framed his face with her palms. "That's awful. How could you live with that kind of constant pressure to perform?"

Max was genuinely amused by her concern. "I'm used to it. The flip side is that I don't screw up very often."

Cleo shook her head wonderingly. "No, I don't suppose you do. But you thought you had when you came home without Ben, didn't you?"

"Yes."

Cleo smiled sadly. "I'm sorry you felt that way. I had no idea you believed your welcome here was contingent on whether or not you brought Ben home. But I've got to admit I'm a little relieved to hear your explanation."

Max searched her face. "Why?"

"Because I'd come to my own conclusion about why you'd packed your bag before you left."

"What conclusion was that?" Max asked.

Cleo ducked her head and kissed his mouth lightly. "Promise you won't laugh?"

"I promise."

"I thought it was just barely possible that you weren't coming back because you'd finally realized I didn't know where those Luttrell paintings were."

Max's gaze turned fierce. "What the hell are you saying?"

"I thought maybe the paintings were all you cared about." Cleo smiled tremulously. "It crossed my mind, Max, that you might have just possibly seduced me primarily to see if you could get me to tell you where I'd stashed your Luttrells. Your old pal, Garrison Spark, didn't help matters when he told me you were quite capable of using that kind of tactic."

Max's fingers tightened abruptly around her waist. His dark lashes veiled his eyes. "You believed that?"

Cleo felt herself growing warm, but she did not lower her gaze. "After you made love to me you asked me about the paintings one last time. Don't you remember? You said something like 'You really don't know where the Luttrells are, do you?' "

"Cleo, I told you I'd come back."

"I know," she admitted.

"But you didn't believe me?"

"I didn't know what to believe. All I could do was cross my fingers and hope you'd return, with or without Ben."

Max watched her intently. "Cleo, what if I told you that it did occur to me that seducing you might be the easiest way to see if you were telling the truth about the Luttrells?"

She grinned. "I'd say you were teasing me."

"You think so?"

"Yep." She touched the edge of his mouth with her fingertip. "We both know you didn't seduce me just to find out where the paintings are. If that was all you wanted from me, you would never have tracked Ben down and talked to him. And you would never have come back here to the inn. Right?"

Max's hand closed tightly around hers. He brushed his mouth across the inside of her wrist in an incredibly gentle, almost reverent kiss. "I guess you're right."

"And before you say anything more, let me remind you that you've got no business lecturing me about my lack of faith in you."

"No?"

"No." Cleo folded her arms on top of his chest. "You displayed the same lack of faith in me and the rest of the family. I can't believe you didn't know we'd want you to come back regardless of whether or not you were successful. We like you because you're you, Max, not because you have a reputation for never screwing up."

"Hardly ever screwing up." Max brought her face close to his and kissed her with rough passion. When he released her, his eyes were gleaming, hard and fierce.

Cleo smiled slowly. "I guess we've both learned something about each other from all this, haven't we?"

Max's answering smile was laced with lazy sensuality. "Well, I'm convinced that you aren't hiding my Luttrells. I knew the first night I met you that you were either one of the most formidable opponents I had ever encountered or . . . Never mind."

"What do you mean, never mind?" Cleo said. "Finish the sentence."

"Or you were one of the nicest, sweetest, most innocent women I had ever met," Max concluded smoothly.

Cleo glowered at him. "That's not what you originally intended to say, was it? What did you really think that first night? That if I wasn't extremely shrewd, I was probably not too bright? Is that what you thought?"

"I can't even remember what I thought that first night. Too much has happened." Max rolled her over onto her back and sat up beside her. He opened the drawer next to the bed and reached inside.

"What are you doing?" Cleo asked, straining to focus on whatever it was he was removing from the drawer. "What's that? It looks like a scarf."

"That's exactly what it is." Max shook out the large square of yellow and blue silk.

"What are you going to do with it?"

"I'm going to try something I read about in chapter five of *The Mirror.*" Max took hold of opposite corners of the scarf and stretched the fabric into a taut, narrow rope.

Cleo's eyes widened even as the first tremors of excitement flowed through her. "Max, you wouldn't."

Max's eyes gleamed with warm, sexy amusement. "Relax, Cleo. I rarely screw up, remember?"

"Yes, I know, but *Max.*" Cleo was suddenly hot all over.

Max slowly eased the hem of her chaste, flower-printed flannel gown up to her waist. Then he slid the strip of yellow and blue silk beneath her buttocks and drew it up between her thighs as if it were a thong-style bikini. He gently pulled it taut.

"Max." Cleo could feel the strip of silk working its way into the moist, heated folds of her feminine flesh. She grabbed fistfuls of the sheet in both hands.

Max tightened the scarf slowly until it was gliding over the delicate bud hidden in the triangle of dark hair. The sensation left Cleo gasping. The feeling was one of tantalizing torment, just as she had imagined it would be when she had written the scene in *The Mirror.*

When Max embellished the original version and used his mouth to dampen the silk between her legs, Cleo came apart in his hands.

She knew Max was watching her in rapt fascination as she surrendered to the climax. For some reason that only made the final sweet convulsions all the more exquisitely exciting.

Max opened one eye a long time later to find Cleo sitting up in bed, leaning over him. She had a speculative expression on her face as she shook out the yellow and blue scarf.

"What do you think you're going to do with that?" he asked with sleepy unconcern.

"Experiment. You never know. Someday I might write a sequel to *The Mirror.*" Cleo started to drape the silk square over him. "From a man's point of view."

Max started to smile. Then he sucked in a deep breath as his recently satisfied body reacted to the sensual touch of the silk. "Sounds interesting."

"Yes, I think it will be."

The phone rang just as Cleo was starting to do some truly creative things with the length of silk. Max swore as he reached for the receiver beside the bed.

"Fortune here."

"Max?" George sounded wide awake for once. "This is me. George. At the front desk."

"What's wrong, George?"

Cleo halted the process of tying the narrowed scarf into a bow around an extremely rigid portion of Max's anatomy. She leaned across him to fumble for her glasses on the nightstand.

Max groaned as her soft stomach pressed against his decorated manhood.

"There's a guy down here says he knows you, Max. Says he wants to talk to you right away. He's threatening to tear the place apart if you don't get down here."

Max sat up against the pillows. "Who is it?"

"He says his name is Roarke Winston."

"Hell, that's all I needed. I'll be right down." Max tossed the phone back into its cradle. He reached for the cane he had propped against the wall.

"What's wrong?" Cleo demanded. She was already off the bed, searching for her jeans.

"Winston's here." Max got out of bed and went to the closet.

"Kimberly's husband?"

"Right." Max started to pull on his trousers and stopped when he noticed that the silk scarf was still tied around him in a wispy, languid bow. He cautiously removed it.

"What's he doing here?" Cleo swiftly buttoned her oxford cloth shirt.

"How the hell should I know? Maybe he's looking for Kimberly." Max tossed the scarf aside with genuine regret.

"Why ask for you?"

Max cocked a brow as he led the way to the door. "Damned if I know. We'll find out soon enough."

He went down the two flights of stairs with Cleo hard on his heels. When he walked into the lobby, he knew there was going to be trouble.

Roarke Winston, patrician-featured, well-dressed, and normally brimming with the subtle arrogance that came from old money and solid family connections, was in a towering rage.

He swung around as Max entered the room. "Fortune, you son of a bitch. Where's my wife?"

"I don't know," Max said calmly. "She's not here."

"You're lying." Roarke started forward, his hands clenched at his sides. His handsome face was mottled with fury. "She's here. I know she is. You talked her into coming here with you, didn't you? You're sleeping with my wife, you bastard."

"Take it easy, Winston," Max said.

"What made you think I'd let you get away with having an affair with my wife?" Roarke closed the distance between himself and Max with long, swift strides.

"Stop it," Cleo yelped in alarm. "Max isn't having an affair with Kimberly."

"The hell he isn't." Roarke's voice rose. "He's wanted to get his hands on Curzon from the start. He figures seducing Kim is one way to do it."

"That's not true," Cleo said. She turned toward the front desk and glared at George. "You're the night desk man, George. Do something."

George gazed at her helplessly and then banged the bell that sat on the front desk. Apparently pleased with that decisive maneuver, he banged it again.

"Oh, for heaven's sake," Cleo muttered.

Roarke came to a halt less than two feet away from Max. "You don't love her. You never did love her. You're just trying to use her. I'll be damned if I'll let you do it."

He swung wildly.

"No," Cleo shouted. "Don't hit him. He didn't do anything."

She leaped in front of Max just as Roarke's fist came crashing toward its target. At the last instant, Max realized that the blow was going to strike Cleo.

He grabbed Cleo's shoulder and spun her aside, out of the path of Roarke's fist. Unfortunately the maneuver did not give him time to use the cane in self-defense. Instead it took him straight into the path of the punch.

Cleo stumbled and fell. In an effort to avoid hitting her, Roarke obviously tried to pull his punch at the last second. But it was too late. His fist clipped the side of Max's jaw.

Max staggered, lost his balance, and sprawled back against the front desk. As he slid gracefully to the floor, he saw Cleo reach for the vase that sat on the corner stand. She grabbed it with both hands and took aim at Roarke's head.

Max didn't know whether to laugh or curse. He was not accustomed to having anyone leap to his defense. It was a pleasant novelty, but enough was enough. If things went any further, someone was going to get hurt.

"Put the vase down, Cleo." Max sat on the floor, propped against the desk in what he hoped was a suitably dramatic fashion. He groaned and gingerly fingered the side of his jaw. "I quit, Winston. You're the winner."

Roarke stood over him, breathing heavily. "Bastard."

"Don't you dare touch him," Cleo said to Roarke. "Get away from him." She set the vase down on the stand and dashed across the room to Max's side. "He's not sleeping with your wife."

"How do you know?" Roarke demanded.

"Because he's sleeping with me." Cleo touched Max's face with gentle, questing fingers. "Isn't that right, Max?"

"Right," said Max.

The sound of running footsteps overhead made everyone, including George, look toward the staircase.

Ben came thundering down the stairs first. His hair was tousled, and his shirt was unbuttoned. He was trying to fasten his jeans. Trisha was right behind him. She was tying the belt of her robe as she hurried down the steps.

Sylvia and Sammy brought up the rear. Both were in their night-clothes. Sammy was yawning.

"What's going on down here?" Ben scanned the lobby scene quickly. "Cleo? Max? Are you guys okay?"

"No," Cleo said.

"Yes," Max said, overriding her. "Allow me to introduce Roarke Winston. He's Kimberly's husband. He was under the mistaken impression that I was spending the night with his wife."

Ben glared at Roarke. "No way, man. Max isn't messin' around with your wife. He and Cleo are like a couple, y'know?"

"Is that right?" Roarke asked with cold disbelief.

"Damn right," Ben said authoritatively. "In fact, they're going to get married."

"Uh, Ben," Cleo began carefully.

Ben ignored her. "Isn't that right, Max?"

Max knew a turning point when he saw one. "Right."

Twelve

"Okay, so maybe we jumped the gun a little," Ben said.

"We?" Max eyed the pipe joint that was less than four inches above his head. He was not in a good mood, and his bad attitude this morning had nothing whatsoever to do with the fact that he was sprawled on his back beneath the bathroom sink in room one-oh-one.

"So I kind of rushed the announcement," Ben admitted.

"You think so?" A drop of water from the leaking pipe fitting hit Max on the forehead. "Dammit."

"Give me a break, Max, I had to think fast last night. That guy Winston was really pissed. He looked like he was going to take the place apart."

"Hand me the other wrench."

"Look, I know you got clipped, but you weren't really hurt." Ben stooped down and thrust a wrench into Max's hand. "Besides, I'll bet you walked right into Winston's punch."

"I did not walk into it. Hand me a rag."

"You sure?" Ben crouched down on his haunches and handed Max a scrap of an old inn towel that was frayed and torn. "He's no fighter. He's too soft. You can't tell me he took you with a sucker punch."

"I was unable to duck because I was too busy trying to shove Cleo out of the way," Max said with great dignity. He wiped the dripping joint with the rag and adjusted the new wrench.

"Yeah? Is that how it happened?" Ben frowned at the pipe joint. "I thought maybe you deliberately took the punch so Cleo would feel sorry for you and fuss and stuff. Which she did."

"Not for long." Max took a grip on the wrench handle and tightened the pipe fitting with ruthless force.

The fact that Cleo had not hovered very long last night after discovering that he was unhurt was one of the chief reasons for Max's foul temper this morning.

She had not only failed to play the ministering angel for more than a few brief minutes, she had not returned to his room after the uproar had died down. Nor had she invited him to hers.

Cleo had recovered her professional innkeeper aplomb almost immediately. She had risen from Max's fallen body, checked the confused Winston into one of the inn's best rooms, and sent everyone back to bed. She had then retired to her own bedroom without so much as a good-night kiss for Max.

"Take it easy or you'll strip the threads," Ben warned.

"You want to take over?"

"No, that's okay. I've fixed a lot of leaking pipes. I know how it's done. You're supposed to be getting experience, remember?"

"You're supposed to be giving helpful advice, remember?"

"Hey, you're doin' okay, man. A real natural. Anyhow, about last night."

"What about it?" Max surveyed the pipe fitting. Another drop of water oozed out of the metal joint.

"Well, I know we all kind of rushed things by making that big announcement about you and Cleo getting married."

"Yes." Max gave the wrench another twist. "You did."

"But it's not like you aren't planning to marry her, or anything like that," Ben pointed out earnestly.

"Is that right?"

Ben scowled. "What the hell's that supposed to mean?"

"Maybe it means I want to take off for a few days and go work in a gas station while I think things over." Max wiped the joint again. It looked dry.

"Come on, Max, that was a cheap shot. We both know you aren't going to take off the way I did. You aren't spooked."

"No, but I think Cleo is. Turn on the water."

"Huh?"

"I said, turn on the water."

"I heard that." Ben got to his feet and turned on the faucet. Water gushed into the sink. "What did you mean about Cleo being spooked?"

"You saw her last night." Max watched to see if the joint was going to start dripping again. "After she figured out that I wasn't dying, she did a damn good job of pretending I didn't exist. She couldn't wait to send everyone, including me, off to bed."

"I guess she was a little embarrassed." Ben turned off the faucet. "You guys hadn't announced anything yet."

"We hadn't announced anything because there wasn't anything to announce. I think this thing is fixed. For your information, Cleo and I have not discussed marriage."

"You sure?"

"Yes, I'm sure. It's not leaking at all now." Max was aware of a pleasing sense of satisfaction. He was getting good at this plumbing business. "Dry as the Sahara." He started to work himself out from the tight confines of the sink cabinet.

"Shit, Max, will you stop talking about the damn pipe?" Ben's face was tight with worry. "Why haven't you asked Cleo to marry you? We all know you're sleeping with her."

"What's that got to do with it?" Max flattened one palm on the countertop and levered himself to his feet. He winced at the twinge in his thigh.

"What do you mean?" Ben demanded. "You know damn well what I'm talking about. We've all known Cleo for a long time. As far as anyone in the family knows, you're the first guy she's ever been serious about."

"What makes you think she's serious about me?" Max turned on the faucet full force again and leaned down to study the pipe connection under the sink. There was no sign of moisture around the fittings.

He realized it was probably idiotic to take so much satisfaction out of the knowledge that he had repaired the leak, but he couldn't help it. Nothing like a little immediate, short-term gratification to take a man's mind off bigger problems, he thought.

"Don't give me that," Ben said. "Cleo wouldn't be sleeping with you if she weren't serious about you. Come on, Max, quit jerking my chain. You're going to marry her, aren't you?"

"Yes." Max turned off the faucet and wiped his hands on the rag. "But first I've got to talk her into it, which might be a lot harder than you seem to think."

"Why?" Ben looked baffled.

"Because you and the others put her under a lot of pressure last night when you made your big announcement," Max said with a patience he did not feel. "She was just getting used to me. She was nowhere near ready to talk about marriage. Now the whole family is acting like it's a fait accompli."

"What's a fait accompli?"

"A done deal."

"Oh." Ben frowned. "You think she's really upset?"

"As I said, she's feeling pressured. People do weird things when they're under pressure."

Ben looked suitably alarmed. "Like what?"

"Like dig in their heels and make life difficult for the people they think are trying to pressure them."

Ben nodded in sober comprehension. "But you can handle her, can't you?"

"First I've got to get her to start talking to me again." Max tossed the wet rag into the tool kit.

Ben brightened. "That shouldn't be any problem. Cleo likes to talk."

Trisha whisked dirty plates and glasses off one of the dining room tables and stacked them in a plastic tub. "Do you want to talk about it, Cleo?"

"No." Cleo bundled up a tablecloth and the used napkins from another table. The familiar routine of clearing the dining room after the small breakfast crowd had departed was doing nothing to soothe her nerves this morning. She had spent a sleepless night, and she felt as if she were walking an invisible tightrope.

"We know you're a little upset, Cleo," Sylvia said from the other side of the empty dining room. Dishes clattered cheerfully as she removed them from a table. "But I'm sure you'll feel better if you talk about it."

"What is there to say?" Cleo jerked another tablecloth off a table with enough force to make it snap in the air. "I have been humiliated, embarrassed, and generally mortified beyond belief."

Andromeda appeared in the doorway. "Now, dear, there's no need to be so agitated. We all know how you feel about Max."

Cleo scanned the expectant faces of her friends. "You do? Well, that's just ducky. I'm glad somebody does, because I don't."

Sylvia smiled gently. "Cleo, let's get real here. You're sleeping with him."

"So what?" Cleo said.

Trisha exchanged a glance with the others. "Between us, we've known you for over three years, Cleo. This is the first time any of us has seen you really interested in a man."

Andromeda smiled serenely. "This is definitely the first time you've had an affair during the whole time I've been acquainted with you, dear."

Sylvia dropped another stack of plates into the bin. "Admit it, Cleo, Max is something special."

"That doesn't mean he wants to marry me," Cleo muttered.

Trisha glanced at her, astonished. "What are you talking about? He said he was going to marry you. I heard him myself."

"So did I," Sylvia said quickly.

"I am so sorry I missed the big scene." Andromeda sighed. "It sounds wonderfully romantic."

Cleo whirled around, her arms full of dirty tablecloths. "It was not romantic. It was a disaster. Max was lying there on the floor, injured. Roarke Winston had accused him of sleeping with Kimberly and was getting ready to hit him again. All George could do was slam the desk bell like a crazy person. Things were in complete chaos."

"And that's when Ben and the others arrived?" Andromeda asked cheerfully.

"Yes." Cleo dumped the dirty tablecloths into a pile. "And that's when Ben, in his infinite wisdom, announced that Max was going to marry me."

"And Max agreed," Andromeda concluded happily.

"It was not like he had a lot of choice under the circumstances," Cleo said. "The man was under enormous pressure. After all, Roarke Winston was threatening to beat him to a pulp."

Andromeda looked thoughtful. "Somehow I don't think pressure bothers Max too much."

Sylvia nodded. "Andromeda's right. Max wouldn't say something like that, regardless of the circumstances, unless he meant it."

"I agree," Trisha said.

Cleo felt trapped. "I don't care if he did mean it." She picked up the basket of dirty tablecloths. "Just because Max agreed to marry me doesn't mean I intend to marry him."

Andromeda frowned. "Whatever are you talking about, dear?"

Cleo lifted her chin. "Don't you understand? There are two things wrong with this situation. First, Max has never asked me to marry him. Two, I'm not at all sure I would marry him even if he did ask me."

Sylvia, Trisha, and Andromeda stared at her. In the ensuing shocked silence, Daystar emerged from the kitchen. She stood, hands on hips, and eyed Cleo speculatively.

"Why wouldn't you want to marry him?" Daystar asked bluntly. "It's as plain as the nose on your face that you love him."

"That does not mean that Max Fortune is good husband material," Cleo said through gritted teeth.

"I disagree," Andromeda said calmly. "I'll admit I had a few qualms about him at first, but that was only because we didn't know much about him."

"Well, now we know a lot more about him, don't we?" Cleo retorted. "And a lot of what we've learned lately makes me have real doubts about marrying the man."

"Cleo, Max loves you," Sylvia said quietly.

Cleo tightened her grip on the basket of dirty tablecloths. "Don't be too sure of that. To be perfectly frank, I'm not sure Max knows how to love."

"Oh, dear," Andromeda murmured. "Whatever do you mean?"

Cleo sighed. "Max knows how to collect the things he wants, and I think that he does want me. At least for the moment. But wanting isn't the same thing as loving, and I have no wish to become a part of Max Fortune's collection of fine art."

Trisha stared at her. "Cleo, I'm sure you're wrong."

"Am I? I'm the one who's been sleeping with him. I know him better than any of you, and I'm here to tell you that Max has never once said anything about love. Kimberly Curzon-Winston may be right. He may not know the meaning of the word *relationship.*"

"How would Ms. Curzon-Winston know anything about Max?" Sylvia demanded.

"Because she was engaged to him at one time."

They all stared at her in amazement.

Satisfied with the effects of her small bombshell, Cleo headed for the swinging door. When she reached it, she turned around and backed through it.

She collided with Roarke Winston, who was on his way out of the kitchen into the dining room. The impact sent the tablecloths in the bin flying in a variety of directions.

"Excuse me." Roarke disentangled himself from a tablecloth. He smiled ruefully. "I seem fated to crash into you, Ms. Robbins. Sooner or later, I'm going to do some damage."

"Don't be ridiculous. And please call me Cleo." She quickly collected the fallen tablecloths. "What were you doing in the kitchen, Mr. Winston? Or should that be Curzon-Winston?"

Roarke's eyes darkened with annoyance. "No, it damn well is not Curzon-Winston. My wife can call herself anything she likes, but my name is just plain Winston. I'd rather you called me Roarke. And the answer to your question, Cleo, is that I went in there looking for you. Someone said you were helping to clear the dining room. I was on my way to find you."

"I see. What can I do for you?" Cleo put down the bin of tablecloths.

Roarke glanced at the ring of interested faces behind Cleo. He lowered his voice. "I wanted to apologize to you for that damned farce I conducted last night in your lobby."

"Forget it. No harm done."

"I promise you I don't generally go around making a fool of myself on a regular basis. But I've been under a lot of stress lately."

"Haven't we all?" Cleo was aware of Sylvia, Daystar, Trisha, and Andromeda listening intently as they stacked dishes. She appealed to them with a silent look.

They took the hint and, one by one, quietly vanished back through the swinging door into the kitchen.

"I suppose so." Roarke's face turned red. "As I said, I just wanted to apologize."

Cleo took pity on him. "Don't worry about it." She opened the linen cupboard and removed a stack of clean tablecloths. "I understand how you must have felt."

"Do you?" Roarke's eyes were bleak.

"Yes," Cleo said gently. "I think so." She smiled. "As long as you're just standing around, why don't you give me a hand with these?"

"What?" Roarke glanced at the stack of tablecloths. "Oh, sure." He smiled. "Not exactly my line of work, but I think I can handle it."

"I don't need any more hotel industry experts around," Cleo muttered. "I've had enough of them lately."

Roarke slanted her a strange glance. "Just between you and me, you're marrying one of the best. Max Fortune is one hell of an expert. Dennison Curzon will do anything to get him back. As you've already discovered, the son of a bitch will even stoop to using Kim."

Cleo hesitated. "Kimberly was anxious to convince Max to return. She told me her father insisted on it."

"He did. As the new chairman of the board of Curzon International, Dennison is having a great time throwing his weight around. For years he lived in Jason's shadow. Now he's determined to show everyone he's even better at running a hotel empire than his brother was."

"Why does he want Max to come back?"

Roarke unfolded another tablecloth and arranged it neatly on a table. "Because the truth is, Dennison is not the natural leader that Jason was. He hasn't got the talent to run Curzon International, and deep down I think he knows it."

"He thinks he can use Max to help run the company?"

Roarke nodded. "He's decided that Jason's secret weapon was Max Fortune. Dennison figures that if he can persuade Fortune to come back, everything will be like it was before, except that Dennison will be in charge this time."

Cleo glanced at Roarke. "Where does Kimberly fit into all this?"

Roarke's jaw set in rigid lines as he whipped open another tablecloth. "My wife has spent most of her life trying to please her father. She's still struggling to be the son Dennison never had. I knew it was a problem when I married her, but I thought we could work it out. Now she feels torn, and part of me is afraid she's going to choose Daddy instead of me."

"One of these days," Max said coldly from the hall doorway, "Kim is going to have to figure out that she can never please Dennison, no matter what she does. Or whom she marries."

Cleo spun around, startled. It was the first time all morning that she had come face to face with Max. He looked even more fierce than he usually did. "Max, I'm warning you, I don't want any more scenes."

Max's brows rose. "I'm not the one who started that scene last night."

"Nor do I want to see any finger-pointing," she added primly.

"Too bad," Roarke said. "I was just getting ready to put in my two cents' worth."

Max smiled without any trace of genuine humor. "Maybe Winston and I had better finish this discussion in private. What do you say, Winston?"

"Not a chance." Roarke snapped open another tablecloth. "I'm not going to volunteer to step outside so that you can beat my brains out."

Cleo was horrified. "Max wouldn't do anything like that."

"No?" Roarke looked distinctly skeptical.

"Of course not." Max gave Roarke a dangerously polite smile. "What I want to discuss is the possibility of getting all you Winstons and Curzons and Curzon-Winstons out of my life on a permanent basis."

"What a strange coincidence. I've got exactly the same goal." Roarke eyed him. "How do you plan to accomplish it?"

"I think it could be arranged if Kim challenged Dennison Curzon for control of the board."

Roarke's jaw dropped. "Are you crazy? Kim could never pull that off."

"She could with your help. You're on the board. Jason appointed you a member the day you married Kimberly."

"Yes, but you know as well as I do that I'm only on the board because I'm one of the family through marriage. It was understood from the start that I'm not supposed to actively interfere with Curzon operations."

"Jason's gone, and the situation has changed," Max said. "We all know that Dennison hasn't got what it takes. Left to his own devices, he'll probably drive Curzon into the ground within three years. Kimberly knows that, too."

Roarke's expression was grim. "She knows it, but she's still trying to please her daddy."

"She only thinks she wants to please Dennison. What she really wants to do is prove she's as good as any son he might have had."

Roarke eyed him thoughtfully. "Is that a fact? You're a shrink?"

"No, but I hung around the Curzon family for twelve years. I know them all fairly well. If Kim takes a good hard look at the situation, I think she'll realize that what she really wants to do is show him that she's capable of running Curzon International just as well as the son Dennison always wanted and never got," Max said softly.

Roarke folded his arms across his chest and watched Max with the respect and wariness of one predator sizing up another.

Cleo was fascinated.

"What makes you an authority on Kim? Your famous six-week engagement?" Roarke asked finally.

"Try to be objective, Winston. Why do you think Kim let herself get talked into getting engaged to me three years ago?" Max showed no sign of emotion. He sounded as if he were talking about an excruciatingly boring incident in the past.

"I've often wondered what she saw in you," Roarke said dryly. "You're not exactly her type."

"I'm aware of that," Max said.

"You were, however, Jason's best friend and confidant. You knew more about the inner workings of Curzon management than anyone else in the whole damn company, including the Curzons."

"That was as far as it went. I wasn't quite good enough to become a member of the family."

"Hell." Roarke gave him an unconcealed look of surprise. "Do you think the Curzons are crazy? If they'd made you a member of the family and put you on the board, you'd have taken complete control of the company in about one month."

Max said nothing. Cleo noticed, however, that no denial sprang instantly to his lips. With a chill she realized that Roarke was right, and Kimberly's fears were not entirely groundless. In one way, Max would have been a serious threat to the Curzons if he had gotten a seat on the board. He would have taken control of the company. His talents and aggressive instincts would have made that outcome inevitable.

What the Curzons had not understood, Cleo thought, was that, as a member of the family, Max would have been one-hundred percent on their side—more of a Curzon, in fact, than any of the rest of them. He would have used his power to protect the family and its holdings.

Cleo knew in that moment of shattering insight that Max cared far more about belonging to a family than he did about making money or running a company.

"Don't give me any bullshit," Roarke said into the sudden silence. "We both know that the only reason you wanted to marry Kim was so that you could get your hands on Curzon."

Max continued to gaze at him impassively. "You're entitled to your own opinion, of course."

Roarke appeared almost amused. "Damn right I am. I know that all you ever wanted from Kim was the chance to control Curzon International. Hell, I don't even blame you, if you want to know the truth."

"No?"

Roarke lifted one shoulder in a negligent shrug. "For all intents and purposes, you were second-in-command for years. Everyone knows it was you who helped Jason turn Curzon into what it is today."

"Thank you," Max said. "I'll assume that's a compliment."

Roarke smiled briefly. "Hey, I'm not arguing that you had a right to try to grab the whole shooting match when the opportunity arose. But don't expect me to approve of the way you tried to use Kim to get what you wanted."

"I think," Max said, "that we're going down a dead-end road as far as this topic of conversation goes. Why don't we get back to our original subject?"

"You want me to help Kim pull a coup and unseat her father? Nice idea, but it's pure fantasy."

"I disagree. Nothing says you're limited to the role of a rubber-stamper on the Curzon board. You can take action. I never noticed you having any problem controlling your own board of directors."

"Damn it, I don't particularly want to get involved with running Curzon. I've got my hands full with my own company."

"This would be a very short-term arrangement. Help Kim take control of the board. Once she's been elected CEO, you can retreat gracefully from active management and let her take over completely. You can start rubber-stamping her projects the same way you used to rubber-stamp Jason's."

Roarke rubbed his jaw. "Kim's brilliant and gutsy. She's got what it takes to run Curzon, doesn't she?"

"Once she's no longer worried about trying to placate Dennison, she'll do fine. She doesn't need me. What she needs is help taking the company away from her father. You can be the one to give her what she wants most in the world." Max paused and smiled slightly. "Think how grateful she'll be."

Roarke narrowed his eyes. "She'd never go up against her old man."

"I think you could convince her to do it," Max said.

Roarke looked briefly intrigued. Then he shook his head. "I don't know. Even if I could talk her into trying to stage a coup, I doubt we could pull it off. Kim would have me on her side, but that still leaves a couple of cousins and her aunt. They'd follow Dennison because they're used to taking orders from his brother."

"You can handle the cousins, and that's all you need," Max said quietly. "If you and Kim show a united front, they'll start taking their lead from you two, rather than Dennison."

Roarke considered that for a moment. "Maybe. It just might work. I don't want to look a gift horse in the mouth or anything, but would you mind telling me what's in this for you, Fortune? What do you want for being so damn helpful?"

"All I want is your guarantee that you and Kim and everybody else with the last names of Curzon or Winston will quit showing up here at the inn at unexpected and inconvenient moments," Max said softly.

"I think I'm getting the picture." Roarke looked at Cleo, and then he met Max's eyes. "You want us out of your way."

"Yes," Max said. "I do. And I'd really appreciate it if you'd start the process immediately."

Roarke slanted another glance at Cleo and smiled. "I can take a hint. It's a long drive back to Seattle. Guess I'd better get started."

Thirteen

That was a cozy little scene I walked in on just now," Max growled as the door of the dining room swung closed behind Roarke. He gave the stack of folded tablecloths that Roarke had left behind a disgusted glance. "Thinking of taking on additional help?"

"Why not? Hotshot executive material is all over the place these days. I might as well take advantage of some of it." Cleo concentrated on spreading another cloth on a table.

Max sat down at one of the tables in the far corner near the window. He propped his cane beside his chair and watched Cleo with brooding eyes. "We have to talk."

"About what?"

"Last night would probably be a good place to start," Max said.

"I've got a better idea. Let's talk about this morning, instead."

Max's eyes darkened. "What about this morning?"

"Did you really try to marry Kimberly in order to get your hands on Curzon International?" Cleo asked in what she hoped was a tone of mild curiosity.

There was a long silence from the table in the corner. "What do you think?" Max finally asked.

Cleo threw him a glare as she whipped open another tablecloth. She looked away quickly because his eyes were burning with an emotion she could not define.

"I think you must have had a very good reason for asking her to marry you," Cleo said in a subdued voice. "Either you were in love with her, which everyone including you seems to seriously doubt, or you wanted something from her. What was it, Max?"

"It's been three years since the engagement ended." Max absently rubbed his thigh. "I believe I've forgotten what it was that convinced me I wanted to marry her."

"Don't give me that." Cleo approached his table with the last of the unfolded cloths. "You told me that she represented a lot of things you wanted. What were those things, Max?"

He looked at her. "Whatever they were, they don't matter anymore."

"You don't want Curzon International?"

"No."

"You don't want Kimberly Curzon-Winston?"

"No." Max watched Cleo unfold the last tablecloth. "I want you."

"Hmm." So much for trying to get him to put his quest into words. She understood, then, that his need for a family of his own was an inchoate longing that he probably did not even fully comprehend himself, let alone want to analyze.

The risk here was excruciatingly clear, Cleo thought. She was in danger of playing the same role in Max's life as Kimberly had played. He did not love her, at least not in the way Cleo wanted to be loved. What Max really wanted were all the things that came with her.

"Why did you insist on going back to your own room last night, Cleo?"

"I wanted to think."

"About us?"

"I suppose so." Cleo refused to be drawn. She did not trust her own mood this morning. She was edgy and unsettled. There were moments when she thought she could see all the way to Max's shadowed soul. But there were other times when he seemed more of an enigma than ever.

Max leaned forward, his expression intent. "Cleo, let's get out of here for a couple of days. We need to be alone together for a while."

She shot him a quick, wary glance. "Why?"

"So that we can talk, damn it."

"We're talking now."

"But not for long." Max glanced toward the door. "Sooner or later someone will interrupt us. You can bet on it. It's damned tough to find any privacy around here, isn't it?"

"Doesn't bother me," Cleo said blithely.

"I noticed. I think you're trying to hide behind the family. Don't be afraid of me, Cleo."

That annoyed her. "I'm not afraid of you."

"Then why have you been avoiding me since last night?"

"I'll give you one guess."

"Because of Ben's announcement." Max smiled persuasively. "Don't blame him. He and everyone else here knows that you're sleeping with me, and they all know that you don't make a habit of having affairs. It's logical that they would conclude we're serious about each other."

"Are we?"

Max's smile vanished. "Yes, damn it, we are."

Cleo lost her precarious temper. "You might be interested to know that I do not blame Ben for embarrassing me last night. I blame you. You went right along with his announcement. You told everyone we were getting married."

"Under the circumstances, it seemed the gentlemanly thing to do. It would have been a lot more awkward for everyone if I'd denied it."

"I don't think you went along with the program just because it was the gentlemanly thing to do," Cleo stormed. "I think you saw Ben's announcement as an extremely convenient opportunity to prevent poor Roarke Winston from beating you to a pulp. You used me."

Max's jaw tightened ominously. "You really believe that?"

Cleo fiddled a bit with her glasses. "Yes, I do."

"You really have an attitude problem this morning, don't you?"

"You think so?" Cleo tilted her head to one side and narrowed her eyes. "Actually, I thought I was behaving with remarkable restraint, given the circumstances."

"That's not how I see it," Max said.

"Too bad." Cleo frowned sharply as she saw his hand move on his thigh. "Why are you massaging your leg? Is it bothering you this morning?"

"Forget my leg. Look, Cleo, I understand that you're feeling as if you've been backed into a corner. I realize we hadn't actually talked about marriage."

"Oh, good." Cleo gave him a bright, brittle smile. "For a while there I thought I was just getting forgetful. It happens when someone is under stress, you know."

"Stop being so waspish. I'm trying to have a rational conversation here."

"In that case you'd better find someone else to have it with," Cleo said. "I'm not feeling very rational at the moment."

"Damn it, Cleo—" Without any warning Max slammed his palm flat against the table in a small explosion of violence that graphically communicated his own anger.

The sharp crack of sound startled Cleo. She jumped and took a step back as Max started to rise from his chair. The dining room door burst open.

"Cleo?" Sylvia's voice was laced with concern. "What's going on here?"

"I knew someone would come in at the wrong moment." Max dropped back into his chair with an air of resigned martyrdom. "No privacy at all."

"That's family life," Cleo said sweetly.

She swung around to face the door. Sylvia stood there, gazing anxiously at the pair near the window. She was not alone. Sammy was with her and so was a very large stranger.

The newcomer was a mountain of a man with the endearingly homely face and sad eyes of a basset hound. He wore a loud green and orange plaid sport coat and a pair of brown polyester slacks. His tie was studded with red polka dots.

"Are you mad at Cleo, Uncle Max? You look mad." Sammy scampered over to Max's chair and gazed up at him with worried eyes.

"Cleo and I were having a private discussion," Max said. "It was a very serious talk."

Cleo raised her brows at the gruff reassurance in his voice. "Don't let him fool you, Sammy. He's mad at me."

Already satisfied by Max's response, Sammy giggled. "But not really, really mad, I bet."

"No." Max scowled at Cleo. "Not really, really mad."

"He's right, Sammy," the stranger said in a deep, rumbling voice that matched his size, "I've known Max for quite a while now, and I can say for sure that when Fortune's really, *really* mad, no one can even tell until it's too late."

Sammy looked at the man in the doorway. "So if he just looks mad, what does that mean?"

"It means he's feeling a tad grumpy." The man sauntered into the dining room. "Probably hasn't had his morning coffee." He looked at Max. "Hi, Max."

"About time you got here, O'Reilly." Max glanced briefly at the polka-dot tie his friend was wearing. "Where did you get that tie?"

"Bought it from some guy who sells them off the back of a truck in an alley between Third and Fourth avenues in downtown Seattle," O'Reilly said proudly. "Heck of a deal. I'll introduce you to him next time you're in town."

"Don't bother."

"We can't all afford to buy our clothes in Europe," O'Reilly said easily.

"I like O'Reilly's tie," Sammy said. "It's nice. Mommy thinks so, too, don't you, Mommy?"

Cleo was astonished to see the faint blush that warmed Sylvia's cheeks.

"Stunning," Sylvia murmured.

O'Reilly grinned at her. The smile transformed his face. "I'm glad someone around here has good taste." He turned back to Cleo. "Allow me to introduce myself. I'm O'Reilly. Compton O'Reilly of O'Reilly Investigations."

"I'm pleased to meet you," Cleo said politely.

"Presumably Max has told you all about me. How brilliant I am. How resourceful and clever. How fearless, tireless, and tenacious, et cetera, et cetera."

Cleo smiled reluctantly. "Max said you were very good at what you do."

A strange twinge of fear went through her as she acknowledged the introduction to Compton O'Reilly. It loosed a flock of butterflies in her stomach and made her feel light-headed.

The arrival of a private investigator brought home the reality of what was happening. Max was taking the recent troubling incidents very seriously. The realization that he was doing so made them suddenly all the more disturbing.

"That's Max for you," O'Reilly said. "Always the master of the understatement. When he says I'm good at what I do, he really means I'm terrific."

Max looked at Cleo. "Did I tell you how modest he was?"

It was Sylvia who answered. "I think Mr. O'Reilly's modesty is self-evident."

O'Reilly grinned at her again. "Thank you, ma'am."

Sylvia turned slightly more pink. She looked at Sammy. "Why don't you come with me, dear? We'll see if we can find Mr. O'Reilly a cup of coffee in the kitchen."

"And some cookies," Sammy said eagerly.

"Now that's one of the better ideas I've heard today," O'Reilly murmured. "I prefer chocolate chip, if you've got them."

Sammy clapped his hands in delight. "So do I."

"Great minds move in the same paths," O'Reilly said. He looked pleased.

"We'll be back in a few minutes," Sylvia promised as she took Sammy's hand.

O'Reilly watched the pair disappear through the swinging doors into the kitchen. Then he turned and gave Max a slow, perusing examination. "What the heck have you gotten yourself into out here, Max, old buddy? And what's this I hear about you being engaged?"

"Rumors." Cleo cleared her throat. "Rumors, innuendos, and lies."

"Is that right?" O'Reilly stuck his hands in his pants pockets and regarded her with a gravely interested expression. "Nothing to all those rumors, innuendos, and lies?"

"Of course not." Cleo ignored Max's annoyed gaze. "Max, here, hasn't even bothered to ask me to marry him, so how could there possibly be a real engagement?"

O'Reilly nodded. "Good point."

"Damn it to hell." Max pinned Cleo with a fierce look. "Is that what's made you so prickly this morning? The fact that I haven't formally asked you to marry me?"

Cleo did not deign to answer that. She gave O'Reilly a bland smile. "Ignore him. He's got an attitude problem today."

"Max always has an attitude," O'Reilly said. "Can't you tell by the way he dresses?"

A short while later, fortified with several cookies and a cup of coffee, O'Reilly glanced down at his notebook. He leaned back in the fanback wicker chair and contemplated Max and Cleo, who were seated across from him in the solarium.

"The bottom line here is that there aren't any obvious suspects. As far as you know, you don't have any enemies. No one's got a grudge against you?"

Cleo shuddered. O'Reilly seemed nice enough, but she was still having qualms about getting a private investigator involved in the situation. "Not that I know of. I haven't had any run-ins with anyone, unless you count Tobias Quinton."

"Who's Tobias Quinton?"

Max shifted slightly. "Forget him. He's not a factor in this."

O'Reilly gave him a level look. "You're sure?"

"I'm sure. Just a slightly disgruntled inn guest. Stayed one night and left the next morning," Max explained.

O'Reilly turned back to Cleo. "Pardon the personal questions, but I need to know the answers. Any possibility you've got an ex-boyfriend who might have become a little too possessive? Especially now that Max is in the picture? Max sometimes makes enemies, I'm sorry to say."

"I wasn't in the picture when the incidents started," Max pointed out. "Nolan Hildebrand was. But he and Cleo had nothing more than a casual dating relationship."

O'Reilly peered at him from beneath bushy brows. "You're positive about that?"

"He wasn't sleeping with her, if that's what you want to know," Max said coolly. "And before you ask, the answer is, yes, I'm sure of that."

"Max." Cleo felt herself turn bright red. "I can answer Mr. O'Reilly's questions on my own." She gave O'Reilly an embarrassed smile. "Nolan and I really were just friends, although I have reason to believe that he might have been thinking of marriage."

"That sounds as if things were more than just friendly between the two of you," O'Reilly said quietly.

"Well, I never actually knew for certain that he had marriage in mind," Cleo said, feeling unaccountably reckless, "because he never actually *asked* me, you see. He had been making certain *assumptions,* apparently. Just like someone else I could name."

"Cleo." Max's voice was laced with dark warning.

"The first I knew of Nolan's plans," Cleo continued, "was when he sort of casually tossed the concept of marriage at me one morning when he was under a lot of stress." She glared at Max. "Men tend to do that a lot around me, too."

"Ignore her, O'Reilly," Max advised. "She's in a bad mood today for some reason."

"Uh-huh." O'Reilly looked at Cleo. "Maybe we ought to talk a little more about Nolan Hildebrand."

Cleo shrugged. "As I told you, there isn't much to talk about. He was very upset when he found out I'd written *The Mirror,* but only because he felt that it disqualified me from being the wife of a future senator."

"He wasn't weird about it, then?" O'Reilly asked. "He didn't act like he had been assigned some holy mission to rid the world of people who write sexy books?"

Cleo blushed again, but she kept her voice cool. "No, just annoyed at having wasted time dating me. Trust me, the only thing Nolan is obsessed with is launching his political career."

"What about this Adrian Forrester you mentioned?" O'Reilly asked.

Cleo wrinkled her nose. "Forget Adrian. My relationship with him was even more casual than the one I had with Nolan."

O'Reilly smiled briefly. "Okay. That will do it for now. Once I've had a chance to talk to your staff and take a look around Harmony Cove, I'll probably have more questions, but I've got a few other angles to check first."

Cleo, weary from the long, intensive session, straightened in alarm. "Wait, what do you mean? You can't run around Harmony Cove asking questions about me and my book."

"Why not?" O'Reilly asked.

"Because no one here knows I wrote it," Cleo said impatiently. "I told you I did it under a pen name. Only the family knows I'm the author."

"That's not true, Cleo," Max said quietly. "Nolan Hildebrand knows, and whoever is staging these incidents knows. It probably won't be long before a lot of other people discover you're the author of *The Mirror.*"

Cleo laced her fingers together very tightly. "I didn't want outsiders to know about *The Mirror*. It's such a personal book."

"Max is right," O'Reilly said. "I'm afraid the secret is out. There's not much point trying to keep your identity hidden any longer. It's to your benefit right now to go public."

"Why?" she demanded.

"In a small town like Harmony Cove news travels fast," O'Reilly explained. "Sure, people will talk about the book. But they'll also talk about the fact that someone is threatening you. That process could turn up some new information."

Max looked thoughtful. "He's right, Cleo. You're well liked in town. That won't change when people find out you wrote *The Mirror*. Most of the people in Harmony Cove are going to be angry on your behalf about the threats that have been made. It's possible that someone knows more than he or she realizes."

"People will be alert for strangers or unusual actions. That will provide some protection for you." O'Reilly smiled reassuringly at Cleo. "I'll talk to your police chief first. We'll get him in our corner and go from there."

Cleo bit her lip, aware that it was useless to argue in the face of such relentless masculine logic. Max and O'Reilly simply didn't understand. They couldn't know how much she dreaded the invasion of privacy she would face once her secret was widely known. It was one thing to be known as a writer of romantic-suspense; it was quite another to be known as the author of something as deeply personal and intimate as *The Mirror*.

She flopped back onto the wicker lounge chair and glared at the bubbling fountain. "I'm not sure it's worth all this fuss. Maybe the incidents are nothing more than someone's idea of a practical joke."

"That note we found in your car was more than a joke," Max said. "And whoever followed you through the fog was either trying to frighten you or worse. I want this business stopped before it goes any farther."

Cleo saw the unshakable intent in his eyes and knew there was no point staging a protest. Besides, she was getting scared herself. She turned back to O'Reilly. "You really think it has to be someone here in Harmony Cove? You said that none of the people who were here the weekend of the motivational seminar looked suspicious?"

"I didn't turn up any red flags when I ran the names of your guests through my usual computer checks," O'Reilly said. "But that doesn't mean one of them isn't nuttier than a fruitcake. However, I don't think we'll find our rabid book critic in that crowd. After all, according to what you told me, the incidents started before any of them arrived at the inn."

"There was the anonymous letter that came through your publisher last month," Max reminded Cleo. "Someone put a copy of the book in Hildebrand's mailbox while the motivational seminar group was at the inn, but none of that crowd was around when that jerk stalked you in the fog."

"I suppose you're right. It must be someone here in Harmony Cove. My God, that's a strange thought." Cleo wrapped her arms beneath her breasts and hugged herself. "To think that it's someone I *know.*"

"It often is in cases like this," O'Reilly said.

Max looked at Cleo. "I think the best thing for us to do is get you out of town for a couple of days while O'Reilly starts asking his questions."

Cleo glanced up sharply. "Leave town? I can't do that. I've got a business to run."

"You're not heavily booked this week," Max said. "Sylvia, Andromeda, and the others can handle things for a couple of nights."

He was right, but Cleo did not want to admit it. "I'd rather stay here."

Cleo watched, annoyed, as O'Reilly exchanged man-to-man glances with Max. Then the detective smiled at her. "Might be easier if you took off for a couple of days. It would give me a chance to break the news to everyone about *The Mirror* and what's been happening to you. By the time you get back, the initial uproar will have had a chance to die down. Your friends here at the inn can field the first round of curiosity seekers for you."

Cleo stirred uneasily. Logically speaking, she knew that the hubbub that would ensue when O'Reilly started asking his questions would be relatively mild compared to what she had gone through four years earlier. At least the gossip would focus on her sex life, she thought ruefully, not death and destruction.

But then there would be all those questions about the obsessed critic who was pestering her. Patty Loftins at the beauty shop would probably read *The Mirror* and speculate to her customers on what the stalker would do next. The pimply-faced kid who worked at the drugstore would watch to see if she bought any birth control supplies the next time she shopped for shampoo. Chuck, the gas station attendant, would wonder if she practiced any of the techniques in *The Mirror* when she went out on a date. He'd probably ask her out the next time she stopped in to fill her tank. Cleo winced at the thought.

"Maybe it wouldn't hurt to leave town for a day or two," Cleo said.

"We'll go to Seattle for a couple of days," Max said, as if everything was settled.

"Seattle?" She slanted him a wary glance.

Max achieved a remarkably earnest expression. "It will give you a real change of scene. O'Reilly will keep an eye on the family for you."

"No problem," O'Reilly said cheerfully. "As long as your kitchen keeps pumping out chocolate chip cookies, I'll be happy to hang around forever."

Max glanced casually at his watch. "We can leave in an hour."

Cleo scowled at him. She knew perfectly well what he was doing. The tendrils of his willpower were forming an invisible net around her, dragging her slowly but inevitably in the direction he wanted her to go. Max was a difficult man to resist when he put his mind to getting what he wanted. In fact, according to Kimberly, he was unstoppable.

"Well . . . ," Cleo said hesitantly.

"Let's get you packed." Max gripped his cane and levered himself to his feet. He looked at O'Reilly. "You've got my number in Seattle. Call me if you learn anything."

"Right." O'Reilly stuffed his notebook into his pocket and rose from the wicker chair. "I'll start talking to the staff here at the inn this afternoon. We'll see where it goes from there."

"Hold it a minute." Cleo held up a hand. "I think we'd better discuss your fee before we go any farther, O'Reilly."

"Fee?" O'Reilly looked as though he were unfamiliar with the concept.

"Yes, fee." Cleo frowned. "I hired a private investigator once. The man spent months on the project. He sent me a bill for nearly fifteen thousand dollars and never turned up a single useful piece of information. I don't want a repeat of that experience."

Max and O'Reilly stared at her as if she'd just announced that she was from Saturn. Max recovered first.

"Why in hell did you hire a private investigator?" he demanded.

Cleo watched the water froth in the fountain. "I wanted someone besides the police to look into the deaths of my parents."

"You told me the cops said it was a case of murder-suicide," Max said very quietly. "Your father killed your mother and turned the gun on himself."

Cleo continued to stare at the fountain. She was intensely aware of O'Reilly's silent, questioning gaze. "I also told you that I've had a hard time accepting that conclusion. Last summer I decided to hire someone to look through the old records of the case and see if there was any reason to think something had been mishandled or overlooked."

"Mind telling me who you hired?" O'Reilly asked in a neutral tone. "Professional curiosity. I might know him."

"His name was Harold Eberson. He had an office in Seattle."

"Yeah." O'Reilly nodded. "I've heard of him. Did he turn up anything for you?"

Cleo put her hands between her knees and pressed them together. "No. He strung me along for a couple of months. He told me he had found a few odd things about the case that he was checking out. But it was all a scam."

"Scam?" O'Reilly repeated.

Cleo nodded, embarrassed at the memory of her own gullibility. "I kept paying his bills until one day they just stopped coming. I called his office to ask what was happening. I got a recording saying the number was no longer in service."

O'Reilly glanced at Max and then looked back at Cleo. "Eberson died in a car accident in October. The reason you never heard any more from him was that no one took over his business. He worked alone. When he died, the business died, too."

"Was he a con man?" Cleo asked bitterly. "How badly did I get taken?"

"Eberson was a small-time operator." O'Reilly shrugged. "If he billed you for fifteen grand, I think it's safe to say you were probably the biggest client he ever had."

Cleo frowned. "But do you think he deliberately ripped me off?"

O'Reilly met her eyes. "I never heard that he was crooked. He just wasn't very big-time. Probably didn't have a head for the business side of things."

"I see." Cleo felt stiff. She started to rub the back of her neck.

Max put his hand on her shoulder and squeezed gently. His thumb moved across the tense muscles. The strength in his fingers felt very good. Cleo could feel the warmth in his hand seeping into her.

"Let's get out of here, Cleo," Max said.

"What about O'Reilly's fee?" she said stubbornly. "I think I need a contract or something. I told you, I don't want another fifteen-thousand-dollar surprise."

"I'll take the same deal you gave Max, here," O'Reilly said. "Minimum wage plus tips and room and board while I'm here."

Cleo wrinkled her nose. "He told you about that?"

"Yeah."

Cleo gave Max a disgusted look. "I suppose you thought it was all very funny, Mr. Hotshot hotel executive."

"No," said Max. "I thought it was the best deal I'd been offered in a long, long time."

Fourteen

The old brick mansion had never seemed so cold. Max checked the thermostat before he went downstairs into the wine cellar to find his best California Cabernet. It was a cold night, but the house should have been comfortably warm. The temperature was set at seventy-four degrees. Max frowned and nudged the setting up to seventy-six. It occurred to him that his attic room at the inn had never seemed chilly.

He knew it was not the mansion that was cold, it was him. It was a familiar sensation. He had felt like this several times before in his life. The first occasion was when a social worker had explained to him that he was going to live with a very nice family. The last time had been when Jason had died.

Tonight was another turning point. He could sense it. A fine tension had set all his nerve endings on red alert.

This time the feeling was the worst it had ever been. This time there was too much at stake. Always before he had been able to walk away from what he knew he could not possess. He did not know how he would walk away from Cleo if she refused his offer of marriage.

On his way back to the kitchen he paused to glance uneasily into the vast living room. Cleo stood with her back to him in front of the broad expanse of windows that overlooked the city and Elliott Bay. She was studying the lights of the downtown high-rises, which gleamed like bright jewels in the rain.

Max watched her, aware of a deep sense of longing inside himself. She had been far too quiet during the drive from the coast. He had made several attempts to start a conversation, only to have each effort flounder.

Cleo had been polite since they left the inn, but she seemed to be off somewhere in a world of her own. Max could not tell what she was thinking, and that fact was making him extremely edgy.

He carried the Cabernet into the kitchen and uncorked it carefully. Long ago Jason had explained to him that a good Cab had to be treated with reverence.

Max experienced a few qualms about his choice of wine as he poured the ruby-colored liquid into two glasses. Maybe he should have chosen champagne, instead. His mouth curved wryly as he realized that, despite Jason's teaching, there were still times when he was unsure of the proper thing to do.

"What are you smiling about?" Cleo asked from the kitchen doorway.

Startled by the question after several hours of near-silence, Max managed to screw up the deft little twisting movement that was designed to prevent the wine bottle from dripping. Two blood-red drops splashed on the polished granite countertop. He looked at them as he set down the bottle.

"I was just thinking that there's one hell of a difference between being born into money and having to battle your way into it," he said. He reached for a paper towel to wipe up the small drops of wine.

"What's the difference?" Cleo asked, her gaze unreadable.

Max shrugged. "A sense of assurance. The certainty that you always know the right thing to do or wear or serve." He handed her one of the glasses. "When you're born into money, you absorb that kind of confidence from the cradle. When you fight your way into it, you never really acquire it."

"I suppose you're right." Cleo delicately tasted her wine. Apparently satisfied, she took a swallow. "On the other hand, when you become successful the hard way, you have the confidence that comes from knowing you earned it."

Max met her eyes. "It's not quite the same thing."

"No, it's a much more impressive sort of assurance. It's the kind of deep-rooted arrogance that comes from knowing that if you lost everything tomorrow and had to start over, you could make your way to the top again. You radiate that kind of confidence, Max."

"That's different. I wasn't talking about that kind of assurance."

"Why not? It's much more interesting than the other kind," Cleo said coolly. "In fact, it can be downright intimidating at times. It's probably most intimidating to someone who comes from a background of wealth. When you're born into money, deep down you don't really know for certain if you could make it on your own. But, Max, you know you can. You've proved it to yourself and the world."

Max smiled. "But the guy who was born with a silver spoon in his mouth wouldn't have to worry about whether to serve champagne or a good Cabernet in a situation like this. He'd know the answer."

"Oh, dear." Cleo's eyes sparkled behind the lenses of her glasses. "Were you suffering a great deal of angst over the matter?"

"Don't worry, I wasn't going to let it ruin my whole evening."

"Because you knew I wouldn't particularly care whether you served champagne or Cabernet or diet cola, right?"

"Right." Max came to a decision. Glass in one hand, cane in the other, he went toward the door. "Come on, I want to show you something."

"What?" She got out of his way and then turned to follow him.

"Come with me." He went down the dark, paneled hallway to the steel door that guarded his treasures. He thrust the glass into Cleo's hand. "Hold this for a minute."

She took the glass and watched curiously as he punched in the code that opened the door. "What's in there?"

"Some things that are important to me." Max opened the door. The lights came on automatically, revealing a stairwell.

Cleo studied the stairs with interest. "Say, you aren't going to do anything real weird to me down there, are you?"

"That depends on what you consider real weird."

Max led the way down the stairs and opened the second steel door at the bottom. Another bank of lights came up as the barrier swung open to reveal his gallery. Max heard Cleo suck in her breath as she stepped into the chamber.

"My God, Max. Is this stuff all genuine?"

The question irritated him. "Hell, yes. Do you think I'd bother to collect fakes?"

She shot him an odd glance. "No, I guess not." She drew a finger along the top of the room's single chair. "Nice chair."

"It's an original," Max said dryly. "English. Early nineteenth century."

"Naturally." She walked to the center of the chamber and turned slowly in a circle, examining the masterpieces of modern art that were hung on the white walls. "I don't see a single picture with a dog or a horse in it."

He couldn't tell if she was teasing him or not. "No seascapes, either."

She looked at him. "I'll give you a couple of the seascapes that Jason painted. You can hang them in your room at the inn next to Sammy's picture."

"Thank you," Max said. "I'd like that."

Cleo paused as she spotted the blank space on the north wall. "Why isn't there anything there?"

"That's where I'm going to hang the Luttrells when I find them."

"Oh, yes. I forgot." Cleo walked over to the bookcase and scanned the shelves. She read the titles on the spines of several leather-bound volumes. "Gosh. Real Latin. Real old. Real impressive. I'll bet the local libraries hope you remember them in your will."

"I did," Max said.

Cleo stopped short when she came to a series of narrow, tattered books. "What's this? *Dr. Seuss? The Hardy Boys?* Max, what are these doing in here?"

"They were the first things I ever collected."

Cleo glanced at him, her eyes gentle. "I see."

"Cleo, will you marry me?"

She went still.

Max realized he suddenly could not breathe.

"Where do you intend to put me?" Cleo asked softly.

A rush of bewildered anger swept through Max. "What the hell are you talking about?"

"I was just wondering where you would hang me in your gallery. I'm not sure I would fit in here, Max." Cleo walked slowly around the room, peering at his collection. "I'm not a very good example of modern art. I might work better in someone's butterfly collection or maybe an exhibit of carnival glass."

"I said I wanted to marry you, not collect you," Max whispered savagely. He put his wine glass down carefully on the small inlaid table near the Sheraton chair. He was afraid that if he kept the fragile crystal in his hand he would snap the stem. He was gripping the carved hawk on his cane so tightly that the muscles in his wrist ached.

"Is there a difference in your mind?" Cleo asked.

"Yes, damn it. Cleo, you said you were angry this morning because I hadn't asked you properly. I'm trying to do it right."

"It wasn't just that you hadn't asked."

"Cleo."

Max took a step toward her and stopped abruptly when he saw her move back a pace. *She was going to refuse.* Anguish ripped through him. He felt more pain than he had ever known in his life. He could feel it gnawing at his vitals, eating him alive. This was worse than when Jason had died.

Cleo's eyes were wide and luminous. When he took another step toward her, she held up a hand as if she were warding off the devil himself.

"Max, why do you want to marry me?"

"Because I want you." The words were torn from him, leaving a raw, gaping wound. He wondered if he would bleed to death right there on the Oriental rug.

Cleo's gaze seared Max's soul for a moment longer, and then, with a small, soft cry, she went into his arms.

"All right," she said into his shirt. "I'll marry you."

Max felt the wound inside him start to close. He was going to survive, after all. He let the cane fall to the rug as he folded Cleo tightly against him. The volatile emotions that had been raging through him were transmuted into a wild, desperate hunger.

He needed her more than he had ever needed anything in his life.

As if she sensed his need, Cleo raised her face to his. Max kissed her heavily. When he felt her response, he groaned and pulled her down onto the rug.

"Max."

He tugged at her clothing, pulling off her shirt and yanking open the fastening of her jeans. He managed to get the denims off together with her silver shoes. Then he fumbled awkwardly with the zipper of his trousers. He didn't even bother trying to take them off. He knew he wouldn't be able to manage the task.

Cleo reached up for him, parting her legs and opening her mouth for him. He fell on top of her like a starving man on a feast.

A moment later he was where he needed to be, deep inside Cleo. She was warm and soft and snug, and he was home.

Cleo opened her eyes and looked up at the canvases that peered down at her like so many dark, tormented eyes. Max's taste in art definitely did not tend toward the sweet or sentimental.

The pictures that hung on the walls of his secret lair exhibited the same riveting combination of savagery and civilized polish that he did. And they were just as complicated and enigmatic as he was.

Cleo knew that, for better or worse, she had just allowed herself to be collected by Max Fortune.

The only things in this room that gave her hope were the inexpensive copies of the children's books that she had discovered amid the valuable tomes in his bookcase. She smiled.

"Cold?" Max sat up slowly. His eyes darkened with satisfaction as he moved his hand possessively along the curve of her thigh.

"A little." Cleo looked up at him. "It's chilly in here."

"The room is climate controlled."

Cleo sat up and reached for her shirt. "To protect the canvases and the books?"

"Yes." Max watched her closely. "Cleo, I want to be married immediately."

She paused in the act of buttoning her shirt. "What's the rush?"

"You know damn well what the rush is." Max used the cane to get to his feet. He reached down to catch hold of her hand. "I don't want you changing your mind."

"I've got news for you, Max." Cleo allowed herself to be pulled to her feet. "You won't be allowed to marry me in some hurried little ceremony at the courthouse. The family won't stand for it. Sylvia, Andromeda, and the others will want it done right. And we can't preempt Trisha and Ben's wedding. It wouldn't be fair to steal the limelight from them."

Max zipped up his trousers. "I was afraid you'd say that."

Cleo made a face at him as she finished dressing. She was vastly relieved to see that his expression was once again one of general irritation. He was no longer wearing the stark, cold mask he'd worn an hour ago when he had asked her to marry him.

She could deal with Max's irritation, Cleo thought. She could handle anything except that terrible, bleak look that had been in his eyes when she'd hesitated to give him the answer he wanted. She'd seen that look in her own eyes often enough in the mirror during the months following her parents' death. It was the look of a person who has lost everything that mattered.

But Max hadn't lost his dreams, Cleo thought. After all, the man had read Dr. Seuss and the Hardy Boys. He couldn't be all ice and iron.

"Cleo? You have a strange expression on your face. What are you thinking about?"

"Dinner," she said.

Max relaxed visibly. "I almost forgot about dinner. I think I've suddenly developed an appetite."

"Me, too. You can fix the scallops. I'll make the salad."

"I meant what I said, Cleo." Max's fingers closed gently but very firmly around her wrist. He brought her palm to his mouth and kissed it. "I want us to be married as soon as possible."

She touched his cheek lightly with her fingertips. She knew he was thinking of how Kimberly had reneged on the engagement six weeks after Max had asked her to marry him.

"It's all right, Max. I'm not going to change my mind."

He veiled his glittering eyes with his lashes. "Word of honor?"

"Word of honor."

Cleo waited until after dinner to call home. Max lounged beside her on the sofa, his eyes on the night-shrouded city, as she dialed the number.

"Robbins' Nest Inn."

"Sylvia? It's me."

"What a surprise." Sylvia chuckled. "Hang on a second." Sylvia cupped her hand over the receiver. "I win," she hissed to someone in the background.

"What's going on? Are you busy?" Cleo asked quickly. "I can call back later if you've got people checking in."

"Nope, we're not busy," Sylvia said cheerfully. "I just had a small bet on with O'Reilly that you'd be unable to resist checking on us this evening. He bet that Max would be keeping you too busy to call. I said that nothing, not even a proper proposal of marriage, could keep you from fretting about how things were going out here."

Cleo shot a quick glance at Max. "Well, you were right."

"About you fretting? That's no big revelation."

"No," Cleo said softly. "About the proper proposal."

"Aha." Sylvia's voice held great satisfaction. "I knew it. And you said yes, right?"

"Right."

"That makes it all nice and official then," Sylvia crowed. "We'll start making plans for the wedding as soon as we get Trisha and Ben married off. I'm sure Sammy will want to be in this ceremony, too. O'Reilly can give the bride away."

"O'Reilly?"

"Sure. He's going to practice on Trisha."

Somewhere along the line, Cleo realized, O'Reilly had become a member of the wedding party. At this rate he was going to become one of the family, just like Max. "Okay."

"Don't worry, Cleo. Andromeda, Daystar, and I will take care of everything."

"Thank you." Cleo didn't know what else to say. "Uh, so how are things going there?"

"Believe it or not, we're managing to scrape along without you. Had a few new reservations for the weekend. Oh, by the way, good old Herbert T. called to book another corporate seminar."

"I thought Mr. Valence was annoyed with us because we lost power the last time he used the inn. Remember how upset he got when he couldn't show his video?" Cleo could still hear Valence's angry protest. *I've got a reputation for flawless performance.*

"He says that in spite of the electrical difficulties, our inn still makes a good background for his seminars. I booked him for the weekend after next. A group of fifteen from some computer firm this time."

"Good," Cleo said. "That will give us a nice crowd. Jason was right when he suggested we start promoting the inn for corporate retreats and seminars."

"Yes, he was. Hey, I'm sure you've got better things to do than chat with the home office. Say hello to Max. We'll see you both in a couple of days."

Cleo hung up the phone and looked at Max. "They're doing just fine without us."

"Don't worry," Max said. "They couldn't get by for long on their own."

"You're sure?"

He smiled. He put his arm around her shoulders and drew her down onto the couch. "I'm sure. I, on the other hand, can't get by for more than a few minutes without you."

The dream came as a shock in the middle of the night. Blood-spattered walls whirled around Cleo, closing in on her. She tried to scream, but, as always, no sound emerged from her horror-constricted throat. She could not move her arms. Her legs were pinned by some heavy object.

"Cleo. Wake up. Wake up, damn it."

Cleo awoke drenched in sweat. Max was crushing her against him. He was holding her tightly, trapping her with the weight of his body as if he could hold her back from the invisible tentacles that reached out for her.

"I'm okay," she whispered. Little wonder she had been unable to move in her dream, she thought wryly. She couldn't move in real life, either. Max's grip was so fierce she could barely breathe.

"The dream again?" Max released her slowly, his eyes shadowed in the darkness.

"Yes. That's the second time in a week." Cleo rubbed her eyes. "I wonder what's happening."

"Stress. Tension. Worry." Max massaged her shoulders. "There's plenty of explanation for the bad dreams you've had lately."

"Do you ever get nightmares?"

"Everyone gets nightmares occasionally."

She relaxed against his chest. Max's hands were warm and strong and comforting. "What are yours like?"

"Some of them are hanging on the walls of my gallery downstairs," he said calmly.

Cleo shuddered. There were a lot of private, secret places in Max Fortune.

"Cleo?"

"Hmm?" She was feeling drowsy again. The last traces of her dream had already retreated to the dark recesses of her mind. Max was good at banishing nightmares, Cleo reflected.

"We could get married the week after Trisha and Ben have their wedding. Your family can arrange to have another reception that soon, can't they?"

She was torn between laughter and exasperation. He was not going to stop pushing until she had set a date. "I've already told you that I'll marry you. Do we have to pick the day and time tonight?"

"I'd like to get the details nailed down."

"Okay, okay. One week is a little fast. We've got the inn to run, you know. How about two weeks after Trisha and Ben's reception?" She felt the exultant relief sweep through him. "We may have to delay the honeymoon for a while," Cleo warned. "I've got a couple of small conventions scheduled next month."

Max's fingers tightened around her shoulders. "I don't give a damn about the honeymoon."

Cleo chuckled. "Thanks a lot."

"You know what I mean. I just want to get everything settled."

Cleo lifted her head and kissed Max lightly on the mouth. He fell back onto the pillow and pulled her down on top of him.

"There's just one thing you should know, Max." Cleo touched the tip of her tongue to the corner of his mouth.

"What's that?"

"It's not *my* family that is going to arrange our wedding reception. It's *our* family."

"You're right. Our family." Max twisted his fingers in Cleo's hair and dragged her face down to his.

"What do you want to do today?" Max asked the next morning. He watched contentedly as Cleo made waffles in the gleaming iron positioned on a table in the breakfast room.

"I don't care. I don't get to Seattle very often anymore. I guess I'd like to do the usual tourist things. Visit the Pike Place Market. Do some shopping. Take in a few good bookstores."

"I've got a better idea. Why don't we shop for a ring?" Max glanced out the window. The downtown high-rises sparkled after the night's rain. "It looks like it's going to be clear for a while. I know a couple of good jewelers."

Cleo smiled ruefully. "It shouldn't take long to find a ring. We'll do the other stuff later." She popped out a waffle and dropped it onto a plate.

The doorbell chimed.

Max looked irritated. He seized his cane and got to his feet. "Whoever that is, I'll get rid of him."

Cleo poured maple syrup on the waffle and listened to Max make his way down the hall.

Max's house was awfully big for one person, she thought. It took forever just to get to the front door. The mansion needed a butler. She wondered why he had bought such a place. Maybe he had been under the impression that if he spent enough money, he could buy a home. Cleo wondered how long it had taken him to discover his mistake.

Cleo heard Kimberly's voice just as she forked up a bite of waffle. She stifled a small groan of dismay when she heard the other woman's high heels on the terrazzo floor of the hall. So much for Max's being able to get rid of his unexpected caller.

"Max, I have to talk to you," Kimberly said in a cool, businesslike tone as she came down the hall. "This is extremely important."

"How did you know I was in town?"

"I called Robbins' Nest Inn. I was told you were here with Cleo. Max, you can't put me off. This is absolutely critical. I've talked to Roarke. He told me you suggested that he and I try to take over the Curzon board. Were you serious?"

"Why not? Looks like the logical move."

"Roarke seems convinced it could be done," Kimberly said slowly.

"The two of you can do it together."

"But my father—"

Max cut her off abruptly. "The only way you're going to prove to your father that you're as good as the son he never had is to take Curzon from him."

"Do you really think so?" Kimberly asked.

"Yes."

Kimberly hesitated. "That isn't the only thing I want to talk to you about. Max, give me five minutes. That's all I'm asking."

"All right," Max said impatiently. His cane thudded softly on the tile as he led Kimberly into the breakfast room. "Five minutes, but no more. Cleo and I have things to do today."

"Such as?" Kimberly asked dryly.

"Such as shop for a ring," Max said. "Cleo and I are engaged."

"Well, isn't that interesting," Kimberly murmured. She looked at Cleo. "I can't say I'm surprised."

"Thank you," Cleo said around a mouthful of waffle. "I think."

"Max was always very good at arranging advantageous engagements for himself," Kimberly said.

"If you're going to make cracks like that, Kim," Max said calmly, "you can leave now."

Kimberly looked at him. "What's the matter, haven't you told her why you've gotten yourself engaged to her?"

Max sat down and regarded Kimberly with cobra eyes. "Say whatever it is you came here to say and then leave."

Kimberly walked over to the sideboard and helped herself to a cup of coffee with the ease of a woman who was familiar with her surroundings. She smiled bleakly at Cleo.

"Has he told you yet that he's negotiating with an outfit called Global Village Properties?" Kimberly asked. "They've offered him the same deal Curzon has, but Max wants more. He wants the CEO position."

"No," Cleo said. She looked at Max. "He didn't mention that."

"Damn," Max said. "I knew I shouldn't have opened the door this morning."

Fifteen

Cleo forked up another bite of waffle and ate it in silence. She was aware of Max's gaze on her as Kimberly talked.

"It's all true," Kimberly said not unkindly to Cleo. "My sources tell me that Max recently met with Turner and Sand, two point men for Global Village Properties."

Cleo glanced at Max. "Is that right?"

"Yes," Max said. His eyes did not leave her face.

Kimberly looked grimly satisfied. She started to pace the breakfast room with the elegant, restless stride of a racehorse that had been penned for too long. Cleo wondered how she could stand wearing high heels all day.

"I only know of one meeting," Kimberly said. "But that doesn't mean he hasn't been negotiating with them since he left Curzon last month. I'm told that they made him a very generous offer."

Cleo glanced at Max. "Did they make you an offer?"

"Yes," Max said.

Kimberly shot him a knowing glance. "The rumor I heard is that the offer included a vice presidency and a seat on the Global Village board. But as I said, Max wants the CEO slot. So he's told them that he's going independent unless they can make it worth his while not to do so."

"What's that supposed to mean?" Cleo asked curiously.

"It means he's allowing everyone to believe he's going into business on his own."

"Unless he receives a better offer from Global Village? Is that what you're saying?" Cleo watched Kimberly carefully.

Kimberly gave a sigh that held a trace of genuine sympathy. "Try not to feel too bad about it, Cleo. Max has a reputation for getting the job done and for using whatever means he thinks are necessary to do it. People who are far more savvy about business than you will ever be have gotten ground to dust beneath his chariot wheels."

"A colorful image." Cleo ignored Max's silent, brooding stare and kept her attention on Kimberly.

Kimberly looked briefly disconcerted. She flicked a quick, searching glance at Max and then frowned at Cleo. "The point I'm trying to make here is that Max is using you to add an element of realism to the picture he's painting for Global Village. Getting engaged to you will convince everyone he's serious about going independent."

"And that will make Global Village surrender to his demands?" Cleo asked.

Kimberly shrugged. "Probably. They want him very badly."

Cleo looked at Max. "Nice to be wanted, isn't it?"

"Depends on who wants you." Max's gaze was unwavering.

Kimberly stopped pacing for a moment. "I wondered why Max turned down my father's offer to come back to Curzon. Now I know why. The CEO slot at Global Village probably looks a good deal more tempting. Max likes to be in charge. At Curzon he'd always be battling the family for control. But at Global Village he can be the one in command."

Cleo used a linen napkin to blot a drop of syrup from the corner of her mouth. When that didn't do the trick, she used the tip of her tongue. "When did you first talk to Global Village, Max?"

"The day I went into town with Ben to get some stuff at the hardware store." His eyes willed her to believe him.

Cleo took a deep breath. "That would be about a week after you had accepted my offer of employment."

"Yes."

"What did you say to them?"

"That I wasn't interested in any position at Global Village," Max said quietly.

"Not even the CEO slot?" Cleo asked.

"No. Not even the CEO slot."

Cleo smiled tremulously. "I guess that means you're still working for me, doesn't it?"

"Yes." Max's eyes were brilliant with an emotion that was not reflected in his voice. "I'm still working for you. I have no plans to quit."

"I thought so," Cleo said. "Well, that settles that little problem, doesn't it? Stop worrying, Kimberly. Max isn't going to work for the competition."

She got up to pour herself a cup of coffee. She wanted to make the action look as nonchalant as Kimberly had earlier, but that plan went out the window when she had to hunt for a cup.

"Second cupboard on the left," Kimberly said coldly.

Cleo set her teeth. "Thank you."

"I can't figure you out." Kimberly eyed her warily. "Originally I thought you were just naive and rather unsophisticated. But right now I'm starting to wonder if there's more to you than meets the eye."

"You mean you're wondering if I'm as dumb as I look?" Cleo asked innocently. "Max had a problem with that in the beginning, too. I wonder what it is about me that gives that impression? Do you think it's the sneakers?" She glanced down at the silver sneakers she was wearing. "Maybe I should do something about my image."

"What sort of game are you playing, Cleo? Do you really think you can control Max?" Kimberly's gaze was bright with speculation. "If you're planning to use him to build an empire for you, I'd advise caution. If Max creates an empire, you can bet he'll be the one who owns and runs it. In the end you'll be left with nothing."

Cleo blew on her coffee. "I'm not trying to build an empire. I'm just trying to run an inn. Good help is hard to find. I was lucky to get Max."

"Don't give me that. We both know you can't possibly afford him."

"All I know is that the offer I made to him was accepted." Cleo looked at Max. "Wasn't it?"

Max smiled faintly for the first time since Kimberly had arrived. His eyes were gleaming. "Yes."

Kimberly scowled at Cleo. "Damn it, what's going on here? There's no way you could match an offer from Global Village or Curzon International."

"You're wrong," Cleo said softly. "Robbins' Nest Inn has something to offer Max that neither you nor Global Village can possibly match."

Kimberly's smile was laced with scorn. "And just what would that be, Cleo? You? Do you really think that Max would walk away from a CEO slot or a vice presidency with corporations like Global Village or Curzon for you or any other woman?"

"No," Cleo said. "Not just for me alone. But I think he'd do it for what comes along with me."

"Robbins' Nest Inn?"

"No," Cleo said. "A family."

"You're out of your mind." Kimberly stared at her in astonishment. "What would Max want with a family?"

"For one thing," Cleo said, "he won't have to worry about the occasional screwup."

"What are you talking about?" Kimberly looked at her blankly.

Cleo took a sip of coffee. "With us Max knows that even if he fails to live up to his amazing reputation once in a while, we'll still want him around. He's one of us whether he screws up or not."

Kimberly's mouth opened on a soundless exclamation. When she could not find the words she sought, she turned to Max.

"All right," she said, "I give up. I can't figure out what's going on here, but it's obvious you've got things in the palm of your hand, as usual. I assume that sooner or later we'll all find out what your agenda is, Max."

"There's no hidden agenda," Max said quietly. "Cleo told you the truth. I'm working for her. I'm not open to outside offers. You may congratulate me on my engagement, and then you may leave."

Kimberly gave him a disgusted look. "Congratulations." She turned around and walked to the door.

Silence descended on the breakfast room.

Max looked at Cleo. "Thanks."

"For what?"

"For everything."

"Sure." Cleo ladled up another spoonful of batter. "Want a waffle?"

"Among other things," Max said. His glance went to the pot of honey that sat in the middle of the table.

Cleo gave him a severe frown. "Don't get any ideas. That scene with the honey in *The Mirror* was pure fantasy."

"My specialty is turning fantasy into reality."

"Forget it. Too sticky."

"Let me worry about the technical details." Max smiled slowly. He picked up the pot of honey.

Cleo forgot about the next waffle.

A cold rain began to fall just as Max and Cleo emerged from an antiquarian bookshop in Pioneer Square. Cleo flicked open her umbrella. Her silver sneakers were getting soaked.

"It's pouring. Let's go back to your place," she suggested.

"I've got a better idea." Max took the umbrella from her and held it aloft so that it shielded both of them. When his fingers brushed against hers he glanced with approval at the emerald ring he had put on her finger an hour earlier. "There's an interesting little gallery around the corner. We can get out of the rain for a while in there."

"I'll bet this gallery doesn't hang any nice pictures of dogs or horses or seascapes," Cleo muttered. They had already been in three other galleries, and none of them had featured the sort of art she liked. All the owners knew Max on sight.

"The day this place hangs a picture of a spaniel will be the day I stop buying art here." Max took a possessive grip on Cleo's arm and shepherded her into the white-walled gallery.

Cleo studied the collection of mostly dark, mostly bleak, mostly gray and brown paintings with an unimpressed eye. She wrinkled her nose at Max. "I really don't understand what you see in this stuff."

Max took in the paintings on display with a single, sweeping glance. "If it's any consolation, I don't see anything at all in this batch."

"Good." Cleo grinned. "There's hope for you yet."

A shining, bald head popped up from behind the counter. "Max, my friend." A heavy-set middle-aged man dressed entirely in black smiled widely. "Long time, no see. Where have you been? I've left half a dozen messages with your office telling you to call me as soon as possible. Did you get them?"

"No," Max said. "I'm no longer working for Curzon. Walter, I'd like you to meet my fiancée, Cleo Robbins. Cleo, this is Walter Stickley. He owns this gallery."

"How do you do?" Cleo said.

"My pleasure." Walter's eyes lit with curiosity. He glanced at Max. "Engaged, did you say?"

"Yes."

"Congratulations. And you say you've left Curzon?"

"That's right. I'm with another firm now."

"That explains why I haven't been able to reach you. I'm glad you decided to drop in today." Walter rubbed his palms together. "I was just about to start making a few phone calls to other clients."

"What have you got to show me?" Max gave the paintings on display another dismissing glance. "I don't see anything very interesting here."

Walter chuckled. "You know I always keep the good stuff in the back room. Follow me."

He came out from behind the counter and led the way down a short hall to a closed door. He opened it and waved Cleo and Max inside.

Cleo took a quick look at the large canvas leaning against the wall and rolled her eyes. This picture was bleaker, more savage, and admittedly more interesting than the ones that were hanging in the outer room, but she didn't like it any better than she had the others.

"Yuck," Cleo said.

Walter shot her a scathing glance. "Philistine."

"She likes pictures of dogs and horses," Max said absently. He was staring at the painting with rapt attention.

"And seascapes," Cleo added. "I'm very fond of seascapes."

"I don't carry that sort of thing," Walter said stiffly.

"I noticed." Cleo watched Max. "You okay, Max? You look a little strange." She wondered uneasily if he were looking into one of his own nightmares.

"I'm fine," Max said softly. "Who's the artist, Walter? I don't recognize the style."

"A recent discovery of mine," Walter said smugly. "His name is David Verrier. What do you think?"

"I'll take it. Can you get it delivered this afternoon? I'm leaving town tomorrow."

"No problem." Walter rubbed his hands together and chortled knowingly. "Thought you'd like it. Five years from now Verrier is going to be worth a mint."

"Yes," Max said. He was still gazing into the painting. "Call me as soon as you get anything else from him. I'll leave you my new number."

"Of course," Walter said happily. "Yours will be the first name on my list."

"Mine will be the only name on your list," Max said.

Walter cleared his throat. "Uh, yes. The only name. But see here, Max. Verrier needs a chance to gain some exposure. You can't grab everything he does and lock it up before the art world has an opportunity to see his work. I want to be able to give him some shows. He deserves the recognition."

Max did not look pleased, but he nodded reluctantly. "All right. You can show his pictures. But I get first crack at whatever he produces."

"It's a deal."

Cleo tipped her head to one side and studied the canvas from a different angle. When that didn't make it any more cheerful, she walked to another corner of the room and peered at it from there. Then she crouched down and tried again from another vantage point.

"Okay, Max, tell me what you see in that picture," she said. "It looks like the bottom of a bucket of black paint to me."

Walter cringed. "Did you say you're going to marry this . . . this *person,* Max?"

"Yes." Max finally tore his gaze away from the picture. He smiled. "She doesn't know much about art, but she knows what she likes."

"I see." Walter's eyes glittered. "By the way, Max, there are rumors floating around."

"Rumors about what?" Max asked without any real show of interest.

"About five Amos Luttrell paintings that have recently disappeared," Walter said softly. "You wouldn't know anything about them, would you?"

"I know that they belong to me," Max said.

"Uh, yes. I suspected you'd say something like that." Walter pursed his lips. "But there appears to be some question of ownership."

Max's mouth curved in a humorless smile. "There's no question at all about who owns the Luttrells, Walter."

Walter cleared his throat. "The story I heard involves Garrison Spark. Word is, he's on the trail of the Luttrells. He's got a client who will pay a quarter of a million for them. He's also got a bill of sale from Jason Curzon. He claims it predates the will."

"The bill of sale, if it exists, is a forgery." Max's eyes met Walter's. "We both know it wouldn't be the first forgery Spark has handled, don't we?"

Walter smiled wryly. "Point taken."

The following afternoon Cleo sat beside Max in the Jaguar and watched with trepidation as Harmony Cove came into sight. "I wonder if the city council will have roadblocks up at the entrance to town to prevent me from coming back."

"Relax, Cleo. No one's going to be upset about the fact that you wrote a book."

"Nolan was."

"Nolan's an ass."

"Yes, well, I'm afraid he's not the only ass in Harmony Cove." Cleo twisted the ring on her finger. She was very conscious of its weight. "By now I suppose O'Reilly has talked to everyone."

"Probably. O'Reilly is very thorough."

"I don't know if this was such a good idea, Max."

He slanted her a sidelong glance. "You think letting that stalker get closer and closer is a better idea?"

"Well, no, but I have to live here in Harmony Cove after this is all over. I don't want people staring at me. I had my fill of curiosity seekers after my parents died."

"I'll keep the curiosity seekers at bay," Max promised softly.

She saw the grim line of his jaw and knew he meant every word. Cleo relaxed slightly. With Max by her side no one was going to give her too much trouble. "I may have to give you a raise."

"I'll take it out in Daystar's corn bread muffins."

Max slowed the Jaguar as they drove through Harmony Cove's block-long downtown district. A woman waved at them from the entrance to the grocery store.

Cleo waved back. "At least Mrs. Gibson doesn't look like she wants to paint a large red A on my forehead."

"Who's Mrs. Gibson?"

"She owns the little bookshop on the corner."

Max smiled. "She's probably ordered several copies of *The Mirror* in anticipation of the rush."

"Oh, geez, Max. This is going to be awful." Cleo fiddled nervously with the car phone.

"Put down the phone and stop panicking." Max slowed the Jaguar still further and turned into the grocery store parking lot.

"What are you doing?" Cleo yelped in alarm.

"We're going to get the worst of this over with in a hurry so you'll stop working yourself up into a lather."

"Max, I don't need anything at the grocery store."

"We'll find something." Max slid the Jaguar neatly into one of the parking spaces and opened the door on his side.

Cleo made no move to unfasten her seatbelt. Max walked around to her side of the car and opened the door.

"Come on, Cleo. This isn't going to be that bad."

"I don't want to deal with this yet."

"You're going to have to deal with it sometime."

"I know. But I don't want to do it today," Cleo insisted.

"Get out of the car, Cleo," Max said gently, "or I will peel you out of there and carry you inside the damn grocery store."

She looked at him with mute defiance. Max's expression was even more stubborn than her own. She knew he was right. Sooner or later she was going to have to face the people of Harmony Cove.

"All right, let's get this over with." Cleo unbuckled the seatbelt and exploded out of the car. She stormed past Max.

"That's my brave Cleopatra," Max muttered.

Already halfway to the door, Cleo stopped and glanced back over her shoulder. She scowled when she realized that she had left Max behind in the dust.

"I'm not going in there alone," she said.

"Then you'll have to slow down a bit." Max reached her side and took her arm. "I don't run except in cases of acute emergency and this is not one of those cases."

"You can move fast enough when you want to," Cleo grumbled. "I've seen you go up and down the stairs at the inn as rapidly as any of the rest of us. Max, are you sure we have to do this?"

"I can't believe you're this nervous about it." Max pushed open the glass door of the grocery store and shoved her gently ahead of him. "You're here for milk."

"We don't need milk. We get a dairy delivery twice a week at the inn," Cleo muttered.

"Today you need milk."

Cleo felt the eyes as soon as she stepped into the familiar surroundings of the store. Everyone from the stock boy to the counter clerk looked at her as if they had never seen her before in their lives. They all waved enthusiastically.

Cleo ducked her head and hurried toward the dairy case.

The young man stocking milk and cottage cheese smiled tentatively at her. "Hi, Ms. Robbins."

"Hi, Tom. How are you today?" Thankful for Max's reassuring presence, Cleo opened the glass door and yanked out a quart of skim.

"Fine. I heard someone was pestering you on account of you wrote a book. Is that true?"

Cleo's fingers trembled around the carton of milk. "Yes."

"Real sorry to hear someone's bothering you. Hope they catch him."

"Thank you, Tom."

"Say, I was, uh, wondering." Tom cast a surreptitious look up and down the aisle and sidled closer.

Cleo steeled herself. "What were you wondering, Tom?"

"About the book you wrote."

Cleo's stomach tightened. "Yes?"

"I, uh, I've been thinking about writing a book myself."

Cleo blinked. "You have?"

Tom nodded urgently and turned a bright shade of red. "Yeah, it's science fiction, y'know?"

"I see," Cleo said uncertainly. "That's great. Good luck with it."

Tom brightened at the encouragement. "It's an alternate world story, see. There's a lot of stuff in it that's similar to our world, but the basic laws of science are different. More like magic, y'know."

"Uh-huh." Cleo took a step back.

Tom eagerly closed the space between them. "My main character is this guy from our world who finds himself stranded in this alternate world. At first he thinks he's dreaming. Then he realizes he's trapped there. He has to learn how to survive or he'll get killed."

"Very clever," Cleo said weakly. She retreated another step.

Tom followed. "He's a computer nerd on earth, so when he's caught in this weird world run by magic, he's really confused for a while."

It dawned on Cleo that Tom the stock boy had no interest at all in *The Mirror*. Convinced he had found a soul mate, he was going to regale her with the plot of his entire book right there in front of the dairy case.

"And then he meets this character who's like a sorcerer, y'know . . ."

"Interesting," Cleo said. She inched back down the aisle, aware of Max's silent amusement. Tom followed her every step of the way.

"Then there's this other sorcerer who's like crazy, y'know? He's discovered some new law of magic. I haven't quite decided what that's going to be yet, but whatever it is, it threatens the whole alternate world . . ."

"That's absolutely fascinating," Cleo said. She glanced at her watch. "I'd love to hear the rest, but I've really got to run."

"Huh?" Engrossed in his tale, Tom frowned, puzzled. "Oh, sure. Look, maybe I could stop by the inn sometime and tell you the rest?"

"We'll see." Cleo turned and fled toward the checkout counter. She did not look back to see if Max was following.

The gray-haired woman at the checkout counter smiled broadly. "Oh, hello, Cleo. Heard someone's been making a nuisance of himself because you wrote a book. I didn't know you were a writer."

"I've only had one book published so far," Cleo muttered. She set the milk down on the counter.

"That's all right, dear, I'm sure you'll write some more. You know, I haven't read a book in years. Just never had the time, what with TV and all. Milk?"

"Yes, please, Ernestine."

"Thought you got dairy deliveries out there at the inn."

Cleo groped for an explanation as Max arrived at the counter. "Ran short."

"Oh." Ernestine whisked the milk through the checkout routine. "You know you and I should get together one of these days."

"We should?"

Ernestine beamed. "I could tell you all about my family history. You could write a book about it. I'm sure people would want to read it. Some real fascinating stuff in my family's history. Did I ever tell you that one of my relatives came out West on a wagon train?"

"I don't believe you ever mentioned it, Ernestine."

"That was Sarah Hill Montrose, I believe." Ernestine assumed a contemplative look. "Her story would make a terrific book. Then there was my great-grandfather, Morton Montrose. He used to farm over in eastern Washington. Raised turkeys, too. Used to tell the funniest stories about those birds. Dumb as bricks, they are."

"Is that right?" Cleo looked at her milk, which was standing forgotten on the counter.

"Eugene Montrose, that's my grandfather, was probably the most interesting of the lot. He fished."

"You don't say. Could I please have my milk, Ernestine?"

"What's that?" Ernestine glanced down at the milk. "Oh, yes. The milk. Here, I'll put it in a bag for you." She stuffed the milk into a sack.

"Thanks." Cleo snatched up the milk, aware that Max's eyes were brilliant with laughter. "See you around, Ernestine."

"Just let me know when you've got time to write that book about my family," Ernestine said cheerfully. "I've got lots of old newspaper clippings and photos and such."

"I'll let you know if I ever get a free minute," Cleo promised. "But I'm pretty busy these days."

She was halfway out the door, with Max still following faithfully behind her, when another familiar figure loomed in her path. Cleo was forced to come to a halt. She clutched the milk close and smiled weakly.

"Hello, Adrian."

Adrian Forrester glowered at her from beneath dark brows. He had a large manila envelope in his hand. "Heard you had a book published."

"Yes, I did." Cleo glanced uneasily at the envelope he was holding. She was afraid she knew what was inside. She'd received her share of rejections before she'd sold *The Mirror*.

"I suppose you had an agent?" Adrian demanded.

"Well, no, I didn't, although I'm thinking of getting one for the next book."

"Know someone in publishing?"

"Uh, no. I didn't know anyone, Adrian. I just sent the manuscript off to a lot of different publishers, and someone finally bought it."

"So you just got lucky."

"Right," Cleo said. "I just got lucky."

"It's because you're writing women's stuff," Adrian said in an aggrieved tone. "That's why they published you instead of me. New York is only interested in women's books these days. Romance, self-help, glitz, erotica. It's all aimed at women. Hell, even the mystery market is skewed toward women."

"What about all the thrillers and science fiction and horror stuff that's published?"

"They're putting relationships in them, too." Adrian looked at her as if it were all her fault.

"Gosh, I don't really think . . ."

"Do you know what this rejection letter says?" Adrian waved his manuscript aloft. "It says they're not interested in hard-boiled detective mysteries featuring male protagonists. The editor suggests I turn my hero into a female private eye."

"Gee, Adrian, I can't imagine why the editor would suggest a thing like that. Unless, of course, it's because a lot of women like to read and are willing to spend their money on books that feature stories they enjoy."

Adrian's glare would have frozen lava. "I'll tell you something. If they weren't putting out books like yours, they'd be publishing my stuff."

Cleo's temper overcame the last vestiges of her fear of being identified as the author of *The Mirror*. "You think so?" she asked.

Max apparently recognized the dangerous sweetness of her tone and finally bestirred himself to intervene. "I think we'd better be on our way, Cleo. The family will be waiting." He took her arm and started toward the Jaguar.

Cleo dug in her heels. "Wait a second. I want to give Adrian some publishing advice."

Max grinned. "I don't think Forrester wants your advice, do you, Forrester?" He wrapped an arm around Cleo and dragged her toward the car.

"She just got lucky," Adrian snarled.

"You think so? Well, maybe it was more than luck," Cleo shouted as Max stuffed her into the front seat of the Jaguar. "Maybe I write better than you do. Maybe my book was better than yours. Did you ever think about that possibility?"

"It's because it was a woman's book," Adrian yelled. "That's the only reason it got published. The women's market is taking over, I tell you."

"So get a sex change operation," Cleo yelled back.

"Good Lord," Max muttered as he slammed the car door shut, "I've created a monster."

Sixteen

"You can stop laughing now," Cleo muttered as Max drove along the bluffs toward Robbins' Nest Inn.

Max glanced at her, unable to suppress his grin. She was sitting with her arms folded in a gesture of complete disgust, her gaze fixed on the winding road.

"Sorry," Max said.

"You're not the least bit sorry. I can tell."

"Come on, Cleo, admit the whole thing was funny. You've been terrified of what everyone in town would think when they found out you wrote *The Mirror*. But being discovered wasn't so bad, was it?"

"I don't think any of them even bothered to read it." She sounded disgruntled.

"I'd say that's a fairly safe assumption. If our recent unscientific survey holds true, we can assume that the vast majority of the people you meet will never actually read your books. But they'll want to talk to you about publishing. People are fascinated with publishing."

"You mean they'll want to tell me the plots of their own books or suggest I write their family's history or complain because I got published instead of them."

"Yes."

Cleo started to smile. "It was sort of funny, wasn't it?"

"Very," Max said softly. "Especially the look on Forrester's face."

"When I think about the way he used to drone on and on about his own book and how it was going to take the publishing world by storm—" Cleo broke off and started to grin.

She burst first into giggles and then into full-blown laughter.

Max watched her out of the corner of his eye and smiled to himself. "I'm not saying you won't get the occasional critic," he cautioned. "But I think you can handle it if someone comes up to you and tells you he thinks your book was trash."

"The way Nolan did?" Cleo's mouth twisted wryly. "Yes, I think so. I've been anxious about having people pry into my private life, but the truth is, all that most of them really wanted to talk about was themselves. This isn't anything like what happened to me after my parents died."

"Of course not."

"I guess I'd let my imagination run away with me."

"You do have a first-class imagination," Max conceded.

The laughter died in Cleo's eyes. "I just wish the stalker was a product of my imagination."

Max watched the road. "So do I."

Cleo turned to him with an expression of intrigued speculation. "Hey, you don't suppose Adrian is the stalker, after all, do you? Maybe his jealousy has gotten the better of him. Maybe he's trying to punish me because I got published and he didn't."

Max shook his head with grim certainty. "No. It's obvious Adrian only recently found out that you'd published *The Mirror*. The incidents started over a month ago. He'd never have been able to keep his jealousy under wraps this long."

Cleo lounged back in the seat. "I'm not so sure about that. Maybe he knew all along and just pretended that he didn't."

Max took one hand off the wheel and reached out briefly to touch her leg. "We'll find out who's trying to scare you, Cleo."

"I hope so."

Max put his hand back on the wheel and drove in silence for a while. There was less than a mile to go until they reached the inn. He and Cleo would be home soon.

Home.

In spite of his concern about the incidents that had been plaguing Cleo, Max was aware of the pleasant sense of anticipation that was simmering deep inside him.

For the first time in his life he felt as if he belonged somewhere. Best of all, he had a woman who wanted him, a woman who had waited her whole life for him.

"What are you thinking about, Max?" Cleo asked softly.

"I was wondering if Ben took care of that dripping shower head in two-sixteen."

Cleo smiled.

The early darkness of a winter night was descending on the coast. Heavy clouds overhead promised more rain before dawn. Max drove around the last bend in the road and saw the lights of Robbins' Nest Inn blazing in the distance.

"Cleo?"

"Hmmm?" Cleo was studying the mostly empty parking lot with an innkeeper's professional frown of concern.

"I want us to have a baby."

She jerked her gaze away from the lot. "A what?"

"A baby." A baby would make everything more secure, Max thought. It would be another bond linking him to Cleo and her friends.

"Why?"

Max hesitated. "Why does anyone want a baby?"

"There are a lot of reasons why someone might want a baby. Not all of them are good reasons. Why do you want one?"

"Is this a test?" Max asked.

"Probably."

He felt the tension in his jaw as he searched for a way to put his certainty into words. "It's time." He concentrated. "I'm going to be thirty-five next month. I've got a secure income from the investments I've made over the past few years. I've got a stable lifestyle now that I'm working for you. And I've got you."

"I'm not sure those reasons are good enough," Cleo said quietly.

Fear surged through him. His fingers clenched around the steering wheel. "What the hell is that supposed to mean?"

Cleo bristled. "Having a baby is a major decision. There are a lot of things to consider. We're talking about a serious commitment."

"You and I have already made a serious commitment."

"I know, but still . . ."

"What's the risk?" Max asked swiftly, sensing a weak point. "Are you afraid I'm going to walk out on you in a year or so, the way Sylvia's husband did to her and Sammy?"

Cleo turned her head to gaze at him with perceptive eyes. "No." Her voice was very soft and very certain. "No, I don't think you would walk out on your family."

"You think I'd make a lousy father, is that it? Look, I know a man with my kind of background probably doesn't seem like a good bet as a father. But I think I could handle the basics. You once told me you didn't have to jump out of a plane in order to figure out what it would do to your insides."

"What do you think are the basics of fatherhood?" Cleo asked with genuine curiosity.

Max flashed her a quick glance. "Being there. Sticking around to do the job."

"Where did you learn that?" Cleo asked.

"From my own father," Max said roughly.

"He spent a lot of time with you?"

"No," Max said. "I never met him. He left before I was born."

"Oh." There was a wealth of understanding in her voice.

"My strategy for being a father is to do just the opposite of everything that was done to me when I was growing up."

Cleo touched his thigh. "Max, I think you'd make a terrific father."

Relief washed over him. He had pushed hard and won again. "You do?"

"Yes." She gazed through the windshield at the warm lights of the inn. "I do."

"Then it's settled." Max turned the Jaguar into the parking lot. "We'll get started right away."

"Could we wait until after dinner?" Cleo asked. "I'm sure the family will have a lot of questions, and Ben and Trisha will probably want to talk about their wedding plans. I'd like to have a chance to go through the new bookings, and maybe O'Reilly will have some news for us."

Max smiled ruefully. "If you insist, I guess we can wait until after dinner."

Everything was going to be okay, he thought. So why did he feel this disturbing sense of unease beneath the satisfaction he was experiencing, he wondered.

But even as he asked the question, he knew the answer. He was still on dangerous ground. After all, he knew better than anyone else that he had pushed Cleo into the engagement just as he had once pushed Kimberly. And now he had pushed Cleo into another commitment.

Maybe he was pushing too hard in his effort to force his way into her life. He knew that he didn't have a good track record when it came to this kind of thing. It was the one area in which he always screwed up.

He probably should have held back, Max thought, suddenly worried about his own successful pressure tactics. Something was wrong.

The things he wanted most in life always seemed to elude him just as he was reaching for them.

Three hours later Max watched, amused, as O'Reilly put his feet up on a wicker footstool in the solarium and lounged contentedly in one of the fanback chairs.

"Playing pasha?" Max asked.

O'Reilly looked at him with knowing eyes. "I think I've finally figured out why you changed jobs, Max. Just be careful you don't put on weight eating chocolate chip cookies."

"I'll work it off. There's always something that needs doing around an old place like this."

"Yeah. Found that out fast. I helped Ben with a couple of leaking faucets while you were gone. Ben thinks you leap tall buildings in a single bound, by the way."

"I don't know why," Max said. "I haven't leaped any lately."

"I guess we all have to find our heroes where we can." O'Reilly grinned. "Sammy supervised the plumbing repairs."

"Sammy's good at supervision."

O'Reilly looked pleased. "He's a great little kid, isn't he?"

"Yes."

"Smart as a whip," O'Reilly said.

"Talented, too," Max said, remembering the crayon drawing that was hanging in the attic.

"What kind of a father would run off and leave Sammy and a fine woman like Sylvia on their own?" O'Reilly asked.

"A real jerk of a father."

"Some guys don't know when they've got it made, do they?" O'Reilly mused.

"No," Max said. "Some guys don't."

O'Reilly gave him a level look. "But some guys, guys like you and me, for instance, are a little brighter. We know a good thing when we see it."

Max's attention was caught by the unfamiliar undercurrent he thought he detected in O'Reilly's voice. He had known the other man for a long time. Since the death of O'Reilly's wife and child, it had been rare to hear any emotion other than unrelenting, completely superficial amusement in his voice.

"Yes," Max said. "Some of us know a good thing when we see it." He glanced toward the French doors as they opened. Ben walked into the room. "Come on in, Ben. We've been waiting for you."

"What's up?" Ben glanced at Max and then at O'Reilly. "You said we needed to have a strategy session?"

"Right. Sit down." Max waved him to a seat. "I figure this is something the three of us should discuss before we talk to the rest of the family. I don't want everyone worrying unnecessarily."

O'Reilly chuckled. "Translated, that means Max thinks this is a job for the men of the household. I'm warning you, the ladies will have a fit if they find out we're making plans behind their backs."

"Gotcha." Ben dropped down on a nearby seat, obviously proud to be included in the strategy session. "I take it we're going to talk about what you found out while Cleo and Max were gone?"

"I've got my notes here somewhere." O'Reilly rummaged around in his pants pockets and pulled out a small notebook. "I'd better bring Max up to speed first."

Max watched him intently. "Anything interesting?"

"Nothing for certain, but when you lay it all out some intriguing questions arise."

Before Max could ask what those questions were, the French doors opened again.

"What's going on in here?" Cleo demanded from the doorway. Trisha and Sylvia hovered to one side, looking half irritated and half anxious. Andromeda and Daystar were standing just behind Cleo.

Max looked at the phalanx of women and swore softly.

"So much for trying to have a war council with just us guys," O'Reilly said dryly. "Come on in, ladies."

"Thank you." Cleo stalked into the room. The others followed with determined expressions. "We intended to do just that."

"Who's watching the front desk?" Max asked.

"George is on duty," Sylvia said. "He'll keep an eye on the handful of guests in the lounge." She sat down next to O'Reilly. "Don't worry, gentlemen, everything is under control. Now, what are you up to in here?"

"I was merely about to give my report," O'Reilly said mildly. "Such as it is."

"You said earlier that you hadn't turned up much." Cleo sat down next to Max. "What's to report?"

O'Reilly flipped open his notebook. "The way I see this, there are three possible explanations for the incidents. The first is the one you and Max came up with, which is that we're dealing with a deranged critic out to punish you for writing *The Mirror*."

Max looked up, frowning. "You don't sound like you think that's the most likely explanation."

"I don't think it is," O'Reilly said. "Mostly because as near as I can tell, no one in town had read the book until I started asking questions about it two days ago. The local bookshop didn't even have it in stock."

"It was a rather small print run," Cleo said apologetically.

"What about the possibility that it's someone from out of town who's read the book and tracked Cleo down?" Trisha asked.

O'Reilly shook his head. "The only place a stranger could be staying here in Harmony Cove is at this inn, Cosmic Harmony, or the motel on the other side of town. None of those establishments has had any repeat customers in the past couple of months."

Ben considered that. "So there was no one person who kept showing up around here each time there was an incident, is that it?"

"That's it," O'Reilly said. "Now, I'm not saying someone couldn't have snuck into town and staged the incidents, but he would have had to know his way around. He would also have had to know something about Cleo. The fact that she was dating Nolan Hildebrand, for example. The time of night she usually goes upstairs to bed. Which room is hers. The fact that she often visits Cosmic Harmony. That kind of thing."

"Good heavens," Andromeda said uneasily. "It sounds like someone has researched Cleo."

"Exactly," O'Reilly said. "That kind of detail can only be learned by studying a person's routine over a period of time."

"All of which means that whoever is doing this knows a great deal about what goes on around here." Max picked up his cane and got to his feet. He ignored the protesting twinge in his thigh as he walked to the window.

It was raining outside, but Max felt warm and comfortable and replete. It had been a pleasant homecoming. Andromeda and Daystar had fixed a special meal of clam chowder, barley salad, and homemade bread. There had been new drawings by Sammy to admire on the refrigerator door. Everyone had exclaimed over Cleo's ring and had instantly begun making plans for the future. It was a future that included Max.

A man could get used to this kind of life real fast, Max thought. But a smart man would never take it for granted. He prided himself on being a smart man.

"Like I said," O'Reilly continued, "it could be a complete stranger, but whoever it is has spent time in and around Harmony Cove. My gut feeling is that someone would have noticed him in a small town like this. Trust me. When we find out who's behind the incidents, the first words out of everyone's mouth will be *'But he seemed like such a nice guy.'* "

"Or girl," Cleo murmured.

O'Reilly nodded. "Or girl."

Max braced both hands on the cane. "All right, what's the next possibility?"

O'Reilly glanced down at his notes. "There's a clear connection between the start of these incidents and the death of Jason Curzon."

Cleo and the others went very still.

"Damn." Max gazed out into the rain. "You're right, O'Reilly."

"I usually am," O'Reilly murmured.

"I should have seen that for myself," Max said, disgusted.

"What on earth are you saying?" Andromeda asked anxiously. "How could Jason's death have anything to do with this?"

"Because he left a quarter of a million dollars' worth of art unaccounted for," Max said grimly. "And everyone seems to think Cleo knows where the paintings are."

"Everyone meaning you and Garrison Spark?" O'Reilly asked dryly.

Max set his back teeth. "I know Cleo doesn't know where the Luttrells are. But Spark still believes she does. He's already tried to talk her into turning them over to him for a fraction of what they're worth."

"You wouldn't believe how many people think I'm not real bright," Cleo said. "My theory is that my choice in foot attire gives the wrong impression."

O'Reilly ignored her. "You think maybe these incidents are part of some sort of elaborate ploy to terrorize Cleo into producing the paintings, Max?"

"It's a possibility," Max said. "As you pointed out, the timing fits. They started shortly after Jason died."

O'Reilly hesitated. "Then why hasn't she received any notes warning her to sell or else?"

Cleo held up a hand for attention. "Maybe Mr. Spark or whoever is behind this wants to get me really spooked first. When I'm totally traumatized and scared to death, he'll zing me with a demand to turn over the Luttrells."

"Maybe," O'Reilly agreed. He didn't look convinced. He tapped his notebook with the tip of his pen. "Something else I wanted to mention while we're on the subject of the paintings. Nolan Hildebrand has to be counted as a suspect."

"Nolan?" Cleo's eyes widened. "Are you crazy? Nolan wouldn't stage those incidents."

"You can't be sure of that," Max said. "He tried to get you to help him find the paintings so that he could collect Spark's finder's fee, remember?"

Cleo grimaced. "Yes, but I just don't see Nolan as the sort who would concoct all those stagey incidents. Besides, he was genuinely shocked when he found out I'd written *The Mirror*. I know he was. He couldn't have known about it earlier."

"His shock could have been an act," Max said. "He might have been trying to deflect suspicion from himself."

"I don't know." Cleo's expression was dubious. "Nolan just isn't that convoluted in his thinking processes, if you know what I mean."

"You mean he's simpleminded?" Daystar asked bluntly.

Cleo scowled. "Not quite. I just don't see him as the type to put together a real devious scheme like this."

"Maybe," O'Reilly said. "Maybe not. I still think we have to consider him as a possibility."

Cleo threw up her hands in surrender. "Okay, okay. Nolan is a suspect. In that case, you might as well add Adrian Forrester to the list. The same logic applies. But I want you all to know that I'm going on record with my own private, personal opinion that neither one of them is behind the incidents."

Max looked at her. "You were willing enough to consider Forrester as a suspect earlier."

Cleo sighed. "I know, but I was annoyed with him at the time. I've had a chance to calm down, and I have to admit that I really can't see him doing this kind of thing."

Max considered that. He had to allow for the possibility that she was right. Cleo could see into people the way he could see into paintings. He should know. She had looked into him and seen what he had wanted most in the world. And she had given it to him.

A twinge went through his thigh. Max stirred, changing position slightly. The long drive from Seattle was taking its toll. He pushed the old, familiar ache to the back of his mind and concentrated on the problem at hand as he walked to the fountain.

"If Spark is behind these incidents," he said quietly, "I think we can squelch the problem fairly easily."

Everyone stared at him.

"How?" Sylvia asked.

"I'll call him tomorrow and arrange a meeting." Max gazed into the turquoise blue fountain. "I'll tell him to forget the Luttrells. I'll also tell him that I want him to vanish."

O'Reilly eyed him in cool appraisal. "We're talking about a quarter of a million bucks here. What makes you think Spark will back out of the scene quietly when there's that kind of money involved?"

"He'll go," Max said.

No one said a word. They all sat in tense silence, staring at him. Max felt their silent questions hammering at him, but he did not volunteer an explanation of just how he would get rid of Spark.

"Okay," O'Reilly finally said in a brisk, businesslike voice, "that takes care of the Spark angle. Which leaves us with a third possible explanation to consider."

Max met O'Reilly's eyes. "I think I like this one the least."

Cleo frowned. "You haven't even heard it yet."

O'Reilly smiled wryly. "Max has a very analytical brain. He's already figured out that the third possibility is a rather nasty one."

"What is it?" Trisha asked uneasily.

Max looked down into the bubbling fountain water. "That there is something in Cleo's past that has triggered someone into coming after her."

"Shit," Ben whispered, awed. He looked at Max. "Are you serious?"

"Yes." Max looked at Cleo, then continued. "I know we talked about this possibility briefly and then let it drop. I didn't want you worrying about it. But it looks like we need to look into it further."

"What is there to look into?" Cleo asked. "I've already told you that I don't have any strange, obsessive men in my past. Nothing bizarre has ever occurred in my life except for the deaths of my parents."

"Your parents died in a very unusual manner," Max said quietly.

"Yes, but there was a logical explanation for it," Cleo reminded him. Her eyes turned bleak. "At least according to the authorities there was a logical explanation."

O'Reilly glanced at Max. Then he turned to Cleo. "I think this is as good a time as any to tell you that I did a little checking into the death of that investigator you hired last summer."

Cleo's gaze swung to O'Reilly. "You looked into Mr. Eberson's death? Why?"

"Because you mentioned that he was working on your case at the time, and because I am a very thorough investigator myself," O'Reilly said.

"Well?" Cleo waited expectantly. "Was there anything strange about his car accident?"

"Not officially. The records indicate that it was an accident. But when I phoned the insurance salesman who took over Eberson's office space, he mentioned that he'd had to wait quite a while before he could move in."

Max watched O'Reilly's face closely. "Why?"

"Because there was some fire damage that had to be repaired first." O'Reilly closed his notebook with a snap. "It seems that there was a small blaze caused by faulty wiring in the office. It completely destroyed Eberson's files."

"Is that so?" Max asked softly.

Cleo wrapped her arms around her knees. Her eyes were huge with worry as she gazed at O'Reilly. "What are you saying? Do you think that Eberson had uncovered something about my parents' death that may have gotten him killed?"

O'Reilly held up a hand. "Cleo, I will tell you honestly that I don't know where this is going to lead. It could very well be a dead end. In fact, in all likelihood, it is a dead end. But it's something that needs to be checked out."

"What are you going to do?" Ben asked.

"I'm going to resume the investigation that was dropped when Eberson died," O'Reilly said. "Now that Max is here to keep an eye on all of you, I'm going to Seattle to start looking into the background surrounding the death of Cleo's parents."

Max saw Cleo go absolutely rigid.

"I'm not sure that's a good idea," she whispered. "What if there is some crazy person out there?"

"Then we'd better find out who he is, hadn't we?" O'Reilly asked calmly. "Before he does any more damage."

Sylvia shifted uneasily in her chair. "I don't want you to take any risks, O'Reilly."

Max noted the very personal note of concern in Sylvia's voice.

O'Reilly beamed reassuringly. "Hey, I'm good at this. It's what I do."

"Sylvia's right," Cleo said quickly. "If there's something dangerous going on here we should call in the police."

"There's no point doing that at this stage," O'Reilly said. "We haven't got enough to go on. Like I said, we're probably chasing a dead-end lead. I just want to be sure we've covered all the bases."

Andromeda frowned. "You still think Spark is the most likely suspect, don't you?"

"That's exactly what I think," O'Reilly said. "The timing of the incidents and the amount of money involved make that the most likely possibility."

"I don't like this," Cleo whispered. "I'm getting a weird feeling."

"What kind of feeling?" Trisha asked.

"I don't know. It's just weird."

Max reached down to take her hand and pull her to her feet. "I think it's time we all went to bed." She didn't resist when he tugged her up off the chair, but the coldness in her fingers worried him.

Trisha looked at O'Reilly. "You're going to leave in the morning?"

"Afraid so." O'Reilly glanced at Sylvia.

"But you'll be coming back, won't you?" Trisha asked. "You said you'd be here for the wedding on Friday."

"Wouldn't miss it for the world," O'Reilly said. "I'll definitely be back on Friday. With my best suit."

"God help us," Max muttered.

Andromeda beetled her brows at him. "I'm sure O'Reilly's best suit is very nice."

"It's green, and it's made out of polyester," Max said. "Need I say more?"

Seventeen

The following night, Cleo put her hands behind her head and gazed up at the shadowed ceiling of the attic. "I'm going with you tomorrow when you talk to Spark."

"No," Max said from the other side of the bed. "For the last time, I don't want you there."

The argument had been festering since four o'clock that afternoon, when Cleo had discovered that Max had made arrangements to talk to Garrison Spark the next day. She had immediately announced her intentions of confronting Spark with Max. Max had put his foot down with a forcefulness that had not only startled her, it had hurt her.

"Max, this is all happening because of me. I have a right to be there with you when you talk to Spark."

"Cleo, stop pushing. I told you, I'm going to handle this."

She sat up in bed, exasperated to the point of anger. "Why are you being so bloody-minded about it? Give me one good reason why I shouldn't be there."

"You don't know anything about handling someone like Spark."

"And you do?"

"Yes."

"What makes you an expert?" she snapped.

"I told you, I once worked for Spark. I know how he thinks. I also know how he operates."

"So?" Cleo challenged.

"So I don't want you anywhere around when I talk to him about what's been happening."

"I'm not an idiot, Max. I won't mess up your plans, whatever they are."

"I never said you were an idiot."

"I am also not as naive as everyone seems to think." Cleo paused suddenly. "Max, does it strike you that we're having our first major quarrel?"

"We're not quarreling."

"Sure sounds like a quarrel to me."

"We are not quarreling, damn it."

Cleo was taken aback by the fierce insistence in his voice. "Okay, so we're having a heated discussion. Whatever you want to call it, I think the time has come for you and me to clear up a little communication problem we seem to have developed."

"What communication problem?" he asked warily.

Cleo took a breath. "You once noted that you and I have different styles of management. Well, those two styles have just collided, and they will probably do so again in the future. We need to learn how to deal with each other when that happens."

"Damn. The last thing I need tonight is a conversation like this."

"Tough. We're having it." Cleo touched his shoulder. "I think you and I need to get something settled here, Max. You can't walk into this family and just start throwing your weight around the way you apparently did when you worked for Curzon International. If you and I are going to make this relationship work, we're going to have to learn to work as a team."

Max did not move. The new tension radiating from him was palpable. "What's that supposed to mean?"

Cleo watched him uneasily. She had the feeling that she had accidentally stepped into a minefield. "I'm just trying to talk about our mutual problem."

Max moved without any warning. He shoved the covers aside and sat up on the edge of the bed. He reached for his cane and got to his feet. "Are you telling me that if we don't do things your way, our relationship, as you call it, is over?"

"Max." Cleo clutched the sheet to her breast. "For heaven's sake, I never said that. I just said we needed to iron out some of our communication problems."

"Communication problems sounds like code for *I'm having second thoughts about marrying you, Max."*

"That's not true," Cleo retorted. "We're having a little trouble relating to each other, that's all."

"Don't give me a lot of pop-psych communication theory." Max looked down at her with dangerous eyes. "Just cut to the bottom line."

"There is no bottom line." Cleo was bewildered by his reaction. "I'm only trying to tell you that you can't expect me to meekly step aside and let you take over running the family and everything else in sight. Good grief, no wonder Kimberly was afraid to give you a seat on the board. She knew you'd take over Curzon if you got half a chance."

Max looked as if she'd slapped him. His hand clenched around the handle of his cane. "Is that what you think I'm trying to do? Take control of your family and your inn?"

Cleo was horrified. "Of course not." She scrambled to a kneeling position in the center of the bed. "Max, you're getting this all wrong."

"Is that right? What part am I getting wrong? It all sounds very clear to me. You think I'm taking over, and unless I handle things the way you want them handled, you're going to back out of the marriage. Did I miss anything?"

"I am not going to back out of the marriage. Will you please stop putting words in my mouth?"

"I'm using the words you used."

Cleo lost her temper. "What on earth is the problem here? Why don't you want me with you tomorrow when you talk to Spark?"

"Because I don't want you there. Isn't that reason enough?"

"No, damn it, it's not."

Max moved to the window and stood looking out into the darkness. "It's all the reason you're going to get. And if that's not good enough, you'll have to make your own decision about what to do next."

The bleakness in his voice was Cleo's undoing. His words echoed with a cold, aloof loneliness that tore at her heart. She wondered how many times in his life Max had waited for others to make the decisions that would send him down the road to the next temporary home.

With a soft exclamation of pain that was as deep as his own, Cleo leaped off the bed and ran across the room to where he stood at the window. She threw her arms around him and leaned her head against his bare chest.

"Max, I've got news for you. It doesn't work like that now."

He touched her hair with a hesitant hand. "What do you mean?"

Cleo raised her head to meet his eyes. She framed his hard jaw between her palms. "You don't get kicked out of this family just because you are occasionally as stubborn as a mule and have an annoying tendency to govern by fiat."

"I don't?" He searched her face with eyes that mirrored both grim acceptance of his fate and a tiny flame of hope.

"No." Cleo stood on tiptoe and kissed him lightly on the mouth. "You're one of us now. It doesn't matter if you occasionally screw up, remember?"

Max's eyes were more enigmatic than Cleo had ever seen them. "You're sure?"

"I'm sure." Cleo grinned. "Of course, in return, you have to learn to accommodate some of my little foibles, which may tend to irritate you now and again. For instance, I am not going to give up on this matter of going with you when you confront Spark. But that's family life for you. A little give and take. What the heck. Nothing's perfect."

There was no answering amusement in Max's expression. "Cleo . . ."

"Yes?"

"Never mind."

Max pulled her against him and held her so tightly Cleo thought her ribs might crack. But they didn't.

After a while Max led her back to bed.

A long time later Max stirred and rolled reluctantly off of Cleo. "You can come with me tomorrow," he said.

Cleo wondered why he sounded like a gambler who had just bet everything on a long shot.

The meeting had been arranged on neutral territory. Spark had suggested that Max meet him at a small motel located forty miles from Harmony Cove. Max had agreed.

He had thought about the meeting most of the night, but he was still not fully prepared for the flood of memories that assailed him when Spark opened the door of his small motel suite. No matter how he sliced it, Max thought, there was no getting around the fact that he owed Spark a great deal.

It was Spark, after all, who had first made it possible for Max to indulge his grand passion for fine art. It was Spark who had allowed him to handle some of the most brilliant paintings that had been produced by West Coast artists in the past twenty years. It was Spark who had provided Max with the opportunity to meet Jason Curzon.

"Well, well, well." Spark's expression was one of cool, half-amused appraisal. "It's been a long time, Fortune. You seem to have done rather well for yourself. Hard to believe that once upon a time you made a living running errands for me."

Spark had changed little during the past twelve years, Max thought. He looked as polished and sophisticated as ever. He still had the supercilious curl of the lip and that expression of bored condescension that was so useful for intimidating timorous collectors.

"There's no point wasting time reminiscing," Max said. He tightened his grip on Cleo's arm. "You've met my fiancée, I believe."

"Fiancée?" Spark's smile was rueful. "I'm sorry. I hadn't realized you had actually made the mistake of falling in love with Fortune, my dear. What a pity. Do come in."

Cleo glared at him as she walked into the room. "We're here to discuss the paintings, Mr. Spark. I suggest we skip the small talk."

"Ah, yes. The Luttrells." Spark motioned Max and Cleo to chairs and then sat down himself. He crossed one leg languidly over the other. "I must admit to being rather startled when I got your call yesterday, Max. May I assume that you are ready to deal?"

"There is no deal," Max said. "If and when the Luttrells are found, they belong to me. I have no intention of selling them."

"I have a bill of sale from Jason Curzon." Spark's eyes were speculative. "It clearly shows that he sold the Luttrells to me shortly before he died."

"That bill of sale is as phony as the Maraston you sold to that collector down in Portland last year," Max said calmly.

Spark's eyes narrowed. "You can't prove that painting was a forgery."

Max smiled faintly. "Sure I can. I own the original."

A flash of annoyance appeared in Spark's eyes. It vanished almost instantly. "You're lying."

Max shook his head with weary patience. "No, Spark, I'm not lying. We both know that I never bluff. I picked up the original three years ago. It's been hanging in my vault ever since. If you insist on producing your bill of sale, I'll contact the Portland collector and suggest he have his Maraston examined by an expert."

"You're the leading authority on Maraston's work."

"Exactly." Max shrugged. "I'll be only too happy to volunteer my expertise in this instance. I imagine the Portland collector will be very grateful. I think it would be safe to say that he'll probably want his money back from you. He will undoubtedly never buy anything from you again, and neither will anyone else who hears the story, which I imagine would spread like wildfire in certain circles."

"Bastard," Spark said, but he sounded more resigned than outraged.

Spark was, at heart, a businessman, Max reflected. He knew when to cut his losses. "I'm surprised you're still peddling the occasional forgery. I would have thought you'd have given up that sideline by now. After all, you do just fine handling the real thing. What's the matter? Still can't resist a quick buck?"

"Some of us never change, do we, Fortune?" Spark's answering smile was tinged with poison. "I see you're still as much of an opportunist as ever. I'm amazed that you've stooped to seducing nice young women in order to get what you want, however. Even in the old days you had some rather irritating standards."

The standards hadn't been all that high, Max reflected. The arrangement he'd had with Spark was a simple one. In exchange for being allowed to handle the art he craved more than food, Max had agreed not to voice his opinions to Spark's clients.

Unless those clients asked for his opinion.

Jason Curzon was the only one who had ever asked Spark's rough-edged errand runner and odd-job man for an opinion.

Out of the corner of his eye, Max watched Cleo's expression. His insides were twisted into a cold knot of anticipation. He had known what would happen if he brought Cleo with him to this confrontation. That was why he had fought so hard to keep her away from the meeting.

But in the end she had destroyed his defenses in her own gentle fashion. At some point last night Max had realized he would have to take his chances. He did not know how she would react to this glimpse into his less-than-savory past, but he accepted the fact that his fate was in her hands.

"Do we understand each other, Spark?" Max asked quietly.

"I think so." Spark turned to Cleo. "Did your fiancé ever tell you precisely what he did for a living when he worked for me, Ms. Robbins?"

Cleo shot a quick glance at Max. "He said he did odd jobs for you."

"That he did." Spark looked pleased. "Some very odd jobs. His duties included picking up extremely valuable works of art from certain sources that were, shall we say, less than reputable. Fortune carried a gun when he worked for me, Ms. Robbins. That should tell you something of the nature of his responsibilities."

Cleo frowned. "I imagine that transporting expensive art requires some security precautions."

"Oh, yes, yes, indeed." Spark chuckled. "Especially when some of that art was purchased from collectors who had ties to the underworld. And then there were the occasions when Max delivered paintings which had rather cloudy provenances."

"You mean they were fakes?" Cleo demanded.

"Excellent fakes, Ms. Robbins." Spark contrived to look offended. "Max can tell you that when I deal in forgeries, I make certain I deal in only first-class forgeries. Ninety-nine percent of the time no one can tell the difference between a good Spark forgery and the original."

"Except Max?" Cleo asked.

Spark sighed. "Unfortunately, yes. Max has what amounts to a preternatural talent for telling the real from the fake. At times it was an extremely useful skill. At other times, it was rather annoying."

"You mean you used Max's talent to make certain you didn't get burned yourself," Cleo concluded. "But you worried that when you burned others, he might spill the beans?"

"Precisely, Ms. Robbins." Spark's eyes glittered. "To my knowledge, however, he experienced an attack of integrity only once during the course of our association. That was when he delivered a certain painting to Jason Curzon. In retrospect I'm inclined to believe that it was not integrity but sheer opportunism that overcame him. Max saw a chance to better himself, didn't you, Max?"

Max kept his gaze steady. "We had a deal, Spark. I told you I wouldn't lie about a painting if one of your clients asked my opinion. Jason asked."

"And shortly thereafter Max resigned his position as my odd-job man to accept a more lucrative offer with Curzon." Spark smiled thinly at Cleo. "Once again I advise you to be cautious around Fortune, Ms. Robbins. Once he has his hands on those Luttrells, he'll be gone."

"That's enough, Spark. I think we understand each other, don't we?" Max got to his feet.

Spark lifted one shoulder in an elegant shrug. "We always did understand each other rather well, Fortune."

"One more thing. Make sure that you notify Nolan Hildebrand that you are no longer in the market for the Luttrells."

"If you insist."

Max folded his hands on top of the hawk and looked at Cleo. The deep sense of foreboding was eating him alive. "Let's go, Cleo."

Without a word, she rose from the chair and walked toward the door. Max followed.

"Fortune," Spark murmured softly behind him.

Max glanced back over his shoulder. "What is it, Spark?"

"I urge you to reconsider. I have a client who will pay a quarter of a million for those Luttrells. I'll split it with you, fifty-fifty. Think about it."

"They're not for sale," Max said.

"I was afraid you'd say that." Spark raised a hand. "Take yourself off. I trust we won't run into each other again any time soon."

"That will be just fine with me. By the way, you probably ought to know that my attorney has a sealed letter which is only to be opened if I suffer an unfortunate accident. The letter contains a short list of the more prominent forgeries that are presently hanging on the walls of some of your clients' homes."

"You always were an ungrateful wretch." Spark's mouth twisted wryly. "Never fear. I shall light candles for your continued good health."

"Thank you. The deal we made still stands, as far as I'm concerned, Spark. You stay out of my way, and I'll stay out of yours."

Spark looked at him. "It's going to be interesting to see how you adjust to married life."

Cleo turned at the door. "He's going to do just fine, Mr. Spark."

Max saw the warmth in her eyes. The tension inside him evaporated at last. It was going to be all right. Cleo was not going to hold his past against him.

Max followed her out into the hall and closed the door of Spark's room. Without a word he took Cleo's arm. Together they walked out of the motel and into the cold, misty rain.

"Well, that's that," Cleo said as Max opened the door of the Jaguar. "What do you think?"

"About Spark?" Max watched her intently. "I think the same thing I thought before. He's not the one behind the incidents. But if I'm wrong and he is the one who's been harassing you, or if he put Hildebrand up to doing it, it will stop now."

"You're sure?"

"Yes. Spark and I understand each other. He knows I'll destroy him if he gets in my way. But he also knows that I'll leave him alone if he leaves me alone."

Cleo shuddered. "Why on earth did you go to work for that man in the first place?"

"I needed a job."

Max shut her door and went around the nose of the Jaguar. He got in behind the wheel and turned to look at Cleo. He didn't know what to say.

Cleo looked thoughtful. "I think I know now why you didn't want me to come along with you this morning."

"I used to pride myself on never screwing up," Max said quietly. "But now when I look back, it seems to me my whole life was a screwup."

"Nah," Cleo said. "You're just feeling a little depressed this morning. You'll get over it."

"You think so?"

"I'm sure of it," Cleo said. She leaned across the seat and kissed him.

"I give up." Ben grimaced at his image in the mirror. "I can't figure out how to tie this stupid bow tie. I've never tied one of these things before in my life."

"Hang on a second, I'll get to you as soon as I've finished with Sammy." Max concentrated on adjusting Sammy's tie. "Hold your chin up, kid. That's it."

Sammy lifted his chin obediently as Max tied the black bow tie that complemented his tiny tuxedo. "Can I take Lucky Ducky?"

"You won't have any place to put him during the ceremony. You're supposed to be guarding the rings, remember?" Max finished his task and surveyed his work with a critical eye.

Sammy was wearing a perfect miniature version of the black and white formal attire that he and Ben were wearing. Max was well aware that this was the first time either Ben or Sammy had been exposed to the fine art of wearing a tux. He had told them it was never too soon to start.

"You look good, kid." Max nodded once, satisfied with the effect. "Your mom isn't going to recognize you."

Sammy studied himself in the mirror. "I look just like you and Ben, huh, Max?"

"You sure do." Max picked up the little black jacket and stuffed Sammy's arms gently into it. He straightened the tiny cummerbund. "Now, whatever you do, don't get any dirt on this outfit until after the ceremony, understand?"

"Sure, Max. I'll be careful. Do you think O'Reilly will be here in time?" Sammy looked worried. He had been fretting about O'Reilly's belated arrival for the past hour.

"He said he'd be here," Max reminded him. "If O'Reilly says something, you can count on it."

The truth was, Max was beginning to fret a bit, himself, although he had no intention of revealing the fact. O'Reilly was normally close to compulsive when it came to matters of punctuality. There was no denying he was pushing the limits today. Max glanced at his watch for the fourth time in the past twenty minutes. The ceremony at Cosmic Harmony was scheduled to begin in an hour.

Ben fiddled with the ends of his tie. "Maybe he had a flat tire." His eyes met Max's in the mirror, reflecting a trace of the unease Max was feeling.

"Could be," Max agreed. "But he's got a car phone. He'd have called if he were going to be late. Here, let me take care of that tie. If you keep fooling with it, we'll have to get it ironed again."

"I don't know why we had to get all gussied up like this," Ben muttered. "Waste of time. I feel like an idiot in this suit."

"It'll be worth it when you see the look in Trisha's eyes. Women are suckers for men in tuxes."

"Yeah?" Ben looked intrigued by that notion. "You really think Trisha will like it?"

"Trust me." Max took charge of the black tie, expertly shaping a perfect bow. "She's going to be swept off her feet."

Ben fingered his starched white shirt. "I'm not sure about these little pleats. You don't think they look like something a girl would wear, do you?"

"Men have been wearing little pleats like this for nearly two hundred years. You're in good company."

"You sure I don't look like a waiter in a fancy restaurant?" Ben asked doubtfully.

"You look like James Bond," Max assured him.

Ben scowled. "I'd rather look like you," he said gruffly. "That way I'd know I don't look like an idiot. You always look like you're supposed to look, y'know?" He groped for words. "You always look right."

Max felt a peculiar twist of emotion. He could not recall anyone ever wanting to emulate him. "Just remember to wear the clothes with an attitude that says you're a lot sharper than they are."

"If you say so." Ben watched in the mirror as Max worked on the tie. "Where'd you learn to do this?"

"Jason taught me."

Old memories swept through Max as he finished the bow and adjusted the points of Ben's collar. Twelve years ago he had been as dubious about the whole process of wearing a tux as Ben was today. Jason had tied the tie for him and had even had to show him how to wear the cuff links.

There was something satisfying about handing on the manly art of dressing for a formal occasion to another young man who was just as rough and unsophisticated as he had once been, Max thought.

"There, that does it. Let's take a look." He stepped back to survey his work. "Perfect. You look like you've been wearing tuxes for years."

Ben studied himself in the mirror. A pleased expression gleamed in his eyes. He straightened his shoulders. "I look older or something, don't I?"

"Cool," Sammy proclaimed. "You look cool, Ben."

"Yeah, I do, don't I?" Ben tugged on the jacket of the tuxedo.

"Just like Max," Sammy said. He picked up Lucky Ducky and tucked the plastic duck under his arm.

"So, I guess we're ready, huh?" Ben turned away from the mirror. There was a slight but definite swagger in his step.

Sammy was instantly alarmed. "We can't go anywhere until O'Reilly gets here."

"We'll wait for O'Reilly," Max assured him. "Go to the window and keep an eye out for him, Sammy."

"Okay." Sammy raced for the window.

Max looked at Ben. "There's one more thing we've got to take care of before we leave for Cosmic Harmony." Max reached into the pocket of his jacket and drew out an airline ticket folder.

"What's that?" Ben asked, momentarily distracted.

"Your honeymoon trip." Max opened the lapel of Ben's jacket and stuffed the ticket folder into the inside pocket. "You're going to Hawaii for a week. It's a gift from the family."

Ben's jaw dropped. *"Hawaii.* I thought me and Trisha were going to Seattle."

"There's been a change in plans. You're driving to Seattle this afternoon, but instead of checking into a hotel downtown, you're going to the airport." Max's mouth curved. "You'll stay the night at a hotel there. Your plane leaves at seven tomorrow morning."

"Hawaii." Ben looked dazed. "But we can't afford to go to Hawaii."

"Like I said, it's a gift from the family." Max briefly checked his own reflection in the mirror and tweaked the bow of his tie. "Now pay attention, Ben. When you reach Honolulu, there will be a limo waiting. The driver will have a card that has your name on it."

"A limo. Holy shit. Trisha won't believe this."

"It's all been paid for in advance. You don't even tip the driver, got that?"

"Yeah, sure. No tip."

"The limo will take you to the Curzon Paradise. It's right on the beach. You'll have one of the honeymoon suites."

"A honeymoon suite?" Ben was clearly overwhelmed. "But that must cost a bundle."

It did, Max reflected, but he had no intention of telling Ben that. "The manager of the hotel is a friend of mine," he said easily. "He owes me a favor." What he owed Max was his job, but that was not important. In any event, Max was paying full price for the suite. Now that he was no longer working for Curzon, he wanted no favors from the corporation. "You sign for everything, got that?"

"Everything?"

"The hotel bill, the meals you eat in the hotel, the snorkeling equipment, and the Hawaiian dress you're going to buy for Trisha. Everything."

"Damn, I can't hardly believe this," Ben said. "Does Trisha know?"

Max smiled and slowly shook his head. "No. You'll get to tell her all about it on the way to the airport this afternoon."

"She's gonna freak," Ben said. "She's gonna be so happy."

"That's the whole point," Max said.

"Shit, Max. This is something else." Ben stared at him. "I don't know how to thank you."

"I told you this was a gift from the family, not just me. And if you want to thank us you can do it by taking good care of Trisha and the baby."

"I will," Ben vowed.

"And by getting back here as soon as the honeymoon's over, so that you can rescue me from whatever home repair disaster I happen to be involved in at the time."

Ben grinned. "Don't worry, I'm not gonna abandon you to the plumbing. Hot damn, this is too much. *Hawaii*. Man, I hope I don't screw up at the airport or make a fool out of myself in that fancy hotel."

Max put a hand on his shoulder. "Listen to me, my friend, I am going to give you some words of wisdom that I want you to remember for the rest of your life."

Ben sobered and looked at Max with an intent expression. "I'm listening."

"It is okay to screw up once in a while," Max said. "Got that?"

"Yeah." Ben started to grin again, but his eyes stayed serious for a moment longer. "I think I can remember that."

"He's here, he's here!" Sammy shouted. "I see O'Reilly! He's just getting out of his car."

"Wearing his green suit?" Max asked.

"Nope. He's got a tux on, just like us. And he's carrying a big present all wrapped in shiny paper."

"We're all set, then," Max said. "Let's go." He picked up his black jacket and shrugged into it. Then he turned to take one last look at Ben and Sammy. He smiled slightly. "We're going to wow the ladies, my friends."

Ben and Sammy exchanged grins.

O'Reilly was pacing back and forth in the lobby and glancing nervously at his watch when Max, Ben, and Sammy arrived downstairs a few minutes later. George, who had come in early to cover the office while the family went to the wedding, smiled.

"What kept you?" Max asked O'Reilly.

"Tell you later," O'Reilly said quietly.

"Hi, O'Reilly." Sammy ran up to O'Reilly and stopped short right in front of him. "I was afraid you weren't coming."

O'Reilly went down on his haunches in front of Sammy. He grinned. "I told you I'd be here, didn't I?"

"Uh-huh." Sammy's eyes reflected his enormous relief. "Ben said maybe your car broke or something."

"Nope, I just had some business to take care of. Hey, let me look at you, kid. Aren't you all spiffed up? I can see Max has been at work. He's the only guy I know who actually knows how to tie a bow tie. Mine is pretied."

"Max says I have to look good on account of I'm supposed to guard the rings," Sammy explained.

"A very important job," O'Reilly said. He got to his feet and nodded at Ben. "So this is the big day. You ready?"

"Ready as I'll ever be," Ben said, but his eyes were eager. "The family is sending me and Trisha to Hawaii. Can you believe it?"

O'Reilly slanted a glance at Max. "Yeah, I can believe it." He handed his gift to Ben. "This is for you and Trisha."

"Hey, thanks." Ben gave the package to George. "Put this with the others, okay? Trisha says we'll open the presents when we get back."

"Will do," George said. He stashed the gift behind the desk. Then he regarded Ben with approval from beneath his bushy brows. "Best of luck to you, Ben."

"Yeah, well thanks." Ben looked at Max. "I guess this is it, huh?"

"This is it." Max took one last assessing look at his charges. He frowned briefly when he saw that Sammy had a smudge on the tip of his nose. "How did you get that?" he asked as he grabbed a tissue from the box behind the front desk.

"I dunno." Sammy stood still while Max rubbed off the smudge. "Maybe from Lucky Ducky."

"Right. I should have known." Max tossed the tissue into a small trash can behind the desk. "Everyone in the car."

Sammy raced out the front door. Ben followed at a slightly slower but no less enthusiastic pace.

Max waited until they were out of earshot before he looked at O'Reilly. "How serious?"

"I wish to hell I knew the answer to that," O'Reilly said. "I'll give you the whole story later. In the meantime, I don't think Cleo should be left alone for even a few minutes."

Max's insides froze. "Christ, O'Reilly, you can't just drop that on me and then say you'll tell me the rest later."

"It's a long story. I don't want to talk about it in front of Ben and Sammy."

"It has something to do with the death of her parents, doesn't it?"

"Maybe. I just don't have all the answers yet, Max. I'm sorry."

"Goddamn it to hell." Max took a savage grip on his cane and went toward the Jaguar.

"Would you believe this is the first wedding I've been to since my own?" O'Reilly asked an hour and a half later as he stood with Max near the buffet table.

"That's two more weddings than I've attended." Max bit into an exquisite salmon canapé that he had just plucked from the table.

"Could have fooled me," O'Reilly said. "You looked like you knew just what you were doing when you took up the position of best man."

"It's the clothes." Max swallowed the canapé. "A man who wears the right clothes for the job always looks like he knows what he's doing, and that's half the battle."

"That sounds like one of Jason Curzon's bits of wisdom."

"It is."

Max scanned the crowd, searching for Cleo. She stood with a group that included a number of townspeople as well as Andromeda and Daystar. Cleo's hair was swept up in a chignon that was more tightly secured than the usual careless knot she wore. The style was decorated with a row of yellow roses that were a beautiful contrast to the deep red highlights in her dark mane.

She looked achingly feminine in her low-necked, tight-waisted yellow gown, Max thought. But, then, the sight of her always made him ache. He wondered if the need for her would ever diminish. He doubted it. He suspected it would only intensify over the years.

The women of Cosmic Harmony had turned the graceful old resort lodge into a fantasy extravaganza done in yellow and white. All the stops had been pulled out for the wedding. In the center of the room a glowing Trisha, dressed in a floor-length creamy white gown and a tiny hat and veil, stood near Ben. Ben looked as if he had just been crowned king of the world. He caught Max's eye and grinned.

Sammy was dashing here and there in the crowd and helping himself to everything that looked like it contained sugar.

"The kid's going to be overstimulated tonight," O'Reilly observed. "Where the hell do they get so much energy at that age?"

Max turned his head at the wistful tone in O'Reilly's voice. "Damned if I know. Let's have the whole story, O'Reilly. Take it from the top."

O'Reilly stuffed a canapé into his mouth. "I took a second look at everything I could find that dealt with the death of Cleo's parents. She's been right about one thing all along; her father wasn't the kind who suddenly ups and shoots his wife and then himself."

"That's what everyone always says after it happens. *He seemed like such a nice man.*"

"Yeah, I know, but in this case, Cleo has a point. Neither Mr. nor Mrs. Robbins had a history of violent outbursts. Neither appeared to suffer from depression or suicidal tendencies. There had been no recent financial reverses for them. Neither had been diagnosed with a fatal illness."

"In other words, no obvious motivating factors." Max watched Cleo. "No wonder she hasn't been able to buy the story the authorities gave her. She knew them too well to believe it."

O'Reilly scowled thoughtfully. "I think there's a real possibility that there was something else going on, and when Eberson started looking into the situation, he triggered a response."

"From someone who did not want the situation investigated?"

"Yeah. Maybe. I just don't know yet, Max."

"Had Robbins recently fired someone who might have been crazy enough to murder him in retaliation?"

O'Reilly shrugged. "He was a businessman, owned a good-sized electronics firm. He had fired a few people over the years. Part of the job. But I couldn't find any evidence to indicate that any of them were deranged or had made threats. The police probably checked that angle at the time, too."

"Anything else?"

"The only other thing I turned up was that Robbins had testified for the prosecution at a murder trial two years before he was killed. I don't know if there was any connection, but I do know that the guy was convicted and sent to prison."

"A long shot."

"I know, but it's all I've got at the moment." O'Reilly glanced at the buffet table. A strange expression lit his eyes. "What the hell is that thing floating in the punch bowl?"

Max followed his gaze. "That's Lucky Ducky. He can swim anywhere. You wouldn't believe some of the places he turns up."

"No kidding?"

"No kidding. I suppose I'd better get the duck out of the punch before someone notices." Max started toward the large crystal bowl.

"Max?" Cleo called.

He stopped and turned around. "Right here, Cleo."

"Oh, there you are." Cleo emerged from the crowd looking cheerfully harried. "I've been looking all over for you and O'Reilly. The photographer is ready to take the next batch of pictures. Come on, let's go before Sammy runs off again."

"Photos?" Max looked at her, bemused. "Of O'Reilly and me?"

"Of course. And the rest of us, too." Cleo smiled brilliantly as she took his hand. "The photographer has finished the portraits of the wedding couple. We're ready to do the family photos now."

"Family photos?" Max looked at O'Reilly.

"Don't mind him," O'Reilly said to Cleo. "Max isn't used to being included in pictures of a family."

"Well, he'd better get used to it," Cleo said dryly. "Daystar is thinking about taking up photography as a hobby."

"You sure you want me in the shot?" O'Reilly asked.

"Sammy and Sylvia insisted," Cleo said.

"Yeah?" O'Reilly looked inordinately pleased.

"Yeah," Cleo said. She grinned.

Ten minutes later Max found himself standing together with Cleo, Andromeda, Daystar, Sylvia, O'Reilly, and Sammy. They formed a tight, warm circle around Ben and Trisha.

"Big smiles, everyone," the photographer ordered unnecessarily.

"Wait," Sammy yelped. "I forgot Lucky Ducky."

"He's in the punch bowl," Max said. "You stay here. I'll get him."

A short while later the photographer finally snapped the picture. The family portrait was complete with a rubber duck.

Eighteen

"I trust you have my usual room ready for me, Ms. Robbins?" Herbert T. Valence asked brusquely as he filled out the registration slip in his precise handwriting. "I don't care to be shifted around from room to room."

"Yes, I know, Mr. Valence. Two-ten is ready for you." Cleo maintained her best professional smile as she handed the key to Valence. "And you may use the parlor for your seminars, just as you have in the past."

Valence clicked his pen five times before replacing it neatly in his jacket pocket. "I hope there won't be any problems with the electricity this time."

"Let's keep our fingers crossed that we won't get any severe storms this weekend," Cleo said with determined cheeriness.

"I don't believe in luck," Valence said. "I've already checked the forecast, and it's supposed to be clear most of the weekend."

"Wonderful. Well, it looks like you've got a nice crowd this time. We've checked in fifteen people who say they're here for your workshop."

"Fifteen is the ideal number of people for my seminar. I can't guarantee results if I'm forced to deal with a larger crowd. And I am known for getting results. I have a reputation to maintain, you know."

"Yes, Mr. Valence. So you've said." Cleo told herself that it was worth putting up with Valence's odd little ways because of the business he brought to the inn. But occasionally she wearied of his cold, inflexible personality and small, obsessive mannerisms. "I hope you enjoy your stay."

Valence frowned as he turned away from the desk. "I am not here to enjoy myself, Ms. Robbins. I am here to conduct business."

Cleo wrinkled her nose at his back as he walked briskly toward the stairs. "You know something, Sylvia? I think Mr. Valence is getting worse. He seems awfully tense tonight."

Sylvia stuck her head out of the office and smiled. "Think of the money."

"I know. Maybe he's just overmotivated. Does it strike you that Max and Herbert T. Valence have something in common?"

"Like what?"

"A reputation."

Sylvia chuckled. "You've got a point. But there's a big difference between Max and Herbert T."

"What's that?"

"You love one, and you're not particularly fond of the other."

Cleo froze. Then she spun around. "What did you say?"

"You heard me. You love Max."

Cleo looked at her anxiously. "Is it that obvious?"

"You've given him everything he wanted, including yourself. You're a generous woman, Cleo, but you've never been that generous with any other man. You've always protected yourself on some level. Except with Max."

"I knew he was different the minute I saw him. He was the man in the mirror," Cleo whispered. "The one in my book."

"I had a hunch that was exactly who he was."

Cleo ran her fingertips along the polished edge of the front desk. "I've become part of his collection."

"Fair's fair, isn't it? You've made Max a part of your family."

Cleo hesitated. "I'll tell you something I haven't told anyone else. Sometimes I'm a little afraid, Sylvia."

"Afraid of Max? I don't believe it. You can trust Max with your life, and you know it."

"That's not what I mean." Cleo gripped the edge of the desk. "I'm afraid that he won't let himself love me. He knows how to go after what he wants, and he knows how to hang on to it. But he's been protecting himself for a lot longer than I've been protecting myself. He's got it down to an art. You should pardon the expression."

"Have you told him that you love him?"

"No." Cleo shook her head quickly. "I didn't want to push him. I guess I've been waiting for him to wake up one morning and realize he's in love with me. But sometimes I'm not sure he'd recognize love if it whapped him in the face. Men can be so dense sometimes."

"You may have to make the first move, Cleo. I'm not sure Max can." Sylvia ducked her head into the office.

Cleo stared at one of the three seascapes left on the lobby walls. The other two were now upstairs in the attic.

But she did not see Jason's foamy seascapes when she gazed at the nearest painting. Instead she looked into the phantom mirror where her deepest secrets were hidden. The figure in the silvery reflection was no longer a mysterious shadow. He was Max, the man she had been waiting for all her life. He had walked into her life and set her free.

But Cleo knew that she had not yet returned the favor. Max was still trapped in the mirror. She had not yet succeeded in freeing him.

Cleo and Max did not climb the stairs to the attic room until nearly midnight.

Cleo was exhausted. The crowd that had checked in for Valence's seminar had been more motivated to party than to study the five steps to success and prosperity. They were still making a lot of noise downstairs in the lounge, but George had assured her he could handle the situation.

"Any more groups like this one and Mr. Valence can take his show on down the road." Cleo flopped on the edge of the bed, pulled off her silver shoes, and removed the clip from her hair.

"I think this bunch is already fairly well motivated." Max watched her shake her hair free. He smiled the faint, enigmatic, utterly sensual smile of the man in the mirror. "And so am I."

"You've had a hard day."

"The hardest part is yet to come." He made his way across the room. When he was standing directly in front of her, he set aside his cane and framed her face with his hands. "But I think I'll rise to the occasion."

"Since when did you become the master of the double entendre?"

"Since I read chapter fifteen." Max eased her onto her back and came down on top of her. "Funniest chapter in *The Mirror.*"

"I'm glad you enjoyed it." He was warm and heavy and deliciously male. Cleo felt her tiredness slip away. It was replaced by a sense of deep anticipation.

Max looked down at her. His eyes darkened. "I enjoy everything about you, Cleo." His mouth covered hers.

She smiled slowly beneath his kiss. Then, rousing herself slightly, she pushed him gently off of her and got to her feet. She took off her glasses and put them down on the side table. Feeling wonderfully wicked, she started to unbutton her oxford cloth shirt.

"Did you read chapter sixteen, by any chance?" she asked.

"Another one of my favorites." Max rolled onto his back and folded his arms behind his head. The faint smile edging his mouth was full of lazy, seductive challenge. "Going to act it out for me?"

"If you like."

"I like." His voice was husky with desire. "Go slow. I don't want to miss a single word of the story."

Emboldened by the sensual encouragement that she saw in his eyes, Cleo slowly finished undoing her shirt. She let the edges hang over her breasts, concealing and revealing.

"Don't forget the mirror," Max said softly.

Cleo walked over to the mirror and looked at her slightly blurred reflection. Her hair was flowing free and wild around her shoulders. Her eyes were shadowed and mysterious. She looked intriguing and exotic, she thought.

She was the fantasy, but she was also the creator of the fantasy. She was both seducer and seduced. A sense of her own power as a woman flowed through her.

Max did not stir on the bed. Cleo knew he was watching her as she watched herself in the mirror, willing her to plunge them both deeper into the world behind the silvered glass.

Her fingers trembled a little as she undid the fastenings of her jeans. She eased the denim slowly down over her hips, leaving her filmy panties in place.

Her eyes never left the mirror as she stepped out of the jeans. Her shirttails fell to the top of her thighs, barely covering the curve of her buttocks. She could see the dark thatch of curling hair through the silk of her panties and knew that Max saw it, too. She sensed the smoldering wildfire of his desire and knew a sweet, singing joy that she could create this reaction in him. It gave her a heady sense of feminine power and at the same time made her feel infinitely generous.

"I'm on my knees," Max assured her softly.

She met his gaze in the mirror and knew that the power she was feeling was inextricably linked to the power in him. It could not be savored to the fullest unless it was in the presence of an equal and opposite force.

Max radiated his own power, and she was as bound by it as he was by the power in her.

"So am I," she whispered.

Max's mouth curved in a smile that made Cleo's knees weak. "That should make it even more interesting."

It also created a bond between herself and Max that was unlike anything she had ever known. She wondered if Max felt the strength of the connection.

Cleo raised her hands and removed her shirt with a gentle shrug. It pooled on the floor at her feet. She saw the rosy crests of her own breasts in the mirror and felt the heat of Max's gaze.

"Imagine that I'm touching you," Max said.

Cleo met his eyes in the glass. "But you aren't touching me."

"Look into the mirror and pretend that I'm standing right behind you. My hands are on your breasts. I can feel your nipples beneath my palms. They're small and firm, like raspberries."

"Raspberries?"

"Raspberries and cream. Very sweet," Max said. "Very fresh. I want to taste them. Can you feel my tongue on you?"

A wave of heat flowed through Cleo. Her nipples became hard and full. She closed her eyes, but the sensation only intensified. "Yes. I can feel your mouth on me."

"What does it feel like?"

Cleo concentrated. "Hot. Wet. Powerful."

"You make me powerful, Cleopatra. Where do you want me to touch you next?"

"Lower." Cleo opened her eyes again and stared at her slightly unfocused image. "I want your hands to go lower."

"There, between your legs?"

"Yes." She shuddered as she felt the coiling, tensing sensation radiating up through her.

"You feel so good, Cleo. Soft and warm." Max paused, as if he were actually exploring her with his fingers. "You're getting wet for me, aren't you?"

"Yes." Cleo felt the dampness between her thighs. She looked into the mirror with a knowing expression. "You're getting hard for me, aren't you?"

"I'm going out of my mind," Max said. "Put your hands on top of my fingers."

"Where are your fingers now?"

"Wherever you want them to be."

"Here," Cleo whispered. She brushed her fingers lightly over her silken panties. Then she drew them up across her belly. Slowly and deliberately she cupped her breasts and offered them to the man in the mirror.

"I think I've had about all the fantasy I can handle tonight," Max muttered. "I don't know about you, but I need the real thing very badly."

"So do I." Shivering with her need and excitement, Cleo turned away from the mirror and walked over to the bed. "There's something that I've been meaning to tell you, Max."

He looked up at her with eyes that were dark with soul-shattering desire. "What's that?"

"I love you."

Without a word, Max reached up and pulled her down on top of him. He captured her head in his hands and crushed her mouth against his own.

Cleo awoke hours later, aware that she was alone in the bed. She turned her head on the pillow and saw Max across the room. He loomed near the window, a ghostly shadow silhouetted against the blackness of the night. She knew from the angle of his body that he had both hands folded on top of the hawk on his cane.

"Max?"

"It's all right, Cleo. I'm just doing some thinking. Go back to sleep."

"I can't sleep with you prowling around the room," she grumbled. "Is something wrong?"

Max was silent for a moment. "I don't know."

She had never heard that tone in his voice. Cleo sat up quickly. "What is it, Max?"

"Remember the feeling you said you had that day when someone stalked you in the fog?"

"I remember it," she said. "I believe it's called a sense of impending disaster."

"It's also called having the sensation that someone just walked across your grave."

"My God, Max." Cleo was unnerved. "Is that how you feel right now?"

"Yes."

She wondered gloomily if her declaration of love earlier had caused this disturbing air of unease around him. He had never responded to her confession, although he had made love to her with an intensity that had shocked her senses.

It had been a risk. She had realized that at the time. Max was not accustomed to love, she reminded herself. There had been no way of knowing how he would react to being told that he was loved.

Cleo tortured herself on the altar of *perhaps*.

Perhaps being loved made Max feel trapped. Perhaps he did not want that kind of pressure. Perhaps he was ambivalent about being the one who was loved. Perhaps all he really wanted was to belong to the Robbins' Nest Inn family. Perhaps he only wanted Cleo because she could give him a home.

Perhaps he didn't really love her at all in the way she wanted to be loved.

Perhaps she had been the one who had screwed up tonight.

Cleo rested her chin on her updrawn knees. "What do you want to do?"

"I don't know. I've felt like this once or twice before in my life. There was trouble every time." Max turned away from the window. "I think I'll give O'Reilly a call."

"Now?" Cleo squinted at the clock. She was so relieved that he didn't seem to be dwelling on her unwelcome declaration of love that she had trouble following the conversation. "It's two in the morning."

"I know." Max reached for the phone, apparently having no trouble seeing its dark shape in the shadows. He picked up the receiver and then froze.

"Max?"

He put the receiver slowly back into the cradle and stared out across the cove. "Christ."

"Max, what is it?" Cleo scrambled out of bed and went to stand beside him. She squinted when she saw the strange orange glow in the distance. "What on earth is that?"

"Cosmic Harmony," Max said. "It's on fire." He turned abruptly away from the desk.

"Oh, my God." Panic welled up in Cleo. "Andromeda and Daystar and the others will be asleep. We've got to get to them." She whirled around, scrabbling about frantically for her glasses.

"Calm down, Cleo." Max was halfway across the room, heading toward the closet. "First, make sure the fire department is on its way."

"Yes. Yes, of course." Cleo grabbed the phone and realized she couldn't see well enough to punch out the emergency number. She fumbled with the light switch and finally found it. She pushed her glasses onto her nose with shaking fingers and stabbed at the phone.

"Forget it," Max said as he pulled on his shirt. "They've already got the word. Hear the sirens?"

Cleo listened to the shrill howl in the distance. "Thank God. Max, we've got to get over there."

"I'll go. You stay here." Max was already dressed. He yanked up his zipper.

"No, I'll come with you." She grabbed her jeans.

Max looked at her, eyes grim. "I want you to stay here."

"Why?"

"Because something is wrong."

"I know something is wrong. Cosmic Harmony is on fire." Cleo had her jeans on and was frantically trying to button her shirt. She realized she was shaking so much that she could barely find the buttonholes.

Max unlocked his leather carryall and removed an object from inside. Cleo froze when she saw that it was a revolver.

"Where did you get that?" she whispered as she watched him load it.

"I've been keeping it handy since that day someone stalked you in the fog." Max looked up. "Don't worry, I'll get rid of it when this is all over. I don't want to keep a gun in the house any more than you do."

"Oh, Max." Cleo shivered.

He moved to stand in front of her. He caught hold of her shoulder with one hand. "Listen to me, Cleo. I want you to stay here at the inn. Do you understand me? You'll be safe here. There are people downstairs. George is here. Sylvia is in her room. There are plenty of lights on in the place. *I want you here.*"

She stared at him, momentarily stunned by the implications of what he was saying. "You're worried about me? But it's Cosmic Harmony that's in trouble."

"I don't like this, Cleo. A fire at Cosmic Harmony at this particular time is too damn weird. I want you where I know you'll be safe while I check out what's happening on the other side of the cove." He released her and went to the door.

"But, Max . . ." Cleo raced after him.

"Stay here, Cleo." Max opened the door.

She instinctively reacted to the command in his voice. For an instant she was immobilized. By the time she could move a few seconds later, Max was already out in the hall. He closed the door in her face.

She heard the familiar squeak of the hall floorboard, and then he was gone.

Cleo made up her mind. She would go downstairs and awaken Sylvia. Together they could discuss the wisdom of going to Cosmic Harmony.

The phone rang on the desk.

Cleo jumped. She paused, her hand on the doorknob, and glanced at the instrument as if it had come alive. It rang again, an urgent summons that sent a thrill of fear down her spine. Reluctantly she went toward it and picked it up.

"Hello?"

"Cleo? It's O'Reilly. I'm on the car phone. I'm on my way to the inn."

"O'Reilly." Cleo felt weak with relief. "Max was just about to call you."

"That doesn't surprise me. Sometimes that guy is downright psychic when it comes to trouble. Is he there?"

"No, he just left. He's on his way to Cosmic Harmony. There's a fire over there."

"Damn it to hell," O'Reilly muttered. "You sure?"

"We can see the flames from here."

"Cleo, listen to me." O'Reilly's voice was suddenly cold and tense. "You stay put, do you hear me?"

Cleo grimaced. "That's what Max just said. Give me one good reason."

"Because something has finally turned up, and I don't like it at all."

"What is this all about, O'Reilly? I'm already scared enough tonight."

"Cleo, did you know your father was a witness at a murder trial two years before he died?"

"Sure, I knew about it." Cleo's fingers clenched around the phone. "He saw a man leaving a building where the police said a murder had been committed. He identified the man on the stand. What has that got to do with anything?"

"That man's name was Emile Wynn. He was a professional hit man. A couple of small-time hoods gave evidence against him, but it was your father's testimony linking him to the scene of the crime that tipped the case in the prosecution's favor. Wynn went to prison."

"I know. O'Reilly, what is this all about? Please hurry. I want to go see what's happening at Cosmic Harmony."

"Three months before your father and mother died, Wynn was released on a technicality."

"What?" Cleo stared at the flames on the other side of the cove. "We were never told about that."

"It wasn't exactly news. Happens every day. At any rate, Wynn disappeared almost immediately. The authorities believed that he had left the country. It was a logical assumption. But I'm beginning to think that Wynn may have changed his identity instead."

Cleo sank down onto the chair. "You think he may have killed my parents out of revenge?"

"It's a real possibility. Cleo, there were a couple of things about Wynn that were noted at the trial. The first was that he had a reputation, and that reputation meant everything to him. He was a fanatic about it."

Cleo rubbed her temple, trying to think. "What sort of reputation?"

"He never failed, and he never left any evidence. He was a professional, and he was obsessive about it."

"Sort of like Max," Cleo whispered.

"Max? What the hell are you talking about?"

"He never screws up."

"Yeah, well, Wynn screwed up that last time, and your father saw him. Now your father is dead. It's possible that Wynn killed him and then murdered your mother simply because she was on the scene at the time."

Cleo squeezed her eyes shut. She felt sick to her stomach. "No witnesses."

"Right. Wynn never left witnesses. Listen, Cleo, this is all conjecture at this point, but I think you may have triggered Wynn back into action when you hired Eberson last summer."

"No," Cleo said softly. "Oh, no."

"I think Eberson did some digging around and came up with some of the same conclusions that I've come up with. He may have been careless and accidentally alerted Wynn to the fact that someone was looking into the case again. Wynn may have decided that his new identity was at risk."

"You think Wynn killed Mr. Eberson, too?"

"I think it's a real possibility. Cleo, do you understand what I'm saying here?" O'Reilly asked tightly. "If I'm right, then you're Wynn's target now. Don't leave the inn."

"But what has all this got to do with the threats I've received concerning my book?"

"Wynn was noted for being very thorough. He did his research carefully. He preferred to make his jobs look like accidents or, as in the case of your father, suicide. He had a reputation for going to a lot of trouble to set up the scene of the hit."

"You think he did some checking on me, found out I'd written *The Mirror,* and decided to set up the scenario that would make people think I was murdered by a deranged reader?"

"He probably knows how much Cosmic Harmony means to you. I don't like the sound of this fire. A little too coincidental."

"That's what Max said."

"Max is on his way to the cove now?"

"Yes."

"Good. You stay put, Cleo. Don't step foot outside the inn until he gets back."

Cleo gave up trying to argue. "All right. I'll go downstairs and wake Sylvia. She and I and Sammy will circle the wagons and wait for the men to do their thing."

"I'll be there in another hour or so." O'Reilly paused briefly. "Tell Sylvia I'm on my way, will you?"

"She'll be waiting for you. We'll all be waiting."

"That's nice to know," O'Reilly said. "Been a long time since I had anyone waiting for me. Listen, I've got to get off the phone now. I'm going to call your police chief. I want to let him know what's going on."

"We've only got a one-man force, O'Reilly. Harry will be out at Cosmic Harmony right now."

"Hell, that's the trouble with small towns. Okay, sit tight. Max and I will handle everything."

Cleo put down the phone.

Her parents had been killed. Murdered. Shot by a cold-blooded hit man.

But all she felt was relief.

As horrible as the truth was, it was infinitely preferable to the explanation that the authorities had insisted upon all these years. Her father had not gone mad and killed her mother and himself. Her parents' love for each other had not been tainted by a foul sickness in her father's mind. The bond between them had been pure and clean, wholesome and steadfast. Just like her love for Max.

In spite of the situation, Cleo felt as if a dark weight had been lifted from her soul.

She rose slowly and started for the door. She wanted to talk to Sylvia.

The flames in the distance caught her attention once more. She paused to glance out the window. It was impossible to tell if it was the main lodge that was on fire or one of the smaller buildings.

The hall floorboard squeaked.

Cleo went perfectly still.

I have a reputation to maintain.

Her own words to Sylvia a few hours earlier came back to her. *Does it strike you that Max and Herbert T. Valence have something in common?*

A reputation.

A reputation.

Cleo leaped for the door. It opened before she could lock it. Herbert T. Valence stepped into the room. He had a pistol in his hand. There was something odd about the shape of the barrel, Cleo realized. Perhaps that was what a silencer looked like.

"Well, Ms. Robbins." Valence smiled his thin, humorless little smile. "We meet properly at last. Allow me to introduce myself. My real name is Emile Wynn. Perhaps you've heard of me. Your father ruined me professionally."

Cleo tried to speak and realized that she could not find her voice. She took a deep breath, the same kind she took when she meditated. She had to say something, anything, in order to break the paralysis.

"You bastard." Her voice was only a squeak. But rage swept through her without warning, driving out the fear. *"You killed my parents."*

Valence frowned as he closed the door behind himself. "I had no choice. Your father's testimony destroyed my reputation. I could not rest until he had paid for it. A man's reputation is everything, Ms. Robbins."

"My mother . . . ," Cleo began in a choked voice.

"Had to go, too, I'm afraid. I plan my little dramas with exquisite care, and I had determined that a murder-suicide seemed most appropriate for that particular situation."

"You've come after me because you knew I'd find you sooner or later," Cleo said.

Valence looked at her with a strangely troubled gaze. "You hired a second-rate investigator last summer. He was a very unprofessional sort, Ms. Robbins. I realized almost immediately that he was nosing around, and I took appropriate steps. But I also knew then that I had to do something about you."

"In other words, you knew I might decide to hire someone else, and next time I might get my money's worth." Cleo took a step back.

Valence did not appear to know that O'Reilly had already learned who he was. Whatever happened here tonight, she must not betray O'Reilly or Max. Valence would surely go after them next.

"Unfortunately it became clear that you were going to be a nuisance, Ms. Robbins." Valence followed her movement with the pistol. "But I must confess that one thing puzzled me. If you had suspicions about your parents' death, why did you wait nearly four years before you hired an investigator?"

"It took me all that time to recover to a point where I could deal with it." Cleo had never known such primitive rage. It consumed her. She was no longer afraid of Valence. "You destroyed my family, you stupid, crazy little man."

"Don't call me crazy." Valence's eyes glittered with an evil light. "Those idiot psychiatrists in prison called me crazy. But they were wrong. You're all wrong. I was a professional with a perfect track record. I never made mistakes. I never failed. Your father destroyed my reputation."

"He didn't destroy it. You screwed up."

"Don't say that." Valence took another step forward. "It's not true. I never screw up, as you so crudely put it, Ms. Robbins."

Cleo edged back toward the mirror. The only defense she could think of at the moment was to keep him talking. The man was insane. It occurred to her that a genuinely professional hit man would have killed her by now. "You're going to try to make people think I was murdered by some deranged person who hated my book, aren't you?"

Valence scowled. "Even if I did not have my personal reasons for terminating you, you deserve to be punished for writing *The Mirror.*"

He was even nuttier than she had first thought, Cleo decided. "Why do you say that?"

"You are the author of a pornographic novel, Ms. Robbins," Valence chided with the outrage of an evangelist. "You're no better than a whore. You write filth, and every decent person knows it."

"Decent person?" She looked at him in disbelief. "You consider yourself a decent person?"

"I am a clean man, Ms. Robbins." Valence's fingers flexed around the grip of the pistol. "My mother made certain that I did not dirty myself in the gutter of sexuality. I am proud to say that I have not had carnal knowledge of a woman since she showed me how obscene the act was."

"Let me guess. You're the product of a dysfunctional family, right?" Cleo did not know if taunting Valence would keep him talking or push him over the edge, but she couldn't think of anything else to do.

"My mother was a pure woman," Valence said savagely. "And she kept me pure."

"By keeping you for herself? I'll bet those prison shrinks had a field day with that, didn't they?"

"Shut up," Valence snarled. "You created a work of filth. No one will think it strange that some clean person took it upon himself to punish you."

Cleo realized with shock that Valence believed what he was saying. "You've got a lot of nerve condemning me for writing erotica. You're a hit man, for God's sake. What does that make you?"

"It makes me a professional." Valence drew a length of red ribbon from his jacket pocket. "A professional with only one stain upon my spotless reputation. But I will soon rub out that stain."

He started toward her. Cleo saw the glint of the wire entwined in the ribbon. She knew that he was going to put it around her neck. The same way the man in the mirror put the ribbon around the throat of the woman in *The Mirror*.

Valence was going to strangle her with the scarlet ribbon.

She opened her mouth to scream, knowing Valence would probably shoot her before she could make herself heard. Perhaps if she made enough of a racket before she died he would not escape undetected.

At that instant the lights flickered and went out.

"Goddamn it," Valence shouted in intense agitation. "Don't move. I'm warning you."

Cleo ignored him and dove for the floor. Valence was as blind as she was, and she knew the room far better than he did. She crawled toward the door, knowing it would take several seconds for Valence's eyes to adjust to the sudden darkness.

A soft, hissing sound overhead told her that Valence had fired the silenced pistol. The bullet splintered wood.

At the same instant the floorboard outside the door squeaked. A draft of air from the hallway told her that someone had opened the door and entered the room. She looked up and thought she could see a dark shadow moving against the deeper shadows of the attic.

Max.

Her hand touched the base of the mirror stand.

Another soft, hissing sigh seared the air in the room. Cleo surged to her feet, grabbed the mirror and its frame, and hurled it toward the spot where she knew Valence was standing.

The mirror struck something solid and fell to the floor. Glass shattered. Valence cried out, revealing his location.

The bright rays of the powerful flashlight that Cleo always kept behind the front desk snapped into life. They pinned Valence in a beam of blinding light.

"Get away from me," Valence screamed. He held out one hand as if in supplication, aimed the pistol toward the source of the light, and pulled the trigger.

The crack of an unsilenced revolver shot rang out at the same instant. Valence slumped to the floor, motionless.

The flashlight fell to the floor, its beam still illuminating Valence's body.

"Max," Cleo shouted as she dashed across the room. "Max, answer me."

"Shit," Max said. "The same damn leg."

Nineteen

Valence was dead, but the following morning Max decided he was still pissed at him and would be for a long time. Every time Max felt the lancing pain from the new stitches in his thigh, he was reminded of how close he had come to losing Cleo. Rage and fear had surged through him last night as he had made his way up the stairs to the attic. The damned cane had never felt so clumsy in his hand. Trying to manage the revolver and the flashlight had been a difficult task. He had never resented his bad leg so much.

But Cleo was safe now, and Max intended to keep her that way even if he had to put a leash on her.

Ensconced in a bed in the local community hospital, Max studied the ring of anxious faces gathered around him. He was still not accustomed to having people fuss over him, he reflected. He wondered if he would ever get to the point where he would take such concern on his behalf for granted. He doubted it. When you had spent most of your life looking for something, you weren't likely to treat it casually when you finally stumbled into it.

The whole family, with the exception of Ben and Trisha, who were still blissfully unaware of events, was hovering at Max's bedside. Cleo had insisted on spending what was left of the night in a chair in his hospital room. The others, who had been sent home by the staff a few hours earlier, had crowded back in right after breakfast.

The nurses had already complained twice that there was no room for them to carry out their duties. The doctor, a smiling woman in her mid-fifties, had told Max that it looked like he was in good hands.

"Does your leg hurt real, real bad?" Sammy clutched Lucky Ducky and gazed at Max with wide-eyed concern.

Max considered the matter closely. Getting shot had been a definite screwup. When he'd gotten a fix on Valence's location, thanks to Cleo, he'd switched on the flashlight with the intention of blinding Valence.

Knowing that Valence would fire toward the beam of light, Max had taken pains to hold the light well off to the side while he aimed his own weapon. Unfortunately, crazy as he was in some ways, Valence had still been enough of a cool-headed professional to shoot to the left of the light. Most people, after all, were right-handed. It was a safe bet that whoever had entered the room would be holding a gun in his right hand and the flashlight in his left. If that person was thinking, he would be holding the flashlight as far from his body as possible.

Valence had been right on all counts. Max had taken the bullet in his left thigh. He would have another scar two inches away from the first one. The doctor had assured him that it was only a flesh wound. Unfortunately, that didn't make the stitches any more comfortable.

"It doesn't hurt real, real bad," Max said. "Just sort of bad."

"Hey, could have been worse." O'Reilly grinned. "Could have been the other leg this time, and then you would have had to use two canes."

"You're a real ray of sunshine, O'Reilly." As it was Max knew he was going to be on crutches for a while. He looked at Cleo, who was standing at the head of the bed. She had such a fierce grip on his hand that the ring on her finger was leaving an imprint on his skin. It felt good. "You're sure you're okay?"

"For the hundredth time, I'm okay." She leaned down and kissed his cheek. "Thanks to you."

"You're a hero, Max," Andromeda told him proudly. She poured some of her special tea out of a thermos she had brought with her. "The local newspaper wants to do a feature on how you rescued Cleo from that horrid Mr. Valence."

Max grimaced as he took the mug of tea from Andromeda. "I don't want to talk to any reporters."

"It's just Bertie Jennings from the *Harmony Cove Herald,"* Daystar assured him. "Don't worry. I've already told him that he can't talk to you until you're back on your feet."

"Thanks." Max scowled. "Maybe by that time he won't want to do the story." A thought occurred to him. "How much damage did the fire do?"

"The meditation center is gone, but the lodge is fine. So are the guest quarters," Daystar said. "We're in good shape, considering what might have happened. But, then, O'Reilly says that destroying Cosmic Harmony was not really Valence's goal. He just wanted to use the fire as a means of causing confusion."

"Valence set the fire using timed fuses so that he could get back to the inn before the blaze started," O'Reilly explained.

"Poor Nolan," Cleo said. "To think we once suspected him of being behind the incidents."

Max did not like the sound of "*poor* Nolan," but he nobly chose to ignore the reference. He could afford to be generous, he told himself. He had Cleo. All Hildebrand had was a budding career in politics, to which he was more than welcome as far as Max was concerned.

"Valence knew a fire at Cosmic Harmony would create chaos not just there but also at the inn," Sylvia said.

"He'd stayed at the inn often enough to know how important Cosmic Harmony was to me," Cleo agreed.

"He obviously figured one of two things would happen when the fire was discovered," Max said. "The first possibility was that Cleo would rush to the scene. If that happened, he no doubt intended to follow and try to get at her in the confusion and darkness while everyone concentrated on the fire."

"The other possibility was that you would leave her safely behind at the inn while you went to see what was happening," O'Reilly concluded.

Max swore softly. "It was a logical plan. Either way Cleo would be vulnerable for the first time since that day Valence had stalked her in the fog."

"He must have realized that Max was keeping an eye on you, Cleo, because of the incidents that had been occurring," Sylvia said. "It was no secret, especially after O'Reilly started talking to people in town about them."

"That's right," Daystar said. "Valence knew he would somehow have to separate Max and Cleo. Trying to get at Cleo while Max was protecting her would have complicated things no end for him."

"He was very proud of his research and planning," Cleo whispered. "And absolutely obsessive about his reputation."

Max felt the shudder that went through her. He tightened his grip on her hand. She smiled tremulously at him. The love in her eyes was bright and clear, and he knew it would last him his whole life.

No one had ever looked at him the way Cleo did. Last night when she had told him that she loved him, he had been so shaken by his good fortune that he had been unable to sort out his emotions. He had only known that he wanted her more than ever, that he had to protect her. She was the most important thing in his world.

This morning when he had awakened to find Cleo sitting beside his bed, he had taken one look at her and finally understood what had happened to him.

"When did it hit you that the fire might be a diversion?" Andromeda asked.

Max pulled his thoughts back to the subject at hand. "When I was about a quarter of a mile down the road. I turned around and drove straight back to the inn. But I had a feeling that something had really gone bad. I started to call Cleo on the car phone, but O'Reilly called me first."

"He was just pulling back into the parking lot when I reached him," O'Reilly said. "I told him what I had told Cleo about a psychotic killer who had a thing about his reputation and who always planned his hits with military precision. The last thing I heard Max say before he hung up was that he knew who the guy was."

"I came to the same conclusion Cleo did," Max said quietly. "Valence was the obvious suspect. He'd been in and out of Harmony Cove all winter giving his damn seminars. He'd had plenty of opportunity to see how things worked at the inn. Plenty of time to set things up."

"We didn't think of him when we drew up that list of guests who had been at the inn the night the ribbon was left on my pillow," Cleo said ruefully.

Max exchanged glances with O'Reilly. "I put him on the list," he said.

"You did?" Cleo was startled.

O'Reilly made a face. "Valence was on the list, and I checked him out, but there were no red flags. The guy had a nice, clean background. Everything was in order." He held up his hands. "What can I say? Valence was a pro."

Max looked at Cleo. "All I could think of was that I had left you alone. I knew that group of seminar attendees had all had too much to drink and were probably sound asleep. When I reached the lobby, George was also asleep, just as he had been when I'd left. I went to Valence's room, and it was empty."

"So he came to my room," Sylvia said. "He woke me up and told me to run down to the basement and throw the main circuit breaker while he climbed the stairs to the attic."

"I was hoping that having the lights go out without warning would throw Valence off stride for at least a few seconds," Max explained. "I recalled how he'd reacted that time when he lost power during one of his seminars."

"I remember that," Sylvia said thoughtfully. "He really got upset, didn't he? It disrupted his carefully orchestrated seminar."

"Earlier this evening when he checked in, he made a point of saying that there were no storms expected this weekend," Cleo mused. "He probably had planned everything so that there would be no rain to put out the fire too quickly at Cosmic Harmony or cause a power failure."

"A real thorough kind of guy," O'Reilly mused. He put his arm around Sylvia. "But not real flexible."

"I think that Valence had gotten so crazy that every little alteration in his schedule threw him into a turmoil," Cleo said.

A commotion out in the hall made Max and everyone else in the crowded room glance toward the door.

"I'm afraid you can't go in there, sir," a nurse said in a loud, authoritative voice. "Mr. Fortune already has far too many visitors."

"I came all this way to see Fortune, and I damn well intend to see him," a man answered in a voice that was louder and more commanding. "I have business with him."

"But he's been seriously injured," the nurse said.

"He's used to it."

"Just what I needed," Max muttered as a familiar figure came through the door. "Another well-wisher. What the hell do you want, Dennison? I'm not supposed to have any visitors. Just family."

Dennison Curzon had the same autocratic attitude Jason had had. He also had the same silver hair and the strongly etched features that characterized the rest of the Curzon family. But his eyes lacked the penetrating, analytical intelligence that had characterized Jason's gaze.

Dennison swept the faces of the small group gathered around Max and dismissed them all. He glowered at Max.

"What's going on here, Fortune? I hear you've gotten yourself shot again."

"I'm recovering nicely, thank you," Max said. "Dennison Curzon, meet the family."

"Family?" Dennison's forehead furrowed in confusion and annoyance. "What family? You don't have a family."

"He does now," Cleo said quietly. She kept her grip on Max's hand as she surveyed Dennison with a curious, searching look. "Jason was your brother?"

"Yes, he was." Dennison switched his attention briefly to her. "Who are you?"

"My fiancée," Max said before Cleo could respond. "Congratulate me, Dennison. Cleo and I are going to be married."

Dennison ignored the announcement and, with typical Curzon single-mindedness, zeroed in on his main target. "Listen, Max, we've got to talk." He cast an irritated glance at Cleo and the others. "Do you think we could have some privacy around here?"

"No," Cleo said.

Nobody made a move toward the door.

Max grinned at Dennison. "Guess not."

"What the hell?" Dennison took a closer look at Cleo. "Who did you say you were?"

"I told you, she's my fiancée," Max said.

"I am also Max's employer," Cleo said crisply.

"The hell you are." Dennison stared at her. "Fortune works for Curzon International."

"No, he doesn't," Cleo said. "Not anymore."

"He works for Cleo," Sammy announced.

Dennison scowled. "Now, see here, I am Dennison Curzon of Curzon International. Max Fortune has worked for my company for twelve years."

"I believe he resigned when your brother died," Cleo murmured. "He now works for me."

"Quite right," Daystar said in her no-nonsense way. "Max has been on the payroll of Robbins' Nest Inn for some time now. He's doing an excellent job."

"Yes, indeed. He's one of the family," Andromeda said.

"Bullshit." Dennison looked at Max. "I don't know what game you're playing here, Fortune, but I need you at Curzon. My daughter and that damned husband of hers took over my board of directors yesterday."

"Kim will do a good job with Curzon," Max said. "She's got what it takes. My advice is don't fight her."

"I'll fight anyone who tries to take over my company. I've waited all these years to take command, and I'm going to do it. I want you in my corner. Let's cut the bullshit, Fortune. Name your price."

"For what?" Max asked.

"For coming back to Curzon as my personal troubleshooter." Dennison narrowed his eyes. "I'll give you the same deal my brother did plus a ten percent increase in salary and bonuses. In return I want your guarantee that you report to me and to me alone."

"I've already got a job," Max said.

"All right." Dennison's expression was taut. "If you come back, I'll consider giving you that seat on the board that Jason wanted you to have."

"No, thanks. I seem to have developed an aptitude for plumbing and home repairs," Max said.

"You heard him," Cleo said. "He doesn't want to work for you. Mr. Curzon, I think you had better leave. Max has had a very rough night, and he needs his rest." She turned to Max. "Don't you need your rest?"

"I need my rest," Max said equably.

"He needs his rest," Sylvia said.

Andromeda and Daystar nodded in agreement.

O'Reilly looked as though he was going to explode with laughter at any second.

Dennison rounded on Cleo. "Don't you dare try to kick me out of here, young lady. Max Fortune belongs to me."

"He most certainly does not." Cleo released Max's hand and took a step toward Dennison. "He belongs to me. And to the rest of us." She looked around at the others. "Isn't that right?"

"Oh, yes," Andromeda murmured. "No question about it."

"He's one of the family," Sammy said loudly. "You can't have him."

Daystar glowered at Dennison. "I'm afraid you're wasting your time and ours with all this nonsense, Mr. Curzon. Why don't you leave?"

"Nonsense? You call this nonsense?" Dennison turned on her with an air of appalled outrage. "Are you out of your mind, lady? Curzon is a multinational corporation. Do you have any idea how much Fortune can earn in a year working for me?"

"No," Daystar said honestly. "But I don't see that it matters."

"Believe me, it matters," Dennison snarled. "Curzon has made Fortune a wealthy man. He can become even wealthier if he comes back to work for me."

"Piffle," Andromeda said. "Max already has a perfectly good job at Robbins' Nest Inn. Isn't that right, Max?"

"Right," said Max.

Dennison looked at him. "This is a joke, isn't it?"

O'Reilly grinned. "Face it, Curzon, it's not a joke. You can't match the benefits that Max has found in his new job."

"Can't match them?" Dennison glared at O'Reilly. "I can pay Fortune enough in one year to enable him to buy that damned inn."

"The man hasn't got a clue," O'Reilly said cheerfully.

Sammy clung very tightly to Lucky Ducky as he gazed up at Dennison. "Go away."

"Yes," Cleo said. "Go away."

"Drive carefully," Andromeda said brightly.

"You're becoming a pest, Mr. Curzon," Daystar said. "I do wish you would take yourself off."

Dennison looked at Max with disbelief and desperation. "Think about this, Fortune. There's a good chance I can talk Kimberly into leaving Winston. I don't think she's been all that happy with him lately. You and my daughter would make a hell of a combination."

"You didn't think so three years ago," Max said. "And you know something? You were right. I owe you for talking Kimberly out of the engagement. In exchange, I'm going to give you some good advice. Don't get in her way now. She'll be the best thing that's ever happened to Curzon International."

"She's taking over, don't you understand?"

"I understand," Max said. "And you're all going to get even richer with her at the helm. If you behave yourself, maybe she'll give you some grandkids."

"That sounds lovely." Andromeda smiled kindly at Dennison. "Wouldn't you love some grandchildren?"

Dennison stared at her and then looked at Max with a baffled expression. "You're serious about this, aren't you? You aren't just playing a game in order to jack up your price?"

"I'm serious, all right," Max said. "You couldn't meet my price in a million years. Go away, Dennison."

Cleo scowled at him. "You are becoming extremely offensive, Mr. Curzon. Only family is supposed to be in this room until the regular visiting hours. Please leave, or I will summon someone from the hospital staff to deal with you."

Dennison gave her one last bewildered glare, and then he turned around and stomped out of the room.

An acute silence descended.

"I want to go home," Max said.

Cleo awoke at dawn the next morning. It wasn't the gray, wet light of the new day that had brought her up out of her slumbers. It was the knowledge that Max was not in bed beside her.

Worried, Cleo sat up abruptly. "Max?"

There was no sign of him. Cleo glanced across the attic room and saw that his crutches were missing. She frowned. Max was still getting accustomed to using the crutches. She didn't like the idea of his navigating the stairs without her assistance.

She heard the floorboard squeak on the other side of the door just as she was about to push aside the covers and go in search of the invalid.

The attic door opened softly, and Max maneuvered himself cautiously into the room. He was wearing a pair of trousers and nothing else. Andromeda had opened the seam on the left pant leg to accommodate the bandage on Max's thigh.

Max concentrated intently, his attention on the floor as he angled the crutches into position. The stem of a white rose was clenched between his teeth.

Cleo stared at the rose, a great joy welling up inside her. *Red for seduction; white for love.*

"Max?" she breathed, hardly daring to believe what she was seeing.

Max looked up quickly. "You're supposed to be asleep," he mumbled around the rose stem.

Cleo smiled brilliantly. She recalled the last chapter of her book very clearly. The man in the mirror, freed at last, had awakened the narrator with a single white rose. Seduction had been transformed into love.

"I'd rather be awake for this, if you don't mind," Cleo whispered.

Max started across the room. His eyes never left Cleo. "I don't mind."

Out of the corner of her eye, Cleo saw something yellow. She glanced down and noticed that Sammy had left Lucky Ducky lying on the floor after paying a visit to Max's bedside last night.

Cleo's eyes widened in alarm as she saw Max's right crutch come down on top of the toy.

"Max, *look out.*"

It was too late. The crutch skittered off the rounded edges of the rubber duck and went out from under Max.

"Hell." Max made a valiant effort to steady himself with the left crutch, but it was hopeless.

Max unclenched his teeth from around the stem of the rose and let it fall.

"That damned duck," Max said as he crashed to the floor.

With a cry of dismay, Cleo leaped out of bed and rushed to his side. "Are you all right? Max, Max, speak to me."

Flat on his back, Max glared at her. "Everything's just ducky."

"Do you think your stitches have come undone?" Cleo bent over his bandaged thigh. "Maybe we should get you to the clinic."

"Forget the leg. Cleo, I love you."

Cleo's hand rested on his leg. Tears misted her eyes. "I'm so glad."

She threw herself down on top of him, careful not to hurt his injured thigh. Max's arms closed tightly around her, holding her close.

"I should have known right from the start," Max said into Cleo's hair.

"It's not your fault you didn't recognize love when you found it," Cleo said against his chest. "You haven't had enough of it to know it when you see it."

"I know it now," Max said, his voice laced with raw wonder. He abruptly went very still.

"Max?" Cleo raised her head and looked down at him in concern. "Are you sure you're all right?"

Max started to smile. "Look up, Cleo."

"At what?"

"At Jason's seascapes."

Cleo craned her head and stared up at the two seascapes hanging on the wall. "What about them?"

"There's something strange about the frames. I never noticed it when I looked at the pictures before, but from this perspective you can see that the frames are too wide." Max levered himself up into a sitting position and reached for one of the fallen crutches.

"What are you doing?"

"Help me get one of those things off the wall."

"I'll handle it." Cleo got to her feet and hefted one of the seascapes. She took it down off the wall and carried it across the room to the bed.

Max made his way over to the desk, opened one of the drawers, and removed the screwdriver he had bought at the Harmony Cove hardware store. "Ben was right. You never know when you're going to need a good screwdriver."

Max crossed the room to the bed, sat down beside the seascape, and went to work on the back of the frame with the screwdriver.

Cleo watched, fascinated. "Max, do you really think that Jason . . . ?"

"Hid the Luttrells behind his seascapes?" Max's mouth curved with satisfaction as he undid the last of the screws. "Yes."

He lifted the back of the frame and set it aside. Then, with great reverence, he removed a white, flat board out of the frame. There was a note attached to it. Max opened it.

> Now that you've found this one, Max, you know where to find the others. I never could paint worth a damn, and I figured that sooner or later you'd wonder why I had bothered with these lousy seascapes. The Luttrells are only a portion of your inheritance, son. I trust you found the rest of it at Robbins' Nest Inn. How does it feel to have a family of your own?
>
> Love,
> Jason

Max turned the board over. Cleo looked at the canvas that was fastened to the other side.

It was a dark, elegantly savage painting full of swirling shapes and abstract tension, and yet it was not entirely bleak. Even to Cleo's untrained eye, it was a work of art perfectly suited to Max. The painting seemed to radiate both the potential for despair and the possibility of love.

Cleo smiled softly. "Good old Lucky Ducky. I wonder why Jason went to the trouble of hiding the paintings if he wanted you to have them."

Max glanced up from the Luttrell. His eyes were brilliant. "Jason wanted me to find something else first. Something that was a lot more important than any painting."

"Did you?" Cleo asked.

"Yes," Max said with absolute certainty. He smiled, his love for her plain to read in his eyes. "I did."

Absolutely, Positively

For Edna and J. L. Krentz,
With love and affection

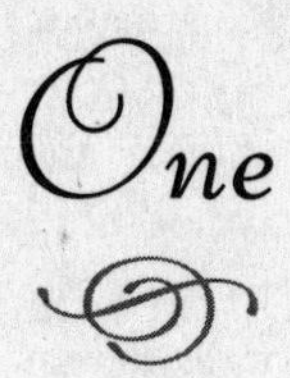

Harry Stratton Trevelyan allowed himself few certainties in life, but during the past month he had become absolutely, positively sure of one thing. He wanted Molly Abberwick. Tonight he intended to ask her to have an affair with him.

This was a major decision for Harry. But then, most decisions were major for him.

The opening sentence of his latest book could have served as his personal motto: *Absolute certainty is the greatest of all illusions.*

As a general rule he applied that principle to his work and to his personal life. A man had only one reliable defense against illusions in both arenas, and that defense was caution. Harry made it a habit to be very, very careful.

Harry's past as well as his current occupation combined to ensure that he viewed the world with what some people called a marked degree of cynicism. He preferred to call it intelligent skepticism, but the result was the same.

The good news was that he rarely got conned, scammed, or fleeced.

The bad news was that a lot of people thought that he was cold-blooded. That, however, did not bother Harry.

By training and inclination, Harry demanded hard, solid proof in virtually every arena of his life. He had a passion for it. He preferred a logical approach to all things.

Once in a while, however, his finely tuned brain seemed to skip the usual methodical steps and leaped straight to an insight so shatteringly perceptive that it sometimes scared him. *Really* scared him. Nevertheless, for the most part, he took satisfaction in exercising his razor-sharp intelligence. He knew that he was much better at thinking than he was at handling relationships.

Thus far he had moved slowly and carefully toward his goal of beginning an affair with Molly. He did not intend to make the mistake he had made with his ex-fiancée. He would not become involved with another woman in a desperate attempt to seek an answer to the dark questions about himself that he could not, would not put into words.

He would settle for sex and companionship this time.

"Will that be all, Harry?"

Harry glanced at his part-time housekeeper. Ginny Rondell, a plump, pleasant-faced woman in her late forties, hovered on the other side of the long granite counter that separated the kitchen from the living room of the high-rise condominium.

"Yes, thank you, Ginny," Harry said. "An excellent meal, by the way."

Molly Abberwick, seated on the black sofa facing the wall of windows, smiled warmly at Ginny. "It was fantastic."

Ginny's broad face suffused with pleasure. "Thank you, Ms. Abberwick. The tea is ready, Dr. Trevelyan. Are you sure you don't want me to serve it?"

"Thanks, I'll handle it," Harry said.

"Yes, well, I'll say good night, then." Ginny came around the edge of the long counter and trundled toward the green-marble-tiled hall.

Harry waited with an unfamiliar sense of gathering impatience as Ginny opened a closet door and removed her purse. He waited while she put on her sweater. At last she let herself out through the front door.

An acute silence fell on the condominium.

Alone at last, Harry thought, wryly amused at his own eagerness. He hadn't felt this way in a long, long time. He could not even recall the last occasion. It had no doubt occurred at some point in his youth. He was thirty-six, but he had been feeling very ancient for the past eight years.

"I'll get the tea," he said as he got to his feet.

Molly nodded. There was an expectant look in her wide, sea green eyes. Harry hoped the expression boded well for his plans for the evening. He had turned off *both* phones for the night, an unheard-of course of action. Ginny had been astounded.

True, he generally switched off the business line in the evenings or when he was engaged in intensive study, but he never threw the switch on the family line when he was at home. He was always available to both sides of his feuding clans.

Harry got to his feet and walked to the granite counter. He picked up the tray containing the pot of tea and two cups. He had ordered the very expensive Darjeeling after having made it his business to discover Molly's personal preference. No sugar. No milk. Harry was good with details.

Covertly, he studied Molly as he carried the tea tray to the glass table in front of the sofa. There was definitely an undercurrent of excitement stirring in her. He could almost feel it lapping at him in tiny waves. His own anticipation surged.

Molly sat somewhat primly on the sofa, her attention caught by the lights of the Pike Place Market down below and the dark expanse of Elliott Bay. It was summer in the Northwest, and the days seemed to last forever. But it was after ten o'clock, and night had finally arrived. Along with it had come Harry's opportunity to begin an affair with his client.

This was not the first time Molly had seen the sights from Harry's twenty-fifth-floor downtown condo. He worked out of his home, and Molly had come here often enough on business during the past month. But this was the first time she had ever seen the lights at night.

"You have an incredible view from up here," she said as he set the tea tray down on the coffee table.

"I like it." Harry sat down beside her and reached for the teapot. Out of the corner of his eye he saw her smile. He took that to be another good sign.

Molly had a very expressive face. Harry could have watched her for hours. The angle of her brows reminded him of a bird on the wing. The image was a good metaphor for Molly. A man who wanted to catch her would have to be very fast and very smart. Harry told himself that he was both.

Tonight Molly was dressed in a businesslike, moss green pantsuit complete with a one-button jacket and softly pleated trousers. She wore a pair of demure, suede pumps. Harry had never before paid much attention to women's feet, but he found himself captivated by Molly's. They were perfectly arched with delicate ankles. All in all, a marvel of engineering design, he thought.

The rest of Molly was well designed, too.

Having given the matter a great deal of close consideration in recent days, Harry had finally concluded that Molly was slender, but definitely not skinny. She practically radiated health and vitality. He was extremely healthy, himself. He had the reflexes of a cat, and he actually felt turbocharged when Molly was in the vicinity.

There was an appealing roundness to certain portions of Molly's anatomy. The jacket of the pantsuit skimmed over high breasts that Harry knew would fit nicely into his hand. The pleats of the trousers flared to encompass full, womanly hips.

Although he found her figure eminently interesting, it was Molly's vibrant face that commanded Harry's most serious attention. She was spectacular, he thought with satisfaction. Not spectacularly beautiful, just spectacular. She was unique. Special. Different.

Intelligence shimmered in her green eyes. Harry acknowledged that he was a sucker for brains in a woman. There was strength and fortitude and character in the delicate yet determined lines of her nose and high cheekbones. Her honey brown hair had a mind of its own. It exploded around her head in a short, thick, frothy mass. The style emphasized the tilt of her fey eyes.

It occurred to Harry that with those eyes, Molly could have made her living as a carnival fortune-teller. It would have been a simple matter for her to convince any likely mark that she could see straight into his past, present, and future.

The realization sparked a flash of renewed caution in Harry. The last thing he needed was a woman who could see deeply into his soul. That way lay madness.

For the space of perhaps three heartbeats he seriously questioned the wisdom of getting involved with a woman whose gaze held such a disconcerting degree of perception. He did not do well with women who were inclined to probe his psyche. His disastrous experience with his ex-fiancée had proved that much. On the other hand, he had no patience with bimbos.

For a few seconds Harry let his future hang in the balance as he contemplated his next move.

Molly gave him a questioning smile, revealing two slightly crooked front teeth. There was something endearing about those two teeth, Harry thought.

He took a deep breath and consigned his qualms to hell with a breathtaking recklessness that should have alarmed him. It would be okay this time, he told himself. Molly was a businesswoman, not a psychologist. She would take a rational, levelheaded approach to what he was about to offer. She would not be inclined to dissect him or try to analyze him.

"I would like to discuss something with you." Harry poured tea into her cup with calm deliberation.

"Yes." Molly gave a little shriek, made a small fist, and pumped it wildly. Her eyes glowed. "Hot damn, I knew it."

Harry looked up, startled. "You did?"

She grinned as she picked up her teacup. "It's about time, if you don't mind my saying so."

Enthusiasm was a good thing in a woman, Harry assured himself. "Uh, no. No, I don't mind. I just hadn't realized that we were on the same wavelength here."

"You know what they say about great minds thinking alike."

Harry smiled. "Yes."

"I realized when you invited me to dinner tonight that this was a special occasion, not an ordinary business consultation."

"Right."

"I knew that you had finally made a decision."

"I have, as a matter of fact." He eyed her closely. "I've given the matter a great deal of thought."

"Naturally. If I've learned one thing about you during the past few weeks, it's that you give everything a great deal of thought. So you finally concluded that Duncan Brockway's grant proposal is worth funding. About time."

Harry blanked for a split second. "Brockway's proposal?"

Molly's eyes sparkled with satisfaction. "I knew you'd approve that one. I just *knew* it. It's so original. So intriguing. And the potential is absolutely unlimited."

Harry narrowed his eyes. "This has nothing to do with Brockway's grant proposal. I wanted to talk about another matter."

The excitement in her eyes dimmed slightly. "You did look it over, didn't you?"

"Brockway's proposal? Yes, I did. It's no good. We can go into the details later, if you like. But right now I want to discuss something more important."

Molly looked honestly baffled. "What's more important than Duncan Brockway's grant proposal?"

Harry set his teacup down with great precision. "Our relationship."

"Our *what?*"

"I think you heard me."

Molly's cup crashed back into its saucer. "That does it, I've had it."

Harry stilled. "What's wrong?"

"You have the nerve to ask me what's wrong? After telling me that you're not going to approve Duncan's proposal?"

"Molly, I'm trying to conduct an intelligent conversation here. However, it seems to be falling apart. Now, about our relationship—"

"Our relationship?" Molly erupted from the sofa with the force of a small volcano. "I'll tell you about our relationship. It's a complete, unmitigated disaster."

"I wasn't aware that we even had one yet."

"We most certainly do. But it's ending here. Now. Tonight. I refuse to continue to pay for your services as a consultant, Harry Trevelyan. Thus far, I have not received one damn thing for my money."

"There seems to be a misunderstanding here."

"I'll say there is." There was green sheet lightning in Molly's eyes. "I thought you invited me to dinner tonight to tell me that you'd approved Duncan Brockway's grant proposal."

"Why in hell would I invite you to dinner just to tell you that Brockway's proposal is a scam?"

"It's not a scam."

"Yes, it is." Harry was not accustomed to having his verdicts questioned. He was, after all, a leading authority in his field.

"According to you, every single one of the one hundred grant proposals that have been submitted to the Abberwick Foundation have been scams."

"Not all of them." Harry preferred accuracy to gross generalizations. "Some were just plain bad science. Look, Molly, I'm trying to discuss something else entirely here."

"Our relationship, I believe you said. Well, it's over, Dr. Trevelyan. This was your last chance. You're fired."

Harry wondered if he had accidentally stepped into a parallel universe. This was not going according to plan.

He had made his decision regarding Molly with great care and consideration. True, he had wanted her from the start, but he had not allowed himself to be swept away by physical desire. He had worked from a very basic premise. Following the demise of his engagement over a year ago, he had given his future sex life a great deal of serious contemplation. He had concluded that he knew exactly what he needed in a woman. He wanted a relationship with someone who had a lot of interests of her own, someone who would not require constant attention from him.

He required a woman who would not take mortal offense when he was consumed with his research. A woman who would not care if he locked himself in his office to work on a book or an investigation. A woman who could tolerate the demands of his personal life.

Most of all he wanted an affair with a woman who would not question his moods or suggest that he get therapy for them.

Molly Abberwick had appeared to fit the bill. She was twenty-nine years old, a competent, successful entrepreneur. From what Harry could determine, she had virtually raised her younger sister single-handedly after her mother's death several years earlier. Her father had been a genius, but as was usually the case with the obsessively creative type, he had devoted his time to his inventions, not his children.

From what Harry could discern, Molly was no fragile flower, but a strong, sturdy plant that could weather the worst storms, perhaps even those that occasionally howled across his own melancholy soul.

As the proprietor of the Abberwick Tea & Spice Company, Molly had proven her ability to survive and flourish in the tough, competitive world of small business. In addition to running her shop, she was the sole trustee of the Abberwick Foundation, a charitable trust established by her father, the late Jasper Abberwick. Jasper's inventions were the real source of the wealth in the Abberwick family. It was the business of the trust that had brought Molly to Harry a month ago.

"You don't want to fire me," Harry said.

"It's the only thing I can do," she retorted. "There's certainly not much point in continuing our association. Nothing is getting done."

"What, exactly, did you expect from me?"

Molly threw up her hands in exasperation. "I thought you would be more helpful. More positive. More *excited* about the various grant proposals. No offense, but waiting for you to approve one is like watching trees grow."

"I don't do excited. I take a deliberate approach to my work. I thought you understood that. That's why you hired me in the first place."

"You're deliberate the same way a stone wall is deliberate." Molly clasped her hands behind her back and began to pace the carpet in front of the windows with long, angry strides. "Our association has been a complete waste of time."

Harry watched her, fascinated. Molly's whole body vibrated with outrage. The volatile emotion should have worried him, but it only seemed to add yet another intriguing dimension to her riveting face.

Riveting? Harry frowned at the thought.

"I knew you would probably be difficult." Molly turned her head to glower furiously at him over her shoulder. "But I didn't think you would be impossible."

Definitely riveting, Harry decided. He could not recall the last time he had been *riveted* by a woman. *Rivet* was a word he generally reserved for other areas of interest. A discussion of Leibniz's claim to the invention of the calculus was *riveting.* Charles Babbage's design for an analytical engine was *riveting.* The ramifications of Boole's work in symbolic logic were *riveting.*

Tonight Harry knew beyond a shadow of a doubt that Molly Abberwick had to be added to the list of things that could rivet him. The knowledge made him deeply uneasy even as it fed his hunger for her.

"Look, I'm sorry that you think I'm difficult," Harry began.

"Not difficult. Impossible."

He cleared his throat. "Don't you think that's an overly personal way to characterize my professional decisions?"

"Calling Duncan Brockway's grant proposal fraudulent is an overly personal way to characterize poor Duncan."

"Forget Brockway's proposal. I only did what you pay me to do, Molly."

"Is that right? Then you're overcharging me."

"No, I'm not. You're overreacting."

"Overreacting? *Overreacting?"* Molly reached the granite counter. She whirled around and started back toward the opposite wall. "I'll admit that I'm fed up. If you want to call that overreacting, fine. But it doesn't change anything. This relationship of ours is not working out at all the way that I thought it would. What a disappointment. What a waste of time."

"We don't exactly have a relationship," Harry said through his teeth. "We have a business association."

"Not any longer," she announced triumphantly.

From out of nowhere, Harry felt the dark, brooding sensation descend on him. He should have been thanking his lucky stars for a narrow escape, he thought. A relationship with Molly would never have worked.

But instead of a sense of relief, he knew a hint of despair. He recalled the day Molly had walked into his office-study for the first time.

She had announced that she wished to hire him as a consultant for the Abberwick Foundation. The trust had been established by her father to make grants to promising inventors who could not get funding for their work. Jasper Abberwick had known the problems such people faced all too well. He and his brother, Julius, had labored under financial difficulties for most of their careers. Their cash flow problems had not been resolved until four years ago, when Jasper had succeeded in patenting a new generation of industrial robots.

Jasper had not been able to enjoy his newfound wealth for long. He and his brother, Julius, had both been killed two years ago while experimenting with their latest creation, a prototype design for a man-powered aircraft.

It had taken a year to get the Abberwick Foundation up and running. Molly had invested the money very shrewdly and was now eager to use the income to make the kind of grants her father had wanted her to make.

As the foundation's sole trustee, she was required to handle a wide variety of problems. She was adept at dealing with the vast majority of them, specifically the ones that involved financial decisions. But, unlike her father, she was a businesswoman, not an engineer or a scientist.

Evaluating the merits of the grant proposals submitted by desperate inventors required a sound, working knowledge of scientific principles and cutting-edge technology. In addition, it demanded historical perspective. Such judgments could only be rendered by a trained mind. The Abberwick Foundation had required the services of someone who could judge a proposal not on the basis of its potential for immediate industrial application, but for its long-term value.

Beyond that, Molly had also needed someone who could weed out the frauds and con artists who circled wealthy foundations such as hers like so many sharks in the water.

Molly had many impressive credentials, Harry acknowledged, but she did not have a strong technical background. She was a woman with half a million dollars a year to spend, and she needed help. Specifically she needed Harry Stratton Trevelyan, Ph.D.

Thus far Harry had perused over a hundred grant proposals for her. He had not approved a single one. He was chagrined to realize that he had not understood how impatient Molly had become during the past few weeks.

His attention had obviously been focused on other things.

He had been curious about her from the moment she had made the appointment to interview him as a consultant. He had recognized her last name immediately. The Abberwick family had produced a long string of eccentric but undeniably gifted inventors over the years.

The Abberwick name was not exactly a household word, but it was certainly a familiar one in the commercial world. There it was associated with a variety of machine tools, control system components, and, in recent years, robotic devices.

As an authority in the esoteric field of the history and philosophy of science, Harry had had occasion to learn something about the various Abberwick contributions to technology.

The family had a history as old as the nation itself. One early colonial Abberwick had made a significant improvement to printing press machinery. That particular device had made it possible to double the output of certain inflammatory tracts and newspapers, which had, in turn, helped shape public opinion concerning a revolution in the American colonies.

In the 1870s another Abberwick had made a major advance in steam engine design. The result had been increased efficiency for the railroads, which had, in turn, influenced the development of the western regions of the United States.

In the late 1930s an Abberwick had invented a control mechanism that had made assembly lines more efficient. The increased efficiency had impacted wartime production of tanks and airplanes.

And so it went. The Abberwick name was sprinkled about the history of American invention like so much popcorn on the floor of a theater. And it was noticed in much the same manner. One didn't really see it until one stepped on it.

But Harry had made a career of stepping on such odd bits of information. Invention shaped history, and history shaped invention. Harry frequently studied the way in which the two meshed, mingled, and influenced each other.

He gave lectures on the subject at various universities and colleges. He wrote books that were considered classics in the field of the history of science. And somewhere along the way, he had become an authority on scientific fraud.

Harry frowned as he watched Molly fume. It alarmed him that he was still looking for an excuse to pursue an affair with her. An intelligent man would back off at this point, and he was nothing if not intelligent.

"Let's be realistic here, Molly," he said. "Firing me would be an extremely foolish move on your part. We both know that."

She spun around, brows beetled. "Don't you dare call me a fool."

"I didn't call you a fool. I merely said that it would be foolish to end our business arrangement. You need me."

"I'm beginning to have serious doubts about that." She aimed a finger at him. "You're supposed to advise me, but so far all of your decisions can be summed up in a single word. And that word is *no.*"

"Molly . . ."

"It doesn't take any great talent to say no, Dr. Trevelyan. I'll bet that I can find lots of people who can say it. Some of them probably charge a good deal less than you do, too."

"But will they say yes when they should say it?" he asked softly.

"All right, so maybe another consultant will screw up now and then, and I'll make some grants to the wrong people." She dismissed that possibility with a wave of her hand. "You know what the French say, you can't make an omelette without breaking a few eggs. At least something will get done."

"Half a million dollars a year is more than a few eggs. You're assuming that you can even find another academic specialist here in Seattle who possesses the historical perspective as well as the scientific and engineering expertise to advise you."

She looked down her strong, assertive little nose at him. "I don't see why it should be so difficult to find someone else to do this kind of consulting."

Harry realized with a sense of amazement that he was actually getting angry. He quickly suppressed the sensation. He would not allow Molly to set a match to his temper.

"You're welcome to try, of course," he said politely.

Molly's soft mouth tightened. She tapped the toe of one suede pump and regarded him with an expression of simmering irritation. Harry said nothing. They both knew that her odds of finding anyone else with his peculiar combination of qualifications was bleak.

"Damn," Molly said eventually.

Harry sensed a minor victory. "You're going to have to be patient, Molly."

"Says who? I'm the sole trustee of the foundation. I can be as impatient as I want."

"This argument is degenerating."

"Yes, it is, isn't it?" Molly brightened. "And you know what? It feels good. I've been wanting to say a few things to you for days, Dr. Trevelyan."

"Harry will do."

She smiled grimly. "Oh, no, I wouldn't dream of calling you just plain Harry. Harry doesn't suit you at all, Dr. Harry Stratton Trevelyan, Ph.D., author, lecturer, and noted detector of scientific fraud." She threw out a hand to indicate the three copies of his latest book that sat on a nearby shelf. "You're much too pompous and arrogant to be a mere Harry."

Harry became aware of a faint, unfamiliar staccato sound. He looked down and discovered that he was drumming his finger against the arm of the sofa. With an effort of will he made himself stop.

He was an idiot even to contemplate trying to salvage his tenuous connection with Molly. He had enough problems in his life.

But the thought of never seeing her again suddenly conjured up an image of a glass bridge stretched over an abyss. It was an old and terrifying mental picture. He pushed it back into the shadows with every ounce of will at his command.

"Why don't you sit down, Molly?" he said, determined to regain control of the situation. "You're a businesswoman. Let's discuss this in a businesslike manner."

"There's nothing to discuss. You said no to Duncan Brockway's grant proposal, remember? And your opinion seems to be the only one that counts around here."

"I vetoed this particular funding request because it's clearly a scam. It's an obvious attempt to defraud the Abberwick Foundation of twenty thousand dollars."

Molly folded her arms beneath her breasts and regarded him with belligerent challenge. "You really believe that?"

"Yes."

"You're certain?"

"Yes."

"Positive?" she asked far too sweetly.

"Yes."

"It must be nice to be so sure of yourself."

Harry did not respond to that goad.

Silence fell.

"I really liked Duncan's proposal," Molly said finally.

"I know."

She flashed him a quick, searching look, as if sensing weakness. "There's no hope at all?"

"None."

"Not even a shred of a possibility that Brockway has hit upon a fundamentally new concept?"

"No. I can run the proposal past a friend of mine at the University of Washington who is an expert on energy sources, if you want confirmation. But he'll back me up. There is no valid scientific basis for Brockway's concept of generating power from moonlight in any manner that is even remotely analogous to the collection of solar power. The technology he proposes to use does not exist, and the theory behind the whole project is pure bull."

Amusement briefly replaced the anger in Molly's eyes. "Pure bull? Is that some kind of specialized technical jargon?"

"Yes, as a matter of fact, it is." Harry was thrown off-balance by her sudden shift of mood. "Very useful jargon. It can be applied to any number of situations. Save the foundation's money for a more deserving applicant, Molly. This Duncan Brockway character is trying to take you for twenty grand."

Molly gave a resigned-sounding groan and threw herself back down onto the sofa. "Okay, I surrender. Sorry I lost my temper. But I'm really getting frustrated, Harry. I've got a lot of things to do. I can't spend all of my time trying to get grant proposals past you."

The storm was past. Harry did not know whether or not to breathe a sigh of relief. "Being a trustee of a foundation is time-consuming."

"Brockway's plan seemed like such a brilliant idea," Molly said wistfully. "Just think, a battery that can generate power from moonlight."

"Con artists aren't brilliant. They just have an incredible amount of audacity." Harry eyed her with sudden speculation. "And charm."

Molly winced. "All right, so I liked Duncan Brockway. He seemed very earnest and sincere when I interviewed him."

"I don't doubt that." So the bastard had tried to sweet-talk her into giving him the money, Harry thought. It came as no surprise. Nevertheless, it annoyed him. "Brockway was very earnestly and sincerely trying to get twenty thousand dollars from the Abberwick Foundation."

Molly scowled. "That's not fair. Duncan's an inventor, not a con man. Just a dreamer who wanted to make his dreams come true. I come from a long line of such people. The Abberwick Foundation exists to help them."

"You told me that the mandate of the foundation is to fund serious inventors who can't get government or corporate backing for their projects."

"I believe that Duncan Brockway is serious." Molly lifted one shoulder in an elegant little shrug. "So maybe his plans were somewhat overenthusiastic. That's not unusual in an inventor."

"And he seemed like such a nice man," Harry muttered.

"Well, he did."

"Molly, if there's one thing I know, it's con artists. You hired me to weed them out for you, remember?"

"I hired you to help me select the best grant proposals and to choose funding applicants who present innovative concepts."

"And to ferret out the scams."

"Okay, okay. You win. Again."

"This isn't supposed to be a battle," Harry said wearily. "I'm just trying to do my job."

"Sure."

"I know that the foundation money is burning a hole in your pocket, but there will be plenty of opportunities to give it away."

"I'm beginning to wonder about that."

"You don't want to be too hasty. Selecting legitimate applicants takes time. It should be done cautiously and deliberately." The same way a man should select a lover, Harry thought.

"Uh-huh." Molly glanced at the crammed bookcases that covered two walls of the large living room. "How long have you been doing this kind of consulting?"

"Officially? About six years." Harry frowned at the sudden change of topic. "Why?"

"Just curious." She gave him a sublimely innocent smile. "You've got to admit it's an unusual career. There aren't a lot of people who specialize in detecting fraudulent grant applications. How did you get started?"

Harry wondered where this was going. The woman changed directions faster than alternating current. "A few years ago an acquaintance who was overseeing a government-funded project became suspicious of some of the test results. He asked me if I would take a look at the methodology the grant recipient claimed to be using. I did. It was immediately clear that the outcome of the experiments had been rigged."

"Immediately clear?" Molly's eyes widened with sudden interest. "You realized the guy was a fake right away?"

"Yes."

"Just like that?" She snapped her fingers.

Harry did not want to go into a detailed explanation of just how it had become evident to him that an elaborate fraud had been perpetrated. "Let's just say I have a feel for that kind of thing."

"A feel for it?" Molly sat forward, obviously intrigued. "You mean you're psychic or something?"

"Hell, no, I'm not psychic." Harry grabbed the teapot and forced himself to pour more of the Darjeeling into his cup. He was pleased to see that not so much as a single drop splashed on the glass table. His hands were as steady as ever. "That's a crazy thing to suggest. Do I look like the kind of person who would claim psychic powers?"

Molly settled back against the sofa. A thoughtful expression lit her eyes. "Sorry. Didn't mean to offend you."

Harry assumed his best professorial tone. "I'm a student of the history and philosophy of science."

"I know."

He gave her a hooded look. "In addition to my doctorate in that field, I have undergraduate degrees in mathematics, engineering, and philosophy."

She batted her lashes. "Wow."

Harry ground his teeth. "My background gives me insights which those who have specialized in only a single field tend to miss."

"Ah, yes. Insights."

"Exactly. As I was saying . . ."

"Before you were so rudely interrupted," she murmured.

"To answer your question concerning my career path," Harry plowed on steadily, "one consulting job led to another. I now do a handful every year, provided that they don't get in the way of my research and writing projects."

"Your research and writing are more important to you?"

"Absolutely."

Molly propped one elbow on the arm of the sofa and rested her chin on the heel of her hand. "So how come you agreed to work for me? I'm sure I'm not paying you nearly as much as you can get from a contract with the government or a big corporation."

"No," he agreed. "You aren't."

"Why, then, are you bothering to consult for the lowly little Abberwick Foundation?"

"Because you're willing to do what government and industry won't do."

She tilted her head to one side. "What's that?"

"Waste money on interesting, intriguing projects that don't have any immediate, obvious application. You're willing to invest in the unknown."

Her brows rose. "That's why you agreed to work for me?"

"That's why I agreed to consult for you," he corrected coolly.

"Same thing."

"Not quite."

She ignored that. "Why are you so eager to fund a bunch of crazy inventors?"

Harry hesitated and then decided to try to explain. "I've spent my entire career studying the history of scientific and technological progress."

"I know. I read your latest book."

Harry was so surprised by that revelation that he nearly choked on his tea. "You read *Illusions of Certainty?*"

"Uh-huh." Molly grinned. "I won't pretend it was the hottest bedside reading that I've ever done, but I admit that I found it unexpectedly interesting."

Harry was amazed to discover that he felt flattered. He glanced at the book on the nearby shelf.

Illusions of Certainty: Toward a New Philosophy of Science was not the sort of volume that made best-seller lists. A lengthy, meticulously researched discussion of historical and societal constraints on scientific and technological progress, it was aimed squarely at the academic market. It had sold very well as a college text for students in the history of science, but it had not been meant for the average reader. Of course, Molly Abberwick was hardly average, he thought ruefully.

"*Calculated Deceptions: A History of Scientific Frauds, Swindles, and Hoaxes* was much more popular," Harry said, striving for modesty. *Calculated Deceptions* had been his first stab at writing for the lay market. It had done surprisingly well.

"I read that one, too."

"I see." Harry got to his feet, embarrassed. He went to stand at the window. "Well. Thank you."

"Don't thank me. I was doing research on you."

"Research?"

"I was trying to decide whether or not to hire you as my fraud detective."

Harry winced. He gazed out into the night and tried to reassemble his fragmented bits of logic. So Molly was not quite what he had expected. So there were some unplumbed depths in her. Some surprises. So what? He was thirty-six years old, but his Trevelyan reflexes were still very good. He could handle an affair with Molly, he decided.

"Go on," she prompted.

"What?"

"You were about to tell me why you're taken with the idea of funding inventions that don't offer any obvious payback."

Harry contemplated the night on the other side of the wall of windows. "I told you, I've made a career of studying the history of invention and discovery. In the course of that study I often find myself asking certain questions."

"What kind of questions?"

"Questions such as what would have happened if Charles Babbage had gotten funding to build his analytical engine in 1833, for example."

"The history of the computer would have to be rewritten?" Molly suggested.

"Undoubtedly. If he had been able to create his vision, the world might have headed into the computer age a hundred years earlier. Just think how much farther along we'd be by now." Harry turned away from the window, suddenly caught up in the passion he felt for his subject.

"There are a thousand other examples of brilliant concepts that languished for lack of money and encouragement. I could name—"

He broke off as the front door opened.

"What in the world?" Molly glanced toward the glass-block barrier that divided the front hall from the living area. "I think someone's coming in, Harry."

Harry started forward. "Ginny must have forgotten to lock the door on her way out."

The intruder suddenly appeared. He was a tall, lanky young man dressed in jeans and a blue workshirt. He stopped when he saw Harry, braced his feet apart, and raised his arm. Light gleamed on the steel blade in his right hand.

"This is the end, Trevelyan," the newcomer snarled. "I've finally tracked you down. You won't escape this time."

"My God." Molly leaped off the sofa. "He's got a knife."

"So he does." Harry paused.

The intruder drew back his hand with a lethal, practiced movement.

"Look out." Molly grabbed the teapot.

"Hell," Harry muttered. "Some people have no sense of timing."

The intruder hurled the blade.

Molly shrieked and threw the teapot in the general direction of the glass blocks.

First things first, Harry thought. He grabbed the teapot as it went sailing past.

"Do something," Molly yelled.

Harry smiled wryly. He cradled the teapot in one hand and opened his other hand to show her the knife he held.

Molly stared at him, open-mouthed. Her gaze went from the knife to the intruder's empty hands.

"You snatched that knife right out of thin air," Molly whispered.

Harry glanced down at the gleaming blade. "Looks that way, doesn't it?"

Two

Nice, Cousin Harry." The stranger clapped appreciatively. "Very nice. Your timing is as great as ever."

"Unfortunately, I can't say the same about yours." Harry set the teapot and the knife down on a nearby table. "I'm trying to conduct a business meeting here."

Stunned by the quick shift of events, Molly stared at Harry. "What's going on? Who is this?"

"Allow me to introduce my cousin, Josh Trevelyan." Harry eyed his relative with resigned disapproval. "He has a flair for the dramatic entrance. It runs in the family. Josh, this is Molly Abberwick."

"Hi," Josh said cheerfully.

Molly found her voice. "Hello."

Josh was young, Molly realized, perhaps two years older than her sister, Kelsey. That made him twenty at the most. He bore more than a passing resemblance to Harry. Same midnight black hair, although Josh's was not yet showing the hint of silver that marked Harry's. Same lean, elegant build. True, Josh had not yet developed Harry's look of sleek, controlled strength, but Molly had a hunch that would come with time.

The chief difference between the two men, other than their ages, was in their faces. It was a significant discrepancy. Josh Trevelyan was undeniably handsome in the traditional sense established by Hollywood.

With his long black lashes, dark, romantic eyes, and finely chiseled nose and mouth, he could have walked straight off the silver screen.

Harry's features, on the other hand, were unabashedly, gloriously fierce. He had the face of a hardened ascetic, a man who had spent years gazing into the depths of an alchemist's seething flask in search of arcane truths.

Harry looked like a man who had practiced self-control and self-denial for so long that those qualities had been absorbed into his very flesh and bone. It seemed to Molly that some very old fires burned in Harry's amber eyes. His powerful, long-fingered hands promised the possibilities of both great art and great despair.

"Next time, try knocking," Molly suggested. She sank down onto the arm of the leather sofa. She could not have remained standing a moment longer. Adrenaline still surged unpleasantly through her veins.

"I'm sorry about this, Molly." Harry looked at his young cousin. "Ms. Abberwick is a client of mine. She's got a point. Next time, knock first."

Josh chuckled, apparently oblivious to Harry's irritation. "Didn't mean to scare the daylights out of you."

"I'm delighted to hear that," Molly grumbled.

Still shaken by what she had just witnessed, she looked at Harry for an explanation. His ferociously intelligent eyes met hers with an expression of rueful chagrin. She got the distinct impression that he was not quite sure what to do next.

Molly was briefly intrigued by that insight. At no time during the past month had she ever seen him betray so much as a hint of uncertainty. Until tonight he had exhibited an almost Zen-like self-assurance. It was a little unnerving.

His unshakable control and bird-of-prey patience together with his undeniable brainpower had combined to make Molly wary. And deeply, inexplicably curious. A moth and flame sort of thing, she had concluded. Very dangerous. Especially for a woman who had always been too burdened with responsibilities to take risks.

She had been flabbergasted to discover that she was attracted to Harry. As soon as the realization had hit her—a momentous event that had occurred the day she met him—she had made a valiant effort to conceal it. She had needed time to decide how to handle it. She was still working on the problem.

Harry Stratton Trevelyan could have been a swordsman, an artist, a monk, or a vampire. With such a range of career options, Molly found it intensely interesting that he had chosen a scholarly vocation.

At first she had rationalized Harry's impact on her senses as a function of the fact that she was just not getting out enough these days. Aunt Venicia, her sister, Kelsey, and her counter assistant, Tessa, were forever telling her that she ought to get a life.

Easy for them to say, Molly thought. What with raising Kelsey, running her business, sorting out the complex legal tangle of her father's affairs, and establishing the Abberwick Foundation, there was not a lot of room for a private life. There never had been.

Molly dated occasionally when she had the time and the opportunity. A year ago she had thought she might finally settle down into a contented relationship with Gordon Brooke, the owner of an espresso shop located near Abberwick Tea & Spice. She and Gordon had a lot in common, and Gordon was an attractive man. But that possibility had evaporated months ago.

For quite a while now, Molly had found herself far more consumed by her busy routine than she was by thoughts of passion. Lately even her quarterly business tax forms seemed more interesting than the men she met. She had begun to wonder if her female hormones had gone into permanent hibernation.

That particular concern had vanished the day she had looked straight into Harry's amber eyes. All of her hormones had sat bolt upright and immediately launched into a stirring rendition of the Hallelujah Chorus.

Her common sense did not join in the refrain, however. It had several pithy things to say on the subject of Harry Trevelyan. They all boiled down to a loud warning to stand clear. Unfortunately, while she had not inherited the family genius for invention, she had gotten a full measure of the other infamous Abberwick family characteristic: curiosity.

And Molly had never been more curious about anything in her life than she was about Harry.

She scowled at him. "Do you Trevelyans always greet each other in such a heartwarming fashion?"

Harry looked pained.

Josh laughed as he sauntered forward. "That bit with the knife is part of an old carnival act that Harry and I run through once in a while just to stay in practice."

"Carnival act?" Molly took several deep breaths to finish metabolizing the remainder of the adrenaline in her bloodstream. She looked at Harry. "What you just did was impossible."

"Not for Cousin Harry," Josh assured her. "Fastest hands in the family."

"What on earth does that mean?" Molly asked.

"Pay no attention to him." Harry put down the teapot. "Snatching a knife out of midair is nothing more than an illusion. My father taught me the routine. I taught it to Josh. Which, upon reflection, may have been a mistake."

"My grandfather says Harry's dad had one of the best working knife acts in the business," Josh said. "Harry knows all of his secrets."

Molly glanced at Harry. "It's just a trick?"

"Yes," Harry said.

Josh gave him a reproachful look. "It's a lot more than a trick." He glanced at Molly. "Hasn't Harry told you about his great gift?"

"No, actually, he hasn't." Molly raised one brow. "I have a feeling that there's a lot Harry hasn't told me."

"Cousin Harry has the Trevelyan Second Sight," Josh confided. His eyes gleamed with laughter at Harry's expression.

"Second sight?" Molly turned back to Harry.

"Josh has a distorted sense of humor," Harry said. "Take my word for it, the knife-catching trick is an illusion, pure and simple."

"Hah. That's just where you're wrong, Harry." Josh smiled wickedly. "It's definitely not simple. You gotta be fast. And you're very, very fast." He winked at Molly. "He's also got the Trevelyan reflexes, y'know."

"Fascinating," Molly murmured. Coming from a family of inventors, as she did, she was accustomed to odd pranks and unusual practical jokes, but this one was definitely unique.

Harry gave Josh a disgusted look. "Show Molly the knife that she thought she saw you throw."

Josh was genuinely horrified. "I can't do that. It's against the rules."

"I make the rules around here," Harry said. "Show her the knife."

"Only if you promise that you won't tell Cousin Raleigh or Aunt Evie."

"Believe me, you have my word on it," Harry said.

"Right." With a theatrical flourish Josh plucked a gleaming blade from beneath his shirtsleeve. He grinned at Molly. "Now you see it." The blade disappeared under his cuff. "Now you don't."

"Amazing." Molly was impressed. "I could have sworn I saw you throw it."

"That's the whole idea," Josh said.

Molly turned to Harry. "Where did you get the knife that you pretended to catch in midair?"

"From an ankle sheath that he wears," Josh explained.

Molly stared at Harry. "Good grief. You carry a knife?"

"Family tradition on his side of the clan," Josh said easily. "Show her, Harry."

"This is not how I had intended to spend the evening," Harry muttered.

Molly watched, fascinated, as he crouched in one of those incredibly fluid movements she had come to associate with him. He calmly slipped the knife into a small leather sheath strapped to his ankle and brushed the cuff of his trousers over it.

Molly shook her head in wonder. "I never even saw you remove it."

Harry shrugged. "You were distracted by Josh's grand entrance."

Molly studied him intently. "Are you two ex-stuntmen, by any chance?"

"Not exactly." Josh slid Harry a sly glance. "Sounds as though my cousin hasn't told you much about us Trevelyans."

"No, as a matter of fact, he hasn't."

"Harry's father, my Uncle Sean, used to own an amusement show," Josh explained.

"Those days," Harry said softly, "are long gone."

"Don't let Aunt Evie hear you say that," Josh cautioned. "She's already pissed off enough as it is because of the way you turned your back on your heritage."

"What heritage?" Molly asked, enthralled.

"Good question," Harry said.

"Come on, now, Harry, I'm shocked at your lack of respect for the Trevelyan traditions." Josh turned to Molly. "Trevelyans have been doing carnival psychic acts and motorcycle stunts, telling fortunes, throwing knives, and racing cars for generations."

Molly was dumbfounded. The notion of Harry Stratton Trevelyan, Ph.D. and all-around know-it-all, as a descendant of a long line of carnies, stuntmen, and race-car drivers was mind-boggling. "This is a joke, right?"

"It's no joke," Josh assured her. "Look at me. I'm carrying on the proud tradition, myself. At least until the end of summer. I go back to the University of Washington in the fall."

"What's your summer job?" Molly asked.

"I set up and operate rides in the Smoke & Mirrors Amusement Company," Josh said. "Aunt Evangeline owns the business. Several members of my family work in it. My grandfather travels with the show, too."

"Your grandfather?"

"Right. Grandpa's been involved in racing all of his life." Josh glanced briefly at Harry. "Smoke & Mirrors is doing a fair in Hidden Springs at the moment. There's stock car racing in the evenings. Grandpa is one of the best mechanics around. He works in the pits."

"I see," Molly said. "Where's Hidden Springs? I don't think I've ever heard of it."

"That's because it's so well hidden," Josh said smoothly. "It's about an hour's drive from here. North and slightly east toward the Cascades. Farm country. Smoke & Mirrors always does well there. The poor townies haven't had any real excitement since we played their local fair last summer."

"Speaking of which," Harry interrupted. "What are you doing here tonight? You're supposed to be working."

"Aunt Evangeline said I could sneak over to Seattle to see you, Harry." The good-natured amusement faded in Josh's eyes. "I wanted to talk to you about some stuff. Sorry I interrupted your evening."

"You should have called," Harry said.

"I tried." Josh shrugged. "I got the answering machine."

Harry's mouth twisted slightly. "I turned off the phones."

Josh looked surprised. "Yeah? You always take calls from family when you're home."

"I made an exception tonight, okay?" Harry said coolly. "Why didn't the doorman use the intercom to tell me you were on the way up?"

"I told Chris that I wanted to surprise you," Josh said.

"Hey, don't worry about it," Molly said quickly before Harry could continue to grill his cousin. "I was about to leave, anyway."

Harry's amber eyes gleamed with impatience. "There's no need for you to leave. We haven't finished our business."

Molly winced. "No problem. We can discuss it tomorrow."

She'd hoped that in the excitement of Josh's arrival Harry had forgotten that she'd lost her temper and fired him. What in the world had gotten into her? she wondered. Firing Harry meant never having an excuse to see him again.

That thought sent a chill through her bones. She got to her feet.

"Don't leave on my account." Josh backed hastily toward the front door. "I'll just go down to the lobby and read or something. Chris won't mind. He likes the company."

"Nonsense." Molly briskly straightened her jacket. "It's nearly eleven. You two obviously have personal things to discuss, and I need my sleep. I've got a business to run. Harry, will you call a cab?"

Harry's jaw tightened. "I'll drive you home."

"There's no need. A cab will be fine."

"I said, I'll see you home," Harry repeated evenly.

Molly met his implacable eyes and thought better of debating the subject. "If you insist."

"I insist."

Maybe he had decided to let her fire him after all, Molly thought. She wracked her brain for a way to forestall that possibility.

He was irritating, arrogant, and downright stubborn, but for some reason the last thing she wanted to do was fire Harry.

Molly's home was on Capitol Hill, some twelve blocks from Harry's downtown condo, but the short drive through the city streets was one of the longest trips she had ever made. She could not decide if Harry was angry or merely brooding.

Whatever his mood, Harry drove the sleek, hunter green sports car with graceful precision. Molly was unfamiliar with the make and model. She had, however, been raised in a family of mechanical geniuses, and she knew expensive engineering design when she saw it. She made a note to ask Harry about his car. But not tonight.

At the moment, she was enthralled not with the car, but with the way Harry handled the gear shift and clutch. She realized that he derived a subtle, sensual pleasure from the smooth, perfectly timed manipulation of the vehicle's controls. He drove the car the way he would have ridden a horse.

"Did you actually travel with a carnival?" Molly finally asked when the silence lengthened.

"No. My father did. As Josh told you, he owned an amusement show.

But he sold it shortly after he ran off with my mother. He took the money and opened a dive shop in Hawaii. That's where I grew up."

"I guess I sort of assumed that you came from a long line of academics."

The streetlights revealed Harry's bleak smile. "I'm the first member of the Trevelyan clan since the first Harry Trevelyan to make a living doing something other than telling fortunes, racing cars, or throwing knives."

"When did the first Harry Trevelyan start the tradition?"

"Early eighteen hundreds."

"And your mother?" Molly asked.

"She was a Stratton."

The significance of his middle name finally clicked. "One of the Seattle Strattons? The commercial real estate development family?"

"Three generations of money, business influence, and political clout," Harry agreed in a voice that lacked all expression.

Molly thought about that. "An unusual combination," she said delicately. "Your father and your mother, I mean."

"A carny and a socialite? *Unusual* is one word for it. The Trevelyans and the Strattons have used a whole thesaurus full of other words. Most of them unprintable."

"I take it neither family approved of the match?"

"That's putting it mildly. The Trevelyans were furious because after the marriage my father sold the show. As far as they were concerned, he'd turned his back on his family, most of whom were working in said show at the time. The new owner had his own crew."

"Instant unemployment for the Trevelyans, hmm?"

"Right."

"And the Strattons?"

"Let's just say that my mother was supposed to marry a wealthy, well-connected Stanford grad. Instead she ran off with a carny." Harry slanted Molly a derisive glance. "How do you think most families would have reacted under those circumstances?"

"Not very enthusiastically, I suppose."

"You've got that right."

"So? What happened?"

Harry's brows rose slightly. "You're very curious."

"Sorry." Molly was embarrassed. "It's a family failing. I come from a long line of inventors, remember."

"I know."

"Look, you certainly don't have to answer if you'd rather not. I didn't mean to pry."

"The Strattons did everything they could to dissolve the marriage. Parker Stratton, my grandfather, tried to force an annulment. When that failed, he pushed for a divorce. One of the reasons my parents moved to the islands was so that they could put a large chunk of ocean between themselves and their families. It was the only way they could get some peace."

"Did things cool down after you arrived?"

"No. The feud continues to this day."

"And you're caught in the middle?"

Harry's shoulder lifted slightly. "That's the way it goes sometimes."

On the surface, he sounded incredibly casual, even dismissive of the family situation. But Molly flinched against the pain implied by his words. It hit her in a wave that made her catch her breath. Whatever Harry felt toward the Strattons and the Trevelyans, it was anything but indifference. But she also understood that he kept his emotions relating to that subject under lock and key.

"Do your parents still live in the islands?" Molly asked.

"My parents are dead. They were murdered by a couple of armored car thieves nine years ago."

Harry's voice was infinitely soft and infinitely cold. But Molly stilled beneath the deluge of powerful emotions that emanated from him. She could not even begin to identify the complex and dangerous brew. Rage? Despair? Remorse? All those and more, yes. This was the stuff of nightmares.

"My God." Molly could not think of anything else to say. "My God."

Harry was silent.

"I'm so sorry," Molly offered, feeling helpless.

"Your folks are both dead, also," he pointed out, as if they had that much in common.

"Yes." It was Molly's turn to fall silent for a while.

Her feelings were not nearly as complicated as Harry's. Whenever she thought about her parents these days, she experienced a straightforward sense of wistful loss. The initial grief had faded over time. So had the anger and fear that she'd once had difficulty admitting to herself. She no longer lay awake at night wondering how she would make the mortgage payment and see her sister safely raised. She had managed to shoulder the responsibilities that had once seemed so overwhelming.

Molly peered through the windshield as the lights of what her sister mockingly called "the Abberwick family mansion" appeared. "Well, here we are. Thanks so much for seeing me home."

"I'll take you to your door." Harry brought the car to a halt in front of the massive wrought-iron gates.

Molly hastily rummaged around in her purse for the card key. When she found it, she handed it to him. Harry lowered his window and inserted the card into the lock. The heavy gates swung inward.

"Good security," Harry remarked.

"My father designed it." Molly tilted her chin to indicate the night-shrouded gardens. "He designed the sprinkler system, too. He was always tinkering with things around the house. My sister, Kelsey, is following in his footsteps. She got the Abberwick genius for scientific and technical stuff."

"What about you?"

Molly chuckled. "I got the bills."

Harry drove slowly along the curving driveway and stopped in front of the steps. He switched off the engine, removed the keys from the ignition, and opened his door. A brief smile came and went on his hard face as he surveyed the old, ramshackle mansion.

Molly had no trouble guessing his thoughts. Her home looked like the work of a seriously deranged architect. It was a bizarre collection of Gothic arches and Victorian flourishes. The perfect setting for a mad scientist.

"Interesting," was all Harry said as he opened Molly's car door.

She smiled as she got out. "Be honest, it bears a striking resemblance to Dr. Frankenstein's castle. What can I say? It's home."

"Were you raised in this house?"

"Yes, indeed. You're looking at the ancestral manor. My parents bought it during a brief spell of Abberwick prosperity thirty years ago. Dad had just patented some new machine tool. He fell in love with this place. Said he needed the space for his workshops. The money didn't last long, of course. It never did with Dad. But somehow we managed to hang on to the house."

"I see."

Molly gave Harry a second card key. He took it from her as they went up the steps to the front door.

Molly tried to think of a polite way to end the evening.

"We didn't finish our earlier conversation," Harry said as he opened the door.

"No, we didn't, did we? But we can conclude it some other time. I'm sure you're anxious to get home so that you can chat with your cousin."

"He'll keep." Harry surveyed the vast hall. "I believe you misunderstood something I said earlier about our relationship."

Molly stepped over the threshold and turned to face him with her brightest smile. "Don't worry. I've decided not to fire you."

Harry propped one shoulder against the doorjamb and folded his arms. "Is that a fact?"

"Yes, it is," Molly said briskly. "You're right when you say that there's not a lot of choice when it comes to the sort of consulting expertise that I require."

"I'm glad to know that you're aware of that."

"So it appears I'm stuck with you."

"Nothing like feeling needed."

"However, I want to make it clear that things cannot continue to go on as they have for the past month. We must make some real progress."

"I agree." Harry moved.

Molly was in his arms before she even realized his intention. He covered her startled mouth with his own and crushed her close to his lean, hard body.

For an instant she was too surprised to react. She inhaled the warm, male scent of him. It acted like a powerful drug on her senses. She could feel the strength in his arms and the sleek power in his body. She could also feel the hard bulge in his close-fitting trousers.

Harry wanted her.

The knowledge inspired the choir of female hormones that had been humming inside Molly all evening. They burst into full-throated song once more.

Molly wrapped her arms around his neck and leaned into the kiss with a soft sigh of delight. Harry groaned softly and tightened his hold on her. Excitement welled up within her. A delicious warmth stole into the lower portions of her body.

"Inside," Harry muttered into her mouth. He urged her back through the doorway.

Molly grabbed his shoulders to steady herself.

"Let me get the door closed," Harry said hoarsely.

Molly ignored him. He was nibbling on her ear, and it felt wonderful. Nothing had ever felt so terrific. She heard the door finally crash shut.

Harry swung her around and crowded her up against the nearest wall. He leaned over her and planted his strong, elegant hands on either side of her head, caging her. He kissed her throat and the hollow of her shoulder.

"Molly. I knew it would be good, but I didn't realize . . . God, I want you." Harry deepened the kiss.

Molly thought she would collapse. Harry thrust his foot deliberately between her ankles, easing her legs apart. Molly felt herself grow damp even though he still had his hands flattened against the wall. She shivered.

She was quivering. Trembling. The sensation awed her. She had never actually trembled with desire. She had assumed the phrase was nothing more than poetic imagery. Harry seemed to be shaking a little, himself, which was even more interesting.

He trailed kisses along the line of her jaw all the way to her ear. "Take off your jacket." His voice was that of the devil at midnight, dark, seductive, infinitely compelling. "Please."

Molly nearly went under for the third time. Somewhere in the distance the rational part of her brain was struggling to be heard. She thought it was yelling something along the lines of *get a grip,* but it was difficult to be certain. An utterly alien sensation of pure, wild recklessness held her.

Years of being careful, responsible, and generally too exhausted to take a chance washed away in an instant.

She lifted her hands to ease her jacket off her shoulders. All she could think about was getting closer to Harry.

A soft whirring noise sounded in the hall.

"What the hell?" Harry broke off the kiss. He swung around with feline speed.

The small dusting robot rolled to a halt less than twelve inches away from Harry's foot and beeped in an aggrieved tone. Its sensors seemed to glower at the object in its path. It waved its dusting sponge as though seeking a target.

Harry fitted his hands to his hips and studied the plastic and metal household robot for a long moment. Then he switched his attention to Molly. "Your chaperon?"

Molly giggled. She *never* giggled, she thought, appalled. She was actually feeling giddy from the effects of Harry's kisses. She swallowed and took a deep breath in an effort to regain some semblance of self-control.

"It's a patented Abberwick Duster," she explained. "There's one on each floor. My father designed them. I set it to dust while I was out this evening. It's just finishing the baseboards. You're in its way."

"Too bad. There's only room for one of us in this hall, and I'm not ready to leave."

"I'll take care of it." Molly hastily bent down and punched a button to send the duster back to its closet.

The little machine obediently swiveled around and hummed off down the hall.

Harry watched it disappear. "Sort of takes the magic out of the scene, doesn't it?"

"To tell you the truth, I'm so accustomed to the cleaning robots that I hardly notice them. I grew up with machines like that around. Every year while my father was alive there were newer and fancier models. My sister continues to experiment with them. Frankly, I wouldn't know how to keep house without them."

Harry exhaled slowly. The ancient fires in his eyes still burned, but he had turned the heat down to a bearable level. "Maybe the interruption was for the best. I've been trying to have a discussion about our relationship all evening. I'll be damned if I'm going to go home without finishing it."

Molly's mouth fell open. "You were talking about this kind of relationship? You? Me? Us?"

"Yes." Harry eyed her with moody consideration. "Us. A relationship."

"Good grief." Molly put a hand on the wall to steady herself. She started making her way very cautiously toward the kitchen. "I had no idea. I thought you were referring to our, uh . . . well, you know."

"You thought I was talking about our business relationship. I'm not. I'm talking about this kind of relationship. Does that really strike you as such a bizarre concept?"

"Uh, well . . ."

"Correct me if I'm wrong, but I got the impression from that kiss that you might have done some preliminary thinking about the possibilities."

Molly's flush deepened. Fantasy was one thing. Reality was quite another. "Well . . ."

Harry ran a beautifully sculpted hand impatiently through his dark hair. "Look, I know we're not exactly a perfect match."

Molly finally located her tongue. "You can say that again. I'm from the business world. You're the scholarly, academic type."

He nodded, obviously in total agreement. "I'm analytical and logical by nature. You're inclined to shoot from the hip."

"You're stubborn."

"You're impulsive."

"You're slower than a turtle when it comes to making decisions," Molly said, getting into the spirit of the discussion. "You wouldn't last five minutes in the business world. The competition would devour you."

"Is that so?" Harry eyed her thoughtfully. "For your information, you wouldn't have made it in the academic world. Don't get me wrong, you've got the basic intelligence, but your thinking processes are undisciplined."

"I say *tomayto* and you say *tomahto,"* she chanted in a singsong voice.

"What?"

"Never mind." Molly contemplated the tantalizing prospect of having the floor-cleaning robot assault him with a mop. "We seem to have established that we were not meant for each other. That didn't take long. Now, then, what was your point, Dr. Trevelyan?"

He frowned. "My point was that I would like to suggest that you and I have an affair."

"You're serious, aren't you?"

"Yes."

She stared at him in disbelief. "I don't believe this. What about that little duet concerning tomatoes that we just sang together? We're opposites."

He shrugged. "Opposites attract."

"Come off it, Dr. Trevelyan. Don't give me that nonsense. I expect better logic from someone with a Ph.D."

"It's not nonsense. It's a basic principle in the science of magnetism."

Molly lifted her eyes toward the high ceiling. "We are not a couple of magnets."

"Look, I'm not suggesting that we get married," Harry said quietly. "I'm suggesting an affair. What's so damned difficult about that idea?"

"You don't think it sounds just a tad cold-blooded?"

Harry hesitated, as though he sensed that he was on dangerous ground. "I think it sounds like a rational way to establish a relationship. We're obviously attracted to each other physically."

"Yeah, but we don't communicate too well, do we?" Molly retorted with grim relish. "If nothing else, I think we established that fact this evening."

"What of it? According to the shrinks, men and women rarely do communicate well."

Molly was intrigued. "You read those pop-psych books?"

"I was engaged to a psychologist for a while a year and a half ago. You hang out with shrinks, you pick up a few things."

"Nothing contagious, I trust. Look, Harry, I don't think your idea is a particularly brilliant one."

"Why not?"

She sighed. "Because I'd probably drive you crazy."

An odd, unreadable expression flashed in Harry's eyes. It was gone in the next instant. "I've thought about that possibility," he said dryly. "But I think that I can handle the situation."

"Gosh whiz, I can't tell you how relieved I am to hear that." She glowered at him. "What about me? You're just as likely to make me crazy, too."

"Are you telling me that you don't think you can cope with my pompous, arrogant, stubborn ways?"

For some reason, that annoyed her. "If I can cope with business competition, rude customers, and the mountain of tax forms I'm required to file just to keep my shop running, I can probably cope with you."

"Is there someone else?" Harry asked softly.

She grimaced. "No." She paused to slant him a sidelong glance. "I take it you're not involved with anyone else, either, or we wouldn't be having this conversation."

"You're right. There's no one else. There hasn't been for quite a while."

"Same here. Doesn't sound like either of us leads an exciting social life, does it?"

He smiled. "I'm hoping to change that."

"You're right, you know," Molly said with a sigh of regret. "We've got absolutely nothing in common. What on earth would we talk about on a date except the Abberwick Foundation?"

"I don't know. Want to find out tomorrow night?"

Molly felt as though she were standing on the brink of a giant, bottomless whirlpool. She was gathering the nerve to dip one toe into the swirling currents when she suddenly remembered a previous engagement. She was amazed at the degree of disappointment she felt.

"I'm busy tomorrow night. I'm going to take my sister shopping for her college wardrobe. She starts her freshman year in the fall."

"Friday night?"

Molly took a deep breath and prepared to jump into the whirlpool. "All right." Panic set in almost immediately. "But this will be just a test date. First, we find out whether or not we're going to bore each other silly over dinner. Then we'll decide what to do after that."

Harry smiled. "I won't rush you into anything. I'm the slow, methodical type, remember?"

Except when you're plucking knives out of thin air, Molly thought.

Three

Josh wandered into the kitchen shortly after seven. He was dressed in jeans and a green pullover. His hair was still damp from the shower. He yawned, dropped onto one of the black wire-frame chairs in front of the granite counter, and reached for the French press coffee pot. The rich aroma of the Gordon Brooke Special Dark City Roast blend wafted through the air.

" 'Morning, Harry. Sorry about interrupting things last night."

"Forget it." Harry spread the *Post Intelligencer* out on the counter. He handed the sports section to Josh and then turned to the headlines.

Both men fell into a companionable silence as they munched cereal, drank coffee, and read the morning paper. The routine was a familiar one. They had observed it together ever since Josh had come to live with Harry at the age of twelve.

The pattern had altered when Josh had started college at the University of Washington. He could have continued to live at home with Harry and commute to the UW, but both of them had known that it was time for Josh to have his own place.

Nevertheless, the condominium was still home. Josh showed up at the front door during school vacations, some weekends, and not infrequently in the evenings if he happened to be at loose ends or wanted to talk about his studies. The unplanned appearances were rarely a problem. Harry was almost always home alone with his books. Last night had been an anomaly.

But Harry was no longer irritated by Josh's unannounced arrival the previous evening. To his quiet astonishment, he was feeling remarkably cheerful in spite of the fact that it had taken him much longer than usual to get to sleep. The prospect of tomorrow night glimmered on the horizon, casting a pleasant glow over the entire day.

Josh finished his first cup of coffee. He looked up from the sports page, a speculative gleam in his dark eyes. "Been a while since I've come home unexpectedly and found you making out with a date."

"I was not making out with her." Harry frowned over an article on inflation. "We were discussing business. I told you, Molly's a client."

Josh helped himself to a second cup of coffee. "I got the feeling she's more than a client. You two been seeing each other long?"

"I've been doing some consulting work for her for about a month."

"Consulting?"

"Right." Harry turned the page.

"Help me out here, Cousin Harry." Josh grinned. "I'm a little confused. Are you dating her or not?"

"Since when did you become so interested in my love life?"

"Since I discovered that you had one again. It's been over a year, if my calculations are correct. Congratulations."

Harry said nothing.

"It's about time you started dating again." Josh's tone grew serious. "You've been living like a monk since Olivia broke off the engagement."

"How would you know? You aren't here most of the time these days."

Josh waved his fork in a vaguely menacing manner. "Ve haf vays of knowing these things."

Harry frowned. "What ways?"

"I recognize that box of condoms stashed in the bathroom cupboard. It's been there ever since you stopped seeing Olivia. The same number of little packets inside, too."

"Hell, I don't believe this." Harry sank his teeth into a slice of toast. "Talk about an invasion of privacy."

"I worry about you, Harry. You have a tendency to brood."

"I don't brood. I contemplate things for long periods of time. There's a difference."

"Call it what you want." Josh shoved bread into the toaster. "I know you better than you think."

"That possibility makes my blood run cold."

Josh's eyes widened innocently. "I only have your best interests at heart."

"I'll console myself with that thought."

"Molly Abberwick seems nice."

"She is."

"You got back here early last night after you took her home."

"Yes."

"Going to see her again soon?"

"As a matter of fact," Harry said, "I'm taking her out to dinner tomorrow night."

"Aha. Don't forget to move the box of condoms back into the drawer beside your bed."

Harry refolded the paper with painstaking care. "Last night you said you wanted to talk to me. Is something wrong?"

The amusement vanished from Josh's eyes. "It's Grandpa."

"Again?"

"Yeah. He's giving me static about going back to school in the fall. Says I'm wasting my time. Two years is enough college for any Trevelyan. He wants me to join his pit crew."

"That sounds familiar."

Josh buttered a slice of toast. "I was wondering if you would talk to him. Make him understand."

Harry gazed absently at the clouds that were moving across Elliott Bay. "I'll talk to him, but I can't promise to change his mind, Josh. You know that. He's stuck in a time warp."

"Yeah, but he'll listen to you. I tell myself it doesn't matter what he thinks. I'm going to finish college and go on to grad school regardless of his opinions." Josh shrugged. "But sometimes he gets to me."

"I know."

"If Dad were still alive things would be different. It would sort of take the pressure off me. But as it stands, I'm all Grandpa has left."

Harry said nothing. Unlike Josh, he had no illusions on that score. He knew that there would have been more, not less pressure on Josh if his father had still been alive. But Wild Willy Trevelyan, daredevil motorcycle stunt driver, ladies' man, and unofficial poster boy for the macho, hard-living lifestyle, was dead.

Wild Willy had been killed seven years earlier when he had tried to ride his overpowered cycle across a mountain of cars that had been set ablaze. A thousand spectators, including his twelve-year-old son, Josh, had witnessed the engine explosion that had caused Wild Willy's death.

Josh had gone into a state of shock. No one in the family knew what to do. Josh's mother had been killed in a carnival accident shortly after he was born. His reckless, embittered grandfather, Leon Trevelyan, was no fit parent for a young, deeply traumatized boy. Most of the other Trevelyans were too broke to assume the responsibility of an extra mouth to feed.

Newly arrived in the Northwest, Harry had also been present in the audience the day Wild Willy had been killed. He had recognized the dazed look in Josh's eyes. In the months since the death of his own parents, Harry had grown accustomed to seeing that same expression every time he had looked into a mirror.

Harry had brought Josh back to Seattle after the funeral. No one in the family had argued about the decision. They had all been vastly relieved to have Harry take charge of the boy.

Josh had eventually begun to recover from his grief, but it was obvious by the end of that first summer that there was nowhere for him to go. Fall was approaching. Harry registered him in a Seattle school.

It became clear very quickly that Josh was highly intelligent. Under Harry's guidance he had developed a passion for math and science.

For his part, assuming responsibility for his young cousin had given Harry a badly needed sense of focus. Things had settled into a stable routine that had worked surprisingly well for several years.

Then, one day shortly after Josh's sixteenth birthday, Leon Trevelyan had appeared at the front door of Harry's condominium.

Leon had wanted his grandson. He intended to teach the boy how to drive a race car.

Fortunately, Josh had been at school that day. Harry had taken his uncle Leon into his study, closed the door, and proceeded to wrestle with the devil.

Harry had known from the outset that he could not afford to lose. Josh's future had been at stake. Failure would have meant consigning the boy to the path his father and grandfather had traveled. It was a dead-end road.

Harry had won the battle.

He pushed aside the old memories. "Don't worry," Harry said. "I'll deal with Leon."

Josh looked enormously relieved. "Thanks."

Harry went back to his paper.

"About this date you've got for Friday night," Josh said.

"What about it?"

"No offense, Harry, but from what I saw last night, you're a little rusty."

"Rusty?"

Josh grinned. "In exchange for getting Grandpa off my back, I am prepared to give you some advice."

"I don't think I need any advice."

"Don't be too sure of that," Josh said. "It's a jungle out there these days."

Tessa Calshot was refilling a glass container of whole cloves when Molly walked into Abberwick Tea & Spice Company on Thursday morning.

" 'Morning, Molly." Tessa hoisted the plastic sack of cloves. The sleeve of her faded, 1930s vintage thrift-shop dress fell back to reveal the elaborate tattoo that decorated her right arm. "Be careful when you go into your office. Kelsey's in there. She's experimenting with a new version of her ground spice dispenser."

"Thanks for the warning."

"Ever vigilant, that's me. Especially so since that little episode with her tea-brewing gizmo." Tessa shook the last of the cloves out of the sack. "Took me most of the morning to clean up after the explosion, if you will recall."

"Only too well." Molly grinned at her assistant.

Tessa spent her nights playing lead guitar for an all-female band called Ruby Sweat, but as far as Molly was concerned, her true talent lay in the marketing and merchandising arena. She had a natural genius for the field, although few traditional businesspeople would have recognized it. Tessa was not exactly the conservative type.

Her spiky hair was rarely the same color two days in a row. This morning it was neon green. Her lipstick was brown. She favored pre–World War II era dresses that hung oddly on her short, sturdy frame. She paired them with large, clunky platform shoes and a number of small steel chains. There was a gold ring in her nose and another through her eyebrow.

Molly wouldn't have cared if Tessa came to work stark naked. Tessa was a natural saleswoman. She could have made a fortune in commissions at Nordstrom if she had been willing to dress to suit the corporate image of the sophisticated fashion store. Fortunately for Molly, she refused even to consider the notion.

Tourists, who comprised a large share of Molly's customers, found Tessa fascinating. They frequently asked to take her picture after they had made their purchases. They couldn't wait to show the photos to their friends back in Kansas. Pictures of Tessa constituted proof positive that things really were different out on the Coast.

Seattleites, on the other hand, long accustomed to the colorful offbeat *barristas* who operated the city's innumerable espresso machines, felt comfortable with Tessa. She reminded them of the counter assistants who sold them their daily lattes. The connection between the familiar world of the Seattle coffee culture and that of the more exotic realm of tea and spices was a subtle one, but it was effective. Molly and Tessa had deliberately exploited it.

"How did the meeting with T-Rex go last night?" Tessa asked as she closed the glass container.

"It got complicated," Molly said.

Tessa leaned her elbows on the counter. "So? Did you fire him like you promised?"

"Not exactly."

Tessa looked surprised. "You mean he finally approved a grant proposal?"

"Not exactly."

"What, exactly, did happen?"

"Let's just say I changed my mind."

"No kidding?" Tessa arched black brows that appeared to have been drawn with a wide-nibbed marking pen. "When you left here yesterday afternoon you swore that T-Rex would get no more chances to savage one of your precious grant proposals. You said that turning down the Wharton Kendall proposal was the next-to-the-last straw. I distinctly heard you say that if Trevelyan nixed Duncan Brockway's grant, the man was definitely road kill."

"Things change." Molly decided there was no point being secretive. "I've got a date with him tomorrow night."

Tessa's eyes widened in shock. "A date with T-Rex?"

"Kind of a stunner, isn't it?" Molly paused beside a shelf to rearrange a collection of designer teapots. "You know, maybe it's time to stop calling him T-Rex."

"You told me he was cold-blooded and utterly ruthless. You said he shredded the work of innocent inventors as if it were so much raw meat. You said that hiring him to help you vet grant proposals had been the equivalent of hiring Tyrannosaurus Rex to baby-sit small, furry mammals."

Molly thought about Harry's mouth on hers. She could still feel the heat he had generated. It was more intense than any of the thirteen different varieties of chile peppers she stocked.

"Let's just say I was definitely wrong about one thing," Molly said. "He's not cold-blooded."

"I don't believe it." Tessa shook her head. "The guy talked you into a date?"

"Sort of."

"Aren't you worried that you'll die of boredom?"

"I don't think boredom will be a problem," Molly mused. "And that's another distinction that must be made between T-Rex and Harry Trevelyan. From all accounts, dinosaurs had tiny little two-watt brains. The same cannot be said of Dr. Harry Trevelyan. He's what they call a polymath these days."

"What's a polymath?"

"The modern term for a Renaissance man. Well-versed in a wide variety of subjects."

"Oh." Tessa looked dubious. "Brainpower does not necessarily make a man an interesting dinner companion."

"Harry is plenty interesting, believe me." Molly inhaled the scents of fine teas and fragrant spices. She glanced around the shop with proprietary pride. Automatically, she checked to see that all was in readiness for the day.

The ritual was a familiar one. She had been going through it faithfully since the first morning she had come to work. That had been when she was twenty years old, the year her mother had died. Molly had been forced to drop out of college to support herself, her sister, and her father.

The Abberwick fortunes, never stable, had taken another serious downturn that year. Jasper had borrowed twenty thousand dollars to finance the development of a new invention, and the bank wanted its money back. The loan officer had been under the impression that Jasper had intended to use the cash to make household improvements. He did not take kindly to the discovery that the money had been poured into a failed design for robotic control systems.

Jasper had been educated as an engineer, but he was constitutionally incapable of holding down a regular job. The compulsion to design and invent always got in the way of even the most liberal corporate routine. Jasper had chafed under any sort of restriction. He had to be free to pursue his dreams.

Molly's mother, Samantha, had loved her husband with patience and understanding. She had also been practical. It was Samantha's steady paycheck that had kept the family afloat during lean times.

Things changed with Samantha Abberwick's death in a car accident. Kelsey had been only nine at the time. The family had been devastated, both emotionally and financially.

Molly had missed her mother desperately, but there was scant time to grieve. Too many things had to be done. Kelsey was Molly's top priority. And then there was the family's fragile financial situation. Without the income from Samantha's job to rely upon, disaster loomed.

Jasper Abberwick was the epitome of the absentminded inventor. In the days following his wife's death, he could not deal with the realities of the family's cash flow problems. He took refuge in his basement workshop, leaving Molly to confront the crisis.

Molly had assessed the situation, and then she had done what had to be done. She had left college for the working world.

The shop she now owned had not been named Abberwick Tea & Spice in those days. It had been called Pipewell Tea in honor of its owner, Zinnia Pipewell.

It had been located in a dingy hole-in-the-wall near the Pike Place Market. Business had not been what anyone would have called brisk. Seattle was a city addicted to coffee, not fine tea. Zinnia could barely afford an assistant.

Molly had suspected from the start that the older woman had felt sorry for her. She knew Zinnia had hired her in the middle of a recession out of compassion, not because she actually needed a counter assistant.

Molly had been determined that her new employer would not regret her act of generosity. She had plunged into the task of working full-time with the same energy and enthusiasm that she had once reserved for her studies. There had been no other option.

Within a week of working at Zinnia's tea shop, Molly had realized that unless something was done, the business would not last the year. With it would go her job. After some research, Molly suggested that Zinnia add a full line of spices to be sold in bulk. Zinnia had gone along with the plan.

Seattle was what gourmets and restaurant reviewers liked to call a *foodie* town. Molly knew that exotic spices were of interest to a lot of people. After locating and contracting with various sources for a steady supply of everything from dried New Mexican chiles to Spanish saffron, Molly had turned her attention to packaging and advertising. The shop changed its name to Pipewell Tea & Spice.

Instead of opting for a trendy, Euro-modern image, which the espresso bars favored, Molly had chosen an old-fashioned, antique design for the shop. The result had been a store that captured the feel of an early nineteenth-century tea and spice traders' dockside warehouse.

Business had picked up rapidly.

Molly expanded carefully. She offered a mailing service so that out-of-town customers would not have to carry their purchases home in their baggage. She provided recipe books and prepackaged dip mixes. She developed catalogs. She installed a tea bar in the front window.

Molly capitalized on the new research reports that promoted the healthful aspects of tea drinking. She pursued health food junkies and jaded coffee drinkers with clever marketing schemes. When that proved profitable, she started marketing to the New Age and meditation crowd. She hired an instructor to give lessons in the ancient art of the Japanese tea ceremony.

The bank got its money. Jasper borrowed more. Life went on. Somewhere along the line Molly realized that she was never going to go back to college to finish her studies.

Zinnia made Molly a partner in the business. With a view toward her own retirement, she had suggested that the name of the shop be changed to reflect the future. Molly had never forgotten the thrill of pride she had experienced the day the Abberwick Tea & Spice Co. sign had gone up over the door of the shop.

A year later, Molly bought out Zinnia's half of the business. The lease was up for renewal. Molly decided to move to a new location. She chose spacious, airy premises midway up a broad flight of fountain-studded steps designed to channel tourists to the waterfront. It was a perfect location for attracting both the tourist crowd and the office workers who often ate their brown bag lunches on the steps.

Zinnia went on a long cruise.

Jasper finally managed to take out a lucrative patent on his industrial robot systems. At Molly's suggestion he had licensed the rights to an aggressive young Oregon firm. Money had poured into the Abberwick family coffers.

There was suddenly so much money that even Jasper and his brother could not manage to blow it all before they were killed in their man-powered aircraft experiment.

Jasper left his daughters a sizable patent royalty income that promised to continue for years. He had left the huge headache that became known as the Abberwick Foundation to Molly.

Tessa busied herself brewing tea for the window service bar. "Tell me more about this hot date with Trevelyan."

"There's nothing to tell," Molly said. "I haven't gone out with him yet."

"Ruby Sweat is playing the Cave on Friday night," Tessa said ingenuously. "You could take him there for an evening of fun and frolic."

"Somehow I don't think the Cave is Harry's kind of place."

"I still don't get it. What made you decide to date—"

A thundering crash interrupted Tessa's question.

Molly spun around to gaze at the closed door of her office. "Oh, no, not again."

She rushed forward and threw open the door. Her sister, Kelsey, looked up from the wreckage of her latest prototype device, a gadget designed to dispense ground spice. Molly could barely see her through the cloud of powdery sage.

"What happened?" Molly demanded.

"There was a small problem with the design," Kelsey gasped. "Cover your nose, quick."

It was too late. Sage wafted through the air. Molly started to sneeze. Tears formed in her eyes. She hurried into her office and slammed the door shut behind her to prevent the spice from getting into the outer shop. She seized a tissue from the box on her desk and breathed through it while she waited for the finely ground sage to settle.

"Sorry about this." Kelsey sneezed into a tissue. "I was real close this time. Next time for sure."

Molly had heard those words a thousand times over the years. Her father and her uncle, Julius, had both used them like a litany. *I was real close this time. Next time for sure.* Molly had considered inscribing those words over the door of the Abberwick mansion as a sort of family motto.

The thing was, with an Abberwick, those infamous words occasionally proved true.

"Situation normal," Molly muttered. She sneezed again. Her eyes watered. She sniffed loudly and yanked more tissue from the box.

Kelsey wiped her own eyes and gave Molly an apologetic smile. The perfect grin revealed the results of several thousand dollars' worth of orthodontia, which Molly had sprung for a few years earlier. Molly briefly admired her investment. The family had not been able to afford such luxuries when she had been in her teens. The result was that Molly had two slightly crooked front teeth.

"You okay?" Kelsey asked.

"This will certainly clear my sinuses for the next six months." Molly brushed sage powder off her chair and sat down. She gave the spice dispenser device a brief glance.

The machine was composed of a series of plastic tubes and levers designed to control the release of dried and ground spice. The small motor that powered the dispenser lay in smoking ruins on the corner of the desk.

"What went wrong?" Molly asked.

Kelsey bent over the wreckage with the air of a police pathologist examining a dead body. "I think the ground sage somehow got sucked into the motor and clogged it."

"I see." There was no point getting upset over this sort of thing, and Molly knew it. Failed experiments were a way of life for Abberwicks. She leaned back in her chair and studied her sister with a mixture of affection and resignation.

Kelsey had definitely inherited the family genius and a talent for tinkering. She had been fiddling with things since she was five. From her dollhouses to her bicycles, nothing was safe. Molly still shuddered whenever she recalled the day she walked into Kelsey's room and found her little sister with a light bulb, an extension cord, and a pair of pliers. Kelsey had intended to turn her toy oven into a real, working model.

Although Kelsey had gotten the Abberwick curiosity and a flair for invention from her father, she had received her blue eyes and coppery red hair from her mother. She had also been blessed with Samantha Abberwick's fine cheekbones and delicate jaw. The orthodontia had provided the pièce de résistance. Molly wished her mother had lived to see just how lovely her youngest daughter had become.

She also wished that her absentminded father had not been so preoccupied with his endless plans and schemes that he had failed to notice Kelsey following in his footsteps.

It had been up to Molly to try to fill in for both missing parents. She had done her best, but she knew a part of her would always fear that she had not done enough or done it right. She could only give thanks that Kelsey did not seem to mind her lack of proper parenting.

"I just need to design a filter." Kelsey studied the ruins of her spice dispenser. "That shouldn't be too difficult."

Molly glanced around the office. "First you'd better figure out a way to clean up this sage powder."

"Don't worry, I'll use the vacuum robot I installed in here last year." Kelsey reached for a screwdriver. "What did T-Rex think of Duncan Brockway's dippy idea for generating power from moonlight?"

Molly sighed. "You knew it was a dippy idea?"

"Brockway's proposal was based on wishful thinking, not good science."

"That's pretty much what Trevelyan said. Why didn't you tell me the proposal was unsound?"

"I didn't want to rain on your parade. I figured that was Trevelyan's job. It's why you pay him."

"Thanks a lot," Molly muttered. "You'd rather I look like an idiot to Harry than clue me in?"

"I'm sure he doesn't think you're an idiot. He knows that technology isn't your strong point." Kelsey looked up from the injured motor. "Hey, what's this? You're calling him Harry now? For the past month he's been T-Rex, Savage Predator. Destroyer of grant proposals."

"I'm trying to break that habit before I go out on a date with him. It could be embarrassing."

"A date." Kelsey stared at her. "You're going out on a date? With T-Rex?"

"His name is Dr. Harry Trevelyan," Molly said primly. "And he's taking me out to dinner tomorrow night."

"I don't believe this."

The phone warbled before Kelsey could recover from her shock. Molly sneezed as she reached for the receiver. "Abberwick Tea & Spice."

"Molly, dear, is that you?"

"It's me, Aunt Venicia." Molly sniffed into the tissue.

"You don't sound well. Do you have a cold?"

"I'm fine. Kelsey had a little accident with her new ground-spice dispensing device."

"No harm done, I take it?"

"My sinuses will never be the same, but other than that, everything's okay."

"Well, that's all right then." Venicia dismissed the incident with the ease of long practice. She had, after all, been married to an Abberwick for thirty years before being widowed in the accident that had killed Molly's father. "I wanted to ask you what you thought of green and gold?"

"Green and gold what?"

"For the wedding colors, dear. Aren't you listening?"

"I'm listening. Green and gold sound lovely."

"Silver might be better." Venicia paused. "But somehow I can't see green and silver together, can you?"

"I've never actually thought about it." Molly brushed sage powder off the morning mail and began to sort through the stack of envelopes and sales brochures.

Venicia launched into a detailed analysis of the virtues of pairing gold rather than silver with green. Molly listened with only a portion of her attention. She was very fond of her aunt, but it was quite possible to do two things at once when Venicia talked about the plans for her upcoming wedding.

Kelsey gave her a sympathetic grin when Molly carefully slit open an envelope.

". . . I told Cutter that would be fine," Venicia said. "There's no problem, is there, dear?"

Molly realized she had missed something. "What's that, Aunt Venicia?"

"I said I told him that I was quite certain you would be able to join us for dinner on Friday night. Weren't you listening, dear?"

"Yes, of course I was." Molly exchanged a wry look with Kelsey. "I was just checking my calendar. It looks like I'm going to be busy on Friday."

"At night?" Venicia sounded startled.

"I know, it's a shock to me, too, but I've actually got a date."

"Why, dear, that's absolutely wonderful. I'm so pleased. Anyone interesting?"

"Harry Trevelyan."

"Your consultant?" Much of the enthusiasm vanished from Venicia's voice. "I thought you didn't care for Dr. Trevelyan."

"I've discovered there's more to Trevelyan than I first thought."

"Well, I suppose that any sort of date is better than nothing at all." Venicia did not sound entirely convinced. "Heaven knows that I've been quite concerned about your lack of social life for some time."

"That's the spirit, Aunt Venicia. Look on the bright side."

"Oh, I am, dear, I am," Venicia assured her. "I'm so glad to hear that you've got plans for tomorrow night. Who knows where it might lead? Why, when I first met Cutter on that cruise, I never dreamed we would fall in love."

"I'm not planning to fall in love with Harry," Molly said quickly. "We're not really each other's type."

"One never knows, dear. Opposites attract."

Molly winced. "I've never really believed in that old saying."

"Listen, I'll ask Cutter to arrange to have dinner with us some other evening. How about Saturday?"

"Saturday will be fine."

"Wonderful. Have fun tomorrow night, dear."

"I'll do that." Molly replaced the receiver with a sense of relief.

Kelsey did not look up as she unscrewed the motor housing. "What's the latest on the wedding plans?"

"Green and gold."

"What happened to blue and gold?"

"That was last week's color scheme." Molly slit open another envelope and removed an order form that had been torn out of her newest catalog. "I'll be glad when this wedding is finally over."

"I know. Aunt Venicia is kind of obsessing on it, isn't she?"

"I'm glad for her." Molly studied the list of spices that had been ordered by a customer in Arizona. "After all those years with Uncle Julius, she deserves a nice, attentive man like Cutter Latteridge."

"A nice, comfortably well-off man like Cutter Latteridge," Kelsey amended dryly. "That house on Mercer Island and that yacht of his didn't come cheap."

"There is that." Molly placed the order form in a stack on her desk. "At least we don't have to worry that he's marrying her for her money. But the important thing is that he pays attention to her. She deserves it."

"Uncle Julius wasn't so bad. He was a lot like Dad."

"Exactly." Molly reached for another envelope. "Half the time Dad forgot he even had a wife. Uncle Julius wasn't any better. Aunt Venicia told me once that in the entire thirty years of their marriage, Uncle Julius never once remembered their wedding anniversary, let alone her birthday."

Kelsey gazed deeply into the guts of the clogged motor. "Just like Dad."

Molly said nothing. Kelsey had said it all. Years of benign neglect were summed up in that simple statement. Jasper Abberwick had loved his family in his own way, but he had always loved his work more. Even the wonderful mechanical toys that he had built for his daughters years ago had been designed primarily as prototypes for the robotic devices he later developed.

Molly loved the old toys. They were stored in the basement workshop. Every six months she faithfully checked the special long-life batteries that Jasper had designed for them. At one time she'd thought that her own children would play with them someday. But lately that possibility had begun to seem more and more remote.

The office door opened. Tessa peered warily around the corner. "Everything okay in here?"

"I think we've survived another of Kelsey's experiments," Molly said.

"Great." Tessa walked into the office. There was a determined gleam in her eyes. "In that case, it's time we talked about your hot date with T-Rex."

Molly slit open another envelope. "What's to discuss?"

Kelsey put down her screwdriver. "Tessa's right. We need to talk. It's been a long time since you went out on a real date. Since you stopped seeing Gordon Brooke, in fact."

"That's not true. I had dinner with Eric Sanders just last month."

"Eric is your accountant," Tessa pointed out. "It was a working dinner. You told me the two of you spent the evening discussing your tax returns."

"So?"

Kelsey frowned. "He didn't even kiss you good night, did he?"

Molly blushed. "Of course not. He's my accountant, for heaven's sake."

"I knew it." Kelsey looked at Tessa. "She's a naive, innocent little lamb."

Tessa made a *tut-tut* sound. "We've got a lot of work ahead of us before we can risk letting her go out on a real date."

Molly eyed them both cautiously. "What are you two talking about?"

"It's a jungle out there," Tessa said. "But don't worry, Kelsey and I will give you a crash course in surviving modern dating."

Harry saw the strange black box sitting in front of Molly's door as soon as he got out of the car. Absently, he shifted the yellow roses he had brought with him to the crook of his left arm. He studied the box curiously as he went toward the front steps of the ramshackle mansion.

His first thought was that someone had tried to make a delivery earlier and had left the box in front of the door when no one had answered the bell.

His next thought was that if no one had answered the door, it could only mean that Molly was not home. *She had forgotten the date.*

Fierce disappointment gripped him. He should have called her again this afternoon to confirm, he told himself.

And then he saw the black wire. It ran from the cover of the black box to the doorknob. The top of the box would be yanked off when the door was opened.

Harry wondered if the arrangement was someone's idea of a practical joke. Perhaps a jack-in-the-box puppet on a spring would pop out when the lid was removed.

Harry climbed the steps slowly, his attention focused on the box.

No joke.

A tingle of awareness went through him. Something was very wrong.

There was a faint, scratching sound from the other side of the heavy door. Molly knew he was here. She was about to open the door.

Harry dropped the roses and leaped toward the box.

"Don't open the door," he shouted.

"Harry?" Molly appeared in the widening crack of the doorway. "Is that you? What's wrong?"

The wire that linked the box to the door went taut. The lid was jerked off the black box. There was a whirring sound. Harry saw a pistol mounted on a metal pedestal rise into the air.

The barrel of the gun was aimed at Molly.

Four

Harry heard a soft, deadly snick even as he launched himself at the pistol assembly. His left hand struck the box, toppling the entire contraption just as the pistol fired.

The sensation of *wrongness* hit him in a shimmering wave at the instant his fingers made contact with the deadly looking mechanism. Harry had no time to react to the feeling. It vanished in a heartbeat.

A split second later, propelled by the momentum of his charging dive, Harry came up hard against the wall of the house. He recovered his balance automatically and watched as the pistol box clattered and banged its way down the front steps onto the drive.

Something soft unfurled from the barrel of the pistol. It fluttered limply as it hit the ground.

"What in the world is going on out here?" Molly looked down at the black box and its contents. She raised startled eyes to meet Harry's. "You do move quickly, don't you?"

"When I feel like it."

Harry straightened his jacket with a shrug and went slowly down the steps to stand over the fallen pistol assembly. A white flag had emerged from the barrel. There were letters printed on it in red. He used the toe of his shoe to spread out the strip of cloth so that he could read the words.

BANG. YOU'RE DEAD.

"Somebody's idea of a bad joke." Harry took a slow, deep breath. He looked at Molly. "Are you all right?"

"Of course. What about you?"

"I'm fine."

"I can see that." She grinned. "You have an original method for overcoming the social awkwardness of a first date."

"As Josh recently pointed out to me, it's been so long since I've had a date, I've forgotten the usual routine." Harry glanced down at the flag pistol. "But this wasn't from me. I brought flowers."

"You did?" Molly spotted the fallen roses. She smiled in delight. "So you did. They're beautiful. How did you know yellow roses are my favorite?"

Harry followed her glance to where the bruised roses lay scattered on the drive. "Lucky guess."

He watched her hurry down the steps to collect the flowers. The roses had been a last-minute suggestion from Josh, but Harry saw no reason to mention that. He told himself he would have thought of them on his own if Josh hadn't brought up the subject. He was out of practice, but he wasn't stupid.

It struck Harry that Molly looked wonderful tonight. She had on a dashing little scarlet dress trimmed with gold buttons. The matching cropped jacket had a snappy, mock-military style. Her rambunctious hair was inadequately confined behind each ear with small gold clips. A pair of strappy black dress sandals emphasized the graceful arch of her feet. Harry realized that he had never before seen Molly in anything except business attire. It was a pleasant change of pace.

"I think most of them survived." Molly stooped to retrieve the roses.

"Forget the flowers. They're ruined."

"No, they're not. One or two are a little crushed, but that's all."

Harry decided not to argue the point. The drooping blooms spoke for themselves. He turned his attention back to the black box and its wicked-looking gun.

"Any idea who left you this?" he asked.

"No." Molly gave the gun assembly a dismissive glance as she walked back up the steps. "It looks like the handiwork of one of my sister's friends. She runs with an inventive crowd. Some of the boys are still a little immature, even though they're all starting college in the fall."

Harry recalled the fleeting but unmistakable sense of *wrongness* that had assailed him when he had reached out to knock the box onto its side. He swiftly suppressed the flash of recognition. There was nothing unusual in such a reaction, he told himself. The sight of a gun aimed at Molly was reason enough to explain the nasty feeling that had hit him at that moment.

"Your sister has friends who play jokes like this?" he asked.

"Kelsey got the family talent for invention." Molly smiled wryly. "She hangs out with a brainy bunch who have similar interests. They're all really very nice for the most part, but some of them have very strange notions of what constitutes humor. They've been known to spend weeks planning very elaborate, very clever pranks to play on each other."

Harry flexed his fingers. Some of the tension eased out of his muscles. "Sounds as if you've been through this sort of thing on previous occasions."

Molly wrinkled her nose. "If you grow up in a household like mine, you learn to take surprises in stride. Come on inside while I put these roses in water."

Harry hesitated, and then he went down on one knee to gather up the bits and pieces of the broken pistol assembly. He braced himself as he touched the fake pistol. A sense of relief went through him when he realized he felt nothing other than plastic and metal beneath his fingertips. It was okay. Just his imagination.

He frowned at the flag that hung from the barrel of the pistol. "Are you sure this was the work of one of your sister's friends?" he asked as he got to his feet.

"What else could it be?" Molly smiled at her armful of yellow roses. "Probably a farewell gag. Kelsey is leaving town on Sunday. She's going to her new college in California to attend a special month-long summer workshop for students in the sciences."

"I see."

With the broken pistol assembly cradled in his arms, Harry followed Molly into the cavernous hall. She led the way into a bizarre kitchen.

Harry gazed around with interest. Everything was familiar but ever so slightly skewed in appearance, as if the contents of the kitchen had all been taken from the galley of the *Starship Enterprise.* The countertops and appliances were fashioned of stainless steel and plastic shaped into innovative forms. A control panel was embedded in the wall.

Molly opened a cupboard door and removed a vase. Harry carried the broken pistol assembly to a polished steel table near the window and set it down.

"Where is your sister tonight?" he asked as he poked among the remains of the black box.

"Out with friends."

"Which of her friends didn't know that she was going out this evening?"

"I have no idea." Molly turned off the water and adjusted the roses in the vase. "Could have been any number of people. Why do you ask?"

Harry picked up the pistol and turned it in his hand. "Whoever set up this contraption must have thought that she would be home this evening."

Molly frowned over a broken rose. "I suppose so." She reluctantly removed the bloom and dropped it into a strange-looking steel container. There was a soft whoosh. The damaged flower vanished from sight.

Harry took off his jacket and hung it on the back of a chair. He sat down at the table and pulled the box toward him. He glanced up and frowned at the odd apparatus that hung from the ceiling. "How do I turn on the light?"

"Red button in the center of the table."

Harry studied the small panel of buttons embedded in the steel table. He touched the red one experimentally. An even, nonglaring light struck the surface of the table. "Nice."

"Thanks." Molly stepped back to survey her flower arrangement. "Well, that takes care of the roses. They really are wonderful, Harry. I can't recall the last time anyone brought me flowers. Thank you."

Harry made a mental note to thank Josh for reminding him of the old-fashioned gesture. "You're welcome."

"If you'll excuse me, I'll get my purse. Be back in a minute."

"Take your time." Harry leaned forward to examine the spring mechanism that had been used to elevate the pistol platform.

He heard Molly leave the kitchen. Her high-heeled sandals sounded in the hall. She would be a few minutes, he decided. He unfastened his cuffs, rolled up his sleeves, and began to dismantle the platform assembly.

Molly returned a short time later. "Harry? I'm ready."

Harry did not look up from his work. He had the spring out of the box. The components of the platform assembly were spread out on the table in front of him. "I'll just be a couple of minutes here."

"Hmm," Molly said.

The artichoke and sun-dried tomato pizza Molly selected from the patented Abberwick Food Storage and Preparation Machine emerged forty minutes later. She chose a sturdy Washington State cabernet from the Abberwick Automated Wine Cellar to go with it. After some additional consideration, she ordered romaine lettuce and blue-cheese salads from the produce section of the Food Storage and Preparation Machine. The device sang softly to itself as it rinsed the fresh romaine and spun it dry.

On a whim, Molly decided to arrange the chunks of blue cheese on the lettuce leaves by hand. The decision to add the final touch with her very own fingers probably had something to do with having a man in the house, she thought.

Some primal female urge, no doubt. It would almost certainly disappear by morning, she assured herself. Such impulses never lasted long.

By the time she was ready to serve, Harry had all the various parts of the black box contraption spread out across the kitchen table. There was no room for the plates and glasses.

Molly covertly studied Harry's forbidding features as he bent over the table. He was fully engaged in the process of dissecting the pistol assembly. The image of an alchemist at work in his laboratory popped into her mind once more. She could literally feel the intensity of his concentration.

She wondered if Harry made love with the same degree of complete, all-consuming attention. The thought made her blush furiously.

Fortunately, Harry did not notice the pink in her cheeks. He was occupied with a small, battery-powered motor he had removed from the box.

Molly pressed a button. A second stainless-steel surface unsealed itself from the wall and unfolded next to the one Harry was using as a workbench. It locked itself into position.

"Well? What do you think?" Molly set the pizza and salads down on the new table.

Harry looked up at last. He blinked as though to clear his brain. Then he glanced at the pizza and salads.

"What's that?"

"Dinner," Molly announced cheerfully. "I don't know about you, but I'm starving."

Acute alarm flickered in Harry's amber eyes. "Hell." He scowled at his watch. "I've got reservations for seven-thirty."

"You *had* reservations for seven-thirty." Molly handed him a napkin. "I'm sure they gave our table to someone else sometime after eight o'clock."

Harry groaned. "I don't believe this. Sorry." He started to rise from the chair. "I'll give the restaurant a call and see if they can fit us in at eight-thirty."

"Forget it. The pizza's ready now and I'm hungry. Hope you like artichoke and sun-dried tomatoes. I felt like experimenting tonight."

Harry gazed at the pizza with masculine appreciation. "You made this?"

"Sort of. I chose the ingredients." Molly punched a button to produce the flatware from a drawer concealed beneath the table. "The Abberwick Food Storage and Preparation Machine did all the work. Except for sprinkling the blue cheese on the salads," she added modestly. "I did that all by myself."

Harry studied the massive stainless-steel device that occupied one kitchen wall. "Amazing. One of your father's patents?"

"Yes. He tried to sell it to every single one of the major appliance manufacturers. They all told him he was crazy. They explained to him that the whole idea was to sell the consumer lots and lots of different machines to do various kitchen tasks, not one single, efficient device that would do everything and last for years."

Harry sank back down into the chair. His mouth quirked ruefully. "That's the story of a lot of interesting inventions." He picked up a wedge of pizza and took a large bite. He chewed in silence and then swallowed. "I tend to get preoccupied when I'm working on an interesting project," he said apologetically.

Molly grinned around her pizza. "I'm familiar with the syndrome."

"Because you come from a family of inventors?"

Molly shrugged. "That and because I, myself, have been known to get a tad overinvolved with a project."

"That's true, isn't it?" The hard lines of Harry's face relaxed slightly. "I've seen you get consumed by some of those grant proposals."

"I get that way about my business, too, at times."

"That makes me feel a little better about tonight," Harry said. "But I don't look forward to explaining to Josh what happened."

"Why? What's Josh got to do with our date?"

"He gave me a pithy little talk on modern dating practices. He seemed to think I had been out of the loop so long, I wouldn't know how to handle myself. Judging by this little fiasco, he may have had a point."

Molly nearly choked on a bite of pizza. She managed to swallow as the laughter bubbled up inside her. "You, too?"

One black brow rose in inquiry. "What's that mean?"

"I got the same lecture from my sister and Tessa, my assistant."

"Irritating, isn't it?" Harry took another bite of pizza. "Personally, I think Josh enjoyed holding forth. I suspect it was repayment for all the cautionary little chats I had with him while he was in high school."

"He spent a lot of time with you when he was younger?"

"He came to live with me after his father died. Josh was twelve. His mother had been killed in an accident during the setup of a carnival ride when he was a baby."

Molly put her pizza down slowly. "You raised Josh from the age of twelve?"

"I'm not sure *raised* is the correct word." Harry shrugged. "I didn't have any idea of what I was doing, but luckily for me, Josh was a great kid. He turned out all right in spite of my lack of experience."

"Mom died when my sister, Kelsey, was just a kid. Dad loved us both." Molly smiled wistfully. "He made us some incredible toys when we were younger. But he was the classic absentminded inventor."

Harry nodded in understanding. "The urge to invent can be an obsession."

"Tell me about it. Sometimes it seemed as if Dad forgot he even had a family. It got worse after Mom died. I think he used his work as an antidote for his grief."

Harry studied her with a perceptive look. "So you tried to fill in for your parents as far as Kelsey was concerned?"

Molly smiled. "I can still see her rolling her eyes whenever I gave her the cautionary lectures."

"Josh did the same thing, but he survived in spite of my interference. He'll be starting his junior year in college this fall. He plans to go on to grad school."

"Following in your footsteps?"

"What can I say? The kid's got a brain on his shoulders."

"So does Kelsey." Molly was unable to conceal her pride. "The workshop she was invited to attend this summer is open to only the most promising high school graduates. I know she'll take to college like a duck to water."

"Josh sure did. Three-point-nine grade average last year."

Molly couldn't help it. She started to laugh.

"What's so funny?" Harry asked.

"Listen to us. We sound like a couple of middle-aged parents discussing the brilliant accomplishments of their offspring."

"I've got an excuse for sounding middle-aged," Harry said dryly. "I'm thirty-six. You're still in your twenties."

Molly made a face. "I turn thirty at the end of the month." She shook her head. "My God, where does the time go?"

Harry munched pizza in silence for a while. "Ever been married?" he finally asked.

"No. Eighteen months ago I thought maybe . . . Well, it didn't work out. You?"

"I was engaged about a year and a half ago, too."

Molly stilled. "What happened?"

"She changed her mind. Married one of my cousins on the Stratton side of the family. Brandon Stratton Hughes."

"I see." Molly wasn't sure what to say to that. "I'm sorry."

"It was for the best. With the advantage of twenty-twenty hindsight, I think I can safely say that the marriage wouldn't have worked."

"Why not?"

"Olivia and I weren't well matched. She's a clinical psychologist. She was always trying to analyze me." Harry hesitated. "I don't think she liked what she found."

"I see." Molly felt the surge of unspoken communication like an undertow to his seemingly casual explanation. There was much more to the story, she thought. "I wonder what Olivia's view of your relationship was."

"I think Olivia's feelings toward me can best be summed up by the expression 'hours of boredom broken by moments of stark terror.' "

Molly stared at him, dumbfounded. It took her a few seconds to find her voice. "Terror, huh?"

"Nothing rough. Maybe nothing very interesting. Olivia would probably call it kinky." Molly wasn't sure, but it looked like Harry was blushing.

"Hm. Kinky might not be so bad. I wouldn't know, I've never tried it." Molly strove to sound blasé.

Harry looked up, and he wasn't blushing anymore. "Is that a fact?"

Their eyes met and held.

The last wedge of pizza trembled in Molly's hand as a rush of shimmering excitement flashed through her. An awareness that was so intense it bordered on pain jolted her nerve endings. She tried to dampen the unfamiliar surge of sexual energy with sheer willpower. When that failed, she decided she had better keep talking. She cleared her throat carefully.

"So," she said.

"So what?"

Molly rallied her brain and thought quickly. "So, would this kinky stuff have anything to do with the Trevelyan Second Sight that Josh mentioned the other night?"

The amusement evaporated instantly from Harry's eyes. It was replaced by a cold, shuttered expression. "I told you, that garbage about the Trevelyan Second Sight is nothing more than an old family show gimmick."

Molly considered that. "Women have believed in female intuition for eons. Most of us simply accept it as a reality. It seems perfectly natural that some men may possess it, too. Maybe there are particularly strong veins of it in some families. Some kind of genetic thing, perhaps."

"More like some kind of bullshit."

Molly blinked. "Well, I guess that tells us where you stand on the subject."

"Sorry." Harry's fierce, ascetic features were a grim mask. "But I've been living with that crap about the Trevelyan Second Sight all of my life, and I can tell you there's not so much as a grain of truth to it."

Molly glanced at the bits and pieces of the black box that lay scattered on the table. "Are you sure? Maybe it's some sort of intuition that's making you so concerned about this silly pistol prank."

Harry glanced at the array of parts spread out on the table. "It doesn't take any special sixth sense to figure out that whoever rigged this has a lot of pent-up hostility."

"You don't know my sister's friends. They're not hostile. But like I said, some of the boys are still immature."

"Someone put a lot of time and energy into setting up the box and gun. And it was aimed at you," Harry said bluntly.

"I told you, it was probably meant to startle my sister."

"I'm not so sure of that." Harry picked up a wire spring and turned it slowly between his lean, powerful fingers. "I think whoever left the box on your step probably knew that you were the person most likely to open the door."

"That's crazy," Molly assured him. "I don't have any enemies. I told you, this is the work of one of my sister's nerdy friends. It was meant as a joke, nothing more."

Harry put down the spring. "You may have more enemies than you think."

"Give me a break. What kind of enemies would I have?"

"You've written over a hundred letters of rejection during the past month. All of them to disgruntled, disappointed inventors."

Molly was startled. "Surely you don't believe that one of them would have retaliated like this?"

"It's a possibility." Harry examined another piece of the black box mechanism. "I think the police should be notified."

"Good lord. Now you're going over the top." Molly was horrified at the prospect of involving the police. Kelsey would be mortified if her friends were questioned. "Nothing happened. It was just a tasteless prank."

"All the same, it might be a good idea to file a report." Harry broke off at the sound of the front door opening.

"That must be Kelsey." Molly sprang to her feet, relieved at the interruption. She went to stand in the arched opening that connected the kitchen to the long front hall.

"Hi, Kelsey. How was the film?"

"Molly." Kelsey's blue eyes widened in astonishment. "What are you doing home this early? What happened to the hot date with T-Rex? Don't tell me he stood you up after we went to all that trouble to find the right dress."

"T-Rex?" Harry murmured behind Molly.

Heat rose in Molly's cheeks. She gave her sister a warning scowl. "Harry is here. We decided to eat in tonight."

"Oops." Kelsey grimaced as she walked down the hall toward her sister. "Sorry about that."

"Come and meet him," Molly said.

Kelsey peered around Molly. She regarded Harry with grave curiosity. "Hi."

"Hello." Harry got to his feet. "I know I'm going to regret asking, but would you mind telling me where I picked up the nickname?"

"T-Rex?" Kelsey gave him an unabashed grin. "Molly started calling you that because of the way you tore apart all those grant proposals. And because your last name starts with the letter T. Trevelyan Rex. Get it?"

"Got it." Harry slanted Molly a speculative glance.

Molly closed her eyes and hoped that she had not actually turned the color of a ripe tomato.

"Hey, didn't mean to interrupt," Kelsey continued blithely. "I came home right after the film instead of going to Robin's house so that I could finish packing. I'm leaving for California on Sunday morning."

"So I hear," Harry said. "A summer workshop in the sciences?"

"Right." Kelsey's gaze fell on the mechanical parts scattered across the table. "What's that?"

"It's the remains of a very unpleasant little prank that one of your friends played on me tonight," Molly said briskly. "I suspect either Danny or Calvin. A fake gun was set to fire when I opened the door. Instead of a bullet, a flag appeared."

"Weird." Kelsey walked toward the table. She frowned at the array of parts. "But I don't think Danny or Calvin is responsible."

Harry's gaze sharpened. "What makes you so certain?"

"Well, for one thing, Danny and Calvin both outgrew this kind of stunt when they were juniors in high school." Kelsey examined the spring mechanism more closely. "And . . ."

"And?" Harry prompted.

Kelsey raised one shoulder in casual dismissal. "This isn't their style. Danny is into computers. Anything he rigged would have been based on some sort of electronic device. Calvin is into chemistry. His stunts always involved chemicals."

Harry smiled slightly. "Excellent reasoning."

Kelsey beamed. "Thanks."

"The workmanship on this thing was sloppy," Harry said. "Are any of your friends inclined to take the quick-and-dirty approach to their projects?"

"Well, Robin is a little casual when it comes to building her prototypes." Kelsey chewed thoughtfully on her lower lip. "But I can't see her setting up something like this. Lucas might have done it. He's kind of young for his age, if you know what I mean. I'll call him in the morning and see if he knows anything about this."

"I'd appreciate that," Harry said.

"Look," Molly said firmly, "I'm sure this is the end of the matter. I suggest we all forget about it."

Kelsey and Harry looked at her.

"Anyone for ice cream?" Molly asked with determined enthusiasm.

Harry glanced at his watch. "I should be going."

"Hey, don't leave on account of me." Kelsey held up both hands and started to back out of the kitchen. "I can vanish upstairs. You'll never even know I'm there."

"That's not necessary." Harry glanced at Molly. "What with one thing or another, I seem to have ruined this evening."

"Not true," Molly assured him. She thought of all she had learned about Harry tonight and hugged the intimate information to herself. "I had a very interesting time."

Harry looked skeptical. "In that case, can I talk you into re-scheduling?"

Molly didn't hesitate. "Absolutely."

"Saturday night?"

Molly started to accept and then recalled that she had other plans. "I'm having dinner with my aunt and her fiancé."

Harry accepted that. "I'll be out of town all day Sunday. I'm driving to Hidden Springs to see Josh's grandfather." He hesitated. "I don't suppose you'd like to come with me?"

Molly shook her head. "Thanks, I'd love to, but Kelsey leaves for California Sunday morning. I'm going to take her to the airport."

An unreadable expression came and went in Harry's eyes. "Hidden Springs is only an hour's drive. I can wait until you've seen Kelsey off."

"Take him up on it," Kelsey advised. "You could use a day off."

"All right." Molly smiled. "Can we go to the fair while we're in Hidden Springs? I haven't been to one in years."

"Why not?" Harry said.

"Sounds like fun," Kelsey said. "When was the last time you rode a Ferris wheel or ate cotton candy, Molly?"

"It's been years," Molly admitted.

Harry looked pained. "Please, anything but cotton candy."

Molly laughed. "Okay, okay, I'll stick to popcorn. But only if you'll promise to win me one of those big stuffed animals."

"No problem," Harry said. "As long as we play a game that's operated by one of my relatives. Without an inside connection, the probability of winning a large stuffed animal approaches infinity."

"Are those carnival games all rigged?" Kelsey asked.

"Let's just say they're not set up to favor the players," Harry said dryly.

Molly batted her lashes. "I bet you could win, regardless, Harry."

The momentary humor disappeared from his harsh face. His gaze grew disturbingly intent. "Remember the hours of boredom before you get too excited about the other stuff."

"I don't bore easily." Molly felt her pulse beat strongly in her veins. She looked into Harry's eyes and was suddenly light-headed. She said the first words that came to her. "If worse comes to worse, I can always amuse myself."

Harry's smile was slow and infinitely seductive. "I trust it won't come to that."

Saturday morning Harry stood alone in the cool, hushed darkness of the Seattle Aquarium. He frequently came here when he wanted to think.

He watched an electric eel as it dozed on the bottom of its tank. The creature fascinated Harry. He found it almost as strange and improbable as the fact that he had asked Molly to go with him to Hidden Springs.

Half an hour ago, driven by a deep restlessness that had made it difficult to concentrate on his work, he had walked down to the waterfront. He needed to think about what he had done the previous evening.

He had intended to keep his relationship with Molly separate from the complications of his family life.

The feud between the Strattons and the Trevelyans rarely broke out into open conflict for the simple reason that Harry made certain that the two clans never came into contact with each other. Harry was the only connection between the two families. Both sides had made it excruciatingly clear that they wanted the situation kept that way.

The Strattons considered the Trevelyans, with the exception of Harry, a lower form of life. They had never forgiven Sean Trevelyan for daring to marry Brittany Stratton, the family princess. The fact that Brittany had run off with Sean of her own free will did not seem to make any difference to the Strattons.

The Trevelyans took an equally dim view of the Strattons, whom they considered patronizing, effete snobs. In their considered opinion, it was the Stratton influence that had caused Harry's father to turn his back on his family.

When Harry had initially planned the affair with Molly, he had never intended to expose her to his difficult relatives. He did not understand the impulse that had made him invite her to Hidden Springs, and that worried him. He had spent a good portion of the night thinking about it.

His brain usually worked in clear, crisp, orderly patterns. The sole exceptions were his occasional *insights.* The realization that his feelings for Molly might be as inexplicable as those rare, traumatic flashes of *knowing* disturbed Harry.

A menacing shiver went through the eel. The creature's cold, emotionless gaze met Harry's through the glass barrier of the tank. Harry contemplated the primitive evolution of the eel's brain with something that could have been envy.

Nothing was complicated for the eel. There were no messy family problems, no sense of being caught between two warring worlds. No melancholy moods. *And no fear of a deep, clawing hunger for a soul-searing bond that could not even be explained, let alone consummated.*

Someone came up to stand in front of the tank. Harry turned his head and gave the newcomer one brief glance before he returned to his contemplation of the eel. He was mildly surprised to see his cousin, Brandon Stratton Hughes.

"I assume this is not a coincidence," Harry said.

"I stopped by your condo." Brandon pitched his voice very low. He looked quickly around the sparsely populated display room, obviously checking to make certain that no one could overhear him. "Your housekeeper said you had walked down here. Kind of an expensive way to kill a little time, isn't it? That ticket at the front door wasn't cheap."

"I've got an annual pass. I like to come here when I want to think."

"You would."

Harry's relationship with Brandon had never been close, but then, with the exception of Josh none of his relationships with the various members of his family could be described as close.

He and Brandon had almost nothing in common except a shared gene pool from the Stratton side of the family.

Brandon was four years younger than Harry. He had the athletic build, blue eyes, fair hair, and aristocratic good looks that had characterized the Stratton males for several generations. Brandon also had a secure position as a vice president in Stratton Properties, the family-held commercial real estate development firm.

"Well?" Harry said. "You must have wanted to talk to me very badly to make it worth paying the entrance fee to the aquarium just to find me."

"I'll get straight to the point. Has Olivia called you today?"

"No."

"What about my mother?"

"I haven't heard from Aunt Danielle today, either." Harry glanced at Brandon. "Why?"

Brandon's face tightened. "They're both a little upset."

"About what?"

Brandon drew a deep breath. "You may as well be among the first to know. I've decided to leave Stratton Properties. I'm going out on my own. I'm setting up a commercial property management firm."

Harry whistled soundlessly. "I'll bet that's been a popular decision."

"You know damn well it's going over like a lead balloon. I made the announcement last night. The whole family is in an uproar. My mother is frantic. Granddad is pissed. Uncle Gilford has already chewed me up one side and down the other."

"I'm not surprised." Harry paused. "And Olivia?"

"Olivia thinks I'm making a big mistake." Brandon gazed glumly at the eel. "She says my decision is not based on a logical assessment of the situation. She says it's a function of my wish to rebel against a controlling grandfather and an overprotective mother."

"You've got one of each," Harry pointed out. "And the rest of the family isn't exactly laid-back, either."

"Damn it, Harry, I'm going to do this." Brandon made a fist with one hand. "I want out of the family business."

"It won't be easy."

"You managed it. You told Granddad to go to hell when he tried to force you to join Stratton Properties. You walked away from your inheritance that day. Granddad cut you out of his will, and you just turned your back on the Stratton money as if it meant nothing."

"The price he wanted me to pay was too high," Harry said softly. "Parker wanted me to pretend that I wasn't a Trevelyan."

Brandon swung around to face him. "I'm going to get out from under the family thumb, too."

"Okay."

"What's that supposed to mean?" Brandon demanded.

"What do you want me to say?"

"I don't want you to say anything," Brandon muttered. "But I want your word that you won't get involved if my mother or Olivia asks you to convince me not to leave the company."

"I won't try to stop you from leaving Stratton Properties," Harry promised. "Why should I? If you want to walk away from a cushy job at the company, that's your business. Just remember that nothing comes for free when you're dealing with Strattons. You'll pay a price."

"You mean Granddad will cut me out of the will, just as he did you?"

"Probably."

Brandon squared his shoulders. "I can live with that."

Harry heard the bold words. He also heard the underlying insecurity. "What does Olivia think of that possibility?"

"Olivia is my wife," Brandon said tightly. "She loves me. When the chips are down, she'll back me."

Harry said nothing. He was no judge of Olivia's affections. He had certainly misread her a year and a half ago, when he had convinced himself that Olivia had loved him.

Five

"Well, Molly, did you carry out your threat to fire your so-called consultant?" Cutter Latteridge sliced into the thick, rare steak that took up half of his plate. Blood red juices ran onto the nearby baked potato.

"I've decided to give Trevelyan another chance." Molly averted her gaze from the sight of the bleeding steak. She looked at her aunt, who was sitting next to Cutter on the other side of the table. "It's not like there's a lot of choice. People with his sort of expertise are few and far between."

"Yes, I know, dear, but you did say he was being awfully difficult," Venicia reminded her. "You told me he hadn't approved a single grant proposal."

"True," Molly admitted. "But I have hopes."

"I trust you do." Venicia made a *tut-tut* sound. "Pity to think of all that money sitting around waiting to go to a worthy cause. Jasper would have been so disappointed."

"I know." Molly smiled.

She was very fond of Venicia. Her aunt had always been part of her life. Venicia had offered comfort and support in the traumatic period following the death of Molly's mother. Years later, in the wake of the failed experiment that had taken the lives of the Abberwick brothers, Molly, Kelsey, and Venicia had grieved together and consoled each other.

Venicia was a slightly plump, energetic woman in her mid-fifties.

Shortly after the patent royalty checks had begun arriving on a regular basis, she had discovered an abiding enthusiasm for trendy fashion. Tonight she was wearing a gold-studded, purple silk jumpsuit, huge purple and gold earrings, and several pounds of gold necklaces.

"Not much point in having a well-endowed foundation if you can't find anyone to fund," Cutter observed. His bushy gray brows bounced as he chewed vigorously on his steak.

"Jasper is probably turning over in his grave," Venicia murmured. "He and Julius were both so eager to help out other financially strapped inventors. They both spent most of their lives scrounging for cash for their projects. They wanted to make it easier for others who found themselves in their position. I wonder why it is that so many inventors are unable to handle finances."

Cutter shook his head sympathetically. "Unfortunately the same brilliant mind that can focus so keenly on invention is often not very good with the financial aspects of the work."

"How true." Venicia sighed. "Neither Jasper nor my husband could be bothered with such concerns. Jasper was worse than Julius, truth be known. He really got into deep trouble with the banks on a couple of occasions, didn't he, Molly?"

"Yes." Molly concentrated on her spicy Thai-flavored pasta. It made her uncomfortable to discuss Jasper's lamentable money habits outside the family. And although it appeared that he soon would be a member of the clan, Cutter Latteridge had not yet made the transition.

"I do believe Jasper's family would have wound up on food stamps after Samantha died if it hadn't been for Molly," Venicia told Cutter. "Poor girl had to drop out of college to go to work in order to keep a roof over their heads."

"Dad more than made up for it in the end," Molly reminded her quietly. "That patent he took out for the industrial robotic systems will provide a large, steady income for years."

"But the money came too late for you, my dear," Venicia said wistfully. "You had already made a success of your tea and spice shop by the time the royalties started arriving."

Molly shrugged. "Depends on your point of view. I had the satisfaction of achieving my success with my own efforts."

"An excellent attitude." Cutter gave her an approving look. "And you should be commended for not squandering the income from those patents on frivolous things. I'm sure Jasper Abberwick would be pleased to know that you've channeled so much money into his foundation."

"She's done exactly what Jasper would have wanted," Venicia said proudly. "Goodness knows she's been generous to me, and she's taken excellent care of Kelsey. There's plenty left over for the foundation."

Cutter assumed a grave expression. "Excellent cause. Never enough money for invention, sad to say. Even at the corporate level, research and development funds are always lacking. This country needs to invest much more into its inventive brains if it wants to maintain a competitive edge in the global economy."

Molly politely tuned him out, as she often did. She had nothing against Cutter. It was hard not to feel tolerant if not downright friendly toward him. He was an affable man who enjoyed playing host. He was gallant and solicitous toward Venicia. But he did have a tendency to pontificate.

Odd, how she never really minded when Harry launched into a lecture, Molly thought, amused. Harry never bored her. Admittedly, he occasionally tried her patience, but he never bored her. Even sitting in her kitchen watching him dismantle the black box that had been left at her front door had been anything but boring.

Cutter was another matter. He was a retired engineering executive who had a tendency to hold forth on whatever subject was being discussed. He considered himself an expert on everything.

Cutter was in his late fifties, a year or two older than Venicia. Balding and blunt-featured, he had the ruddy looks and sturdy build that hinted of a childhood spent on a farm.

Molly had once asked him why he had retired at such an early age. He had given her a kindly smile and allowed as to how he'd come into some family money. In addition, he'd taken advantage of a very generous early retirement plan offered by his firm. Life was short, he'd explained. He had wanted to enjoy it while he was still relatively young and in good health.

After he and Venicia had met on the spring cruise, they had been inseparable. Their engagement had been announced a month ago.

". . . Don't you agree, Molly?" Cutter asked.

It was the note of concern in his voice that brought Molly's attention back to Cutter. She gave him an apologetic smile. "Sorry, I didn't catch that. What was your question?"

"I said," Cutter repeated patiently, "don't you think it's a little strange that your high-priced grant proposal consultant can't seem to find any worthwhile projects for you to fund?"

"I've discussed the problem with him."

"How many proposals has the foundation received?"

"About a hundred."

"And this Dr. Trevelyan hasn't approved a single one." Cutter frowned. "Odd. Very odd. My experience in the corporate world suggests that at least five or ten percent of those proposals should have been solid."

Venicia looked at him with some surprise. "Five or ten?"

Cutter hacked off another chunk of beef. "At least. I'm not saying one would want to fund all five or ten, but there should have been that many that warranted serious consideration."

"Statistics can be tricky," Molly said. For some reason she felt compelled to defend Harry's decisions. "One hundred grant proposals isn't a very large sample."

"Quite true," Cutter agreed. "Still, one does wonder what this Dr. Trevelyan is up to."

"Up to?" Molly gave him a sharp look. "What do you mean?"

"Nothing, I'm sure," Cutter said soothingly. "Nevertheless . . ."

"Nevertheless, what?" Molly demanded.

"I would advise caution, my dear," Cutter said.

"Caution?"

"You're new at this sort of thing." Cutter put down his knife and regarded her with a slightly troubled frown. "Bear in mind that there is always a great deal of money to be made in the administrative end of any charity operation. An unscrupulous person in Trevelyan's position could make himself a tidy fortune in consulting fees over a period of time."

"I don't believe Harry would use his position to con me." Molly realized that she was inexplicably incensed by what had been nothing more than a reasonable warning from a man who had seen more of the world than she had. "I'm aware that there is no shortage of embezzlers and frauds hanging around waiting to take advantage of foundations such as mine, but I can promise you that Harry Trevelyan isn't one of them."

Cutter raised his heavy brows. "The more charming they are, the more clever they are, my dear."

"Harry isn't particularly charming," Molly muttered. But he had given her very similar advice, she reminded herself.

"No offense," Cutter said gently, "but he does appear to have you eating out of the palm of his hand."

"That's nonsense," Molly said.

Venicia touched her napkin to her lips and gave Cutter a worried look. "Do you think that Dr. Trevelyan might be milking the foundation with outrageous consulting fees?"

"I'm not making any accusations," Cutter said.

Molly's fingers tightened on her fork. "I should hope not. Besides, Harry's fees aren't outrageous."

Venicia and Cutter both looked at her.

"Okay, they're on the high side," Molly admitted. "But they're within reason. Especially given his qualifications."

Cutter snorted politely and went back to his steak.

Venicia glanced at him and then turned to Molly with an uneasy expression. "I do hope you haven't gotten yourself tangled up with someone like that dreadful Gordon Brooke again, dear."

Molly winced. "Trust me, Harry Trevelyan has nothing in common with Gordon Brooke."

Cutter cleared his throat to draw Molly's and Venicia's full attention. "As I said, administrative costs are difficult to control in any organization, especially a nonprofit foundation. A trustee in Molly's position must be on her guard."

"Harry Trevelyan is not a thief or a swindler," Molly said fiercely.

Cutter sighed. "I never said he was. I'm merely suggesting that a charitable trust is very vulnerable to abuse. Anyone can call himself a consultant, after all."

Venicia nodded sagely. "Cutter is quite right. One reads about charities and foundations being defrauded all the time. You will be cautious with your Dr. Trevelyan, won't you, Molly?"

Molly stabbed her fork into a heap of pasta. She'd been forced to be cautious all of her adult life. She'd had too many responsibilities weighing on her to allow her the luxury of taking a few chances. She was nearly thirty years old, and there was finally a glimmer of excitement on the horizon. What's more, she was free to explore that glimmer.

Molly smiled blandly. "You know me, Aunt Venicia. I'm the soul of caution. I'll be careful."

Molly scrutinized Kelsey one last time as the passengers began to file on board the plane. "Are you sure you have everything you're going to need?"

Kelsey rolled her eyes. "If I've forgotten anything, you can send it down to me."

"I'm fussing, aren't I?"

"Yes, you are." Kelsey chuckled. "I'm only going to be gone for a month."

"I know." Molly gave her sister a misty smile. "But this is a sort of trial run for me. A taste of what it's going to be like when you leave for college in the fall."

Kelsey's expression grew serious. "I've been giving that some thought. I talked to Aunt Venicia. We both think you should sell the house, Molly."

Molly stared at her in amazement. "Are you kidding?"

"No, I'm not. The mansion is too big for you to live in all by yourself."

"It's no trouble to keep up, thanks to Dad's cleaning robots. I know how to maintain them."

"That's not the point," Kelsey insisted. "The Abberwick mansion will be just too much house for you when you're there all alone. And it's filled with the past, if you know what I mean."

"I understand, Kelsey, but I don't mind that part."

"I think you will when you're rattling around in that big old house all by yourself. Promise me you'll at least consider selling it. You could get yourself a modern downtown condo."

"But it's our home. It's always been our home."

"Things will change when I leave for college."

Molly looked at the sister she had raised to womanhood and saw the future in Kelsey's intelligent eyes. "Believe me, I realize that."

Of course things would change. Molly told herself she had always known that this moment would arrive. Kelsey was about to start her own life. Her talent and brains would take her far from the crazy old ramshackle Abberwick mansion. It was the way of the world.

"Please, Molly, don't cry."

"Wouldn't think of it." Molly blinked very rapidly to clear the moisture from her eyes. "Listen, have a great time at the workshop."

"I will." Kelsey shifted her backpack and started toward the gate. She looked back once. "Promise me you'll think about selling the house, okay?"

"I'll think about it."

Molly waved good-bye until Kelsey disappeared from view down the ramp. Then she reached for a tissue. When she realized that a single tissue wasn't going to be sufficient for the task at hand, she headed for the women's room.

It wasn't her promise to her sister that was on Molly's mind later that afternoon as she and Harry drove toward Hidden Springs. It was the one she had made to her aunt the previous night at dinner.

I'll be careful.

She did not know which should concern her the most, the safety of the Abberwick Foundation assets or the safety of her own heart. She had a nasty suspicion that she was falling in love with Harry Trevelyan.

Maybe it was just sexual attraction, she reassured herself.

She slanted a sidelong glance at him. His powerful, elegant hands appeared relaxed and yet in complete control as they gripped the wheel. Quiet competence radiated from him no matter what the circumstances, she thought. There was a core of strength in him that compelled respect on a very primitive level.

If this was just passion, it was heady, potentially dangerous stuff.

I'll be careful.

Right. She would be careful the way a mountain climber was careful when approaching Everest. Careful the way a spelunker was careful when descending into a deep cave. Careful the way an astronaut was careful when stepping out into space.

"What kind of car is this?" Molly asked curiously. "I don't think I've ever seen one quite like it."

"You haven't. It's one of a kind at the moment. It's a Sneath P2. One of a series of prototypes. Friend of mine designed and built it. It's got the aerodynamics of a racing car, the strength of a well-made European touring car, and an engine which is supposed to go for years at a time without a tune-up."

"Amazing. Why did your friend give it to you?"

"I helped him obtain the venture capital he needed to build the prototypes."

Molly gave him an inquiring glance. "I think of you as an academic type, but I suppose in your line of work you come into contact with investors all the time."

"Yes," Harry said evenly. "But unlike the Abberwick Foundation, they all want to back projects that show real potential for repaying the investment."

Molly chuckled. "Me, I just want to throw the money away."

"How did things go at the airport this morning?"

"Fine." Molly was startled by the quick change of subject. "Why do you ask?"

"It feels strange when they leave home, doesn't it? I know your sister is only going away for a month this summer, but in the fall, it will be for real. That's when you realize that things have changed forever."

Molly smiled wryly. "Okay, so I cried my eyes out in the rest room after she left. I'm all right now."

"Glad to hear it. Try to look on the bright side. No more rock music posters in their bedrooms and no more lying awake at night waiting until they finally come home. Look at me. I've been teen-free for two years now, and I'm a new man."

He understood, Molly thought. He was trying to make light of the turning point she had faced that morning, but he knew what it had been like for her. Harry had been through the same experience, accepted the same responsibilities.

"I'll take your word for it," she said. *Oh, my God. This is getting serious.*

Harry lapsed back into silence. The beautifully tuned engine of the exotic car hummed to itself. Molly settled down into the leather seat and watched the lush farmlands speed past the window. In the distance the Cascades rose toward a clear, blue sky. The future, which had seemed to be shrouded in mist a few hours ago, began to look bright once more.

The silence lengthened. Molly stirred and glanced at her watch. She realized that Harry had not said a single word for nearly twenty minutes. It wasn't the lack of conversation that had begun to bother her. It was the gathering tension she felt. It was radiating from him.

"Is something wrong?" she asked.

"No." Harry did not look away from the road. "I was just doing some thinking."

"You're not looking forward to this trip, are you?"

"Not especially."

"This may sound like a dumb question, but why are we driving all the way to Hidden Springs if you aren't anxious to see your relatives?"

"I told Josh I'd have a talk with his grandfather," Harry said. "Leon is giving him a hard time. He's leaning on Josh. Trying to convince him that he doesn't need to finish college."

"Josh's grandfather would be your uncle, right?"

"Right. My father's younger brother."

Molly thought about that. "Why didn't he take charge of his grandson after Josh's father was killed?"

"That would have been difficult. Uncle Leon was in jail at the time."

"Jail?" Molly turned her head to stare at him. "For heaven's sake, why?"

Harry slanted her an unreadable glance. "He was awaiting trial on charges resulting from a dispute he had with a county sheriff."

"I see." Molly digested that news. "What sort of dispute?"

"Uncle Leon was screwing the sheriff's wife. He and the lady were discovered by her husband in a motel room. The sheriff was understandably pissed."

"Oh." Molly hesitated. "I can see why the sheriff was angry, but an affair doesn't constitute grounds for arrest."

"The sheriff nailed him for auto theft, not for messing around with another man's wife."

"Auto theft?" Molly repeated weakly.

"Uncle Leon and the lady used the sheriff's car to drive to the motel."

"Good grief. That wasn't very smart."

"No, it wasn't. But then, as far as I'm concerned, Josh is the first member of that branch of the family to show any brains in three generations." Harry's hand flexed on the steering wheel. "I'll be damned if I'll let Leon pressure him into leaving college."

"Why would Leon want to do that in the first place?"

"Leon used to make his living driving race cars at county fairs. His son—my cousin Willy and Josh's father—was a motorcycle stuntman. He was killed doing a stunt. Every few years Leon gets the harebrained notion of encouraging Josh to follow in the family footsteps."

"Whew. I can see why you're concerned. Doesn't sound like a career path loaded with potential."

"It's a dead end." Harry moved his right hand to the gearshift as he prepared to turn off the highway. "Literally, in Willy's case. I'm not going to let Josh get sucked into that lifestyle."

"How will you convince your uncle to leave him alone?"

"The same way I did the last time." Harry's mouth was a grim line. "Sweet reason."

Molly did not press the matter. It was Trevelyan family business, after all. But she could not resist one last question. "What happened to Leon when he went to trial for auto theft?"

"The charges were dropped."

"He must have had a good lawyer."

"He did. I hired him myself."

The Ferris wheel came into view first. It rose majestically above the midway, a venerable, graceful, glittering contraption that still had the power to enthrall young and old alike. The engineers who designed exotic rides for the new high-tech theme parks had invented far more elaborate thrill machines over the years, but nothing would ever replace the Ferris wheel on a carnival midway.

Harry did not enjoy Ferris wheels, or any of the other rides, for that matter. He told himself that it was because he'd come from a carny family. Although his father had sold his amusement show before his son was born, Harry had spent several summer vacations traveling with his Trevelyan relatives. He had learned to set up, operate, and tear down the rides. No one who worked the midway got a kick out of the machines. It was a business, after all.

But Harry had always suspected that his personal dislike of the whirling, churning, stomach-wrenching devices went deeper in him than it did in other people involved in the world of the carnival. The real truth was that he hated the lack of control he experienced when he was trapped inside one of the small, spinning carriages.

He had struggled too long to develop a sense of self-mastery. He could not willingly surrender that control to anyone or anything else, not even for a three-minute amusement park ride.

Molly twisted in her seat to get a better view of the fairgrounds. "Where are we going?" she asked as Harry drove past the main parking lots.

"Around back to where the carnies and the fair people park their vehicles. Uncle Leon will be there somewhere."

The motley collection of trucks, vans, trailers, and motor homes stood on the far side of the fairgrounds. They were shielded from the view of the fairgoers by a fence lined with the colorful booths and tents of the midway.

Harry parked near a stand of trees and got out. A light wind blew toward him across the fairgrounds. The combined scent of grease, popcorn, and corn dogs hit him, as it always did, with a tidal wave of memory.

Molly came to stand beside him. "Something wrong?"

"No." Harry pulled his thoughts back to the present. "That smell always reminds me of the summers I spent with my Trevelyan relatives."

Molly held a wisp of hair out of her eyes and regarded him with an intently curious expression. "I'll bet you're not a big fan of popcorn and hot dogs."

"No, I'm not." He took her hand and started toward a cluster of aging trailers. "Look, this interview with Uncle Leon is not going to be pleasant. Do you think you can find something else to do until it's over?"

"No problem. I'll tour the exhibits."

"Don't get conned into buying any of the juicer-grater-slicer-dicer machines from the guys who do the demonstrations. The gadgets are all junk."

"Don't be silly," Molly said. "I'm a businesswoman, remember? I'm not likely to be taken in by someone else's sales pitch."

Harry gave her a pitying look. "Haven't you ever heard that the easiest person to sell to is a person who is in sales?"

"Hah. I don't believe it. I've never heard that particular bit of wisdom. It sounds like more of your paranoid philosophy, and I am not going to listen to it. Now, how will I find you after you've finished speaking to your uncle?"

Harry smiled faintly. "Somewhere on the midway you'll find a fortune-teller's tent. Look for a sign advertising Madam Evangeline. I'll meet you there around one o'clock."

"Got it." She touched his arm in a light, fleeting gesture, and then she walked off toward the gate.

Harry waited until she disappeared into the crowd. He still didn't understand why he had brought her with him today, but he was glad he had.

He walked through the encampment until he found the aging trailer Leon called home. It was parked near a tree. Leon's old truck stood nearby.

Harry pounded on the screen door of the trailer. "Leon, you inside?"

"Who the hell . . . ?" Leon came to the door of the trailer. He squinted against the sunlight. When he saw Harry his teeth flashed in the Trevelyan grin. "Shit. So you finally got here. You're late. Figured you'd show up yesterday."

"If I'd known you were so eager to see me again, I'd have waited a little longer."

"The hell you would have waited." Leon opened the screen door. "When it comes to this kind of thing, you're as predictable as the sunrise. One of your bad habits, boy. Come on in."

Harry stepped into the shadowy confines of the trailer. The blinds were shut. It took a brief moment for his eyes to make the transition from the sun-drenched parking lot to the close darkness inside the metal hulk.

"Beer?" Leon asked casually from somewhere off to the left.

The cold, damp can came hurtling out of the gloom before Harry could reply. He opened his hand without thinking about it. The beer can landed firmly in his grasp. Things had a way of doing that.

"Thanks," Harry said absently.

Leon grinned. "Still fast as ever, I see. Damn shame you didn't use those talented Trevelyan hands for something a little more useful than writin' dull books."

Harry peeled back the ring on the beer can. "Reflexes have a way of going on a man as he gets older. I prefer to rely on my brains."

"That Stratton blood of yours ruined you." Leon sprawled on the battered sofa that was built into the curved rear wall of the trailer. He gestured with his beer can. "Have a seat."

Harry sank down onto the ripped vinyl bench that framed the eating nook. He glanced around without much interest.

Little had changed, either in the decor or in Leon, over the years. Trailer and owner appeared to have bonded in some indefinable manner. The stained linoleum on the floor had a counterpart in Leon's faded shirt and ancient, low-slung jeans. The torn curtains on the small windows smelled of tobacco and booze. So did Leon.

Harry decided that, on the whole, Leon was holding up better than his trailer. That was due to the sturdy Trevelyan genes, not anything resembling good health habits.

Leon was in his sixties, but he still possessed the lean build and broad shoulders that were characteristic of Trevelyan males. He was as handsome as Harry's father had been. Harry knew Leon still traded shamelessly on his looks. His uncle went through women as though they were lollipops. Willy had had the same approach to the opposite sex.

Harry was satisfied that Josh was not going to follow in their footsteps in that regard. For all his good-natured teasing about the unused box of condoms in the bathroom cupboard, Josh had more common sense and innate integrity about such matters at twenty than his father and grandfather had ever had in their entire lives. Harry had made sure of it.

Leon took a long, deep swallow of beer. "So how's the soft life in the big city?"

"Fine." Harry waited. He had learned long ago that it never paid to reveal urgency or eagerness with Leon. Leon liked to goad people until he provoked them into doing something stupid.

"Shit. I still don't know why you want to live like that," Leon mused. "Where's your Trevelyan spirit?"

"Beats me." Harry took a short sip of the beer.

"No guts, no glory, son. Haven't you ever heard that bit of wisdom?"

"I hear it every time I have a conversation with you, Uncle Leon."

"Josh tells me you're seeing some mousy little shopkeeper."

Harry did not move. "Did Josh call her mousy?"

"No, but I got the picture. Runs a tea shop, Josh said. I know the type. Prissy, uptight little business suit, right?"

"Not quite," Harry said softly.

Leon ignored him. "Hell, your pa at least had the gumption to run off with a rich man's daughter. Your ma was a real beauty, and everyone knows the Strattons have enough money to float a battleship."

"So they say."

"You're a damn fool for turning your back on all that cash, by the way."

"So I'm told."

Leon squinted at him over the beer can. "Hell, you ain't the best-lookin' Trevelyan to come down the road, but you're still a Trevelyan. Thought you could do better than a dull little shopkeeper."

"When did you develop this abiding interest in my private life?"

"Got to take an interest in it. Worried about Josh."

Harry steeled himself. "What does my private life have to do with Josh?"

"Simple." Leon grimaced. "You're a bad influence on the boy. All he talks about is goin' to college forever and a day to get some fancy science degree. Says he wants to do research, for cryin' out loud. Next thing you know, he'll be dating boring little shopkeepers, too."

"And you'd rather he got himself killed trying to make a motorcycle fly through a ball of fire?"

"Bastard." Leon flung his empty beer can against the wall of the trailer. He sat forward, his fists bunched on his knees. "I want him to be a man, like his father was. Like I am. Like your father was. I don't want him turnin' into a goddamned, overeducated wimp like you."

"How much?" Harry asked without inflection.

"What's that supposed to mean?"

"You know what it means. How much do you want in exchange for laying off Josh for the summer?"

"You think you can buy anything, don't you? That's the damned Stratton blood in you talkin'. Well, I've got news for you. This is my grandson's future we're discussin'. He's all I got left in this world. Blood of my blood, fruit of my loins. I want to see him become a man I can be proud of. You think you can put a price tag on that kind of thing?"

"No problem."

Leon's face worked furiously. "This is about family, damn you. It's not about money."

"Don't give me that crap," Harry said wearily. "We both know this isn't about Josh or his future. It's about making a deal."

"Son-of-a-bitch."

"It's okay, Uncle Leon. I'm willing to negotiate one more time. Now, how much do you want?"

Leon glowered at him for a few more seconds. Then he fell back against the couch and closed his eyes. "I need a new truck. Old one won't go another mile. Evangeline's got a whole summer of fairs lined up. Got to have reliable transportation."

Harry whistled softly. "A new truck, huh? Congratulations, Uncle Leon. You're learning to think big."

Leon slitted his eyes. "We got a deal?"

"Sure." Harry put his unfinished beer down on the table. He got to his feet. "Same deal as last time."

"Like I said, you're as reliable as the sunrise. Got to watch that, Harry. Bad habit like that'll get you into a lot of trouble."

Harry went to the door of the trailer. He looked out across the grassy parking lot. "I meant what I said, Leon. We have the exact same deal as last time."

"Yeah, yeah. I heard you."

Harry opened the screen door and went down one step. He glanced back over his shoulder. "You stop pressuring Josh to leave college, and I'll pay for your new truck."

"Like I said, we got a deal."

"Yes." Harry met his uncle's eyes. "Break your end of the bargain, Leon, and you know what happens."

"Don't threaten me, boy. You'd never go through with it. You haven't got the guts to do it, and we both know it."

Harry said nothing. He just held Leon's gaze. The sounds of the fairground receded into the distance. A great silence gripped the trailer. The shadows within seemed to thicken.

Leon appeared to shrink in on himself. "Yeah, yeah. A deal's a deal. Go on, get outa here. I got to get down to the pits. Racing starts at seven-thirty tonight."

Harry let the sagging screen door clatter shut behind him.

He walked toward the fairground entrance. The smell of grease and popcorn and the aroma of the animal barns washed over him.

He suddenly wanted to find Molly.

Clutching an armful of purchases, Molly paused outside the red, gold, and turquoise striped booth. She looked up to read the words on the sign overhead.

Madam Evangeline
Learn the Secrets of the Past, Present, and Future
ADVICE ON MATTERS OF LOVE AND MONEY
Discretion Assured

Molly studied the beaded curtain that closed the entrance to the booth. She did not believe in palmistry, card readings, or crystal balls. The last thing she wanted to do was get her fortune told. She wondered if Harry intended to meet her outside or inside the booth.

She turned to scan the length of the midway, hoping to catch sight of him in the crowd. All she saw was an endless stream of people, their hands full of popcorn, candy apples, and hot dogs, wandering from booth to booth.

As Molly watched, a young man strolled past carrying a huge stuffed panda bear. He caught her eye and grinned.

"I won it for my girlfriend," he said proudly.

"Nice." Molly eyed the panda wistfully. "Was it hard to win?"

"Nah. You could probably win one for yourself."

"Do you really think so?"

"Sure," the young man responded very smoothly. "Why not give it a try? Only costs a quarter a toss. The booth is right across the way. See it?"

"Yes. Thanks. Maybe I'll give it a whirl."

"You won't be sorry," the young man promised. He strolled off down the midway.

Molly was about to make her way through the crowd to the coin toss game when she heard the fortune-teller's curtain snap open behind her.

"Madam Evangeline sees the past, present, and future," a throaty voice declared. "Come inside and learn your fate in love and fortune."

Molly swung around in surprise. A handsome, statuesque, middle-aged woman with silver-shot black hair stood amid the clattering beads. Fine brown eyes, a classic nose, and high cheekbones composed a face that would be striking until the woman was well into her nineties.

The fortune-teller was dressed in an ankle-length gown made of several layers of variously colored and patterned fabrics. Her long, graceful fingers were sheathed in rings. A massive necklace hung with gold and amber pendants accented an impressive bosom.

"Hello," Molly said politely. "I'm supposed to meet someone here."

The woman looked deep into Molly's eyes. "I think you have already met him."

"I beg your pardon?"

The woman inclined her head in a regal gesture. "I am Madam Evangeline. Come inside, and I will show you your future."

Molly shifted the packages in her arms. "That would be pointless. I don't believe in fortune-telling, Madam Evangeline. And, quite frankly, I wouldn't want to know my future, even if you could see it for me. Thanks, anyway. If you don't mind, I'll just wait out here."

"Please come inside," Evangeline murmured in an insistent tone. "I will not tell you anything that you do not wish to know."

Molly hesitated, her curiosity piqued. She glanced around once more to see if she could spot Harry in the crowd. There was no sign of him. She turned back to Evangeline.

"Actually, there is something you could tell me," she said.

Evangeline bowed. "I am at your service. Come inside and tell me what it is you would discover." Bells tinkled as she beckoned Molly into the tent.

Molly stepped cautiously through the dancing beads. A shadowy gloom filled the interior. The floor was covered in a midnight-blue carpet dotted with yellow stars and a moon. Yards of dark, heavy fabric cascaded down all four sides of the tent.

When her eyes adjusted to the low light, Molly was able to make out a table draped in maroon velvet. An opaque, softly glowing glass ball stood in the center. Beside it was a deck of cards. A shallow, silver bowl filled with water was placed on a nearby shelf.

"Please sit down." Evangeline gestured toward one of the two chairs that were positioned on either side of the table. "You may put your packages on the floor over there, if you wish."

"Thanks. They're getting very heavy." Molly set her burdens down and heaved a small sigh of relief. "I had no idea I'd find so many useful items in the exhibit halls."

Evangeline smiled. "Many people have had the same experience."

"I can believe it." Molly brushed her frothy, windblown hair back behind her ear. "You should have seen the crowds I had to fight in order to get this stuff. One lady actually tried to snatch my new Ace Wondermatic All-Purpose Kitchen Appliance right out of my hands."

"Amazing. Do sit down."

"All right." Molly glanced toward the beaded curtain. "But I don't want to miss my friend. He should be along at any minute."

"I guarantee that he will find you."

"If you're sure." Molly obligingly sat down and surveyed the glass ball and the deck of cards with some interest.

"Now, then, we shall begin." Evangeline cupped the glass ball in her hands. Her heavily made-up eyes met Molly's. "Tell me what it is you wish to know."

"Well, since you ask, what I'd really like to know is how this all works."

Evangeline blinked. "How it works?"

"The tricks of the trade, so to speak." Molly leaned closer. "I've heard that professional fortune-tellers are very good at guessing things about their clients' personal lives. How do you do it?"

"You want to know how I do it?" Evangeline looked scandalized.

"Exactly. Not quite my field, of course, but I'm curious. What are the clues that you use? Clothes? I expect you can tell a lot from people's clothing. But so many folks just wear name-brand jeans and sport shoes these days. What can you tell about people wearing that kind of thing?"

Evangeline's expression congealed. "I do not use tricks. I am gifted with a touch of the second sight. It runs in my family, you see."

"Hmm."

"My powers are very real. And even if I were a charlatan who used cunning to deduce facts about my clients, I would not tell you my secrets."

Molly wrinkled her nose. "I was afraid of that. Oh, well, it was worth a try."

"Look here," Evangeline muttered, "I can tell you anything you wish to know about your love life."

"I doubt it. I don't have one."

"Well, you soon will." Evangeline picked up the cards and began to lay them out, one by one on the table. "Aha. See the blue king?"

Molly glanced at the card. "What of it?"

"He represents a man you have recently met. This man is tall. He has dark hair and eyes the color of the ancient amber in my necklace. They are the eyes of a man of power. A man who will change your destiny."

Molly laughed. "I see you're acquainted with Harry Trevelyan. I'll bet you're his aunt. I believe Josh mentioned an Evangeline Trevelyan. How did you identify me, though? Did you figure out who I was when I told you that I was waiting for someone, or did Josh describe me to you?"

Evangeline gave her an exasperated glare. "I figured it out because I'm a fortune-teller. It's my business to know things like that. Now, let's get on with this, shall we?"

Molly shrugged. "What's the point? Now that I know who you are and you know who I am, I'm not going to be amazed or astounded by anything you tell me about Harry."

"What if I told you that I do not know who this Harry is?"

Molly grinned. "Come off it, you know Harry. Admit it."

"You're making this extremely difficult," Evangeline said brusquely. "Let's take it again from the top. You have recently met a tall, dark-haired man with amber eyes. This man—"

"You forgot handsome."

Evangeline looked up from her cards with a ferocious scowl. "I beg your pardon?"

"Aren't you supposed to say that I've recently met a tall, dark-haired, *handsome* man?" Molly pursed her lips. "I always thought it was tall, dark, and handsome. Yes, I'm sure that's the way it goes."

Evangeline tapped one long, crimson nail against the table. "All right, so he's not so handsome. I wouldn't be too choosy, if I were you. What are you? Thirty? Thirty-two? Time's running out, friend."

"I wasn't complaining about Harry's looks. I just said you're wrong. He is tall, dark, and extremely attractive."

Evangeline eyed Molly as if she had serious doubts about her IQ level. "You think Harry's good-looking?"

"Well, maybe not in the traditional sense," Molly admitted. "But, then, I'm not much of a traditionalist. In my family we tend to go for the unusual. Harry is definitely not the boy next door. He's one of a kind."

"You can say that again," Evangeline grumbled. "Don't know how he turned out the way he did. His father was one of the most handsome men I've ever laid eyes on, and his mother looked like a fairy-tale princess. Something obviously went haywire when the two sets of genes combined."

Beads jangled softly.

"Cut me some slack here, Aunt Evie." Harry glided into the tent. "Can't you fake it a little on the tall, dark, and handsome bit? You owe me that much, at least."

Molly spun around in her chair, relieved to see him. "Hi, Harry."

"Hello." Harry let the beaded curtain close behind him.

Evangeline's eyes gleamed with amusement as she rose from her chair. "As I was just explaining to your friend, I never falsify these things. I have my professional standards to uphold. But I will concede that handsome is as handsome does, and beauty is in the eye of the beholder, et cetera."

Harry laughed. "How are you, Aunt Evie?"

"The arthritis has been acting up again, but other than that, I can't complain. Good to see you. Josh said you were going to pay us a visit." She walked around the table, arms outstretched, bells jingling.

Harry accepted Evangeline's enveloping hug with equanimity.

Molly tried to read his face in the gloom. As usual, his expression gave no clue to his feelings. It was impossible to tell how well the interview with his uncle had gone.

Harry glanced at the stack of packages on the floor as his aunt released him. "Not hard to tell where Molly's been. I was afraid of this."

"I found some really terrific kitchen gadgets," Molly said. "Wait until you see them. One slices carrots into cute little baskets, which you can fill with olives and things for an hors d'oeuvre tray. And there's another one that makes little boats out of cucumbers."

Harry's mouth kicked up at the corner. "When was the last time you felt an overpowering urge to make carrot baskets and cucumber boats?"

Evangeline chuckled. "Don't tease her, Harry. I'm sure she'll enjoy her gadgets."

"Not likely. She's got a kitchen full of high-tech gadgetry that puts this stuff to shame." He glanced at Molly with an indulgent expression. "I warned you not to get suckered by the sales pitches in the exhibition halls."

"Must you be so negative?" Molly retorted. "Not everyone is a con artist, you know."

Harry smiled coolly. "I'm not negative, I'm realistic."

"Sounds like the same thing to me. And for your information, I did not get taken in by fancy sales pitches," Molly said. "I examined the products and watched the demonstrations. I liked what I saw, so I bought some of the items."

"Those hucksters sell nothing but useless junk. Everyone knows that."

"Hah. Every single item is guaranteed for life," Molly informed him triumphantly.

"Is that a fact? And just how are you going to collect on the guarantees?" Harry asked. "When the fair closes, the product demonstrators will vanish. And so will the guarantees."

Molly raised her eyes toward the heavens. "You know what your problem is, Harry? You think everyone in the whole world is out to deceive and defraud."

Evangeline looked at Harry. "You two know each other fairly well, I take it?"

"I know Harry better than he thinks I do," Molly said darkly.

"We've known each other a month," Harry told his aunt. "Molly has a lot to learn."

Evangeline chuckled. "Being the gifted seer that I am, I know who she is. But why don't you introduce us properly?"

"Sorry about that," Harry said. "Evangeline, meet Molly Abberwick. Molly, this is Evangeline Trevelyan. One of my aunts. Best fortune-teller in the family."

"Nice to meet you," Molly said.

"A pleasure." Evangeline sat down at the table, picked up the cards, and reshuffled them. "Let me see, where were we?"

"You were telling her that I was tall, dark, and ugly, I believe." Harry pulled aside a heavy bit of drapery at the back of the tent. He plucked a folding chair out of the shadows.

"What I really wanted to know was how a fortune-teller makes such accurate guesses about her clients," Molly explained. "I realize that some fortunes are generic. Most people want to hear that they'll come into money or find true love. And I suppose it's always safe to say that a client is about to go on a journey since nearly everyone travels at one time or another."

Evangeline's smile twisted wryly. "Your friend has natural talent, Harry."

"What can I say?" Harry crossed the tent with the chair in one hand. "She's smart. A sucker for a sales pitch, maybe, but basically smart."

"Such flattery will get you nowhere." Molly turned back to Evangeline. "I want to know how a fortune-teller or psychic goes beyond the obvious clues. How do you personalize a fortune?"

"She's also got a streak of curiosity a mile wide." Harry dropped the folding chair lightly down next to the table, opened it, reversed it, and straddled it. He rested his arms along the back of the chair. "I'm told it runs in her family."

"Interesting," Evangeline murmured. "Well, my dear, I'm afraid I can't satisfy your curiosity in the matter of telling fortunes. What can I say? There are no secrets. It's a gift."

"Are you talking about the Trevelyan Second Sight?" Molly asked.

"No," Harry said coldly. "She isn't. Because there is no such thing."

Evangeline cocked a disapproving brow. "You should have a bit more respect for the Sight, Harry. After all, you've got more of it than anyone else in the family."

"The hell I do," Harry said.

Molly studied Evangeline intently. "If you won't tell me the tricks of the fortune-telling trade, tell me about the Trevelyan Second Sight."

"Damn," Harry muttered.

"It runs in the family," Evangeline said smoothly. "Harry won't admit he's got a full measure of it. He used to spend some of his summers with us, and I can tell you that I've seen flashes of it in him since he was about twelve. And of course there are the reflexes. He can't deny he got those, too. A genuine throwback to the first Harry Trevelyan."

"Harry told me that his ancestor lived in the early eighteen hundreds," Molly said.

"That's right." Evangeline shuffled the cards with a thoughtful air. "He was sort of an early private investigator. He used to solve crimes and find missing people."

"Did he claim to have psychic powers?" Molly asked.

"No," Evangeline admitted. "He apparently failed to understand his own talent. He wanted to deny it for some reason. But family legend records that he had the Sight. He also had excellent reflexes. We know that because there are some fascinating stories of how he saved his own life and the lives of others when he was confronted by some violent people in the course of his work."

"Fiction," Harry said. "Pure fiction."

Molly ignored him. "Did anyone else in the family become a private investigator?"

"No," Evangeline said. "No money in it. The Trevelyans took their psychic talents to the stage, instead. Mind readers, daredevils, knife throwers. That kind of thing. Every Trevelyan since the first Harry has wanted to believe that he had a touch of the Sight. Some did. Some didn't. The talent tends to skip around a lot."

Molly gave Harry an appraising look. "This Harry does have good reflexes."

"And here I thought you admired me for my brain," Harry said.

Evangeline reshuffled the cards. "In the Trevelyans, the reflexes have always been linked with the gift. The faster the hands, the keener the Second Sight, Granny Gwen always said." She scowled at Harry. "And you have more speed than anyone else in the family, Harry. It broke Granny Gwen's heart when you refused to follow in the Trevelyan tradition."

"In case you haven't guessed," Harry said to Molly, "my sainted great-grandmother, God rest her soul, had a real talent for laying guilt trips on people who didn't do what she wanted them to do. She was mightily irritated when I decided to go after a Ph.D. Granny Gwen wanted me to make a career out of throwing knives or racing cars or jumping off tall towers into little pools of water."

Evangeline gave him a reproving frown. "You're not being fair to your great-grandmother, Harry. It wasn't the fact that you wanted an education that angered and hurt her. It was your refusal to acknowledge the gift of the Sight. She was convinced that you were the first Trevelyan to be born with a complete dose of it since Harry the First."

"Sounds a bit like the Abberwick family talent for invention," Molly mused. "It skips around, too. My sister got it. I didn't."

Harry gave her an odd look. "I'm not so sure of that. Your energy was channeled into building up your business because your family needed a stable income. But I think that successful entrepreneurship is a form of inventive genius. Most people fail at it. You didn't."

Molly was so stunned by the unexpected compliment that she couldn't think of anything to say. She gazed at Harry, aware of a fierce warmth in her face. He smiled his faint, mysterious smile, and the heat descended straight into her lower body.

Evangeline glanced from one to the other with a perceptive gaze. "I think that's enough on the Trevelyan Second Sight. How did it go with the old man, Harry? I know Leon's been sniping at Josh all summer."

"Uncle Leon hasn't changed a bit," Harry said. "But he and I arrived at another one of our little understandings. He'll back off. At least for a while."

Molly heard the ice in his voice. It sent a small shiver through her, melting the sensual warmth.

Evangeline seemed blissfully unaware of the dark chill in Harry's words. She winked at Molly. "Harry has a way of dealing with Leon that none of the rest of the family can match. For some reason Leon will listen to him."

Molly smiled. "Maybe Harry does have some genuine psychic ability." She raised her hands in mock threat. "You know, the power to fog up men's minds, or whatever."

Harry gave her a disgusted look.

"Why do you say that he might actually have the Sight?" Evangeline asked with startling intensity.

Molly leaned back in her chair and shoved her hands into the pockets of her jeans. "It seems to me that Harry changed his own future. And then he changed Josh's. That's got to be a gift of some kind, don't you think? How many people do you know who alter their own destinies and the destinies of others?"

Harry stared at her.

Evangeline slanted him a sidelong glance. "You know, I hadn't thought of it quite that way. She's got a point, Harry."

"The only kind of power I exerted over my future and Josh's was the power of common sense," Harry said.

Molly grinned. "Whatever, it's a heck of a lot more impressive than mumbo jumbo."

Amazingly, Harry turned a dull shade of red.

"Well, now." Evangeline's mouth curved in a knowing smile. "Let's see about the future of your love life, Molly."

"Forget it," Molly advised.

Evangeline ignored her. She peeled a card off the top of the deck and laid it down, face up. "Aha. Here's the blue king again. He's not going to disappear, it seems. When he turns up twice in a row, one must pay attention. It means your love life is about to become very interesting."

"Coincidence. Or a very skillful job of shuffling." Molly got to her feet. "I told you, I'm not interested in having my fortune read." She swept out a hand and scooped up the cards in a single motion.

"Coward," Evangeline murmured.

"No." Harry laughed as he got to his feet. "She's smart."

"Thank you," Molly said demurely.

Evangeline spread her hands in a gesture of surrender. "Very well, I give up. If Molly doesn't want to know about her love life, that's her decision. Harry, when do you intend to start back to Seattle?"

"There's no rush." Harry glanced at his watch. "I want to say hello to Cousin Raleigh and his wife and a few of the other members of the family."

"Raleigh's handling the Ferris wheel." Evangeline idly shuffled the cards. "A word of warning. He wants to borrow money. He and Sheila have a baby on the way."

"I stand warned. Come on, Molly, I'll introduce you to some more of the family."

"All right." Molly looked at Evangeline. "I hope I'll see you again one of these days."

"Something tells me you will," Evangeline said with serene confidence.

Harry helped Molly gather up her packages. Then he paused beside the fortune-telling table. "Take care of yourself, Aunt Evie."

"I will." She smiled up at him. "You do the same. By the way, I'm going to give you a call next week. I want to talk to you about updating the video arcade. It's one of our biggest draws, and you know how quickly those darn games go out of date."

Something indefinable—resignation or perhaps even pain—came and went in Harry's gaze. It vanished immediately, leaving behind a cool, shuttered expression. Molly wanted to reach out and put her arms around him. She wanted to offer comfort, but she was not sure why.

"You know where to reach me, Aunt Evie."

Molly came to a halt beside the table. "Are you sure you won't tell me how you got the blue king to come up twice in a row, Evangeline?"

"Aunt Evie will never reveal a trade secret." Harry picked up the deck of cards and began to shuffle them with practiced grace. "I, on the other hand, have absolutely no professional ethics when it comes to this kind of thing. Here, I'll show you how to make one particular card come up over and over again."

"No, you most definitely will not." Evangeline snatched the deck back from him and put it down on the table. "Not with my cards. Off with you, Harry. You never did have any respect for the business."

"You're right, I never did," Harry agreed.

"You've ruined this deck," Evangeline grumbled as she fingered the cards. "Now I'll have to reorganize it."

Molly studied the deck. "Does that mean that the blue king is no longer on top?"

"Right," Harry said. "I shuffled it the old-fashioned way. If the blue king is on top this time, it's due to pure chance, and the odds are staggeringly against it." He reached down and flipped over the top card to demonstrate.

It was another king, but this one was not blue. It was red.

"Hell," Harry said very softly. The laconic amusement disappeared from his eyes as he looked at the colorful card.

"Oh, dear," Evangeline whispered. She stared at the red king, her attention riveted.

Molly frowned. "What's wrong? It's not the blue king. It's another card altogether."

"Yes, it is." Harry did not take his eyes off the king.

"What's the big deal about the red king?" Molly asked.

"Just a fluke," Harry said quietly.

Evangeline shook her head slowly. "There are no flukes when you deal the cards."

"All right, just for the sake of argument, let's assume that my love life may be about to improve," Molly said, trying to lighten the atmosphere. "Why so glum?"

Evangeline sighed. "This is not the blue king. It's the red king. It has nothing to do with your love life, Molly. When it's the first card in the deck it indicates something else entirely."

"What?" Molly was exasperated.

"Danger." Evangeline switched her veiled gaze to Harry. "Great danger."

Molly scowled. "I don't believe it."

"Very wise of you," Harry said. "It's superstitious nonsense."

"I wouldn't put too much credence in it, myself," Evangeline admitted with surprising honesty. She paused, then said, "If it hadn't been for the fact that it was Harry who shuffled the cards. Promise me that you'll be careful, Harry."

Molly frowned at the red king.

Harry touched her shoulder. "Relax, Molly. It's all an illusion. Smoke and mirrors. Like catching knives or reading minds. Let's go."

Seven

"I saw you write that check for your cousin Raleigh," Molly said as she buckled her seat belt. It was early evening, the summer sun still bright on the horizon.

"Did you?" Harry put on a pair of sunglasses that were so dark they appeared black.

"Yes, I did. You can't deny it."

Harry rested an arm along the back of the seat and turned his head to survey the chaotic parking lot traffic. "Then you know why I don't like to spend a lot of time at the carnival," he said as he eased the Sneath P2 out from under the trees where he had parked it earlier in the day. "Costs a fortune."

Molly smiled. "It was very nice of you."

"Raleigh's okay. He and Sheila aren't very good with money, but they're hard workers."

"How did things go with your uncle?"

"Let's just say we reached an understanding. With any luck it will hold until Josh graduates from college. By then Josh should be able to deal with the old man on his own."

Molly hesitated and then gave in to the compelling curiosity. "I know this is none of my business, but just how did you talk Leon into backing off?"

Harry's eyes were unreadable behind the black sunglasses, but his mouth quirked in a humorless fashion. "A combination of bribery and threats."

"Bribery I can understand. But what sort of threat did you use?"

"One that has enough teeth in it to scare even Leon." Harry shifted gears with a fluid snap and accelerated toward the exit.

Molly opened her mouth to ask for further details, but the words melted away when she saw the grim set of Harry's jaw. Even the force of her Abberwick curiosity was not strong enough to overcome that *no trespassing* warning.

"I see," Molly said.

Harry did not respond. He was wholly absorbed in his driving, as though he were an integral part of the vehicle as well as its master. The black sunglasses gave him a remote, alien quality.

Molly was beginning to recognize the signs. Harry was in one of his moods. He was walking through the dark jungle of his own thoughts, contemplating something he could not or would not discuss with her.

Molly sank back into the seat and watched the rural landscape rush past the windows as the sleek, exotic sports car plunged straight toward the center of the late sun.

After a while she turned and reached behind the seat to scoop up the package of kitchen gadgets she had purchased at the fair. She settled back to read the operating instructions for the Ace Wondermatic All-Purpose Kitchen Appliance.

Seattle was bathed in the last, fading light of the June evening when Harry exited Interstate Five. He drove into the heart of the city, heading toward First Avenue. Slowly he roused himself from the brooding mood that had settled on him.

When he stopped for a red light at Stewart and Third Avenue, he glanced at Molly. He had been comfortably aware of her presence beside him for the last hour, but it suddenly struck him that she hadn't said a word since she had asked him about his meeting with Leon. Then again, he had not been much of a conversationalist, himself.

Damn.

A much belated alarm bell sounded somewhere in Harry's brain. Women did not tolerate long silences well. He had learned that lesson from Olivia. Toward the end of the engagement she had complained increasingly about his long bouts of contemplation. The more she had berated him for them, the longer the silences had grown.

Harry wondered if he had screwed up royally this afternoon by failing to carry on a lively conversation during the drive from Hidden Springs. He tried to think of a smooth way to recover whatever ground he had lost through the extended silence.

He cleared his throat when the light changed. "It's nearly eight o'clock." He shifted gears gently. "I'll park the car in the building garage. We can walk to one of the market restaurants for dinner."

Molly turned to look at him, her gaze contemplative rather than accusing. Then she smiled slightly. "All right."

Harry breathed a sigh of relief. He couldn't tell what she was thinking, but at least she was not sulking. He was greatly cheered by the realization that Molly was not the type to hold a little silence against a man. Nevertheless, he felt compelled to apologize for his mood.

"Sorry I haven't been a great conversationalist on this trip." He turned into the alley behind his condominium building and used the remote to open the steel gate. "I was thinking."

"I know. It really bothers you, doesn't it?"

He removed his sunglasses as he drove into the garage. "What bothers me?"

"The way your family insists that you have the famous Trevelyan Second Sight."

"It's damned annoying at times." Harry parked in a numbered slot. "But bear in mind that I only get that nonsense from my Trevelyan relatives. The Strattons think it's total bunk. Which it is."

"But you don't laugh it off." Molly studied his profile as he switched off the ignition. "Whenever the subject comes up, it either angers you or it sets you to brooding."

He shoved open the car door. "If this is a roundabout way of telling me that I bored you to tears on this trip . . ."

"It's not." Molly opened her own door and got out. She faced him across the Sneath's roof. "It's merely an observation. The topic of the Trevelyan psychic gifts makes you irritable. Are you going to deny it?"

"I agree it irritates me." In fact, he was getting irritated all over again at this very minute, Harry realized. He made himself shut the car door with exquisite care.

"Do you know why?"

"Because it's so much stupid nonsense." *And because sometimes I'm afraid that it's not nonsense. Sometimes I wonder if it's for real and if the knowing will drive me mad.* Harry drew a deep breath and shoved that chilling thought back into the deepest recesses of his mind.

Molly watched him from the far side of the car. "I think there's more to it than the fact that it violates your sense of academic reason and logic."

Harry's whole body tightened as though preparing for combat. He had known from the beginning that he was taking a risk with this woman.

"Such as?" he asked very casually.

Molly's vivid, intelligent face was thoughtful. "Perhaps all the talk about the Trevelyan family talent reminds you too much of a world that you feel you barely escaped. The world of fake fortune-tellers and daredevils."

Harry relaxed slightly. He rested his arms on the roof of the car. "You may have a point. But I'll let you in on a little secret."

"What's that?"

"If you think I brood whenever the topic of the Trevelyan Second Sight arises, you should see me when I have to listen to one of my Stratton relatives lecture me about how I failed to follow four generations of Stratton men into the corporate world. The real world, where real men are sharks and wolves and other assorted predators and measure their worth by the size of their investment portfolios."

She blinked in astonishment. Then she laughed softly. "How awful. I take it you haven't bothered to please either side of your family?"

"No." Harry was captivated by the amusement dancing in her green eyes. The last ghostly remnants of his latest mood evaporated. He smiled. "The Strattons don't have any more respect for the academic world than the Trevelyans do. Both families think I deliberately chose an effete, ivory-tower life devoted to meaningless academic research and study merely to annoy them. The fact that I've made money at it just irritates them even more."

"We all have our little motivations. So what if it took an overriding desire to annoy your relatives to turn you into a leading authority on the history of science?"

"On the whole, the Stratton complaints about my choice of careers aren't any worse than the Trevelyans'," Harry said. "Uncle Leon takes it a step farther, however. He worries about the genetic implications."

"The genetic implications?"

Harry smiled fleetingly. "He's convinced that my Stratton blood has unmanned me. He thinks it's turned me into a weak, prissy wimp."

"Good grief. No wonder you were feeling a bit moody on the drive home. Have you been juggling the Strattons and the Trevelyans all your life?"

"Yes." He held up a hand to forestall the inevitable question. "Don't ask me why I bother."

"I don't have to ask. None of us chooses our relatives."

Harry reached into the car to collect Molly's purchases. "I'll put these in the trunk while we get something to eat."

After dinner he would find a way to convince Molly to come back to the condo with him for the night, Harry thought as he opened the trunk. There had to be a way to manage that feat. He wanted her more tonight than he ever had. The need in him had metamorphosed into a gnawing hunger.

Perhaps if he had Molly in his bed tonight he would not lie awake thinking about the red king that he had dealt from Evangeline's deck of cards. He hated it when things like that happened.

Intent on furthering his plans for the evening, Harry whisked Molly into the elevator and tapped the lobby button.

A moment later the doors opened to reveal the building lobby. The first thing Harry saw was his ex-fiancée, Olivia. She was striding restlessly back and forth in front of the doorman's station.

"Damn," he said softly.

This situation constituted positive proof that he lacked any shred of psychic talent, he thought grimly. If he'd actually possessed a touch of the Trevelyan Second Sight, surely he would have had a premonition of trouble on the way up from the garage.

At the sight of him, Olivia came to a halt. Her fingers tightened on the strap of her expensive taupe leather shoulder bag. "Harry."

He eyed her warily. Olivia was impeccably turned out, as always. Her tendency toward perfectionism had been one of the things he had admired about her at the start of their relationship. It had implied self-control. It had implied that she was a woman who had answers.

Today she was dressed in a cream silk blouse, soft, rust-colored trousers, and a lightweight beige silk jacket. Her golden hair was drawn back into a refined twist. Her beautiful features were strained with tension. Her gray eyes were shadowed with concern.

Harry heroically resisted an urge to retreat back into the elevator. "Hello, Olivia." He tightened his grip on Molly's hand as he came to a halt in the middle of the lobby. "I'd like you to meet Molly Abberwick. Molly, this is Olivia Hughes. My cousin Brandon's wife."

"How do you do?" Molly said. She gave Olivia a polite smile.

Olivia nodded stiffly. "Hello."

"We were just on our way out to dinner, Olivia," Harry said. "Will you excuse us?"

Olivia's fine brows came together in a determined frown. "Harry, I've been waiting for you for hours. Your housekeeper left at five. She told me that she was sure you'd be home this evening."

"I am home, as you can see, but I've got plans."

Olivia spared another brief glance for Molly and then dismissed her presence. "I want to talk to you. Family business."

"Some other time, Olivia." Harry made to go around her since Olivia showed no indication of moving out of his path.

"Harry, this is very important."

Molly tugged on his arm. "Uh, Harry?"

Olivia's mouth tightened. "I really must speak with you, Harry. The matter won't wait."

Molly gently disengaged her fingers. She smiled very brightly at Harry. "This looks serious. Don't worry about me. I'll take a cab home."

"Damn it, Molly, whatever it is, it can wait. You and I are going out to dinner."

"No." Olivia's voice cracked. "Brandon's future is on the line, Harry. And it's all your fault. You're responsible for this mess. You've got to clean it up."

"Me?" Harry stared at her.

" 'Bye, Harry." Molly backed quickly toward the glass doors. "Thanks for an interesting day."

He started to go after her. Olivia put a restraining hand on his arm.

"I have got to talk to you about this situation," Olivia said urgently. "It won't keep."

"It's okay," Molly called from the glass doorway. "Really. No problem."

Harry looked from one woman to the other. He knew when he was defeated. "I'll have Chris get you a cab, Molly."

"Sure thing, Mr. Trevelyan." Chris, the evening doorman, reached for the phone.

"No need." Molly was halfway out the door. "There's one right across the street. I can see it from here."

Harry took another step toward her and stopped. His hands tightened at his sides. He did not want her to go home alone. He wanted her here with him.

"I'll call you later," he said.

"Don't worry, we'll be in touch," she assured him. "All the kitchen gadgets I bought at the fair are still in your car trunk."

She waved. The heavy glass door swung shut. Harry watched as she scurried across the intersection to the waiting cab.

Molly was gone. He could feel the darkness settle around him.

"You're in one of your moods, aren't you?" Olivia sounded vaguely petulant as Harry ushered her through his front door. "It's depression, you know. You might as well stop pretending it isn't. Denial serves no therapeutic purpose."

"I am definitely in a mood, and it is not a good one." He closed the door and went to stand at the window. The last fragment of the setting sun disappeared behind the Olympics. Night closed in on the city. The old-fashioned round globes of the Pike Place Market streetlights down below cast a golden glow.

Harry tried to spot the cab that was carrying Molly toward the weird old mansion on Capitol Hill, but it was long gone.

"Damn you, Harry, must you always be so self-absorbed? I came here to have a serious conversation with you. The least you can do is pay attention. This is all your fault in the first place."

Harry did not turn around. "I assume this is connected to the conversation I had with Brandon yesterday morning?"

There was a brief, startled pause.

"Brandon talked to you?" Olivia sounded tentative.

"Yes."

"Well? Did you make an effort to convince him not to leave Stratton Properties?"

"He's a full-grown adult. It's his future. His decision. Why should I get involved?"

"Because he would never have come up with this little scheme if it hadn't been for you," Olivia exploded softly. "Damn it, Harry, he's doing this to prove something, not because it's the best thing for our future. I've tried, but I can't get him to take a rational view of the situation."

Harry glanced at her over his shoulder. "What do you think he's trying to prove?"

"That he's as strong and independent as you are." Olivia tossed her purse down onto the sofa with an angry movement of her hand. "He's jealous of you, Harry."

"Jealous? Why the hell should he be jealous? You left me to marry him."

Olivia swung around furiously. "Must you bring that up?"

"Look, I wasn't trying to rehash the past. I was merely pointing out that if there was a competition going on between Brandon and me, he won it."

Olivia flushed. "This isn't about me, it's about stupid masculine pride. Machismo. Balls. Whatever you men call it. It's a potentially destructive urge on Brandon's part. He wants to prove to himself that he's got the same kind of guts you have. He's always secretly admired you for the way you turned your back on the Stratton money. Now he's determined to see if he can make it outside the family, too."

"So? Let him give it a whirl. Where's the harm?"

Olivia's eyes narrowed in outraged fury. "The harm is that his grandfather will punish him for following in your footsteps. We both know it. Parker will cut Brandon out of the will. Danielle is on the edge of a nervous breakdown because of this. She sacrificed a great deal for Brandon's sake, and now it's about to go up in smoke."

"I didn't know people still had nervous breakdowns," Harry mused. "I thought you psychologists had more modern terms for that condition."

Olivia's face was tight and bleak. "This is not a joke, Harry."

"And this is not my problem."

"It most certainly is. You caused it by being a role model for Brandon."

"I didn't set out to be anyone's role model," he said very softly.

Olivia flinched. "Please, Harry, don't speak to me in that tone of voice. You know it upsets me."

Harry drew a deep breath. "I thought I was being remarkably civil under the circumstances."

"When you're in one of your moods, every word you utter sounds as though it had been dug out of a glacier."

Harry clasped his hands behind his back. "Just what do you expect me to do, Olivia?"

"Talk to Brandon. Make him see that leaving Stratton Properties is not a wise move."

"He's not likely to listen to me if he's in the middle of trying to prove something."

"The least you can do is try to talk him out of this. Harry, you've got to do something before he goes too far with his plans. Parker will never forgive him if he walks away from Stratton Properties the way you did. Danielle will be crushed. And Brandon will ultimately be sorry he made a mistake of this magnitude."

So that was the ex-fiancée.

Molly sat down at the kitchen table with a plate of spinach ravioli laced with Parmesan, fresh basil leaves, and olive oil. She forked up two of the ravioli and considered the stack of new grant proposals in front of her.

Surely she could find one out of this lot that would pass muster with Harry.

Olivia was certainly pretty. No, that was putting it mildly. She was lovely.

Molly munched ravioli and wondered what had gone wrong between Harry and Olivia.

Hours of boredom broken by moments of stark terror.

Olivia had not appeared terrified of Harry this evening. She had looked like a woman who had a claim on his time and attention. Molly wondered what had drawn the two together in the first place. Olivia certainly didn't look to be Harry's type. Of course, Molly reflected, her own opinion on that subject was definitely biased.

She took another bite of ravioli and turned a page. It was pointless to speculate. The bottom line was that in the end Olivia had married Harry's cousin, Brandon Stratton Hughes.

It was certainly interesting that Olivia had come to Harry for help with whatever family problem had caused her so much concern, though.

Molly pushed the haunting thoughts aside. She forced herself to concentrate on the summary page of the grant proposal that lay open on the table in front of her.

The old house hunkered down for the night with a sigh and a few creaks and groans. A distant hum from the floor above indicated that a cleaning robot was going about its duties.

After a while Molly took a break to put her dishes onto the conveyer belt that would whisk them through the patented Abberwick Dishwasher. When the machine was finished, the dishes would all be automatically stacked and stored.

Molly was concentrating on a proposal for an emission-free engine design when the cleaned dishes emerged from the machine. She did not look up as the rubber-coated mechanical arms stacked the plates neatly in the adjacent cupboard.

"Are you seriously involved with Molly Abberwick?" Olivia asked as she picked up her purse.

Harry turned away from the window. "Yes."

"You're sleeping with her?"

"That's none of your business," Harry said.

Olivia had the grace to look embarrassed. "No, I suppose it isn't. I just wondered if there were any, uh, complications."

"Complications?"

"The sort you and I had," Olivia said brusquely.

"Ah, yes. That sort. As I recall, you said I made you nervous."

"There's no need to be sarcastic. I'm only trying to help."

Harry eyed her with some surprise. "How?"

"I've told you that I think you're suffering from posttraumatic stress disorder because of the manner in which your parents died," Olivia said quietly. "It's not an unusual reaction to serious trauma. I wish you would call Dr. Shropton. He's had a lot of experience treating the disorder. And there's medication that can help."

"I'll keep that in mind."

"You're not going to do a damn thing about it, are you?" Olivia asked in a burst of fresh anger. "You won't seek professional help. You won't discuss your dysfunctional behavior. You won't even admit you have a problem."

"Look, Olivia—"

"Let me tell you something, Harry. As a professional, I can guarantee you that your problems won't get any better if you persist in denying their very existence. They'll ruin your relationship with Molly Abberwick, just as they ruined our relationship."

"Thanks for the warning," Harry said. "But I don't think we can blame my personality defects entirely on the fact that our relationship fizzled."

"Don't you dare try to tell me that you ever loved me, Harry. Whatever you felt for me, it wasn't love."

He stilled. "Did you love me?"

"I tried," Olivia whispered valiantly. "I really did try, Harry."

"Noble of you." He knew of no way to tell her that he had tried to love her, too. She would never comprehend that it was his very attempt to do so that made her flee the engagement. *Moments of stark terror.*

"It was hopeless," Olivia said. "You're not free to love anyone, Harry. For a while I thought perhaps we could work things out. I thought if you would only learn to communicate. If you could develop some empathy. Share your feelings. Get out of denial. But it was impossible."

"Yes, I suppose it was."

"And then the sex got . . . well, it got weird, Harry. You know it did."

Harry felt his insides grow cold. "I'm sorry." There was nothing else to say.

"I know you didn't intend to scare me, but you did. At first you were so distant, so cold in bed. I felt as if a robot were making love to me, not a man."

Harry closed his eyes.

"And then, that last time that we were together, you seemed to lose control or something. It was overwhelming." Olivia groped for words. "Terrifying, if you want the truth. I realized afterward that we had to end the engagement."

Harry vowed he would not make the same mistake with Molly.

He was well aware that women who became involved with him labeled him difficult. Over the years he had heard all the tearful accusations. He was too distant, too remote, too uncommunicative, too cold.

Until Olivia, Harry's infrequent relationships had all floundered on the rocky shoals of boredom or exasperation. But with Olivia, he had given in to a growing sense of desperation. He was in his mid-thirties. The longing for a true bond with a woman had grown so strong within him that he had succumbed to temptation. He had carefully, cautiously, opened himself ever so slightly to Olivia.

The result had been a disaster. She was right. The sex got weird.

Harry knew it was his own fault. So long as he maintained a certain emotional distance in the relationship—so long as things were limited to the physical and the intellectual—he could keep matters under control.

But there were those bleak moments when he craved something else, something he could not name. And those moments came with increasing frequency of late. More than any vampire hungering for blood, he longed for a dark consummation that he could not even comprehend.

Not only were the moments of need coming over him more often, plunging him into darker moods than any he had known in the past, they were more intense. A fear that had once been remote and easily repressed, the fear of going insane, was beginning to surface with alarming regularity. Each time it appeared it took more strength of will to crush it.

The kitchen phone rang just as Molly finished the last page of the final grant proposal. She reached across the table and picked up the receiver.

"Hello?"

"Did you get dinner?" Harry asked without preamble.

Molly smiled. "Yes, thanks. I'm perfectly capable of feeding myself."

"I know."

Molly frowned. "Are you all right? You sound weird."

"Do me a favor and don't call me weird. Call me arrogant, pedantic, stubborn, or any of the other things you like to call me, but not weird, okay?"

"Okay. You don't sound weird. You sound weary. That's what I meant to say. Weary. What's wrong?"

"Olivia left a few minutes ago."

"Hmm."

"My cousin Brandon has decided to quit his job with the family firm. She wants me to talk him out of it."

"I see." Molly hesitated. "Can you do that?"

"I doubt it. I'm not sure I should even try. Can we reschedule dinner for tomorrow night?"

Molly hesitated.

"Please," Harry said quietly.

"Fine. I'll look forward to it. Oh, by the way, Harry, I just finished going through the newest stack of grant proposals, and I think I've found some really exciting prospects. I can't wait for you to take a look at them."

"Neither can I."

"You don't sound genuinely enthusiastic."

"I will be by tomorrow night."

"Right. It's been a very long day."

"Yes. Good night, Molly." Harry paused. "Thanks for making the trip to Hidden Springs with me."

"I had a great time. I think Kelsey is right. I should get away more often. Good night, Harry."

Molly hung up the phone very slowly. She sat quietly for a while, listening to the sounds of the house. They were comfortable, familiar, soothing sounds. They were the sounds of home.

She thought about Kelsey's advice to sell the mansion. It was probably the logical thing to do. But for some reason Molly could not envision such a move.

After a time she put the last grant proposal on the pile and rose from the table. The lights in the kitchen winked off as she walked out of the room.

She climbed the curved staircase and went down the hall to her bedroom.

A short time later, she slipped into bed. She folded her arms behind her head and gazed up into the shadows for a long time. Eventually she turned on her side and fell asleep.

Her dreams were an eerie collage of red kings, knives, and unseen menace. A muted whirring sound broke into them, exacerbating the sense of threat.

It took Molly's sleep-drugged brain a few seconds to register the fact that the noise was not part of her dream. When she finally realized that something was wrong, fear sliced into her consciousness, bringing her fully awake.

Molly opened her eyes in an instant of explosive terror. A dark figure cloaked in layers of black fabric was rising from the floor beside her bed. She had a glimpse of a skeletal face, yawning holes where eyes should have been, and a clawed hand.

Molly was paralyzed. A scream got trapped in her throat.

The figure leaned over the bed. The mechanical whirring grew louder. The clawed hand lifted in a jerky fashion.

The instinct for survival unlocked Molly's frozen limbs. She shoved aside the quilt and managed to roll off the far side of the bed.

She hit the floor with a jarring thud, scrambled to her feet, and ran for the door.

The hall lights came on automatically in response to her frantic movements. Molly glanced back over her shoulder to see how close her pursuer was.

That was when she realized that the thing from under the bed had not moved to follow her. It still hovered over the rumpled sheets, clawed hand frozen in midair. The whirring sound ceased abruptly, as though a switch had been turned off.

"Oh, no," Molly whispered. "Not again."

Eight

The shrill ringing of the phone cut into a dream in which Harry was dealing from a deck of cards that contained nothing but red kings. He knew he had to find the queen or all was lost. But the damn phone kept interrupting his concentration.

He stirred and reached for the receiver with a mixture of irritation and foreboding. He glanced at the clock. It was nearly one in the morning. Calls at this hour invariably meant trouble.

"Trevelyan here." He hauled himself up against the pillows. At least he was out of the dream. *For a while.*

"Harry, it's me. Molly."

The breathless tremor in her voice had the impact of cold water on all his senses. Harry was suddenly wide awake. Every muscle in his body hardened with battle-ready tension. "What's wrong?"

"Something very strange has just happened. Remember the fake gun that someone left outside my door the other evening?"

"Hell, yes."

"Well, I think that whoever set up that prank has just played another one on me."

"Bastard," Harry whispered. He tightened his grip on the phone. "As bad as the first?"

"It was similar to the first one, but I have to admit this one was a lot more effective. I don't think I've ever been so frightened in my entire life."

"Are you all right?" Harry was already out of bed, heading across the room toward the closet.

"Yes, I'm fine. It was harmless. Just very scary." Molly hesitated. Her voice dropped to a low, apologetic mumble. "Sorry for bothering you. I don't know why I called you. I dialed your number without really thinking about it."

"It's all right." Harry cradled the phone between his shoulder and ear while he yanked open the closet door.

"I shouldn't have called at this hour."

"I said forget it. I'm on my way." Harry pulled on the first pants he found, a pair of olive-green chinos. "I'll be there as soon as I get the car out of the garage."

"Thanks." Relief was audible in Molly's voice.

"This time we notify the cops."

"Now, Harry, I don't want to do anything rash. I'm sure this is just another practical—"

"I'll see you in a few minutes." He tossed the phone into the cradle, grabbed a shirt, slid his feet into worn running shoes, and headed for the door.

He refused to think about the red king.

The streets were empty. Within ten minutes of leaving his garage, Harry drove through the massive wrought-iron gates that guarded the aging monstrosity Molly called home. The gates had been unlocked from inside the house.

He surveyed the old house as he shut off the engine. Light glowed in every window, including the peaked attic. Molly must have gone through each room and switched on every single lamp.

Whoever had pulled this stunt had definitely succeeded in scaring Molly. The perpetrator had probably not counted on the secondary effect he'd achieved, Harry thought as he loped up the front steps. The bastard had not yet realized that he'd also gotten her consultant's full attention.

He would not leave Molly here alone tonight, Harry promised himself. He didn't care how much she argued. She was coming back to his condominium until he could decide how to deal with the situation.

The front door opened just as he raised his hand to pound on it. Molly stood there, silhouetted by the hall light. She clutched the lapels of an oversized white terry-cloth bathrobe in one hand. Her hair looked as though it had been through an explosion. Her eyes were huge and shadowed.

"Harry." She stared at him for an instant as though not quite certain what to do next.

Before Harry realized her intent, she hurled herself straight into his arms and buried her face against his shoulder.

He caught her close.

She had called him. She needed him. She was right here in his arms. Where she was supposed to be.

The dark longing gathered within him, seeking that which it could not have, that which it would inevitably destroy.

Harry sucked in air. With a savage act of will he got a grip on himself and the wild emotions that threatened to sweep through him. He would not allow the hunger to gain control. There was too much at stake. He could not risk terrifying Molly. He must not lose her.

"It's all right. I'm here." Gently he set Molly away from him. It was not easy. Her arms seemed to be locked around his neck.

Reluctantly Molly raised her face to look at him. "Thank you for coming. I really appreciate it. I shouldn't have bothered you."

"Forget it." Harry searched her eyes and relaxed slightly. She was flushed, but not with fear of him.

He saw that her robe had parted, revealing an incredibly innocent-looking white nightgown trimmed with a delicately scalloped neckline. Her breasts rose gently above the scallops. Her nipples, visibly erect, were pressed against the gossamer fabric. Harry flexed his hands and listened to his blood as it roared through his veins.

Molly glanced down, blushed, and hastily secured the robe. "Come in. I'll make some tea."

Harry realized his fingers were trembling slightly. He stepped across the threshold and closed the door.

"It's every kid's worst nightmare. The monster under the bed." Molly poured tea from a white earthenware pot. The one thing she took care to prepare by hand was tea. There was something about good tea that demanded the personal touch. No machine, not even one of her father's kitchen appliances or Kelsey's gadgets, could prepare tea properly. "And I reacted just like a kid. Scared the beejeebies out of me."

"Someone got the effect he wanted." Harry surveyed the remains of the mechanical horror that he had spread out on the stainless-steel kitchen table.

Molly had watched as he dissected the creature with the finesse of a jeweler removing precious stones from a necklace. One by one Harry had taken apart the pieces of the device that had rolled out from under her bed.

Displayed in the bright kitchen light, the cheap black fabric, Halloween mask, and assorted mechanical components did not look very frightening. Molly was a little chagrined.

"I guess I overreacted," she said. "The pistol prank didn't bother me very much, but this one really got to me."

"It was meant to get to you." Harry held a gear up to the light to study it. "This thing was more of a threat than the pistol. It was right inside your house. Inside your bedroom. I think whoever is behind these incidents is deliberately trying to rev up the fear factor."

Molly shuddered. She searched Harry's grim face, trying to determine just how serious he was.

The answer was clear. He was very serious. She could feel the waves of focused energy emanating from him.

"I still can't believe that these incidents are meant to be anything more than nasty pranks, though," Molly said. She poked at the awkwardly constructed steel claw. It was composed of five metal rods thrust through holes cut in the fingers of a tattered black glove. "I wonder how he got into the house to set it up?"

"Did you check for open windows or unlocked doors?"

Molly huddled deeper into her robe. "I went through every room before you got here. There's no sign of forced entry. All the doors and windows were locked. The security system was on."

"The device was probably installed under your bed earlier today. Which leaves us with a couple of possibilities." Harry picked up the Halloween mask. "Whoever is doing this either knows you well enough to know your security code—"

"Impossible," Molly said quickly. "Kelsey and I have always been extremely careful. She wouldn't give out the code to anyone, not even a friend. And neither would I."

Harry got to his feet. "Then we're looking for someone who's good enough to bypass your household security system."

Molly looked up at him. "Good enough?"

"I guess I should say bad enough. Whoever he is, he's caused enough trouble tonight. Go upstairs and pack a bag. I'm taking you home with me."

"Home." She shot up out of her chair so quickly that it started to topple over backward.

"Right." Harry deftly caught the chair before it clattered to the floor. He righted it without even glancing at it. "Home to my place. You can spend the night there. In the morning we'll talk about what to do next."

Molly was torn. A part of her dreaded the prospect of spending the rest of the night by herself. But another part was reluctant to admit that things had become so serious that she had to leave her home.

"I appreciate the offer, but I don't want to put you to any trouble," she said. "I doubt if it's necessary. This was probably just another stupid prank. I can't believe that whoever set this thing would actually come back here tonight."

"Trust me." Harry urged her gently but determinedly toward the hall stairs. "It's necessary."

"Why?"

"For my peace of mind," Harry said.

"Oh." She couldn't think of an adequate rebuttal to that.

"I want to think on this for a while tonight. In the morning we'll file a report with the cops."

"Fat lot of good that's going to do. Investigating stupid practical jokes must rank right at the bottom of their list of priorities," Molly muttered.

"I know. But I want this incident on record."

He did not elaborate, but Molly knew what he was thinking. Harry wanted the prank reported because he believed that there would be more of them and that they might become increasingly dangerous.

An hour and a half later Harry stood alone in his darkened living room. He listened carefully, but there was no sound from the guest bedroom. Molly had finally gone to sleep.

He gazed out through the wall of windows that separated him from the night and considered the small gear assembly he held in his hand. It seemed to smolder with a heat only he could detect.

He prepared to concentrate. Really concentrate.

He had not wanted to do this. He had not opened himself to this kind of intense contemplation since the day Wild Willy Trevelyan had been killed in the motorcycle stunt. Harry reminded himself that he had not liked the truth that his *insights* had revealed on that occasion. He might not like whatever truth he gleaned from tonight's contemplation, either.

He certainly did not relish the sensation that he knew would accompany the exercise. He felt excruciatingly vulnerable whenever he experienced even small flashes of insight. The deeper exploration he intended to try for tonight would be far worse. He could expect to question his own sanity before it was over. He hated the fear that was waiting for him in the darkness of his own mind.

But he had to take the chance. His need for answers was stronger than his terror of going mad.

Harry plunged himself into the deepest level of thought. It was akin to sinking into a whirling void, a place at the farthest reaches of the galaxy. The trick was to avoid traveling too far into the darkness. Somewhere out there the abyss awaited him.

His concentration became so intense that he lost all sense of his surroundings. He was no longer in his own living room. He was part of the night outside the windows.

The metal burned into his palm. Something inside him screamed a silent warning, not about the mechanical gear he held, but about what was happening to his personal fortifications. He had forged those internal barriers over a period of years, working by instinct alone, not fully aware of what he was trying to accomplish.

It was not until he was well into his twenties that he had begun to comprehend that he was attempting to build a wall at the edge of the abyss.

He had done his work well, considering the fact that he had no model from which to work. Over the years he had learned to use the shallow reaches of the intense state of concentration that his mind was capable of producing. For the most part, he pretended not to see the dark depths below.

But tonight he was going to reach down into them in a search for answers.

Carefully, cautiously, he dismantled the barriers that protected him from the dangers of the abyss.

There were few things Harry feared in life, but the feeling that descended upon him now was definitely one of them. The lack of control that accompanied the complete eradication of his inner fortress was the price he had to pay to accomplish his aims.

He stood at the window, staring out into the night, and let the vibrations of awareness flood his mind. He gave himself up to the process of *knowing.*

The darkness on the other side of the window flowed into the living room and wrapped itself around him.

Harry closed his eyes and tightened his grasp on the small gear in his hand. There was something important here. Something he needed to comprehend in order to help Molly.

He saw the abyss. And the glass bridge that spanned it. He could not see the other side. He had never been able to see it. He had never allowed himself to cross the bridge. Only rarely had he even risked stepping out onto it.

He did not know what awaited him on the far side of the abyss, but he knew with great certainty that madness lay below. He took a tentative step out onto the glass bridge. *Don't look down,* he told himself. *Just don't look down.*

"Harry?"

From out of nowhere the hunger rose within him, devastating his severely weakened defenses.

"Harry, are you all right?" Molly's voice was a whisper of sound in the distance. It reached through the endless night that surrounded him.

She was here in the living room. Right behind him.

No. Leave. Go back to your bed. For God's sake, don't come near me. Not now.

But the words were trapped in his mind. He could not utter them aloud.

"Is something wrong, Harry?"

Yes. Yes. Yes.

He could not form the words with his tongue. His body would not obey his commands. Harry staggered as he turned to face Molly.

He watched her walk toward him through the shadows and knew a savage despair. He was too far out on the glass bridge. He could not control the desperate, questing need within himself.

Balanced on the knife-thin edge of glass, Harry glimpsed the opposite shore of the abyss. He suddenly understood why he had always crushed any speculation of what might await him there. It was better not to contemplate too closely that which he could not possess.

Longing, fierce and intense, clawed his insides.

"Are you all right?" Molly came to a halt in front of him. She was cloaked in the white robe she'd brought with her. Her hair was loose and gloriously wild. Her eyes were crystal clear, fathomless pools in the moonlight.

Harry gathered himself for a Herculean effort. He finally managed to get his tongue to function. "Go back to bed."

"Good heavens, there is something wrong, isn't there?" She raised her hand to touch his face with sensitive fingertips. "Lord, you're burning up. I think you've got a fever. You should have said something earlier. I had no idea you were ill. You had no business coming to my rescue in this condition. You should be in bed."

"No," he croaked. The glass on which he was so precariously balanced shuddered beneath him. He could not retreat. He could not go forward. In another few minutes the bridge would surely shatter. "I'm okay. Leave me alone."

"Don't be silly. I can't do that." She took his free hand and turned to lead him down the hall. "I'm going to put you to bed and find a thermometer. Why didn't you tell me you weren't feeling well?"

"I'm. Not. Sick."

She paid no attention to his weak protest. She started toward his bedroom. Harry was helpless to resist the gentle tug on his hand. It drew him as surely as if she had bound him with magic.

He struggled to regain his normal, rational level of awareness. But it was too late. Molly's touch had drawn him farther out over the abyss. The hunger to discover what lay on the other side was too strong to deny.

"Here we are." Molly guided him into his bedroom. She released his hand to turn down the bed.

She had her back to him. Harry was enthralled by the nape of her neck. Never had he seen anything so lovely. He was literally entranced by the delicate curve. He took a step toward Molly, hand outstretched to touch her.

And stumbled over his own feet.

"Now I know you really are ill," Molly said as she steadied him. "Usually you move like one of those fish in the aquarium in your study."

"A fish?" Anguish flared in him. Fish were cold and emotionless creatures. Maybe Molly thought he was incapable of a normal human response. Maybe she had already seen the craziness in him.

"You know." Molly waved a hand. "You sort of glide along very slowly as if you were floating through the sea. Then, every once in a while, *flash,* you move so fast it startles me."

"Flash." Relief seared him. She was talking about the way he moved, not his mental state.

"In the whole time I've known you, I've never seen you lose your balance or stumble until tonight. Don't worry, I'm sure it's just the fever upsetting your equilibrium. You'll be fine in the morning."

Harry shook his head. He could not even begin to explain what was happening to him. He did not understand it himself. Thus far Molly seemed oblivious to the savage battle he was waging, but he knew that stage would not last long. In a few more minutes she would understand that there was something strange in him.

Molly reached out to switch on a light beside the bed.

He stood there, swaying slightly, and fought to regain his self-control. But the hunger was too strong. Molly looked more inviting than any woman had ever looked since Eve.

She was the woman who waited for him on the opposite side of the abyss.

Harry's insides were raw with the churning need.

Molly finished fussing with the bed. She turned toward him, her spectacular eyes shadowed. The concern was for him, he realized with a sense of wonder. She was not yet afraid of him. She was worried about him.

He could do nothing now to stave off disaster. He knew that in another few seconds she would begin to sense the overwhelming desire in him. She would know that it was unnatural, even though it felt completely natural to him.

She would be terrified. She would pull away from him as though he were some alien monster.

Molly would run from him as Olivia had, and because he was so very vulnerable tonight, Harry was not certain that he would survive her complete and total rejection. He would fall from the glass bridge and fall forever.

He was doomed.

"Let me help you with your shirt." Molly's hands moved lightly over his chest, seeking buttons.

Harry shuddered violently as she touched him.

"You're shivering." She paused briefly to study him more closely. "Are you cold?"

"No. Hot. Very hot." *And getting hotter.*

"I'll get you something to drink in a minute." She bent her head as she resumed the task of removing his shirt.

Her tousled hair tickled his nose. It was the most delightful sensation Harry had ever experienced. He inhaled the flowery scent of her shampoo. He took a deeper breath and drew in the underlying fragrance of her body. It was the essence of femaleness, and it riveted everything that was male in him.

She was seducing him as surely as if she had dressed in seven veils and thumped a tambourine, but she did not have a clue.

Harry groaned. An object fell to the carpet with a soft thud. He realized dimly that he had dropped the gear that he had carried from the front room. There had been something important about that gear. Something he needed to know.

But Molly had his shirt undone now, and he could no longer think about the gear. Her fingers were brushing against his bare chest. *God, such sweet, warm, soft fingers.* She was branding him with her touch.

"Molly." Her name was a plea, a prayer, and a curse. The last because he knew that his fate was sealed. He would surely lose her tonight.

"It's all right," she murmured gently. "You'll be fine. Did this fever come on quite suddenly?"

"Yes." And it was going to be the death of him.

She pursed her lips in a considering expression. "It may be food poisoning."

There was only one cure now for the fire that would soon consume him. The glass edge shivered again beneath his feet. Disaster loomed.

Molly's fingers went to his shoulders now to ease aside his shirt. Her touch warmed his bare skin to the flash point. His hands shook. The searing heat rose within him. He was harder than he had ever been in his life.

His shirt fluttered to the carpet.

Molly looked into his eyes. "You're so warm. I'd better get that glass of water."

Harry seized the chance to break the dangerous spell she had woven so unwittingly. "Yes."

"I'll get it. Sit down, Harry, before you fall down. No offense, but you look terrible."

"Yes." She hated the way he looked. It was starting. Soon she would fear him. Despair seized Harry.

He sank down on the edge of the bed and tried to pull himself together while Molly went into the adjoining bath. He lowered his head into his hands and strove to center himself.

Get off the glass bridge. Rebuild the walls.

Water ran in the sink.

Faster, you fool. You'll lose her.

But he could not retreat. It was too late.

"Here you are," Molly said softly. "Drink this, and then get straight into that bed."

Harry opened his eyes. He did not lift his head. The first thing he saw through his splayed fingers was the drawer in the bedside table. Early this morning, in an optimistic moment, he had taken the box of condoms from the bathroom and put it into the little drawer.

Molly moved to stand in front of him, blocking his view of the drawer. She thrust a glass into his fingers.

He very nearly dropped it.

"Careful," Molly said.

He managed to down the water, but it did nothing to assuage the fire. He wished it had been whiskey or brandy. Alcohol might have taken the edge off the erection that threatened to rip a hole in his pants.

"Thanks." He realized his voice sounded as if his tongue had been dragged across sandpaper.

"Maybe I should call the emergency room to get some advice."

"No. No, please. Don't call anyone."

"Okay." She knelt in front of him to untie his shoes.

Harry stared at the folds of the white robe as it eddied around her. It made him think of a bridal gown. Molly looked both sensuous and chaste. The combination was electrifying.

"I know you're the independent type." Molly tugged off one shoe. "But you may as well accept the fact that you need help tonight. You're sick, Harry."

"So they tell me."

It struck him that the reason she had not taken to her heels yet was because she still attributed his odd behavior to a bad case of food poisoning.

The sight of Molly kneeling in front of him was the most erotic vision Harry had ever had. He imagined her unzipping his pants, lifting him free with her hands, dampening his hot skin with her tongue.

"Take it easy, Harry." Molly slipped off the other shoe. "We've almost got you into bed."

"Yes." It would be his coffin by dawn. He could not survive what was bound to happen.

"You'll feel better in the morning."

"No."

"Of course you will." She paused suddenly, staring at the small leather sheath strapped to his ankle.

Harry wanted to explain the knife. He wanted to tell her that it was more than family tradition. He wanted to tell her everything. But that meant telling her the full truth about his parents and how they had died and how he'd been too late to save them. He could not even begin to tackle that subject in his present state. He wondered if the sight of the blade would turn her away from him.

Without a word, Molly unbuckled the sheath and put it on the bedside table. Then she rose, put one hand on his shoulder, and pushed him gently backward.

He fell against the pillows with all the light, airy grace of a bull elephant going over a cliff. He lay there and watched helplessly as Molly bent over him. The white robe parted slightly, revealing a bit of the scalloped neckline of her gown. He licked his dry lips and fought for words.

"Please." It was all he could say.

"What is it?" she asked. "What do you want?"

"You."

She blinked. A fiery flush crept into her cheeks. "Harry, you're ill."

"No. I'm not sick. Not the way you mean. I want you. Please."

She leaned over the bed to put her hand on his forehead. "It's the fever. You're delirious."

"No. Touch me." He flung out an arm. He managed to capture her wrist before she could remove her hand from his head. "Here." He moved her fingers to his erection. "Make love to me."

She went very still.

She would run from him now, Harry thought. This was it. The end.

"Harry?" Her eyes were green gems warmed by an inner fire.

"This is what's wrong with me," he whispered harshly. "Not food poisoning. I want you so much. So damned much."

"Oh, Harry."

She was about to panic. Harry was sure of it. In another instant she would flee. He could do nothing to stop her.

"Don't go," he whispered.

Her fingers closed tentatively over the bulge in his pants. Harry thought he would go up in flames. Then she straightened slowly. Her eyes never left his face. This was it, he realized bleakly. She had finally seen the weirdness in him. She would leave him here alone in the darkness.

The white robe fell to the carpet. It was followed by the white nightgown.

Harry drank in the sight of Molly's nude body. The vision threatened to swamp all his senses. Moonlight gleamed softly on the curves of her small, high breasts and the lush flare of her thighs. The dark triangle of hair that shielded her secrets mesmerized him.

She came to him.

She came to him.

For a split second Harry did not understand. He had been so certain she would run.

"Molly?" he gasped.

She settled slowly on him like soft, warm tropical rain. She brushed her mouth gently, tentatively across his. He could feel her breasts pressed against his chest.

She was making love to him.

The last remnants of his control vanished. Harry broke into a headlong run across the glass bridge, heedless now of the threat that lay below. All he cared about was reaching the opposite shore of the abyss.

He wrapped Molly in his arms, turned her, and crushed her into the bedding. He heard her soft, startled cry, and then she was clinging to him, clutching wildly at his shoulders. He felt her nails on his back.

He reached down between her legs, thrust his fingers through the soft hair and found her hot and wet and ready for him. He vaguely recalled the condom in the drawer beside the bed. He groped for the knob of the drawer. He could not seem to get hold of it.

Clumsy. So impossibly clumsy. Not like him. "Damn."

"I'll get it." Molly sounded breathless as she reached out to open the drawer for him.

He fumbled around inside. Found the box. Found the packet.

Foreplay. The voice inside his head was very insistent. Women liked foreplay. Lots of foreplay.

"What's wrong?" Molly sounded frantic, but eager.

Definitely eager. Not terrified.

"Foreplay," Harry muttered. "Supposed to be foreplay."

"We can do it later, can't we? Make it afterplay." She yanked at his zipper. "Harry, I can't wait. I've never felt like this."

He sucked in his breath as she jerked open his pants. But no damage was done. His hand shook so violently he could not unroll the condom. Molly had to help him.

He watched her frown intently over the task. Her sweet awkwardness was electrifyingly erotic. Each tug, each touch, each delicate fumble translated into a caress that threatened to make him explode.

Then he was finally, achingly ready, and she was waiting for him, reaching for him. She wanted him.

The wonder of it stole his breath. She wanted *him,* weirdness and all.

Molly lifted herself, opening for him, inviting him into her warmth. The hot, moist, womanly scent of her body took him on a journey to the heart of creation.

Harry covered her mouth with fierce urgency. Her lips parted for him. He drove himself into her body, pushing past the resistance of her delicate muscles. She was tight. Unbelievably tight. Then he was inside, and she was holding him so snugly that he could not tell where his body ended and hers began.

He moved within her, sinking deeper and deeper into her welcoming heat. Her legs closed around him. He felt her nails score his shoulders.

Molly screamed softly, a passionate cry of release that Harry knew he would never forget as long as he lived. It was the most beautiful song in the world.

But there was little time to savor the erotic notes. The tiny tremors of her climax tugged at him, demanding that he follow her into the vortex.

He could not have resisted even had he wanted to try. And resisting Molly's sweet summons was the last thing he wished to do.

Harry raced off the far end of the glass bridge and landed on the opposite shore of the abyss.

He was safe. Molly was there with him.

This was what came of taking chances.

Molly opened her eyes to a wall of morning light. It poured through the windows, flooding the bedroom.

So that's what making love with Dr. Harry Stratton Trevelyan felt like.

She smiled. Then she grinned. There was nothing quite so deeply fulfilling for an Abberwick as having her curiosity satisfied.

Molly suppressed an exuberant giggle with some difficulty. She had certainly never had her curiosity satisfied the way it had been last night. Her whole body seemed to be purring this morning.

She stretched, propped herself on one elbow, and regarded Harry as he slept beside her. The intimate sight sent a shiver of excitement through her. He was spectacular. A magnificent male beast. Of course he wasn't handsome. Handsome did not even begin to describe him. Handsome was a ridiculously weak, soft, trivial word for such an outstanding specimen of manhood. He was wonderful. He was the most fascinating man on earth.

Even sprawled facedown amid the rumpled sheets, Harry retained an aura of masculine grace. The muscles of his shoulders and back were sleekly contoured with unmistakable strength. His alchemist's hands looked powerful against the white linens. The harsh, exotic lines of his face were etched with the potential for passion and relentless will, even though his brilliant eyes were temporarily veiled behind closed lashes.

Molly laughed silently at her own extravagantly romantic flight of fancy. She was obviously falling in love. Probably already there. So what? she thought. She had waited long enough for the right man to come along, long enough to take a chance.

The responsibilities that had been a part of her for years suddenly seemed weightless. She had never felt more free in her life.

She reflected on the revelations the night had brought. She now knew for certain that Harry's capacity for passion and his seemingly inexhaustible, implacable will were tempered by a startling vulnerability.

She would never forget the look in his eyes last night when he had pleaded with her to make love to him. He obviously had not realized the depth of her feelings, or he would have known that there was no need to beg. He would have to be insensate not to know it now.

She recalled the stoic lack of hope that she had seen in him during those first fragile moments. The bleakness in his gaze had baffled her. It still did. It was as though he had offered himself to her with the expectation of being rejected.

A man like Harry did not willingly make himself vulnerable. He had been in a very strange mood, even for him, last night.

She thought about the damp sweat that had glistened on his forehead and the strained lines of his face. The intense heat of his body had alarmed her initially. When she had found him standing alone in the darkness she had been convinced he was ill. Yet he had denied it. Then he had proven just how healthy he was by making love to her with driving vitality.

Odd. Very odd.

Molly considered the situation. Granted, her experience in these matters was somewhat limited, but common sense told her that, whatever had been wrong with Harry last night, he had not been suffering from food poisoning.

The precise instant when he had surged into her for the first time would be engraved on her memory forever. It seemed to her that it had been far more than a simple act of passion. It was as if he had bound himself to her in that moment.

The experience had exhausted both of them. They had fallen asleep immediately after their bodies had trembled and shuddered together in the climax.

Then again, perhaps her imagination had just gone off the deep end, Molly thought. That was a very likely possibility under the circumstances.

Unable to lie quietly in bed when she was feeling so energized, Molly pushed aside the covers. She was careful not to awaken Harry as she got to her feet.

The first step made her draw a sudden breath. She winced slightly at the subtle tug of muscles that had been strained by unaccustomed nocturnal activity. She recovered quickly and padded barefoot across the gray carpet.

Midway to the bathroom, she paused to collect her nightgown and robe, which lay in her path. Then she went into the white-tiled bath.

She hung her robe and gown on a hook, turned on the water in the glass-framed shower, and stepped beneath the hot spray. It felt wonderful. But, then, she had a hunch everything would feel terrific today. She was in a fabulously good mood.

She was lathering herself with a huge bar of plain, unscented soap when the glass shower door opened without warning. Steam billowed out into the room.

Molly turned quickly, blinking water out of her eyes. Harry loomed in the opening. Misty tendrils of vapor swirled around him. He stared at her with an intensity that made her blush from head to toe. Instinctively she lowered her hands to cover the dark thatch of hair at the apex of her thighs. It was an ancient, utterly pointless gesture. Harry had seen everything there was to see of her last night.

He certainly did not suffer from a similar false modesty, Molly noted with interest. He had come straight from the bed without bothering to don a robe. His body was heavy with arousal. His amber eyes were starkly, sensually aware.

But something about him was vastly different this morning, Molly realized. Then she saw that his gaze no longer held the desperate vulnerability that had been so evident last night. He looked at her now with ferocious attention, as if amazed to find her in his shower.

She managed a tremulous smile. "Hi. You look as though you've just seen a ghost or something."

"Not a ghost." Harry stepped into the shower and closed the door. "You."

"Who were you expecting?"

"No one." His voice was low and husky. He grasped her slick shoulders and pulled her gently, deliberately against his rock-hard erection. "I thought it had all been a dream."

Molly drew a quick, steadying breath as he pressed against her. Then she grinned. "I hope you're not going to tell me that you thought I was just a wet dream?"

"Not just an ordinary wet dream," he whispered against her throat. "A really, really good wet dream. Better than any wet dream I've ever had in my life."

She trembled in his arms. "Oh, well, that's different, I suppose."

"Yes, it is. You're different." He bent his head and took her mouth with a slow thoroughness that had not been a part of last night's feverish lovemaking.

Molly shivered beneath the warm water. Her body responded immediately, just as it had during the night. She wrapped her arms around his neck and returned the kiss with hot urgency.

Harry laughed softly against her mouth. "Not so fast. What with all the excitement last night, we forgot something important."

"What was that?"

"Foreplay."

"Oh, that. To tell you the truth, I don't think it was necessary. I didn't miss a thing."

"Maybe it's not strictly necessary." Harry slid one hand down her back, tracing the line of her spine. Then he cupped her buttocks and squeezed gently. "But I think it's going to be a lot of fun."

Molly felt her knees weaken. She sighed and leaned into his strength, glorying in the hard lines of his body. This was not the time to ask him about his strange mood last night. He was no longer vulnerable. The barriers of his self-control were firmly back in place. He would not welcome her questions, no matter how subtle.

She felt his long fingers dip lower, gliding straight into the dark cleft that divided her soap-slick derriere.

"Harry."

"Like I said. A lot of fun."

A long time later Molly opened the refrigerator door and surveyed the contents. After due deliberation she selected a carton of eggs, milk, and some butter. She set all of the items on one long granite countertop while she rummaged through various cupboards in search of syrup. There was a bottle of pure Canadian maple on a shelf near the refrigerator.

She discovered a heavy, unsliced loaf of fresh sourdough bread securely wrapped in a plastic bag. Further research turned up several fry-ing pans in various sizes. Uncertain of which would be best for her intended purpose, she set out three of them. Next, she began a search for a suitable bowl.

When she was through, she stepped back to survey the array of items she had set out on the counter. Now, all she needed was a cookbook.

It was oddly pleasant to putter around Harry's kitchen. There was a satisfying intimacy implicit in the process of making breakfast for the two of them, even without the aid of the Abberwick Food Storage and Preparation Machine.

Perhaps during the meal there would be an opportunity to ask Harry the questions that were uppermost in her mind this morning. She wanted to know what he had been thinking last night when she had found him standing in front of the window staring out into the night.

To her surprise, she found several cookbooks in a corner cupboard. She wondered if Harry had collected them or if his housekeeper, Ginny, kept them on hand. After due consideration, Molly selected one subtitled *Simple Steps to Gourmet Delights.* She flipped the pages to the index.

She looked up from her task when she heard Harry's footsteps in the hall. "I hope you like French toast," she called. "I haven't done much cooking without the Abberwick Food Storage and Preparation Machine, but I think I can cope."

There was no response. She sensed that something had changed yet again in Harry's mood before he appeared.

He came to a halt in the doorway. One glance told her that this was not the time to ask him intimate questions about the vulnerability she had seen in him last night. Her playful shower companion had disappeared. In his place was the grimly serious man she had seen so often during the past month.

His hair was still damp. He was dressed in a pair of khaki trousers and a black cotton shirt. His eyes were hooded and thoughtful. One of his hands was clenched tightly at his side.

Molly closed the cookbook very slowly. "Harry, what's wrong?"

"I think I know him."

"What on earth are you talking about?"

He held out his clenched hand and opened his fingers to reveal the gear assembly he held. "I think I know whoever was responsible for making this."

"That's impossible."

"No." He walked to the counter and set the gear down on it. He studied the mechanism the way a hawk studies a mouse. "I started to realize it last night. But it was vague and distorted. And then you came into the front room. I got sidetracked."

Molly raised her brows. "That's one way of putting it."

He ignored her weak humor. His attention was riveted on the gear. "A few minutes ago I found it on the carpet as I was getting dressed. I must have dropped it last night."

"So?"

"So it all came flooding back to me the minute I picked it up." He raised his eyes to meet hers. There was cold speculation in his gleaming gaze. "Only this time the feeling wasn't mushy or unclear. It was clean and sharp."

"I don't understand. What's all this about mushy feelings?"

"Forget it." Harry scowled, as if he'd said more than he'd intended. "Just an expression. What I meant was that I—"

Molly held up one hand. "Hold on here. Harry, are we talking about your infamous Trevelyan Second Sight?"

"Don't get silly on me now, Molly. You're too smart for that kind of nonsense. Let's just say that things clicked in my head a couple of minutes ago when I took a second look at this gear."

"Aha. One of your insights, then?"

"Something like that," he allowed coolly. "I would have figured it out last night, but my thinking got a little fuzzy due to very understandable reasons."

"What reasons?" she demanded.

He looked briefly amused. "You seduced me."

"Oh, that." She blushed. "I thought you meant something else. All right. So it clicked. What was it?"

"I realized something I should have understood immediately. I know the man who made this gear assembly." Harry frowned. "Or, at least I know his work. It's almost the same thing."

"You're losing me, Harry."

"Remember how your sister took one look at the fake pistol device and announced that at least two of her friends were innocent?"

"She said it wasn't their style."

"Exactly." Harry sat down on a counter stool. "There's a certain style to this kind of thing. The fake pistol and that damned hobgoblin that was put under your bed were not off-the-shelf items. The devices were individually built and tailored to their particular tasks."

Molly eyed the gear. "I think I'm beginning to see where this is going."

"It defies the laws of probability to believe that two different people would have designed precisely the same gear assemblies, using the same jury-rigged motor and battery design and the same sloppy elevation mechanisms."

"All right, so it was probably the same person who built both the gun and the goblin," Molly said. "We already assumed as much. What makes you think you know him?"

"I've seen these sloppy designs somewhere else."

Molly stared at him. "You're sure?"

Harry smiled slightly. "That's what I'm trying to tell you. I know this person's work. Now all I have to do is figure out where I've seen this particular style of crude engineering design."

"How do you intend to research the problem?"

"That's easy," Harry said. "I'll start by going back through all one hundred of those grant proposals I told you to reject."

The implications of what he was saying hit Molly so hard that she had to grasp the edge of the counter for support. "Oh, my God. You don't think it's one of those inventors, after all, do you?"

"Yes," Harry said. "That's exactly what I think. It looks like one of the people whose grant proposals we turned down has decided to take some revenge."

Molly sighed heavily. "My father's foundation has caused me nothing but trouble. I wish he had thought of something else to do with his money."

"Well," Harry said slowly, "there are two schools of thought on that subject."

"There are?"

"One, as you just suggested, is that the Abberwick Foundation is a headache."

"Uh-huh." Molly raised her brows. "What's the other point of view?"

"The other side of the issue is that I would never have met you if your father hadn't appointed you sole trustee of the foundation."

"Hmm." Molly cheered at that observation. "There is that."

"Yes." Harry's eyes gleamed with sensual memories. "There is that." He glanced at the cluttered counter. "What are you doing here?"

"I'm going to make us some breakfast. French toast, to be exact." Molly selected a large knife from a drawer and prepared to attack the loaf of sourdough.

"When was the last time you cooked without the aid of the Abberwick Food Storage and Preparation Machine?"

Molly frowned in thought as she began to saw through the end of the loaf. "I think I was eighteen or nineteen. Why?"

"Maybe you'd better let me give you a hand."

"Nonsense. Any fool can make French toast." At that moment the wide-toothed bread knife hit a rough spot in the sourdough. Molly bore down with grim determination.

Too much determination. And at a bad angle. The acrylic bread board suddenly skidded across the granite countertop. Molly yelped in surprise. Instinctively she yanked the knife out of the loaf. It came free with unexpected speed and flew out of her hand. She stared in dismay as it soared and wheeled in the air and then plunged down toward the granite, point first. She wondered how much a fine-quality bread knife cost.

With a deceptively easy motion that was almost too fast for the eye to follow, Harry reached across the counter and caught the knife by the hilt just before it struck the unforgiving granite. He smiled. "I'll slice the bread for you."

"Thanks. I'd appreciate that."

"And there you have it," Molly said as she concluded her tale two hours later. "The adventures of Molly Abberwick and the mysterious hobgoblin."

"You spent the night with T-Rex?" Tessa paused in the act of replacing a glass canister full of smoky Lapsang Souchong tea on the shelf. "I don't believe it."

Molly gave her a repressive glare. "He was kind enough to let me stay at his place after I was nearly scared out of my wits by that stupid goblin prank."

"Kind? He doesn't look like the kindly type to me." Tessa narrowed her eyes. "And why do I have this feeling that you did not sleep on the couch?"

"Now, Tessa, you know I don't believe in discussing my personal life."

"That's because you haven't had a personal life to discuss for ages," Tessa retorted. "What's going on here? Are you and Trevelyan having an affair?"

"I'd hardly call it that."

"Damn. You are having an affair." Tessa looked at her with worried eyes. "Do you think that's smart? You said yourself that the two of you have absolutely nothing in common. You said he's stubborn and difficult and arrogant. You said—"

"I'll be in my office if anyone needs me." Molly strode through the opening and slammed the door behind her.

She dropped into her desk chair. The door promptly opened again, and Tessa stuck her head around the corner. "All right, forget the juicy personal stuff. I'll worm the truth out of you later. What's Trevelyan going to do about that goblin thing that someone put under your bed?"

"I'm not sure. He seems to think he recognizes the guy's work. He says it's sloppy. He's sure that he can identify the same style of design in one of the grant proposals."

Tessa's eyes widened. "He thinks that whoever is behind this is one of the inventors you rejected?"

"Uh-huh."

"Shouldn't you be talking to the police?"

"We will, as soon as Harry gets a lead on a likely suspect. At this point all we've got are a couple of nasty pranks and an unlimited pool of possible perpetrators."

"I see what you mean. No one's been hurt. There's no evidence of forced entry. So far they're just pranks."

"Right. I'm afraid that if we go to the cops now they'll think one of Kelsey's friends is responsible, just as I did. Lord only knows where that assumption would take the police. Assuming they have time to investigate such a minor event in the first place."

Tessa looked troubled. "What are you going to do?"

"There's nothing I can do at the moment. We'll have to wait and see if Harry can come up with anything useful. In the meantime, I've got a business to run. Let's get to work."

Gordon Brooke strode into Abberwick Tea & Spice at five minutes before noon. Molly was in the process of measuring out a half pound of Keemun tea for a customer. She stifled a groan of dismay.

Gordon had a file folder tucked under one arm. Stylish as always, he was clad in a pair of loose-fitting, multipleated stone-colored trousers and an open-throated coffee-colored shirt with wide, billowing sleeves. A rakish embroidered vest completed the ensemble. He would have looked at home sitting in a sidewalk café in Paris or Rome.

Molly made a show of being very busy with a flurry of new customers who wandered into the shop at that moment. Tessa did the same. Gordon lounged against a display of gift-boxed spice sets and waited. Molly hoped that he would become bored and leave before the rush of customers did, but her luck was out. Gordon did not budge.

Tessa exchanged a commiserating glance with Molly as the crowd gradually dwindled.

When the customer base was down to two, both of whom were still browsing the shelves, Molly reluctantly turned to Gordon. He gave her his most endearing grin, the one that put a dimple in his cheeks.

"Got something to show you, Molly." He held up the folder he had brought with him.

Molly eyed the folder with deep suspicion. "What?"

Gordon straightened and started forward. "Let's go into your office."

He disappeared inside before Molly could think of a polite excuse. She trailed slowly after him. Tessa rolled her eyes.

When Molly reached the door of her office, she saw that Gordon had already made himself at home. He was sitting in the chair behind her desk. He had the folder open in front of him.

"I want you to see my projections for the next three years, Molly."

"Gordon, if this is about a loan, you're wasting your time. We went through this three months ago."

"Just take a look at these numbers. That's all I'm asking. They're solid as a rock. The only thing I need to make it come together is a little infusion of cash."

"I told you, I'm not going to finance your expansion plans, Gordon."

He looked up from the papers he had spread out on her desk. "Think of it as an investment, because that's exactly what it is. A hell of a better investment than some zany invention cooked up by a crackpot inventor, for God's sake."

Molly planted her hands on the desk. "I will say this one more time, and that's it. I am not interested in making you a loan."

Without any warning, the warm, persuasive charm on Gordon's face disappeared. "Goddamn it, Molly, you've got to listen to me."

Startled by the outburst, Molly took a quick step back. "What do you think you're doing?"

Frustration and rage flashed in his eyes. "I've got too much riding on this. Do you think I'm going to let all of my plans go down the tubes just because you're harboring a grudge?"

"I'm not harboring any grudges."

"The hell you aren't." Gordon surged to his feet. "You're still pissed because of what happened between us."

"Are you nuts? That was eighteen months ago. Believe it or not, I've had better things to do in the meantime than nurse a broken heart or carry a grudge."

"Then stop letting your emotions get in the way of good business," Gordon shot back. "Don't you understand what's at stake here?"

"Sure. Your reexpansion plans. Do you think I care about financing a half-dozen Gordon Brooke Espresso Bars? I've got my own business to worry about."

"This isn't about expansion for the sake of expansion. This is life and death."

Molly's mouth fell open. "Life and death?"

"No joke, Molly. I'm sitting on the brink of bankruptcy." Gordon's hands clenched into fists. "I have to have fresh money, or Gordon Brooke Espresso is going to go under. All of it. Everything I've worked for will come crashing down around my ears."

Molly closed her eyes briefly. "I'm so sorry, Gordon. I didn't realize things were that precarious."

"You can save me." He started around the desk with renewed determination. "I need you, honey. For old times' sake, say you'll help me."

She bit her lip. "Please, don't make this a personal thing. You said it was business. And as a businesswoman, I don't want any part of it. I'm into tea and spices, not coffee."

He took a step toward her. "Molly, what happened between us is old news. You and I can start over. We'll be partners this time. We've got so much in common."

Molly felt the hair stir softly on the nape of her neck. She knew without turning around that the door to her office had just opened. She also knew who had entered.

"Am I interrupting anything important here?" Harry asked with a dangerous chill in his voice.

Molly whirled around, relieved to see him. She gave him an overly bright smile. "Not at all."

Gordon's expression turned thunderous. "I'm trying to have a business conversation with Molly."

"Too bad. I've got an appointment with her, myself." Harry glanced at his watch. "For lunch. You'll have to excuse us."

Gordon's jaw resembled a concrete reinforcing bar. "I don't think I've met you."

Molly leaped into the awkward silence that fell between the men. "That's right, you two don't know each other. Gordon, this is Dr. Harry Trevelyan. He's a noted authority on the history of science. He's consulting for the Abberwick Foundation. Harry, this is Gordon Brooke of Gordon Brooke Espresso. You've probably had some of his coffee."

Harry said nothing.

Gordon scowled. "You're the guy who's helping Molly select funding projects for the foundation?"

"Yes." Harry looked at Molly. "Ready?"

"Let me get my purse." Molly hurried around the corner of her desk.

Gordon put out a hand to catch hold of her arm. "Damn it, Molly, this is important. Let me finish what I've started here."

"Some other time." Molly ducked his outstretched fingers. She pulled her purse out of a drawer. "Harry's right. He and I have an appointment to discuss some foundation business."

"Yeah, I'll bet you do." Gordon gave Harry a fulminating look. "I know all about you so-called foundation consultants."

Harry cocked a brow. "You do?"

"Sure. You latch onto people like Molly who handle the funds for a foundation or a charity. You convince them that they need you in order to get the job done, and then you milk the operation for all the fees and associated costs you can get. It's nothing more than a legal scam."

Molly was shocked. "Gordon, stop it. I don't want to hear another word."

"It's the truth. Guys like Trevelyan here are the reason so many charities wind up with such high administrative and management costs and so little cash for their projects."

Molly gripped the strap of her purse. "Please leave, Gordon. Now."

"Hell." Gordon's eyes slitted in sudden comprehension. "He's screwing you, isn't he? I should have guessed." He gathered up his papers and crammed them into the folder. "He'll bleed your precious foundation dry, Molly. And then he'll dump you. Don't say you weren't warned."

Gordon stormed toward the door. Harry stepped politely out of his path.

Ten

It had been a very near thing, Harry thought later as he waited in line at the sidewalk window of a waterfront café. A chill went through him whenever he thought about the events of the night. He felt as if he'd been standing in the path of an onrushing train and had somehow, inexplicably, managed to escape certain disaster.

He still did not comprehend his good fortune, but he was profoundly relieved to know that he had not scared the living daylights out of Molly. In fact, she seemed virtually unruffled by his behavior during the night.

Perhaps a little too unruffled. Harry frowned. She acted as if she hadn't noticed anything strange or even slightly out of the ordinary during last night's lovemaking.

Memories of her passionate, exquisitely feminine response to him returned in a heated rush. She had come to him, made love to him, taken him deep inside her warm, tight, fiercely welcoming body. He had actually *felt* the joyous delight in her, frothy as fine champagne. It was as though she had been waiting for him all of her life.

And for the first time in his life, he had known true sexual satisfaction. Last night the relentless hunger, the craving for an incomprehensible consummation that had been growing so strong during the past few years had been assuaged, temporarily, at least. He would never forget the experience. It was far more profound than any physical release he had ever known.

But as glorious as it had been, there was no getting around the fact that Molly's reaction still baffled him. He was sure that she had been exposed to a full onslaught of that part of him he had fought to conceal even from himself. Yet she hadn't seemed fazed by it. Olivia had caught only the merest glimpse and had been convinced that he was more than a little crazy.

He had been lucky, Harry told himself. Very, very lucky. Molly had attributed his behavior to a fever. Or perhaps she had simply been too shaken by the malicious prank that had been played on her earlier in the evening to be aware of the weirdness in him. Whatever the reason, he had not terrified her the way he had Olivia. But he had certainly scared the hell out of himself.

The whole thing had been too damn close. He would make certain that he did not take such risks a second time. From now on he would be careful.

From now on he would be in control whenever he made love to Molly.

Harry paid for two cups of chowder. He picked up the cardboard tray and walked across the pier to where Molly was sitting at an umbrella-shaded table.

He was braced for the sight of her, but the euphoric thrill that he had experienced this morning, when he had discovered that she had not left him, struck again. He realized with some chagrin that he was getting hard just looking at her. He could only hope that his pants concealed his uncontrollable physical reaction. He wondered if he would be forced to take deep breaths every time he saw her, or if he would gradually grow accustomed to the sudden clench of excitement in his gut.

Molly's attention was on the gulls that soared and swooped like miniature fighter planes in pursuit of stray french fries and bits of fried fish. The soft breeze played with her hair the way an electric beater played with egg whites.

Wistfully, Harry studied the graceful line of the nape of Molly's neck. The deep hunger throbbed within him. He could almost feel her warm, silken skin. More hot images of the night drifted through his head. It was only about the thousandth time that day that they had interfered with his concentration. His hands tightened on the tray. Fortunately he had a lot of concentration.

Harry put the tray of chowder down on the table. "Lunch is served. Red for you and white for me. Did I get it right?"

Molly held a tendril of tawny hair out of her eyes and surveyed the two cups of chowder. "Right. How can you stand that thick, white, pasty stuff, anyway?"

"Just one more point on which we differ," Harry said equably as he sat down. It would probably be a good idea to remind himself more frequently of how little they had in common, he thought. It would help restore a certain crucial distance. "I like New England–style clam chowder. You prefer the red kind which amounts to nothing more than some clams and potatoes floating around in tomato juice."

"A matter of opinion," she said loftily. "Any luck with the grant proposals?"

"No. It's going to take time to find what I'm looking for. If I have to go through all of the proposals it could take several days. The sort of details I'm after aren't obvious. They're subtle."

Molly tapped her plastic spoon impatiently against the rim of her chowder cup. "Days?"

He looked up from his chowder. "You'll stay with me until we nail the bastard."

"I will?"

"Do you really want to go back to that big old spooky house by yourself every night and stay there all alone? Wondering what the son-of-a-bitch's next little trick will be?"

"It's not spooky." Molly closed her eyes and shuddered. "But, you're right. I'm not sure I want to stay there alone at the moment." Then she eyed him through her lashes. "I could stay with my aunt."

"And draw the prankster's attention to her house?"

A shocked expression lit Molly's eyes. "Oh, my God. I can't do that."

"You'll be safe at my condo. The doormen are on duty twenty-four hours a day. They won't let anyone into the building who isn't supposed to be there."

"If you're sure," she said hesitantly.

"I'm sure."

"Well, maybe just until we identify the prankster," she clarified.

"Right. Until we know who's behind this." It was settled. She would stay with him. Harry suppressed a rush of pleasure. "I'll start looking for our rejected inventor immediately."

"You really think you can pick his work out of that pile of grant proposals?"

"Given time, yes."

Molly shook her head. "Amazing. It'll take hours of work."

"I know you're not the patient type," Harry said quietly.

"But you are?"

He shrugged. "It usually pays off."

"Just another little example of how different we are?" she asked smoothly. "Like our different tastes in clam chowder?"

"Out of curiosity, which type of chowder does Gordon Brooke prefer?" Harry asked before he could stop himself. "Red or white?"

"Gordon?" Molly wrinkled her nose. "Red, I think."

"Naturally."

"Why do you say that?"

"It strikes me that you and Brooke have a lot in common."

"Not really," she said much too swiftly.

"You're both entrepreneurs." Harry knew for certain now that he was on to something important. "You both sell similar products to a similar market base. Seems like you two would have a lot to talk about."

"Like what?"

"Business problems," Harry suggested. "Taxes. City government regulations on small businesses. That sort of thing."

"Okay, so we have some business problems in common. Big deal."

"You're both single," Harry pointed out.

"So?"

"So, I sensed a certain informality between the two of you," Harry said dryly.

"What is this? The Trevelyan Inquisition? All right, Gordon and I have known each other for a couple of years. We don't have so much in common, however, that I intend to loan him fifty grand from the Abberwick Foundation."

Damn, Harry thought. *So that's what this is all about. The sucker is trying to use her.* He ripped open a tiny packet of pepper. "Fifty thousand?"

"Uh-huh." Molly concentrated on her chowder.

"That's a lot of money."

"Gordon needs cash. He got overextended. He says he's in financial trouble. He's already had to close two of his espresso bars."

"Talk about raw nerve." Harry dumped the pepper onto his chowder and tossed the empty packet aside in disgust. "He actually tried to convince you that his business plans qualify as an invention worthy of the backing of the Abberwick Foundation?"

"Something like that." Molly's brows drew together in a small frown. "He's been after me for several weeks now, but he didn't tell me that he was actually on the brink of bankruptcy until today."

"He probably saved the sob story for the last-ditch effort."

Molly's fingers tightened on the handle of her spoon. "He must be desperate to confess that he's in danger of losing his business. I know him well enough to realize what that admission cost his pride."

Harry did not like the note of sympathy that had crept into her voice. "Just how well do you know him?"

"As you said, Gordon and I have some business interests in common."

"And you both like the same kind of chowder."

Molly glowered. "And his shop is right across the steps from mine. What of it?"

"That well, huh?"

"Sheesh, all right, already. I surrender. A year and a half ago Gordon and I were involved for a while. I'm sure you've guessed as much. Now, are you satisfied?"

"You can't blame me for being a little curious," Harry said.

"The heck I can't."

"It's only natural under the circumstances. You grilled me a bit on the subject of my ex-fiancée, if you will recall."

Molly blushed. "I guess that's true. Okay, now we're even."

"Not quite," Harry murmured. "What happened between you and Brooke? Why did you two stop seeing each other?"

Molly lifted one shoulder in an elaborately casual shrug. "You know how it is. A year and a half ago I was very busy with the legal and investment work required to set up my father's foundation. I was also running my own business. And there was Kelsey to worry about. She was still in high school. What with one thing and another, there wasn't much time left over for a personal life. Gordon and I just drifted apart. It's over."

"How did it end? With a bang or a whimper?"

Molly gave him a frosty look. "We're not talking about the end of the universe as we know it. We're talking about a casual dating relationship that sort of petered out."

"Petered out? An interesting expression, given the topic."

The frost in her eyes turned to ice. "You're being difficult, Trevelyan."

"So how did it end?"

"Good grief, you're the most persistent man I've ever met."

"Part of my charm," Harry said humbly.

"Is it?" A glint appeared in Molly's eyes. "If you must know, it ended with a hiss."

Harry paused, his spoon halfway to his mouth. "A hiss?"

Molly's smile was grim. "The sort of hissing shriek an espresso machine makes when the steam is forced through the ground coffee."

"I see. That kind of hiss."

"Exactly."

Harry considered the matter for a short time and then decided to push for the rest of the story. "Would you mind explaining the hiss?"

Molly sighed. "Gordon and I had been dating for nearly two months. I thought things were going rather well. As you noted, we had a lot to talk about. But one day I walked into his shop shortly before closing time. The place was empty. The young woman who was usually on duty behind the counter was not around, but . . ."

"But?"

"But I thought I heard the sound of an espresso machine. The noise was coming from the storage room at the back of the shop."

"Ah," Harry said. "I believe I begin to perceive the ending of this tale."

"It certainly doesn't take ESP to do that," Molly muttered.

Harry stilled. He searched her face but saw no sign that she had intended any veiled references to last night. He relaxed slightly. "Go on."

"To make a short story even shorter, I went into the storage room expecting to find Gordon testing out a new espresso machine. But he was testing out his counter assistant, instead. The two of them were going at it on top of a pile of sacks full of Gordon Brooke's Special Espresso Roast Costa Rican Blend."

"I can understand how an encounter like that would have left an indelible impression."

"Enough to put one off espresso for life," Molly assured him.

"And the hissing sound?"

Molly grimaced. "That was Gordon. He sounded just like one of his machines."

"You didn't, uh, recognize the noise?" Harry asked carefully.

"Our relationship had, thankfully, not progressed to that stage."

"You weren't sleeping with him?"

"No." Molly smiled wryly. "Now, are you satisfied?"

"Almost," Harry said.

Molly glowered. "You're impossible. Do you have to pursue every little detail?"

"I like to collect odd scraps of information."

"This isn't exactly an interesting footnote in the history of science. Why do you want so much information on Gordon?"

"I figure it's to my benefit to learn as much as I can about him."

She regarded him with deep suspicion. "Why?"

Harry watched a dozen gulls dive toward the same french fry. The bird that got to it first seized the morsel and climbed swiftly skyward to escape the competition. "I like to plan ahead. When did you and Gordon first start dating?"

Molly was silent for a moment. Harry sensed that she was choosing her words with great care. He wondered why the subject of Gordon Brooke required such extreme caution.

"We met about two years ago. I told you, we started going out together about eighteen months ago," Molly said finally.

"That would have been about six months after your father died?"

"Yes."

"About the time you took the first legal steps to establish the Abberwick Foundation?"

"Uh-huh." Molly studiously spooned up more chowder.

Harry whistled softly. "So it took Brooke that long to figure out that you were in control of a five-hundred-thousand-dollar-a-year foundation? He must be a little slow. No wonder he's on the verge of bankruptcy."

"That's it." Molly slammed her spoon down onto the table. "I knew you'd say something like that. I just *knew* it."

"What did I say?"

"Don't you dare try that innocent expression with me, Dr. Trevelyan. You know perfectly well that you just implied that Gordon tried to use me eighteen months ago."

"Now, Molly—"

"You virtually accused him of having his eye on the Abberwick Foundation assets, not me. The implication is that I was too naive and too gullible to realize it until I saw him going at it with his assistant."

"I'm sorry," Harry said.

"Hah. I don't believe that for one single minute. You think I'm soft in the head when it comes to financial matters, don't you?"

"Not in the least," Harry said, surprised by her conclusion.

"Yes, you do. You no doubt gained that unfortunate impression because I seem too eager to make grants to the various inventors who have applied for them."

"I think you've got a soft spot for inventors, yes. But that's another issue."

"You bet it is." Molly aimed her spoon at him as though it were a ray gun. "Bear in mind, Dr. Trevelyan, that I did not make Abberwick Tea & Spice a successful business enterprise by being stupid about money."

"True," he conceded.

"Nor am I naive and gullible when it comes to investments. The fact that I got my father's foundation up and running is proof of that."

"Absolutely."

"So maybe I am a little softhearted when it comes to inventors. What of it? It's a family trait. Abberwicks have spent generations looking for funding for their inventions. It's only natural that I would feel for others who are in the same position my father and uncle were in for most of their lives."

"I understand. I apologize."

Molly abruptly collapsed against the back of her chair with a disgruntled expression. "Why should you be sorry? It's the truth. Gordon did try to use me to get money for his damned espresso bars. I hoped you wouldn't find out. It's embarrassing."

"I doubt if it was any more embarrassing than discovering that my ex-fiancée was in love with my cousin," Harry said.

Molly looked briefly nonplussed. Then her mouth kicked up at one corner. "You've got a point. I'll bet that was a little rough, wasn't it?"

"It didn't do a lot for my ego, but I survived."

Molly's hair bounced in the wind as she leaned forward and folded her arms on the table. "Maybe you and I have more in common than we first thought."

Harry gazed into her shatteringly clear eyes and felt the desperate hunger rise within him. He fought savagely to squelch it. He could not take any more risks. He had gotten lucky last night because Molly had believed him to be ill. He must not lose his control again. At least not until he was absolutely, positively certain that she would not fear the strangeness in him.

"Maybe we do," Harry agreed.

"Eighteen months ago Gordon wanted cash to expand," Molly said quietly. "When he didn't get it from me, he talked a bank into making him a loan. He opened five new locations within three months. He moved too quickly. Now things have started to implode. He needs more money to stay afloat, and the bank won't give him another dime."

"So he's come to you."

"Uh-huh."

"But this time," Harry said carefully, "you know what he's after."

"Yes."

Harry looked out across Elliott Bay. "Ever wish things had worked out differently between you and Brooke?"

"I think I can state with great certainty that Gordon and I would not have lasted very long as a couple."

Harry glanced at her and saw the fresh mischief in her eyes. "Why not?"

"I hate to sound picky, but going to bed with a man who makes noises like an espresso machine during intimate moments is out of the question. I have my standards."

Relief poured through Harry. "I'll try not to hiss at the wrong time."

Harry studied the drawings attached to the grant proposal that was spread out on his desk. The sketch was for a device that would supposedly collect energy from the sun and use it to power an automobile. Harry had nixed the grant on the grounds that the inventor's theories and technological ability were both equally mundane. The proposal embodied no original thinking. Nor did it exhibit the level of mechanical engineering expertise required to carry it out.

But whoever had set up the fake gun and the hobgoblin was not a truly original thinker, Harry reminded himself. Clever but not original. There was a vast difference.

The disgruntled inventor had used ordinary ideas and well-worn technology to create his malicious devices. Technically speaking, whoever had submitted the solar-powered automobile proposal could have been the creator of the pranks. But there was something that did not quite fit. Something did not feel right.

Harry set the proposal aside and turned to the next one on the pile. He had worked his way through nearly half of the hundred documents stacked on his desk. He intended to keep going until he found the one he was searching for. It was here, somewhere. He was convinced of it.

Molly, seated at the glass table next to the aquarium, looked up from her small computer. "Any luck?"

"No." Harry scanned the cover page of the next proposal. "But I'll find it. I'm a patient man."

Molly made a face. "I do not want to hear that patience is a virtue."

"I'll skip the lectures tonight. I've got better things to do."

"Thanks." Her expression sobered. She regarded him with a shadowed look. "This is really going above and beyond the call of duty, Harry. No one's paying you to find this guy."

"Forget it," Harry said. "That bastard is here somewhere, and I'm going to dig him out." He turned the page of the proposal and concentrated on the drawing of a wind-driven generator.

Molly returned to her computer.

A companionable silence settled on the study. Harry realized absently that he was starting to take such silences for granted. He no longer worried about offending Molly when he sank into his thoughts. She always seemed to have plenty to do herself. She did not have to be entertained. Nor did she pester him with questions about his moods.

The buzz of the lobby intercom jarred Harry out of his concentration a few minutes later. He glanced at his watch. It was nearly ten o'clock.

"We've got a visitor," he said.

"Who in the world would drop by for a visit at this hour?"

"Family."

"Ah, yes. Of course."

Harry got to his feet and went across the room to the intercom panel. He punched the button. "This is Trevelyan."

"You have a visitor, Mr. Trevelyan," Chris, the doorman, announced. "Mrs. Danielle Hughes is here to see you."

Harry closed his eyes in brief resignation. "Send her up, Chris."

"Sure thing, Mr. Trevelyan."

Harry released the intercom button. "My Aunt Danielle. Brandon's mother."

"Ah."

He turned to Molly and saw empathy in the jeweled depths of her gaze. It was an odd sensation to know that she somehow understood his feelings at that moment. He was not entirely sure that he comprehended them himself. It was always like this when he dealt with his family.

Molly started to close the top of her computer. "You'll probably want to talk to your aunt alone in here. I'll go out into the living room."

"No, stay where you are. No sense allowing Danielle to disrupt your work as well as mine. I'll introduce you to her, and then I'll talk to her in the front room."

"Whatever you want. I take it this is going to be an unpleasant conversation?"

"Let's just say I think I know what Danielle wants." Harry walked toward the door. "Experience tells me that the sooner I give it to her, the sooner I'll be able to get back to work."

"Good luck."

The doorbell chimed. Harry went to answer the imperious summons. Danielle was standing in the outer hall. Her handsome, patrician features were set in an expression of steely determination. The anxiety in her eyes was real. Harry knew her well enough to realize that in this mood, she would not be easily deterred.

Although his mother and Danielle had been sisters, there was little more than a superficial resemblance between the two women as far as Harry was concerned. Both had been beautiful in their youth, and their fine bone structure had accepted age well. But Harry remembered his mother as a happy, energetic woman whose eyes had sparkled with an exuberant love of life and an easy, affectionate spirit.

Harry could not recall ever having seen Danielle in a genuinely cheerful mood. She could be coolly pleasant and gracious when the occasion demanded, but that seemed to be her limit. The shadows of her miserable marriage to Dean Hughes still clung to her, even though Dean had had the decency to get himself killed in a car accident several years earlier.

"Harry, I must talk to you about Brandon." Danielle swept into the condominium. She came to an abrupt halt and looked straight down her nose at Molly, who was standing in the doorway of the study. "Who's this?"

"Hello," Molly said politely.

"I didn't realize you had company, Harry." Danielle glanced at him as if she expected him to dismiss Molly the way he would have dismissed a servant.

"This is Molly Abberwick. Molly, my aunt, Danielle Hughes."

"Danielle Stratton Hughes," Danielle corrected coldly.

"How do you do?" Molly murmured.

"You must be Harry's new little friend," Danielle said. "Olivia mentioned that she had met you."

"Harry's little friend?" Molly pursed her lips. Amusement danced in her eyes. "Somehow I never thought of myself as any man's *little friend.* What a concept."

It did not take the Trevelyan Second Sight to know trouble when it was about to explode in his face, Harry thought. "Ms. Abberwick is a client, Danielle."

Molly looked more amused than ever. "A little friend and a client."

Danielle made a show of looking at the diamond-framed watch she wore. "It's rather late to be doing business, isn't it?"

"Depends on the business," Molly said.

Danielle lifted her chin. "If you will excuse us, I have family matters to discuss with my nephew."

"You bet. No problem." Molly backed into the study. "Take your time. I won't bother you at all. You won't even know I'm in here."

She winked at Harry just before she closed the study door.

Danielle gave the closed door a disdainful look as she went past it into the living room. "Really, Harry, you're not going to tell me that woman is a client of yours."

"You didn't come here to discuss my relationship with Molly."

"Don't be rude." Danielle settled onto the sofa. "I'm in no mood for it. I've got problems enough on my hands."

Harry went to stand at the window. He looked out into the night. "What do you want, Danielle?"

"You've spoken with Brandon?"

"Yes. And with Olivia."

"Then you know about Brandon's ridiculous scheme to go into business on his own?"

Harry glanced briefly at her over his shoulder. "Yes."

"You've got to talk him out of it, Harry."

"Why should I? Brandon's smart, and he's willing to work hard. Let him follow his dream."

"That's impossible, and you know it," Danielle said tightly. "My father will never allow him to go out on his own. Especially since you refused to join the company. Brandon has to stay with Stratton Properties. You know that as well as I do."

"It's the money, isn't it? You're afraid Parker will cut Brandon out of the will if he leaves the company."

"That's exactly what he'll do, and we both know it. You know how Father feels about the firm."

"Parker's feelings aren't as important as Brandon's in this instance," Harry said. "He wants to try his wings. Let him go, Danielle. If you don't, he'll only resent you for not having any faith in him."

"Don't you dare lecture me on how to deal with my son. You've done enough damage already."

"Me?" Harry swung around to confront her. "What the hell have I done?"

"You know perfectly well that you're the one who put the idea of leaving Stratton Properties into Brandon's head."

"Olivia tried to tell me that. Damn it, Danielle, this is not my fault."

"Brandon was perfectly content to stay with Stratton Properties until you came along. After you walked away from your Stratton inheritance, I realized that Brandon actually envied your streak of foolish independence. It got worse after he married Olivia. Now he's convinced himself that he must go out on his own."

Harry slowly massaged the back of his neck. "You think Brandon is leaving the company in order to prove something? Maybe he just wants to start his own business. What would be so unusual about that? He's a Stratton. Business is in his blood."

"He's jealous of you, don't you understand?" Danielle stood up abruptly. "God knows why, but he is. He wants to prove to himself and to Olivia that he's as strong and self-reliant as you are. In the process he's going to ruin his life."

"I think that's overstating the situation."

"No, it's not," Danielle said. "It's the truth. If Brandon doesn't stay with Stratton Properties, my father will disinherit him. I know he will."

"You can't be sure Parker will go that far."

"I am sure of it," Danielle retorted. "He disinherited Brittany when she ran off with Sean Trevelyan, didn't he? And he disinherited you, too, when you refused to join the company. He swore you'd never see a dime of the Stratton money. He means it, Harry."

"I don't doubt it, but the circumstances are a little different."

"I wish I could believe that, but I can't risk it. You must do something. Just because you don't want the Stratton money, that doesn't give you the right to influence Brandon. I will not stand by and see my son deprived of his inheritance because of you. Do you understand me, Harry?"

"Even if I admit, for the sake of this idiotic discussion, that I am guilty of inadvertently persuading Brandon to leave Stratton Properties, what the hell do you expect me to do about it now?"

"Talk him out of it." Danielle turned on her expensively shod heel and went down the hall.

Harry closed his eyes in weary resignation as Danielle went through the door and shut it behind her.

After a moment he heard the study door open quietly. He looked across the room to where Molly stood watching him.

"I couldn't help overhearing." Molly propped one shoulder against the jamb. "Your aunt's voice carries."

"Tell me about it." Harry massaged the back of his neck. "I'm sorry you had to sit through that."

"Did your grandfather really offer to reinstate you in his will if you joined the family firm?"

"Yes."

"And you turned him down, of course."

"Parker Stratton uses money to control people. It's as natural for him as breathing." Harry went into the kitchen to find the bottle that he kept in a cupboard next to the refrigerator. "Can I interest you in a little medicinal brandy?"

"Sure." Molly unpropped herself from the jamb and came forward. "What happens now? Will you try to talk Brandon out of leaving the family firm?"

"No." Harry splashed brandy into two glasses. "I'll talk to Parker. See if I can convince him to let Brandon go out on his own without reprisals."

Molly accepted the brandy snifter. "Do you think that's possible?"

"Maybe." Harry smiled humorlessly. "With a little luck, I think I can convince Parker to do the right thing."

Molly's eyes were very green as she regarded him over the rim of the brandy glass. "The way you convinced your uncle Leon to lay off Josh?"

"Something like that, yes."

"Correct me if I'm wrong, but I get the impression that everyone on both sides of your family seems to think it's your job to solve all of their problems."

"Not all. Just some of them."

Molly was silent for a while. "How did you get into this situation, Harry?"

He did not pretend to misunderstand the question. "Damned if I know."

"Harry, this is me, Molly, remember? You can't brush me off with that kind of answer. I'm too smart."

He smiled reluctantly. "Granted. And you've got the Abberwick curiosity. I mustn't forget that."

"Look, if you don't want to tell me why you put up with scenes like the one you just went through with your aunt, that's fine. It's your business. And it is a family matter. I have no right to pry."

"It's not that I don't want to explain the situation." Harry contemplated his brandy. "I'm just not sure of the answer. No one's ever asked me that particular question before."

"Leave it to an Abberwick," Molly said lightly. "We're inquisitive by nature."

Harry thought about it for a good thirty seconds before he made his decision. He looked up from the brandy and found Molly watching him with calm perception and something that might have been sympathy.

"I got into this mess because I had some damn fool notion of ending the feud between the Strattons and the Trevelyans," Harry said eventually.

"Ah." Complete understanding lit Molly's eyes. "Of course."

"The only thing my parents wanted from either side of the family was peace. It was the one thing no one would give them."

"And as the one who has blood from both sides flowing in his veins, you decided to try to build a bridge between the Strattons and the Trevelyans."

Harry swirled the brandy in his glass. "That was the general idea."

"It was to be your tribute to the memory of your parents, wasn't it?"

"Something like that." He wasn't surprised that she understood it all, in one single gulp. What startled him was the odd sense of relief he experienced now that he had confided his quixotic dream to her.

"You're committed to ending the feud just as I'm committed to my father's foundation."

"Yes," Harry said. "But just between you and me, I think you're going to be a lot more successful with the Abberwick Foundation than I'm going to be with ending the Trevelyan-Stratton feud."

"Really?"

"After all these years, both sides of my family look at me and still see the past, not the future. Each wants me to make a choice between the two families, and neither will be satisfied until I do."

"And you won't do that."

"I'm half Stratton and half Trevelyan. How can I choose?"

"I notice that the feud doesn't stop anyone on either side of your family from using you," Molly said dryly. "It's weird, isn't it, Harry?"

"What is?"

"That even though you're the family outcast, in a way you've managed to become the head of both clans?"

"I'm not the head of the families," Harry said. "I'm just the fool who got stuck in the middle. There's a big difference."

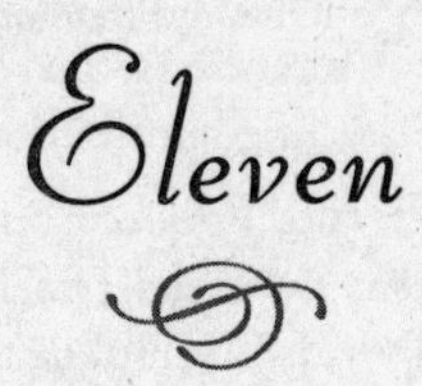

Molly could not stand the ravishing torment any longer. She was so buffeted by the endless waves of pleasure that she could hardly catch her breath. Harry's stunningly intimate touch left her shivering with need. He made love to her with an enthralling thoroughness. His powerful, elegant hands were gentle and sure and utterly relentless. He coaxed the climax from her as if he were mining liquid diamonds. His long fingers glistened in the moonlight.

"Harry. Oh, my God, Harry. Please. No. I can't . . . I can't . . ."

"Jump," he whispered against her skin. "I'll catch you."

The delicious tension exploded inside her. She clenched her fists in his dark hair and surrendered with a wordless gasp of wonder. He held himself back, waiting until she was trembling in the heart of the storm before he pushed deeply into her body. Molly trembled at the impact.

She wrapped Harry close and clung to him as he shuddered heavily in the throes of his own release.

It wasn't until he sprawled on top of her, the skin of his shoulders damp with perspiration and the elemental scent of sex thick in the air, that Molly realized the truth.

It had been good. Better than good. It had been a fantastic, deliciously erotic, incredibly sensual experience. But something had been different this time.

Something had been missing.

She lay awake for a long while afterward. Granted, she did not have a great deal of experience, which made logical comparisons difficult. But last night her body had been tuned to Harry's in some way she could not explain. Tonight everything within her, each nerve and muscle, had tried to recapture the experience. She had come close, but it had not been the same.

The sense of resonance was missing.

Last night Harry had opened a locked door and invited her into a secret chamber. Tonight that door had remained firmly closed. Molly knew she would not be fully satisfied until he unlocked it again.

She awoke alone in the big bed. For a few drowsy seconds it seemed entirely normal to have the bed to herself. Then she opened her eyes and saw the unfamiliar expanse of night sky outside the wall of windows. Her first clear thought was that there was too much darkness. Then she remembered that she was in Harry's bed, and she should not be alone. Harry should have been there with her.

She stirred and peered at the clock. The illuminated numbers informed her that it was nearly three in the morning. It didn't take ESP to figure out that Harry had left the bed to go back to the stack of proposals in his study.

Molly folded her hands behind her head and contemplated what she had learned about Harry. A pattern was emerging.

He had come to Seattle within a year after the deaths of his parents. She had no doubt but that he had told himself he wanted to make peace between the families in honor of his mother and father. But Molly suspected there was more to the story than that. Perhaps more than even Harry himself knew.

He'd had every right to turn to the Strattons and the Trevelyans after he'd found himself completely alone in the world. They were his blood kin. They had accepted him, but Molly was learning that the acceptance had come at a high price. Everyone wanted something from Harry.

Molly sat up abruptly and threw aside the covers. She got out of bed, tugged on her robe, and padded, barefoot, down the hall to Harry's study.

A shaft of light was visible through the half-opened door. Molly walked quietly into the room.

She knew that she had not made a sound on her way down the hall, but Harry must have heard her approach. He was seated behind his desk, watching the door, waiting for her. He was wearing a dark gray terrycloth robe. The pattern of intensely contrasted light and shadow from the halogen lamp etched his stark features. His midnight dark hair was tousled from the pillow. His amber eyes glowed with the anticipation of a raptor that is just about to sink talons into prey.

Molly knew at once what had happened. "You found the proposal you were looking for?"

"About three minutes ago. Take a look."

Molly crossed the room to the desk and glanced at the papers spread out in front of Harry. "I remember that one." She craned her head to read the cover page. *"Proposal for the Construction of a Device to Measure Paranormal Brain Waves,* by Wharton Kendall. I liked it, but you vetoed it, the same way you did all the others."

"Paranormal brain waves? Give me a break." Harry shot her a disgusted look. "Kendall is the kind of inventor who gives other inventors a bad name. A classic crackpot. No solid scientific training. No formal technical background. No originality or true insight. And to top it off, he's into this damn paranormal garbage. I should have remembered this guy right off."

"Hmm." Molly tapped one finger absently on the desk. "What makes you think Kendall's the person who played those nasty pranks on me?"

Harry turned the proposal document around so that she could see one of the diagrams more clearly. "Take a look at his design for the gearing mechanism that he planned to use on his crazy brain wave gadget."

Molly studied the drawing of an elaborate machine composed of myriad wires and an electronic panel mounted on a movable platform. "So?"

"Phony, pseudoscientific aspects of the project aside, the design is inelegant, unoriginal, and uninspired. Exactly like the designs of the fake gun and the goblin contraptions. The whole device has a jury-rigged look, just as those machines did. And this gear assembly," he pointed to a small section of the drawing, "is our smoking gun. Kendall's our man, all right."

"I'm amazed that you remembered such small details, Harry. This was one of the first proposals I showed you and, as I recall, you glanced at it for all of ten seconds."

"That was nine seconds more than it deserved." Harry's mouth quirked wryly. "But that was early on in our association, and I was still trying to play the polite consultant. I hadn't yet realized that you and I were going to go toe-to-toe over each and every off-the-wall grant proposal the foundation received."

"You mean, before I realized how stubborn and picky you were going to be?"

"Something like that." Harry lounged back in his chair and surveyed her with a thoughtful expression. "The question now is, what do we do about Kendall? I don't have any hard evidence here. Certainly not enough to take to the police."

Molly searched his face curiously. "Are we talking about a conclusion reached on the basis of your famous intuition?"

"We are talking about one of my insights, which, in turn, was produced by years of experience and trained observation," Harry said coolly.

"Have you ever noticed that you get downright snappish whenever there's a reference to intuition or psychic stuff?"

"I have no patience with that kind of nonsense."

Molly smiled. "You have patience for just about everything else."

"Every man has his limits."

"I see. Well, even if you did have convincing proof that Kendall had pulled those stunts, we're not dealing with attempted murder or even real mayhem here. I doubt that the cops could do much except issue a warning."

"Something I can do myself," Harry said very softly.

Molly was instantly alarmed. "Now, Harry—"

He picked up the drawing and examined it intently. "I wonder if Kendall is still at this address. I don't recognize the name of the town."

"I don't like that look in your eye."

Harry's head came up so swiftly that Molly was startled into taking a step back.

He pinned her with a fierce gaze. "What look?"

"Take it easy." Molly spread her hands. "It was just an expression."

"Sorry." Harry was silent for a moment. "My ex-fiancée used to make similar comments about my expressions. She said I made her nervous."

"Do I look nervous?"

Harry studied her closely. "No."

"Bear in mind at all times, Harry, that I am not your ex-fiancée."

He blinked slowly and then he smiled. "Don't worry. I won't ever confuse you with Olivia."

This time the amber in his eyes was so warm Molly could almost feel the heat. She cleared her throat and pulled her attention back to the matter at hand. "Now, then, what I meant to say was, I am not sure I approve of your plans to confront Wharton Kendall. What, exactly, do you intend to do?"

"Pay a personal call on him to discuss the little matter of nasty pranks."

Molly pursed her lips. "He'll probably deny everything."

"I don't plan to give him the chance to deny anything. I'm going to convince him that I have proof that he's the one behind the pranks and that if he tries anything else, I'll go to the cops."

"In other words, you're going to try to put a scare into him?"

"Yes."

Molly contemplated that. "Think you can do it?"

Harry looked up from the drawing. All of the warmth had drained out of his gaze. "Yes."

Molly was suddenly aware of a distinct chill in the room. Instinctively she raised a hand to pull the lapels of her robe more closely together. "I'll go with you."

"No, you will not." Harry went back to studying the drawing.

Molly stopped clutching her robe. She planted her hands on the desk and narrowed her eyes. "You are not a lone crusader, Dr. Trevelyan. You are working for the Abberwick Foundation. That means you take orders from me. I will accompany you when you visit Wharton Kendall. Is that clearly understood?"

Harry glanced up once more from Kendall's drawing. He gave her a long, thorough assessment, and then his mouth twitched at the corner. "Understood."

"Good." Molly straightened.

"There's just one small problem."

"What's that?"

"Finding Kendall may take some time." Harry indicated the cover page of the proposal. "There's no phone number. He gives his address as a post office box in a place called Icy Crest."

"Where's that?"

"I don't know. First we have to find the town, and then we have to find Kendall. It's going to take at least a full day to track him down and talk to him once we've located him. You probably don't want to be out of town on a work day. I know how important your business is to you."

"Oh, no," Molly said swiftly. "You're not getting rid of me that easily. I can arrange to leave Tessa in charge for a day."

"You're sure?"

"Absolutely, positively certain, Dr. Trevelyan."

"Have I ever told you that I don't like to be called Dr. Trevelyan?" Harry asked conversationally.

"No." Molly grinned. "I figured out weeks ago that it irritates the heck out of you."

Icy Crest proved to be little more than a blip on the map. It was located deep in the Cascade Mountains, at the end of a narrow, twisting, two-lane road. It was several miles from Interstate 90, which linked eastern and western Washington.

Molly studied the scruffy little town through the windshield of Harry's sleek car and wondered why she was suddenly consumed by a deep sense of unease.

The tiny mountain hamlet possessed the usual accoutrements of small rural villages everywhere, namely a single gas station, a dreary-looking grocery called Pete's, a café, and a tavern. A small sign in the dirty window of the grocery store declared that the post office was located inside.

A handful of men clad in worn denims, boots, and billed caps lounged in front of the store. Molly noticed that all of the caps bore the colorful logos of various farm equipment manufacturing companies. Malevolent eyes watched as Harry parked the car and switched off the ignition.

"Something tells me this may not be as simple as it sounded," Molly said.

Harry surveyed the men hanging around in front of the store. "What gives you that impression?"

"I'm not sure. I think it's the hats." Molly nibbled on her lower lip. "I don't know, Harry. I don't like this."

"It's a little late for second thoughts. You were the one who insisted on coming along."

"I'm aware of that. Usually I enjoy small towns. But there's something about this one—" She broke off, unable to put her qualms into words.

"What about it?"

She slanted him a quick, sidelong glance. "What would you say if I told you that I had an unpleasant feeling about this place?"

"I'd say that's an eminently reasonable feeling to have under the circumstances. We're here to see a man who's been trying to scare you to death, remember. Why would you feel enthusiastic about coming face-to-face with him?" Harry opened the door and got out.

Molly followed quickly. Harry was right. Given the situation, there was nothing odd about her troubled mood. She smiled tentatively at the cluster of men watching her. None of them smiled back.

Harry looked straight at the small crowd gathered in front of the store and inclined his head slightly. To Molly's surprise, one or two of the men gave him a stiff response. The others shifted their booted feet and found something else besides Molly to engage their attention.

Harry took Molly's hand and walked into the grocery store.

Molly took in the shelves of dusty canned goods, packages of toilet paper, and assorted household necessities. Neon beer signs hung in the windows. A soft drink machine hummed to itself in the corner.

Harry released Molly's hand, slipped some change out of his pocket, and crossed the room to the pop machine. He dropped the coins into the slot and punched in his selections. Machinery whirred. Cans clanked.

A massive figure appeared in the doorway behind the front counter. Molly caught a glimpse of a vast, hairy stomach draped over the waistband of a pair of old, sagging jeans. She quickly averted her eyes from the sight.

"Can I help ya?" The voice was unexpectedly high and nasal for such a large man. There was a distinct lack of welcome in it.

Harry picked up the soft drink cans that had rolled into the tray. "Are you Pete?"

"Yeah."

"I'm Harry. This is Molly."

Pete squinted at Molly. She smiled brightly. He gave her a grudging nod and snapped his gum. Then he turned back to Harry.

"Somethin' you wanted, Harry?"

"We're looking for a man named Wharton Kendall. We understand he lives here in Icy Crest."

Pete chewed gum and squinted in thought. "Used to." There was an air of challenge in the statement, as if he dared Harry to ask for more details.

Molly was acutely aware of the tension in the air. It was probably nothing more than the natural reluctance of a small town resident to provide information to a stranger, but it was uncomfortable.

Harry seemed oblivious to the atmosphere. He popped the top on one of the cans and took a long swallow. Then he looked at the big man behind the counter. "How long has Kendall been gone?"

"Not long. Coupla days."

"Did he live nearby?"

Pete's broad face set in lines of mulish resistance. It was apparent that he did not intend to answer any further questions.

Harry just looked at him for a long time. The silence thickened. Molly had an urge to run out of the store. She stood her ground only because she could not leave Harry alone.

The strain of the extended silence finally broke Pete's resolve to say nothing further on the subject of Wharton Kendall.

"Rented a cabin from Shorty for a while." Pete went back to work on his chewing gum.

Harry took another swallow of his soft drink and continued to study the big man with cold, unblinking eyes. "Any idea where Kendall went?"

Pete stirred restlessly beneath Harry's gaze. His obvious discomfort reminded Molly of the reactions of the men out in front of the store.

"Shorty told me the crazy son-of-a-bitch was headed for California. No loss. Guy was weird, y'know? Kendall a friend of yours?"

"No." Harry did not elaborate. "Who's Shorty?"

"Runs the tavern next door."

"Thanks."

"Sure. Right." Pete scratched the large portion of his stomach that was not covered by his shirt.

Harry handed the unopened soft drink can to Molly. "Let's go see Shorty."

"I can't believe you pulled that off," Molly said half an hour later as Harry halted the Sneath in the drive of an aging cabin.

"Pulled what off?" Harry rested his arms on the wheel and examined the cabin with close attention.

"The way you convinced Pete and Shorty to give us the information we wanted. You have an interesting effect on people, Harry. Have you ever noticed?"

He glanced at her in mild surprise. "What makes you think Pete and Shorty weren't happy to give us the information about Kendall?"

"Hah. Don't give me that. You know perfectly well you somehow intimidated Pete, and you bamboozled Shorty." She held up the key in her hand and dangled it in front of him. "So we're interested in renting a cabin, are we?"

"It was as good a line as any." Harry opened his door and got out.

"You're as smooth as silk when you want to be, Harry." Molly scrambled out of the car and walked around the front of it to join him. "Do they teach the fine art of concocting outrageous stories in graduate school?"

"As it happens, I got that talent from the Trevelyan side of the family."

"You do know what Shorty thinks, don't you?"

"I can take a wild guess." Harry took the key from her fingers and started toward the front door of the cabin.

"I'll just bet you can, since you're the one who put the idea into his head." Molly hurried after him. "He thinks we're looking for a secluded cabin far from the city in order to conduct an illicit weekend affair."

"Yes."

"Somehow," Molly said very deliberately, "Shorty got the impression that one or both of us is married."

"Well, it wouldn't be an illicit affair if we were both free, now, would it?" Harry fitted the key into the lock of the cabin door.

"I'm not sure I like having my reputation trashed just for the sake of a peek inside Wharton Kendall's cabin."

"Relax." Harry pushed open the cabin door. "If Shorty ever sobers up long enough to talk to Pete, he'll realize that we were more interested in checking out Kendall than we were in using this place as a love nest."

"That should confuse him no end."

"It won't matter," Harry said. "By then, we'll be long gone."

"I know, but—" Molly stopped talking abruptly, her attention captured by the interior of the cabin. "Good grief. I'd say *what a dump,* but I think someone else has already used that line."

From the eroded rug in front of the hearth to the layered stains on the linoleum floor of the kitchen, the cabin was a disaster. The smell of old cooking grease and rotting garbage permeated the air.

Harry surveyed the scene. "Looks like Kendall cleared out quickly."

"This," Molly declared, "is not just evidence of a hasty departure. A mess like this is weeks, even months in the making. This is the work of a born slob."

Harry smiled briefly. "I told you Kendall was a sloppy thinker."

"It shows." Molly walked cautiously through the clutter. "I wonder where he did his work."

"Must have been right here in the living room. Unless he converted the bedroom into a workshop. I'll take a look." Harry crossed to the short hall and glanced around the corner of the bedroom door.

"See anything in there?" Molly called.

"Just a broken-down bed that only a truly desperate couple forced to conduct their illicit love affair here in Icy Crest would find romantic."

"That lets us out." Molly went to peer over his shoulder. "We're not desperate, and we're not illicit."

The bedroom was no cleaner than the living room and kitchen. Tattered curtains hung limply over the single grimy window. The mattress had the uniform gray patina and unpleasant stains that only long years of hard use could provide. The closet doors stood open. The interior was empty except for a broken shoelace and a sock on the floor.

"He's definitely gone," Harry said. "I wonder why."

Molly shrugged. "Shorty said that Kendall told him he was going back to California. Maybe that was the simple truth."

"Maybe." Harry looked unconvinced. "Or maybe he's back in Seattle planning another prank."

"Maybe he'd had enough of revenge," Molly suggested, feeling quite optimistic now that it was obvious Kendall was gone.

"Possible." Harry moved into the center of the room. He went down on one knee to look under the bed. "Or maybe he realized he'd pushed his luck a little too far. Any way you cut it, there are a lot of maybes."

Molly watched as Harry rose and went into the bathroom. "What are you looking for?"

"I'm not sure. I'll know it when I see it."

"It looks like Kendall took all of his possessions."

"Yes." Harry walked out of the bathroom and headed for the front room. "But he packed in a hurry. And he was sloppy, remember?"

"So?"

"So, it's possible he overlooked something in his haste to get out of Icy Crest." Harry began systematically to open and close the kitchen cupboard doors.

"Such as?"

"An address. The phone number of someone he knows in California. Whatever. Anything that will give me a lead."

Molly's uneasy mood had begun to lift, but Harry's words sent it plunging once more. "But he's gone. It's over. He can't continue his stupid revenge scheme from California."

"Something tells me it would be good policy to know exactly where he is. I don't like the idea that he's drifting around out there in the ether. I want to get a handle on him."

"I think you're being overly cautious here," Molly said.

"It's my nature. I do things methodically and logically, remember?"

"Yeah, sure."

Molly gingerly raised a couch cushion to see what evil lurked underneath it. When she discovered the decomposing remains of several crushed potato chips, she eased the cushion back into place. She cautiously continued the search, but all she discovered was further evidence that Wharton Kendall had subsisted on junk food.

In an effort to demonstrate that she, too, could be systematic and orderly, she knelt on the couch and peered down into the darkness behind it. She was surprised to see a notebook wedged between the wall and the back of the couch.

"Aha," she said.

Harry glanced at her from the other side of the small room, where he was going through a desk. "Aha, what?"

"I see something." Molly scrambled off the couch and tried to shove the massive relic away from the wall. It didn't budge. "This sucker is heavy."

"Hang on, I'll give you a hand with that." Harry crossed the room and took a firm grip on one arm of the couch. He shoved it away from the wall as easily as though it were made of cardboard.

Molly sidled into the opening and plucked the notebook off the floor. "It's probably nothing at all. But my father used to keep his notes in three-ring binders like this."

Harry stood behind her and watched as she flipped open the notebook. He frowned at the crude drawings inside. "Looks like more of his wild designs for paranormal instrumentation. The guy is really out there on the fringe. And you were ready to give him ten grand to finance his loony project."

"That is very unfair. You know perfectly well that I did not argue with you when you turned down his proposal. I was still at the point in our association where I was trying to show due respect for your technical expertise."

"That stage didn't last long," Harry said absently. "Wait, turn the page back."

Molly obediently flipped back to the previous sheet of paper. She studied the sketch that had caught his eye. "Well?"

"Don't you recognize it?"

"No. Should I? It looks like a box with a jumble of mechanical stuff inside."

"It's the box that housed the fake gun assembly," Harry said with soft certainty. "This is it. This is our proof that Kendall was behind the pranks."

Half an hour later Molly experienced a quiet surge of relief as the unfriendly town of Icy Crest vanished behind a curve in the road. She adjusted her seat belt, settled back, and picked up Wharton Kendall's notebook. She began to turn the pages with casual interest.

"Do you still think it's necessary to track Kendall down?" she asked as she studied one of the sketches.

"Definitely. I want him to know that we're on to him and that we've got enough evidence to call in the police, if necessary." Harry accelerated smoothly out of a tight curve. "But the more I think about it, the more I'm convinced that you're right. It's going to be tough to convince the cops to get involved in this."

"There's been no real violence, and he's apparently left the state. I can't see anyone getting too worked up about Kendall except you and me."

"With any luck, Kendall has abandoned his revenge in favor of trying to find some fresh funding in California."

"Think he'll convince someone down there to back him?"

"We're talking about California." Harry glanced in his rearview mirror. He frowned slightly and then returned his attention to the road. "No shortage of nuts down there who will be more than willing to finance one of his flaky paranormal inventions."

"I suppose you're right." Molly heaved a small sigh. "Well, since the dynamic duo of Abberwick and Trevelyan seems to have solved the mystery of the malicious pranks, I guess I'll be able to move back home."

"I've got plenty of room."

"Yes, I know, but if I stay at your place much longer I will cross that invisible line that separates houseguest from roommate."

"Feel free to cross it."

"I can't stay with you indefinitely," she said gently.

"Why not?"

She gave him an exasperated look. "Because I can't, that's why not. Our arrangement was that I would stay with you until we located Kendall."

"Which we have not yet done."

"Harry, I have a home of my own."

"I don't see—" Harry broke off abruptly.

"What's wrong?" Molly asked without glancing up from the notebook.

"Nothing. Why?"

"I don't know. I just had a feeling that something was bothering you." She turned another page and paused to examine a sketch of what appeared to be a helmet with wires attached to it. "This is interesting. Harry, maybe we shouldn't have been so quick to dismiss Kendall's research."

"What research? There's no research behind his crackpot ideas. Just fantasy." Harry eased his foot down on the pedal. The car picked up speed.

Molly closed the notebook with a snap. "What is it? What's wrong?"

"Some fool in a blue Ford is coming up behind us too fast for this road."

Molly turned in the seat and glanced through the rear window. She saw a late-model blue car emerge from the last curve. It was moving swiftly. Too swiftly for the winding road. The Ford's tinted windows made it impossible to see the driver's face.

"Looks like the impatient type. Better let him pass, Harry."

"There's no passing lane and nothing but a series of curves for the next ten miles."

"You could pull over to the side." A sense of urgency gripped Molly as the Ford drew closer. "Do it, Harry. The guy may be drunk."

Harry did not argue. He started to downshift.

The Ford leaped ahead, moving out to pass.

"He's going to go around us," Molly said, relieved at this evidence of the Ford's obvious intentions.

The Ford was abreast of them now. It made no move to shoot past them. Instead, as Molly watched in horror, it edged closer to the front fender of Harry's sleek sports car. She suddenly realized that the driver of the Ford intended to force them off the road.

There was no place to go. A sharp, tree-studded incline waited on the other side of the all-too-fragile guard rail.

"Harry."

"Hang on," Harry said softly.

Molly held her breath. Some part of her knew that they could not possibly escape the Ford now. It was too close. And the next wicked curve loomed ahead. Close. Much too close. She waited for the impact.

What happened next was a blur to Molly. Braced for the crash, she was unprepared for the sudden, violent deceleration of the sports car as Harry braked abruptly. Molly heard the tires scream in protest. The Sneath went into a slide.

She was dimly aware of the blue Ford flashing past as it overshot its target. It swerved frantically as the driver fought to recover control before he entered the next curve.

And then it was gone.

Molly waited for the sliding Sneath to crash through the guard rail.

Twelve

Harry ended the controlled slide and brought the Sneath to a clean stop in the right-hand lane. He automatically checked the rearview mirror to make certain there was no one coming out of the curve behind him. Then he surveyed Molly. She was safe within the cocoon of her seat belt and shoulder harness. Her face was strained, but she appeared astonishingly calm.

"Are you all right?" Even to his own ears his voice sounded as rough as a lava field. He couldn't help it. The impact of the realization that Molly could have been killed would take a while to wear off. Maybe a lifetime.

"I'm fine, thanks to you." She turned her head to look at him. Her eyes were enormous. "That was an incredible piece of driving. I thought we were going over the side."

"Good car."

Molly shook her head. "Good driver. Anyone else would have lost control. Josh was right. You do have terrific reflexes."

Harry dredged up a smile that he knew very probably resembled the skeletal grin of a Halloween mask. "We all have our little talents."

"Your little talent just saved both our lives," she said with great depth of feeling. "If I weren't so terrified of unfastening my seat belt while we're sitting in the middle of this road, I'd give you a big, wet, squishy kiss."

"I'll take you up on that later." Harry checked the mirror once more and then put the engine in gear.

He could have caught up with the blue Ford, he thought with fleeting regret. He would have liked very much to do just that. And if he had been alone, he would have done it. There was little doubt but that he had a distinct advantage on a road full of curves such as this one. His reflexes and the handling characteristics of the Sneath guaranteed it. But it would have been a risky chase, and he was not about to put Molly in further danger.

"Do you think we should report that car to the highway patrol?" Molly asked after a minute.

Harry shrugged. "Sure. But I doubt that anything will come of it. Near misses aren't uncommon. Especially on back roads like this."

"We can describe the car. It was a late-model blue Ford."

"Yes, but there were no plates."

"No license plates?" Molly stared at him. "I guess that in all the excitement I didn't even notice. I hate to ask, but do you think it was a deliberate attempt to run us off the road? Or do you think the driver was under the influence, and we happened to be in the wrong place at the wrong time?"

"I don't know," Harry said honestly. "But I don't like coincidences."

"The guy was probably drunk."

"Maybe."

Molly slanted him an assessing look. "You're not thinking what I think you're thinking, are you?"

"That the driver of the Ford was Wharton Kendall?"

She sighed. "I knew it. You're thinking the same thing. It's highly unlikely, isn't it? I mean, Kendall is supposed to be in California by now."

"That's where he's supposed to be. But there seems to be a general consensus that the bastard is nuttier than a fruitcake. Who knows where he is."

"Why would he sneak around Icy Crest waiting to see if someone came looking for him? It doesn't make sense. He moved out of Shorty's cabin. Where would he sleep?"

"In his car."

"Where would he eat?"

"He could have a supply of junk food stashed in the trunk of the Ford."

"How would he know when and where to watch for us?"

Harry thought about that one for a couple of seconds. "He could have hidden in the woods in order to keep an eye on the cabin. Waited to see if anyone came looking for evidence. Or someone in Icy Crest might have done the legwork for him. Maybe good old Pete or Shorty or one of the men standing around out in front of the grocery store called Kendall and let him know someone was in town looking for him."

Molly looked thoughtful. "That implies he had a phone available."

"Cellular car phones aren't exactly a novelty these days."

She made a face. "You have an answer for everything, don't you? The thing is, the good folk of Icy Crest all seemed to dismiss Kendall as a weird kook. I don't think they liked him very much."

"Even weird kooks have money. Someone in town might have been willing to take his cash in exchange for providing information."

Molly frowned. "Wharton Kendall doesn't have a lot of money. If he did, he wouldn't have had to apply for funding from the Abberwick Foundation."

"I don't think it would take more than fifty bucks to tempt any of those men who were hanging around Pete's store. Hell, Pete himself would probably turn in his own mother for twenty-five dollars and a shirt that was a couple of sizes larger."

"You could be right. Damn. This mess is getting more and more complicated, isn't it? Things could go on like this for a very long time." Molly became very quiet.

Harry understood quiet. He was accustomed to sinking into his own personal pools of deep silence for hours on end. He had been around Molly long enough to know that she was quite capable of occupying herself with her own thoughts. But the remote expression on her face now made him uneasy. There was an important issue he wanted settled before they reached Seattle.

"Molly?"

"Hmm?"

Harry flexed his hands on the wheel. He had to handle this carefully. "This incident today settles one matter. You're definitely going to stay with me until we get this thing sorted out."

She looked slightly startled. "How did you know that I was thinking about moving back into my own house?"

"Because I can read your mind," he shot back, irritated by her stubbornness.

"Read my mind?" She flashed him one of her brilliant, laughing smiles. "Ah, yes, the infamous Trevelyan Second Sight."

"It was a joke, Molly."

"I know." Her smile vanished. She touched his arm briefly. "I was just teasing you."

He opted for the logical, well-reasoned approach. It was what he did best. "You would feel safer, and I would worry a whole lot less, if you stayed with me until I've located Kendall."

"That could take a while. And what happens if you can't find him? What if he's just vanished?"

The implications of the question took Harry's breath away. It ignited a fantasy that had been smoldering deep inside him. What if Molly came to live with him for good?

He would eventually find Kendall, of course. The man was too sloppy and too disorganized to disappear without a trace. Harry would locate him and take steps to make certain that he never bothered Molly again.

But what if Molly did not move out?

"Would that be a problem?" he asked softly.

She crossed her arms beneath her breasts and focused intently on the road. "As I was saying before we were so rudely interrupted by the blue Ford, I can't stay with you indefinitely."

"Why not?"

"You have to ask me that? Harry, at the beginning of our relationship, you're the one who took great pains to point out to me just how many things we do *not* have in common."

"You added a couple of things to the list," he reminded her. "Something about tomatoes. Look, maybe we both overestimated the number of areas of disagreement. We seem to be able to deal with the ones that do arise."

She turned her head quickly to look at him. Harry could feel the intense curiosity and the sensual awareness emanating from her. He struggled to find the logical, reasoned words that would convince her that moving in with him for good was the right decision. But his excellent brain failed him in his hour of need. He could not pressure her. He could only ask.

Ask. Plead. Hope. That was not his way. He knew better than to risk asking others for what he needed. What the hell was happening to him?

A shock of recognition went through him. What he was experiencing now as he waited for Molly's answer was all too familiar. It was akin to what he had felt the other night when he had been caught up in the vortex of intense concentration and she had come to him dressed in bridal white. He was vulnerable in a way he did not understand. It was a terrifying sensation.

"Staying with you for a few days is one thing," Molly said gently. "Staying indefinitely means we're living together."

Yes, it does, he thought. *You'd be in my bed every night. You'd be sitting across from me at the breakfast table every morning.*

"Well . . ."

"Just until we find Wharton Kendall and deal with him," he said.

She tensed. Then she gave him another brief, searching glance. "All right. If you're sure this is what you want."

It's what I need, he thought, still numbed by the shock of realization. "It's the only logical way to go," he said aloud.

"Right. Logical."

The following morning Harry got off the elevator on the thirty-first floor of the downtown high-rise office tower. The massive, gleaming brass letters on the wall across from the bank of elevators spelled out the name of the company that had made the Strattons a family of movers and shakers in Seattle.

STRATTON PROPERTIES, INC.
COMMERCIAL REAL ESTATE
AND PROPERTY DEVELOPMENT

Harry turned to the right and went down the plushly carpeted corridor to the reception desk. An attractive, neatly suited woman in her twenties looked up with a smile of immediate recognition. Harry did not appear in the offices of Stratton Properties very often, but the staff knew him on sight. His visits tended to be memorable.

"Good morning, Mr. Trevelyan. What can I do for you today?"

"Good morning, Verna. Would you please tell my grandfather that I want to see him for a few minutes?"

"Certainly." Verna pressed the intercom button on her desk. "Mr. Stratton?"

"What is it, Verna?" Parker Stratton's voice was gravelly with age, but it had lost none of its authority.

"Mr. Trevelyan is here to see you."

There was a brief pause. Then Parker's voice came back through the intercom in a low growl. "Tell him I'm busy. Give him an appointment for next week."

Harry nodded pleasantly to the receptionist and started past her desk. "Thanks, Verna. Hold all his calls until I leave."

"But, Mr. Trevelyan," Verna called anxiously. "Mr. Stratton says he's busy at the moment."

"He can't be busy. He's officially retired." Harry went around the corner, past the tasteful display of art glass that occupied one wall. He opened the door of Parker's office without bothering to knock.

Parker was seated behind his desk. He had a gold pen in one gnarled hand. He still had a finger on the intercom button. He glowered at Harry. "You've got the manners of a damned Trevelyan."

"I am a Trevelyan." Harry closed the door and took a chair. "Unfortunately for you, I'm also a Stratton."

"I assume you didn't barge into my office to discuss genealogy. What do you want?"

"I'm here to talk about Brandon's plans to go into business for himself."

"Damn it to hell." Parker tossed aside the gold pen. "I knew sooner or later you'd interfere in this fiasco. Did Danielle go crying to you? Or was it Olivia?"

"I've talked to both of them. I've also talked to Brandon."

"What the hell is it with you, Harry? Why do you always have to get involved in family stuff like this?"

"Beats me. Maybe it's because I am family." Harry stretched his legs out in front of him and contemplated his grandfather.

A few years ago at the age of seventy, Parker had reluctantly turned over the day-to-day operation of Stratton Properties to his son, Gilford. Nothing short of an act of God, however, could keep Parker from going into his office every day. Stratton Properties was his life.

Parker had lived and breathed business from the cradle, and the diet had served him well. He used a cane when his arthritic knee bothered him, but other than that, he was in excellent health. He looked at least ten years younger than his chronological age, thanks to his fine Stratton bone structure. His doctor had told him that he had the heart and lungs of a man twenty years younger.

Stratton Properties was a part of Parker, as necessary to him as the very air he breathed. The day he died, he would be seated behind his desk.

"I'll get right to the point," Harry said. "I think you should give Brandon his chance. Tell him you're behind him. Tell him there will be no reprisals."

Parker aimed a finger at him. "You stay out of this, by God. As far as I'm concerned, you're the reason he's taken this damn fool notion into his head in the first place."

Harry held up both hands, palms out. "Scout's honor, I never once encouraged him to try his hand at commercial property management. He came up with the idea all on his own."

"The hell he did. He saw how you walked away from your Stratton heritage, and he's decided to show everyone else in the family that he's just as goddamned stubborn and independent as you are."

"I think you're giving me entirely too much credit," Harry said.

"I'm not giving you any credit." Parker's eyes turned fierce. "I'm giving you the full blame for this stupid situation. If you hadn't come along, Brandon would never have thought about leaving the firm."

"You can't be sure of that."

"I am sure of it, damn it," Parker insisted. "You've been a bad influence on him."

"He wants to spread his wings a little. Why not let him do it?"

Parker's hand clenched into a bunched fist. "He won't survive a year out there on his own."

"You don't know that for certain. After all, he's got Stratton blood in his veins. Your blood. Who knows what he can do?"

"You've got Stratton blood in your veins, too." Parker's eyes narrowed. "But it wasn't enough to turn you into a businessman."

"We both know that I wasn't cut out for the corporate world," Harry said mildly.

"You mean you weren't cut out to face the real world. You prefer to hide in your damned ivory tower. You'd have been a vice president today if you'd joined the company when you first came to Seattle."

"Not likely," Harry said. "You and Gilford would have fired me within three months. I would never have fit in around here."

"Because you lack the discipline to fit in," Parker retorted. "That's your problem, Harry. You're too damned arrogant and bullheaded. It's your father's fault. He deliberately turned you against your heritage. It was his way of thumbing his nose at all things Stratton. It was his final revenge against me, that's what it was."

"I think we've covered this territory fairly thoroughly in the past."

Parker's jaw was rigid. For a moment it looked as though he was prepared to continue the old argument. Then he lounged back in his chair. "What's this I hear about you having a new lady friend?"

Harry raised his brows. "Word gets around. Her name is Molly Abberwick."

"Danielle says she appears to have moved in with you."

"She has. For a while."

Parker scowled. "You know I don't approve of that kind of thing."

"I know." Harry steepled his fingers. "Let's get back to the subject of Brandon."

"There's nothing to discuss. Don't expect me to encourage him in this idiotic scheme to go into business for himself. He has a duty to his family."

"Danielle is afraid that you'll disinherit Brandon if he goes off on his own."

"I will," Parker said immediately. "Told him as much the other day."

"Skip the threats. Give him your blessing, Parker."

"Why the devil should I?"

"Because he's going to go off on his own, anyway, and because it would be a lot less nerve-wracking for Danielle if you tell her it's okay by you."

"Why should I make it any easier for anyone?"

Harry waited a heartbeat or two until he knew he had Parker's full attention. "You owe Danielle this much."

"I owe her? Are you crazy? I've given my daughter everything. Given everyone in the family too damn much. That's half the problem around here. They're all spoiled." Parker beetled his brows. "What do I owe her?"

"She helped you save your precious company after your oldest daughter ran off with my father," Harry said evenly. "She did what my mother was supposed to do for you. She married Dean Hughes. Because of her you got the infusion of cash you needed so badly at the time. And you got the Hughes connections. They were worth even more than the money, weren't they?"

Parker stared at him, openmouthed, for a few seconds. Then his teeth snapped together. "How dare you imply that I forced Danielle into that marriage! As if I could. This isn't the Middle Ages."

"It might as well be, as far as you're concerned. You're still trying to run people's lives as if you were some feudal lord."

"I have a right to run a few things around here. I built this company. If it wasn't for me there would be no Stratton Properties, Inc."

"You had a little help along the way," Harry said softly. "Specifically from your daughter Danielle. She stepped into the breach when my mother ran off with my father. You owe her, Parker."

"I don't owe her a damn thing."

"You owe her big time, and you know it. She endured a hellish marriage for the sake of the family business. If it hadn't been for her, Stratton Properties would have gone under thirty-five years ago. It's payback time."

"What's this sudden concern with whether or not your aunt had a happy marriage? Most people don't have happy marriages, you know."

"My parents did," Harry said softly.

Parker flushed with rage. "Sean Trevelyan stole my little Brittany from her family. He seduced her, by God. He came like a thief in the night. He took her away from her home and her heritage and everything that was rightfully hers."

"And he kept her happy."

"He never gave her what she should have had, what she deserved."

Harry met his eyes. "If you want to see what would have happened to my mother if she had been married to Dean Hughes for a few years, take a look at Danielle."

"How dare you!" Parker roared. "At least she would still be alive."

Harry felt as if all the air had suddenly been sucked out of the room. *He was too late. They were both dead. And now he was going to die, too. He would never reach the surface in time. Too late. Too late.*

Emotion howled like a cold north wind across his soul. For a moment the barriers that protected him from the abyss wavered and threatened to dissolve. Harry could see straight through them to the endless darkness, and it beckoned with a terrible seductiveness. It would be so easy just to let himself fall into the depths and be lost forever.

And then an image of Molly appeared. She smiled at him from the opposite side of the abyss. Reality solidified around him.

Harry looked at Parker. "Like I said, you owe Aunt Danielle. Give her the one thing she really wants. The one thing that only you can give her."

"What's that?"

"Peace of mind about Brandon's future. Brandon doesn't need it, but she does. Danielle hasn't had much peace of mind in her life. She's been too busy trying to please you."

Parker's hands bunched into fists on the arms of his chair. "Who the hell appointed you avenging angel in this family?"

"Damned if I know." Harry opened the door.

"You can be a real SOB, Harry, you know that?"

Harry looked back over his shoulder, met and held his grandfather's eyes. "Runs in the family. Both sides."

He went out the door and closed it quietly.

He was not particularly surprised to find his uncle, Gilford Stratton, waiting for him in front of the art glass display. Harry smiled bleakly. This was not going to be one of his lucky days.

Gilford was forty-nine, the youngest of Parker's three offspring. With his aristocratic bones, fair hair, and hazel eyes, he was as handsome as the rest of the Strattons. Fifteen years ago he had married Constance Heeley, the daughter of a prominent Northwest shipping family. They had two children.

Luckily for the Strattons, Gilford had inherited more than just the family looks. He had also inherited the Stratton business talents. Stratton Properties was thriving under his administration.

"What are you up to now, Harry?" Gilford watched him with cool caution. Then understanding blazed in his eyes. "Damn it, you've upset Parker again, haven't you?"

"It doesn't take much. You know as well as I do that Parker gets annoyed at the very sight of me. But don't worry, he'll survive our latest discussion."

Gilford took a menacing step forward. "You talked to him about Brandon's stupid plan to leave the company, didn't you?"

"Yes."

"Stay out of this. You know how the old man feels about anyone in the family leaving the firm."

"I know," Harry said.

"I'm warning you, Harry, don't get involved in this. Let Parker handle it."

"His refusal to let Brandon go gracefully is tearing Danielle apart."

Gilford's expression tightened. "I know. I'm sorry about it, but that's the way it goes. It's not your problem. For once, try not to meddle in family business." He turned on his heel and strode off down the corridor to his corner office.

Harry watched him go, and then he made his way back through the reception area to the bank of elevators. The good news was that Molly was coming home for lunch.

Molly folded her hands on top of her desk and regarded the sober, serious countenances of her aunt and Cutter Latteridge. She knew they both meant well, but their concern was irritating, nonetheless.

"Don't worry about me, Aunt Venicia. I'll be fine at Harry's place."

"But, dear, if you don't feel comfortable staying in your own home, you can stay with me." Venicia, dressed in a flowing orange and fuchsia dress, was as bright as any of the tropical fish in Harry's aquarium. But her eyes were troubled. "I really don't know if you should be moving in with Harry Trevelyan like this. You hardly know him."

"Believe me, I'm getting to know him better every day," Molly said.

Venicia straightened her shoulders with a determined air. She slanted a quick glance at Cutter and then frowned at Molly. "Dear, Cutter and I have discussed your Dr. Trevelyan, and we feel there is something not quite right about this whole situation."

"Not quite right?" Molly repeated.

Cutter cleared his throat meaningfully. "I know this isn't any of my business. I'm not exactly a member of the family yet." He paused to reach out and lightly touch Venicia's hand. "But I feel as if I'm almost one of the clan, and I must speak up here."

"Cutter, please," Molly said. "Don't worry."

"I can't help it, my dear." Cutter assumed the pontificating air he did so well. "I'm extremely concerned about this entire matter. If odd things have been happening to you lately, and if you're sure that the pranks are not the work of one of your sister's friends, I urge you to let the police handle the situation."

"As a matter of fact, Harry talked to the police yesterday," Molly said. "There's not much they can do, especially if Wharton Kendall has left for California."

"But surely they can do something about that car that tried to run you off the road," Venicia said.

"They couldn't do anything except make a note of it and promise to keep an eye out for a blue Ford driven in a dangerous manner," Molly explained. "Harry and I can't even be certain there's a connection between the attempt to sideswipe us and Wharton Kendall. Personally, the more I think about it, the more I doubt that there is. We were probably just the near victims of a drunk driver."

Cutter gave her a considering look. "Why do you believe there's no connection?"

"Because until now, Kendall's idea of revenge has been to scare me with childish pranks," Molly said. "He certainly hasn't tried to hurt me."

Cutter's eyes narrowed. "If this Wharton Kendall fellow is responsible for the incidents, he's obviously a sick man, my dear. His insane rage may escalate. He could be very dangerous. Your aunt is right. You probably ought to move in with her until this is all over."

"I'll be safe at Harry's," Molly insisted. She did not want to point out that if Kendall was pursuing her, the last thing she wanted to do was put Venicia in jeopardy.

Venicia sighed. "My dear, I hate to sound old-fashioned, but you really must think about how this looks. People will wonder what Dr. Trevelyan's intentions are."

Molly rolled her eyes. "Aunt Venicia, please. We're not living in the last century."

Cutter looked grim. "I think we can guess Trevelyan's intentions."

Molly scowled at him. "What's that supposed to mean?"

"It means," Cutter said, "that there may be more to this than meets the eye. I realize that you are attracted to the man, my dear, but you must keep a level head. You are responsible for a great deal of money."

Molly unclasped her hands and braced them against the edge of her desk. "Are you still concerned that Harry may be interested in me only because he intends to skim a fortune in consulting fees off the foundation assets?"

"Don't be angry, dear," Venicia said quickly. "Cutter and I are both worried about this unusual relationship that seems to have sprung up between you and Dr. Trevelyan."

"I hate to say this," Cutter added ominously, "but it has struck me that your Dr. Trevelyan may be taking advantage of this Wharton Kendall situation."

"That's outrageous," Molly said.

"Is it?" Cutter looked unconvinced. "It appears to me that he's drawing you deeper and deeper into his web. Trevelyan has convinced you that you need his protection in addition to his expertise. You've become emotionally involved, my dear."

"For the last time," Molly said through her teeth, "I know what I'm doing."

Cutter shook his head. "Anyone who is the trustee for a well-endowed foundation must question such a personal relationship with someone who stands to profit from that foundation. No, my dear, the way I see it, you've got two distinct threats to worry about. The possibility that an unstable inventor is out for revenge, and the equally unwelcome prospect of working with an unscrupulous consultant."

Molly realized she was seething. "If Harry was so interested in getting his hands on a fortune, he wouldn't have walked away from the Stratton money."

Cutter studied her with a sympathetic expression. "He didn't exactly walk away from it, my dear. According to my sources, he and his grandfather, Parker Stratton, quarreled bitterly. Harry refused to go to work for the firm. Stratton cut him off from the family money. And there's something more. Something you may not know."

"What's that?" Molly demanded.

Cutter hesitated. "I hate to say this, but I have heard a rumor to the effect that Harry Trevelyan may not be a well man, mentally speaking."

"*What?* Where on earth did you hear that?"

Cutter sighed. "An acquaintance of mine once worked for Stratton Properties. He knows people there. Apparently Trevelyan's fiancée broke off her engagement to him when she discovered that he had some sort of psychiatric disorder. She's a psychologist, I understand, so she understood the implications."

Molly leaped to her feet. "That is absolutely, positively untrue. Harry is not crazy."

"Please, Molly," Venicia soothed. "You must be rational about this."

Molly glowered at her. "Just what do you suggest I do?"

Venicia smiled reassuringly. "Actually, I have an idea, Molly."

"What's that?"

"You could turn the trusteeship of the foundation over to me," Venicia said. "I know it's been a trial to you from the start. Let me handle things for you. If I took over, you would be able to step out of the picture entirely."

Molly stared at her. "Turn the foundation over to you?"

"It's a thought," Cutter said slowly. "Wharton Kendall would soon realize that you no longer hold the purse strings. The knowledge might cool his obsession with revenge. And Dr. Trevelyan would no longer be a risk, either."

"He's not a risk," Molly whispered.

"Look at it this way," Cutter said gently. "If his romantic interest in you is genuine, he won't care if you're no longer in charge of the foundation."

"You'll discover soon enough if his intentions are honorable," Venicia put in helpfully.

Molly shook her head. "Aunt Venicia, you don't want the task of running the foundation, believe me. It's a constant headache."

"Well, no, I don't want the job," Venicia said honestly. "But I'm willing to undertake the responsibility. It's the least I can do. Cutter could assist me. He's got a strong background in engineering. He could sort through the proposals and make selection decisions."

"I must admit, I would find the work interesting," Cutter said thoughtfully. "Keep the old brain sharp."

"We're both retired," Venicia reminded Molly. "We have the time for charity work."

"Give the matter some consideration, Molly." Cutter rose to his feet and took Venicia's hand. "Turning the reins of the foundation over to your aunt might solve all of your problems. Now, you must excuse us. Venicia and I have an appointment with our travel agent. Got a honeymoon to plan, you know."

"That reminds me," Venicia said. "You won't forget that you promised to come with me when I shop for my wedding gown, Molly?"

"I won't forget," Molly said.

Venicia and Cutter turned toward the office door. They halted abruptly when they saw that it was open. Harry lounged there, one shoulder against the jamb.

"Don't let me get in the way," he said softly.

Cutter bristled. "We don't intend to." He conducted Venicia through the doorway.

A moment later the front door of the shop closed behind them.

Molly swallowed. "I didn't hear you come in."

"Why is it," Harry asked, "that every time I walk into your office lately I find someone trying to convince you that I'm a threat to the Abberwick Foundation assets? First Gordon Brooke and now your aunt and her fiancé."

"I'm sorry you overheard that. Venicia and Cutter are concerned, that's all. It's the Wharton Kendall thing."

"It sounded like more than that," Harry said. "I thought I heard something about honorable intentions."

Molly blushed. "Aunt Venicia and Cutter are a little old-fashioned."

"What a coincidence." Harry's eyes were unreadable. "I just came from a meeting with someone else who takes an old-fashioned view of two people living together without benefit of a marriage license."

Molly gave him a very bright smile. "Luckily for us, we're both modern thinkers."

Thirteen

"He goes by the name of Wharton Kendall," Harry said into the phone. He paced the floor of his study as he talked to Fergus Rice. "I want you to find out where he is now and where he might have been yesterday, if possible."

"I'll do my best. Fax me what you've got from that grant proposal you said he wrote and anything else that looks interesting."

"I will."

There was a pause accompanied by soft clicking sounds on the other end of the line. Harry knew that Fergus was making notes on his computer.

Fergus Rice was a private investigator. One of the best. Harry had used his services occasionally in the past when he had needed practical information to supplement his own scholarly deductions in the course of an investigation into scientific fraud.

Harry was an expert when it came to studying the academic and technical evidence, but he was not a trained investigator in the old-fashioned, gumshoe sense of the word. He could have learned the craft, but he preferred not to spend his time in the mundane task of checking addresses and phone numbers. He paid other people to do that for him when necessary and billed the client for the expense.

"Is that it?" Fergus asked when he'd finished his notes.

"For now. If I come up with more, I'll let you know. Put a rush on this, will you, Fergus? The man's getting flakier by the day. The first two practical jokes were not lethal, but if that was Kendall in the blue Ford yesterday, he's definitely become dangerous."

"I'll get right on it."

Harry tossed the phone down into the cradle and went to stand in front of the large saltwater aquarium. He contemplated the angel fish as they cruised the miniature reef and wondered how many more people were going to get in line to convince Molly that she should not put her trust in him.

He had a reputation for being able to identify swindlers and charlatans of the most sophisticated kind, Harry thought. Large corporations and the government sought out his services when scientific fraud was suspected. He had written a book on the history of scientific hoaxes and another volume on the perils of scientific and academic illusions.

It seemed to him that his entire life had been devoted to the study of deception. His Trevelyan birthright had given him the skills to detect hustlers, liars, and cheats. His Stratton blood had provided him with sound business instincts. His academic training had endowed him with the knowledge and insight that enabled him to spot high-tech flimflammers.

Always he had been on the side of truth. Always he had been the one to expose the deceivers. Always he had taken the righteous stance and pointed the finger at those who sought to deceive.

Now people were telling Molly that he was very probably trying to deceive and defraud her. And he had no way to prove his innocence.

So far she seemed to trust him. How many times would she have to hear him accused of sleeping with her in order to get his hands on the Abberwick Foundation assets before she began to put some credence in the notion, he wondered.

He also wondered how many times she could listen to someone label him crazy before she began to believe it.

There was a soft sound from the hall.

"Brooding again?" Molly asked cheerfully from the doorway.

Harry turned swiftly to face her. "I didn't hear you come home."

"I arrived just as Ginny was leaving." Molly crossed the study to put her arms around his neck.

He folded her close and bent his head to kiss her. It felt good to have her here at the end of a long day, he thought. It felt right. He did not want to think about what might happen if she listened to the accusations and warnings.

Molly leaned her head back and searched his face with her gem-green eyes. "Want to talk about dinner?"

He smiled slightly. "What did you have in mind?"

"I think we should go out this evening. You're in one of your morose phases. Probably the full moon. Dinner out might help you shake off the mood."

"All right." A shiver of unease went through him. He wondered if his periodic bouts of solemn contemplation were starting to bother her. The possibility darkened his already bleak frame of mind. He struggled to strike an upbeat note. "You choose the restaurant."

"Why don't we go across the street to that new place featuring Pacific Rim cuisine?" She paused as one of the two phones on the desk burbled. "Oops. Private line. Must be family." Her hands dropped away from his neck.

"Damn." Harry eyed the phone with misgivings. For a few seconds he actually thought about ignoring the call. He did not want to deal with any more family problems today. Then he reached for the receiver.

"This is Harry."

"Harry, it's me, Josh."

The urgency in Josh's voice fueled Harry's gathering gloom as nothing else could have done. "What's wrong?"

"Grandpa is in the hospital here in Hidden Springs. He crashed his new truck an hour ago."

Harry closed his eyes briefly. "How bad?"

"Bad. The doctor warned us that the next few hours are critical." There was a desperate, disbelieving note in Josh's voice. "He said Grandpa might not make it through the night."

Harry glanced at his watch. "I'll be there as soon as I can. Don't give up the ship. Leon is one tough old bird."

"He's not really that old. He's not even seventy, you know. Lots of people live a lot longer."

"Take it easy, Josh."

Josh paused. When he spoke again, his voice was very subdued. "There was a fire at the scene, Harry. Just like there was when Dad was killed."

"I'm on my way, kid."

"Thanks."

Harry put down the phone. He looked at Molly. "I'm sorry. I've got to drive to Hidden Springs tonight. Leon managed to smash up his new truck. And, being Leon, he managed to make a spectacular mess of the situation."

"I'll go with you," Molly said.

Harry was startled at his reaction to her quiet offer. He was so accustomed to dealing with Trevelyan and Stratton family crises on his own that he did not immediately recognize the sense of relief that he felt.

Molly stood near the window of the hospital room and listened to the beeps, pings, and clicks of the machines that kept Leon Trevelyan from slipping through death's trapdoor. Leon was not aware of her presence. His attention was equally divided between his pain and Harry.

Harry was alone at Leon's bedside. A variety of Trevelyans, including Josh and Evangeline, hovered in the waiting room down the hall. The nurse had refused to allow them all into Leon's room at the same time.

Molly had seen the way the entire family had turned toward Harry when he had walked into the hospital a short while ago. It was as if they expected him to take charge. And in some subtle but unmistakable manner, he had done just that.

He had first conferred quietly with the doctor. Then he had announced that he wanted to talk to Leon for a few minutes. Molly had started to take a seat near Josh, but Harry had looked at her, and she had known that he wanted her to accompany him into the room.

"Well, Leon, you nearly did it this time, didn't you?" Harry said quietly.

"Shit. Who sent for you, Harry?" Leon's voice rasped in his throat. "I don't need you here."

"Believe me, there are a number of other places I'd rather be."

"Me, too." Leon paused as if to gather energy. "Where's Josh?"

"Out in the waiting room."

"Send him back in here, damn it."

"I will in a few minutes. We need to talk first."

"Why?"

"I spoke to the cops," Harry said. "They told me that you wrapped the truck around a tree. It was raining. Driving too fast in unsafe conditions, according to the report."

"Son-of-a-bitch," Leon muttered. "I'm dyin', and you want to give me another one of your damned safety lectures."

Molly saw Harry's jaw tighten, but his expression did not alter. It remained implacable. She knew then that he had a very specific goal, and he would do whatever he had to do in order to achieve it.

"Not a lecture," Harry said. "I want to make a deal with you. Don't get me wrong. I think you'll probably make it through this. God knows you've made it this far."

"The old Trevelyan reflexes," Leon whispered hoarsely.

"Right. The old Trevelyan reflexes. But just in case you don't come through this time, there's something you should know."

Leon opened one eye and squinted up at Harry. "What's that?"

"Don't expect me to polish your hero image with Josh after you're gone. Not unless you and I reach an understanding here."

"Christ, he's my grandson. He's all I've got left."

"I know. But I'll tell him everything, Leon, if you don't agree to my terms."

"Goddamned blackmailer. That's what you are."

"You and I have been blackmailing each other for years, Leon."

"Bullshit." Leon sucked in air. "It was a rigged game. You always held the winning hand."

"One more deal, Leon. One more deal, and you can die a hero in Josh's eyes. Of course, he'd rather have you live, but that's up to you."

"Jesus H. Christ. What d'ya want from me?"

Harry rested his arms on the raised bed rail and clasped his hands loosely together. He looked down into his uncle's haggard features. From where she stood Molly could see his eyes. They were as hard as polished amber, but she could have sworn she saw pain burning beneath the surface. He did not like what he was doing, but he was going to see it through. Josh was his first priority.

"I'm going to send Josh back in here in a few minutes. When I do, I want you to set him free of the past."

"What's that supposed to mean?"

"It means I want you to tell him that times have changed. The days of wild living and stupid risk taking are gone forever. Tell him that his father would never have wanted him to follow in his footsteps. Tell him that you don't want him to do it, either. Tell him that you want him to continue on the new road that he's chosen. That you're proud of him. Give him your blessing, Leon."

"Christ, Harry. You want me to tell him it's okay to become like you?

You want me to encourage him to turn his back on his heritage?"

"I want you to tell him," Harry said with relentless determination, "that you've been wrong all these years. That you realize now that it's time for the next generation of Trevelyan men to evolve. It's time for them to rely on their brains instead of their guts and their reflexes."

"Why should I do that?" Leon hissed. "You've already convinced him to finish college. Isn't that enough for you?"

"It's not enough for him. He loves you, Leon. He wants your approval. He needs to hear you tell him that you don't think he's a failure as a man just because he's chosen a path that will lead him away from fast cars and hard living."

"Josh doesn't give a damn about me." Leon's voice was strained with bitterness. "You've been his hero for years. Ever since you took him away from his family."

"You're wrong. You're his grandfather, and nothing can ever change that. He needs something from you that I can't give him, Leon. He needs to know you approve of the future he wants to pursue. It will make things a hell of a lot easier for him."

"Five will get you ten I know what the terms of this deal are."

Harry shrugged. "Same as always. If you do this for Josh, I won't tell him about Willy."

"Shit. I knew that was coming."

Leon's face contorted with anguish. He drew another rasping breath. "How do I know I can trust you?"

Harry was silent for a moment. "Have I ever lied to you, Uncle Leon?"

Leon's answer was lost in a wracking cough. When he recovered, he gazed blearily up at Harry. "You win, you SOB. Send him in, and then get outa here. I'll do this in my own way."

"Sure." Harry straightened.

For a few seconds he continued to gaze down at Leon. A wave of intense sadness went through Molly. She knew there was something else Harry wanted to say. Something that would not have been a threat or a form of coercion. Something that might have constituted a gesture of peace, an offer to end what was obviously an old war.

But in that brief moment, Molly also knew that Harry did not know how to claim the truce he wanted. He had asked Leon to set Josh free of the past, but Harry could not ask for a gift of equal value for himself.

Without a word, he turned away from the bed. Molly met his eyes in the shadows. She held out her hand. He took it, his fingers closing fiercely around hers.

Together, they left the room.

"It was weird." Josh picked up the hospital cafeteria tray and carried it toward a small table. "It was as though Grandpa was trying to say goodbye. He was different than I've ever seen him. Not so tough. Much older, if you know what I mean."

"He's been through a lot tonight." Molly sat down and took the plastic cups off the tray. "It's probably given him a great deal to think about."

"Yeah."

Molly was well aware that it was Harry, not the near-fatal truck accident, that had been responsible for whatever philosophical change had come over Leon. Harry had said nothing to her about the scene she had witnessed in Leon's room, but she knew without being told that he did not want Josh to know what had occurred.

It was nearly midnight. She had invited Josh to join her in the cafeteria after he had left his grandfather's side a few minutes earlier.

Harry was occupied with the hospital paperwork and the insurance forms. Everyone seemed to assume that it was his job to take care of those things. The other Trevelyans talked quietly to each other in the waiting room while they took turns maintaining the bedside vigil.

"Cheer up, Josh. Your grandfather has made it this far." Molly sipped the excruciatingly bad tea she had bought at the counter. She hated tea made from a tea bag. It never compared to the freshly brewed product. "The doctor said his condition has stabilized. I'd say his odds of making it until morning are getting better all the time."

"But he talked as if he expected to die. Said he wanted to tell me some things that have been on his mind." Josh stirred his coffee with a plastic stick. "He told me that he'd been wrong all these years when he tried to get me into racing."

"Did he?" Molly kept her voice neutral.

"He said the Trevelyan men have always lived by their guts and their reflexes, but that a lot of 'em didn't live very long. He said the world has changed. It's brains that count now. He said I've got more than my father and he had put together, and I shouldn't waste them."

Molly nodded. "Your grandfather obviously wants a different

future for you than the one he and your father made for themselves."

"Yeah." Josh hesitated. "I've always planned on finishing college and going for my doctorate. I've wanted to do the kind of work Harry does since I was thirteen. But Grandpa always said a man has to prove himself by looking death in the face and spitting in its eye. He said a man has to live on the edge or he'll go soft. He's always said that Harry was a gutless wonder."

"Hmm."

Josh looked up from his coffee. "He said things like that about Harry even after he found out what happened when Harry's folks were murdered."

Molly put down her cup and stared at Josh. "What, exactly, did happen?"

Josh was chagrined. "I take it Harry hasn't told you the full story?"

"No."

"I shouldn't have said anything. Everyone on both sides of the family knows the basic facts. But Harry never talks about it."

Molly shuddered. "I can understand that. But you can't leave me hanging like this. What happened?"

Josh gazed into his coffee as if it were an oracle glass. "The only reason I know the whole story is because one night when I was fourteen, I heard Harry call out in his sleep. I thought something terrible had happened. I went tearing down the hall to his room. He was sitting on the edge of his bed, staring out the window. He looked as though he had just awakened from a nightmare."

"Go on."

"I wasn't sure that he even saw me. I asked him what was wrong." Josh's hand tightened on the cup.

"What did he say?"

"Nothing for a long, long while. It spooked me, if you want to know the truth. I'd never seen him like that. He always seemed strong. So centered. Controlled. But that night I had the strangest feeling that he was pulling himself together. It was like he was picking up various bits and pieces of himself and regluing them back into place, if you know what I mean."

Molly recalled the night she had found Harry staring out the window, Kendall's gear in his hand. She remembered the shockingly vulnerable look in his eyes, so alien for him. "I think I do."

"After a while he started to speak. For some reason, maybe because I'd found him just after he'd awakened from the dream, he talked to me in a way he never had before. I'll never forget it. He sat there on the bed, staring out into the night, and he told me exactly what had happened the day Uncle Sean and Aunt Brittany were killed."

Dread welled up inside Molly. "Harry was there?"

"My aunt and uncle had a dive shop on one of the smaller islands in Hawaii."

"Yes, I know."

"That day they took the afternoon off to go diving. They decided to explore an underwater lava flow cave that they had discovered a few weeks earlier. They were checking out the entrance when they were surprised and killed by two men who had followed them down."

"Dear God," Molly whispered. "But why did the men murder them?"

"Uncle Sean and Aunt Brittany were in the wrong place at the wrong time. There had been an armored car robbery three days earlier in Honolulu. The killers had hidden a fortune in negotiable securities in the cave. I guess the plan was to wait for the search to cool down before they brought the haul back to the surface. In the meantime, they were keeping an eye on the cave. They were posing as tourists. They had rented a boat and dive gear."

"And when they saw Harry's parents diving in the vicinity of the cave, they assumed that they were cops or other thieves who had somehow stumbled onto the hiding place?"

"Apparently." Josh rubbed the back of his neck in a weary gesture that was strangely reminiscent of Harry. "They followed Harry's folks underwater, found them inside the cave, and shot them in the back with spear guns. Uncle Sean and Aunt Brittany never had a chance."

Molly closed her eyes. "How ghastly."

"Yes." Josh paused. "Harry arrived on the scene a few minutes after his folks had been killed."

"Oh, no."

"He had just arrived on the island for a visit. He'd gone straight to the shop and was told that his folks had taken the afternoon off to go diving near the old lava flow. Harry decided to surprise them. He took a boat and some dive gear and went to find them."

Molly could hardly breathe. "He could have been killed, himself."

"Yes. But as it turned out, it was the two armored car robbers who died."

"How?"

Josh raised his eyes to meet hers. "Harry killed them."

"What?" Molly was stunned. "Are you certain?"

"Yes," Josh said. "I'm certain. The night of the nightmare, he told me that when he found his parents' boat and saw the other boat anchored nearby, he knew something was very wrong. He got into his dive gear, took a spear gun, and went down to find out what was happening. The killers were just exiting the cave. Apparently they hoped the sharks would take care of the evidence. Harry said . . ."

"What did he say?" Molly prompted gently.

Josh frowned, as though groping for words. "He said it seemed as if the whole sea had turned red. He said he felt as though he were swimming through an ocean of blood. He told me that he knew what had happened even before he discovered his parents' bodies."

Molly's stomach churned. "I can't even imagine how terrible it must have been."

"He ran straight into the killers. But unlike Uncle Sean, he was prepared. He knew something was wrong. There was a fight. But Harry is fast. Very fast."

"Harry killed those two men?"

"Yes. He nearly died, himself, in the process. I gather one of the murderers cut his air hose during the struggle. Harry brought his parents' bodies to the surface before the sharks came, but it was too late. They were both dead."

Molly blinked back tears. "Dear heaven."

"I don't think Harry has ever forgiven himself," Josh said. "I think that's why he tends to brood sometimes, you know? Olivia told him that he's got posttraumatic stress disorder or something."

"I don't understand. It was a terrible tragedy. But why would Harry blame himself?"

"I think he blames himself for being too late to save his folks." Josh swallowed the last of his coffee. "The night that I found him sitting on the edge of his bed, he told me that if he'd been just a few minutes earlier, he could have saved his parents' lives. He kept saying that he had been too late."

At five-thirty that morning, Harry opened his eyes to see a doctor standing in the doorway of the hospital waiting room.

"Wake up." Harry gently eased Molly's head off his shoulder.

"We've got a visitor." He took one look at the doctor's face and knew at once that Leon was going to live. He was surprised by the force of the wave of relief that went through him. The old bastard was as tough as nails.

Molly opened her eyes and glanced at the doctor. "Something's happened?"

The doctor surveyed Harry and Molly and the weary crowd of half-dozing Trevelyans. He smiled. "Good news. I'm happy to tell you that Mr. Trevelyan's condition has been upgraded to satisfactory. He's out of the woods. I think it's safe to say he'll live to pay off that new truck he cracked up last night."

A weak but heartfelt cheer went up. Josh looked at Harry and grinned.

Evangeline heaved a sigh of relief. "I knew Leon wouldn't go out that easily."

"He always claimed he had nine lives, like a cat." Raleigh grinned weakly. "But by my reckoning, he's used up at least eight."

"You can say that again," Raleigh's pregnant wife murmured wearily. "Someday the old coot is going to take one chance too many."

"But not today, apparently," Harry said quietly.

The doctor looked at him. "He's asking for you."

Harry got to his feet and stretched. Molly stood up beside him. She gave him a questioning glance. He shook his head. "It's okay. I'll go see what he wants. Then we can get some breakfast in the cafeteria and head back to Seattle."

She nodded. "I'll wait here."

Harry went down the hall to Leon's room. Sunlight filtered in through the window. A nurse was just leaving Leon's bedside. She smiled as she went past him.

Harry waited until she was gone. Then he went to the bed.

"Congratulations," he said to Leon. "I had a hunch you'd pull through."

Leon turned his head on the pillow and glared at him. "Yeah? Wish I'd been as certain. If I'd been sure I wasn't going to kick the bucket this time, I wouldn't have let you push me around last night. You took advantage of my weakened condition."

"A deal's a deal."

"Yeah, yeah. You got what you wanted." Leon paused. "How's Josh?"

"Fine. He told everyone what you said to him last night. About how it's time for the Trevelyan men to start using their heads instead of other portions of their anatomies."

"Make him happy, d'ya think?"

"Yes. You took a load off his shoulders." Harry fixed his uncle with a meaningful look. "You gave him something I couldn't give to him. Something he'll have for the rest of his life."

"What's that?"

"The knowledge that you're proud of him and that his father would have been proud of him, too. He no longer feels that he's being a traitor to the Trevelyan heritage."

"Yeah, well, maybe you were right. Maybe it's time for a new heritage, y'know?"

Harry smiled. "What's this? Don't tell me that a little brush with death has given you a new philosophy of life?"

"Nah. It just made me a little more practical. I've never made much money in the racing game, and as for Willy, well, we both know what happened to him. Be good if Josh tries something different."

"You surprise me, Leon. I don't know what to say, except thanks."

Leon squinted up at him. "Now that you mention it, there is something else you can do to show your undyin' gratitude."

"What's that?"

"I'm gonna need a new truck."

Molly glanced at Harry as she buckled her seat belt. She was amused. "Leon wants you to buy him another truck?"

"Leon has never been one to let a golden opportunity slide past without making a grab for it." Harry eased the Sneath out of the hospital parking lot.

He drove out onto the main road with a sense of satisfaction. It was seven-thirty. They would be back in Seattle in an hour. Molly would be at her shop in plenty of time to open it for the day.

"Your uncle is a real piece of work." Molly hesitated. "I couldn't help but notice that you definitely play hardball with him."

"If that's a polite way of saying that I put the screws to him last night when he thought he might die, I plead guilty. From past experience, I've learned that there is no other way to deal with Leon."

Molly was silent for a few minutes. Harry wondered what she was thinking. It occurred to him that she might not approve of the way he handled his relatives.

"I know it's none of my business," Molly said after a while. "But would you mind telling me what it is that you hold over Leon? Is he really afraid that you'll tarnish his image in Josh's eyes?"

"Yes."

"What makes him think you could do that, assuming you would do it?"

Harry flexed his hands on the wheel. She had a right to know, he thought. Maybe that was the real reason he had asked her to accompany him into Leon's room last night. Maybe he wanted to tell her the truth.

"Leon and I share a secret. He and I are the only two people in the world who know that Josh's father died because the mechanic in charge of his motorcycle failed to give the engine a thorough going over the night before Willy did his last stunt. There was something wrong with the fuel lines. Something that the mechanic would have caught if he had done his job properly."

Molly turned slightly in the seat. "Who was Willy's mechanic?"

"Leon."

"I had a feeling you were going to say that. What went wrong? Why didn't Leon check out the engine?"

"Because he was too busy screwing the sheriff's wife in a motel room."

Molly looked stricken. "I remember your telling me something about Leon being in jail the day Willy was killed."

"He was. The sheriff made his arrest around ten that morning. Willy died at one o'clock that afternoon."

"How did you figure out that Leon hadn't done his job as a mechanic?"

Harry concentrated on the road. "Because I examined the wreckage after the accident. When I went over the remains of the engine, I knew that something had gone wrong in the fuel lines."

She gave him a searching glance. "You just knew?"

"I spent a lot of time with the bits and pieces that were left over after the explosion," Harry said carefully.

"You got one of your insights?"

"You could say that."

"Is that what happened the day your parents were murdered?" she asked softly. "When you found their boat and the one the killers had used, did you know that something terrible had happened? Is that why you went down with a spear gun?"

Harry reminded himself to breathe. "Josh talked to you?"

"Yes."

He gripped the wheel so tightly he wondered that it did not crack. "If I'd been just a few minutes earlier—"

"No," she interrupted very calmly. "You had nothing to do with their deaths. You are not responsible for what happened, Harry. Life is full of *what ifs,* but they are meaningless questions. You're a man who has devoted himself to scholarly study and reasoned thinking, you must know how futile it is to ponder the *what ifs.* The answers change nothing."

Harry could not think of any response to that.

"You're also a man who is very much in control of most things in his world," Molly continued. "But some things are out of your control, Harry. You must accept that simple fact or you will drive yourself crazy."

"I sometimes wonder about that possibility." It was the first time he had ever admitted his deepest fear aloud, Harry realized. Doing so made the threat all the more real.

"Don't be ridiculous." Molly smiled slightly. "I was speaking metaphorically. The very fact that you can even wonder if you're going crazy means you very likely aren't crazy. Real nuts don't question their own nuttiness. They think they're the only normal ones. That's why they're nuts."

"That's an interesting way of viewing the current state of the art of clinical psychology," he said dryly.

Molly touched his shoulder. "Remember what you wrote in *Illusions of Certainty?* 'Absolute certainty is the greatest of all illusions.' "

"I remember. What the hell does that have to do with this?"

"Total control is an illusion, Harry. The biggest one of all. You aren't responsible for everything and everyone. You're only human."

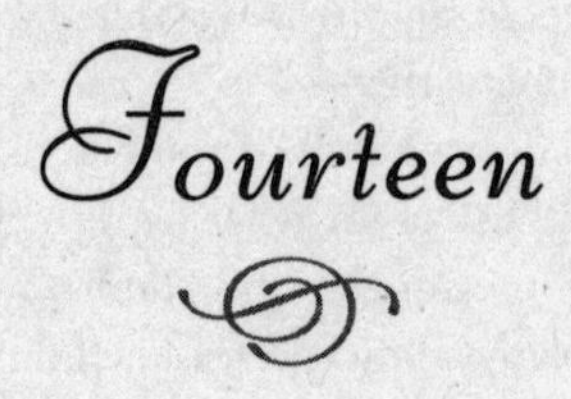

Fourteen

Harry went straight to his study the moment they walked in the front door. Molly, thinking fondly of a hot shower and a bracing cup of tea, trailed after him, yawning. She was learning the patterns of his life, and it had become obvious in the past few days that this particular routine was an indelible one.

She lounged in the doorway of his private sanctum, arms folded, and watched as Harry methodically played back the calls that had come in on his private line.

There were three messages on Harry's answering machine. Molly knew they had all come in sometime during the night. She was not particularly surprised to learn that all three were from Strattons.

> *Harry? It's Brandon. Where the hell are you? Call as soon as you get in. I need to talk to you.*

The machine whirred and clicked.

> *This is your Aunt Danielle, Harry. Call me immediately.*

More clicks from the answering machine.

> *Harry, this is Gilford. If you're screening your calls, pick up*

the phone now. If you're not there, call me as soon as you get this message. Where the hell are you? It's seven-thirty in the morning.

The answering machine pinged to indicate the end of the messages. Harry hit the rewind button. He glanced at his watch and then reached for a pen and a pad of paper.

"Want some advice?" Molly asked softly.

Harry did not look up from the notes he was making, but one black brow rose in inquiry. "What's that?"

"You've dealt with enough family problems in the past few hours. Give it a break."

His mouth curved humorlessly. "Different family."

"No, all the same family. Yours. Harry, you've had a long night with very little sleep. Take a shower. Have a cup of coffee. You can answer those calls later. Much later." Molly paused. "Like maybe this afternoon or tomorrow. Next week might be a good time."

He slowly put down the pen and looked at her. "What's that supposed to mean?"

"It means that you have a right to put yourself first once in a while." She held out her hand. "Come on. Let's go take a shower."

She saw the hesitation in his face, and then, to her intense relief, he took her hand and allowed himself to be led down the hall.

At five o'clock that afternoon, Molly flipped the sign in the shop window so that it read CLOSED and groaned aloud. "I've had it, Tessa. I'm going to stop by my place to check on things and pick up some fresh clothes. Then I'm heading straight back to Harry's. I'm looking forward to putting my feet up and having a nice glass of chilled chardonnay."

"Is that a fact?" Tessa repainted her mouth with heavy brown lipstick.

"I'm getting too old for short nights followed by full work days. I don't know how you do it."

"It's the music." Tessa dropped the lipstick into a huge leather bag as she came around the counter. "It gives me energy. How much longer are you going to stay with T-Rex?"

"I don't know." Molly watched a gaggle of tourists climb the broad steps toward First Avenue. "To tell you the truth, I'm starting to worry a little about the situation. I feel as though I'm living in limbo."

"I'm starting to worry about your situation, too. I understand why you don't want to stay at your own place, but maybe you should move in with your aunt. I don't like this business of you living with Trevelyan. It's not you."

Molly glanced at her, astonished. "What the heck is this? You've been after me for months to get a love life."

"Is that what you've got? A love life?" Tessa's vividly outlined eyes held an old-fashioned expression that was disconcertingly at odds with her nose ring, neon hair, and clashing arm chains. "Or are we talking just a sex life here?"

The question had a strange effect on Molly. She felt as though she had suddenly stepped out into space. Her insides fluttered wildly in the weightless environment. "I wish I knew."

"Damn. I was afraid of this."

"Tessa, it's after five. Begone."

"Look, if you want to talk—"

"I don't. But thanks, anyway."

Tessa hesitated. "Sure. Whatever you say, boss. I'm here if you need me."

"I know. Thanks."

Tessa opened the front door. "Hey, I almost forgot."

"About what?"

"A friend of mine in the band wants to talk to you. She's working on a really strange gadget. I told her about your foundation, and she got excited. She could use the money to help finance her project."

Molly was momentarily distracted from her own problems. "Your friend is an inventor?"

"Yeah. Her name is Heloise Stickley. Plays bass guitar in the band. But her main interest is alternate levels of consciousness."

"How nice," Molly said. "What are alternate levels of consciousness?"

"Beats me. She's got some kind of theory about people who can sense things that the rest of us can't. You know, like colors that go beyond the normal spectrum. Stuff like that. She's working on a machine that detects special brain waves or something."

Molly winced. "Uh, maybe you'd better not encourage her to apply for funding to the Abberwick Foundation. Harry is a little biased against inventors who work in the field of paranormal studies. To be perfectly blunt, he thinks it's all garbage."

"You don't need T-Rex's permission for every single project, do you?"

"Well, no. But I'm paying big bucks for his advice. It would be stupid not to follow it."

"Just talk to Heloise, okay? There's no harm in that, is there?"

"No, of course not." Molly smiled wryly. "You could sell ice in Alaska during the winter, Tessa. Tell Heloise that I'll be glad to talk to her."

"Great." Tessa grinned as she went through the door. "See you tomorrow."

Molly waited until the door had closed again. Then she walked through the shop one last time, going through her evening ritual. She straightened canisters of tea. Checked the special orders file. Pulled the shades in the front windows.

When all was in order, she let herself out the front door and secured it firmly. The steps in front of the shop were still cluttered with people, but the crowd was thinning rapidly. The fountains sparkled in the late afternoon sun.

Molly walked up toward First Avenue, heading toward the nearest bus stop. Gordon Brooke stepped out of the front door of his coffee bar as she went past.

"Molly." He gave her an ingratiating smile. "On your way home?"

"Yes." She paused briefly. "Did you have a good day?"

"Fair. Look, I wanted to apologize for my behavior in your office the other day. I didn't mean to embarrass you in front of Trevelyan."

"Forget it."

Gordon sighed. "I didn't handle that scene very well, but I am genuinely concerned. You seem to be getting serious about him."

"Don't worry about me, Gordon."

"That's just it, I do worry about you." He shoved one hand into the pocket of his fashionable bronze-colored trousers. "If nothing else, we're old friends. I don't want to see you get in over your head with a guy like Trevelyan. He's not really your type."

"Amazing how everyone seems to have an opinion on the subject. You'll have to excuse me, Gordon. I've got a bus to catch."

Molly hurried up the remainder of the steps, crossed the street, and caught a crowded bus to Capitol Hill. There was one empty seat in the middle of the bus, but it was next to a bag lady who had stacked all of her worldly possessions on it. This being Seattle, none of the standing passengers stooped to the incivility of requesting that the woman move her things.

The bus made its way past the eclectic collection of bookstores, cafés, body-piercing parlors, and leather clothing shops that gave the Capitol Hill district its colorful identity. When it lumbered into the old residential district beyond, Molly got off.

She walked along the quiet, tree-lined streets to the Abberwick mansion. The sight of the sprawling old house beyond the iron gates filled her with an unexpected rush of affection. Kelsey was wrong, she thought. She could not sell the mansion. It was home.

The massive front gates swung open when she keyed in the code. She walked up the drive, noting that everything seemed to be in order so far as the gardens were concerned. The perpetual sprinkling system that her father had designed had obviously been working without a hitch.

She went up the steps and let herself into the hall. For a moment she stood there in the shadows, allowing memories to coalesce around her. There were ghosts in this house, but they were part of the family, part of her. She could not abandon them.

After a moment Molly looked down. The wooden floor gleamed. The polishing robot had been at work. She walked into the front parlor. The bookcases had all been recently dusted by the dusting machine.

She left the parlor and went up the massive staircase to the second floor. There, she turned and went down the hall to her bedroom.

No, she definitely would not put the house on the market, Molly thought as she took fresh clothes out of the closet and stuffed them into a patented Abberwick Nonwrinkling Suitcase. The crazy old mansion would never sell, anyway, except possibly to a developer who would tear it down to make room for condominiums or apartments. Only someone who valued the unique and the bizarre would love it the way she did.

She could live here by herself, Molly decided. Granted, the house was technically too big for one person, but her father's endless household inventions would take care of most of the work involved in maintaining the mansion.

What it really needed was a family. A very special sort of family, one with an extraordinary father whose brilliant eyes were the color of ancient amber.

The thought came out of nowhere. Molly stood very still in the center of the bedroom, clutching the red jacket she had just taken off a hanger.

An image of two dark-haired, amber-eyed children materialized in the gloom. The pair, a boy and a girl, were laughing with gleeful anticipation. She sensed that they were eager to run downstairs to her father's old workshop. They wanted to play with the automated toys that Jasper Abberwick had invented years ago for Molly and Kelsey.

For a few seconds Molly could not breathe. *Harry's children.*

The vision faded, but the emotions it had generated inside Molly did not.

After a while she adjusted the cleverly engineered clothes-folding mechanism inside the suitcase and shut the lid. She made a quick tour of the remainder of the rooms on the second floor to make certain that all was in order. Then she went downstairs.

She left the suitcase in the hall while she toured the rooms on the first floor. Nothing was amiss. The only thing left to do was to make her way down to the basement to check the machinery that powered the household robots.

She went down the steps into the windowless rooms below the house. The bright overhead lights winked on in the workshop when she opened the door. Across the room she saw the glowing lights on the control panel that regulated all the various mechanical and electrical systems in the house.

Molly heard the faint creak just as she stepped into the workshop.

Two thoughts struck her simultaneously. One was rational, intellectual, and based on common sense. It held that such creaks and groans were to be expected in an old house.

The second thought was irrational and intuitive. It emanated straight from the most primitive part of her mind, the region charged with the tasks of survival. It told her with grave certainty that she was not alone in the mansion. She was being stalked.

Someone had been hiding in one of the basement storage rooms while she methodically toured the upstairs rooms.

A floorboard groaned.

Panic seized Molly. She glanced back toward the stairs and knew a searing helplessness. She would have to go past a long line of storage rooms in order to escape. Someone waited in one of those rooms.

Even as she contemplated her chances, a door opened at the end of the hall. A man materialized in the shadows. His face was covered with a ski mask. He raised his hand. Molly saw the gun in his fist.

She chose the only option open to her. She dashed through the workshop doorway, whirled around, and slammed the old wooden door closed. She threw the bolt.

Muffled footsteps thudded down the hall. They came to a halt on the other side of the door. The antique glass knob rattled under Molly's hand. Instinctively she jerked her fingers away from it.

Belatedly she realized that it was not smart to stand directly in front of the door. The intruder could easily shoot through the aging wood.

She took several more steps back from the door until she reached the center of the workshop. A heavy, jarring crash shook the door. It rattled on its hinges. The gunman intended to force his way into the workshop. It was only a matter of time before he achieved his goal.

Molly turned in a slow, desperate circle, feeling like a trapped animal. There was no escape from the workshop. The brick walls of the basement loomed around her, confining her in a space that was no larger than the upstairs parlor. There was no place to hide.

Her gaze fell on the brooding, shrouded shapes that lined one wall of the room. The image of two black-haired children with intelligent amber eyes popped into her head again.

The children wanted to play with the glittering, flashing, mechanical toys that Jasper Abberwick had built for his daughters.

There was another thud. The door shuddered and groaned as if it had taken a mortal wound. Molly knew now that the intruder meant to kill her. She felt the menace in her bones. She had to act or else she would die right here in the basement of her own home.

Harry. Harry, I need you.

The silent scream for help shrieked through her head. There was no point calling out. No one would hear her.

The amber-eyed children wanted to play.

Molly gathered herself and hurried across the room to the nearest tarp-covered form. She yanked the canvas aside to reveal the huge, lumbering toy she had once named the Creature from the Purple Lagoon. It was as tall as she was, with a great, gaping, toothy mouth and a long tail. When she had been eight years old she had thrilled to the knowledge that she could control such a grand beast.

Molly steadied the monster on its wonderfully hideous feet and punched a button on the control panel. Her faithful, semiannual attention to the special long-life batteries was rewarded.

Red lights flashed in the creature's eyes. With a hiss of fake steam, the monster cranked slowly into motion. It started forward on its huge, claw-footed legs. The thick tail shifted from side to side.

The door trembled beneath another blow.

Molly jerked the canvas shroud off another one of the mechanical toys. This one was a spaceship. Two large dolls dressed in bizarre costumes manned the ray guns. Molly punched a button. The ship hummed to life. Strobes pulsed around the outer edge. The imitation weapons beamed green rays into the shadows.

There was another jarring crash of noise from the door. Molly uncovered more toys. One by one she powered up the robots, monsters, and vehicles of her small army.

She was working on a miniature glider, a prototype of the machine that had killed her father and her uncle, when she heard the door give way with a splintering crack.

She hit the master switch on the panel that controlled all of the household electricity.

The workshop was instantly plunged into a stygian darkness just as the man in the ski mask came through the door. Molly's mechanical defenders chugged, roared, and hummed through the inky blackness, filling it with a nerve-shattering barrage of flashing lights and whirring, clanking noises.

The toys surged willy-nilly around the room, charging blindly into each other, the walls, and anything that got in their path. Molly ducked down behind a workbench and held her breath.

It was a scene out of a special effects nightmare.

The cavelike darkness was pierced with wildly pulsing strobes. A cacophony of roars, hisses, and grunts created a deafening howl.

"What the hell?" The hoarse shout of surprise from the gunman held a note of raw terror.

Thunder boomed in the lightless chamber. Molly crouched closer to the floor, aware that the intruder had just fired his gun.

"Goddamn it," the intruder yelled.

This time there was pain in the rasping cry. Molly knew the man had collided with one of the war machines in the darkness.

Molly heard the clang of metal on metal and realized that the gunman had swung out blindly in an attempt to ward off another automated attacker. She heard one of the large toys crash to the floor. Its pulsing lights continued to flash in a crazed rhythm that periodically spotlighted its churning claws.

The spaceship turned its ray guns toward the doorway. Green beams lit the darkness as the toy opened fire. Molly glimpsed the strange, jerky movement of the gunman as he was caught in the path of the strobes. She realized that he was struggling frantically to escape.

He tripped over a dinosaur's swishing tail. Screaming in rage and fear, he regained his feet and plunged blindly ahead.

A scattered burst of green beams from the spaceship's armament revealed the doorway. The intruder ran through it into the dark hall. The erratic strobes swung in another direction, and Molly lost sight of the gunman. The toys were creating too much of a racket to enable her to hear the sound of footsteps on the stairs, but a moment later Molly thought she felt impact vibrations from the wooden floor over her head. The intruder was running down the front hall.

Molly waited for a long time behind the milling ranks of her toy defenders. Eventually she made her way by feel to the master control panel. She switched on the household lights with trembling fingers and reached for the phone.

Her first call was to 911. The second was to Harry.

As it turned out, the second call was not necessary. Harry came through the front door of the mansion five minutes later.

"It was that crazy bastard, Kendall." Harry prowled back and forth in front of the wall of windows. He felt as restless and trapped as a lion in a cage. "Had to be him. So much for the theory that he went to California. Damn that son-of-a-bitch. He's really gone over the edge. We've got to find him."

Molly, coiled in a chair, her feet tucked under her, sipped chardonnay. "Harry, stop pacing. You're making me dizzy."

He ignored her. "I keep thinking there's something else I should do."

"You've given the cops everything we've got, and you've called your private investigator, Fergus Rice. What else can you do? Try to relax."

"Relax?" Harry swung around to confront her. "How the hell am I supposed to do that?"

"You could start by doing what I'm doing." She held her wine glass aloft. "Pour yourself a drink. We both need to unwind."

Harry knew she was right. He was almost vibrating with a sense of helpless rage.

Kendall had almost killed her this afternoon. The knowledge churned in his guts. He was in a foul mood, and he knew it. The truth was, he had been sinking into this state slowly but inexorably for several hours. He had been seething with a sense of terrible urgency since shortly after five that afternoon.

The undefined sensation of doom had descended on him with the force of a tidal wave. He had been working in his study, waiting for the sound of Molly's key in the front door lock, when it had hit him. He had suddenly needed to know where she was. Needed to know that she was safe.

He had called her shop, but there had been no answer. It had occurred to him that she had gone to the mansion for fresh clothes. He had started to dial the number.

But for some reason, he had felt an overpowering urge to get the car out of the garage and drive to Capitol Hill. He had fought the illogical need as long as he could before he had finally given in to it.

The open front gate had given the first verifiable proof that there was a basis for his alarm. He had heard the sirens in the distance just as he raced through the front door of the mansion.

There had been no sign of Molly. It was the thundering din in the basement that had drawn him downstairs. His first thought was that some of Jasper Abberwick's machines had run amok.

As long as he lived, Harry knew he would never forget the sight of Molly surrounded by a herd of bizarre mechanical toys. He had taken one look at her stricken face and known, without her having to explain, that she had very nearly died in that workshop.

He had also known that he would have been too late to save her.

Harry came to a halt in front of Molly. He leaned down and gripped the arms of the chair, forcing her to look up at him. "From this moment until Wharton Kendall is in custody, you are not to go anywhere alone. Is that clear?"

"Harry, I know you're a little upset over what happened, but there's no need to overreact."

"I will walk you to work in the mornings. I will pick you up for lunch. I will meet you after work and escort you back here. Understood?"

"I promise I won't go home alone again," she temporized.

He leaned closer. "You won't go anywhere alone."

She bit her lip. "Harry, you'll drive me crazy if you try to make me a prisoner."

"Don't use the word lightly. You don't know what crazy is."

"And you do?"

"Some people," he said very deliberately, "have implied that I may have a nodding acquaintance with the condition."

"But I thought we settled that issue. You're not crazy." She studied him with sudden comprehension. "Ah. You're referring to Olivia, aren't you?"

"She is a professional," he said through set teeth.

"Maybe. But I wouldn't worry about her diagnosis, if I were you."

"Easy for you to say," Harry muttered. "I can certainly testify to the fact that I went a little nuts this afternoon when I realized you weren't home on time and that I had no idea where you were."

Her eyes widened. "Now that is interesting, isn't it?"

"No, it's crazy-making, not interesting. I don't want to go through that again. Ever. And that is why you are not to go anywhere by yourself until Kendall is caught."

She pursed her lips, her eyes thoughtful. "When did you first realize that I was in trouble?"

He was suddenly wary. "I realized you were late around five-thirty."

"That would have been about the time that I wished you were with me. I remember thinking your name very, very clearly."

"Molly, for God's sake, don't try to tell me that you believe there was some extrasensory perception involved here."

"Maybe it was your intuition at work again," she suggested ingenuously.

He released the arms of her chair and straightened abruptly. "Are you serious?"

"Let's look at this rationally."

"Now, that would certainly be a novel approach."

She paid no attention to his sarcasm. "Tell me, how did you know that I'd gone home to pick up some clothes?"

"Hell." Harry resumed his pacing. "Not from any paranormal powers, I can promise you that. It was a perfectly logical deduction under the circumstances."

"Hmm."

"Don't say that."

She gave him a quizzical look. "Don't say what?"

"Don't say *hmm* in that tone of voice."

"Okay. But, Harry, in all seriousness, I'm starting to wonder if there is something to this paranormal stuff."

"For the last time, I do not have any psychic powers. Even those in the family who believe in the Trevelyan Second Sight don't believe it takes the form of the kind of mental telepathy that allows two people to communicate without words. Not even the original Harry Trevelyan believed he could do that."

"Hmm."

Harry glared at her.

"Sorry," Molly said. "I was just thinking. We're back to intuition, I suppose."

"Insight," he said grimly. "Reasoned, logical insight occasionally gives the illusion of being something more than what it actually is."

"So it was reason and logic that enabled you to deduce that I was in trouble at the mansion?"

"For all the good it did." Harry shut his eyes and let the stark truth roll through him. "I was too late to make a difference. Too damn late. If you hadn't had that inspiration to hide in your father's workshop and use those old toys to defend yourself, I would have found you—" He broke off, unable to put the rest into words.

"Yes. It was a useful inspiration, wasn't it?" Molly took another sip of wine. A faraway expression lit her eyes.

"What the hell gave you the idea to use the mechanical toys the way you did?" Harry asked. "Or was it just a case of necessity being the mother of invention?"

"What would you say if I told you that I got the idea to use the toys from a couple of children?"

He scowled briefly. "What children? Are you telling me there were some children involved in this? You didn't say anything about them to the police."

"There was no point," Molly said, oddly wistful. "The children haven't been born yet."

Harry stared at her. She'd been through a lot today, he reminded himself. She was probably suffering from some sort of delayed shock. "Molly, we'd better get you into bed. You need rest."

She smiled. "Harry, have you ever thought about having kids?"

He came to a halt in front of the window. His imagination projected a clear, unmistakable picture of her rounded and ripe with child. His child. An intense longing welled up within him. He took a deep breath. "I think that wine is getting to you. It's probably because of the stress. Come on. I'll help you undress. You need a good night's sleep."

"Hmm."

"Too late."

The hoarse, desperate words were barely audible, but they woke Molly from a dream of huge, marauding mechanical toys. Adrenaline surged through her. She opened her eyes and looked at Harry, who was asleep on the bed beside her.

A broad shaft of moonlight slanted into the room through the wall of windows. The icy light bathed him in silver. There was a damp sheen of sweat on his bare shoulders.

"Too late," he muttered into the pillow. He shifted restlessly. "Can't breathe. Can't *breathe.*"

"Harry, wake up."

"Can't breathe. Too late."

Molly touched him gently. It was as though she had plugged him into a light socket. Harry came awake with shocking suddenness, rolled to the edge of the bed, and got to his feet in one smooth motion. He whirled to look down at her.

In the cold moonlight she could not make out the curious amber color of his eyes, but she had no problem seeing the haunted expression in them. She sat up slowly against the pillows and pulled the sheet to her throat.

"You were dreaming," she whispered.

"Yes." He blinked a few times as though to clear away the ghosts. A shudder went through him. He took a deep breath and seemed to steady himself. "Sorry."

"A nightmare?"

He ran a hand through his hair. "I haven't had one like that in a long time. Years. I'd almost forgotten how bad they were."

Molly pushed aside the covers and stood. She padded quickly around the end of the wide bed and went to him. Wrapping her arms around his waist, she leaned against him, offering the only comfort she had to give.

"It's all right, Harry. It's over."

He stood rigidly in her embrace for a long moment, and then, with a husky, wordless groan, he put his arms around her and held her as though she were the only woman on earth. For a few minutes they stood there quietly in the moonlight.

"It was because of me, wasn't it?" Molly finally dared to suggest. "The incident this afternoon triggered your dream. You feel guilty because you got to me after Kendall had already gone."

"I got to you too late." Harry's voice was uncompromisingly harsh. "You could have been killed."

"The way your parents were?"

Harry went absolutely still. "Yes."

"What happened to me today brought back all the old memories, didn't it?"

"Probably."

"And some old dreams."

"I guess so." He sounded weary all the way to his soul.

"You can't save everyone, Harry. Not even all the people you care about. Life doesn't give us that option. I learned that the hard way, myself. Let it go."

"I don't think I can. Not completely. Not ever."

"Then share it with me." Molly braced herself. "Tell me what it was really like that day your parents were murdered."

"You don't want to hear about it."

Molly was not certain she had the right to pry further, but something within her drove her to push on, even though it was obvious her questions would not be welcome. "You said that you were too late to save your folks that day."

"Too goddamned late." Without warning, rage and pain poured from him in a torrent. It was as if somewhere inside him a dam had burst. "Just as I was too late today. Too late. Always too damned late."

Molly hugged him fiercely. "You went down with a spear gun that day your parents died."

"Christ. Did Josh tell you that part, too?"

"Yes." Molly lifted her head to search his face. His eyes glittered. "You were almost killed, yourself, weren't you?"

"They saw me as they emerged from the cave." The words sounded as if they emanated from somewhere near the outer rings of Hades, the region of unbearable cold. "I knew then what had happened. They came straight toward me. I killed the first man with the spear gun. The other one was on me before I could reload. His shot missed. But he had a knife. Took it from a sheath he wore on his ankle. Sliced through my air hose."

"Oh, God, Harry." She tightened her hold on him.

"I had a knife, too. Dad had given it to me. I killed the bastard with it. But I was out of air. Took a tank off one of the dead men. Used it to swim on down to the cave. But I was too late. They were both dead."

Stark silence fell.

Molly cradled Harry's face between her palms. She sensed that the tale was unfinished, although she did not know what remained to be told. She only knew that he had to tell her everything.

Molly probed cautiously, feeling her way as carefully as though she walked through a minefield. "You said you knew as soon as you arrived on the scene that there was danger. That something terrible had happened?"

Harry gazed past her into the night outside the window. "I saw the second boat anchored next to theirs. I reached out to touch the hull. Everything was wrong. So goddamned wrong."

"I understand."

"I found them. Brought them back to the surface. I couldn't seem to breathe, even though I had a half-full tank of air." Harry rubbed his eyes with one hand. "And the water was a strange shade of red. A trick of the late afternoon light, I think. But it looked like blood."

"It must have been unbearable."

"Yes."

"No wonder you still dream about it. Harry, you couldn't save your parents' lives that day. But you must never forget that your father saved yours."

He pulled his attention away from the night and looked down at her with a scowl of confusion. "What?"

"Your father taught you how to use a knife, didn't he? He gave you the one you wear. The one you used that day."

"He taught me everything he knew. It's the only reason that I survived that fight."

"The skills your father gave you saved your life that day, just as the mechanical toys my father made for me saved my life this afternoon."

Harry was silent for a moment. "Yes."

"Sometimes it's good to remember things like that, Harry. We're all connected to each other. Sometimes we save others. Sometimes they save us. That's the way life is. None of us can do all of the saving, all of the time."

Harry said nothing. But he did not pull away from her embrace.

"Your father fulfilled his responsibility to you by teaching you the things you needed to know in order to survive in that terrible moment."

"Molly, I don't know what you're trying to do here, but if this is your idea of a little amateur psychology, forget it." His mouth twisted bitterly. "Olivia already gave it her best shot, and she's an expert."

"What did Olivia say?"

Harry shrugged. "She talked a lot about the destructiveness of guilt. Said there was medication for posttraumatic stress disorder. I told her that I wasn't interested in rewriting history with a feel-good pill."

Molly gave him a small shake. "What I'm telling you isn't therapy, it's truth. You're the one who's supposed to be the expert when it comes to sorting out reality from illusion. Well, look at this piece of truth I'm giving you, and tell me honestly if you think it's a lie."

"And just what is this truth you want me to see?"

She refused to be intimidated by the anger that was pulsing through him. She knew intuitively that it was good for him to release the emotion. He had kept too many things bottled up inside for too long.

"Listen to me, Harry. Your father saved your life that day, and that is exactly the way he would have wanted it. He was your father, and you were his son. He took care of you that day. It was his right as a father. Your mother would have felt the same way. That's the way it's supposed to be. You repaid the gift by passing it along."

Harry's jaw tightened. "I don't understand."

"What if it had been Josh instead of you who went down that day?

What if he had been the one to encounter those two murderers?"

Harry stared at her with unblinking eyes and said nothing. He did not have to say anything. Molly knew exactly what he was thinking. Harry had raised Josh. He had a father's instincts toward him.

"I agree that a man like you would never be content to rewrite history in order to make himself feel better," Molly continued gently. "That's not the way out. You make things right by balancing the scales. It's not therapy, it's a karma thing."

"I don't believe this. Karma? Don't tell me that you're into that kind of mystical nonsense."

"All right, you're a man of science, think of it in technical terms. Apply Newton's Laws of Motion. For every action there is an equal reaction. Your father saved your life, and you responded by doing the same for Josh."

"What does Josh have to do with this?" Harry asked tensely. "I've never saved his life."

"Yes, you have. You saved him from the legacy of the past. It was a legacy that could easily have gotten him killed or left him washed up and embittered like his grandfather. You gave him a future filled with promise. That was a priceless gift, Harry."

"All I did was make sure he got an education."

"No, you gave him much more than that. You gave him a stable environment. You were a true father to him. You wrestled that old devil, Leon, for his soul, and you won."

Harry leaned his damp forehead against hers in a gesture of unutterable exhaustion. "This is a strange conversation to be having in the middle of the night."

"Josh isn't the only one you've saved," Molly said steadily. "From what I can see, you've made a habit of saving Strattons and Trevelyans during the past few years."

He stilled. "Now what are you talking about?"

"Well, as an example, you've made it possible for Brandon to go out on his own without risking his inheritance."

"Brandon won't thank me for it."

"Maybe not, but that's his problem. I know you've also helped your cousin Raleigh and his wife. I suspect that you had something to do with making it possible for Evangeline to buy Smoke & Mirrors Amusement Company. I have a hunch the list is endless."

"Things like that are different."

"No, they're not. They're important because they help people." She smiled up at him. "And you know what? You did save my life today, although it was indirectly."

His face hardened. "Don't joke about it, Molly."

"This is no joke." She held his eyes with her own, willing him to see the truth. "I told you that I got an inspiration for using my old toys to save myself from Kendall."

"You said you got the idea from a couple of kids."

"The children were yours, Harry."

"Mine?" Harry was thunderstruck. "I thought I was the crazy one here."

"They were your children. I saw them very clearly. A boy and a girl. They had your eyes."

Harry gripped her shoulders, his eyes fierce in the moonlight. "Are you telling me that you had a vision or something?"

Molly smiled tremulously. "Well, maybe it was just wishful thinking."

"Wishful thinking," he repeated blankly.

"I have a very good imagination. It runs in the family. Along with the streak of curiosity."

"Molly—"

She touched his lips with one fingertip. "I think it's time you thought about having kids of your own. You'd make a really fantastic father. You have an aptitude for the job."

His mouth opened. No words came out. He closed it again. Then he wrapped one arm around her neck, bent his head, and kissed her with such seething hunger that Molly went limp in the face of it. Her head fell back against his shoulder.

She was stunned by the wave of sharp, searing need that rolled over her and through her. It left her weak and breathless. And filled with anticipation.

Harry was kissing her now the way he had that first night. She felt like a flower caught in a hurricane. She trembled beneath the impact of the storm and sensed the darkness at its heart. She heard Harry groan. She felt his hands close around her waist. The moonlit room spun around her. Her senses were tumbled into chaos.

The next thing she knew, she was lying flat on her back across the bed. Her legs were splayed wide. The skirt of her nightgown was hiked up to her waist. Harry came down on top of her.

Molly was intensely aware both of her own softness and of the crushing weight of Harry's body. He was fully, heavily aroused. She felt the unyielding hardness of him pressing against her inner thigh.

She gasped for breath when he briefly freed her mouth to kiss her throat. She fought to recover her senses, which were in complete disarray. She was swamped by sensation. Frantically she tried to sort out her impressions. There was something in this that was not coming from her.

She was aware of a deep, raging hunger. A desperate craving that was unlike anything she had ever known. She was in danger of being consumed by an explosive, demanding need that had been tethered too long. The need was fueled by sexual desire, but desire was only a part of the volatile brew.

Harry's hands moved on her body, touching her everywhere. His teeth rasped against her nipple. The urgency in him nearly overwhelmed her.

This wasn't sex, Molly thought, dazed. This was . . . something else. Something more.

The dark storm howled, creating a dangerous vortex. Molly knew that she was in danger of being sucked into the spinning whirlpool of unleashed hunger.

Harry's hunger.

A shock of recognition lanced through Molly. In a blinding flash of certainty, she understood that what she was experiencing was emanating from Harry. The emotions that tore through her, the searing need, the intolerable aloneness, the desperation, it was all coming from him.

And it resonated with something deep inside her.

Molly reacted instinctively. She clung to him, knowing that she could satisfy the clawing need in him, aware that she needed him to satisfy her own newly discovered hunger. "I'm here."

"No." Harry abruptly heaved himself upward as though he would break the current of contact that sizzled between them. He stared down at her, his hands caging her, his face a mask of torment. "Damn it, I never meant to do this. I swore I would not risk it again. I can't."

And suddenly Molly knew that if she was afraid of what was happening, her fear was nothing compared to his own. The knowledge was strangely reassuring.

"It's all right," she whispered. "You're not alone." She sank her fingertips into the perspiration-slick skin of his powerful shoulders and pulled him back down on top of her. She cradled him between her thighs and covered his hard, alchemist's face with hot, fervent kisses.

Harry shuddered in surrender. "Molly." His mouth closed over hers.

She opened herself for him. She sensed that Harry had been struggling with the dark hunger for years. He had chained the driving need with the force of his self-control. But that formidable willpower had been breached tonight. *Just as it had the first time they had made love,* Molly realized. Now she knew what it was that had been different.

"Together," she whispered. "We do this together." She lifted herself, curling her legs around him.

"Molly. God, Molly." Harry reached down between their damp bodies, centered himself. He entered her with a long, shuddering sigh.

He filled her completely, stretching her to the limit. He began to move with deep, powerful, surging strokes. The rhythm was flawless. It was as if he could read her body, understood it, knew what was required to satisfy it. He was tuned to her, just as she was tuned to him.

Molly's climax was upon her with such suddenness that she could not even cry out. She simply gave herself up to it. It went through her in shock waves.

She was vaguely aware of Harry's harsh shout of satisfaction as he shook in the throes of his own release.

He collapsed heavily on top of her. Satisfaction radiated from him. It was a satisfaction that went beyond the physical.

Molly understood his satiated sensation because it reverberated through her.

Wholeness.

Completion.

Consummation.

Hours of boredom broken by moments of stark terror.

The words beat relentlessly through Harry's head until they finally succeeded in waking him. He opened his eyes reluctantly. He was obsessive on the subject of truth, but at that moment he would have traded his soul for a fistful of lies that he could tell himself.

His worst nightmare had come true. Molly had seen the darkness in him. All of it. She had stood beside him, held his hand, and looked down into the abyss.

Olivia's words came back to haunt him.

And then the sex got . . . well, it got weird, Harry. . . .

But Olivia had never even gotten close to the real truth. She had experienced nothing more than a small hint of the reality that Molly had faced. For Olivia, that pale shadow of the true darkness had been more than enough to scare the daylights out of her.

Tonight, Harry knew that he had exposed Molly to the entire production. A shroud of despair settled over him. He had lost everything.

Molly stirred. Harry turned his head on the pillow and made himself look into her moonlit face. He would face the rejection in her. He would confront the full weight of his loss. And know that he had only himself to blame.

Molly smiled with drowsy, dreamy warmth. "So, have you given any more thought to the idea of having kids?"

Harry felt as if the world had fallen away beneath his feet. All of his fine reflexes turned to mush. He could only stare at her, amazed, bewildered, hardly daring to hope. It took him a while to find his tongue.

"Kids?" he finally got out.

"I really think you ought to consider the subject."

"Kids."

"Yes. With me."

"With you?"

She gave him an expectant look. "Probably best not to wait too long. Neither of us is getting any younger."

"Kids. With you." He could not seem to collect his thoughts.

She touched his cheek with gentle, questing fingers. Her eyes were luminous. "I know I'm not exactly your idea of the perfect wife. I remember the list very clearly."

His mouth was dry. He had to swallow. "What list?"

"The list of all the reasons why we aren't well suited. *I say tomayto, you say tomahto.*"

He shook his head, dazed. "Tomatoes were on your list, not mine."

"Were they? Yes, I guess they were, come to think of it. Your list had other stuff on it, didn't it? Boring stuff. Temperamentally different, you said. No interests in common outside of our mutual concern with the grant proposals. Just two ships passing in the night, you said."

"No." Harry levered himself up on one elbow and leaned over her. He curved a hand around her bare thigh, savoring the sleek feel of her. "I never said anything about ships passing in the might. I'd remember."

She reached up to curl a strand of his hair around one fingertip. "Maybe it was something about the fact that I didn't have a Ph.D. to hang on the wall next to yours."

"No. I never said anything about your not having a Ph.D., either."

"You're sure?"

"I'm certain."

"Absolutely, positively certain?"

"Yes," Harry muttered. "Absolutely, positively. Molly, before we got off on this tangent, you said something about kids."

"It was a subtle hint."

He drew a deep, steadying breath. "Are you asking me to marry you?"

"That's what I like about a well-educated man. If he contemplates the obvious long enough, he finally gets a clue." Molly smiled. "Will you marry me, Harry?"

He fought for the words. "What about . . ."

"What about what?"

He clamped his teeth together. "What about the hours of boredom broken by moments of stark terror?"

"What about 'em? So far I haven't encountered any boring parts yet."

"What about the other?" he made himself ask. "Molly, I swear to God, I don't understand what happened when we made love earlier. I don't want to understand it. I just know that sometimes, if I'm caught off guard, I get . . . too intense or something."

"You know what I think? I think there's something to that business about the Trevelyan Second Sight."

He closed his eyes in despair. "You can't be serious."

"Harry, an intelligent person must remain open to all possibilities. I believe a noted authority on the history of science once wrote that it is a dangerous illusion to believe that one can always distinguish the possible from the impossible."

"I wrote that."

"As I said, a noted authority. I happen to agree with you. I come from a long line of flaky inventors who flourished because they refused to be bound by the illusion of certainty. I think we have to consider the possibility that you've got a trace of some kind of paranormal sixth sense."

"No."

She ignored him. "It's possible that when some heavy-duty emotion, such as sexual desire, kicks in, the elevated intensity of your feelings adds energy to your extrasensory abilities."

"Molly . . ."

"In those moments of heightened sensitivity, perhaps it becomes possible for some unusual things to happen. Maybe some of your innermost thoughts can spill over into the mind of whoever happens to be, uh, intimately connected to you."

"That's crazy. Utterly without scientific basis."

"Just a logical explanation for something that cannot otherwise be explained. Now, will you stop muttering and give me an answer to my question?"

Harry took a serious grip on a universe that seemed to be spinning out of control around him. He pulled her down on top of him. Spearing his fingers through her wonderful, unruly hair, he wrapped his hand around the back of her head and held her still for a deep kiss.

His answer was in that kiss, but just in case she had not understood, Harry said the words aloud. "I'll marry you."

Sixteen

"You're going to marry Harry Trevelyan?" Venicia kicked aside the lace-trimmed train of the billowing, white wedding gown. She turned away from her image in the mirror to stare at Molly in stunned amazement. "You can't possibly be serious."

Molly, seated in a small chair, flapped her hand in a small, hushing gesture. "I am. Very serious."

She was aware that the saleswoman behind the counter was eavesdropping. Another customer politely averted her head, but it was obvious that she, too, was all ears.

The boutique, which specialized in bridal gowns and dresses for members of the wedding party, was not very large. Venicia's exclamation of dismay had not gone unnoticed.

"But my dear, you said yourself, you and Trevelyan have absolutely nothing in common," Venicia continued, oblivious to Molly's unsubtle signal for silence. "You said he agreed with you."

"I think he's decided we have more in common than he first thought." Molly studied the lines of the wedding gown with a critical eye. "Are you sure you want to fuss with that long train?"

"What? Oh, the train. I've always wanted to wear a gown with a train." Venicia brightened briefly as she shook out the satin skirts. "I feel like a different woman in this gown. Lord knows, I couldn't even afford a new dress when your uncle and I were married. This time around, I'm going to do it right. Cutter insists."

"Good for you." Molly had a sudden inspiration. "You know something? I think I'll do the same thing."

"What on earth are you talking about?"

"I'm going to pull out all the stops for my wedding, too. Fancy gown, catered reception, the works. I can afford it, and it would be good for Harry."

"Good for Harry?" Venicia's delight in her own plans vanished once more. "I was afraid this would happen. Cutter has been very worried, also. We both feared you were becoming too involved with Trevelyan."

"I'm involved, all right."

"Molly, please listen to me. I'm well acquainted with the effects of romantic chemistry these days. Cutter is an extremely romantic man, after all. But you're old enough to understand that there's a difference between a flash-in-the-pan passion and true love."

"Sure."

"You want what Cutter and I have." Venicia's eyes misted briefly. "True affection and commitment."

"Of course."

"Dear, I really don't think you'll find that sort of thing with Trevelyan. He's not your type at all. You must take a more realistic view of your relationship with him."

"I am taking a realistic view of it." Far more realistic than anyone could possibly guess, Molly thought wistfully.

Realistic meant understanding that Harry was different.

Realistic meant accepting that he had a long way to go before he would allow himself to admit that he was in love, assuming he ever could admit it. He had an abhorrence of that which could not be explained logically. There was no denying that Harry had too much to untangle within himself before he could deal with such an illogical emotion as love.

Realistic meant accepting that Harry was a man at war with his own nature.

Last night in the crucible of the passion that had flared between them, Molly had finally comprehended the deepest truth about Harry. It was not that he was haunted by his parents' deaths, as Olivia had assumed.

Although he would no doubt suffer from occasional nightmares for the rest of his life, Molly sensed that Harry had found ways to deal with the terrible memories. The proof of his resilience lay in the core of willpower and inner strength that had enabled him to live a productive life.

The trauma of that episode had not stopped him from carving out a notable career, nor had it kept him from being a good father figure to Josh. Harry coped with his exacting work and his equally exacting families quite well. He had told Molly that the nightmares had become increasingly rare in the past few years.

No. Although he would never completely escape the lingering sense of guilt he experienced whenever he thought about the way his parents had died, Molly knew that Harry could deal with it. That was not his real problem.

Harry's real problem was that he was being slowly split asunder by the powerful forces of his own nature. It had all become so painfully clear last night.

For a man of learning and logic, a modern-day Renaissance man who prided himself on his intellectual prowess and his self-mastery, there could be no more threatening concept than the idea that he might possess a paranormal sixth sense. A sense that could not be explained or comprehended was anathema.

Harry could not even bring himself to believe in the possibility of paranormal abilities, let alone accept the fact that he might actually be endowed with some.

Realistic meant being patient while Harry struggled to unite the two sharply divided elements within himself. His talent for rationalizing the situation was astounding, Molly thought wryly. With true Trevelyan sleight of hand, he had pulled off the very neat trick of occasionally tapping his sixth sense without admitting to himself that he even possessed it. Insight, he called it.

Insight, my big toe, Molly thought. Whatever Harry's sixth sense was, it was a lot more than reasoned insight. And on some level he knew that. That was what was tearing him apart.

Oh, yes, she was being excruciatingly, painfully, realistic about her relationship with Harry.

Realistic meant accepting that his talent, whatever it was, might very well prevent him from ever experiencing the emotion of love in the same way that normal people experienced it.

Molly was absolutely certain that they shared a bond, and she was sure that Harry realized it. The deep hunger in him was undeniable, as was the satisfaction they found together. But she could not even begin to guess how Harry interpreted the nature of that bond.

She would have given a great deal to have a slightly more unrealistic view of the situation, Molly thought. She was, after all, about to marry a man who had never even told her that he loved her.

Of course, she hadn't told him that she loved him, either.

Venicia seemed unaware of Molly's distracted air. "The thing is," she continued forcefully, "you're not exactly a poor woman, Molly. I hate to say this, dear, but a lady in your situation must seriously question a man's interest in her before she commits herself to marriage. Surely you learned that lesson from your experience with Gordon Brooke."

"You're not living below the poverty line, either, Venicia. But you don't seem concerned about Cutter's interest in you."

"That's different, and you know it. Cutter is quite comfortably well off in his own right. You've seen the yacht and the house on Mercer Island. He has an established background."

"So does Harry."

"I know he's a member of the Stratton family, but you heard Cutter explain that he's not in line for any of the money."

"Harry doesn't want the Stratton money. He's got enough of his own."

"You mean from his books and consulting fees? Dear, that sort of income would hardly make him wealthy. He writes academic tomes, not best-sellers that get made into films. I'm sure the consulting business pays quite handsomely by most people's standards, but it can't possibly compete with your own income. You are a very wealthy woman, Molly."

"Only when you consider the assets of the Abberwick Foundation."

"One can hardly ignore them. You control those assets, my dear. And that's just my point. It was bad enough when Cutter and I were concerned that Trevelyan was planning to skim off exorbitant fees for his consulting services. Now we've got to wonder if he's marrying you in order to get his hands on the foundation income."

"Set your mind at ease," Molly said. "Harry was not exactly pushing for marriage. As a matter of fact, technically speaking, he never even asked me to marry him."

Venicia looked dumbfounded. "He didn't?"

"I'm the one who proposed to him," Molly explained. "And it wasn't easy. I had to drag the appropriate response out of him."

Harry might possess an unusual talent for seeing beneath the surface, Molly thought, but he was blind as a bat in some ways.

"I don't believe this. You're going to marry him?" Tessa's expression was every bit as astonished as Venicia's had been. "I thought this was supposed to be just an affair or something."

"Things change." Molly opened the copy of the *Post-Intelligencer* that was lying on her desk and surveyed the ad for Abberwick Tea & Spice. "This looks great. Terrific placement. Right next to an article on the health benefits of tea drinking."

Tessa glanced at the ad. "My friend at the newspaper told me that the article was planned for today's issue. I got the ad department to cooperate."

"Nice going. Remind me to give you a raise one of these days."

"Will do. Look, are you sure you know what you're doing here, boss?"

"Well, maybe a raise would be overkill. How about a nice letter of commendation for your file?"

"I'm not talking about my raise," Tessa said. "I'm talking about your marriage plans. Your aunt and her fiancé are worried about Trevelyan's intentions. I heard them talking to you the other day."

"They think he's after the assets of the Abberwick Foundation." Molly frowned. "Actually, I think it was Cutter who put the idea into my aunt's head."

"I hate to be the one to say this, Molly, but it's not exactly a paranoid thought. In fact, it's a realistic possibility. The only reason you even met Trevelyan in the first place was because of the foundation."

"I'm the one who found him, remember? He didn't come looking for me."

"Yes, but he certainly moved fast enough after you introduced yourself, didn't he? Molly, let's get real. I know you're a successful businesswoman, and you've done a terrific job raising your kid sister. I realize that you had the full financial responsibility of your family after your mother died."

"So?"

"So, while I'll admit that you've had some experience with harsh reality, you haven't had a lot of experience with the male of the species. Molly, what do you know about this guy?"

"Enough."

"Bull. You knew a lot more about Gordon Brooke, and look how that ended."

"I seriously doubt that I'll ever walk into a room and find Harry boffing a counter assistant on a pile of coffee bean sacks."

Tessa threw up her hands. "Can you be sure of that?"

Molly smiled. "Absolutely, positively."

"But *how* can you be sure?"

Molly considered the matter briefly. She could think of no way to describe the bond she sensed existed between herself and Harry. There was no way to explain that if anything ever happened to sever that bond, she would be aware of it immediately. Things would not get to the counter assistant boffing stage without her sensing well in advance that something had gone dreadfully wrong in the relationship.

But even without that intuitive knowledge, Molly knew that she had logic and reason on her side. Harry's relationships with his difficult relatives proved that he had a history of making commitments and sticking by them, even when he wasn't given much encouragement. And she intended to give him plenty of encouragement.

"Harry's the loyal type," Molly said simply.

Tessa's nose ring quivered as she drew a deep, resigned breath. "Have you told Kelsey?"

"No. She's very busy at that summer workshop. I don't want to distract her. I'll give her the news when she comes home." Molly smiled. "You and Kelsey can both be bridesmaids."

"Don't tell me you're planning a traditional wedding?"

"With all the trimmings," Molly assured her.

Harry wandered slowly through the darkened corridors of the Seattle Aquarium. His attention shifted from one illuminated display tank to the next. Cold, emotionless eyes gazed out at him as though aware of his presence.

A chill moved through him. He could almost feel the creatures on the other side of the glass assessing him. He knew that as far as a fish was concerned, he fell into one of two categories. He was either food or a threat.

The world was simple when one possessed a simple brain governed by simple imperatives, Harry thought. Decisions were easy. Choices were limited. Complex emotions were nonexistent.

One didn't need complicated, disturbing emotions when one was trapped forever in the dark abyss. Only the simple ones were required. Anger. Fear. Hunger. There was no room for hope.

Harry paused in front of a large tank occupied by several cold-eyed denizens. He drew a deep breath, allowing the memories of last night to flood him with warmth.

Molly wanted him. She was not afraid of the darkness in him. She had asked him to marry her. She wanted to have babies with him.

Harry let the knowledge sink into his soul. Flames flickered in the darkness.

He gazed into the display tank for a while longer, and then he turned and walked out of the shadowed passages of the aquarium.

Outside Molly waited for him in the bright sunlight.

He stopped at the entrance and gazed at her with a sense of wonder. She leaned against the pier railing, her honey-colored hair dancing around her vibrant face. She smiled with welcome when she spotted him amid the crowd of joggers, tourists, and lunch-bound office workers.

Harry watched, bemused, as she waved and hurried toward him with the eagerness of a lover. Not just a lover, he thought. His future wife.

"Here I am, Harry."

An indefinable sensation washed through him. As it receded, it left behind traces of raw vulnerability. But for some reason the knowledge did not terrify him the way it would have done a few days ago.

"I'm starved," Molly said breathlessly as she reached him.

"Me, too." He took her arm and walked her toward an outdoor café.

"Something wrong?" she asked.

"I'm not sure."

"What's that supposed to mean?" She gave him a look of anxious inquiry. "Harry? What is it?"

"Probably nothing."

"Uh-oh. You've had another one of your insights, haven't you?"

"Maybe. I'll tell you the details after we get our clams and chips."

Harry realized that he was no longer amazed by her perception. Somewhere along the line he had come to accept the fact that she would almost always recognize his various moods. She would know when he was merely feeling in a contemplative or reflective frame of mind and when he was seriously concerned.

Not even his parents had understood him as well as Molly did. No one had ever understood him so well. It was an unsettling thought.

Ten minutes later they sat down at a small, round table that was protected from the sidewalk traffic by a low, decorative barrier.

Harry drizzled malted vinegar over his fried clams and considered where to begin. "I've been going through Kendall's notebook."

"Find anything interesting?"

"Nothing more than what we already discovered. I've gone through every page of the book. There isn't any other reference to his plans to terrorize you other than those sketches of the machines he used to set up his damn pranks."

"No notes about his desire for revenge?"

"Nothing like that. The brief descriptions of the pistol assembly and the goblin were all very businesslike."

Molly paused in the act of stuffing a french fry into her mouth. "Businesslike?"

"You know what I mean." Harry moved his hand in a vague gesture. "It's as if the plans for those gadgets were nothing more than just designs for ordinary, routine projects."

"Hmm." Molly munched thoughtfully. "No passion in them, is that it?"

Harry considered her succinct description. She had put her finger on what was bothering him. "Maybe that's it. You'd think a man bent on vengeance would display more emotion toward the project. An inventor's sketches are unique to the individual. They convey a great deal to the trained eye."

Molly nodded. "I've seen the differences in my sister's drawings when she's really excited about a project. Lots of strong, positive lines. There's an eagerness and enthusiasm in them."

"Exactly. I was once asked to examine some notebook sketches made by a man who planned to blow up a research lab because he believed the company had stolen his ideas. He had made some drawings of an explosive device he planned to mail anonymously to the research facility."

"And?"

Harry ate another clam. "And there was something in those sketches that was not in his other work. An intensity, an outrage. You could almost feel the anger radiating off the page."

"Insight or intuition?"

He scowled. "Neither. It was similar to interpreting someone's handwriting. You could see the rage and the craziness in it."

"You could see it, but I'll bet very few other people could. What happened to the crazed inventor?"

"He got caught trying to mail the explosive device," Harry said absently.

Molly smiled. "He got caught because you deduced what he was about to do from his sketches and the cops staked him out, right?"

Harry shrugged. "I was asked to give my opinion on the drawings. I told the cops that it was a safe bet the guy intended to kill someone with his device. I also told them that, judging from the skilled details of the sketches, the device would probably work."

"My, you do lead an exciting life, Harry."

"Actually, it was a rather placid existence until you came into it."

Molly grinned. "I don't believe that for a minute."

"To be blunt," Harry said deliberately, "I can do without some of the added excitement you've brought into my life. Unfortunately, I don't foresee it fading until they catch Kendall."

"They'll catch him," Molly predicted. "You heard the detective who talked to us yesterday. They'll track him down now that they know he's truly dangerous. Want to talk about our wedding plans?"

Harry nearly choked on a fried clam. It was the first time she had mentioned the subject of marriage since she had proposed last night. He grabbed his iced tea and took a deep swallow.

Molly frowned in concern. "Are you all right?"

"Yes." He took another slug of tea and set the cup down with great precision. He cleared his throat. "I was thinking of something simple. Vegas, maybe."

"I was thinking of something large and magnificent," Molly said.

Harry eyed her warily. "Do you have a lot of friends to invite?"

"Yes. And then there's all those Strattons and Trevelyans."

Harry raised his brows. "Are you kidding? The Strattons and Trevelyans won't sit in the same room together long enough for a preacher to say the magic words."

"Hmm."

"Forget the fancy wedding. It'll have to be a courthouse marriage or Vegas. Take your pick." Harry paused. "If you're still serious about this, that is."

"Oh, I'm very serious about it," Molly assured him.

Harry's stomach unclenched. He downed the rest of his fried clams with a curious sense of relief.

Molly sat alone in the front room of Harry's condominium the following evening and listened to the silence. It was an unnatural sort of silence. A silence fraught with meaning and portent.

Olivia was in Harry's study. She had been in there alone with him for nearly twenty minutes. The door of the study was firmly closed.

Molly had immediately excused herself when Olivia had made it clear that she wished to speak to Harry alone. Harry had not appeared pleased at the prospect of a private interview with his ex-fiancée, but he had accepted the situation with his usual stoicism.

Molly watched the late summer twilight give way to night and thought about Olivia and Harry. It was difficult to see what Harry had thought he'd had in common with his ex-fiancée other than a Ph.D. It was odd that a man who had a talent for insight had made such a mistake in his personal life. He did appear to have a gift for shooting himself in the foot every time he tried to apply his intellectual abilities to matters of emotion.

Molly glanced at the clock. Another five minutes had passed. She went back to the book she had been trying to read.

The study door opened. Molly put one arm on the back of the couch and turned her head to see Olivia walking toward her. There was no sign of Harry.

"Finished?" Molly asked politely.

"Yes. It was family business."

Molly nodded. "Harry gets a lot of that."

Olivia frowned. "I beg your pardon?"

"Never mind. Inside joke."

Olivia glanced back at the study door with a look of irritation. "Harry's in one of his moods."

"He's probably just thinking. Can I make you a cup of tea?"

"No, thank you. Harry got a business call just as I was getting ready to leave. He's still on the phone."

Molly started to rise. "I'll see you out."

"That won't be necessary." Olivia's smile was cool. "I know my way around here."

"I'm sure you do."

"He tells me that the two of you are going to be married."

"That's right." Molly gave Olivia her most winning smile. "I'm planning a big wedding, by the way."

"Are you?"

"Everyone from both sides of his family will be invited, of course."

"That should be interesting." Olivia hesitated. "I'd like to ask you a personal question, if you don't mind."

"Okay. I can't guarantee an answer, though."

"Are you sure you know what you're doing?"

"Yes, thank you."

Olivia's mouth tightened. She glanced again at the closed study door. "I probably shouldn't tell you this, but in my professional opinion, Harry has some serious problems. He ought to be in therapy."

"Harry is different, I'll give you that. But I don't think a shrink will do him any good."

"I'm sorry, but I know him a great deal better than you do, and I think it's a mistake for him to marry. Any marriage that Harry enters into is bound to fail."

"Are you nuts?"

Olivia gave her a cold stare. "You do realize that I am a clinical psychologist, don't you?"

"Harry told me. I have a great deal of respect for your professional expertise, Olivia, but I don't think you understand Harry very well. He's quite unique."

"He's dysfunctional, not unique," Olivia snapped. "He's very likely suffering from posttraumatic stress disorder and periodic bouts of depression. To be quite honest, he's an excellent candidate for medication."

"A candidate for medication?" Molly wrinkled her nose. "I don't think he's interested in running for that office."

"I'm not joking, Molly. This is a serious matter. I cannot advise you to marry a man with Harry's problems."

"Relax, you're off the hook. I'm not asking for your advice."

Olivia glared at her in obvious frustration. "Look, I'll be frank. You and Harry haven't known each other very long. Your relationship is still in its early phase. I think you should know that sooner or later Harry will demonstrate some clinically significant abnormalities in his sexual relationship with you."

Molly held up a hand. "Hold it right there. I'm not one of your patients. I have no intention of discussing my sex life with you."

"I'm trying to save you from making a terrible mistake."

"You don't have to worry about saving me from Harry."

Olivia narrowed her eyes. "You do realize he's not in line for any of the Stratton fortune, don't you? He quarreled with his grandfather. He won't see a dime."

"Money has nothing to do with this. Good night, Olivia."

"You're either very stupid or very foolish."

Molly grinned. "You mean I have a choice?"

Olivia swung around on her heel and went swiftly down the hall toward the front door. She let herself out without a word of farewell. The door slammed shut behind her.

Molly saw Harry lounging, arms folded, in the entrance of his study. He gazed thoughtfully after Olivia for a long moment. Then he met Molly's eyes.

"Clinically significant abnormalities?" he repeated slowly.

"You heard that, did you?"

"Only the last part. Did she give you her complete diagnosis?"

"Yes, but I wouldn't put too much stock in her theories if I were you. She is one weird shrink. That's why she probably became a shrink in the first place. She was looking for answers to her own problems."

His mouth curved slightly. "I see."

"Which is not to say that I don't believe that one can't get a great deal of help from a good therapist," Molly continued with scrupulous honesty. "But one does need to select one's therapist with great care."

"Care."

"Right. There's all that business with transference and countertransference, you see. One has to find a therapist whose own hang-ups don't get in the way of treating the patient's."

"You sound like an expert."

"I consulted a therapist for a while after my mother died," Molly said. "As a matter of fact, I consulted half a dozen of the little suckers before I found one I could talk to. I went to her a few times. She helped me work through some stuff."

"What kind of stuff?"

Molly hesitated, reflecting back on those difficult days and the dreadful fear she had faced at the age of twenty. "A feeling of being overwhelmed by the responsibilities I knew I had to handle. Some anger at being stuck with those responsibilities. My therapist was good. I only saw her a handful of times because I couldn't afford her for long. But I got a lot out of our little chats."

Harry smiled fleetingly. "I guess that makes you an expert, all right."

Molly eyed him thoughtfully. "It doesn't require expertise, just plain old common sense, to figure out that Olivia is not qualified to diagnose you. She's got her own problems, and they're connected to you."

Acute interest burned in Harry's eyes. "What kind of problems?"

"Isn't it obvious?"

"Not to me."

"The two of you have a history. At the very least, I'd say she feels guilty about having ended the engagement. She's probably rationalized her actions by telling you and herself that you've got psychological problems that make it impossible for you to have a healthy relationship."

"You don't think she might be right?"

"Heck, no." Molly smiled. "You're different, Harry. Definitely one of a kind. But you're going to make a terrific husband and father."

Harry was silent for a moment. "Maybe you have a thing for clinically significant abnormalities," he suggested.

"Maybe I do. Who was that on the phone?"

"Fergus Rice, the private investigator I hired to keep tabs on Kendall."

"Did he discover something?" Molly asked.

"Two hours ago Wharton Kendall drove a blue Ford over a cliff somewhere along Highway One in Oregon. He was apparently heading for California. Kendall was killed in the crash."

It took a few seconds for the significance of that simple statement to sink in. When it did, Molly leaped off the sofa and raced across the room to Harry.

"It's over," she whispered as she threw herself into his arms.

Harry's arms tightened around her. "That's what Rice said."

Seventeen

"All right, that's it. I've had it." Molly sat straight up in bed and turned to glower at Harry. "Enough is enough. What's wrong? Why aren't you asleep?"

Harry slanted her a surprised glance from beneath his lashes. The sheet was crushed to his waist. His arms were folded behind his head. The expression on his savage features was one of intent concentration.

"I'm thinking," he said.

"Your thinking is giving me a severe case of insomnia."

"Sorry. I didn't realize I was keeping you awake."

"How am I supposed to sleep when you're lying there staring at the ceiling?"

"Why should it bother you if I stare at the ceiling?" he asked with what appeared to be genuine curiosity.

"Darned if I know, but it does. It's as if you're humming in my brain or something. It's keeping me awake."

"I can't help it. When I think, I think."

"Nope. This definitely isn't the sort of humming I hear when you're just thinking. I can sleep through that. This humming is more like a seriously-concerned-that-we-may-have-a-very-big-problem-on-our-hands kind of humming."

His eyes narrowed. "What the hell is this stuff about me humming in your head?"

She shrugged. "I can't explain it. It's just sort of a sensation I've been getting lately. Don't you feel it?"

"No." Harry seized the edge of the sheet and started to shove it aside. "Look, if I'm keeping you awake, I'll go into the front room."

"No, you won't." Molly caught him by his bare shoulder and pulled him down onto the pillow. "Stay right where you are."

He relaxed against the pillow without protest, one brow raised in polite inquiry.

Molly punched her own pillow a few times and adjusted it against the headboard behind her. "Now, then, tell me what the problem is."

He hesitated for only a couple of seconds before he seemed to come to a decision. "It's Kendall's notebook."

"You're still worrying about that? But I thought we had decided that our problems are over now that Kendall is dead."

"There's something wrong with that notebook." Harry levered himself up to a sitting position beside her and arranged his own pillow behind his back. "I just wish I could put my finger on it."

"You said that you didn't think the drawings of the gun and goblin mechanisms conveyed a sense of extreme rage."

"Yes, but that's not what's bothering me now."

Molly studied him in the shadows. "What, exactly, is bothering you?"

"It's the way the intruder went after you the other day in your house. There was something about the way he did it that doesn't fit with the designs in Kendall's notebook."

Molly shivered. "It all seemed very efficient to me."

"That's just it," Harry said softly. "It was efficient. Straightforward. Simple. Not very creative. Or personal."

"I guess that depends on your definition of creativity. And I can assure you that I took the attempt very personally." Molly blinked as realization struck her. "Uh-oh. I think I see where you're going with this."

Harry drummed the long, lean fingers of his right hand absently against the sheet beside him. "If a man such as Kendall was bent on murder, he would be inclined to use a gadget of his own design to kill his victim."

"Harry, maybe you're carrying your deductive insights a little too far here."

"He used gadgets to try to terrorize you," Harry said, oblivious to the interruption. "It's logical that he would have come up with something in the same vein if he went so far as to try to murder you."

"Uh, Harry . . ."

"A mechanism that he had designed and built, himself. A device of his own invention, one that would have given him satisfaction when it worked properly. The same logic applies to his use of a car to try to run us off the road. It doesn't fit."

Molly reached out to touch his arm. "Now, hold on here. The blue Ford belonged to Kendall. You said your investigator, Mr. Rice, verified that it was registered to him."

"Yes."

"So it's only logical to assume that it was Kendall at the wheel the other day when that same Ford tried to run us off the road."

"Someone else could have used Kendall's car to try to kill us."

"But no one else has any reason to kill us."

"So far as we know." Harry looked out into the darkness beyond the windows. "I've been lying here wondering if someone else is involved in this."

Molly pulled the bedclothes up to her throat. "All right, let's assume for the moment that there is another person involved. What's his or her motive? We decided Kendall was out for revenge because I turned down his grant proposal."

"It was a logical assumption." Harry pushed aside the covers and got out of bed. "But what if there was another person with another motive?"

Molly watched him as he started to pace the room in front of the bank of windows. She could feel the intensity pooling within him as he focused on the problem at hand. Harry was nude except for a pair of white briefs that hugged his strongly muscled flanks. There was an eerie, spectral quality about him as he moved in and out of the moonlight.

"What other person?" she asked gently. "And what other motive could there possibly be? I've turned down approximately a hundred grant proposals. I suppose we could be dealing with more than one disgruntled grant applicant. But it seems a little unlikely that we'd have two homicidal inventors in the batch."

"Who knows?" Harry paced through a shaft of cold, silver light and on into the deep shadow at the far end of the room.

"It would also imply," Molly continued, thinking through the obvious logic, "that at some point Kendall and this other mystery inventor worked together on their little terrorist project."

"Or it could mean that someone else knew about Kendall's desire for revenge and used it as camouflage for himself."

"Good lord." Molly drew up her knees and wrapped her arms around them. "Are you saying that another, more vicious individual who actually wants to kill me knew that Kendall was angry? And set him up to take the rap once I was dead?"

"There's a certain logic to it." Harry reached the bookcase, turned, and retraced his path toward the opposite end of the room. The force of his concentration was so powerful that it seemed to charge the atmosphere around him.

"I don't know," Molly said doubtfully. "It's awfully farfetched. Chances are that, with Kendall dead, the whole thing really is finished, just as Fergus Rice said."

Harry came to a halt in front of the windows. "It doesn't feel finished, Molly."

She smiled slightly. "Then you'll have to do something about it, won't you? If you don't, neither of us will ever get any sleep."

He looked at her, his eyes bleak. "It's beginning to look that way."

"Any ideas?"

"It might help if I could examine something else that belonged to Kendall," Harry said slowly. "It might give me a fix on whether or not I'm right about his preference for inventing his own weapons."

"It occurs to me that, if there is someone else involved in this mess, Kendall's recent demise might not have been an accident."

"Hell." Icy moonlight turned Harry's face to stone. "You're right. I've been concentrating so much on the possibility that there are two people involved that I didn't consider all the implications. If Kendall had a partner, or if he was being used as a fall guy by someone else, that second person might have gotten rid of him because he had become a liability."

"This is getting very complicated, not to mention nasty."

Harry swung away from the window. "I need to get a look at that blue Ford. Rice can find out where it was taken after the crash."

"It's after one in the morning. Fergus Rice will be sound asleep. He won't be able to do anything at this hour." Molly yawned. "Why don't you come back to bed?"

"I'm in no mood to sleep."

She gave him a smugly angelic smile. "In that case, perhaps we could discuss a few of your significant clinical abnormalities."

Harry, who was halfway across the room, en route to the telephone, spun around. There was a strange glitter in his eyes. "What did you say?"

"Don't you like it when I talk dirty?"

"Molly . . ."

"Come back to bed, Harry." She patted the sheet beside her. "There's absolutely nothing you can do until after breakfast. If you can't sleep, we'll find some way to fill the time."

He hesitated. Then the taut lines of his face relaxed slightly. He walked to the side of the bed and looked down at her with a thoughtful expression that was belied by the extraordinarily brilliant gleam in his eyes.

"Significant clinical abnormalities?" he murmured.

"What can I say? I'm a sucker for 'em. Yes, sir, give me those hours of boredom followed by moments of stark terror, and I'm a happy camper."

Harry's teeth flashed in a lethally sexy grin. He put one knee on the bed and leaned down, trapping her between his arms. "I eat happy campers for bedtime snacks."

"Can't wait." She put her arms around his neck and pulled him down on top of her.

He came to her in a rush of sensual, startlingly playful energy. He seized hold of her and rolled over and over with her until the sheets were tangled and Molly was laughing helplessly.

He finally brought the tumbling game to a halt near the foot of the bed and braced himself on his elbows above her.

Flushed and breathless, Molly looked up and saw the uninhibited joy in him.

"There is nothing quite like the taste of a happy camper," Harry murmured. His eyes gleamed in the shadows as he slid slowly down the length of her body. He settled himself between her legs.

Molly felt his teeth on the inside of her thigh. She gasped and dug her fingers into his shoulders. He parted her gently with his fingers.

"Harry?"

And then she felt his mouth on her in an unbearably intimate kiss.

The world came apart.

Molly shut the refrigerator door and set the box of fresh raspberries down on the counter next to the sink. "You know, Harry, I've been thinking. This condo of yours is nice enough and the view is terrific, but it's not very functional."

"Functional?" Harry echoed absently. He held the kitchen phone in one hand as he prepared to punch in Fergus Rice's phone number.

"You know, efficient. I miss my housekeeping machines. The dusting robots, the dishwasher, and the kitchen clean-up devices. The Abberwick Food Storage and Preparation Machine. Honestly, I don't know how you get along with these old-fashioned appliances. They're straight out of the Dark Ages."

"I've got a housekeeper, remember?" Harry listened impatiently as the phone rang on the other end of the line.

"Yes, I know, but still, it all seems so primitive."

Harry scowled as the phone rang for the third time. "Put that knife down."

"I was just going to slice some English muffins to go with the raspberries."

"I'll slice the muffins when I get off the phone."

"Sheesh. Are you always this grumpy in the morning?"

"Only when I see you with a knife in your hand." The phone continued to ring.

Molly set the knife aside and propped her elbows on the counter. "How do you feel about moving into my house after we're married?"

"The Abberwick mansion?" Harry glanced at the clock. It was nearly eight. Fergus usually went into his office early. "You want to stay in that crazy old house?"

"It's a great place for kids. They'd have Kelsey's and my old toys to play with. And you'd have plenty of room for your books. You could have one whole wing for your offices and library. The kids would be underfoot all the time, of course, but I think you'd like that."

Harry stopped listening to the phone, his full attention suddenly riveted on Molly. "Kids?"

"Sure. How many do you want? I know we're going to have at least two."

"Uh—" Harry broke off at the sound of Fergus's voice.

"Rice here."

"Fergus, it's Harry."

"For crying out loud, Harry, it's two minutes to eight. I just walked in the door. Haven't even had my second cup of coffee."

"I'm calling about the Kendall situation."

"What situation? I thought the accident down in Oregon took care of the problem. The man's dead, Harry."

"I know. But I want to examine his car. Where did the authorities take it?"

"It'll probably be hauled off to a wrecking yard sometime today. Something wrong?"

"I don't know. Have the authorities finished the accident investigation?"

"Sure. Finished it yesterday. It was all very straightforward. Nothing of a suspicious nature. The Ford was totaled, though. That kind of thing can happen to a car when it goes straight over a sheer cliff."

"Can you arrange for me to get a look at it?"

"I don't see why not." Fergus paused to make some notes. "I'll contact the owner of the wrecking yard this morning and set it up."

"Thanks, Fergus. Call me as soon as you've cleared it. I'll fly down to Portland and rent a car to drive to the coast."

"Right."

Harry replaced the receiver and looked at Molly. "He's going to arrange for me to examine the Ford."

"What do you think you'll be able to tell by looking at it?"

"I don't know." Harry watched Molly rinse the raspberries. "Maybe nothing."

She gave him a knowing look. "Or maybe something?"

"Rice says the authorities have already completed their investigation, but since they had no reason to suspect that Kendall was killed, they could have overlooked something."

"Such as?"

"I don't know. Sabotaged brakes. Evidence of an encounter with another car."

Molly nibbled thoughtfully on her lower lip. "You think maybe someone sideswiped Kendall?"

"The idea has a familiar ring to it, doesn't it?" The lobby intercom buzzed, breaking into Harry's chain of thought. "Who the hell could that be at this hour?"

"I'll give you two guesses." Molly gently piled the fragile raspberries into a bowl.

"Two guesses?"

"It's either a Stratton or a Trevelyan. Take your pick."

Harry raised his brows as he depressed the intercom button. "Yes?"

"Mr. Trevelyan, this is George downstairs in the lobby. There is a Mr. Hughes here to see you."

Harry groaned. "At this hour?"

"Yes, sir."

"Tell him this is important," Brandon said in the background.

There was a hard, determined edge to his voice. "Tell him it's a family matter."

"Send him up, George," Harry said. He released the intercom button.

"Want me to get lost?" Molly asked.

"No." Harry thought about his conversation with Olivia the previous evening. "Stay right where you are."

A few minutes later the front doorbell chimed discreetly. Harry reluctantly went to answer it. He was not feeling enthusiastic about the prospect of dealing with any of his relatives this morning. He had other things on his mind.

He opened the door. Brandon, dressed in a lightweight sweater and slacks, stood glowering in the hall.

"Good morning," Harry said mildly.

Brandon strode into the hall without a greeting. His expression was thunderous.

"Want a cup of coffee?" Harry asked as he closed the door.

Brandon ignored the polite inquiry. He swung around to confront Harry. "Olivia came here to see you last night."

"Yes."

"Damn it, I told her I didn't want her getting involved in this. I told my mother the same thing. Why the hell won't they stay out of it?"

"Probably because they're worried about you."

"I don't need anyone worrying about me. I can handle this thing just fine all by myself." Brandon stalked into the front room. He came to an abrupt halt when he saw Molly behind the kitchen counter. "Who are you? A new housekeeper?"

"No," Molly said. "I'm Harry's fiancée."

"His fiancée?" Brandon stared at her. "Olivia said something about Harry getting engaged to the trustee of the Abberwick Foundation. I didn't believe it."

"This is Molly Abberwick," Harry said, annoyed by the expression of amazement on Brandon's face. "Molly, this is my cousin Brandon Hughes. Aunt Danielle's son. Olivia's husband."

Molly nodded. "How do you do, Brandon? We're just about to eat. Have you had breakfast?"

"Yes. Thanks." Brandon's eyes narrowed. He glanced speculatively at Harry. "So this engagement is for real?"

"It's real, all right." Harry took his seat at the counter.

"Sort of sudden, isn't it?" Brandon asked.

"Time is relative." Molly gave Brandon a smile that was sweeter than the sugar she was spooning lightly over the berries. "Harry and I feel we know each other well enough to commit to marriage. Don't we, Harry?"

"Yes," Harry said. "Why don't you sit down, Brandon?"

"I'd rather talk to you in your study."

"Too bad. I'd rather eat breakfast." Harry glanced at the bowl of raspberries Molly had set in front of him. "Give me those muffins and the knife."

Wordlessly, Molly handed him the requested items. Harry went to work slicing the muffins.

"If you won't have coffee, how about some tea, Brandon?" Molly asked. "I'm making a pot for myself."

"No, thanks. Look, Harry, this is a personal matter." Brandon shot a quick look at Molly. "Family business."

"From now on," Harry said softly, "Molly is family. My family. Anything you want to say to me can be said in front of her."

Brandon's mouth compressed into a thin line. "The two of you are engaged, not married."

"Same thing as far as I'm concerned." Harry handed the neatly sliced muffins across the counter to Molly. "Talk if you want to talk. Otherwise, you can leave. I've got a busy day ahead."

Brandon took a step closer and lowered his voice. "Harry, let's be realistic here. Given your track record, I don't think you should be counting chickens until they're hatched."

"What the hell is that supposed to mean?" Harry asked.

"You want me to spell it out?"

"Yes."

"You know damn well what I'm trying to say." Brandon glanced uneasily at Molly, who smiled brightly in return. He turned back to Harry. "Look, this is a little awkward. Let's go into your study."

"No."

Brandon lost his temper. "I can hardly be expected to discuss sensitive matters in front of a stranger."

"I told you, Molly's not a stranger. She's going to be my wife."

Brandon reddened. "Not according to Olivia. She thinks this engagement isn't any more likely to survive than your other one did. And she should know."

"Think so?"

"She knows people, Harry. It's her job, remember?" Brandon had the grace to give Molly an apologetic look. "My wife is a clinical psychologist. One of the best in the city."

"Yes, I know," Molly said demurely. "We've met. She was kind enough to give me some free advice."

Brandon turned back to Harry. "I'm sure Molly is very discreet, and I have absolutely nothing against her. But until you actually get yourself married, I'm not prepared to discuss my business in front of an outsider."

Harry reached the end of his patience. He came up off the stool in a movement that caused Brandon to take a hurried step back.

"You came here to talk," Harry said very softly. "Say what you want to say or leave."

"All right, if that's the way you're going to be," Brandon said stiffly, "I'll come back later."

"I may not be here later," Harry said. "I've got plans for the day."

"You're doing this deliberately, aren't you? You're trying to make this as difficult for me as possible. What do you want me to do? Grovel to you just because you convinced Granddad to let me go out on my own?"

"Why don't you ask Olivia? She seems to think she's an authority on my motives." Harry sat down again and picked up his spoon.

"Whoa. Time out." Molly formed a referee's T with her hands. "I vote we call a truce here." She put a cup and saucer on the counter. "Here, have some coffee, Brandon. Gordon Brooke's finest. It's his Dark Seattle Roast."

Harry looked up from his raspberries. He was irritated. "I didn't know we were drinking a Gordon Brooke blend."

"Not me. You. Personally, I never touch the stuff. And don't look at me that way. Your housekeeper bought it."

"Remind me to have Ginny buy another brand." Harry went back to his raspberries. "Either sit down or leave, Brandon. I don't like having you hover while I eat."

Brandon fumed for a minute longer, and then he subsided onto a stool. He picked up the coffee cup Molly had given him and took a long swallow. When he was finished he set the cup down with a soft crash. "Okay, let's talk."

"I'm listening."

"I'm here because I want to discuss the financing of my new plans. Granddad has agreed to let me leave the company without any repercussions, which is a great relief to Mother and Olivia, but he won't help me."

"Hold it right there," Harry said. "I'm not a bank. I talked to Parker for you, but that's as far as I can go."

"That's not true. You know people, Harry." Brandon fiddled with his coffee cup. "I'm aware that you arranged financing for one of your Trevelyan relatives when she decided to buy that carnival amusement company."

"That was different."

"Yeah? How was it different? Don't your Stratton relatives count?"

"My Stratton relatives are all rich."

"Not all of them," Brandon said meaningfully. "When I leave Stratton Properties, I'm going to be on my own."

"Olivia charges her patients as much as a good tax attorney charges her clients. You won't starve."

"It's true, we'll have Olivia's income to live on until I establish myself," Brandon said. "But she can't afford to capitalize an operation the size of the one I'm planning. You know that as well as I do."

"So?" Harry could feel Molly watching him from the other side of the counter.

"So the banks won't touch me unless Stratton Properties is involved in the loan. Even if I could talk Granddad or Uncle Gilford into backing me, I'd rather not," Brandon said. "You know that if they're involved, they'll try to take over."

"True."

Brandon frowned. "I think I know why you never joined Stratton Properties."

"My interests lie in other areas."

"Tell me something. Did you know that when you came to live here in Seattle, the whole family was convinced that you were out to take your Stratton relatives for whatever you could get?"

Harry set his spoon down with great care. "That was evident from the start."

"Granddad said it was the Trevelyan blood in you. He said you would try to con us Strattons out of what you figured was your rightful inheritance. He said he wouldn't give you a dime unless you proved that you were a true Stratton."

"Which meant joining the company," Harry finished wearily. "Brandon, this is old history. What do you want from me?"

Brandon straightened his shoulders. "You've got some contacts with venture capitalists because of the technical consulting work you've done. I want you to introduce me to some of the money people. I'm not asking you to go out on a limb for me. I just want the introductions. I'll take it from there."

Harry looked at Molly. She gave him a wry, understanding smile but said nothing. He turned to Brandon. "I'll see what I can do."

Relief flared in Brandon's eyes. "Thanks." He got to his feet. "You won't regret this, Harry. Like I said, I'll make my presentations to the investors and take my chances. Just put me in touch with people who are interested in making sound investments."

"On one condition," Harry temporized.

"What's that?"

"Give me your word of honor that you'll do your best to stop Olivia from handing out her professional opinions of my psychological profile to all and sundry. It's getting to be annoying."

Brandon was plainly startled. He started to scowl, and then a spark of reluctant amusement lit his gaze. "I'll try, but it might not be easy."

"I know." Harry caught Molly's eye. "But I'd appreciate it if you could convince her to keep her diagnoses to herself. Just tell her some people don't mind hours of boredom broken by moments of stark terror."

Brandon looked mildly baffled. But he shrugged it off and turned to leave. Then he stopped and smiled at Molly. "Thanks for the coffee."

"You bet," she said. "Oh, by the way, Brandon, Harry and I are planning a big wedding. Everyone in both families will be invited. We'll expect you and Olivia, of course."

"Olivia and I will attend," Brandon said slowly. "But I wouldn't count on any of the others from the Stratton side of the family unless you can guarantee that none of the Trevelyans will be there."

"Everyone will be there," Molly repeated coolly.

Brandon glanced at Harry. Harry said nothing. He knew as well as Brandon did that there was no hope of getting all of the Strattons and Trevelyans to attend the wedding. Sooner or later, Molly would have to face that simple fact of life.

"Right, well, I'd better get going," Brandon said hastily. He headed toward the door, his step a good deal lighter than it had been when he entered earlier.

Eighteen

"How the hell can you be certain that Trevelyan's not marrying you in order to get his hands on the foundation assets?" Gordon grumbled as he scooped up the papers he had spread out on the counter. "That's all I want to know. How can you be so damned sure?"

Molly regarded Gordon with an acute sense of irritation. It was shortly after five. Tessa was in the storage room, finishing some labels for a mail order shipment. Harry would be here any moment. It was time to close the shop and go home.

Home.

It struck her that she was home when she was with Harry. She wondered if he felt the same way when he was with her. She hoped he did. He needed a sense of home more than any man she had ever known.

Gordon had appeared at the door of Abberwick Tea & Spice just as Molly was turning the CLOSED sign in the window. He had stuck one foot in the door and made another pitch for financing. Molly had allowed him to ramble on about his new expansion plans as she tidied the shop for the night. When he had finished his arguments in favor of using Abberwick funds to promote Gordon Brooke Espresso Bars, she had politely refused. Again.

Gordon had turned quite red in the face. He seemed unable to accept either her unwillingness to finance him or her engagement to Harry. The two seemed to be linked together in Gordon's mind, and for some reason it was the latter that apparently annoyed him the most.

"I just don't get it, Molly." Gordon dumped the papers into a leather file. "Why are you so sure you can trust him?"

"It's none of your business, is it?"

Gordon contrived to appear hurt. "We've known each other a long time. It's only natural that I'm concerned about you."

"Let's be honest here." Molly leaned against the spice counter and regarded Gordon with an impatience she did not bother to conceal. "What you're really asking me is how do I know that Harry is not another you, isn't it? How do I know I won't discover the hard way that he has a taste for pretty counter assistants?"

Gordon flushed. "Don't twist my words."

"I don't owe you any explanations," she continued. "But the truth is, I'm absolutely, positively certain that Harry is not another Gordon Brooke. How do I know this? I think it has something to do with the way he hums."

Gordon ignored that. "It's not a joke, damn it. I'm just trying to keep you from making a big mistake. One that could cost you a fortune."

"I doubt if it will cost me as much as financing several new Gordon Brooke Espresso Bars."

"The espresso bars would be an investment," Gordon insisted. "That's a whole different matter. This is your future I'm concerned about. Molly, you control a lot of money through the Abberwick Foundation. Chances are the assets will continue to grow through the years. How can you be sure that you'll be able to keep it out of Trevelyan's hands? You've made him your technical consultant, for Christ's sake."

"So?"

"So he'll be making all the important decisions."

"No, he won't. I will be making the important decisions." Molly was thoroughly irritated now. "Why does everyone assume that I'm a complete idiot when it comes to the Abberwick Foundation? What makes you think that I'm going to turn control of the assets over to Harry or anyone else?"

Gordon waved his hands in a soothing gesture. "Take it easy. Calm down. I was just trying to point out the facts."

"The heck you were. You're trying to undermine my relationship with my fiancé. I'm not going to listen to another word."

"Okay, okay. If that's the way you're going to be about it, fine. But don't blame me when you wake up some morning and discover the assets of the Abberwick Foundation have vanished sometime during the night."

"Out. Now."

"I'm leaving." Gordon clutched his file of papers and started to back toward the door. "But if you had an ounce of common sense, you'd—" He broke off abruptly as he collided heavily with Harry, who had just opened the door. "Ooph."

Harry didn't flinch under the impact, but Molly noticed that Gordon bounced a little.

Gordon recovered and swung around to see who was standing behind him. "What the hell are you doing here, Trevelyan?"

"I'm engaged to Molly, remember?" Harry said.

"You could have knocked," Gordon muttered.

"The door was unlocked."

"Gordon was just leaving." Molly gave Gordon a steely look. "Isn't that right?"

"Yeah, yeah, I'm on my way," Gordon grumbled.

"Don't let me stop you." Harry moved politely out of the doorway.

Tessa emerged from the storage room. "The labels are done, Molly. I'm off."

Molly stilled. She glanced at Tessa, and then she looked at Gordon.

"Gordon?" she said softly.

"What?" He turned to scowl at her from the doorway.

"Want some advice?"

He looked distinctly wary. "What sort of advice?"

Molly tapped one finger on the counter, thinking swiftly. "You put out a good product. I don't care for coffee, but I know that yours is some of the best in the city."

"So?"

"You got into trouble with your espresso bars because you expanded too rapidly," Molly said. "If you're serious about salvaging your business, you're going to have to pay closer attention to the basics of running your operation. You need professional advice regarding marketing techniques, packaging, and advertising."

"Yeah?" Gordon glared, half-defiant, half-intrigued. "Where do you suggest I get that advice?"

"From Tessa," Molly said.

A startled hush fell on the shop.

Tessa reacted first. "What are you talking about, Molly? Are you saying I should give Gordon the benefit of everything I've learned working for you?"

"Only if he's willing to pay for it," Molly murmured.

Tessa was incensed. "You actually want me to help the competition? You want me to show him how to beef up his advertising program? Redesign his packaging? Tell him how to handle suppliers? What would that make me?"

"A consultant," Harry said.

Tessa blinked. Then she met Gordon's eyes across the room.

"A consultant." Tessa savored the word.

"I couldn't afford much in the way of consulting fees," Gordon warned.

"That's okay," Tessa said smoothly. "I'll take a percentage of the profits."

"There aren't any at the moment," Gordon said.

Tessa glanced at Molly and then smiled. "There will be."

Gordon hesitated. "You want to go have a latte and talk about it?"

"Sure," Tessa said. "What have I got to lose?" She grabbed her oversized backpack and followed him out of the shop.

Harry raised one brow as the door closed behind the pair. "Should I be concerned about this sudden show of compassion for Brooke?"

Molly was surprised by the question. "I didn't do that for Gordon's sake. I did it for Tessa."

"I see."

"Tessa has a feel for sales and marketing," Molly said. "She's a natural, but she'll never fit in with corporate America. I've been worrying about her future. She can't work as my assistant forever. She needs to find a specialized niche where she can develop her talents. It occurred to me that Gordon Brooke Espresso Bars may be a good place to start."

Harry's eyes gleamed. "Know what I think?"

"What?"

"I think that, in addition to the Abberwick curiosity, you also got the family urge to tinker. It just so happens that you do your tinkering with people rather than inanimate objects."

"Never mind Tessa and Gordon. Any news from your investigator?"

The wry humor vanished from Harry's gaze. "Rice phoned twenty minutes ago. He finally located the car and made arrangements with the owner of the wrecking yard. I'm going to take a look at Kendall's Ford in the morning."

"You're going to fly to Portland tomorrow morning?"

"First thing."

"I'll go with you," Molly said.

"What about your shop?"

"Tessa can handle things here tomorrow. She can bring in one of the other women in the band if she needs help."

Harry gave her a considering look. Then he nodded once. "All right. Maybe it would be better if you came with me."

Molly was pleased. "You think I might be able to give you some helpful advice?"

"Not exactly," Harry said. "I think that if Kendall really was murdered by someone who was trying to cover his tracks, I'd rather have you where I can keep an eye on you."

Molly made a face. She collected her shoulder bag and started toward the front door. "Always nice to feel wanted."

At ten o'clock the following morning Harry stood with Molly amid the carcasses of a herd of dead automobiles. A formidable steel fence topped with frothy coils of barbed wire surrounded the remains of the deceased vehicles. The sign at the entrance of the metal graveyard bore the name Maltrose Wrecking.

It was a suitable day for viewing the departed. A leaden sky promised rain at any moment. A brisk sea breeze snapped at the sleeves of Harry's shirt. It had already whipped Molly's hair into a fluffy froth. She had to hold the stuff out of her eyes with one hand.

The owner of the junkyard, one Chuck Maltrose, stood next to Harry. He was a big man who looked as if he had once played football and lifted weights. His glory days appeared to have ended at some point in the distant past, however. Much of the muscle had turned to fat over the years.

"This the one you wanted to see?" Chuck glanced at Harry.

Harry eyed the remains of the blue Ford and then glanced at the notes he had made during Fergus Rice's last phone call. "This is it."

"Take your time," Chuck said. "You're welcome to look all you want for your fifty bucks."

"Thanks."

"Let me know when you're finished. I'll be in my office."

"Right." Harry did not glance at Chuck as the bulky man trundled off toward the aging trailer that served as an office. He could not take his attention off the Ford.

He had not even touched the car, but already he could tell that there was something not quite right about it. Despite its crumpled condition, the Ford should have felt familiar. Only a few days ago it had been used in an attempt to force his Sneath P2 over a cliff. Admittedly, he'd only seen it in a series of disjointed snapshots, first in his rearview mirror and then as it flashed past the Sneath. He'd had his hands full with the task of keeping his vehicle from jumping the guard rail. But still . . .

"What is it, Harry?" Molly asked.

He glanced at her. "I don't know yet. Maybe nothing except the obvious."

She hugged herself. "It's a mess, isn't it? We're looking at a car that went over a cliff. A man died in that Ford. It gives me chills just to look at it."

Harry said nothing. The knowledge that Wharton Kendall had died in the car was not what was making him so uneasy. Something else was niggling at him. The wrongness emanated from the car in subtle waves.

And he wasn't even in one of his moods of intense concentration.

It occurred to Harry that the part of his brain that was good at what he preferred to call *reasoned insight* had become unaccountably more sensitive lately. Ever since he had started making love to Molly, to be precise.

The realization dumbfounded him. He stared at the blue Ford and wondered what was happening to him. His imagination was running wild, that was the problem. Or maybe it was much worse, much more ominous than that.

The old dread unfurled deep inside. Maybe he really would go crazy one of these days.

"Harry?" Molly touched his arm. "Are you okay?"

"Of course I'm okay. Why shouldn't I be?" Harry willed the old fear back into its hiding place. He summoned up Molly's reassuring advice on the subject. *The very fact that you can even wonder if you're going crazy means you aren't crazy.* He took a savage grip on his self-control. "I'm trying to think."

"Sorry."

Harry deliberately turned away from the concern he saw in her eyes. He would apologize later for his short temper. He would also put off worrying about the possibility of being fitted for a straitjacket until some later time. He had been postponing that particular concern for years. It could wait a little longer.

He made himself take a careful look at the ruined Ford. The guts of the dead beast were exposed to view. The hood had been ripped off in the crash. The doors hung open at odd angles, as though the bones inside the metal skin had been broken. The windows were empty of glass. They reminded Harry of sightless eyes.

He walked slowly around the Ford.

"What are you going to do?" Molly asked.

Harry rolled up his sleeves. "Just look things over."

"Everything was smashed when the car went over the cliff. How will you know if any damage you discover today was done before the accident?"

Harry leaned over the fender and studied the dented valve cover. "I'm not sure I'll be able to tell a damned thing. I just want to take a close look."

"Sort of get a feel for the situation?" Molly suggested innocently.

Harry ignored her. Very cautiously he allowed himself to concentrate as he leaned farther over the crumpled fender.

The sense of wrongness eddied around him, lapping gently at his senses. But it was not coming from inside the engine compartment. He stepped back from the fender. He tried to be subtle as he took a deep breath, but he could feel Molly watching him very intently.

Something was definitely not right.

After a few seconds, when he was sure he had himself firmly under control, he got into the driver's seat. He surveyed the damage to the interior. The steering wheel was gone. The glass cover on the instrument panel was a spider's web of tiny cracks. He bent down to examine the brake pedal.

Again the wrongness assailed him. But it was not as strong inside the car as it had been when he had been standing near the front fender.

"Something wrong with the brakes?" Molly asked expectantly.

"I don't think so." Harry wrapped himself in the armor of his willpower and gingerly touched the brake pedal. Experimentally he depressed it.

. . . and simultaneously sharpened his concentration.

It was so damn tricky. This matter of trying to think with this degree of utter clarity was so useful and yet so dangerous.

"What is it?" Molly asked. "What do you feel?"

"I don't *feel* anything," Harry muttered. "The brakes are all right."

"Are you sure?"

"As sure as I can be under the circumstances." He was almost positive that no one had cut the brake lines. There was still plenty of resistance in the system.

"I guess discovering something as dramatic as severed brake lines would have been a little too obvious."

Harry glanced sharply at her. "You sound disappointed."

She shrugged. "I've seen my share of old movies."

"That kind of sabotage only works well on film," Harry said absently. "It's too unpredictable in real life. The problem is that the person who cuts the lines has no way of knowing for certain just when the last of the fluid will bleed out."

"You mean there would be no way to time it so that the brakes would fail on the right curve?"

"Exactly." Harry thought about it. "It's a very uncertain way to kill. And our man, assuming there is someone other than Kendall involved in this, prefers more straightforward, predictable methods."

"What makes you say that?"

"Think about it, Molly. The guy tried to run us off a road, and he attempted to kill you with a gun."

"I see what you mean." Her brow furrowed delicately. "He takes the blunt approach."

"Only when it comes to the actual murder attempt," Harry said slowly. "He's certainly been extremely subtle when it comes to setting his scene and choosing his fall guy. In fact, he's a lot better at that end of the business than he is at closing the deal."

"What do you think that means?"

Harry looked at her as his mind tore into the problem. "It may mean that whoever's behind this has had a lot more experience with setting the stage than he's had with murder. Killing people may be new to him."

Molly shivered visibly. "But why would he have had more experience with establishing his camouflage?"

"Maybe," Harry said, "because that's all he's had to do until now in order to accomplish his objectives. When it comes to the backdrop of his operation, he thinks like a con man with a lot of experience."

"A con man?"

"It's possible that he's got a background in fraud or embezzlement or some other nonlethal crime."

"So he's clever with that part but not so skilled when it comes to murder." Molly closed her eyes briefly. "Thank God."

"Yes."

"Well, now that we know this definitely wasn't an accident, it would be very interesting to discover exactly how Kendall's car was sabotaged," Molly said thoughtfully.

"We don't know for certain that it wasn't an accident. We're making an assumption."

"Your assumptions are more in the nature of inspired guesses, Harry. You know it and I know it."

Harry heard something click and realized it was the sound of his back teeth coming together. He was irritated by Molly's certainty that Kendall had been murdered. He knew that she was picking up on his own sense of the situation and that she trusted his instincts.

The knowledge that Molly had developed such unquestioning faith in his insights worried him. It was as though her belief in his abilities rendered those abilities even more suspect. It made it seem all the more probable that there really was something abnormal involved.

Harry got out of the car and cautiously put a hand on the front fender. The wrongness hit him again, more insistent this time. He bent down to take a closer look at the crushed metal.

The impact of the crash had scraped and scarred the blue paint all the way to bare metal in places. Harry moved his fingers along the huge gouges that had been left in the fender. He stopped abruptly when his fingertips touched a deep dent near an empty hole that had once been occupied by a headlight. He stilled.

Molly hurried over to where he stood. "What did you find?"

"Blue paint."

"What's so strange about blue paint? The Ford is painted blue."

"I'm aware of that." He fingered a small fragment of paint. Something about it bothered him.

Harry took a deep breath and centered himself mentally as best he could. Slowly, carefully, he allowed himself to consider the flecks of blue enamel in all their tiny, varied aspects.

He tried to assign only a limited portion of his concentration to the task. He did not want to lose control. *Let the information seep in,* he cautioned himself. *Just a little bit at a time. Think about it. Look for the inconsistencies.*

Harry took a cautious step out onto the glass bridge.

The wind off the sea sharpened suddenly, whipping at his clothing, threatening to topple him into the abyss.

He fought to keep his balance. If he lost control, he would fall into the deepest, coldest canyon at the bottom of the darkest part of the sea.

"Harry?" Molly's voice was soft, gentle, questioning. Concerned.

The glass shuddered beneath his feet. He lifted his fascinated gaze from the endless darkness beneath him and looked toward the opposite side of the chasm.

Molly waited there. She held out her arms.

He regained his balance and started toward her. Each step was steadier, more certain.

He was wide open to sensation and awareness. The world around him was a thousand times more vivid than it had been a moment ago. The overcast sky was no longer a uniform gray. Instead it was a hundred variegated shades of light and shadow. Molly's smile was brighter than any sun, and her eyes were green jewels.

The paint beneath his fingers screamed at him.

Harry sucked in his breath.

"Take it easy, Harry. I'm here."

He lurched the last few steps across the glass bridge. Reached for Molly with desperate hands. She came into his arms, warm and comforting and alive. He was not alone out here in the darkness.

Harry closed his eyes and held Molly with all the strength that was in him.

The world steadied swiftly, returning to its natural shades and intensities. The force of the sea wind lessened. The bridge and the abyss beneath it vanished.

Harry opened his eyes. Molly peered anxiously up at him from within the circle of his arms.

"Are you okay?" she asked gently.

"Yes." He focused on her concerned expression as he fought for breath. "Yes, I'm okay."

"You look terrible."

"I'm all right."

"You were burning up a minute ago." She put a hand on his forehead. "You feel a little cooler now. I wonder if men have hot flashes."

Harry gave a choked groan, caught between old fear and fresh laughter. His mixed emotions warned him that he was not yet back in full control.

She studied him closely. "What did you see there on the fender?"

"I told you, blue paint." Harry crouched beside the front wheel. "But not from this car."

"What?" Molly's mouth fell open. She hunkered down beside him. "Blue paint from another car?"

"I think so." He looked at her. "Blue on blue. The differences in the two colors is so slight that the investigating officers would never have noticed it. But there is a difference."

"So there was another car involved."

"Yes." Harry rose to his feet. "What's really interesting is that it was probably from the same blue Ford that tried to force us off the road. Because this is not the same car that we encountered outside of Icy Crest."

"Oh, my God. Two blue Fords."

"I told you, this guy is very good at setting up the scenery for his little plays. He's had plenty of experience in that department."

"This isn't just one of your logical insights, is it?" Deep curiosity burned in Molly's eyes. "You can actually *feel* that there's something wrong with that streak of blue paint on the fender, can't you?"

"I can *see* the small differences in it. I've trained myself to observe tiny details. It's one of the reasons I'm good at what I do."

"Don't play games with me," Molly said quietly. "Or yourself. You knew something was wrong with this car the instant you took a close look at it. Why not admit it?"

Under normal circumstances, he would have reacted to her insistent prodding with cool sarcasm or a show of irritation. But even though he was feeling more or less back in control, he was still raw around the edges.

The result was that Molly's questioning ignited the dark fear in him. He fought the dread with the only weapon he had, a firestorm of rage.

"Damn it, what the hell do you want me to say?" The anger, fed by the fear, beat in his veins. "That I really do think I've got some kind of sixth sense? I might as well announce to the world that I'm crazy."

"You are not crazy. I've told you that."

"What are you? Some kind of authority?"

Molly did not flinch beneath the storm. "Harry, if you do have some sort of paranormal ability, you'd better acknowledge it and deal with it. It's a part of you, whatever it is."

"You're the one who's nuts if you think I'm going to go around claiming that I've got extrasensory perception. People who believe they've got paranormal powers end up on serious medication." Harry closed his eyes. Visions of psychiatric asylums danced in his fevered brain. "Or worse."

"You don't have to admit the truth to anyone except yourself." Molly smiled bleakly. "And to me, of course. You can't hide it from me."

"There's nothing to admit."

"Listen to me, Harry. I've got a feeling that if you don't accept the reality of your abilities, whatever it is, you'll never figure out how to control them. You can't repress them forever."

"I can't repress what doesn't exist."

"You're a man who deals in truth. Admit the truth to yourself. Think of this sixth sense, or whatever it is, the same way you do your excellent reflexes. Just a natural, inborn ability. A talent."

"Natural? You call that paranormal crap natural? Molly, you're starting to sound nuttier than Olivia thinks I am."

"That's not fair to Olivia. She doesn't think you're nuts. She believes that you're suffering from posttraumatic stress disorder and maybe some periodic depression."

"Trust me, she thinks I'm ready for the psycho ward."

"But, Harry—"

He took a step toward her, his hands clenched at his sides. The wind picked up once more. The sky darkened. "I swear to God, Molly, I don't want to hear another word about this psychic stuff. Do you understand me? Not another damned word."

She put her hand on his shoulder. "Listen to me."

"We will not discuss this matter again," Harry said through his teeth. Her fingers were warm. He could feel them through the fabric of his shirt. The anger seeped slowly out of him, leaving a great weariness.

"Hey, am I interruptin' something here or what?" Chuck Maltrose heaved into Harry's field of vision.

Harry drew a deep, steadying breath and switched his attention to the owner of the wrecking yard. "We were discussing a private matter."

"Sure. No problem." Maltrose held up one hand, palm out. "I'm not one to get into the middle of a private squabble. Just wondered if you were finished with your look-see."

"I believe Harry's finished here, Mr. Maltrose," Molly said crisply.

Harry watched her give Maltrose one of her brilliant smiles.

Chuck Maltrose was not so sanguine. He shot Harry a covert, wary look.

Harry wondered if the crazy stuff actually showed in his eyes, or if Maltrose was merely reacting to the remnants of anger that were undoubtedly still evident. He just needed a few more seconds to pull himself together, Harry thought. He would be fine in a minute.

Fortunately Molly took immediate charge of Chuck Maltrose. Harry listened as she chatted with him about the impending storm. By the time they had concluded that the rain would hit fairly soon, Harry had himself back under control.

"So now we know there's another blue Ford out there somewhere," Molly said as she slid into the passenger seat of the rental car. "What do we do next, Sherlock?"

"I'll stop at a pay phone and put in a call to Fergus Rice." Harry turned the key in the ignition. "He can notify the cops."

"There must be a zillion blue Fords."

"Yes, but with any luck, there won't be that many with a dented right front fender."

"Still, it seems like a long shot." Molly flopped back against the seat. "This thing just doesn't make sense anymore. The motive doesn't seem logical."

"I've been thinking about that. There may be another motive." Harry frowned as he pulled out onto the road. "One we haven't considered."

"There are only so many motives in the world. Revenge, passion, and greed sum up almost the entire list."

"So far we've been concentrating on revenge," Harry noted.

"I find it hard to believe that I'm the target of two disgruntled inventors," Molly said flatly. "One, maybe. But two? And we can forget about passion. My life simply has not been that exciting until recently."

"That leaves us with greed."

Molly wrinkled her nose. "Killing me isn't a real good way of getting the foundation to finance someone's grant proposal."

Harry stared at the road ahead as it all started to come together in a rush of crystal clear perfection. The theory assumed form and substance with such speed that he could only marvel at how he had overlooked the obvious for so long.

"Last night," he said carefully, "when I walked into your shop, you were assuring Brooke that you wouldn't be idiotic enough to turn control of the foundation assets over to anyone else."

"Darn right."

"Molly, what does happen to those assets if you're out of the picture?"

"Huh?"

"You heard me. If something happened to you, would Kelsey become the trustee of the Abberwick Foundation?"

"Not until she's twenty-eight. I drew up the papers that way because I didn't want her to get stuck with the burden of running the foundation until she'd had a chance to finish school and get started on a career."

"Who becomes the trustee if you're gone?"

"Aunt Venicia."

Harry whistled soundlessly. "I should have seen it from the beginning."

"What on earth are you talking about? Surely you aren't about to accuse Aunt Venicia of plotting to murder me? That's ludicrous. She could care less about running the foundation."

"Not her. The man she's going to marry."

Molly stared at him, stunned. "Oh, my God. Cutter Latteridge."

Nineteen

Molly panicked. "Stop the car. I have to get to a phone. I've got to warn Aunt Venicia."

"Take it easy," Harry said. "Venicia is safe enough for the moment. Cutter isn't married to her yet. If he harms her now, she's useless to him. He needs her alive until after the wedding."

"That's true, isn't it? He doesn't stand a chance of getting his hands on the foundation until after the marriage." Molly closed her eyes in a silent prayer of gratitude. "Thank heavens Aunt Venicia insisted on a big wedding that takes weeks to plan."

"Yes."

"But what are we going to do?"

"Nothing for the moment." Harry's elegant hands flexed on the wheel. "We haven't got a dime's worth of proof that Latteridge is behind this. We need background information on him. If he's an expert, he'll have a history. I'll get Fergus on it immediately."

Molly began to calm down. As soon as she was thinking clearly again, the questions descended in a flood. "This is wild. How on earth could Cutter have planned and carried out such a bizarre scenario?"

"Whoever he is, he's set up elaborate schemes before. This isn't the work of an amateur. He knows how to take care of the details." Harry's expression became very intent. "At least when it comes to the window dressing part. He's not so good at murder."

"For which we can thank our lucky stars."

"All right," Harry continued, "we're dealing with a professional con artist. As I said, he's probably got a record of some kind. We'll find it and use it to focus the attention of the authorities on him."

Molly considered. "He knew about the Abberwick Foundation. Only someone who is familiar with the world of inventors and invention would have been aware of my father and the fact that he had made arrangements to establish the foundation."

"True. He could have met your father or your uncle at one time."

"I doubt it."

"Why?" Harry asked. "I certainly knew about your father's work long before I met you. A lot of people involved in the commercial application of robotic devices were aware of Jasper Abberwick."

"I suppose so," Molly agreed.

The storm that had been threatening for the past few hours finally struck. Rain splashed on the windshield. Harry switched on the wiper blades.

The drive toward Portland continued in silence for several miles. Molly glanced at Harry from time to time, aware that he had fallen into one of his thoughtful moods. She knew that he was examining the problem of Cutter Latteridge from every possible angle. She could almost feel his razor-sharp intellect dissecting the situation.

"When, precisely, did Latteridge first appear on the scene?" Harry finally asked.

"I told you, Aunt Venicia met him on a cruise that she took in the spring. Why?"

"I'm trying to figure out the timing," Harry said. He lapsed back into silence.

A few miles later he spoke again. "I think I've got enough to give Rice. I'm going to find a phone."

A short while later a gas station loomed in the mist. Harry slowed the car and eased it off the road and into a parking area. He shut off the engine and opened the door.

"I'll be right back." He got out, shut the door, and loped through the rain to the limited shelter of the phone booth.

Molly watched him through the rain-washed windows. From time to time ghostly ripples, an unfamiliar awareness of danger, went through her. At first she did not understand. She knew that she was scared and extremely worried about Venicia's safety, but this other sensation felt as though it emanated from outside herself.

It wasn't until she saw Harry replace the receiver and start back toward the car that she realized she was picking up a distant echo of *his* own awareness of the danger they faced.

It was not unlike the sensation she experienced more and more often when she was in bed with Harry. Alien, yet familiar.

Harry broke into her disturbing thoughts when he opened the car door and got in behind the wheel. "It's pouring out there." He ran his fingers through his damp hair to get rid of the moisture. He scowled when he saw Molly's face. "What's wrong?"

Molly cleared her throat. If he had felt anything at all during the past few minutes, he was not about to acknowledge it. "Nothing." She managed a weak smile. "I'm just a little anxious, that's all."

"Not surprising under the circumstances." Harry turned in the seat, his expression intent. "I talked to Rice. Told him to start looking into Cutter Latteridge's background. With any luck he'll have some preliminary information for us by the time we get back to Seattle."

"But what are we going to do about Aunt Venicia? We can't allow her to continue to date a murderer."

"If you try to warn her about Latteridge, you'll put both her and yourself in extreme danger." Harry reached across the seat to squeeze her hand. "Let me handle it, Molly."

"You always seem to end up in this role."

He released her fingers and put the car in gear. "What role?"

"Playing the hero. It hardly seems fair. Someday someone ought to save you."

He gave her an odd glance as he drove out of the parking lot. "I'm no hero."

"Yes, you are. Trust me, I know one when I see one."

The green light on Harry's answering machine was blinking frantically when he walked into his study late that afternoon. There were three messages.

"Your private line," Molly observed. "Must be family calls."

"With any luck one of them will be from Fergus Rice." Harry punched the playback button. "I told him to use the private number."

The first call was from Josh. He sounded upbeat.

Harry? It's Josh. Thought you'd like to know that the hospital discharged Grandpa this morning. He's on crutches, but he swears he'll be back in the racing pit tomorrow night.

The second call was from Danielle.

Harry, this is your aunt. I understand you're going to give Brandon a list of venture capitalists. He says he's determined to go outside the family for financing. I don't think it's wise for him to do that. Please give me a call. I want to discuss this with you.

"I knew Aunt Danielle would start acting like a nervous hen when her only chick tried to leave the nest," Harry said.

Molly glanced at him. "What will you do?"

Harry scrawled Danielle's name on a pad of paper. "Talk to her. Persuade her to lay off Brandon." He waited for the next voice, hoping it would be Fergus Rice with information. It was.

Harry, it's Rice. Give me a call as soon as you get in. I've got some news that I think will interest you.

Harry reached for the phone and punched in the number. Fergus answered on the first ring.

"It's Harry. What have you got?"

"The good news is that I got lucky right off the bat, thanks to your guesswork. I started by checking a couple of charitable foundations which operate along the same lines as the Abberwick Foundation. You know, the kind that make grants for scientific and technical work."

"What did you find?"

"It looks like Cutter Latteridge is an alias for a con man named Clarence Laxton. He's had a half-dozen different names during the past five years. He specializes in scamming foundations. Been pretty successful at it from what I can tell, but he got caught by investigators a year ago."

"Any jail time?"

"No. He literally vanished hours before the authorities moved in. When they got to his office, it had been cleaned out. There was no trace. He covered his tracks very well. You'll be interested to know that until now there's been no indication that he's ever resorted to violence."

"I think the violence is new for him," Harry said. "His original goal may have been to work himself into a position of trust."

"In other words, he would have eventually offered his consulting services to Molly?"

"Exactly. Maybe he figured he could persuade her to turn the day-to-day running of the foundation over to him. After all, he was about to become a member of the family, and he had a working knowledge of engineering technology."

"He probably thought that he could drain the assets and then disappear," Fergus agreed. "But when she hired you, he panicked and concocted another plan. One that required him to get rid of Molly altogether."

"He used Wharton Kendall, a rejected inventor, as a stalking horse."

"Makes sense," Fergus said. "This guy has a reputation for doing his research. He would have known who you were and that you were a potential threat to him."

"So what's the bad news?" Harry asked.

"I'm not sure if it's good or bad. Sort of depends on your point of view," Fergus said. "It looks like Latteridge left the country this afternoon."

Harry felt everything inside him go very still. "You're sure?"

"As sure as I can be under the circumstances. A man answering Latteridge's description was on the two-thirty flight to London. He had a passport, luggage—the works."

"The passport was in Latteridge's name?"

"According to my sources. I've talked to my friends in the police department. The problem is, we don't even have proof of fraud, let alone murder or attempted murder."

Harry put his hand over the receiver to speak to Molly. "Latteridge got on an international flight at SeaTac earlier today."

Molly's eyes widened. "He's gone?"

"Looks like it." Harry heard Fergus say something on the other end of the line. "What's that?"

"I said, it looks like this thing is over, Harry."

"That's what you said when you told me Wharton Kendall had gone over a cliff."

"This times it feels real," Fergus said. "You know these guys. Once the con goes sour, they pull a vanishing act."

"True."

Molly frowned. "I wonder if Aunt Venicia knows he's gone. I'd better call her right away."

Harry shook his head. "We'll go see her in person. This isn't the kind of news you deliver over the phone."

Molly sighed. "You're right."

"Harry?" Fergus sounded confused. "Are you still there?"

"I'm here. I wonder what made Latteridge suspect that someone was getting close."

"I don't know," Fergus said. "Maybe your sudden trip down to Oregon worried him. He would have kept very close tabs on your movements. And he does have a history of getting out of the picture just in time to avoid the authorities."

"A good con man always knows when to cut his losses."

"Exactly," Fergus said. "You want some more of the details?"

Harry picked up a pen. "Let me have everything you've got."

Giving the bad news to Venicia was one of the hardest things Molly had ever done. She was grateful for Harry's solid, steadying presence. He stood beside her in Venicia's newly redecorated mauve-and-green living room while Molly explained that Cutter Latteridge was never coming back.

Venicia's initial reaction of irate disbelief gradually crumpled, first into stunned shock and then into tears. Molly began to cry, too. When she got too choked up to continue, Harry calmly and gently filled in the details.

"But he was a man of comfortable means," Venicia protested as she dabbed her eyes with a tissue. "The house on Mercer Island . . ."

"He took possession of the house with an elaborate scam," Harry explained. "The banks and the realtors are scrambling to put all the pieces together, but it looks like he established a phony line of credit with an East Coast bank and used it to con the real estate agency and the escrow company."

"And the yacht?"

"Same story," Harry said. "The yacht broker is till trying to sort out the mess."

"I don't know what to say." Venicia sniffed sadly. "He was such a gentleman."

"His good manners and charming ways were part of his stock-in-trade," Harry said.

Venicia looked at Molly with woebegone eyes. "I've been nothing but an old fool, haven't I?"

"Wrong on both counts." Molly hugged her tightly. "You aren't old, and you definitely aren't a fool. Cutter or Clarence or whatever his name is conned all of us, Aunt Venicia."

"He's conned a lot of other people, too," Harry said. "He's an expert."

"An expert at hurting people." Venicia stiffened. "What if he returns? You say he's dangerous."

Molly looked at Harry.

"It's not likely that he'll come back to Seattle any time soon, if ever," Harry said. "At heart he's a con artist, not a killer. Fraud is his thing. He needs anonymity to pursue his business. His main goal now will be to bury his Cutter Latteridge identity so that he can go back to work on a new scam somewhere as far from here as possible."

Venicia shrank back into the enfolding cushions of her designer chair. "Now I know why he had begun to pressure me to move the date of the wedding forward. He said he couldn't wait to marry me."

"He was starting to get nervous because of my presence in the picture," Harry said. "He probably sensed that the con was in danger of blowing up in his face."

"I'm supposed to go for one more fitting on my gown," Venicia whispered. "It's so lovely. And it cost a fortune." She reached for a fresh tissue. Then she paused and looked at Molly. "I've just had a thought."

"What's that?" Molly asked.

Venicia smiled with the natural resiliency of a woman who had been married to an inventor for thirty years. "We'll tell the boutique to fit the gown to you, dear."

Ten days later Molly was in the process of measuring out a tiny smidgeon of saffron when she heard the shop bell jingle. She glanced toward the door and saw a young woman dressed in a studded leather belt, black vest, and jeans hovering anxiously in the doorway. The woman had short, spiky hair that had been tinted dead black. Her bare arms were decorated with a variety of tattoos. She wore little round glasses on her nose.

"Are you Molly Abberwick?"

"Yes, I am." Molly smiled. "Can I help you?"

"I'm Heloise Stickley." Heloise glanced at Tessa, who was just returning from the storage room with a sack of green peppercorns. "Hi, Tessa."

"Heloise. You made it." Tessa looked at Molly with an air of determination. "Molly, this is my friend, the inventor. You know, the one who plays bass guitar for Ruby Sweat?"

Molly got a sinking sensation in her stomach. "The one who wants to apply to the Abberwick Foundation for grant money?"

"You got it." Tessa beamed at Heloise. "Did you bring your sketches and notes?"

Heloise nodded. She cast another nervous glance at Molly. "I promise I won't take up much of your time, Ms. Abberwick."

"This is about some sort of device designed to measure paranormal brain waves, isn't it?" Molly said slowly.

Heloise came forward eagerly. "I'm on to something here, Ms. Abberwick. I'd really appreciate it if you'd give me a few minutes to explain my theories. No one else will even listen to me."

Molly sighed. "Come with me."

She led the way into her office. Heloise followed, her face aglow with enthusiasm and excitement.

At three o'clock the following afternoon it dawned on Harry that something in his environment was not functioning in a normal manner. He slowly surfaced from the deep pile of notes he was making for his paper on François Arago's work in light and optics. It took him a moment to figure out what was bothering him. Then it hit him.

The private line phone had not rung all day.

Because he had intended to devote himself to the paper on Arago, he had set the answering machine on his business line to take messages. He had turned off the ringer so that he would not be bothered by incoming calls.

But he had not turned off the private line. Everyone in the family knew that when he was at home, he was available.

There had not been a single call on his private line all day. An unusual turn of events. Harry could not remember the last occasion when he had gone an entire day without a phone call from someone in one or the other of his extended clans.

It was not as if everything had quieted down. On the Stratton side, Danielle was still fretting over Brandon's decision to seek funding from a venture capitalist. Parker was fuming about Brandon's intentions and demanding to have input into the decision-making process. For his part, Brandon was trying to get his grandfather off his back.

Gilford was annoyed because he blamed Harry for having upset Parker. Olivia was dropping dark hints that Harry and Molly should seek couples counseling before they got married. Yesterday she had called to give him the names of two more psychologists.

On the Trevelyan side, Evangeline had begun a campaign to convince Harry to help her find financing for a new thrill ride. Josh had been calling in regular reports of Leon's progress. Raleigh had let it be known that he was out of money again and the baby was due at any moment.

No question about it, Harry thought, the private line phone should have rung sometime during the day. He leaned back in his chair, steepled his fingers, and contemplated the unnaturally silent telephone.

His gaze settled on the phone cord that was discreetly draped over the side of the desk. He followed it with his eye to the point where it disappeared behind a reading chair.

After a moment he got to his feet and walked to the chair. He looked behind it and saw that the phone cord was lying on the floor. Someone had disconnected it from the telephone jack on the wall.

Harry was very certain that he had not accidentally unplugged the phone. He was equally sure that Ginny would not have made such a mistake while cleaning.

It did not take long to narrow the range of possibilities.

Harry reconnected the phone cord to the wall jack. Then he went back to his desk, picked up the receiver, and dialed the number of his business line.

He waited for his own prerecorded message to come on the line. He was not unduly surprised when he heard Molly's voice instead of his own.

> *You have reached the office of Dr. Harry Stratton Trevelyan. If you are calling on a business matter, please stay on the line and leave a message after the beep. If you are a member of his family on either the Stratton or the Trevelyan side, and you are calling this number because you cannot get through on his private line, please dial the following number imme-*

diately. You will receive extremely urgent and vital information which will directly impact your life.

Harry listened to the phone number that Molly rattled off at the end of the message. He recognized it at once. It belonged to the Abberwick Tea & Spice Company.

Molly had found a way to reroute all of his family calls to her shop.

Harry stood quietly for a long time, phone in hand, and wondered what the hell was going on. Life with the daughter of a genius inventor was definitely not going to be dull.

The phone on the desk in Molly's office warbled loudly. She ignored the insistent summons while she finished ringing up a sale. The customer was a writer who lived near Seattle. She came in regularly to buy great quantities of the special blend of tea that Molly had created for her.

"Thanks, Ann." Molly handed over the packet of tea. "See you next month."

Ann smiled. "I'll be back. Can't sit down in front of the word processor without a pot of my special blend."

Tessa leaned through the doorway of the office. "Phone for you, Molly."

"Thanks, Tessa."

Molly hurried into her office and took the receiver from Tessa's hand. "This is Molly Abberwick. How can I help you?"

There was a short, charged silence on the other end of the line.

"Molly?" Olivia's voice reverberated with outrage. "What on earth do you think you're doing? Where's Harry?"

"Harry is busy at the moment."

"Put him on the line. I want to speak with him. This is a family matter."

"Sorry. Harry is not available."

Molly perched on the edge of her desk and idly swung one leg. This was the fourth family call that she had taken since she had unplugged Harry's private line and inserted her own message into the answering machine attached to his business line.

She knew that he had intended to turn off the business line that morning in order to work. But he never turned off the private line. She had, therefore, disconnected it so that any Stratton or Trevelyan seeking to get through to Harry would be forced to try his business line. Whereupon said caller would get her message and call her, instead.

Word was spreading quickly through the Stratton and Trevelyan clans. Thus far she had dealt with Brandon, Evangeline, and Danielle.

"This is ridiculous," Olivia snapped. "What's going on?"

"I'll tell you exactly what I have told the others who called. I'm giving the Strattons and Trevelyans a small sample of the power I shall wield once Harry is married to me."

"Power?"

"Precisely." Molly smiled into the phone. "As his wife I shall be in a unique position to limit access to Harry."

"Is this some sort of stupid joke?"

"I promise you, I am very, very serious," Molly assured her. "Today I merely made it difficult to reach Harry by phone. But if my demands are not met, there will be worse to come. I can and will make it virtually impossible to gain access to Harry."

"Are you out of your mind?"

"What an odd question from someone in your line of work. No, I am not out of my mind, but I am determined to get what I want. Be warned, if the Strattons and Trevelyans fail to comply with my demands, I shall find ways to make it extremely difficult for anyone on either side of his family to get to Harry."

"I don't understand." Olivia was clearly nonplussed now. "This makes no sense at all."

"I shall present my demands to representatives of the Stratton and Trevelyan clans tomorrow at noon. I guarantee that everything will make perfect sense then."

"Harry is going to hear about this," Olivia threatened.

"Not if you and the others want to continue to have reasonably free access to him, he won't," Molly warned sweetly. "As I was saying, I shall present my demands tomorrow. High noon at the vegetarian restaurant around the corner from my shop. Be there or face the consequences."

Molly hung up the phone before Olivia could suggest she get professional psychiatric help.

The Strattons were the first to arrive.

Molly stood at the head of the long table in the alcove of the trendy vegetarian restaurant and watched as Danielle, regal in her disapproval, led the contingent.

"This is an absolute outrage," Danielle declared.

"Good afternoon, Mrs. Hughes." Molly inclined her head. "I'm glad you could make it."

"You were impossibly rude on the phone, Miss Abberwick," Danielle informed her. "As far as I'm concerned, you issued a threat."

"You were right," Molly said. "It was a threat."

She deduced that the two men following Danielle were Parker and his son, Gilford. Their ages and signature bone structure identified them as clearly as a fingerprint. Both men radiated icy anger. Olivia and Brandon brought up the rear. Each wore an expression of great caution.

"Good afternoon." Molly waved the newcomers to the chairs that lined the left-hand side of the table. "Please be seated."

Parker's silvered brows came together in a straight line above his patrician nose. "We know who you are. I'm Parker Stratton."

"Yes." Molly smiled. "We spoke on the phone this morning. You wanted to know what the hell I was up to, I believe."

"Now, you listen to me, young woman," Parker snapped, "I have better things to do with my time than play stupid games. I don't know what you're trying to pull here, but if it's money you're after, you can damn well—"

"It's not about money, Granddad," Brandon said quietly. He watched Molly with speculative eyes. "Whatever this is all about, it's not about cash. Ms. Abberwick has plenty of that at her disposal."

Olivia went to one of the chairs on the left side of the table. "I'll tell you what this is all about. It's about power and control. Isn't that right, Molly? You think you can exert both over the rest of us because of your position as Harry's fiancée."

Molly gripped the back of her chair. She kept her smile fixed determinedly in place. "Have a seat, Olivia. You can psychoanalyze me later to your heart's content. But please don't send me a bill."

"No one controls a Stratton, by God," Gilford said evenly. "Ms. Abberwick, I'm a busy man. I'm here today only because you made it clear that there is some sort of family crisis. You've got exactly five minutes to convince me of that."

Molly looked at him. "Have a seat, Mr. Stratton. I will explain everything." She glanced toward the door as the next group of people arrived.

Danielle opened her mouth to speak and then closed it abruptly as her gaze fell on the newcomers who hovered in the doorway. She stared as if she could not believe her eyes. "My God. How dare they intrude like this."

"What the devil?" Parker swung around to see what had alarmed Danielle. His eyes widened with fury. "Christ Almighty. What are *they* doing here?"

Molly looked at the cluster of Trevelyans who had arrived. She saw at once that she'd managed to get a fairly good turnout. Josh had been no problem, of course. He had agreed to come without hesitation. But she was secretly relieved to see Leon, who was still on crutches, and Raleigh and Evangeline with him.

Evangeline, as statuesque and commanding in a skirted suit as she had been in her colorful fortune-teller's garb, swept through the room full of Strattons. Then she glowered at Molly.

"You didn't say anything about them being here."

"There's a lot I haven't had a chance to explain yet, Evangeline." Molly indicated the chairs on the right-hand side of the table. "But everything will soon become clear. Please sit down."

Parker looked as if he were about to explode. He made for the door.

"I'll be damned if I'll sit across the table from that lot of thieving Trevelyans."

Leon's face twisted with fury. He lifted one crutch and swung it across the doorway, effectively barring Parker's escape. "You're not going anywhere, you old son-of-a-bitch. If us thieving Trevelyans have to sit through this, so do you goddamned prissy, high-toned Strattons."

"Prissy?" Parker beetled his brows at Leon. "Just who are you calling prissy, you bastard?"

"Enough." Molly banged a spoon against the glass in front of her. "You will all sit down right now. I don't particularly care whether or not you eat the lunch I have ordered and paid for, but you will sit and you will listen to me. Or else none of you will ever have ready access to Harry again."

The roomful of Strattons and Trevelyans turned on her, momentarily united in their fury.

"I fail to see why you think that you hold some sort of club over the rest of us," Danielle said. "Harry is a Stratton. He's a blood relative. You can't keep us from contacting him whenever we wish."

"Oh, yes, I can," Molly retorted. "I proved as much yesterday when I disconnected his private line. That was nothing, I assure you. The possibilities are virtually limitless when it comes to cutting you off from Harry. Now sit down. All of you."

They sat. Grudgingly, reluctantly, refusing to make eye contact with the people who sat across from them, both groups sat down at the table.

Molly alone remained standing. She surveyed the irate faces turned toward her. Only Josh looked at her with a trace of amused anticipation in his expression. She took a deep breath. "Thank you."

"Get on with it," Leon muttered.

"Very well." Molly tightened her grip on the back of her chair. "I shall come straight to the point. I have two demands. If they are both met, I shall allow contact with Harry to resume. I cannot promise you that I will not occasionally limit that contact if I feel it has become abusive, but I will not make it impossible for you to reach Harry as I did during the past twenty-four hours."

Parker scowled. "What makes you think that access to Harry is so damned important to any of us?"

"The fact that you're all here makes me think that." Molly released her hold on the chair and began to walk slowly around the long table. "Harry is important to both the Strattons and the Trevelyans. Vitally important. You have all found ways to use him, have you not?"

Olivia eyed her. "What is that supposed to mean?"

Molly clasped her hands behind her back. "Let us return to those forgotten days of yesteryear when Harry first arrived here in Seattle. That would have been about seven years ago, I believe. He had lost his parents less than a year before that. He had no brothers or sisters. He was not married. In effect, he was alone in the world. He came here in search of his blood kin."

"Wrong," Gilford said. "He came here because he got a grant to do research in the history of science at the UW."

Molly glanced at him. "The type of grant which Harry received did not stipulate where he should do his research. He had a choice of several prestigious universities. He came here because he had roots here. The Stratton side of his family has lived in Seattle for three generations. The Trevelyans have made Washington their home base for years."

Olivia drummed her polished fingers on the table. "Harry once told me that he stayed on here after he completed his grant work because he liked Seattle. He said that he had developed a good network of academic contacts in the local colleges and universities. He said it was a good place for him to establish himself professionally."

"He could have done that anywhere." Molly shook her head. "No, he stayed in the area because by the time he had finished his grant, he had found a place for himself in both the Stratton and Trevelyan families."

Parker bridled. "He made it damned clear he wanted no part of his Stratton heritage."

"That's not true," Molly said quietly. "The only thing he didn't want was the Stratton money."

"It's the same thing," Parker grumbled.

"No, Mr. Stratton, it's not. At least, not to Harry." Molly made her way around the end of the table and started up the Stratton side of the room.

Gilford frowned. "When Harry told us that he refused to join the company, he as much as told us that he considered himself more Trevelyan than Stratton."

"He *is* more Trevelyan than Stratton," Evangeline announced triumphantly.

"Damn right," Raleigh put in helpfully. "Got the reflexes. And Granny Gwen always said she thought he had the Sight."

Olivia grimaced. "For God's sake, could we please keep this conversation in the realm of reality? Harry has a disorder, not paranormal abilities."

Evangeline deigned to fix her with a freezing glare. "Just because you don't believe in such things doesn't mean they don't exist."

"I certainly don't believe in that psychic nonsense," Olivia shot back. "No reasonably well-educated person does believe in it, and that includes Harry, himself."

"Now see here—" Leon began.

"That's enough on that topic," Molly interrupted forcefully. "Whether or not Harry has paranormal abilities has nothing to do with this discussion. Harry is in Seattle because he wants to be involved with both his Stratton and Trevelyan relatives. He wants what his parents longed for and never got—an end to the feud."

Leon shot Parker a scathing look. "The Strattons started it."

Parker gave a muffled squawk. "Why you washed up, no-good, sneaky bastard—"

Molly paused to bang on Josh's water glass with a fork. "I'm not finished here."

The Strattons and Trevelyans turned disgruntled faces toward her once more.

"Thank you," Molly said. "Now then, as I was saying. In an effort to find a place for himself in the bosom of his family, Harry has allowed all of you to take serious advantage of him."

Danielle stiffened in her chair. "Are you implying that we use Harry?"

Molly smiled approvingly at her. "Yes, Mrs. Hughes, that is exactly what I'm implying."

Danielle stared at her, open-mouthed, and then she turned red. "That's an outrageous insult, Ms. Abberwick. And I for one object."

Evangeline was equally annoyed. "What's all this about us using Harry?"

"That is precisely what all of you do," Molly said quietly.

"He's a Trevelyan," Evangeline sputtered. "He has a certain responsibility to his family."

Gilford glowered at Evangeline across the table. "His mother was my sister, and don't you forget it. That makes him a Stratton. His responsibility is to his Stratton relatives, not to you freeloading Trevelyans."

Leon climbed to his feet with a roar. "Why you lousy little two-bit wimp. Harry doesn't owe you a damn thing."

"Sit down, Leon. Now." Molly paused to regain everyone's attention. "Listen to me, all of you. I've lived with Harry long enough to hear the kind of messages that come in on his private line. Two or three a day sometimes."

"So?" Gilford challenged.

"So, he's told me about some of your demands, and I've overheard many of you whining to him about various and assorted problems."

"Whining?" Gilford looked scandalized by the accusation.

"Yes, whining," Molly repeated. "All of you who contact Harry seem to have one thing in common."

A hush fell on the room.

Olivia toyed with a spoon. "I suppose you're going to tell us what that one thing is?"

"Yes," Molly said. "I am. The one thing both Strattons and Trevelyans have in common is that whenever you talk to Harry, you all want something from him."

Stunned silence greeted that simple observation. The unnatural hush was immediately followed by an uproar that made conversation impossible. For several minutes Molly could hear nothing above the thundering din of objections, exclamations, and defensive responses.

Josh was the only one who did not leap to his feet or yell in protest. He lounged in his seat with that cool masculine grace that characterized the Trevelyan men and gave Molly a slight, knowing smile. She winked at him.

Eventually, when she deemed the initial explosion over, she raised her hands to regain control of the room.

"People, people, take your seats," she said loudly. "Sit down, all of you, or I'm going to walk out of here right now."

There were a few more angry protests before the Strattons and Trevelyans reluctantly subsided back into their chairs.

"Now, then," Molly said calmly, "for those of you who doubt my interpretation of events, let me list just a small sampling of the many ways in which you all try to use Harry. Shall we begin on the Trevelyan side?"

"Why not?" Parker fumed. "Bunch of lazy, shiftless cons and carnies. That's all they are. They'd take advantage of their own grandmothers."

Leon started to get to his feet. "Why, you—"

"Down, Leon," Molly said quickly. "As I was saying, we shall begin on the Trevelyan side of the family. Evangeline, who did you go to four years ago when you wanted help putting together a financing package for Smoke & Mirrors Amusement Company?"

Evangeline's face tightened in astonishment. "That was business."

"Business which you could not have conducted if you hadn't had help from Harry." Molly held up a finger. "Now, just to keep things even, we shall go to the Stratton side of the family. Brandon, who did you approach when you wanted assistance in setting up your new property management firm?"

Brandon blinked. "That's different. I just needed some names of venture capitalists."

"Names which Harry supplied." Molly held up another finger. "Back to the Trevelyans. Leon, who bought your new truck for you?"

Leon's dark eyes glittered with anger. "That's between me and Harry, damn it."

"Precisely. Harry bought it for you." Molly held up another finger and looked toward the Stratton side of the table. "Gilford, who did you go to when you wanted help convincing Parker that it would be a good idea to expand Stratton Properties into commercial development on the Eastside?"

Gilford looked shocked. "How did you find out about that? That's proprietary information."

"Harry mentioned it," Molly said dryly.

Danielle bristled. "I shall have to speak to Harry about maintaining family confidences."

"Too late, I'm afraid," Molly murmured. "Like it or not, Harry now considers me one of the family. That means the rest of you will have to do the same."

That brought another wave of charged silence. The Strattons and Trevelyans glared at each other and then at Molly.

"Now, then," Molly continued briskly, "since we're talking about confidential Stratton information, perhaps this is as good a time as any to remind you, Mrs. Hughes, of just how much you've relied on Harry during the past few years."

"Me?" Danielle's expression was one of deep indignation. "I'm his aunt. I have every right to discuss certain problems with my nephew."

"Problems which you want him to resolve for you," Molly said. "I'm sure you recall how you went to Harry when you became anxious about Brandon going out on his own?"

"There's no need to bring that up now." Danielle cast a quick, uneasy glance at her father, Parker.

"Fine." Molly turned toward Raleigh. "Maybe we should talk about how useful you find Harry when money runs short?"

Raleigh winced. "I get your point."

"I think we all do," Parker said in a tone of weary resignation. "It's clear where this is going. Ms. Abberwick, you seem to feel that Harry has been imposed upon by both sides of his family."

"It's a little more complicated than that," Molly said carefully. "I believe that he has *allowed* himself to be imposed upon because deep down he wants a connection with both sides of his family, and this was the only way you would allow him to be a part of your lives."

"That's not true," Danielle said. "Naturally we wanted Harry to take his rightful role within the family."

Molly turned to confront her. "Did you? That's not the way it came across to Harry. All his life the Strattons and Trevelyans have tried to make him choose sides in the war between the families."

Olivia grimaced. "That's putting it rather strongly."

Molly ignored her. "You're all guilty of trying to make him declare himself either a Stratton or a Trevelyan. When he refused to deny either side of his heritage, you tried to punish him for it."

Parker narrowed his eyes. "That's your view of the situation, Ms. Abberwick. There's another side to Harry that you don't seem to know about. He's not exactly Mr. Nice Guy when he wants to force one of us to do what he thinks we ought to do."

"You can say that again," Leon muttered. "Harry plays hardball, and that's a fact."

Gilford gave Molly a wry look. "My father and Leon are both right, Ms. Abberwick. Harry doesn't hesitate to resort to blackmail, arm-twisting, or outright threats when he deems it necessary."

Molly smiled complacently. "I don't doubt it. He gets that from both sides of his family, I'm afraid."

Evangeline was irritated. "What's that supposed to mean?"

"It means," Molly said coolly, "that Harry can be just as hard as you force him to be. He's half Stratton and half Trevelyan, after all. The thing is, none of you truly understand him."

Olivia waved one hand in a disgusted, supercilious gesture. "That's an inane thing to say, Molly. I assure you, I understand Harry very well."

"No," Molly said simply. "You don't. You can't."

"I happen to be a professional," Olivia reminded her.

"That's your problem," Molly said. "No offense, Olivia, but you're a prisoner of your own professional training. It forces you to view the behavior of other people from a certain theoretical perspective."

"That perspective happens to be grounded in years of solid scientific research and study," Olivia retorted.

"You've tried to analyze Harry using conventional techniques," Molly said. "But they won't work on him. I don't intend to go into the subject now, but you can believe me when I say that Harry's different."

Olivia gave a ladylike snort. "That ridiculous statement only goes to show how sadly uninformed and willfully naive you are. You have no experience in the field of clinical psychology, Molly. Your opinions are nothing more than examples of wishful thinking."

"Speaking of wishful thinking," Brandon said dryly, "I wish you would get off the subject of Harry's psychological problems, Olivia. I more or less promised the guy that I'd try to keep you from analyzing him at every opportunity."

Olivia flushed. "What are you talking about?"

"It annoys him," Brandon explained. "And I can't say I blame him. You know something? Molly's right. Harry has done me a major favor. The least I can do is keep you off his back. Whatever else you can say about Harry, he's smart. If he wants professional help, let him get it outside the family, okay?"

Olivia was clearly taken aback. She started to say something and then lapsed into silence.

Brandon looked at Molly. "I think we all understand what you're trying to say here. I, for one, have to agree that, from your point of view, it probably does look as if we've all tried to use Harry in one way or another."

"And tried to force him to choose sides in a war he never started," Molly concluded.

"You can say that again," Josh muttered. "I lived with him for years, remember? I know what it's been like for him. Everyone is always after him. Always trying to get him to turn his back on one side of the family or the other. Molly's right. Everyone here has been more than happy to use him when it was convenient."

Danielle lifted her chin imperiously. "I disagree completely. No one has used Harry. He has responsibilities in the family, and he's carried them out from time to time. That's all there is to it."

"Whatever the truth of the matter," Gilford said, "it's obvious that Molly has a different take on the situation. And like it or not, she's the one who's going to be married to Harry. I think she's made her point. None of us wants to have to go through her to get to Harry. As his wife, she's going to have a lot of control over the situation. If she decides to protect him from the rest of us, she's going to be able to do it."

Evangeline gave Molly an assessing look. "What do you want from us?"

"As I told you when you first sat down," Molly said, "I have two demands."

Josh's mouth curved with anticipation. "What are they?"

"First," Molly said, "in honor of his forthcoming marriage, I want a bachelor party for Harry. A real bachelor party. One that will be attended by every able-bodied male on both sides of the family. No excuses will be accepted. Josh and Brandon will organize it."

Everyone seated at the table gaped. Josh and Brandon exchanged wary looks.

"Second," Molly continued, "I want everyone on both sides of Harry's family to attend the wedding. Anyone who is not there will find it extremely difficult to get to Harry at any time during the next fifty or sixty years."

"Good God," Parker muttered.

Molly looked at the stunned faces of Harry's family. "Do I make myself perfectly clear?"

Josh grinned. "Absolutely."

She frowned at him. "One more thing. There will be no naked women jumping out of cakes at Harry's bachelor party. Understood?"

"Yes, ma'am," Josh said. "No naked women in the cakes. Got it."

Molly glanced toward the door where a waiter carrying a large tray had appeared. "Well, that's that. Let's eat. And no food fights allowed."

That night Harry woke up at midnight. He came awake gradually, not with a start. He lay quietly for a few seconds, wondering what had roused him from sleep. He could not put his finger on it. Nothing felt wrong. There had been no nightmares. No strange sounds in the dark.

Then suddenly, inexplicably, he knew that Molly was wide awake beside him. He gathered her close. With a soft little murmur, she snuggled deeper into his arms. He slid one leg between her thighs.

"What's wrong?" he whispered on a yawn.

"Nothing."

"You sure?" He nuzzled the curve of her shoulder. The scent of her warmed him, delighted him, thrilled him. A certain part of him was abruptly wide awake.

"I'm sure. I was just lying here, thinking."

"Humming." He nibbled her earlobe.

"What?"

"You were humming." He slid the sleeve of her nightgown downward to free one delicate breast. She felt so good beneath his hands. Soft. Warm. Exciting. "I heard you."

She ignored that. "Harry, what are you doing?"

"What does it look like I'm doing?" He bent his head to kiss one nipple. It firmed at the touch of his tongue.

"Harry?" She stroked his shoulders.

"Yes?" He flattened his hand on her stomach.

"How does the first of the month sound? That's two weeks from now."

"What happens on the first of the month?" He tangled his fingers in the hair at the apex of her thighs, probing for the warmth and gathering dew he knew he would find there.

Molly sucked in her breath. "Our wedding. Kelsey will be back from her summer workshop by then. I . . . Harry." Her hands clenched in his hair. She twisted, lifting herself against his questing hand.

Satisfaction coursed through Harry. Her response to him seemed to grow stronger, more familiar, more intimate in some indefinable manner each time he made love to her. It was like playing an instrument, he thought. The more they practiced together, the better the music got.

"The first of the month sounds fine," Harry whispered.

"You'll be finished with your paper by then?" She was breathless now.

"Yes." He settled between her silken thighs and entered her slowly. "The sooner the better, as far as I'm concerned."

He did not even bother to fight the urge to sink himself, all of himself, completely into her. This opening of his senses brought such powerful, intense pleasure to both of them.

It was as though he had lived in a shuttered room all of his life until he had met Molly. Now, when he was with her like this, the windows were fully open at last, and he could see the true colors of the world.

A long time later Harry drifted contentedly on the verge of sleep, allowing himself to luxuriate in the deep satisfaction that had come in the aftermath of the lovemaking.

Part of him was dimly aware of the moonlight on the bed, the feel of Molly cuddled against him, and a gentle sensation that had no name.

He considered the sensation with idle curiosity. It was a sort of muted singing, he thought. No, make that a *feeling.* Almost a presence somewhere in his mind.

Molly was humming again.

It wasn't an unpleasant sensation, he decided. In fact it had a certain comforting quality.

"Don't worry about it," Molly murmured sleepily. "You get used to it."

Harry stirred. "Get used to what?"

But Molly did not answer. She was already fast asleep.

Twenty-one

Olivia sipped thoughtfully at the cup of specially blended Assam tea Molly had just finished making. She glanced around the front room of Harry's condominium, which was littered with several packing cartons full of books. "Do you know where they've taken him?"

"No." Molly poured tea for herself and sat back on the sofa. She curled one jean-clad leg under herself and gave Olivia a wry smile. "Maybe it's better that way. I warned Josh about naked women bursting out of cakes, but that still leaves a lot of entertainment possibilities that I'd rather not contemplate too closely."

"Bachelor parties do have a certain reputation."

Molly made a face. "Don't remind me. Talk about an archaic tradition. Must be a leftover from the Medieval days when the male members of the wedding party got the groom drunk and then pushed him into bed with the bride."

Olivia gave her a keen look. "So why did you insist that the Stratton and Trevelyan men throw a party for Harry?"

"I think you can guess the answer to that."

Olivia met her eyes. "Yes. It doesn't take a degree in psychology to figure out that you want Harry to feel that his family cares enough about him to call a truce for his sake."

"It's the one thing he wants from them. The only thing he's ever asked of them."

"And you made certain he got it. I have to admit, I'm amazed. I didn't think there was any force on the face of the planet that could persuade the Strattons and the Trevelyans to put aside the feud even for a short time."

"The Strattons and the Trevelyans aren't so tough. You just have to know how to deal with them."

Olivia studied her with sudden understanding. "You really do love Harry, don't you?"

"Yes."

"Has he—" Olivia broke off and looked away for a brief moment. "I'm sorry, this is a very personal question. You would be within your rights to tell me to mind my own business, but I can't resist asking. Has he told you that he loves you?"

"Not in so many words," Molly admitted.

She was not altogether certain why Olivia had shown up at the door ten minutes ago. It was nearly nine o'clock. An hour earlier Josh had dragged Harry off to the parking garage on the pretext of showing him a brand-new Ferrari that he claimed was lodged in one of the stalls. There was more than enough Trevelyan blood in Harry to make him take a serious interest in that particular lure.

What Harry had not known when he agreed to go downstairs to view the mythical car was that he was about to be abducted in a stretch limousine that Brandon had hired for the evening.

Molly had had a few anxious moments, but the fact that Harry and Josh had not returned to the condominium meant that the plot had been successfully carried out. Pleased at the promising start to her scheme, she had finished the dinner dishes and was about to curl up with a book when Olivia had arrived.

As far as Molly could tell, Olivia simply wanted to talk.

"Doesn't it worry you that he hasn't told you that he loves you?" Olivia asked.

"He'll get around to it." At least Molly hoped Harry would eventually get around to figuring out that what he felt for her was love. "Harry does things in his own time and in his own way. He's different."

"You keep saying that."

"It's true." Molly smiled over the rim of her teacup. "I come from a long line of people who were all a little different. I know 'em when I see 'em."

"Yes, but Harry's differences, as you call them, go rather deep."

"Olivia, do you mind if I ask you a personal question?"

Olivia looked briefly uneasy. "What is it?"

"What did you see in Harry in the first place? It's obvious that the two of you were a bad match."

Olivia sighed. "You may not believe this, but I honestly thought at the beginning that we were a very good match. I met Harry at a small reception in his honor after he gave a talk on the contributions of eighteenth-century Enlightenment thinkers to the development of psychology."

"You figured you had something in common?"

"Well, yes." Olivia frowned. "Harry is very well respected in the academic world. He's intelligent. Well-educated. He seemed well-grounded emotionally. At least he did at first."

"Ah, yes. His infamous self-control." Molly grinned. "When did you discover that it conceals a seething cauldron of dangerous passions and dark desires?"

Olivia went blank. "I beg your pardon?"

"Never mind. I'm just teasing you. When did you decide that the two of you were not cut out for each other?"

Olivia shifted slightly in her chair. "Are you sure you want to go into this?"

"Absolutely. I'm dying of curiosity."

"To be honest," Olivia said, "it became clear very quickly that Harry had a serious emotional disorder which had to be dealt with therapeutically before he would be able to form a healthy, normal relationship with a woman."

"Hmm."

"I tried," Olivia said, grimly earnest. "Lord knows I tried. He wouldn't talk to me. He refused counseling or therapy. I told him there was medication now that could help him. He wouldn't even speak to a doctor about it. And then . . ."

"Then, what?"

"Well, he began to make me nervous, if you want to know the truth."

"Why?"

Olivia gazed out into the night. "I had the feeling that he wanted something from me, something I could not even begin to give to him. I didn't know what it was that he seemed to need. I just knew I couldn't supply it."

"What did you want from him?" Molly asked.

Olivia shot her a swift, searching glance. "A healthy, well-balanced, mutually satisfying relationship, of course. A marriage based on respect and trust and compatibility."

"And you didn't think you could find that with Harry?"

"It was impossible. Harry . . ." Olivia struggled for the right words. "Harry seemed so restrained at first. But toward the end of our engagement he became stranger. He started to *overwhelm* me."

"Overwhelm you?"

"It's difficult to explain. I never really understood it, myself. I had never encountered his particular symptoms in my clinical practice, and I had never studied such a syndrome when I was in school. I'm sure his odd behavior is the result of a posttraumatic stress disorder, but it was not clear what was going on. I became very frightened. I knew that I had to get out of the relationship."

"And Brandon was there, waiting to rescue you?"

Anger flashed in Olivia's eyes. "He didn't rescue me. I rescued myself."

"Sorry."

"Brandon and I had come to know each other during the weeks I was engaged to Harry. I admit that there was a strong attraction between us from the start. We both knew it and tried to ignore it. But Brandon realized that I was becoming increasingly anxious about Harry's bouts of depression and his . . . his intensity."

"You talked to Brandon about Harry's behavior?"

Olivia nodded. "I could talk to Brandon in a way that I could never talk to Harry. It was such a relief."

Molly leaned forward. "Olivia, it's all right. Don't torture yourself any longer with guilt."

"I don't feel any guilt in the matter," Olivia flared. Tears glittered suddenly in her eyes. "Guilt is a paralyzing, destructive emotion. I have no reason to feel guilty."

"No reason at all," Molly soothed. "You and Harry were never meant to be a couple. Trust me on this. I'm absolutely, positively certain of it."

"What makes you say that?" Olivia demanded.

"Harry connects emotionally in ways that you will never be able to explain with any fancy psychological theory. You will never truly understand him. As I keep telling you, he's different."

Olivia's teacup rattled in its saucer. "I tried to help him."

"I know."

"I did everything I could to get him into therapy." Olivia grabbed her purse, reached inside, and snatched a tissue. She blotted her eyes. "Oh, God, you can't possibly understand. It was like watching my father all over again."

"Oh, dear," Molly whispered.

Olivia did not appear to have heard her. She dabbed at more tears. "My father suffered from bouts of depression. They got worse as time went on. Mother tried to get him to see a doctor. So did I. But he refused. One day he went into the woods with a gun. He never came back."

Molly put down her teacup and rose from the sofa in a single movement. She went to Olivia and hugged her tightly. Olivia did not resist the offer. Instead, she turned her face into Molly's shoulder and began to sob.

Molly patted her gently. "Olivia, you're an expert. Surely you don't need me to tell you that you weren't responsible for your father's suicide."

"No. Lord knows, I've had enough therapy in the course of my training to deal with that." Olivia's tears began to subside.

"And you probably don't need me to remind you that Harry is not your father. You don't have to worry about saving him. He's not your problem."

Olivia sniffed once or twice and then raised her head. She managed a tremulous smile. "You know something? I think you missed your calling. You should have studied psychology."

"Thanks. But I prefer the tea and spice business."

"Maybe it's your lack of formal training that makes it easier for you to see the situation more clearly," Olivia mused as she dropped the damp tissue into her purse.

"All I know is that you feel you failed with Harry, and your feelings about that are complicated because you were personally involved with him. I can only imagine what a mess it must have been."

"A mess?"

"Sure. There you were, engaged to a man you were beginning to view as a patient, rather than as a lover. A man whose problems reminded you of your father's problems." Molly waved a hand. "At the same time you were falling in love with another man who happened to be related to your patient-fiancé. To top it all off, your patient was growing increasingly weird, and he refused to go into therapy. No wonder you freaked and broke off the engagement. It was the only intelligent, sensible thing to do."

There was a short, sharp pause.

"We do not generally use the term *freaked* in clinical psychology," Olivia murmured. "But maybe it's apt in this particular instance."

Molly blinked. "Was that a little joke I just heard? A bit of psychiatric humor? Olivia, you surprise me."

Olivia smiled wanly. "I've got a really good one about how many shrinks it takes to change a lightbulb."

Molly started to laugh. "I can't wait to hear it."

Olivia's smile finally reached her eyes. "Maybe you're right. Maybe it's time to let go of the guilt I feel toward Harry. I think he's in good hands."

Parker surveyed the noisy, crowded tavern with a scowl of acute disdain. A country-western band filled the room with a wailing tale of bad love and good liquor. The lead singer was dressed in a skintight silver lamé jumpsuit. None of the men who lounged at the bar had bothered to remove his hat. In the far corner a rowdy group had gathered around a pool table. It was obvious that money was on the line.

"Who the hell chose this place?" Parker demanded.

"We did." Josh glanced at Brandon for backup.

"Thought it would be neutral territory," Brandon said with somewhat forced enthusiasm. He signaled to a woman dressed in rhinestone cowboy garb. "Have a beer, Granddad."

"I drink whiskey," Parker grumbled.

"Matter of fact, so do I." Leon leered at the waitress as she approached the table. "Nice boots, honey."

Raleigh groaned. "Jeez, Uncle Leon. Don't make an ass out of yourself, okay?"

"Like my boots, mister?" The waitress glanced down at the red sequined cowboy boots that matched her hat.

Leon grinned. "Yeah."

"You can have 'em if you want 'em. By the end of the evening my feet are dyin' in these things."

"I could take care of that little problem for you, darlin'." Leon waggled his brows.

"No, thanks." The woman gave him a laconic smile. "I've got someone else who likes to massage my aching feet."

"How big is he?" Leon asked with calculating interest.

"It's a she," the waitress murmured. "And she's five foot eleven, rides a Harley, and wears a lot of leather and metal. Plays the drums in a band called Ruby Sweat. Ever hear of it?"

"Uh, no," Leon admitted. "Probably not my kind of music."

"Probably not. Somehow, I doubt that you and my friend would get along," the waitress said.

Leon winced. "Figures. Go out with a bunch of Strattons and what do you expect?"

Parker glowered at him. "Try not to make an even bigger fool of yourself than you already are, Trevelyan. I've got a reputation in this town."

Leon squinted. "A reputation for what? Flower arranging?"

"Give it a break, Grandpa," Josh hissed.

Unperturbed, the waitress tapped her pen firmly against her little pad of paper in order to get the attention of everyone at the table. "May I take your orders?"

"A beer for me," Josh said hastily.

"Same for me," Brandon said. "And maybe some nachos."

Parker scowled. "If beer is all that's available, I suppose I'll have the same."

Raleigh followed suit. "Me, too."

Gilford frowned in consideration. "Do you have a selection from the local microbreweries, by any chance?"

"Yes, sir, we've got one local brand," the waitress assured him. "Skid Road."

Gilford looked pained. "I don't believe I've ever heard of that one."

"It's from a small brewery that just opened in Pioneer Square," the waitress said.

"All right. I'll try it."

The waitress glanced expectantly at Harry, who sat at the head of the table. "What about you?"

"Skid Road sounds fine," Harry said.

"Make 'em all Skid Roads," Gilford ordered.

"You bet. I'll be right back." The waitress dropped her little pad into the pocket of her short red cowboy skirt and moved off into the crowd.

Leon watched her with a wistful expression. "Cowgirls ain't what they used to be."

"Shut up, you old coot," Parker ordered. "Haven't you heard of sexual harassment?"

Leon feigned astonishment. "Why, no, I haven't. Where do I go to get me some?"

Josh heaved a long-suffering sigh and looked at Harry. "Are we having fun yet?"

Harry considered the men who were seated at the table. The small crowd was composed of virtually every one of his nearest male relatives who was twenty-one or older. It was the first time he had ever seen them all together in one room.

"I assume this bachelor party was Molly's doing?" he said into the silence that had descended on the table.

"Whatever gave you that idea?" Gilford muttered.

"Just a wild guess," Harry said. Out of the corner of his eye he saw the waitress returning with a tray of Skid Roads. He wondered how soon they could all call a halt to this farce and go home.

Raleigh frowned. "Now, Harry, I know what you're thinkin', and it wasn't like that. We all wanted to give you a send-off. Isn't that right, Uncle Leon?"

Leon cocked one brow. "Sure." He leaned back as the waitress set a bottle of beer down on the table in front of him. "Hell, I'm always willin' to party."

Parker picked up his beer. "Would you mind answering one question for me, Harry?"

"What's that?" Harry asked.

"I've got no objections to the idea of you getting married. It's your business. But why in hell do you want to go and marry a bossy little piece like that Molly Abberwick? Son, take it from me, she's going to make your life a living hell."

"You can say that again." Leon shook his head. "I'll tell you something, that lady's got balls."

Harry looked at him. "No balls."

"Huh?" Leon blinked in confusion.

"She's got guts, but no balls." Harry took a swallow of beer. "There's a small but significant difference. Maybe you're not particular, Uncle Leon, but when it comes to things like this, I prefer accuracy."

There was a moment of stunned silence around the table. Everyone stared at Harry. And then Brandon's mouth twitched. A moment later he exploded in laughter. Josh joined in with a howl of amusement. Gilford started to grin.

"Son-of-a-bitch," Leon muttered. Then he started to chuckle.

Parker and Raleigh traded strange looks.

Harry was the only one who noticed the three burly men in denim and leather who sauntered into the tavern at that moment. They appeared no different from many of the other tavern patrons, but something about them sent a stab of unease through him.

The newcomers surveyed the room with expressions of drunken anticipation.

"Damn." Harry set down his beer. "I think it's time to leave."

Raleigh glanced at him. "What's wrong?"

"Nothing. Yet." Harry started to reach for his wallet. He saw the newcomers start toward the Stratton-Trevelyan table.

With an instinct for trouble that had served him well over the years, Leon looked up expectantly. He grinned when he saw the three men bearing down on the table. "Well, well, well."

Parker frowned. "What's going on here?"

"With any luck, the evening is about to liven up," Leon assured him happily.

The three men reached the table. The one in the lead sported a couple of days' growth of beard and a greasy ponytail. He hooked his broad thumbs into a wide leather belt.

"Say, now, this wouldn't be the bunch of sweet-cakes that belongs in that fancy limo parked out front, would it?"

"Who you callin' a sweet-cake?" Leon asked pleasantly.

"Now, see here," Parker said. "This is a private party."

A second man grinned, displaying darkened teeth. "Too bad. We wanna have some fun, too."

Leon gave him a toothy smile. "Not at our table."

"Don't see why not," the first man replied. He swept out a long, hairy arm, caught hold of the edge of the table, and turned it on its side.

Bottles and glasses went flying. Chairs scraped. The Strattons and Trevelyans scrambled to their feet. A shout went up at the nearby tables.

"Son-of-a-bitch." Leon waved one crutch with enthusiasm.

"Oh, shit," Raleigh said. "This is gonna be one fun bachelor party, ain't it?"

Harry seized his beer bottle before it hit the floor. He held it the way he would have held a knife. He caught Josh's eye. "Front door," he ordered. "Now."

"Right." Josh glanced at the makeshift weapon Harry held and grabbed his own bottle. He started to back toward the door.

Gilford looked outraged. An expression of surprise crossed Parker's face. Harry shoved both of them toward the front door.

He didn't see who threw the first punch, but he saw Leon swing a crutch in response. The man with the oily ponytail doubled over with a choked gasp.

In the end it didn't matter who started the fray. The result was entirely predictable by all the known laws of science. The tavern erupted into a free-for-all. Screams, shouts, and curses rang out. The band turned up the volume in a desperate attempt to drown out the crowd.

Intent on getting his relatives to the safety of the limo, Harry moved quickly. He ducked the swinging fist of one of the denim-clad men and came up under the blow to plant a solid punch into a bulging stomach.

The man staggered backward. An expression of astonishment lit his beefy face. Before he could recover, Harry grabbed Parker by the shoulder and launched him in the general direction of the door.

His grandfather, however, was concentrating on other matters.

"No-good hooligan." Parker swung a bottle of Skid Road at one of the three men who had initiated the scene. The bottle shattered on the man's shoulder, eliciting a growl of outrage.

Harry hauled Parker out of harm's way.

Josh and Brandon looked at Harry for direction.

"Josh, take charge of Raleigh," Harry ordered. "Brandon, get Gilford and Parker out of here. I'll handle Leon."

"Right." Brandon took hold of Parker and started toward the door.

Josh seized Raleigh's arm. "Let's get outa here, cuz. Party's over."

"Ah, shoot. The fun was just startin'," Raleigh complained. But he allowed himself to be dragged toward the door.

Harry grasped Leon's collar just as his uncle was winding up for another swing of his crutch.

"What the hell?" Leon scowled at him. "Leggo. I've got business to attend to."

"This is my party," Harry said as he hustled Leon toward the door. "And I'm ready to leave."

"You never were any fun, boy," Leon said as Harry hauled him out into the night. "That's your whole problem in life. You don't know how to enjoy yourself."

Harry ignored him. He did a quick head count as everyone piled into the waiting limousine. There was a brief, awkward moment when Leon's crutch got caught on the door frame, but Harry got the door closed just as the fight spilled out into the parking lot.

"Looks like we're all here." Harry caught the limo driver's eyes in the rearview mirror. "Let's go."

The driver already had the engine running. "My pleasure, sir."

The big car's tires kicked up a storm of gravel as the limousine roared out of the tavern parking lot. Somewhere in the distance sirens wailed, but the limousine was safely on its way.

For a few minutes no one said a thing. The subdued lights in the plush passenger compartment revealed a selection of interesting expressions as everyone looked at everyone else.

Then Leon chuckled and held up several bottles of Skid Road that he had somehow managed to liberate on the way out the door. "Anyone want another round?"

"Hell, yes," Raleigh said. "Give me one of those, Uncle Leon. I need it."

"Personally, I could use something stronger," Parker muttered.

Josh grinned and began to rummage around in the limousine's tiny bar. "I do believe there is a bottle of whiskey here, Mr. Stratton. Yep, here we are." He held up a bottle.

"Thank God." Parker watched Josh pour the whiskey. "I haven't been in a situation like that since I was in the Marines."

Leon looked at him with sudden interest. "You were in the Marines?"

"Yes, I was." Parker took the whiskey from Josh.

"Well, I'll be damned. So was I." Leon stuck out his hand.

Parker hesitated, and then he shook Leon's hand.

Harry was aware of a curious new mood settling on the small crowd in the back of the limousine. He was not certain what it was, but it felt good.

Brandon looked at the others. "Gentlemen, I do believe that this is what my wife, the noted shrink, would call a male bonding experience."

"Don't know what that means," Leon said cheerfully, "but I'll drink to it."

The sound of a key scraping haphazardly in the front door lock roused Molly. Harry was home at last. She sat up on the sofa where she had fallen asleep reading and glanced at her watch. She was surprised to see that it was nearly one o'clock in the morning.

Relief poured through her. The bachelor party must have been reasonably successful to have lasted this long.

She yawned, got to her feet, and went down the hall to greet her husband-to-be. The scratching sound came again. Harry was apparently having a problem unlocking his own front door.

"I do hope you're not soused, Harry," she said as she opened the door. "A little male bonding is one thing, but if those Stratton and Trevelyan relatives of yours got you rip-roaring drunk, I'm going to be very annoyed."

She broke off in horror when she saw who stood at the door.

"I assure you, I'm not drunk, my dear," Cutter Latteridge said. He gave her his most charming smile and showed her the gun in his hand. The barrel was oddly shaped. "And I won't be staying long. There's just one or two things I want to take care of before I start another project."

"Cutter." Molly was too stunned to move. "How did you get in here?"

"Actually, the name is Clarence, but you can call me Cutter." He motioned with the gun. "And to answer your question, I got in through the garage. Garage security is always so lax, isn't it?"

Molly took a step back. Cutter walked into the hall and closed the door behind himself.

"They said you had disappeared," Molly whispered. "They said it wasn't your style to come back after the con went sour."

"Generally speaking, they're right." Cutter heaved a sigh of regret. "I'm not fond of the physical stuff. Entirely too messy. I prefer to make my living with my wits. But in this instance, I feel that I must make an exception."

"You mean another exception, don't you? You killed Wharton Kendall."

"He became unreliable," Cutter said. "There was simply too much money at stake, I suppose. He felt he had a right to more of it than I planned to give him for his services. Amazing how greedy some people can be, isn't it?"

"You'll never get your hands on the Abberwick Foundation assets now," Molly pointed out desperately. "Why take the risk of coming back to Seattle?"

"Because Trevelyan won't give it up." Cutter's face suffused with sudden fury. "He's like a goddamned bloodhound. He's got his investigator rummaging around in my past, looking for evidence, trying to find patterns. And we all have patterns. Sooner or later he'll track me down. I can't have that."

Molly had not realized that Harry had kept Fergus Rice on the case, but the news did not surprise her. "You can't stop Harry."

"I must," Cutter said. "If I don't get rid of him, I won't have any peace for the rest of my life."

Fear seized Molly's insides. "What are you going to do?"

"I'm going to dispense with both you and Trevelyan in one neat, tidy package."

"You can't get away with this. Everyone will realize who murdered us."

"I don't think so." Cutter smiled coldly. "I've spent quite some time planning this project. And I've waited for just the right moment."

"What are you talking about?"

"It will appear that Harry Trevelyan, psychologically disturbed man that he is, went over the edge. He came home drunk and depressed after his bachelor's party. Shot his fiancée, who he mistakenly believed had resumed her affair with her old boyfriend, Gordon Brooke, and then turned the gun on himself. Happens all the time, eh?"

"You're the crazy one if you think this will work."

"It will work, my dear. I'm very good with details." Cutter glanced at his watch. "We may as well sit down. There's nothing we can do until Trevelyan returns home, after all, and I understand that bachelor parties can go on for some time."

Molly knew she would never have a chance to scream aloud. Cutter stood too close, his gun at the ready. He could knock her unconscious or kill her before she could utter a sound.

She recalled the day that Cutter had trapped her in her father's basement workshop. Harry had arrived on the scene within minutes after Cutter had left the house.

He would never admit it, but Molly knew that Harry had come to the Abberwick mansion that day because he had sensed that she was in danger. She had called to him and he had come. Admittedly, he'd arrived a little late, but he had come.

Molly looked into Cutter's cold eyes and saw death. In desperation, she screamed a silent warning into the night.

Harry.

Danger. Death.

Be careful. Be careful. Be careful.

Harry opened the door of the limousine as soon as it pulled into the loading zone in front of his condominium building.

Leon gave him a reproachful look. "You sure you want to go home this early? Night's young, boy."

"It's one-thirty in the morning, and I'm not accustomed to this kind of excitement." Harry got out of the car and looked at his relatives through the open door. "I've had about all the partying I can stand for one night. But I want you all to know that I had a hell of a time."

"Hey, we oughta do this more often," Raleigh said.

"I'm not so sure about that." Brandon grinned ruefully. "I think I'm about ready to call it a night, too."

"Me, too," Gilford said.

Parker snorted. "These youngsters don't have the stamina we did in our heyday, do they, Leon?"

"What d'ya expect?" Leon said. "They've all got it too soft these days."

"That's the truth," Parker agreed fervently.

Harry glanced at Josh. "Make sure Leon doesn't embarrass himself."

"I'll give it my best shot." Josh's grin faded. He searched Harry's face. "Anything wrong?"

"No," Harry said. "I'm ready for bed, that's all." He started to close the limo door.

"Let's hear it for the groom-to-be," Leon yelled. "Man's never gonna be the same again, once he's married."

Harry shut the door on the good-natured cheers.

He watched the limousine cruise off into the night, and then he turned and went swiftly toward the lobby door.

Halfway there, he broke into a loping run.

Something was wrong.

Danger. Be careful. Be careful.

The riveting sense of wrongness had slashed through his good mood a few minutes earlier. His first instinct, born of long habit, had been to repress it.

But the realization that the chilling sensation was somehow connected to Molly crept insidiously into his mind. He had been unable to ignore it.

Danger. Danger. Danger.

Molly's advice came back to him in an overwhelming rush. She had told him not to fight his own nature. She had warned him that the battle would tear him apart. For the first time, Harry acknowledged that she was right. The one sure way to drive himself crazy was to refuse to accept the truth.

He forced himself to relax and cautiously open his senses.

He's here. He's here. Murder. Murder.

Harry staggered under the impact of the silent, screaming blow. He recovered awkwardly and fumbled with his keys. Chris, the night doorman, emerged from his small office and opened the lobby door.

"Evening, Mr. Trevelyan. Late night, huh?"

"Bachelor party," Harry said tersely. He fought for control even as he tried to leave all his senses on full alert.

Chris winked. "Congratulations."

"Thanks." A wave of dizziness hit Harry as he started toward the elevator.

"Anything wrong, Mr. Trevelyan?"

Harry missed the elevator call button on the first attempt. Panic shot through him. *Too late. I'm going to be too late.* "Chris, have there been any visitors to my place while I was out?"

"Just Mrs. Stratton."

"Olivia?" Harry shook his head, trying to clear it.

"Yes, sir. But she left several hours ago."

"No one else?"

"No, sir."

"Do me a favor, will you?" Harry said hoarsely.

"Sure."

"I'm going to play a little joke on Molly."

"A joke?"

"Bachelor party joke."

"Oh. Right. Got it." Chris grinned. "What do you want me to do?"

"Give me a few minutes to get upstairs and then call me on the intercom. When I answer, tell me that Detective . . ." Harry rubbed his forehead and forced himself to think. "Tell me that Detective Foster of the police department is on his way up. Say he's told you it's an emergency."

Chris's brow wrinkled. "Emergency?"

"Yes. Just a joke. Will you do it for me?"

"You bet."

"Thanks, Chris." The elevator door slid open. Harry managed to get himself inside and punch the right button.

As the doors closed, he leaned back against the wall, shut his eyes, and concentrated on finding his balance on the glass bridge that stretched above the abyss.

He was not going to fight the conflicting sensations this time, he promised himself. He would try Molly's suggestion. He would simply sink into his senses. The way he did when he was with her.

Too late. Too late.

A rat named panic was trying to eat into his awareness. Harry forced the creature back into its dark hole.

Just another sense. No different than sight or touch or smell. Just another one of his natural abilities. Like his reflexes. Perfectly normal, Molly had said. For him.

Perfectly normal. All he had to do was accept it. Use it. Be at peace with it. Molly's life might depend on his acceptance of his own natural abilities.

Molly's life.

Harry took a deep breath. He steadied himself on the glass bridge.

From out of nowhere an alert calm stole over him. Harry began to breathe more easily. He knew without experimenting with them that he had regained control of his reflexes. He had stopped trembling. He straightened away from the elevator wall.

The elevator door opened. Harry drew another deep, steadying breath.

He stepped out of the elevator and went down the carpeted corridor to his front door. He shoved the key into the lock and turned the knob.

"Molly?" He slurred his voice and stumbled deliberately as he let himself into the hall. The feeling of impending danger threatened to crush him. "Honey, I'm home. Hell of a party. Should have seen the fight at the tavern."

"Well, well, well. Blind drunk." Cutter Latteridge smiled as he came around the corner into the hall. He grasped Molly's arm in one hand, chaining her to his side. In his other hand he held a silenced gun that was leveled at Harry's chest. "How very convenient."

Twenty-two

"Harry, I tried to warn you." Molly's eyes glittered with tears of despair. "I'm so sorry. I'm so sorry."

Harry peered at her, as though having a problem focusing on a moving image. "What the hell's he doing here?"

"I'm here to set the stage for a proper departure, Trevelyan," Cutter said.

"I'm not going anywhere." Harry staggered toward him, allowing the momentum of his awkward movement to send him careening into a wall. He fetched up against it and started to slide gently toward the floor. "Put that gun away, Latteridge. You can't shoot anyone here. Not your style."

"My style has changed, thanks to you, Trevelyan."

"Harry." Molly tried unsuccessfully to shake herself free of Cutter's grip. "Are you all right?"

"Haven't felt this good in a long time." Harry scrabbled around on the floor. His fingers brushed against his ankle sheath. He made a show of heaving himself back into an upright position. The knife was now tucked into his shirt sleeve. "What's going on here?"

"He wants to make our deaths look like a murder-suicide," Molly whispered. She searched his face as if trying to see past the facade of drunkenness. "Harry, he's going to kill us."

"Nah. He won't do that." Harry floundered forward. "Will you, Latteridge or Laxton or whatever your name is?"

"Stay where you are," Cutter ordered quickly. He backed away, dragging Molly with him.

"Can't shoot me in the chest," Harry explained cheerfully. "Wouldn't look like a suicide, now would it? Got to go for the head or mouth or something."

"Damn you," Cutter hissed. "You really are crazy, aren't you?"

Harry shook his head sadly. "And here I thought a shrink like Olivia was supposed to maintain confidentiality."

"Keep your distance or I'll kill Molly right now," Cutter warned. "Right *now,* do you understand me?"

"Sure, sure." Harry massaged the back of his neck as he lurched to a swaying stop. "I hear you."

Cutter frowned. "I'm delighted to see you drunk, Trevelyan, but I must admit this is beyond my expectations."

"I make it a practice never to live up to other people's expec . . . expectations," Harry said.

Molly's eyes widened with sudden comprehension. He knew then that she had finally realized he was not drunk. He willed her not to give the game away.

"Stay right where you are, Trevelyan." Cutter started to raise the gun.

At that instant the intercom buzzed. Cutter froze.

"Hey, we got a visitor," Harry said brightly. "Party time."

"Don't answer it," Cutter ordered.

"Got to." Harry lifted one shoulder in an elaborate, what-can-I-do shrug that sent him reeling off-balance once more. "Doorman knows I'm up here. He saw me get on the elevator. Knows Molly's here, too."

Cutter scowled furiously, clearly torn. "All right, answer it. But tell him you're going to bed and don't want any visitors. Got that?"

"Sure thing. Headed for bed."

Harry stumbled toward the intercom. As he stretched out a hand to punch the button he gauged the distance to his target. Cutter was holding Molly directly in front of him. From this angle Harry knew that he could hit Cutter's shoulder. But that was not good enough. He needed a shot that would bring Latteridge down before he could fire the gun.

"Yeah, Chris?"

"Sorry to bother you at this hour, Mr. Trevelyan," Chris said in portentous accents, "but there's a Detective Foster from the police department on his way up to see you. He says it's an emergency."

"Police." Cutter, already disconcerted by the interruption, exploded with rage. "Goddamn you, Trevelyan. What's going on here? What have you done?"

"Beats me," Harry said as he turned away from the intercom. He smiled at Cutter. "Looks like we've got company from the police department. Now what do you suppose the police want at this hour? I wonder if I forgot to pay a parking ticket."

"Damn you."

"Don't think the old murder-suicide scenario's going to work tonight," Harry said. "Be a little tough to explain to Detective Foster on your way out, eh?"

Cutter's face worked. He abruptly released Molly, shoved her out of his path, and glanced wildly at the door. "I've got to get out of here."

"There are two elevators," Harry volunteered helpfully. "With any luck you won't get into the same one Detective Foster is about to arrive in."

"Stay back." Cutter swung the gun frantically between Molly and Harry and then concentrated on Harry. "Don't move. I mean it."

Harry raised his arms in a wide arc. "I'm not going anywhere."

"You son-of-a-bitch," Cutter snarled. "This isn't over."

"You sound like my cousin Josh. Kid's got a similar flair for melodrama."

Cutter ignored him. He whirled and ran for the door.

The blade slipped eagerly out from beneath Harry's sleeve. The hilt fit his hand perfectly. He waited for the right moment, knowing beyond a shadow of a doubt that it would come. It was as if he could read Cutter's mind before Cutter himself knew what he was going to do.

There was no paranormal sense involved, just logic and observation. Cutter was in a panic. He was acting emotionally, not logically. Fury would overrule his common sense. He would be unable to resist taking vengeance for all that had gone wrong.

Harry knew that Cutter would turn and try to kill him before he fled.

Sure enough, Latteridge swung around as he wrenched open the door. Rage had screwed his face into a grotesque mask. "You've ruined everything, Trevelyan. Damn you."

He aimed the gun.

Not at Harry. At Molly.

In that instant, Harry was sure that he did go a little crazy. *Too late.*

His reflexes took over. The knife left his hand as though it had a will of its own.

It struck Cutter in the center of his chest. The impact jerked him back a step. A strange, uncomprehending expression replaced the rage in his eyes.

He dropped the gun and clawed at the hilt of the knife. "But I planned it all so carefully," he said hoarsely as he fell to his knees. "Nothing could go wrong this time."

Cutter sprawled facedown on the tile. He did not move.

Harry pulled Molly close. She buried her face against his shoulder. She was crying when she said, "You saved us. You saved both our lives tonight."

This time he had not been too late.

"You knew, didn't you? Before you came through the door, you knew he was here."

Harry tightened his grip on Molly as they watched the soft light of dawn wash away the last of the darkness outside the windows. The police had finally left a short while earlier. Latteridge's body had been removed. The blood on the hall tile was gone.

Neither Molly nor Harry had felt much like going to bed.

"I knew . . ." Harry hesitated, uncertain how to put it into words. "I felt that something was wrong."

"You sensed more than that. You realized that Latteridge was here."

"It was a logical deduction, given the fact that he was the only real source of danger we had encountered recently."

"Don't give me that logic stuff." Molly turned in the circle of his arm. Her emerald eyes gleamed with a knowing expression. "You knew he was here because I'd warned you."

"Did you?"

"Yes, I did, and what's more, you heard me. In your mind, Harry."

He bent his head and brushed his mouth across hers. "Let's just say that I got one of my insights."

"It was a lot more than that." She wrapped her arms around his neck and kissed him soundly. When she was finished she moved her head back a couple of inches and smiled. "One of these days I'll get you to admit it."

"You're safe." Harry eased her back onto the sofa and covered her body with his own. "Dear God, Molly, that's all that matters."

She touched the edge of his mouth with the tip of her finger. "And you're safe, too. That's all that matters to me." Her eyes glowed.

An all-consuming passion exploded within Harry without warning. The rational part of his brain knew that it was very likely a reaction to the aftermath of violence and the fact that he had come very close to losing Molly. But the reasoning was swept aside by the powerful need that seized hold of him.

"Molly," he whispered. *"Molly."*

"Yes." She pulled his mouth down to hers.

Desire roared through both of them, an elemental force that could not be stopped. Harry fumbled with Molly's clothing and then with his own.

Half undressed, they came together in a storm of need.

Need was everything in that moment. Harry did not question its demands. He accepted it, welcomed it, surrendered to it.

He needed to feel the boundless warmth and life and energy in Molly. He needed to experience the incredible sense of sinking into her, of touching the deepest part of her while she touched the deepest part of him.

Molly opened herself to him. He surged into her, seeking arcane mysteries that could not be learned in any other way. He craved the secrets of her soul and yearned to show her his own.

He stepped boldly out onto the glass bridge, knowing that Molly waited for him on the far side of the abyss. As long as she was there, he would not fall.

He was no longer alone in the whirling darkness.

When it was over, Harry lay sprawled in Molly's arms, allowing the warmth of her to seep into his bones, all the way to his soul.

I love you, he thought.

Molly cradled his face between her hands. "I love you, Harry."

It was then that Harry realized that he had never spoken the words aloud. Not once. Incredible. He could not imagine life without her. It was time to tell her what was in his heart.

"I love you, Molly."

She smiled, her eyes bright with laughter and love. "I heard you the first time."

Twenty-three

Harry brought Molly and their newborn son home to the Abberwick mansion on a fine day in spring. He settled both onto the grand Victorian fainting couch in the front parlor and prepared to limit visitors to a reasonable number. It wasn't going to be easy. A long line of Trevelyans, Strattons, and Abberwicks had announced their intention to call upon the new mother and baby. The hall was already filled with gifts.

Harry stood near the couch and gazed down at his son. Awe and a sense of wonder that exceeded anything he had ever felt for the laws of Newton and Einstein soared through him.

"Incredible," Harry whispered. "He's absolutely incredible."

"That's just what I was thinking." Molly gave Harry a tired, but thoroughly satisfied smile. "What do you think of the name Sean Jasper Trevelyan?"

"A little awkward, but what the heck. He'll be able to handle it." Harry gingerly reached out to touch Sean's tiny fingers. "Amazing."

"If you think this one's amazing, wait until you see the next one," Molly said.

"The next one?"

"There will be a little girl, too, you know," Molly predicted happily. "In about two years, I think."

"You've got plans?" Harry asked indulgently.

"I saw her, remember? The day she and little Sean, here, saved my life by reminding me of my father's giant toys down in the workshop. We'll call her Samantha Brittany after our mothers."

Harry grinned. "Anything you say, my love. I certainly don't have the strength to argue with you. I know the doctor insisted on discharging you and Sean today, but I'm still recovering. It's going to be a while before I can go through that again."

"You were wonderful," Molly assured him.

"I was a basket case."

"Not true. You never left my side." Molly touched her son's tiny nose with the tip of her finger. "Or my head," she added very softly.

Harry pretended not to hear that. But the part of him that had once dreaded such comments and the implications buried in them no longer reacted with instant alarm.

Footsteps sounded in the hall. Harry looked toward the door. "I told Ginny to keep the visitors to a minimum today."

"Hi." Tessa stuck her head around the edge of the door. Heloise Stickley hovered directly behind her. "We came to pay our respects to the new member of the family."

"Come on in," Molly said. "Hello, Heloise."

"Hi, Ms. Abberwick. I mean, Mrs. Trevelyan." Heloise smiled shyly. She clutched a large, unwrapped box in both hands. "Cute kid."

"We think so." Molly glanced at the large box. "How nice of you to bring a present, Heloise."

Heloise flushed. "Yeah, well, this isn't exactly a present. I finished my prototype. Thought you'd like to see it."

Harry groaned. "Not today, thanks."

"But it works," Heloise said, enthusiasm replacing her shyness. "At least, theoretically. I haven't had a chance to actually test it yet. I need to find a suitable subject. Someone who gives off the right brain waves."

Harry took a step back, scowling. "Don't look at me."

"Huh?" Heloise cast him a quizzical glance. "I wasn't thinking of using you, Dr. Trevelyan. I need someone who has a history of manifesting some sort of psychic abilities."

"Right." Harry smiled blandly. "Well, I guess that lets me out."

Molly gave him a laughing glance. Then she looked at Tessa. "How's the hotshot espresso bar consultant?"

"We're opening a new Gordon Brooke Espresso Bar in Bellevue in

June," Tessa said complacently. "This time it will be done right. Going to make a killing. And I get a chunk of the profits."

"I think it's time I hired a new assistant," Molly said. "Something tells me I won't be seeing much of you in the future."

"I'll never abandon my roots," Tessa assured her. "But I'm considering having my eyebrow ring removed. What do you think?"

"Don't do anything rash," Molly advised. "You've got an image to maintain."

"True." Tessa looked thoughtful.

A soft knock announced another visitor.

"Okay if I come in?" Josh asked.

"Sure," Molly said. "Meet Sean Jasper."

"Sean Jasper? Great name." Josh ambled into the room and came to a halt near the bed. "Looks like he's going to take after his old man."

"What's that supposed to mean?" Harry asked.

Josh grinned. "Let's just say he's not the best-looking little dude in the Trevelyan clan."

"He's gorgeous," Molly said firmly. "Just like his father."

"Thank you," Harry murmured.

"Beauty is in the eye of the beholder, I guess," Josh allowed. "Maybe when he loses some of those wrinkles he'll look a little better."

More footsteps. Kelsey appeared in the doorway. She was wearing a small backpack. "Molly, I just got in. Plane was a little late. Ginny tells me that I missed the whole thing. Are you okay?"

"We're both okay," Molly said.

"Oh, he's adorable." Kelsey started forward and then came to a halt when she saw Josh. She blushed. "Hi."

"Hi." Josh appeared to be having trouble deciding what to say next. "Haven't seen you since Christmas."

"When you spilled the punch on me," Kelsey agreed.

"Couldn't have been me," Josh said. "I've got great reflexes. Runs in the family. How's school?"

"Terrific," Kelsey said. "What about you?"

"Good," Josh said. "Just fine."

An awkward silence fell. Josh and Kelsey continued to stare at each other as if they were alone in the parlor.

Molly glanced at Harry and raised her brows.

Harry didn't need mental telepathy to know what she was thinking.

Things had been like this between Josh and Kelsey since they had met shortly before the wedding.

"There, I've got it all set up," Heloise announced, oblivious of the sudden hush. "Stand back, everyone, while I turn it on."

"What?" Harry spun around to see that Heloise had removed a strange-looking apparatus from the large box. It consisted of several dangling metal cuffs, a sophisticated electronic control panel replete with various meters and dials, and a long cord. The cord was plugged into a nearby outlet.

"All set?" Heloise asked brightly.

"Hold on just a minute here." Harry started toward the plug with grim determination. "This is no place for that kind of thing."

Heloise flipped a switch. The control panel lit up like a Christmas tree.

"Oh, wow," Heloise breathed. "It's actually registering something. This is the first time I've ever picked up this kind of reaction."

"Holy cow." Kelsey shucked her backpack and went toward the machine. "What is it, what's going on?"

"I'm not sure yet." Heloise began twisting dials and making adjustments.

Josh went to stand behind Kelsey. "What is this thing?"

"It's a device designed to pick up paranormal brain waves." Heloise hunched over her control panel. "I've been working on it for months, thanks to the grant I got from the Abberwick Foundation. Whew. Someone in this room is really emitting some strong vibes."

Harry halted halfway to the plug. "Get that idiot device out of here, Heloise. This is neither the time nor the place for a demonstration."

"Wait, Harry." Cradling Sean Jasper in her arms, Molly pushed aside the blanket and sat up on the edge of the couch. "Let's see what Heloise has come up with."

"You're supposed to be resting," Harry muttered.

"I'm fine. I want to see how Heloise's machine works."

Harry briefly cursed the Abberwick curiosity. He took another step away from the machine. The lights on the control panel did not dim.

"Hang on, everybody." Heloise busied herself with some dangling wires. "I'm definitely getting a reading. This is so exciting. Someone in this room is putting out paranormal brain waves like crazy."

"I hope it's me," Kelsey said. "I'd love to have paranormal brain waves."

Heloise held one of the meters close to her. "No. Sorry. It's not you."

"Try Harry," Josh suggested. "Everyone in the family says he's got the Second Sight."

Heloise looked at Harry.

"Don't come near me with that thing," Harry warned. "You got that grant from the Abberwick Foundation against my professional advice. It was a waste of money, as far as I'm concerned. There is absolutely, positively no scientific rationale for this kind of research."

"Come on, Harry," Molly said. "Let Heloise attach the meter to you. What harm can it do?"

"Yeah," Josh said. "What's the harm?"

"The harm is that it violates every basic principle of the laws of science," Harry said. "And I will not be a party to any such damn fool experimentation."

"Now, Harry, be a sport." Molly paused as Heloise came to an abrupt halt in front of her. "What is it, Heloise? What's happening?"

"I'll be darned." Heloise gazed at the meter with a rapturous expression. "The reading is very strong right here."

"Me?" Molly was delighted.

"No, I don't think so." Heloise cautiously moved her meter around in the vicinity of Molly and little Sean Jasper. "Not you."

"Shoot." Molly grimaced. "I was hoping I might have a few psychic powers."

"The baby," Heloise announced. "The paranormal waves are coming from Sean Jasper."

"Good heavens," Molly whispered. Awe shone in her eyes. "It's hereditary."

Harry stared at his infant son. Then he smiled slowly. "Don't blame me. Something tells me it runs in both sides of his family."

Molly laughed.

And in that moment Harry did not need any special psychic power to catch a glimpse of the love-filled future that lay ahead. He could see that future very clearly in Molly's brilliant eyes.

He was absolutely, positively certain of it.